CRIME AND HORROR IN VICTORIAN LITERATURE AND CULTURE

VOLUME II

Edited by

MATTHEW KAISER

HARVARD UNIVERSITY

Copyright © 2010 by Matthew Kaiser. All rights reserved. No part of this publication may be reprinted, reproduced, transmitted, or utilized in any form or by any electronic, mechanical, or other means, now known or hereafter invented, including photocopying, microfilming, and recording, or in any information retrieval system without the written permission of University Readers, Inc.

First published in the United States of America in 2010 by University Readers, Inc.

Trademark Notice: Product or corporate names may be trademarks or registered trademarks, and are used only for identification and explanation without intent to infringe.

14 13 12 11 10   1 2 3 4 5

Printed in the United States of America

ISBN: 978-1-935551-54-6

www.cognella.com 800.200.3908

To my students

Contents

Introduction	1

Part V: Monstrosity

Edward Bulwer-Lytton (1803–1873) Monos and Daimonos	9
Christina Rossetti (1830–1894) Goblin Market	17
Robert Louis Stevenson (1850–1894) Strange Case of Dr. Jekyll and Mr. Hyde	37
Frederick Treves (1853–1923) The Elephant Man	95
"Jack the Ripper" Letter to Central News Office	103
John Barlas (1860–1914) Terrible Love	105
Stanislaus Eric Stenbock (1860–1895) The True Story of a Vampire	107

Part VI: Hauntings

Leopold Lewis (1828–1890)
The Bells — 117

Margaret Oliphant (1828–1897)
A Beleaguered City — 151

Vernon Lee (1856–1935)
A Phantom Lover — 247

Christina Rossetti (1830–1894)
A Chilly Night — 291
Cobwebs — 293

Lafcadio Hearn (1850–1904)
Furisodé — 295

Part VII: Chaos

Thomas Carlyle (1795–1881)
From The French Revolution — 301

Edward Bulwer-Lytton (1803–1873)
From The Last Days of Pompeii — 307

Alfred Tennyson (1809–1892)
The Kraken — 311

Bithia Mary Croker (ca.1849–1920)
Jack Straw's Castle — 313

Max Nordau (1849–1923)
From Degeneration — 319

Algernon Charles Swinburne (1837–1909)
Hermaphroditus — 329

THOMAS HARDY (1840–1928)
  Hap   333

A. MARY F. ROBINSON (1857–1944)
  Neurasthenia   335

ÉMILE DURKHEIM (1858–1917)
  From Suicide: A Study in Sociology   337

ROBERT LOUIS STEVENSON (1850–1894)
  The Suicide Club   355

PART VIII: Death

ROBERT BROWNING (1812–1889)
  Childe Roland to the Dark Tower Came   421

ALFRED TENNYSON (1809–1892)
  Tithonus   433
  Rizpah   437

CHRISTINA ROSSETTI (1830–1894)
  After Death   443

FLORENCE MARRYAT (1837–1899)
  My First Séance   445

ALEXANDER WILLIAM KINGLAKE (1809–1891)
  Cairo and the Plague   453

EMILY BRONTË (1818–1848)
  Death   469

ACKNOWLEDGMENTS   471

Introduction

horr•ĕō –ēre –ŭī *vt* to dread; to shudder at, shrink from; to be amazed at; *vi* to stand on end, stand up straight; to get gooseflesh; to shiver, tremble, quake, shake; to look frightful, be rough.

To tremble, to get gooseflesh, to feel the hair on one's neck stand on end: these are some of the physical symptoms of the psychological condition called being horrified. From the Latin verb *horrere*, "horror" is more than "fear" or "dread." Horror is a painful awareness of—and acute sensitivity to—the penetrability and thus fragility of our skin: the realization of just how breachable that thin membrane is between the inside and outside of our bodies. We do not typically think about our pulsing hearts, or the quivering pinkness of our glistening viscera. We repress these images, tuck them away in our minds. We stroll cheerfully through daily life—or plod cluelessly, depending on who we are—forgetting to the best of our ability the fleshy world beneath our skin. Horror shatters this forgetfulness. Whether it comes in the form of a violent film, or the evening news, or a grisly car accident we pass in slow motion on our evening commute, horror reminds us that we are, in the end, *meat*.

Not all horror is so bodily. Even the most abstract or metaphysical experiences of horror, however, communicate a sense of crossed or unstable boundaries, a feeling of disorientation or uncanniness, a sense that what was once far away is now close by, or what was once up is now down, or what was once seemingly dead is now all-too-alive, all-too-present. Horror undermines our ease and complacency. It discombobulates us. We feel tense and defensive. Sometimes we turn and run. So terribly deformed was Joseph Merrick, for instance, the Victorian man who was known commonly as the "Elephant Man," and so unrecognizable as human was his face, that trained nurses who had seen it all in their long careers dropped their trays, screamed, and fled when they entered his hospital room for the first time. Merrick was in his mid-twenties when someone, for the first time in his life, smiled at him upon meeting him. So unprepared was he for this smile, for a gesture of kindness that most of us take for granted, that he began sobbing uncontrollably.

That so many Victorian writers and thinkers were fascinated by sensations of spatial and temporal disorientation, by a creeping of the flesh, is due to the fact that the nineteenth century in Great Britain was a time of political, demographic, scientific, cultural, and economic change. Opportunities for horror abounded. Old boundaries blurred and were redrawn. Ancient orders collapsed. Customs died. The world seemed to many to be spinning toward an unfamiliar future. The population of Great Britain, the first industrialized nation on earth, grew at an unprecedented rate; millions of people moved to crowded, unsanitary cities to work in the new manufacturing sector. Extreme poverty, exacerbated by periods of high unemployment and political unrest, existed in proximity to flourishing wealth, to a politically and culturally ascendant middle class, with its disposable income, its moralism and materialism, anxiety and ease. Having fully recovered from the loss of its American colonies in the eighteenth century, Great Britain became, in the wake of its victory over Napoleonic France, the world's foremost military and economic power, transforming itself, by century's end, into the largest and most powerful empire the world had ever seen. By the 1890s, one in every four acres of land on earth was under the British flag; one in every four people on the planet was a British subject. Scientific discoveries and technological innovations—the railroad, photography, telegraphy, for instance, or Darwin's theory of evolution—transformed the country's physical landscape and the geography of the mind, jolting the Victorians into a new world of possibilities and threats. The old narratives—those binding agents that once held society together—seemed to dissolve before their eyes.

The disenchanting and exhilarating sensation of modernity is comparable to feeling out of place. The ground has shifted—and is shifting still—beneath one's feet. Karl Marx described life in the nineteenth century as a queasy state in which "all that is solid melts into air." Looking around in the mid-1880s at an England he barely recognized, so unlike the "old days," Victorian cultural critic John Ruskin likened the modern world to a monstrous, unnatural "storm-cloud" on the horizon, a meteorological phenomenon he had never seen before. Writing in the early twentieth century, E. F. Benson described this storm from the inside. He compares memories of his Victorian childhood to "glimpses seen through the window by night when lightning is about": "The flash leaps out without visible cause or warning, and the blackness lifts for a second revealing the scene, the criss-cross of the rods of rain, the trees shining with moisture, the colours in the flower-beds, and then darkness like a lid snapped down hides all till the next flash flickers." The monsters that creep through Victorian literature are metaphors for the deformities wrought on the Victorian psyche by modernity: misfit thoughts, a lost sense of community, insatiable new capitalist appetites. Likewise, the myriad ghosts that haunt Victorian literature suggest a state of cultural and psychological flux, a porous border between past and present, between this world and the next.

If the Victorians mourned the loss of the old, looked with trepidation upon the rapid approach of the unknown, they also found their footing on the undulant surface of modern life. They survived and flourished. Victorian modernity is an unlikely confection of optimism and anxiety. Masters of the seas and the earth, the Victorians set a tone that persists to this day, shaping in important ways our own globalized world. They saw themselves as reformers, as fixers of a broken world. The idea of "fixing" is a particularly Victorian idea. It suggests repair and renovation, a can-do attitude: world-historical confidence in one's ability to save the world. It also suggests, however, a desire to arrest or control, to regulate or lay down the law, to chase that upstart spirit, chaos, into the shadows. On an increasingly discordant and complex planet, the Victorians sought—with good intentions and with bad—to produce a stabilizing sense of the normal. If they seem to strive a bit too earnestly at times for truth, for epistemological and philosophical certainty, that is because the truths on which they once relied had turned to dust before their eyes, like a corpse in an unsealed tomb.

The Victorians are famous for policing themselves and everyone else, for policing culture and desire, for policing the world. They sought to put everything in its rightful place. They are credited by some with inventing, popularizing, and disseminating—through education, popular culture, political and scientific discourse, and though commonsense—the concept of the normal. Whereas order was once maintained in society through violence or through the unspoken threat of violence, the Victorian middle class attempted to stabilize society, philosopher Michel Foucault suggests, with a far more effective instrument of control: the imperative that one be normal. Socialization became synonymous with normalization. A normalized individual polices herself, measures herself against a norm, conforms. In normalization, we internalize the norm, take it to heart, and make it a cherished part of ourselves. The criminal, the misfit, the oddball, and the freak: the Victorians did not punish or ostracize these people. They used them to define, refine, and ultimately to codify the normal. These people became the exceptions that proved the rule. Just as a disease teaches doctors the nature of health and the workings of the body, so criminal behavior taught Victorian criminologists how successful socialization works. The normalizing impulse in modern culture, then, can be traced to a political and emotional need on our part to find our footing, to orient ourselves, in a world in which "all that is solid melts into air." If the normal is a reassuring concept, it is also a paranoid one. At the root of all horror is a hunger for normality, for the reassurance it provides, for the stability it promises.

The two volumes that comprise *Crime and Horror in Victorian Literature and Culture* offer readers a chance to gaze at the Victorian psyche, at that mixture of paranoia and confidence with which English, Scottish, and Irish writers faced the nineteenth century, made sense of the horror they could not fully repress, the normality they could not quite achieve. Together, these volumes contain one novel, two plays, three novellas, nine short stories, twenty-two poems, and numerous contextualizing examples of nineteenth-century journalism, social criticism, criminology, memoirs, excerpts, and government reports. In a project of this scope, one must abandon the fantasy of a comprehensive account of crime and horror in Victorian literature and culture. For every text included, four or five had to be excluded. Instead, I have opted to provide readers with eight "footholds" in the period, entry points into themes or topics that captivated the Victorian imagination, triggered the sensation of horror, an unsettling awareness of porous or transgressed boundaries. These include: the slum, the criminal essence, the heavy hand of the law, prostitution, monstrosity, hauntedness, chaos, and death. *Crime and Horror in Victorian Literature and Culture* contains numerous voices. Some are familiar: Charles Dickens, Robert Louis Stevenson, Christina Rossetti, and Arthur Conan Doyle. Other voices, however, have been forgotten or neglected in recent years, and are collected here and annotated for the first time in a long time, in some cases, for the first time ever: Octavia Hill, Stanislaus Eric Stenbock, Bithia Mary Croker, among others. I invite readers to explore the varied landscape of Victorian fear. Plunge into its forgotten valleys; scale its daunting heights. For in the twenty-first century, a century shaped in so many ways by the nineteenth, *their* fear is now *our* fear.

A project of this size cannot be accomplished alone. I owe a debt of gratitude to many people. First, I'd like to thank my research assistant Kelly Haigh, who collected biographical data on many of the authors included in this anthology, and who wrote some of the author biographies that follow, as well as portions of others. I am grateful to the staff at University Readers for their commitment to this project and for helping me to complete it expeditiously, especially Mieka Hemesath, Monica Hui, Jessica Knott, Jennifer Bowen, and Toni Villalas. At Harvard University, Rebecca Curtin worked with me to organize and digitize an enormous amount of material, and a Faculty Research Assistance Grant provided the necessary funds. I'd also like to express gratitude to Carol Dell'Amico, Jim Engell, Molly Clark Hillard, Elaine Scarry, Carolyn Williams, Sybil Kaiser, and Ken Urban, for their feedback, assistance, and support.

Part V
Monstrosity

Monos and Daimonos

Edward Bulwer-Lytton

A popular novelist in his day, Edward Bulwer-Lytton (1803–1873) is neglected today. Born in London to a dysfunctional family of means, the debonair Bulwer-Lytton received his education at Cambridge, where he transformed himself into a Byronic playboy, immersing himself in high society, having an affair, at one point, with one of Byron's former mistresses. At twenty-four he married Rosina Doyle Wheeler, a penniless belle. To finance their lavish lifestyle, an increasingly irritable Bulwer-Lytton turned writer, trying his hand, with considerable success, at a variety of novelistic subgenres: the novel of manners, *Pelham* (1828); the Newgate novel, *Paul Clifford* (1830); the historical novel, *The Last Days of Pompeii* (1834); and the domestic idyll, *The Caxtons* (1849). In addition to eleven volumes of poetry and some highly successful plays, Bulwer-Lytton dabbled in science fiction and occult fiction, which led to rumors of his involvement in various secret societies. By the time he embarked on his long career in parliamentary politics, serving first as a Radical and then as a Conservative, eventually becoming Secretary of the Colonies in 1858, Bulwer-Lytton was embroiled in open warfare with his estranged wife, who bitterly attacked him in print, and even heckled him at a campaign rally in 1858, which led to her incarceration in a madhouse for several weeks at his insistence. Plagued by a chronic ear infection contracted earlier in life, from which he gradually became deaf, Bulwer-Lytton died when the infection spread to his brain. The following tale appeared in May 1830 in the *New Monthly Magazine*. In Greek, *monos* means "single"; a *daimon* is an attendant spirit or lesser deity.

I AM English by birth, and my early years were passed in ——; I had neither brothers nor sisters; my mother died when I was in the cradle; and I found my sole companion, tutor, and playmate in my father. He was a younger brother of a noble and ancient house: what induced him to forsake his country and his friends, to abjure all society, and to live in a rock, is a story in itself, which has nothing to do with mine.

As the Lord liveth, I believe the tale that I shall tell you will have sufficient claim on your attention, without calling in the history of another to preface its most exquisite[1] details, or to give interest to its most amusing events. I said my father lived on a rock—the whole country round seemed nothing but rock!—wastes, bleak, blank, dreary; trees stunted, herbage blasted; caverns, through which some black and wild stream (that never knew star or sunlight, but through rare and hideous chasms of the huge stones above it) went dashing and howling on its *blessed* course; vast cliffs, covered with eternal snows, where the birds of prey lived, and sent, in screams and discordance, a grateful and meet[2] music to the heavens, which seemed too cold and barren to wear even clouds upon their wan, grey, comfortless expanse: these made the characters of that country where the spring of my life sickened itself away. The climate which, in the milder parts of —— relieves the nine months of winter with three months of an abrupt and autumnless summer, never seemed to vary in the gentle and sweet region in which *my* home was placed. Perhaps, for a brief interval, the snow in the valleys melted, and the streams swelled, and a blue, ghastly, unnatural kind of vegetation, seemed here and there to mix with the rude lichen, or scatter a grim smile over minute particles of the universal rock; but to these witnesses of the changing season were the summers of my boyhood confined. My father was addicted to the sciences—the physical sciences—and possessed but a moderate share of learning in any thing else; he taught me all he knew; and the rest of my education, Nature, in a savage and stern guise, instilled in my heart by silent but deep lessons. She taught my feet to bound, and my arm to smite; she breathed life into my passions, and shed darkness over my temper; she taught me to cling to her, even in her most rugged and unalluring form, and to shrink from all else—from the companionship of man, and the soft smiles of woman, and the shrill voice of childhood; and the ties, and hopes, and socialities, and objects of human existence, as from a torture and a curse. Even in that sullen rock, and beneath that ungenial sky, I had luxuries unknown to the palled tastes of cities, or to those who woo delight in an air of odours and in a land of roses! What were those luxuries? They had a myriad varieties and shades of enjoyment—they had but a common name. What were those luxuries? *Solitude!*

---

1   Far-fetched.
2   Fitting.

My father died when I was eighteen; I was transferred to my uncle's protection, and I repaired to London. I arrived there, gaunt and stern, a giant in limbs and strength, and to the tastes of those about me, a savage in bearing and in mood. They would have laughed, but I awed them; they would have altered *me*, but I changed *them*; I threw a damp over their enjoyment and a cloud over their meetings. Though I said little, though I sat with them, estranged and silent, and passive, they seemed to wither beneath my presence. Nobody could live with me and be happy, or at ease! I felt it, and I hated them that they could love not me. Three years passed—I was of age—I demanded my fortune—and scorning social life, and pining once more for loneliness, I resolved to journey into those unpeopled and far lands, which if any have pierced, none have returned to describe. So I took my leave of them all, cousin and aunt—and when I came to my old uncle, who had liked me less than any, I grasped his hand with so friendly a gripe,[1] that, well I ween,[2] the dainty and nice member was but little inclined to its ordinary functions in future.

I commenced my pilgrimage—I pierced the burning sands—I traversed the vast deserts—I came into the enormous woods of Africa, where human step never trod, nor human voice ever started the thrilling and intense solemnity that broods over the great solitudes, as it brooded over chaos before the world was! There the primeval nature springs and perishes; undisturbed and unvaried by the convulsions of the surrounding world; the leaf becomes the tree, lives through its uncounted ages, falls and moulders, and rots and vanishes, unwitnessed in its mighty and mute changes, save by the wandering lion, or the wild ostrich, or that huge serpent—a hundred times more vast than the puny boa that the cold limners of Europe have painted, and whose bones the vain student has preserved, as a miracle and marvel. There, too, as beneath the heavy and dense shade I couched in the scorching noon, I heard the trampling as of an army, and the crush and fall of the strong trees, and beheld through the matted boughs the behemoth[3] pass on its terrible way, with its eyes burning as a sun, and its white teeth arched and glistening in the rabid jaw, as pillars of spar glitter in a cavern; the monster, to whom only those wastes are a home, and who never, since the waters rolled from the Dædal[4] earth, has been given to human gaze and wonder but my own! Seasons glided on, but I counted them not; they were not doled to me by the tokens of man, nor made sick to me by the changes of his base life, and the evidence of his sordid labour. Seasons glided on,

---

1 Grip.
2 Think.
3 An enormous monstrous animal.
4 Intricately designed.

and my youth ripened into manhood, and manhood grew grey with the first frost of age; and then a vague and restless spirit fell upon me, and I said in my foolish heart, "I will look upon the countenances of my race once more!" I retraced my steps—I recrossed the wastes—I re-entered the cities—I took again the garb of man; for I had been hitherto naked in the wilderness, and hair had grown over me as a garment. I repaired to a sea-port, and took ship for England.

In the vessel there was one man, and only one, who neither avoided my companionship nor recoiled at my frown. He was an idle and curious being, full of the frivolities, and egotisms, and importance of them to whom towns are homes, and talk has become a mental aliment.[1] He was one pervading, irritating, offensive tissue of little and low thoughts. The only meanness he had not was fear. It was impossible to awe, to silence, or to shun him. He sought me for ever; he was as a blister to me, which no force could tear away; my soul grew faint when my eyes met him. He was to my sight as those creatures which from their very loathsomeness are fearful as well as despicable to us. I longed and yearned to strangle him when he addressed me! Often I would have laid my hand on him, and hurled him into the sea to the sharks, which, lynx-eyed and eager-jawed, swam night and day around our ship; but the gaze of many was on us, and I curbed myself, and turned away, and shut my eyes in very sickness; and when I opened them again, lo! He was by my side, and his sharp quick voice grated, in its prying, and asking, and torturing accents, on my loathing and repugnant[2] ear! One night I was roused from my sleep by the screams and oaths of men, and I hastened on deck: we had struck upon a rock. It was a ghastly, but, oh Christ! how glorious a sight! Moonlight still and calm—the sea sleeping in sapphires; and in the midst of the silent and soft repose of all things, three hundred and fifty souls were to perish from the world! I sat apart, and looked on, and aided not. A voice crept like an adder's hiss upon my ear; I turned, and saw my tormentor; the moonlight fell on his face, and it grinned with the maudlin grin of intoxication, and his pale blue eye glistened and he said, "We will not part even here!" My blood ran coldly through my veins, and I would have thrown him into the sea, which now came fast and fast upon us; *but the moonlight was on him, and I did not dare to kill him.* But I would not stay to perish with the herd, and I threw myself alone from the vessel and swam towards a rock. I saw a shark dart after me, but I shunned him, and the moment after he had plenty to sate his maw. I heard a crash, and a mingled and wild burst of anguish, the anguish of three hundred and

---

1   Sustenance.
2   Resistant.

fifty hearts that a minute afterwards were stilled, and I said in my *own* heart, with a deep joy, "*His* voice is with the rest, and we *have* parted!" I gained the shore, and lay down to sleep.

The next morning my eyes opened upon a land more beautiful than a Grecian's dreams. The sun had just risen, and laughed over streams of silver, and trees bending with golden and purple fruits, and the diamond dew sparkled from a sod covered with flowers, whose faintest breath was a delight. Ten thousand birds, with all the hues of a northern rainbow blended in their glorious and glowing wings, rose from turf and tree, and loaded the air with melody and gladness; the sea, without a vestige of the past destruction upon its glassy brow, murmured at my feet; the heavens without a cloud, and bathed in a liquid and radiant light, sent their breezes as a blessing to my cheek. I rose with a refreshed and light heart; I traversed the new home I had found; I climbed upon a high mountain, and saw that I was in a small island—it had no trace of man—and my heart swelled as I gazed around and cried loud in my exultation, "I shall be alone again!" I descended the hill: I had not yet reached its foot, when I saw the figure of a man approaching towards me. I looked at him, and my heart misgave me. He drew nearer, and I saw that my despicable persecutor had escaped the waters, and now stood before me. He came up with his hideous grin, and his twinkling eye; and he flung his arms round me,—I would sooner have felt the slimy folds of the serpent—and said, with his grating and harsh voice, "Ha! ha! my friend, we shall be together still!" I looked at him with a grim brow, but I said not a word. There was a great cave by the shore, and I walked down and entered it, and the man followed me. "We shall live so happily here," said he; "we will never separate!" And my lip trembled, and my hand clenched of its own accord. It was now noon, and hunger came upon me; I went forth and killed a deer, and I brought it home and broiled part of it on a fire of fragrant wood; and the man eat, and crunched, and laughed, and I wished that the bones had choked him; and he said, when we had done, "We shall have rare cheer here!" But I still held my peace. At last he stretched himself in a corner of the cave and slept. I looked at him, and saw that the slumber was heavy, and I went out and rolled a huge stone to the mouth of the cavern, and took my way to the opposite part of the island; it was my turn to laugh then! I found out another cavern; and I made a bed of moss and of leaves, and I wrought a table of wood, and I looked out from the mouth of the cavern and saw the wide seas before me, and I said, "Now I shall be alone!"

When the next day came, I again went out and caught a kid, and brought it in, and prepared it as before, but I was not hungered, and I could not eat, so I roamed forth and wandered over the island: the sun had nearly set when I returned. I entered the cavern, and sitting on my bed and by my table was that man whom I thought I had left buried alive in the other cave. He laughed when he saw me, and laid down the bone he was gnawing.

"Ha, ha!" said he, "you would have served me a rare trick, but there was a hole in the cave which you did not see, and I got out to seek you. It was not a difficult matter, for the island is so small; and now we *have* met, and we will part no more!"

I said to the man, "Rise, and follow me!" So he rose, and I saw that of all my food he had left only the bones. "Shall this thing reap and I sow?" thought I, and my heart felt to me like iron.

I ascended a tall cliff: "Look round, said I; "you see that stream which divides the island; you shall dwell on one side, and I on the other; but the same spot shall not hold us, nor the same feast supply!"

"That may never be!" quoth the man; "for I cannot catch the deer, not spring upon the mountain kid; and if you feed me not, I shall starve!"

"Are there not fruits," said I, "and birds that you may snare, and fishes which the sea throws up?"

"But I like them not," quoth the man, and laughed, "so well as the flesh of kids and deer!"

"Look, then," said I, "look: by that grey stone, upon the opposite side of the stream, I will lay a deer or a kid daily, so that you may have the food you covet; but if ever you cross the stream and come into my kingdom, so sure as the sea murmurs, and the bird flies, I will kill you!"

I descended the cliff, and led the man to the side of the stream. "I cannot swim," said he; so I took him on my shoulders and crossed the brook, and I found him out a cave, and I made him a bed and a table like my own, and left him. When I was on my own side of the stream again, I bounded with joy, and lifted up my voice; "I shall be alone *now!*" said I.

So two days passed, and I *was* alone. On the third I went after my prey; the noon was hot, and I was wearied when I returned. I entered my cavern, and behold the man lay stretched upon my bed. "Ha, ha!" said he, "here I am; I was so lonely at home that I have come to live with you again!"

I frowned on the man with a dark brow, and I said, "So sure as the sea murmurs, and the bird flies, I will kill you!" I seized him in my arms; I plucked him from my bed; I took him out into the open air, and we stood together on the smooth sand, and by the great sea. A fear came suddenly upon me; I was struck with the awe of the still Spirit which reigns over solitude. Had a thousand been round us, I would have slain him before them all. I feared now because we were alone in the desert, with silence and GOD! I relaxed my hold. "Swear," I said, "never to molest me again: swear to preserve unpassed the boundary of our several homes, and I will *not* kill you!" "I cannot swear," answered the man; "I would sooner die than forswear the blessed human face—even though that face be my enemy's!"

At these words my rage returned; I dashed the man to the ground, and I put my foot upon his breast, and my hand upon his neck, and he struggled for a moment—and was dead! I was startled; and as I looked upon his face I thought it seemed to revive; I thought the cold blue eye fixed upon me, and the vile grin returned to the livid mouth, and the hands which in the death-pang had grasped the sand, stretched themselves out to me. So I stamped on the breast again, and I dug a hole in the shore, and I buried the body. "And now," said I, "I am alone at last!" And then *the sense of loneliness*, the vague, vast, comfortless, objectless sense of desolation passed into me. And I shook—shook in every limb of my giant frame, as if I had been a child that trembles in the dark; and my hair rose, and my blood crept, and I would not have stayed in that spot a moment more if I had been made young again for it. I turned away and fled—fled round the whole island; and gnashed my teeth when I came to the sea, and longed to be cast into some illimitable desert, that I might flee on for ever. At sunset I returned to my cave—I sat myself down on one corner of the bed, and covered my face with my hands—I thought I heard a noise; I raised my eyes, and, as I live, I saw on the other end of the bed the man whom I had slain and buried. There he sat, six feet from me, and nodded to me, and looked at me with his wan eyes, and laughed. I rushed from the cave—I entered a wood—I threw myself down—there opposite to me, six feet from my face, was the face of that man again! And my courage rose, and I spoke, but he answered not. I attempted to seize him, he glided from my grasp, and was still opposite, six feet from me as before. I flung myself on the ground, and pressed my face to the sod, and would not look up till the night came on and darkness was over the earth. I then rose and returned to the cave; I laid down on my bed, and the man lay down by me; and I frowned and tried to seize him as before, but I could not, and I closed my eyes, *and the man lay by me*. Day passed on day and it was the same. At board, at bed, at home and abroad, in my uprising and my down-sitting, by day and at night, there, by my bed-side, six feet from me, and no more, was that ghastly and dead thing. And I said, as I looked upon the beautiful land and the still heavens, and then turned to that fearful comrade, "I shall never be alone again!" And the man laughed.

At last a ship came, and I hailed it—it took me up, and I thought, as I put my foot on the deck, "I shall escape from my tormentor!" As I thought so, I saw him climb the deck too, and I strove to push him down into the sea, but in vain; he was by my side, *and he fed and slept with me as before!* I came home to my native land! I forced myself into crowds—I went to the feast, and I heard music—and I made thirty men sit with me, and watch by day and by night. So I had thirty-*one* companions, and one was more social than all the rest.

At last I said to myself, "This is a delusion, and a cheat[1] of the external senses, and the thing is *not*, save in my mind. I with consult those skilled in such disorders, and I will be—*alone again!*"

I summoned one celebrated in purging from the mind's eye its films and deceits—I bound him by an oath to secrecy—and I told him my tale. He was a bold man and a learned, and he promised me relief and release.

"Where is the figure now?" said he, smiling; "I see it not."

And I answered, "It is six feet from us!"

"I see it not," said he again; "and if it were real, my senses would not receive the image less palpably than yours." And he spoke to me as schoolmen speak. I did not argue nor reply, but I ordered the servants to prepare a room, and to cover the floor with a thick layer of sand. When it was done, I bade the Leech[2] follow me into the room, and I barred the door. "Where is the figure now?" repeated he; and I said, "Six feet from us as before!" And the Leech smiled. "Look on the floor," said I, and I pointed to the spot; "what see you?" And the Leech shuddered, and clung to me that he might not fall. "The sand," said he, "was smooth when we entered, and now I see on that spot the print of human feet!"

And I laughed, and dragged my *living* companion on; "See," said I, "where we move what follows us!"

The Leech gasped for breath; "The print," said he, "of those human feet!"

"Can you not minister to me then?" cried I, in a sudden and fierce agony, "and must I *never* be alone again?"

And I saw the feet of the dead thing trace one word upon the sand; and the word was—NEVER.

---

1 Trick.
2 Physician.

GOBLIN MARKET

CHRISTINA ROSSETTI

The youngest child of an Italian political exile living in England, Christina Rossetti (1830–1894) and her three siblings grew up in a bilingual household steeped in art, culture, and politics. The creative energy and excitement that illuminated Rossetti's childhood was subdued in her adolescence, however, when her father's health declined and the family faced financial difficulties. Rossetti devoted herself increasingly to religion—she broke off two marriage engagements due to irreconcilable religious differences—and became involved in the Anglo-Catholic movement within the Church of England. Her first volume of poetry, *Goblin Market and Other Poems* (1862) reflects both her early artistic exuberance and her spiritual gravity. "Goblin Market" presents itself as a vigorous children's fable but also expresses Rossetti's sober preoccupation with the problems of temptation, sin, and salvation. Other collections followed, including *The Prince's Progress and Other Poems* (1866), *Sing-Song* (1879), and *A Pageant and Other Poems* (1881), which included her famous sonnet sequence, "Monna Innominata." In the final years of her life, Rossetti focused her creative energies, for the most part, on devotional poetry. Throughout her career, however, she explored issues of gender and the sexual exploitation of women, working for a time with "fallen women" at the Highgate Penitentiary. She also criticized members of the Pre-Raphaelite Brotherhood, which her notoriously sensual brother, Dante Gabriel Rossetti, co-founded, for the stagnant conventionality of their depictions of women in art. With a grim lack of confidence in her own prospects for salvation, Rossetti, who contracted Graves' disease in 1871, succumbed to breast cancer at the age of sixty-four.

Morning and evening
Maids heard the goblins cry:
"Come buy our orchard fruits,
Come buy, come buy:
Apples and quinces,
Lemons and oranges,
Plump unpecked[1] cherries,
Melons and raspberries,
Bloom-down-cheeked peaches,
Swart-headed[2] mulberries,   10
Wild free-born cranberries,
Crab-apples, dewberries,[3]
Pine-apples, blackberries,
Apricots, strawberries;—
All ripe together
In summer weather,—
Morns that pass by,
Fair eves that fly;
Come buy, come buy;
Our grapes fresh from the vine,   20
Pomegranates full and fine,
Dates and sharp bullaces,[4]
Rare pears and greengages,[5]
Damsons and bilberries,[6]
Taste them and try:
Currants and gooseberries,
Bright-fire-like barberries,[7]
Figs to fill your mouth,

---

1 Unpitted.
2 Black-headed.
3 Similar to the blackberry.
4 Wild plums.
5 Green plums.
6 Similar to blueberries.
7 Similar to boysenberries.

Citrons[1] from the South,
Sweet to tongue and sound to eye;   30
Come buy, come buy."

Evening by evening
Among the brookside rushes,[2]
Laura bowed her head to hear,
Lizzie veiled her blushes:
Crouching close together
In the cooling weather,
With clasping arms and cautioning lips,
With tingling cheeks and finger tips.
"Lie close," Laura said,   40
Pricking up her golden head:
"We must not look at goblin men,
We must not buy their fruits:
Who knows upon what soil they fed
Their hungry thirsty roots?"
"Come buy," call the goblins
Hobbling down the glen.
"Oh," cried Lizzie, "Laura, Laura,
You should not peep at goblin men."
Lizzie covered up her eyes,   50
Covered close lest they should look;
Laura reared her glossy head,
And whispered like the restless brook:
"Look, Lizzie, look, Lizzie,
Down the glen tramp little men.
One hauls a basket,
One bears a plate,
One lugs a golden dish
Of many pounds weight.
How fair the vine must grow   60
Whose grapes are so luscious;

---

1   Sweet, lemonlike fruits.
2   Bulrushes or cattails.

How warm the wind must blow
Thro' those fruit bushes."
"No," said Lizzie: "No, no, no;
Their offers should not charm us,
Their evil gifts would harm us."
She thrust a dimpled finger
In each ear, shut eyes and ran:
Curious Laura chose to linger
Wondering at each merchant man,   70
One had a cat's face,
One whisked a tail,
One tramped at a rat's pace,
One crawled like a snail,
One like a wombat prowled obtuse and furry,
One like a ratel[1] tumbled hurry skurry.
She heard a voice like voice of doves
Cooing all together:
They sounded kind and full of loves
In the pleasant weather.   80

Laura stretched her gleaming neck
Like a rush-imbedded swan,
Like a lily from the beck,[2]
Like a moonlit poplar branch,
Like a vessel at the launch
When its last restraint is gone.

Backwards up the mossy glen
Turned and trooped the goblin men,
With their shrill repeated cry,
"Come buy, come buy."   90
When they reached where Laura was
They stood stock still upon the moss,
Leering at each other,

---

1 Badgerlike animal.
2 Stream.

Brother and queer brother;
Signalling each other,
Brother with sly brother.
One set his basket down,
One reared his plate;
One began to weave a crown
Of tendrils, leaves and rough nuts brown   100
(Men sell not such in any town);
One heaved the golden weight
Of dish and fruit to offer her:
"Come buy, come buy," was still their cry.
Laura stared but did not stir,
Longed but had no money:
The whisk-tailed merchant bade her taste
In tones as smooth as honey,
The cat-faced purr'd,
The rat-paced spoke a word   110
Of welcome, and the snail-paced even was heard;
One parrot-voiced and jolly
Cried "Pretty Goblin" still for "Pretty Polly;"—
One whistled like a bird.

But sweet-tooth Laura spoke in haste:
"Good folk, I have no coin;
To take were to purloin:
I have no copper in my purse,
I have no silver either,
And all my gold is on the furze[1]   120
That shakes in windy weather
Above the rusty heather."
"You have much gold upon your head,"
They answered all together:
"Buy from us with a golden curl."
She clipped a precious golden lock,
She dropped a tear more rare than pearl,

---

1 Yellow-flowered shrub.

Then sucked their fruit globes fair or red:
Sweeter than honey from the rock.¹
Stronger than man-rejoicing wine,   130
Clearer than water flowed that juice;
She never tasted such before,
How should it cloy with length of use?
She sucked and sucked and sucked the more
Fruits which that unknown orchard bore;
She sucked until her lips were sore;
Then flung the emptied rinds away
But gathered up one kernel-stone,
And knew not was it night or day
As she turned home alone.   140

Lizzie met her at the gate
Full of wise upbraidings:
"Dear, you should not stay so late,
Twilight is not good for maidens;
Should not loiter in the glen
In the haunts of goblin men.
Do you not remember Jeanie,²
How she met them in the moonlight,
Took their gifts both choice and many,
Ate their fruits and wore their flowers   150
Plucked from bowers
Where summer ripens at all hours?
But ever in the noonlight
She pined and pined away;
Sought them by night and day,
Found them no more but dwindled and grew grey;
Then fell with the first snow,
While to this day no grass will grow
Where she lies low:

---

1   "He made him ride on the high places of the earth, that he might eat the increase of the fields; and he made him to suck honey out of the rock, and oil out of the flinty rock" (Deuteronomy 32:13).
2   Pronounced "Jenny."

  I planted daisies[1] there a year ago   160
That never blow.
You should not loiter so."
"Nay, hush," said Laura:
"Nay, hush, my sister:
I ate and ate my fill,
Yet my mouth waters still;
Tomorrow night I will
Buy more:" and kissed her:
"Have done with sorrow;
I'll bring you plums tomorrow   170
Fresh on their mother twigs,
Cherries worth getting;
You cannot think what figs
My teeth have met in,
What melons icy-cold
Piled on a dish of gold
Too huge for me to hold,
What peaches with a velvet nap,[2]
Pellucid grapes without one seed:
Odorous indeed must be the mead[3]   180
Whereon they grow, and pure the wave they drink
With lilies at the brink,
And sugar-sweet their sap."

Golden head by golden head,
Like two pigeons in one nest
Folded in each other's wings,
They lay down in their curtained bed:
Like two blossoms on one stem,
Like two flakes of new-fall'n snow,
Like two wands of ivory   190
Tipped with gold for awful[4] kings.

---

1 The daisy is a traditional symbol of innocence.
2 Fuzzy surface.
3 Meadow.
4 Commanding awe.

Moon and stars gazed in at them,
Wind sang to them lullaby,
Lumbering owls forbore to fly,
Not a bat flapped to and fro
Round their rest:
Cheek to cheek and breast to breast
Locked together in one nest.

Early in the morning
When the first cock crowed his warning, 200
Neat like bees, as sweet and busy,
Laura rose with Lizzie:
Fetched in honey, milked the cows,
Aired and set to rights the house,
Kneaded cakes of whitest wheat,
Cakes for dainty mouths to eat,
Next churned butter, whipped up cream,
Fed their poultry, sat and sewed;
Talked as modest maidens should:
Lizzie with an open heart, 210
Laura in an absent dream,
One content, one sick in part;
One warbling for the mere bright day's delight,
One longing for the night.

At length slow evening came:
They went with pitchers to the reedy brook;
Lizzie most placid in her look,
Laura most like a leaping flame.
They drew the gurgling water from its deep;
Lizzie plucked purple and rich golden flags,[1] 220
Then turning homewards said: "The sunset flushes
Those furthest loftiest crags;
Come, Laura, not another maiden lags,
No willful squirrel wags,

---

1   Irises.

The beasts and birds are fast asleep."
But Laura loitered still among the rushes
And said the bank was steep.

And said the hour was early still,
The dew not fall'n, the wind not chill:
Listening ever, but not catching 230
The customary cry,
"Come buy, come buy,"
With its iterated jingle
Of sugar-baited words:
Not for all her watching
Once discerning even one goblin
Racing, whisking, tumbling, hobbling;
Let alone the herds
That used to tramp along the glen,
In groups or single, 240
Of brisk fruit-merchant men.
Till Lizzie urged, "O Laura, come;
I hear the fruit-call but I dare not look:
You should not loiter longer at this brook:
Come with me home.
The stars rise, the moon bends her arc,
Each glowworm winks her spark,
Let us get home before the night grows dark:
For clouds may gather
Tho' this is summer weather, 250
Put out the lights and drench us thro';
Then if we lost our way what should we do?"

Laura turned cold as stone
To find her sister heard that cry alone,
That goblin cry,
"Come buy our fruits, come buy."
Must she then buy no more such dainty fruit?

Must she no more such succous[1] pasture find,
Gone deaf and blind?
Her tree of life drooped from the root: 260
She said not one word in her heart's sore ache;
But peering thro' the dimness, nought discerning,
Trudged home, her pitcher dripping all the way;
So crept to bed, and lay
Silent till Lizzie slept;
Then sat up in a passionate yearning,
And gnashed her teeth for baulked[2] desire, and wept
As if her heart would break.

Day after day, night after night,
Laura kept watch in vain 270
In sullen silence of exceeding pain.
She never caught again the goblin cry:
"Come buy, come buy;"—
She never spied the goblin men
Hawking their fruits along the glen:
But when the noon waxed bright
Her hair grew thin and grey;
She dwindled, as the fair full moon doth turn
To swift decay and burn
Her fire away. 280

One day remembering her kernel-stone
She set it by a wall that faced the south;
Dewed it with tears, hoped for a root,
Watched for a waxing shoot,
But there came none;
It never saw the sun,
It never felt the trickling moisture run:
While with sunk eyes and faded mouth
She dreamed of melons, as a traveller sees

---

1 Succulent.
2 Balked.

False waves in desert drouth 290
With shade of leaf-crowned trees,
And burns the thirstier in the sandful breeze.

She no more swept the house,
Tended the fowls or cows,
Fetched honey, kneaded cakes of wheat,
Brought water from the brook:
But sat down listless in the chimney-nook
And would not eat.

Tender Lizzie could not bear
To watch her sister's cankerous care 300
Yet not to share.
She night and morning
Caught the goblins' cry:
"Come buy our orchard fruits,
Come buy, come buy:"—
Beside the brook, along the glen,
She heard the tramp of goblin men,
The voice and stir
Poor Laura could not hear;
Longed to buy fruit to comfort her, 310
But feared to pay too dear.
She thought of Jeanie in her grave,
Who should have been a bride;
But who for joys brides hope to have
Fell sick and died
In her gay prime,
In earliest Winter time,
With the first glazing rime,[1]
With the first snow-fall of crisp Winter time.

Till Laura dwindling 320
Seemed knocking at Death's door:

---

1   Coating of ice.

Then Lizzie weighed no more
Better and worse;
But put a silver penny in her purse,
Kissed Laura, crossed the heath with clumps of furze
At twilight, halted by the brook:
And for the first time in her life
Began to listen and look.

Laughed every goblin
When they spied her peeping: 330
Came towards her hobbling,
Flying, running, leaping,
Puffing and blowing,
Chuckling, clapping, crowing,
Clucking and gobbling,
Mopping and mowing,
Full of airs and graces,
Pulling wry faces,
Demure grimaces,
Cat-like and rat-like, 340
Ratel- and wombat-like,
Snail-paced in a hurry,
Parrot-voiced and whistler,
Helter skelter, hurry skurry,
Chattering like magpies,
Fluttering like pigeons,
Gliding like fishes,—
Hugged her and kissed her,
Squeezed and caressed her:
Stretched up their dishes, 350
Panniers, and plates:
"Look at our apples
Russet and dun,
Bob at our cherries,
Bite at our peaches,
Citrons and dates,
Grapes for the asking,

Pears red with basking
Out in the sun,
Plums on their twigs;   360
Pluck them and suck them,
Pomegranates, figs."—

"Good folk," said Lizzie,
Mindful of Jeanie:
"Give me much and many:"—
Held out her apron,
Tossed them her penny.
"Nay, take a seat with us,
Honour and eat with us,"
They answered grinning: 370
"Our feast is but beginning.
Night yet is early,
Warm and dew-pearly,
Wakeful and starry:
Such fruits as these
No man can carry;
Half their bloom would fly,
Half their dew would dry,
Half their flavour would pass by.
Sit down and feast with us,   380
Be welcome guest with us,
Cheer you and rest with us."—
"Thank you," said Lizzie: "But one waits
At home alone for me:
So without further parleying,
If you will not sell me any
Of your fruits tho' much and many,
Give me back my silver penny
I tossed you for a fee."—
They began to scratch their pates,   390
No longer wagging, purring,
But visibly demurring,
Grunting and snarling.

One called her proud,
Cross-grained, uncivil;
Their tones waxed loud,
Their looks were evil.
Lashing their tails
They trod and hustled her,
Elbowed and jostled her, 400
Clawed with their nails,
Barking, mewing, hissing, mocking,
Tore her gown and soiled her stocking,
Twitched her hair out by the roots,
Stamped upon her tender feet,
Held her hands and squeezed their fruits
Against her mouth to make her eat.

White and golden Lizzie stood,
Like a lily in a flood,—
Like a rock of blue-veined stone 410
Lashed by tides obstreperously,—
Like a beacon left alone
In a hoary roaring sea,
Sending up a golden fire,—
Like a fruit-crowned orange-tree
White with blossoms honey-sweet
Sore beset by wasp and bee,—
Like a royal virgin town
Topped with gilded dome and spire
Close beleaguered by a fleet 420
Mad to tug her standard down.

One may lead a horse to water,
Twenty cannot make him drink.
Tho' the goblins cuffed and caught her,
Coaxed and fought her,
Bullied and besought her,
Scratched her, pinched her black as ink,
Kicked and knocked her,

Mauled and mocked her,
Lizzie uttered nor a word; 430
Would not open lip from lip
Lest they should cram a mouthful in:
But laughed in heart to feel the drip
Of juice that syruped all her face,
And lodged in dimples of her chin,
And streaked her neck which quaked like curd.
At last the evil people
Worn out by her resistance
Flung back her penny, kicked their fruit
Along whichever road they took, 440
Not leaving root or stone or shoot;
Some writhed into the ground,
Some dived into the brook
With ring and ripple,
Some scudded on the gale without a sound,
Some vanished in the distance.

In a smart, ache, tingle,
Lizzie went her way;
Knew not was it night or day;
Sprang up the bank, tore thro' the furze, 450
Threaded copse and dingle,[1]
And heard her penny jingle
Bouncing in her purse,
Its bounce was music to her ear.
She ran and ran
As is she feared some goblin man
Dogged her with gibe or curse
Or something worse:
But not one goblin scurried after,
Nor was she pricked by fear; 460
The kind heart made her windy-paced

---

1 A wooded valley.

That urged her home quite out of breath with haste
And inward laughter.

She cried "Laura," up the garden,
"Did you miss me?
Come and kiss me.
Never mind my bruises,
Hug me, kiss me, suck my juices
Squeezed from goblin fruits for you,
Goblin pulp and goblin dew. 470
Eat me, drink me, love me;[1]
Laura, make much of me:
For your sake I have braved the glen
And had to do with goblin merchant men."

Laura started from her chair,
Flung her arms up in the air,
Clutched her hair:
"Lizzie, Lizzie, have you tasted
For my sake the fruit forbidden?
Must your light like mine be hidden, 480
Your young life like mine be wasted,
Undone in mine undoing
And ruined in my ruin,
Thirsty, cankered, goblin-ridden?"—
She clung about her sister,
Kissed and kissed and kissed her:
Tears once again
Refreshed her shrunken eyes,
Dropping like rain
After long sultry drouth; 490
Shaking with aguish fear, and pain,
She kissed and kissed her with a hungry mouth.

---

1 "Whoso eateth my flesh, and drinketh my blood, hath eternal life; and I will raise him up at the last day" (John 6:54).

Her lips began to scorch,
That juice was wormwood[1] to her tongue,
She loathed the feast:
Writhing as one possessed she leaped and sung,
Rent all her robe, and wrung
Her hands in lamentable haste,
And beat her breast.
Her locks streamed like the torch   500
Borne by a racer at full speed,
Or like the mane of horses in their flight,
Or like an eagle when she stems[2] the light
Straight toward the sun,
Or like a caged thing freed,
Or like a flying flag when armies run.

Swift fire spread thro' her veins, knocked at her heart,
Met the fire smouldering there
And overbore its lesser flame;
She gorged on bitterness without a name: 510
Ah! fool, to choose such part
Of soul-consuming care!
Sense failed in the mortal strife:
Like the watch-tower of a town
Which an earthquake shatters down,
Like a lightning-stricken mast,
Like a wind-uprooted tree
Spun about,
Like a foam-topped waterspout
Cast down headlong in the sea,   520
She fell at last;
Pleasure past and anguish past,
Is it death or is it life?

---

1   A poisonous plant with a bitter oil from which the alcoholic beverage absinthe is made.
2   Makes headway against.

Life out of death.
That night long Lizzie watched by her,
Counted her pulse's flagging stir,
Felt for her breath,
Held water to her lips, and cooled her face
With tears and fanning leaves:
But when the first birds chirped about their eaves,   530
And early reapers plodded to the place
Of golden sheaves,
And dew-wet grass
Bowed in the morning winds so brisk to pass,
And new buds with new day
Opened of cup-like lilies on the stream,
Laura awoke as from a dream,
Laughed in the innocent old way,
Hugged Lizzie but not twice or thrice;
Her gleaming locks showed not one thread of grey   540
Her breath was sweet as May
And light danced in her eyes.

Days, weeks, months, years
Afterwards, when both were wives
With children of their own;
Their mother-hearts beset with fears,
Their lives bound up in tender lives;
Laura would call the little ones
And tell them of her early prime,
Those pleasant days long gone   550
Of not-returning time:
Would talk about the haunted glen,
The wicked, quaint fruit-merchant men,
Their fruits like honey to the throat
But poison in the blood;
(Men sell not such in any town:)
Would tell them how her sister stood,
In deadly peril to do her good,
And win the fiery antidote:

Then joining hands to little hands   560
Would bid them cling together,
"For there is no friend like a sister
In calm or stormy weather;
To cheer one on the tedious way,
To fetch one if one goes astray,
To lift one if one totters down,
To strengthen whilst one stands."

    1859

Strange Case of Dr Jekyll and Mr Hyde

Robert Louis Stevenson

Robert Louis Stevenson (1850–1894) lived an adventurous life in the persistent shadow of death. The son of a prosperous Edinburgh civil engineer, Stevenson developed a severe respiratory illness in childhood, which caused him, from the age of thirty, to spit blood. Noted for his lanky figure, his flamboyant garb, and his Bohemian air, Stevenson travelled the world—Western Europe, California, Hawaii, and the South Pacific—in pursuit of a climate conducive to health, and devoting his professional energies to literature, to the initial frustration of his parents. A versatile and innovative writer, Stevenson is the author of travel narratives, poetry, essays, novels, and numerous short stories, of which he is considered a master. His short story triptych "The Suicide Club" was published in 1882 in his collection *New Arabian Nights*. After a halting start, his literary reputation was made with *Treasure Island* (1883), the Scottish adventure novel *Kidnapped* (1886), and *Strange Case of Dr. Jekyll and Mr. Hyde* (1886), his famous tale of split identity. After marrying Fanny Osbourne in 1880, an American divorcée ten years his senior, Stevenson returned to Scotland, moving next to Switzerland and France, then England. Upon the advice of his physician, however, he left England for good in 1887, eventually settling in Samoa, where he turned his literary and political attentions to Polynesian culture, adopting a Samoan name, and becoming a fierce critic of European imperialism.

TO
KATHARINE DE MATTOS[1]

It's ill to loose the bands that God decreed to bind;
Still will we be the children of the heather and the wind.
Far away from home, O it's still for you and me
That the broom is blowing bonnie in the north countrie.[2]

Story of the Door

Mr. Utterson the lawyer was a man of a rugged countenance, that was never lighted by a smile; cold, scanty and embarrassed in discourse; backward in sentiment; lean, long, dusty, dreary and yet somehow lovable. At friendly meetings, and when the wine was to his taste, something eminently human beaconed from his eye; something indeed which never found its way into his talk, but which spoke not only in these silent symbols of the after-dinner face, but more often and loudly in the acts of his life. He was austere with himself; drank gin when he was alone, to mortify a taste for vintages; and though he enjoyed the theatre, had not crossed the doors of one for twenty years. But he had an approved tolerance for others; sometimes wondering, almost with envy, at the high pressure of spirits involved in their misdeeds; and in any extremity inclined to help rather than to reprove. "I incline to Cain's heresy,"[3] he used to say quaintly: "I let my brother go to the devil in his own way." In this character, it was frequently his fortune to be the last reputable acquaintance and the last good influence in the lives of down-going men. And to such as these, so long as they came about his chambers, he never marked a shade of change in his demeanour.

---

1 Stevenson's cousin. The poem is Stevenson's own.
2 That the broom (a flowering shrub) is blooming prettily in the Scottish Highlands.
3 Cain, the son of Adam and Eve, murders his younger brother Abel in a fit of jealousy. Asked by God where his brother might be, Cain snaps, "Am I my brother's keeper?" (Genesis 4:9). Cain's "heresy" refers, in Utterson's case, not to fratricide or to a lack of respect for God, but to feeling apathetic about the fate of one's fellow man.

No doubt the feat was easy to Mr. Utterson; for he was undemonstrative at the best, and even his friendships seemed to be founded in a similar catholicity[1] of good-nature. It is the mark of a modest man to accept his friendly circle readymade from the hands of opportunity; and that was the lawyer's way. His friends were those of his own blood or those whom he had known the longest; his affections, like ivy, were the growth of time, they implied no aptness in the object. Hence, no doubt, the bond that united him to Mr. Richard Enfield, his distant kinsman, the well-known man about town. It was a nut to crack for many, what these two could see in each other or what subject they could find in common. It was reported by those who encountered them in their Sunday walks, that they said nothing, looked singularly dull, and would hail with obvious relief the appearance of a friend. For all that, the two men put the greatest store by these excursions, counted them the chief jewel of each week, and not only set aside occasions of pleasure, but even resisted the calls of business, that they might enjoy them uninterrupted.

It chanced on one of these rambles that their way led them down a by-street in a busy quarter of London. The street was small and what is called quiet, but it drove a thriving trade on the week-days. The inhabitants were all doing well, it seemed, and all emulously hoping to do better still, and laying out the surplus of their gains in coquetry; so that the shop fronts stood along that thoroughfare with an air of invitation, like rows of smiling saleswomen. Even on Sunday, when it veiled its more florid charms and lay comparatively empty of passage, the street shone out in contrast to its dingy neighbourhood, like a fire in a forest; and with its freshly painted shutters, well-polished brasses, and general cleanliness and gaiety of note, instantly caught and pleased the eye of the passenger.

Two doors from one corner, on the left hand going east, the line was broken by the entry of a court; and just at that point, a certain sinister block of building thrust forward its gable on the street. It was two storeys high; showed no window, nothing but a door on the lower storey and a blind forehead of discoloured wall on the upper; and bore in every feature, the marks of prolonged and sordid negligence. The door, which was equipped with neither bell nor knocker, was blistered and distained. Tramps slouched into the recess and struck matches on the panels; children kept shop upon the steps; the schoolboy had tried his knife on the mouldings; and for close on a generation, no one had appeared to drive away these random visitors or to repair their ravages.

---

1   Breadth.

Mr. Enfield and the lawyer were on the other side of the by-street; but when they came abreast of the entry, the former lifted up his cane and pointed.

"Did you ever remark that door?" he asked; and when his companion had replied in the affirmative, "It is connected in my mind," added he, "with a very odd story."

"Indeed?" said Mr. Utterson, with a slight change of voice, "and what was that?"

"Well, it was this way," returned Mr. Enfield: "I was coming home from some place at the end of the world, about three o'clock of a black winter morning, and my way lay through a part of town where there was literally nothing to be seen but lamps. Street after street, and all the folks asleep—street after street, all lighted up as if for a procession and all as empty as a church—till at last I got into that state of mind when a man listens and listens and begins to long for the sight of a policeman. All at once, I saw two figures: one a little man who was stumping along eastward at a good walk, and the other a girl of maybe eight or ten who was running as hard as she was able down a cross street. Well, sir, the two ran into one another naturally enough at the corner; and then came the horrible part of the thing; for the man trampled calmly over the child's body and left her screaming on the ground. It sounds nothing to hear, but it was hellish to see. It wasn't like a man; it was like some damned Juggernaut.[1] I gave a view halloa,[2] took to my heels, collared my gentleman, and brought him back to where there was already quite a group about the screaming child. He was perfectly cool and made no resistance, but gave me one look, so ugly that it brought out the sweat on me like running. The people who had turned out were the girl's own family; and pretty soon, the doctor, for whom she had been sent, put in his appearance. Well, the child was not much the worse, more frightened, according to the Sawbones;[3] and there you might have supposed would be an end to it. But there was one curious circumstance. I had taken a loathing to my gentleman at first sight. So had the child's family, which was only natural. But the doctor's case was what struck me. He was the usual cut and dry apothecary, of no particular age and colour, with a strong Edinburgh accent, and about as emotional as a bagpipe. Well, sir, he was like the rest of us; every time he looked at my prisoner, I saw that Sawbones turn sick and white with the desire to kill him. I knew what was in his mind, just as he knew what was in mine; and killing being out of the question, we did the next best. We told the man we could and would make such a scandal out of this, as should make his name stink from one end of London to the other. If he had

---

1   Huge, unstoppable force crushing everything in its path.
2   In fox hunting, a "view halloa" is the shout given by a hunter when a fox is spotted darting from the bushes.
3   Slang for "surgeon," or "doctor" more generally.

any friends or any credit, we undertook that he should lose them. And all the time, as we were pitching it in red hot, we were keeping the women off him as best we could, for they were as wild as harpies. I never saw a circle of such hateful faces; and there was the man in the middle, with a kind of black, sneering coolness—frightened too, I could see that—but carrying it off, sir, really like Satan. 'If you choose to make capital out of this accident,' said he, 'I am naturally helpless. No gentleman but wishes to avoid a scene,' says he. 'Name your figure.' Well, we screwed him up to a hundred pounds for the child's family; he would have clearly liked to stick out; but there was something about the lot of us that meant mischief, and at last he struck. The next thing was to get the money; and where do you think he carried us but to that place with the door?—whipped out a key, went in, and presently came back with the matter of ten pounds in gold and a cheque for the balance on Coutts's,[1] drawn payable to bearer and signed with a name that I can't mention, though it's one of the points of my story, but it was a name at least very well known and often printed. The figure was stiff; but the signature was good for more than that, if it was only genuine. I took the liberty of pointing out to my gentleman that the whole business looked apocryphal, and that a man does not, in real life, walk into a cellar door at four in the morning and come out of it with another man's cheque for close upon a hundred pounds. But he was quite easy and sneering. 'Set your mind at rest,' says he, 'I will stay with you till the banks open and cash the cheque myself.' So we all set off, the doctor, and the child's father, and our friend and myself, and passed the rest of the night in my chambers; and next day, when we had breakfasted, went in a body to the bank. I gave in the cheque myself, and said I had every reason to believe it was a forgery. Not a bit of it. The cheque was genuine."

"Tut-tut," said Mr. Utterson.

"I see you feel as I do," said Mr. Enfield. "Yes, it's a bad story. For my man was a fellow that nobody could have to do with, a really damnable man; and the person that drew the cheque is the very pink of the proprieties,[2] celebrated too, and (what makes it worse) one of your fellows who do what they call good. Black mail, I suppose; an honest man paying through the nose for some of the capers of his youth. Black mail House is what I call that place with the door, in consequence. Though even that, you know, is far from explaining all," he added, and with the words fell into a vein of musing.

---

1 Coutts & Co., a highly reputable private bank in Great Britain.
2 Height of respectability.

From this he was recalled by Mr. Utterson asking rather suddenly: "And you don't know if the drawer of the cheque lives there?"

"A likely place isn't it?" returned Mr. Enfield. "But I happen to have noticed his address; he lives in some square or other."

"And you never asked about—the place with the door?" said Mr. Utterson.

"No, sir: I had a delicacy," was the reply. "I feel very strongly about putting questions; it partakes too much of the style of the day of judgment. You start a question, and it's like starting a stone. You sit quietly on the top of a hill; and away the stone goes, starting others; and presently some bland old bird (the last you would have thought of) is knocked on the head in his own back garden and the family have to change their name. No, sir, I make it a rule of mine: the more it looks like Queer Street,[1] the less I ask."

"A very good rule, too," said the lawyer.

"But I have studied the place for myself," continued Mr. Enfield. "It seems scarcely a house. There is no other door, and nobody goes in or out of that one but, once in a great while, the gentleman of my adventure. There are three windows looking on the court on the first floor;[2] none below; the windows are always shut but they're clean. And then there is a chimney which is generally smoking; so somebody must live there. And yet it's not so sure; for the buildings are so packed together about that court, that it's hard to say where one ends and another begins."

The pair walked on again for a while in silence; and then "Enfield," said Mr. Utterson, "that's a good rule of yours."

"Yes, I think it is," returned Enfield.

"But for all that," continued the lawyer, "there's one point I want to ask: I want to ask the name of that man who walked over the child."

"Well," said Mr. Enfield, "I can't see what harm it would do. It was a man of the name of Hyde."

"Hm," said Mr. Utterson. "What sort of a man is he to see?"

"He is not easy to describe. There is something wrong with his appearance; something displeasing, something downright detestable. I never saw a man I so disliked, and yet I scarce know why. He must be deformed somewhere; he gives a strong feeling of deformity, although I couldn't specify the point. He's an extraordinary looking man, and yet I really can name nothing out of the way. No, sir; I can make

---

1   British slang for "in financial difficulties."
2   The floor above the ground floor.

no hand of it; I can't describe him. And it's not want of memory, for I declare I can see him this moment."

Mr. Utterson again walked some way in silence and obviously under a weight of consideration. "You are sure he used a key?" he inquired at last.

"My dear sir …" began Enfield, surprised out of himself.

"Yes, I know," said Utterson; "I know it must seem strange. The fact is, if I do not ask you the name of the other party, it is because I know it already. You see, Richard, your tale has gone home. If you have been inexact in any point, you had better correct it."

"I think you might have warned me," returned the other with a touch of sullenness. "But I have been pedantically exact, as you call it. The fellow had a key; and what's more, he has it still. I saw him use it, not a week ago."

Mr. Utterson sighed deeply but said never a word; and the young man presently resumed. "Here is another lesson to say nothing," said he. "I am ashamed of my long tongue. Let us make a bargain never to refer to this again."

"With all my heart," said the lawyer. "I shake hands on that, Richard."

Search for Mr Hyde

THAT evening, Mr. Utterson came home to his bachelor house in sombre spirits and sat down to dinner without relish. It was his custom of a Sunday, when this meal was over, to sit close by the fire, a volume of some dry divinity[1] on his reading desk, until the clock of the neighbouring church rang out the hour of twelve, when he would go soberly and gratefully to bed. On this night, however, as soon as the cloth was taken away, he took up a candle and went into his business room. There he opened his safe, took from the most private part of it a document endorsed on the envelope as Dr. Jekyll's Will, and sat down with a clouded brow to study its contents. The will was holograph,[2] for Mr. Utterson, though he took charge of it now that it was made, had refused to lend the least assistance in the making of it; it provided not only that, in case of the decease of Henry Jekyll, M.D., D.C.L., LL.D., F.R.S.,[3] &c., all his possessions were to pass into the hands of his "friend and benefactor Edward Hyde," but that in case of Dr. Jekyll's "disappearance or unexplained absence

---

1 Religious text.
2 A document written by hand by the person named as its author.
3 Doctor of Medicine, Doctor of Civil Law, Doctor of Laws, Fellow of the Royal Society.

for any period exceeding three calendar months," the said Edward Hyde should step into the said Henry Jekyll's shoes without further delay and free from any burthen or obligation, beyond the payment of a few small sums to the members of the doctor's household. This document had long been the lawyer's eyesore. It offended him both as a lawyer and as a lover of the sane and customary sides of life, to whom the fanciful was the immodest. And hitherto it was his ignorance of Mr. Hyde that had swelled his indignation; now, by a sudden turn, it was his knowledge. It was already bad enough when the name was but a name of which he could learn no more. It was worse when it began to be clothed upon with detestable attributes; and out of the shifting, insubstantial mists that had so long baffled his eye, there leaped up the sudden, definite presentment of a fiend.

"I thought it was madness," he said, as he replaced the obnoxious paper in the safe, "and now I begin to fear it is disgrace."

With that he blew out his candle, put on a great coat and set forth in the direction of Cavendish Square,[1] that citadel of medicine, where his friend, the great Dr. Lanyon, had his house and received his crowding patients. "If anyone knows, it will be Lanyon," he had thought.

The solemn butler knew and welcomed him; he was subjected to no stage of delay, but ushered direct from the door to the dining room where Dr. Lanyon sat alone over his wine. This was a hearty, healthy, dapper, red-faced gentleman, with a shock of hair prematurely white, and a boisterous and decided manner. At sight of Mr. Utterson, he sprang up from his chair and welcomed him with both hands. The geniality, as was the way of the man, was somewhat theatrical to the eye; but it reposed on genuine feeling. For these two were old friends, old mates both at school and college, both thorough respecters of themselves and of each other, and, what does not always follow, men who thoroughly enjoyed each other's company.

After a little rambling talk, the lawyer led up to the subject which so disagreeably preoccupied his mind.

"I suppose, Lanyon," said he, "you and I must be the two oldest friends that Henry Jekyll has?"

"I wish the friends were younger," chuckled Dr. Lanyon. "But I suppose we are. And what of that? I see little of him now."

"Indeed?" said Utterson. "I thought you had a bond of common interest."

"We had," was the reply. "But it is more than ten years since Henry Jekyll became too fanciful for me. He began to go wrong, wrong in mind; and though of course I

---

1 Fashionable square in London's West End, near Oxford Circus.

continue to take an interest in him for old sake's sake as they say, I see and I have seen devilish little of the man. Such unscientific balderdash," added the doctor, flushing suddenly purple, "would have estranged Damon and Pythias."[1]

This little spirt[2] of temper was somewhat of a relief to Mr. Utterson. "They have only differed on some point of science," he thought; and being a man of no scientific passions (except in the matter of conveyancing)[3] he even added: "It is nothing worse than that!" He gave his friend a few seconds to recover his composure, and then approached the question he had come to put. "Did you ever come across a protégé of his—one Hyde?" he asked.

"Hyde?" repeated Lanyon. "No. Never heard of him. Since my time."

That was the amount of information that the lawyer carried back with him to the great, dark bed on which he tossed to and fro, until the small hours of the morning began to grow large. It was a night of little ease to his toiling mind, toiling in mere darkness and besieged by questions.

Six o'clock struck on the bells of the church that was so conveniently near to Mr. Utterson's dwelling, and still he was digging at the problem. Hitherto it had touched him on the intellectual side alone; but now his imagination also was engaged or rather enslaved; and as he lay and tossed in the gross darkness of the night and the curtained room, Mr. Enfield's tale went by before his mind in a scroll of lighted pictures. He would be aware of the great field of lamps of a nocturnal city; then of the figure of a man walking swiftly; then of a child running from the doctor's; and then these met, and that human Juggernaut trod the child down and passed on regardless of her screams. Or else he would see a room in a rich house, where his friend lay asleep, dreaming and smiling at his dreams; and then the door of that room would be opened, the curtains of the bed plucked apart, the sleeper recalled, and lo! there would stand by his side a figure to whom power was given, and even at that dead hour, he must rise and do its bidding. The figure in these two phases haunted the lawyer all night; and if at any time he dozed over, it was but to see it glide more stealthily through sleeping houses, or move the more swiftly and still

---

1   Symbols of undying friendship between men, Damon and Pythias were Pythagorean philosophers from the fourth century BCE. Condemned to death for treason by the tyrant Dionysus I of Syracuse, Pythias begs to return to Greece before his execution to settle his affairs. Dionysus agrees on condition that Pythias's friend Damon remain in Syracuse in his place, acting as human collateral, subject to execution in the event Pythias flees. When Pythias returns on schedule, Dionysus is so touched by his loyalty to his friend, that he makes the two men his court philosophers.
2   Spurt.
3   The transfer of title of property from one person to another, which Stevenson wryly implies amounts to legal "alchemy," that is, the dubious transmutation of one metal into another.

the more swiftly, even to dizziness, through wider labyrinths of lamplighted city, and at every street corner crush a child and leave her screaming. And still the figure had no face by which he might know it; even in his dreams, it had no face, or one that baffled him and melted before his eyes; and thus it was that there sprang up and grew apace in the lawyer's mind a singularly strong, almost an inordinate, curiosity to behold the features of the real Mr. Hyde. If he could but once set eyes on him, he thought the mystery would lighten and perhaps roll altogether away, as was the habit of mysterious things when well examined. He might see a reason for his friend's strange preference or bondage (call it which you please) and even for the startling clauses of the will. And at least it would be a face worth seeing: the face of a man who was without bowels of mercy: a face which had but to show itself to raise up, in the mind of the unimpressionable Enfield, a spirit of enduring hatred.

From that time forward, Mr. Utterson began to haunt the door in the bystreet of shops. In the morning before office hours, at noon when business was plenty and time scarce, at night under the face of the fogged city moon, by all lights and at all hours of solitude or concourse, the lawyer was to be found on his chosen post.

"If he be Mr. Hyde," he had thought, "I shall be Mr. Seek."

And at last his patience was rewarded. It was a fine dry night; frost in the air; the streets as clean as a ballroom floor; the lamps, unshaken by any wind, drawing a regular pattern of light and shadow. By ten o'clock, when the shops were closed, the bystreet was very solitary and, in spite of the low growl of London from all round, very silent. Small sounds carried far; domestic sounds out of the houses were clearly audible on either side of the roadway; and the rumour[1] of the approach of any passenger preceded him by a long time. Mr. Utterson had been some minutes at his post, when he was aware of an odd, light footstep drawing near. In the course of his nightly patrols, he had long grown accustomed to the quaint effect with which the footfalls of a single person, while he is still a great way off, suddenly spring out distinct from the vast hum and clatter of the city. Yet his attention had never before been so sharply and decisively arrested; and it was with a strong, superstitious prevision of success that he withdrew into the entry of the court.

The steps drew swiftly nearer, and swelled out suddenly louder as they turned the end of the street. The lawyer, looking forth from the entry, could soon see what manner of man he had to deal with. He was small and very plainly dressed, and the look of him, even at that distance, went somehow strongly against the watcher's inclination.

---

1   Noise.

But he made straight for the door, crossing the roadway to save time; and as he came, he drew a key from his pocket like one approaching home.

Mr. Utterson stepped out and touched him on the shoulder as he passed. "Mr. Hyde, I think?"

Mr. Hyde shrank back with a hissing intake of the breath. But his fear was only momentary; and though he did not look the lawyer in the face, he answered coolly enough: "That is my name. What do you want?"

"I see you are going in," returned the lawyer. "I am an old friend of Dr. Jekyll's—Mr. Utterson of Gaunt Street—you must have heard my name; and meeting you so conveniently, I thought you might admit me."

"You will not find Dr. Jekyll; he is from home," replied Mr. Hyde, blowing in the key. And then suddenly, but still without looking up, "How did you know me?" he asked.

"On your side," said Mr. Utterson, "will you do me a favour?"

"With pleasure," replied the other. "What shall it be?"

"Will you let me see your face?" asked the lawyer.

Mr. Hyde appeared to hesitate, and then, as if upon some sudden reflection, fronted about with an air of defiance; and the pair stared at each other pretty fixedly for a few seconds. "Now I shall know you again," said Mr. Utterson. "It may be useful."

"Yes," returned Mr. Hyde, "it is as well we have met; and *à propos,* you should have my address." And he gave a number of a street in Soho.[1]

"Good God!" thought Mr. Utterson, "can he too have been thinking of the will?" But he kept his feelings to himself and only grunted in acknowledgement of the address.

"And now," said the other, "how did you know me?"

"By description," was the reply.

"Whose description?"

"We have common friends," said Mr. Utterson.

"Common friends?" echoed Mr. Hyde, a little hoarsely. "Who are they?"

"Jekyll, for instance," said the lawyer.

"He never told you," cried Mr. Hyde, with a flush of anger. "I did not think you would have lied."

"Come," said Mr. Utterson, "that is not fitting language."

The other snarled aloud into a savage laugh; and the next moment, with extraordinary quickness, he had unlocked the door and disappeared into the house.

---

1   Entertainment district in central London, famous for its nightclubs, dancing halls, and houses of ill repute.

The lawyer stood awhile when Mr. Hyde had left him, the picture of disquietude. Then he began slowly to mount the street, pausing every step or two and putting his hand to his brow like a man in mental perplexity. The problem he was thus debating as he walked, was one of a class that is rarely solved. Mr. Hyde was pale and dwarfish, he gave an impression of deformity without any nameable malformation, he had a displeasing smile, he had borne himself to the lawyer with a sort of murderous mixture of timidity and boldness, and he spoke with a husky, whispering and somewhat broken voice; all these were points against him, but not all of these together could explain the hitherto unknown disgust, loathing and fear with which Mr. Utterson regarded him. "There must be something else," said the perplexed gentleman. "There *is* something more, if I could find a name for it. God bless me, the man seems hardly human! Something troglodytic,[1] shall we say? or can it be the old story of Dr. Fell?[2] or is it the mere radiance of a foul soul that thus transpires through, and transfigures, its clay continent?[3] The last, I think; for O my poor old Harry Jekyll, if ever I read Satan's signature upon a face, it is on that of your new friend."

Round the corner from the bystreet, there was a square of ancient, handsome houses, now for the most part decayed from their high estate and let in flats and chambers to all sorts and conditions of men: map-engravers, architects, shady lawyers and the agents of obscure enterprises. One house, however, second from the corner, was still occupied entire; and at the door of this, which wore a great air of wealth and comfort, though it was now plunged in darkness except for the fan-light,[4] Mr. Utterson stopped and knocked. A well-dressed, elderly servant opened the door.

"Is Dr. Jekyll at home, Poole?" asked the lawyer.

---

1   Like a prehistoric caveman.
2   John Fell (1625-1686), Dean of Christ Church College, Oxford, and a strict disciplinarian, about whom his satirical student Thomas Brown (1662–1704) famously wrote:

> I do not love thee, Dr. Fell,
> The reason why I cannot tell;
> But this I know, and know full well,
> I do not love thee, Dr. Fell.

3   Container.
4   Semicircular window above a door, the mullions of which evoke a plaited fan.

"I will see, Mr. Utterson," said Poole, admitting the visitor, as he spoke, into a large, low-roofed, comfortable hall, paved with flags,[1] warmed (after the fashion of a country house) by a bright, open fire, and furnished with costly cabinets of oak. "Will you wait here by the fire, sir? or shall I give you a light in the dining room?"

"Here, thank you," said the lawyer, and he drew near and leaned on the tall fender. This hall, in which he was now left alone, was a pet fancy of his friend the doctor's; and Utterson himself was wont to speak of it as the pleasantest room in London. But tonight there was a shudder in his blood; the face of Hyde sat heavy on his memory; he felt (what was rare with him) a nausea and distaste of life; and in the gloom of his spirits, he seemed to read a menace in the flickering of the firelight on the polished cabinets and the uneasy starting of the shadow on the roof. He was ashamed of his relief, when Poole presently returned to announce that Dr. Jekyll was gone out.

"I saw Mr. Hyde go in by the old dissecting room door, Poole," he said. "Is that right, when Dr. Jekyll is from home?"

"Quite right, Mr. Utterson, sir," replied the servant. "Mr. Hyde has a key."

"Your master seems to repose a great deal of trust in that young man, Poole," resumed the other musingly.

"Yes, sir, he do indeed," said Poole. "We have all orders to obey him."

"I do not think I ever met Mr. Hyde?" asked Utterson.

"O, dear no, sir. He never *dines* here," replied the butler. "Indeed we see very little of him on this side of the house; he mostly comes and goes by the laboratory."

"Well, good night, Poole."

"Good night, Mr. Utterson."

And the lawyer set out homeward with a very heavy heart. "Poor Harry Jekyll," he thought, "my mind misgives me he is in deep waters! He was wild when he was young; a long while ago to be sure; but in the law of God, there is no statute of limitations. Ay, it must be that; the ghost of some old sin, the cancer of some concealed disgrace: punishment coming, *pede claudo*,[2] years after memory has forgotten and self-love condoned the fault." And the lawyer, scared by the thought, brooded awhile on his own past, groping in all the corners of memory, lest by chance some Jack-in-the-Box of an old iniquity should leap to light there. His past was fairly blameless; few men could read the rolls of their life with less apprehension; yet he was humbled to the dust by the many ill things he had done, and raised up again into a sober and fearful gratitude by the many that he had come so near to doing, yet avoided. And then by

---

1 Flagstones.
2 Latin for "on limping or lame foot."

a return on his former subject, he conceived a spark of hope. "This Master Hyde, if he were studied," thought he, "must have secrets of his own: black secrets, by the look of him; secrets compared to which poor Jekyll's worst would be like sunshine. Things cannot continue as they are. It turns me cold to think of this creature stealing like a thief to Harry's bedside; poor Harry, what a wakening! And the danger of it; for if this Hyde suspects the existence of the will, he may grow impatient to inherit. Ay, I must put my shoulder to the wheel—if Jekyll will but let me," he added, "if Jekyll will only let me." For once more he saw before his mind's eye, as clear as a transparency, the strange clauses of the will.

Dr Jekyll Was Quite at Ease

A FORTNIGHT later, by excellent good fortune, the doctor gave one of his pleasant dinners to some five or six old cronies, all intelligent, reputable men and all judges of good wine; and Mr. Utterson so contrived that he remained behind after the others had departed. This was no new arrangement, but a thing that had befallen many scores of times. Where Utterson was liked, he was liked well. Hosts loved to detain the dry lawyer, when the light-hearted and the loose-tongued had already their foot on the threshold; they liked to sit awhile in his unobtrusive company, practicing for solitude, sobering their minds in the man's rich silence after the expense and strain of gaiety. To this rule, Dr. Jekyll was no exception; and as he now sat on the opposite side of the fire—a large, well-made, smooth-faced man of fifty, with something of a slyish cast perhaps, but every mark of capacity and kindness—you could see by his looks that he cherished for Mr. Utterson a sincere and warm affection.

"I have been wanting to speak to you, Jekyll," began the latter. "You know that will of yours?"

A close observer might have gathered that the topic was distasteful; but the doctor carried it off gaily. "My poor Utterson," said he, "you are unfortunate in such a client. I never saw a man so distressed as you were by my will; unless it were that hidebound pedant, Lanyon, at what he called my scientific heresies. O, I know he's a good fellow—you needn't frown—an excellent fellow, and I always mean to see more of him; but a hide-bound pedant for all that; an ignorant, blatant pedant. I was never more disappointed in any man than Lanyon."

"You know I never approved of it," pursued Utterson, ruthlessly disregarding the fresh topic.

"My will? Yes, certainly, I know that," said the doctor, a trifle sharply. "You have told me so."

"Well, I tell you so again," continued the lawyer. "I have been learning something of young Hyde."

The large handsome face of Dr. Jekyll grew pale to the very lips, and there came a blackness about his eyes. "I do not care to hear more," said he. "This is a matter I thought we had agreed to drop."

"What I heard was abominable," said Utterson.

"It can make no change. You do not understand my position," returned the doctor, with a certain incoherency of manner. "I am painfully situated, Utterson; my position is a very strange—a very strange one. It is one of those affairs that cannot be mended by talking."

"Jekyll," said Utterson, "you know me: I am a man to be trusted. Make a clean breast of this in confidence; and I make no doubt I can get you out of it."

"My good Utterson," said the doctor, "this is very good of you, this is downright good of you, and I cannot find words to thank you in. I believe you fully; I would trust you before any man alive, ay, before myself, if I could make the choice; but indeed it isn't what you fancy; it is not so bad as that; and just to put your good heart at rest, I will tell you one thing: the moment I choose, I can be rid of Mr. Hyde. I give you my hand upon that; and I thank you again and again; and I will just add one little word, Utterson, that I'm sure you'll take in good part: this is a private matter, and I beg of you to let it sleep."

Utterson reflected a little looking in the fire.

"I have no doubt you are perfectly right," he said at last, getting to his feet.

"Well, but since we have touched upon this business, and for the last time I hope," continued the doctor, "there is one point I should like you to understand. I have really a very great interest in poor Hyde. I know you have seen him; he told me so; and I fear he was rude. But I do sincerely take a great, a very great interest in that young man; and if I am taken away, Utterson, I wish you to promise me that you will bear with him and get his rights for him. I think you would, if you knew all; and it would be a weight off my mind if you would promise."

"I can't pretend that I shall ever like him," said the lawyer.

"I don't ask that," pleaded Jekyll, laying his hand upon the other's arm; "I only ask for justice; I only ask you to help him for my sake, when I am no longer here."

Utterson heaved an irrepressible sigh. "Well," said he. "I promise."

The Carew Murder Case

NEARLY a year later, in the month of October 18—, London was startled by a crime of singular ferocity and rendered all the more notable by the high position of the victim. The details were few and startling. A maid servant living alone in a house not far from the river, had gone upstairs to bed about eleven. Although a fog rolled over the city in the small hours, the early part of the night was cloudless, and the lane, which the maid's window overlooked, was brilliantly lit by the full moon. It seems she was romantically given, for she sat down upon her box, which stood immediately under the window, and fell into a dream of musing. Never (she used to say, with streaming tears, when she narrated that experience) never had she felt more at peace with all men or thought more kindly of the world. And as she so sat she became aware of an aged and beautiful gentleman with white hair, drawing near along the lane; and advancing to meet him, another and very small gentleman, to whom at first she paid less attention. When they had come within speech (which was just under the maid's eyes) the older man bowed and accosted the other with a very pretty manner of politeness. It did not seem as if the subject of his address were of great importance; indeed, from his pointing, it sometimes appeared as if he were only inquiring his way; but the moon shone on his face as he spoke, and the girl was pleased to watch it, it seemed to breathe such an innocent and old-world kindness of disposition, yet with something high too, as of a well-founded self-content. Presently her eye wandered to the other, and she was surprised to recognise in him a certain Mr. Hyde, who had once visited her master and for whom she had conceived a dislike. He had in his hand a heavy cane, with which he was trifling; but he answered never a word, and seemed to listen with an ill-contained impatience. And then all of a sudden he broke out in a great flame of anger, stamping with his foot, brandishing the cane, and carrying on (as the maid described it) like a madman. The old gentleman took a step back, with the air of one very much surprised and a trifle hurt; and at that Mr. Hyde broke out of all bounds and clubbed him to the earth. And next moment, with ape-like fury, he was trampling his victim under foot, and hailing down a storm of blows, under which the bones were audibly shattered and the body jumped upon the roadway. At the horror of these sights and sounds, the maid fainted.

It was two o'clock when she came to herself and called for the police. The murderer was gone long ago; but there lay his victim in the middle of the lane, incredibly mangled. The stick with which the deed had been done, although it was of some rare and very tough and heavy wood, had broken in the middle under the stress of this insensate cruelty; and one splintered half had rolled in the neighbouring gutter—the other, without doubt, had been carried away by the murderer. A purse and a gold watch were found upon the victim; but no cards or papers, except a sealed and stamped envelope, which he had been probably carrying to the post, and which bore the name and address of Mr. Utterson.

This was brought to the lawyer the next morning, before he was out of bed; and he had no sooner seen it, and been told the circumstances, than he shot out a solemn lip. "I shall say nothing till I have seen the body," said he; "this may be very serious. Have the kindness to wait while I dress." And with the same grave countenance he hurried through his breakfast and drove to the police station, whither the body had been carried. As soon as he came into the cell, he nodded.

"Yes," said he, "I recognise him. I am sorry to say that this is Sir Danvers Carew."

"Good God, sir," exclaimed the officer, "is it possible?" And the next moment his eye lighted up with professional ambition. "This will make a deal of noise," he said. "And perhaps you can help us to the man." And he briefly narrated what the maid had seen, and showed the broken stick.

Mr. Utterson had already quailed at the name of Hyde; but when the stick was laid before him, he could doubt no longer: broken and battered as it was, he recognised it for one that he had himself presented many years before to Henry Jekyll.

"Is this Mr. Hyde a person of small stature?" he inquired.

"Particularly small and particularly wicked-looking, is what the maid calls him," said the officer.

Mr. Utterson reflected; and then, raising his head, "If you will come with me in my cab," he said, "I think I can take you to his house."

It was by this time about nine in the morning, and the first fog of the season.[1] A great chocolate-coloured pall lowered over heaven, but the wind was continually charging and routing these embattled vapours; so that as the cab crawled from street to street, Mr. Utterson beheld a marvellous number of degrees and hues of twilight; for here it would be dark like the back-end of evening; and there would be a glow of a rich, lurid brown, like the light of some strange conflagration; and here, for a moment, the fog would be quite broken up, and a haggard shaft of daylight would glance in between the swirling wreaths. The dismal quarter of Soho seen under these changing glimpses, with its muddy ways, and slatternly passengers, and its lamps, which had never been extinguished or had been kindled afresh to combat this mournful reinvasion of darkness, seemed, in the lawyer's eyes, like a district of

---

1   A reference to the sickening mixture of fog and heavy coal smoke—also called "pea soup"—that darkened the skies of London in the nineteenth and early twentieth centuries, taking days sometimes to dissipate.

some city in a nightmare. The thoughts of his mind, besides, were of the gloomiest dye; and when he glanced at the companion of his drive, he was conscious of some touch of that terror of the law and the law's officers, which may at times assail the most honest.

As the cab drew up before the address indicated, the fog lifted a little and showed him a dingy street, a gin palace,[1] a low French eating house, a shop for the retail of penny numbers[2] and twopenny salads,[3] many ragged children huddled in the doorways, and many women of many different nationalities passing out, key in hand, to have a morning glass; and the next moment the fog settled down again upon that part, as brown as umber,[4] and cut him off from his blackguardly surroundings. This was the home of Henry Jekyll's favourite; of a man who was heir to quarter of a million sterling.

An ivory-faced and silvery-haired old woman opened the door. She had an evil face, smoothed by hypocrisy; but her manners were excellent. Yes, she said, this was Mr. Hyde's, but he was not at home; he had been in that night very late, but had gone away again in less than an hour; there was nothing strange in that; his habits were very irregular, and he was often absent; for instance, it was nearly two months since she had seen him till yesterday.

"Very well then, we wish to see his rooms," said the lawyer; and when the woman began to declare it was impossible, "I had better tell you who this person is," he added. "This is Inspector Newcomen of Scotland Yard."

A flash of odious joy appeared upon the woman's face. "Ah!" said she, "he is in trouble! What has he done?"

Mr. Utterson and the inspector exchanged glances. "He don't seem a very popular character," observed the latter. "And now, my good woman, just let me and this gentleman have a look about us."

In the whole extent of the house, which but for the old woman remained otherwise empty, Mr. Hyde had only used a couple of rooms; but these were furnished with luxury and good taste. A closet was filled with wine; the plate was of silver, the napery[5] elegant; a good picture hung upon the walls, a gift (as Utterson supposed) from Henry Jekyll, who was much of a connoisseur; and the carpets were of many plies and agreeable in colour. At this moment, however, the rooms bore every mark

---

1   Cheap bar.
2   Cheap, lurid paperback novels.
3   Cheap eats.
4   Dark yellowish-brown.
5   Household linen.

of having been recently and hurriedly ransacked; clothes lay about the floor, with their pockets inside out; lockfast[1] drawers stood open; and on the hearth there lay a pile of gray ashes, as though many papers had been burned. From these embers the inspector disinterred the butt end of a green cheque book, which had resisted the action of the fire; the other half of the stick was found behind the door; and as this clinched his suspicions, the officer declared himself delighted. A visit to the bank, where several thousand pounds were found to be lying to the murderer's credit, completed his gratification.

"You may depend upon it, sir," he told Mr. Utterson: "I have him in my hand. He must have lost his head, or he never would have left the stick or, above all, burned the cheque book. Why, money's life to the man. We have nothing to do but wait for him at the bank, and get out the handbills."[2]

This last, however, was not so easy of accomplishment; for Mr. Hyde had numbered few familiars—even the master of the servant maid had only seen him twice; his family could nowhere be traced; he had never been photographed; and the few who could describe him differed widely, as common observers will. Only on one point, were they agreed; and that was the haunting sense of unexpressed deformity with which the fugitive impressed his beholders.

Incident of the Letter

IT was late in the afternoon, when Mr. Utterson found his way to Dr. Jekyll's door, where he was at once admitted by Poole, and carried down by the kitchen offices[3] and across a yard which had once been a garden, to the building which was indifferently known as the laboratory or the dissecting rooms. The doctor had bought the house from the heirs of a celebrated surgeon; and his own tastes being rather chemical than anatomical, had changed the destination of the block[4] at the bottom of the garden. It was the first time that the lawyer had been received in that part of his friend's quarters; and he eyed the dingy windowless structure with curi-

---

1 Locked.
2 Fliers distributed in the manner of a "wanted poster."
3 Various rooms comprising the kitchen area, including pantries and storage rooms.
4 Had changed the building's intended use.

osity, and gazed round with a distasteful sense of strangeness as he crossed the theatre,[1] once crowded with eager students and now lying gaunt and silent, the tables laden with chemical apparatus, the floor strewn with crates and littered with packing straw, and the light falling dimly through the foggy cupola.[2] At the further end, a flight of stairs mounted to a door covered with red baize;[3] and through this, Mr. Utterson was at last received into the doctor's cabinet.[4] It was a large room, fitted round with glass presses,[5] furnished, among other things, with a cheval-glass[6] and a business table, and looking out upon the court by three dusty windows barred with iron. The fire burned in the grate; a lamp was set lighted on the chimney shelf,[7] for even in the houses the fog began to lie thickly; and there, close up to the warmth, sat Dr. Jekyll, looking deadly sick. He did not rise to meet his visitor, but held out a cold hand and bade him welcome in a changed voice.

"And now," said Mr. Utterson, as soon as Poole had left them, "you have heard the news?"

The doctor shuddered. "They were crying it in the square," he said. "I heard them in my dining room."

"One word," said the lawyer. "Carew was my client, but so are you, and I want to know what I am doing. You have not been mad enough to hide this fellow?"

"Utterson, I swear to God," cried the doctor, "I swear to God I will never set eyes on him again. I bind my honour to you that I am done with him in this world. It is all at an end. And indeed he does not want my help; you do not know him as I do; he is safe, he is quite safe; mark my words, he will never more be heard of."

The lawyer listened gloomily; he did not like his friend's feverish manner. "You seem pretty sure of him," said he; "and for your sake, I hope you may be right. If it came to a trial, your name might appear."

"I am quite sure of him," replied Jekyll; "I have grounds for certainty that I cannot share with anyone. But there is one thing on which you may advise me. I have—I have received a letter; and I am at a loss whether I should show it to the police. I

---

1 Operating theatre; the amphitheatre where cadavers were dissected for an audience of medical students.
2 Dome-shaped skylight.
3 Heavy felt fabric, placed on doors to deaden noise.
4 Private office.
5 Glass-door cupboards, often with drawers instead of shelves.
6 A full-length pivoting mirror.
7 Mantle.

should like to leave it in your hands, Utterson; you would judge wisely I am sure; I have so great a trust in you."

"You fear, I suppose, that it might lead to his detection?" asked the lawyer.

"No," said the other. "I cannot say that I care what becomes of Hyde; I am quite done with him. I was thinking of my own character, which this hateful business has rather exposed."

Utterson ruminated awhile; he was surprised at his friend's selfishness, and yet relieved by it. "Well," said he, at last, "let me see the letter."

The letter was written in an odd, upright hand and signed "Edward Hyde": and it signified, briefly enough, that the writer's benefactor, Dr. Jekyll, whom he had long so unworthily repaid for a thousand generosities, need labour under no alarm for his safety as he had means of escape on which he placed a sure dependence. The lawyer liked this letter well enough; it put a better colour on the intimacy than he had looked for; and he blamed himself for some of his past suspicions.

"Have you the envelope?" he asked.

"I burned it," replied Jekyll, "before I thought what I was about. But it bore no postmark. The note was handed in."

"Shall I keep this and sleep upon it?" asked Utterson.

"I wish you to judge for me entirely," was the reply. "I have lost confidence in myself."

"Well, I shall consider," returned the lawyer. "And now one word more: it was Hyde who dictated the terms in your will about that disappearance?"

The doctor seemed seized with a qualm of faintness; he shut his mouth tight and nodded.

"I knew it," said Utterson. "He meant to murder you. You have had a fine escape."

"I have had what is far more to the purpose," returned the doctor solemnly: "I have had a lesson—O God, Utterson, what a lesson I have had!" And he covered his face for a moment with his hands.

On his way out, the lawyer stopped and had a word or two with Poole. "By the by," said he, "there was a letter handed in today: what was the messenger like?" But Poole was positive nothing had come except by post; "and only circulars[1] by that," he added.

This news sent off the visitor with his fears renewed. Plainly the letter had come by the laboratory door; possibly, indeed, it had been written in the cabinet; and if

---

1 Advertisements, junk mail.

that were so, it must be differently judged, and handled with the more caution. The newsboys, as he went, were crying themselves hoarse along the footways: "Special edition. Shocking murder of an M.P."[1] That was the funeral oration of one friend and client; and he could not help a certain apprehension lest the good name of another should be sucked down in the eddy of the scandal. It was, at least, a ticklish decision that he had to make; and self-reliant as he was by habit, he began to cherish a longing for advice. It was not to be had directly; but perhaps, he thought, it might be fished for.

Presently after, he sat on one side of his own hearth, with Mr. Guest, his head clerk, upon the other, and midway between, at a nicely calculated distance from the fire, a bottle of a particular old wine that had long dwelt unsunned[2] in the foundations[3] of his house. The fog still slept on the wing above the drowned city, where the lamps glimmered like carbuncles;[4] and through the muffle and smother of these fallen clouds, the procession of the town's life was still rolling in through the great arteries with a sound as of a mighty wind. But the room was gay with firelight. In the bottle the acids were long ago resolved;[5] the imperial dye[6] had softened with time, as the colour grows richer in stained windows;[7] and the glow of hot autumn afternoons on hillside vineyards, was ready to be set free and to disperse the fogs of London. Insensibly the lawyer melted. There was no man from whom he kept fewer secrets than Mr. Guest; and he was not always sure that he kept as many as he meant. Guest had often been on business to the doctor's; he knew Poole; he could scarce have failed to hear of Mr. Hyde's familiarity about the house; he might draw conclusions: was it not as well, then, that he should see a letter which put that mystery to rights? and above all since Guest, being a great student and critic of handwriting, would consider the step natural and obliging? The clerk, besides, was a man of counsel; he would scarce read so strange a document without dropping a remark; and by that remark Mr. Utterson might shape his future course.

"This is a sad business about Sir Danvers," he said.

---

1   Member of Parliament.
2   Untouched by the light of day.
3   Cellars.
4   Bright red gems, garnets.
5   Separated, mellowed.
6   Color purple associated with ancient Roman imperial robes.
7   Stained glass windows.

"Yes, sir, indeed. It has elicited a great deal of public feeling," returned Guest. "The man, of course, was mad."

"I should like to hear your views on that," replied Utterson. "I have a document here in his handwriting; it is between ourselves, for I scarce know what to do about it; it is an ugly business at the best. But there it is; quite in your way: a murderer's autograph."

Guest's eyes brightened, and he sat down at once and studied it with passion. "No, sir," he said; "not mad; but it is an odd hand."

"And by all accounts a very odd writer," added the lawyer.

Just then the servant entered with a note.

"Is that from Doctor Jekyll, sir?" inquired the clerk. "I thought I knew the writing. Anything private, Mr. Utterson?"

"Only an invitation to dinner. Why? do you want to see it?"

"One moment. I thank you, sir;" and the clerk laid the two sheets of paper alongside and sedulously compared their contents. "Thank you, sir," he said at last, returning both; "it's a very interesting autograph."

There was a pause, during which Mr. Utterson struggled with himself. "Why did you compare them, Guest?" he inquired suddenly.

"Well, sir," returned the clerk, "there's a rather singular resemblance; the two hands are in many points identical: only differently sloped."

"Rather quaint,"[1] said Utterson.

"It is, as you say, rather quaint," returned Guest.

"I wouldn't speak of this note, you know," said the master.

"No, sir," said the clerk. "I understand."

But no sooner was Mr. Utterson alone that night, than he locked the note into his safe where it reposed from that time forward. "What!" he thought. "Henry Jekyll forge for a murderer!" And his blood ran cold in his veins.

---

1 Strange.

Remarkable Incident of Doctor Lanyon

TIME ran on; thousands of pounds were offered in reward, for the death of Sir Danvers was resented as a public injury; but Mr. Hyde had disappeared out of the ken[1] of the police as though he had never existed. Much of his past was unearthed, indeed, and all disreputable: tales came out of the man's cruelty, at once so callous and violent, of his vile life, of his strange associates, of the hatred that seemed to have surrounded his career; but of his present whereabouts, not a whisper. From the time he had left the house in Soho on the morning of the murder, he was simply blotted out; and gradually, as time drew on, Mr. Utterson began to recover from the hotness of his alarm, and to grow more at quiet with himself. The death of Sir Danvers was, to his way of thinking, more than paid for by the disappearance of Mr. Hyde. Now that that evil influence had been withdrawn, a new life began for Dr. Jekyll. He came out of his seclusion, renewed relations with his friends, became once more their familiar guest and entertainer; and whilst he had always been known for charities, he was now no less distinguished for religion. He was busy, he was much in the open air, he did good; his face seemed to open and brighten, as if with an inward consciousness of service; and for more than two months, the doctor was at peace.

On the 8th of January Utterson had dined at the doctor's with a small party; Lanyon had been there; and the face of the host had looked from one to the other as in the old days when the trio were inseparable friends. On the 12th, and again on the 14th, the door was shut against the lawyer. "The doctor was confined to the house," Poole said, "and saw no one." On the 15th, he tried again, and was again refused; and having now been used for the last two months to see his friend almost daily, he found this return of solitude to weigh upon his spirits. The fifth night, he had in Guest to dine with him; and the sixth he betook himself to Doctor Lanyon's.

There at least he was not denied admittance; but when he came in, he was shocked at the change which had taken place in the doctor's appearance. He had his death-warrant written legibly upon his face. The rosy man had grown pale; his flesh had fallen away; he was visibly balder and older; and yet it was not so much these tokens of a swift physical decay that arrested the lawyer's notice, as a look in the eye and quality of manner that seemed to testify to some deep-seated terror of the mind. It was unlikely that the doctor should fear death; and yet that was what Utterson was tempted to suspect. "Yes," he thought; "he is a doctor, he must know his own state and

---

1   Beyond the range or reach.

that his days are counted; and the knowledge is more than he can bear." And yet when Utterson remarked on his ill-looks, it was with an air of great firmness that Lanyon declared himself a doomed man.

"I have had a shock," he said, "and I shall never recover. It is a question of weeks. Well, life has been pleasant; I liked it; yes, sir, I used to like it. I sometimes think if we knew all, we should be more glad to get away."

"Jekyll is ill, too," observed Utterson. "Have you seen him?"

But Lanyon's face changed, and he held up a trembling hand. "I wish to see or hear no more of Doctor Jekyll," he said in a loud, unsteady voice. "I am quite done with that person; and I beg that you will spare me any allusion to one whom I regard as dead."

"Tut-tut," said Mr. Utterson; and then after a considerable pause, "Can't I do anything?" he inquired. "We are three very old friends, Lanyon; we shall not live to make others."

"Nothing can be done," returned Lanyon; "ask himself."

"He will not see me," said the lawyer.

"I am not surprised at that," was the reply. "Some day, Utterson, after I am dead, you may perhaps come to learn the right and wrong of this. I cannot tell you. And in the meantime, if you can sit and talk with me of other things, for God's sake, stay and do so; but if you cannot keep clear of this accursed topic, then, in God's name, go, for I cannot bear it."

As soon as he got home, Utterson sat down and wrote to Jekyll, complaining of his exclusion from the house, and asking the cause of this unhappy break with Lanyon; and the next day brought him a long answer, often very pathetically worded, and sometimes darkly mysterious in drift. The quarrel with Lanyon was incurable. "I do not blame our old friend," Jekyll wrote, "but I share his view that we must never meet. I mean from henceforth to lead a life of extreme seclusion; you must not be surprised, nor must you doubt my friendship, if my door is often shut even to you. You must suffer me to go my own dark way. I have brought on myself a punishment and a danger that I cannot name. If I am the chief of sinners, I am the chief of sufferers also. I could not think that this earth contained a place for sufferings and terrors so unmanning; and you can do but one thing, Utterson, to lighten this destiny, and that is to respect my silence." Utterson was amazed; the dark influence of Hyde had been withdrawn, the doctor had returned to his old tasks and amities; a week ago, the prospect had smiled with every promise of a cheerful and an honoured age; and now in a moment, friendship, and peace of mind and the whole tenor of his life were wrecked. So great and unprepared a change pointed to madness; but in view of Lanyon's manner and words, there must lie for it some deeper ground.

A week afterwards Dr. Lanyon took to his bed, and in something less than a fortnight he was dead. The night after the funeral, at which he had been sadly affected, Utterson locked the door of his business room, and sitting there by the light of a melancholy candle, drew out and set before him an envelope addressed by the hand and sealed with the seal of his dead friend. "PRIVATE: for the hands of J. G. Utterson ALONE and in case of his predecease *to be destroyed unread*," so it was emphatically superscribed; and the lawyer dreaded to behold the contents. "I have buried one friend today," he thought: "what if this should cost me another?" And then he condemned the fear as a disloyalty, and broke the seal. Within there was another enclosure, likewise sealed, and marked upon the cover as "not to be opened till the death or disappearance of Dr. Henry Jekyll." Utterson could not trust his eyes. Yes, it was disappearance; here again, as in the mad will which he had long ago restored to its author, here again were the idea of a disappearance and the name of Henry Jekyll bracketed. But in the will, that idea had sprung from the sinister suggestion of the man Hyde; it was set there with a purpose all too plain and horrible. Written by the hand of Lanyon, what should it mean? A great curiosity came on the trustee, to disregard the prohibition and dive at once to the bottom of these mysteries; but professional honour and faith to his dead friend were stringent obligations; and the packet slept in the inmost corner of his private safe.

It is one thing to mortify curiosity, another to conquer it; and it may be doubted if, from that day forth, Utterson desired the society of his surviving friend with the same eagerness. He thought of him kindly; but his thoughts were disquieted and fearful. He went to call indeed; but he was perhaps relieved to be denied admittance; perhaps, in his heart, he preferred to speak with Poole upon the doorstep and surrounded by the air and sounds of the open city, rather than to be admitted into that house of voluntary bondage, and to sit and speak with its inscrutable recluse. Poole had, indeed, no very pleasant news to communicate. The doctor, it appeared, now more than ever confined himself to the cabinet over the laboratory, where he would sometimes even sleep; he was out of spirits, he had grown very silent, he did not read; it seemed as if he had something on his mind. Utterson became so used to the unvarying character of these reports, that he fell off little by little in the frequency of his visits.

Incident at the Window

IT chanced on Sunday, when Mr. Utterson was on his usual walk with Mr. Enfield, that their way lay once again through the bystreet; and that when they came in front of the door, both stopped to gaze on it.

"Well," said Enfield, "that story's at an end at least. We shall never see more of Mr. Hyde."

"I hope not," said Utterson. "Did I ever tell you that I once saw him, and shared your feeling of repulsion?"

"It was impossible to do the one without the other," returned Enfield. "And by the way what an ass you must have thought me, not to know that this was a back way to Dr. Jekyll's! It was partly your own fault that I found it out, even when I did."

"So you found it out, did you?" said Utterson. "But if that be so, we may step into the court and take a look at the windows. To tell you the truth, I am uneasy about poor Jekyll; and even outside, I feel as if the presence of a friend might do him good."

The court was very cool and a little damp, and full of premature twilight, although the sky, high up overhead, was still bright with sunset. The middle one of the three windows was half way open; and sitting close beside it, taking the air with an infinite sadness of mien, like some disconsolate prisoner, Utterson saw Dr. Jekyll.

"What! Jekyll!" he cried. "I trust you are better."

"I am very low, Utterson," replied the doctor drearily, "very low. It will not last long, thank God."

"You stay too much indoors," said the lawyer. "You should be out, whipping up the circulation like Mr. Enfield and me. (This is my cousin—Mr. Enfield—Dr. Jekyll.) Come now; get your hat and take a quick turn with us."

"You are very good," sighed the other. "I should like to very much; but no, no, no, it is quite impossible; I dare not. But indeed, Utterson, I am very glad to see you; this is really a great pleasure; I would ask you and Mr. Enfield up, but the place is really not fit."

"Why then," said the lawyer, good-naturedly, "the best thing we can do is to stay down here and speak with you from where we are."

"That is just what I was about to venture to propose," returned the doctor with a smile. But the words were hardly uttered, before the smile was struck out of his face and succeeded by an expression of such abject terror and despair, as froze the very blood of the two gentlemen below. They saw it but for a glimpse, for the window was instantly thrust down; but that glimpse had been sufficient, and they turned and left the court without a word. In silence, too, they traversed the bystreet; and it was not until they had come into a neighbouring thoroughfare, where even upon a Sunday there were still some stirrings of life, that Mr. Utterson at last turned and looked at his companion. They were both pale; and there was an answering horror in their eyes.

"God forgive us, God forgive us," said Mr. Utterson.

But Mr. Enfield only nodded his head very seriously, and walked on once more in silence.

The Last Night

MR. Utterson was sitting by his fireside one evening after dinner, when he was surprised to receive a visit from Poole.

"Bless me, Poole, what brings you here?" he cried; and then taking a second look at him, "What ails you?" he added, "is the doctor ill?"

"Mr. Utterson," said the man, "there is something wrong."

"Take a seat, and here is a glass of wine for you," said the lawyer. "Now, take your time, and tell me plainly what you want."

"You know the doctor's ways, sir," replied Poole, "and how he shuts himself up. Well, he's shut up again in the cabinet; and I don't like it, sir—I wish I may die if I like it. Mr. Utterson, sir, I'm afraid."

"Now, my good man," said the lawyer, "be explicit. What are you afraid of?"

"I've been afraid for about a week," returned Poole, doggedly disregarding the question, "and I can bear it no more."

The man's appearance amply bore out his words; his manner was altered for the worse; and except for the moment when he had first announced his terror, he had not once looked the lawyer in the face. Even now, he sat with the glass of wine untasted on his knee, and his eyes directed to a corner of the floor. "I can bear it no more," he repeated.

"Come," said the lawyer, "I see you have some good reason, Poole; I see there is something seriously amiss. Try to tell me what it is."

"I think there's been foul play," said Poole, hoarsely.

"Foul play!" cried the lawyer, a good deal frightened and rather inclined to be irritated in consequence. "What foul play? What does the man mean?"

"I daren't say, sir," was the answer; "but will you come along with me and see for yourself?"

Mr. Utterson's only answer was to rise and get his hat and great coat; but he observed with wonder the greatness of the relief that appeared upon the butler's face, and perhaps with no less, that the wine was still untasted when he set it down to follow.

It was a wild, cold, seasonable night of March, with a pale moon, lying on her back as though the wind had tilted her, and a flying wrack[1] of the most diaphanous[2] and lawny[3] texture. The wind made talking difficult, and flecked the blood into the face. It seemed to have swept the streets unusually bare of passengers, besides; for Mr. Utterson thought he had never seen that part of London so deserted. He could have wished it otherwise; never in his life had he been conscious of so sharp a wish to see and touch his fellow-creatures; for struggle as he might, there was borne in upon his mind a crushing anticipation of calamity. The square, when they got there, was all full of wind and dust, and the thin trees in the garden were lashing themselves along the railing. Poole, who had kept all the way a pace or two ahead, now pulled up in the middle of the pavement, and in spite of the biting weather, took off his hat and mopped his brow with a red pocket-handkerchief. But for all the hurry of his coming, these were not the dews of exertion that he wiped away, but the moisture of some strangling anguish; for his face was white and his voice, when he spoke, harsh and broken.

"Well, sir," he said, "here we are, and God grant there be nothing wrong."

"Amen, Poole," said the lawyer.

Thereupon the servant knocked in a very guarded manner; the door was opened on the chain; and a voice asked from within, "Is that you, Poole?"

"It's all right," said Poole. "Open the door."

The hall, when they entered it, was brightly lighted up; the fire was built high; and about the hearth the whole of the servants, men and women, stood huddled together like a flock of sheep. At the sight of Mr. Utterson, the housemaid broke into hysterical whimpering; and the cook, crying out "Bless God! it's Mr. Utterson," ran forward as if to take him in her arms.

"What, what? Are you all here?" said the lawyer peevishly. "Very irregular, very unseemly; your master would be far from pleased."

"They're all afraid," said Poole.

Blank silence followed, no one protesting; only the maid lifted up her voice and now wept loudly.

---

1   Remnants of cloud.
2   Translucent.
3   Having the properties of lawn, a light, cottony fabric.

"Hold your tongue!" Poole said to her, with a ferocity of accent that testified to his own jangled nerves; and indeed, when the girl had so suddenly raised the note of her lamentation, they had all started and turned towards the inner door with faces of dreadful expectation. "And now," continued the butler, addressing the knife-boy,[1] "reach me a candle, and we'll get this through hands[2] at once." And then he begged Mr. Utterson to follow him, and led the way to the back garden.

"Now, sir," said he, "you come as gently as you can. I want you to hear, and I don't want you to be heard. And see here, sir, if by any chance he was to ask you in, don't go."

Mr. Utterson's nerves, at this unlooked-for termination, gave a jerk that nearly threw him from his balance; but he recollected his courage and followed the butler into the laboratory building and through the surgical theatre, with its lumber of crates and bottles, to the foot of the stair. Here Poole motioned him to stand on one side and listen; while he himself, setting down the candle and making a great and obvious call on his resolution, mounted the steps and knocked with a somewhat uncertain hand on the red baize of the cabinet door.

"Mr. Utterson, sir, asking to see you," he called; and even as he did so, once more violently signed to the lawyer to give ear.

A voice answered from within: "Tell him I cannot see anyone," it said complainingly.

"Thank you, sir," said Poole, with a note of something like triumph in his voice; and taking up his candle, he led Mr. Utterson back across the yard and into the great kitchen, where the fire was out and the beetles were leaping on the floor.

"Sir," he said, looking Mr. Utterson in the eyes, "was that my master's voice?"

"It seems much changed," replied the lawyer, very pale, but giving look for look.

"Changed? Well, yes, I think so," said the butler. "Have I been twenty years in this man's house, to be deceived about his voice? No, sir; master's made away with; he was made away with, eight days ago, when we heard him cry out upon the name of God; and *who's* in there instead of him, and *why* it stays there, is a thing that cries to Heaven, Mr. Utterson!"

"This is a very strange tale, Poole; this is rather a wild tale, my man," said Mr. Utterson, biting his finger. "Suppose it were as you suppose, supposing Dr. Jekyll to have been—well, murdered, what could induce the murderer to stay? That won't hold water; it doesn't commend itself to reason."

---

1   Boy employed to clean cutlery.
2   Get through this task.

"Well, Mr. Utterson, you are a hard man to satisfy, but I'll do it yet," said Poole. "All this last week (you must know) him, or it, or whatever it is that lives in that cabinet, has been crying night and day for some sort of medicine and cannot get it to his mind. It was sometimes his way—the master's, that is—to write his orders on a sheet of paper and throw it on the stair. We've had nothing else this week back; nothing but papers, and a closed door, and the very meals left there to be smuggled in when nobody was looking. Well, sir, every day, ay, and twice and thrice in the same day, there have been orders and complaints, and I have been sent flying to all the wholesale chemists in town. Every time I brought the stuff back, there would be another paper telling me to return it, because it was not pure, and another order to a different firm. This drug is wanted bitter[1] bad, sir, whatever for."

"Have you any of these papers?" asked Mr. Utterson.

Poole felt in his pocket and handed out a crumpled note, which the lawyer, bending nearer to the candle, carefully examined. Its contents ran thus: "Dr. Jekyll presents his compliments to Messrs. Maw. He assures them that their last sample is impure and quite useless for his present purpose. In the year 18—, Dr. J. purchased a somewhat large quantity from Messrs. M. He now begs them to search with the most sedulous care, and should any of the same quality be left, to forward it to him at once. Expense is no consideration. The importance of this to Dr. J. can hardly be exaggerated." So far the letter had run composedly enough, but here with a sudden splutter of the pen, the writer's emotion had broken loose. "For God's sake," he had added, "find me some of the old."

"This is a strange note," said Mr. Utterson; and then sharply, "How do you come to have it open?"

"The man at Maw's was main[2] angry, sir, and he threw it back to me like so much dirt," returned Poole.

"This is unquestionably the doctor's hand, do you know?" resumed the lawyer.

"I thought it looked like it," said the servant rather sulkily; and then, with another voice, "But what matters hand of write," he said. "I've seen him!"

"Seen him?" repeated Mr. Utterson. "Well?"

"That's it!" said Poole. "It was this way. I came suddenly into the theatre from the garden. It seems he had slipped out to look for this drug or whatever it is; for the cabinet door was open, and there he was at the far end of the room digging among the crates. He looked up when I came in, gave a kind of cry, and whipped

---

1 Very.
2 Extremely.

upstairs into the cabinet. It was but for one minute that I saw him, but the hair stood upon my head like quills. Sir, if that was my master, why had he a mask upon his face? If it was my master, why did he cry out like a rat, and run from me? I have served him long enough. And then …" the man paused and passed his hand over his face.

"These are all very strange circumstances," said Mr. Utterson, "but I think I begin to see daylight. Your master, Poole, is plainly seized with one of those maladies that both torture and deform the sufferer; hence, for aught I know, the alteration of his voice; hence the mask and his avoidance of his friends; hence his eagerness to find this drug, by means of which the poor soul retains some hope of ultimate recovery—God grant that he be not deceived! There is my explanation; it is sad enough, Poole, ay, and appalling to consider; but it is plain and natural, hangs well together and delivers us from all exorbitant alarms."

"Sir," said the butler, turning to a sort of mottled pallor, "that thing was not my master, and there's the truth. My master"—here he looked round him and began to whisper—"is a tall fine build of a man, and this was more of a dwarf." Utterson attempted to protest. "O, sir," cried Poole, "do you think I do not know my master after twenty years? do you think I do not know where his head comes to in the cabinet door, where I saw him every morning of my life? No, sir, that thing in the mask was never Doctor Jekyll—God knows what it was, but it was never Doctor Jekyll; and it is the belief of my heart that there was murder done."

"Poole," replied the lawyer, "if you say that, it will become my duty to make certain. Much as I desire to spare your master's feelings, much as I am puzzled by this note which seems to prove him to be still alive, I shall consider it my duty to break in that door."

"Ah, Mr. Utterson, that's talking!" cried the butler.

"And now comes the second question," resumed Utterson: "Who is going to do it?"

"Why, you and me, sir," was the undaunted reply.

"That is very well said," returned the lawyer; "and whatever comes of it, I shall make it my business to see you are no loser."

"There is an axe in the theatre," continued Poole; "and you might take the kitchen poker for yourself."

The lawyer took that rude but weighty instrument into his hand, and balanced it. "Do you know Poole," he said, looking up, "that you and I are about to place ourselves in a position of some peril?"

"You may say so, sir, indeed," returned the butler.

"It is well, then, that we should be frank," said the other. "We both think more than we have said; let us make a clean breast. This masked figure that you saw, did you recognise it?"

"Well, sir, it went so quick, and the creature was so doubled up, that I could hardly swear to that," was the answer. "But if you mean, was it Mr. Hyde?—why, yes, I think it was! You see, it was much of the same bigness; and it had the same quick light way with it; and then who else could have got in by the laboratory door? You have not forgot, sir, that at the time of the murder he had still the key with him? But that's not all. I don't know, Mr. Utterson, if ever you met this Mr. Hyde?"

"Yes," said the lawyer, "I once spoke with him."

"Then you must know as well as the rest of us that there was something queer about that gentleman—something that gave a man a turn—I don't know rightly how to say it, sir, beyond this: that you felt it in your marrow kind of cold and thin."

"I own I felt something of what you describe," said Mr. Utterson.

"Quite so, sir," returned Poole. "Well, when that masked thing like a monkey jumped from among the chemicals and whipped into the cabinet, it went down my spine like ice. O, I know it's not evidence, Mr. Utterson; I'm book-learned enough for that; but a man has his feelings, and I give you my bible-word it was Mr. Hyde!"

"Ay, ay," said the lawyer. "My fears incline to the same point. Evil, I fear, founded—evil was sure to come—of that connection. Ay, truly, I believe you; I believe poor Harry is killed; and I believe his murderer (for what purpose, God alone can tell) is still lurking in his victim's room. Well, let our name be vengeance. Call Bradshaw."

The footman came at the summons, very white and nervous.

"Pull yourself together, Bradshaw," said the lawyer. "This suspense, I know, is telling upon all of you; but it is now our intention to make an end of it. Poole, here, and I are going to force our way into the cabinet. If all is well, my shoulders are broad enough to bear the blame. Meanwhile, lest anything should really be amiss, or any malefactor seek to escape by the back, you and the boy must go round the corner with a pair of good sticks, and take your post at the laboratory door. We give you ten minutes, to get to your stations."

As Bradshaw left, the lawyer looked at his watch. "And now, Poole, let us get to ours," he said; and taking the poker under his arm, he led the way into the yard. The scud[1] had banked over the moon, and it was now quite dark. The wind, which only broke in puffs and draughts into that deep well of building, tossed the light of the candle to and fro about their steps, until they came into the shelter of the theatre, where they

---

1   Windswept clouds.

sat down silently to wait. London hummed solemnly all around; but nearer at hand, the stillness was only broken by the sound of a footfall moving to and fro along the cabinet floor.

"So it will walk all day, sir," whispered Poole; "ay, and the better part of the night. Only when a new sample comes from the chemist, there's a bit of a break. Ah, it's an ill-conscience that's such an enemy to rest! Ah, sir, there's blood foully shed in every step of it! But hark again, a little closer—put your heart in your ears Mr. Utterson, and tell me, is that the doctor's foot?"

The steps fell lightly and oddly, with a certain swing, for all they went so slowly; it was different indeed from the heavy creaking tread of Henry Jekyll. Utterson sighed. "Is there never anything else?" he asked.

Poole nodded. "Once," he said. "Once I heard it weeping!"

"Weeping? how that?" said the lawyer, conscious of a sudden chill of horror.

"Weeping like a woman or a lost soul," said the butler. "I came away with that upon my heart, that I could have wept too."

But now the ten minutes drew to an end. Poole disinterred the axe from under a stack of packing straw; the candle was set upon the nearest table to light them to the attack; and they drew near with bated breath to where that patient foot was still going up and down, up and down, in the quiet of the night.

"Jekyll," cried Utterson, with a loud voice, "I demand to see you." He paused a moment, but there came no reply. "I give you fair warning, our suspicions are aroused, and I must and shall see you," he resumed; "if not by fair means, then by foul—if not of your consent, then by brute force!"

"Utterson," said the voice, "for God's sake, have mercy!"

"Ah, that's not Jekyll's voice—it's Hyde's!" cried Utterson. "Down with the door, Poole."

Poole swung the axe over his shoulder; the blow shook the building, and the red baize door leaped against the lock and hinges. A dismal screech, as of mere animal terror, rang from the cabinet. Up went the axe again, and again the panels crashed and the frame bounded; four times the blow fell; but the wood was tough and the fittings were of excellent workmanship; and it was not until the fifth, that the lock burst in sunder and the wreck of the door fell inwards on the carpet.

The besiegers, appalled by their own riot and the stillness that had succeeded, stood back a little and peered in. There lay the cabinet before their eyes in the quiet lamplight, a good fire glowing and chattering on the hearth, the kettle singing its thin strain, a drawer or two open, papers neatly set forth on the business table, and nearer the fire, the things laid out for tea: the quietest room, you would have said, and, but for the glazed presses full of chemicals, the most commonplace that night in London.

Right in the midst there lay the body of a man sorely contorted and still twitching. They drew near on tiptoe, turned it on its back and beheld the face of Edward Hyde. He was dressed in clothes far too large for him, clothes of the doctor's bigness; the cords of his face still moved with a semblance of life, but life was quite gone; and by the crushed phial in the hand and the strong smell of kernels[1] that hung upon the air, Utterson knew that he was looking on the body of a self-destroyer.

"We have come too late," he said sternly, "whether to save or punish. Hyde is gone to his account; and it only remains for us to find the body of your master."

The far greater proportion of the building was occupied by the theatre, which filled almost the whole ground story and was lighted from above, and by the cabinet, which formed an upper story at one end and looked upon the court. A corridor joined the theatre to the door on the bystreet; and with this, the cabinet communicated separately by a second flight of stairs. There were besides a few dark closets and a spacious cellar. All these they now thoroughly examined. Each closet needed but a glance, for all were empty and all, by the dust that fell from their doors, had stood long unopened. The cellar, indeed, was filled with crazy[2] lumber, mostly dating from the times of the surgeon who was Jekyll's predecessor; but even as they opened the door, they were advertised of the uselessness of further search, by the fall of a perfect mat of cobweb which had for years sealed up the entrance. Nowhere was there any trace of Henry Jekyll, dead or alive.

Poole stamped on the flags of the corridor. "He must be buried here," he said, hearkening to the sound.

"Or he may have fled," said Utterson, and he turned to examine the door in the bystreet. It was locked; and lying nearby on the flags, they found the key, already stained with rust.

"This does not look like use," observed the lawyer,

"Use!" echoed Poole. "Do you not see, sir, it is broken? much as if a man had stamped on it."

"Ay," continued Utterson, "and the fractures, too, are rusty." The two men looked at each other with a scare. "This is beyond me, Poole," said the lawyer. "Let us go back to the cabinet."

---

1   Cyanide smells like almonds.
2   Damaged, unusable.

They mounted the stair in silence, and still with an occasional awestruck glance at the dead body, proceeded more thoroughly to examine the contents of the cabinet. At one table, there were traces of chemical work, various measured heaps of some white salt being laid on glass saucers, as though for an experiment in which the unhappy man had been prevented.

"That is the same drug that I was always bringing him," said Poole; and even as he spoke, the kettle with a startling noise boiled over.

This brought them to the fireside, where the easy chair was drawn cosily up, and the tea things stood ready to the sitter's elbow, the very sugar in the cup. There were several books on a shelf; one lay beside the tea things open, and Utterson was amazed to find it a copy of a pious work, for which Jekyll had several times expressed a great esteem, annotated, in his own hand, with startling blasphemies.

Next, in the course of their review of the chamber, the searchers came to the cheval glass, into whose depths they looked with an involuntary horror. But it was so turned as to show them nothing but the rosy glow playing on the roof, the fire sparkling in a hundred repetitions along the glazed front of the presses, and their own pale and fearful countenances stooping to look in.

"This glass have seen some strange things, sir," whispered Poole.

"And surely none stranger than itself," echoed the lawyer in the same tones. "For what did Jekyll"—he caught himself up at the word with a start, and then conquering the weakness: "what could Jekyll want with it?" he said.

"You may say that!" said Poole.

Next they turned to the business table. On the desk among the neat array of papers, a large envelope was uppermost, and bore, in the doctor's hand, the name of Mr. Utterson. The lawyer unsealed it, and several enclosures fell to the floor. The first was a will, drawn in the same eccentric terms as the one which he had returned six months before, to serve as a testament in case of death and as a deed of gift in case of disappearance; but in place of the name of Edward Hyde, the lawyer, with indescribable amazement, read the name of Gabriel John Utterson. He looked at Poole, and then back at the paper, and last of all at the dead malefactor stretched upon the carpet.

"My head goes round," he said. "He has been all these days in possession; he had no cause to like me; he must have raged to see himself displaced; and he has not destroyed this document."

He caught up the next paper; it was a brief note in the doctor's hand and dated at the top. "O Poole!" the lawyer cried, "he was alive and here this day. He cannot have been disposed of in so short a space, he must be still alive, he must have fled! And then, why fled? and how? and in that case, can we venture to declare this suicide? O, we must be careful. I foresee that we may yet involve your master in some dire catastrophe."

"Why don't you read it, sir?" asked Poole.

"Because I fear," replied the lawyer solemnly. "God grant I have no cause for it!" And with that he brought the paper to his eyes and read as follows.

> My dear Utterson,—When this shall fall into your hands, I shall have disappeared, under what circumstances I have not the penetration to foresee, but my instinct and all the circumstances of my nameless situation tell me that the end is sure and must be early. Go then, and first read the narrative which Lanyon warned me he was to place in your hands; and if you care to hear more, turn to the confession of
>
> Your unworthy and unhappy friend,
>
> Henry Jekyll.

"There was a third enclosure?" asked Utterson.

"Here, sir," said Poole, and gave into his hands a considerable packet sealed in several places.

The lawyer put it in his pocket. "I would say nothing of this paper. If your master has fled or is dead, we may at least save his credit. It is now ten; I must go home and read these documents in quiet; but I shall be back before midnight, when we shall send for the police."

They went out, locking the door of the theatre behind them; and Utterson, once more leaving the servants gathered about the fire in the hall, trudged back to his office to read the two narratives in which this mystery was now to be explained.

DOCTOR LANYON'S NARRATIVE

ON the ninth of January, now four days ago, I received by the evening delivery a registered envelope,[1] addressed in the hand of my colleague and old school-companion, Henry Jekyll. I was a good deal surprised by this; for we were by no means in the habit of correspondence; I had seen the man, dined

---

1 Letter or package that requires the signature of recipient upon delivery.

with him, indeed, the night before; and I could imagine nothing in our intercourse that should justify the formality of registration. The contents increased my wonder; for this is how the letter ran:

10TH DECEMBER, 18—

Dear Lanyon,—You are one of my oldest friends; and although we may have differed at times on scientific questions, I cannot remember, at least on my side, any break in our affection. There was never a day when, if you had said to me, "Jekyll, my life, my honour, my reason, depend upon you," I would not have sacrificed my fortune or my left hand to help you. Lanyon, my life, my honour, my reason, are all at your mercy; if you fail me tonight, I am lost. You might suppose, after this preface, that I am going to ask you for something dishonourable to grant. Judge for yourself.

I want you to postpone all other engagements for tonight—ay, even if you were summoned to the bedside of an emperor; to take a cab, unless your carriage should be actually at the door; and with this letter in your hand for consultation, to drive straight to my house. Poole, my butler, has his orders; you will find him waiting your arrival with a locksmith. The door of my cabinet is then to be forced; and you are to go in alone; to open the glazed press[1] (letter E) on the left hand, breaking the lock if it be shut; and to draw out, *with all its contents as they stand*, the fourth drawer from the top or (which is the same thing) the third from the bottom. In my extreme distress of mind, I have a morbid fear of misdirecting you; but even if I am in error, you may know the right drawer by its contents: some powders, a phial and a paper book. This drawer I beg of you to carry back with you to Cavendish Square exactly as it stands.

That is the first part of the service: now for the second. You should be back, if you set out at once on the receipt of this, long before midnight; but I will leave you that amount of margin, not only in the fear of one of those obstacles that can neither be prevented nor foreseen, but because an hour when your servants are in bed is to be preferred for what will then remain to do. At midnight, then, I have to ask you to be alone in your consulting room, to admit with your own hand into the house a man who will present himself in my name, and to place in his hands the drawer that you will have

---

1   Glass-door cabinet.

brought with you from my cabinet. Then you will have played your part and earned my gratitude completely. Five minutes, afterwards, if you insist upon an explanation, you will have understood that these arrangements are of capital importance; and that by the neglect of one of them, fantastic as they must appear, you might have charged your conscience with my death or the shipwreck of my reason.

Confident as I am that you will not trifle with this appeal, my heart sinks and my hand trembles at the bare thought of such a possibility. Think of me at this hour, in a strange place, labouring under a blackness of distress that no fancy can exaggerate, and yet well aware that, if you will but punctually serve me, my troubles will roll away like a story that is told. Serve me, my dear Lanyon, and save

Your friend,
H. J.

P.S. I had already sealed this up when a fresh terror struck upon my soul. It is possible that the post office may fail me, and this letter not come into your hands until tomorrow morning. In that case, dear Lanyon, do my errand when it shall be most convenient for you in the course of the day; and once more expect my messenger at midnight. It may then already be too late; and if that night passes without event, you will know that you have seen the last of Henry Jekyll.

Upon the reading of this letter, I made sure my colleague was insane; but till that was proved beyond the possibility of doubt, I felt bound to do as he requested. The less I understood of this farrago,[1] the less I was in a position to judge of its importance; and an appeal so worded could not be set aside without a grave responsibility. I rose accordingly from table, got into a hansom,[2] and drove straight to Jekyll's house. The butler was awaiting my arrival; he had received by the same post as mine a registered letter of instruction, and had sent at once for a locksmith and a carpenter. The tradesmen came while we were yet speaking; and we moved in a body to old Dr. Denman's surgical theatre, from which (as you are doubtless aware) Jekyll's private cabinet is most conveniently entered. The door was very strong, the lock excellent; the carpenter avowed he would have great trouble and have to do much damage, if force

---

1 Confused mix.
2 Two-wheel horse-drawn carriage.

were to be used; and the locksmith was near despair. But this last was a handy fellow, and after two hours' work, the door stood open. The press marked E was unlocked; and I took out the drawer, had it filled up with straw and tied in a sheet, and returned with it to Cavendish Square.

Here I proceeded to examine its contents. The powders were neatly enough made up, but not with the nicety of the dispensing chemist; so that it was plain they were of Jekyll's private manufacture; and when I opened one of the wrappers, I found what seemed to me a simple, crystalline salt of a white colour. The phial, to which I next turned my attention, might have been about half-full of a blood-red liquor, which was highly pungent to the sense of smell and seemed to me to contain phosphorus and some volatile ether. At the other ingredients, I could make no guess. The book was an ordinary version book and contained little but a series of dates. These covered a period of many years, but I observed that the entries ceased nearly a year ago and quite abruptly. Here and there a brief remark was appended to a date, usually no more than a single word: "double" occurring perhaps six times in a total of several hundred entries; and once very early in the list and followed by several marks of exclamation, "total failure!!!" All this, though it whetted my curiosity, told me little that was definite. Here were a phial of some tincture, a paper of some salt, and the record of a series of experiments that had led (like too many of Jekyll's investigations) to no end of practical usefulness. How could the presence of these articles in my house affect either the honour, the sanity, or the life of my flighty colleague? If his messenger could go to one place, why could he not go to another? And even granting some impediment, why was this gentleman to be received by me in secret? The more I reflected, the more convinced I grew that I was dealing with a case of cerebral disease; and though I dismissed my servants to bed, I loaded an old revolver that I might be found in some posture of self-defence.

Twelve o'clock had scarce rung out over London, ere the knocker sounded very gently on the door. I went myself at the summons, and found a small man crouching against the pillars of the portico.

"Are you come from Dr. Jekyll?" I asked.

He told me "yes" by a constrained gesture; and when I had bidden him enter, he did not obey me without a searching backward glance into the darkness of the square. There was a policeman not far off, advancing with his bull's eye[1] open; and at the sight, I thought my visitor started and made greater haste.

---

1   Lantern with a planoconvex lens, used as flashlight.

These particulars struck me, I confess, disagreeably; and as I followed him into the bright light of the consulting room, I kept my hand ready on my weapon. Here, at last, I had a chance of clearly seeing him. I had never set eyes on him before, so much was certain. He was small, as I have said; I was struck besides with the shocking expression of his face, with his remarkable combination of great muscular activity and great apparent debility of constitution, and—last but not least—with the odd, subjective disturbance caused by his neighbourhood.[1] This bore some resemblance to incipient rigor,[2] and was accompanied by a marked sinking of the pulse. At the time, I set it down to some idiosyncratic, personal distaste, and merely wondered at the acuteness of the symptoms; but I have since had reason to believe the cause to lie much deeper in the nature of man, and to turn on some nobler hinge than the principle of hatred.

This person (who had thus, from the first moment of his entrance, struck in me what I can only describe as a disgustful curiosity) was dressed in a fashion that would have made an ordinary person laughable: his clothes, that is to say, although they were of rich and sober fabric, were enormously too large for him in every measurement—the trousers hanging on his legs and rolled up to keep them from the ground, the waist of the coat below his haunches, and the collar sprawling wide upon his shoulders. Strange to relate, this ludicrous accoutrement was far from moving me to laughter. Rather, as there was something abnormal and misbegotten in the very essence of the creature that now faced me—something seizing, surprising and revolting—this fresh disparity seemed but to fit in with and to reinforce it; so that to my interest in the man's nature and character, there was added a curiosity as to his origin, his life, his fortune and status in the world.

These observations, though they have taken so great a space to be set down in, were yet the work of a few seconds. My visitor was, indeed, on fire with sombre excitement.

"Have you got it?" he cried. "Have you got it?" And so lively was his impatience that he even laid his hand upon my arm and sought to shake me.

I put him back, conscious at his touch of a certain icy pang along my blood. "Come, sir," said I. "You forget that I have not yet the pleasure of your acquaintance. Be seated, if you please." And I showed him an example, and sat down myself in my customary seat and with as fair an imitation of my ordinary manner to a patient, as the lateness of the hour, the nature of my preoccupations, and the horror I had of my visitor, would suffer me to muster.

---

1 Proximity.
2 Trembling.

"I beg your pardon, Dr. Lanyon," he replied civilly enough. "What you say is very well founded; and my impatience has shown its heels to my politeness. I come here at the instance of your colleague, Dr. Henry Jekyll, on a piece of business of some moment; and I understood …" he paused and put his hand to his throat, and I could see, in spite of his collected manner, that he was wrestling against the approaches of the hysteria[1]—"I understood, a drawer …"

But here I took pity on my visitor's suspense, and some perhaps on my own growing curiosity.

"There it is, sir," said I, pointing to the drawer, where it lay on the floor behind a table and still covered with the sheet.

He sprang to it, and then paused, and laid his hand upon his heart; I could hear his teeth grate with the convulsive action of his jaws; and his face was so ghastly to see that I grew alarmed both for his life and reason.

"Compose yourself," said I.

He turned a dreadful smile to me, and as if with the decision of despair, plucked away the sheet. At sight of the contents, he uttered one loud sob of such immense relief that I sat petrified. And the next moment, in a voice that was already fairly well under control, "Have you a graduated glass?"[2] he asked.

I rose from my place with something of an effort and gave him what he asked.

He thanked me with a smiling nod, measured out a few minims[3] of the red tincture and added one of the powders. The mixture, which was at first of a reddish hue, began, in proportion as the crystals melted, to brighten in colour, to effervesce audibly, and to throw off small fumes of vapour. Suddenly and at the same moment, the ebullition ceased and the compound changed to a dark purple, which faded again more slowly to a watery green. My visitor, who had watched these metamorphoses with a keen eye, smiled, set down the glass upon the table, and then turned and looked upon me with an air of scrutiny.

"And now," said he, "to settle what remains. Will you be wise? will you be guided? will you suffer me to take this glass in my hand and to go forth from your house without further parley? or has the greed of curiosity too much command of you? Think before you answer, for it shall be done as you decide. As you decide, you shall be left as you were before, and neither richer nor wiser, unless the sense of service rendered to a man in mortal distress may be counted as a kind of riches

---

1   Nervous disorder associated with women, one of the symptoms of which is a constricted throat.
2   Laboratory beaker with measurements printed on side.
3   Drops.

of the soul. Or, if you shall so prefer to choose, a new province of knowledge and new avenues to fame and power shall be laid open to you, here, in this room, upon the instant; and your sight shall be blasted by a prodigy to stagger the unbelief of Satan."

"Sir," said I, affecting a coolness that I was far from truly possessing, "you speak enigmas, and you will perhaps not wonder that I hear you with no very strong impression of belief. But I have gone too far in the way of inexplicable services to pause before I see the end."

"It is well," replied my visitor. "Lanyon, you remember your vows: what follows is under the seal of our profession. And now, you who have so long been bound to the most narrow and material views, you who have denied the virtue of transcendental medicine, you who have derided your superiors—behold!"

He put the glass to his lips and drank at one gulp. A cry followed; he reeled, staggered, clutched at the table and held on, staring with injected[1] eyes, gasping with open mouth; and as I looked there came, I thought, a change—he seemed to swell—his face became suddenly black and the features seemed to melt and alter—and the next moment, I had sprung to my feet and leaped back against the wall, my arm raised to shield me from that prodigy, my mind submerged in terror.

"O God!" I screamed, and "O God!" again and again; for there before my eyes—pale and shaken, and half fainting, and groping before him with his hands, like a man restored from death—there stood Henry Jekyll!

What he told me in the next hour, I cannot bring my mind to set on paper. I saw what I saw, I heard what I heard, and my soul sickened at it; and yet now when that sight has faded from my eyes, I ask myself if I believe it, and I cannot answer. My life is shaken to its roots; sleep has left me; the deadliest terror sits by me at all hours of the day and night; I feel that my days are numbered, and that I must die; and yet I shall die incredulous. As for the moral turpitude that man unveiled to me, even with tears of penitence, I cannot, even in memory, dwell on it without a start of horror. I will say but one thing, Utterson, and that (if you can bring your mind to credit it) will be more than enough. The creature who crept into my house that night was, on Jekyll's own confession, known by the name of Hyde and hunted for in every corner of the land as the murderer of Carew.

HASTIE LANYON

---

1   Bulging.

Henry Jekyll's Full Statement of the Case

I WAS born in the year 18— to a large fortune, endowed besides with excellent parts,[1] inclined by nature to industry, fond of the respect of the wise and good among my fellow-men, and thus, as might have been supposed, with every guarantee of an honourable and distinguished future. And indeed the worst of my faults was a certain impatient gaiety of disposition, such as has made the happiness of many, but such as I found it hard to reconcile with my imperious desire to carry my head high, and wear a more than commonly grave countenance before the public. Hence it came about that I concealed my pleasures; and that when I reached years of reflection, and began to look round me and take stock of my progress and position in the world, I stood already committed to a profound duplicity of life. Many a man would have even blazoned[2] such irregularities as I was guilty of; but from the high views that I had set before me, I regarded and hid them with an almost morbid sense of shame. It was thus rather the exacting nature of my aspirations than any particular degradation in my faults, that made me what I was and, with even a deeper trench than in the majority of men, severed in me those provinces of good and ill which divide and compound man's dual nature. In this case, I was driven to reflect deeply and inveterately on that hard law of life, which lies at the root of religion and is one of the most plentiful springs of distress. Though so profound a double-dealer, I was in no sense a hypocrite; both sides of me were in dead earnest; I was no more myself when I laid aside restraint and plunged in shame, than when I laboured, in the eye of day, at the furtherance of knowledge or the relief of sorrow and suffering. And it chanced that the direction of my scientific studies, which led wholly towards the mystic and the transcendental, reäcted and shed a strong light on this consciousness of the perennial war among my members.[3] With every day, and from both sides of my intelligence, the moral and the intellectual, I thus drew steadily nearer to that truth, by whose partial discovery I have been doomed to such a dreadful shipwreck: that man is not truly one, but truly two. I say two, because the state of my own knowledge does not pass beyond that point. Others will follow, others will outstrip me on the same lines; and I hazard the guess that man will be ultimately known for a mere polity of multifarious, incongruous and independent denizens. I for my part, from the nature of my life, advanced infallibly in one direction and in one direction only. It was on the moral side, and in my own person, that I learned to recognise the thorough and

---

1 Abilities.
2 Prominently displayed, bragged about.
3 Parts of himself.

primitive duality of man; I saw that, of the two natures that contended in the field of my consciousness, even if I could rightly be said to be either, it was only because I was radically both; and from an early date, even before the course of my scientific discoveries had begun to suggest the most naked possibility of such a miracle, I had learned to dwell with pleasure, as a beloved daydream, on the thought of the separation of these elements. If each, I told myself, could but be housed in separate identities, life would be relieved of all that was unbearable; the unjust might go his way, delivered from the aspirations and remorse of his more upright twin; and the just could walk steadfastly and securely on his upward path, doing the good things in which he found his pleasure, and no longer exposed to disgrace and penitence by the hands of this extraneous evil. It was the curse of mankind that these incongruous faggots[1] were thus bound together—that in the agonised womb of consciousness, these polar twins should be continuously struggling. How, then, were they dissociated?

I was so far in my reflections when, as I have said, a side light began to shine upon the subject from the laboratory table. I began to perceive more deeply than it has ever yet been stated, the trembling immateriality, the mist-like transience, of this seemingly so solid body in which we walk attired. Certain agents I found to have the power to shake and to pluck back that fleshly vestment, even as a wind might toss the curtains of a pavilion.[2] For two good reasons, I will not enter deeply into this scientific branch of my confession. First, because I have been made to learn that the doom and burthen of our life is bound forever on man's shoulders, and when the attempt is made to cast it off, it but returns upon us with more unfamiliar and more awful pressure. Second, because as my narrative will make alas! too evident, my discoveries were incomplete. Enough, then, that I not only recognised my natural body for the mere aura and effulgence of certain of the powers that made up my spirit, but managed to compound a drug by which these powers should be dethroned from their supremacy, and a second form and countenance substituted, none the less natural to me because they were the expression, and bore the stamp, of lower elements in my soul.

I hesitated long before I put this theory to the test of practice. I knew well that I risked death; for any drug that so potently controlled and shook the very fortress of identity, might by the least scruple of an overdose or at the least inopportunity in the moment of exhibition, utterly blot out that immaterial tabernacle which I looked to it to change. But the temptation of a discovery so singular and profound,

---

1 Bundle of sticks tied together and used for fuel.
2 Large tent.

at last overcame the suggestions of alarm. I had long since prepared my tincture; I purchased at once, from a firm of wholesale chemists, a large quantity of a particular salt which I knew, from my experiments, to be the last ingredient required; and late one accursed night, I compounded the elements, watched them boil and smoke together in the glass, and when the ebullition had subsided, with a strong glow of courage, drank off the potion.

The most racking pangs succeeded: a grinding in the bones, deadly nausea, and a horror of the spirit that cannot be exceeded at the hour of birth or death. Then these agonies began swiftly to subside, and I came to myself as if out of a great sickness. There was something strange in my sensations, something indescribably new and, from its very novelty, incredibly sweet. I felt younger, lighter, happier in body; within I was conscious of a heady recklessness, a current of disordered sensual images running like a mill race[1] in my fancy, a solution of the bonds of obligation, an unknown but not an innocent freedom of the soul. I knew myself, at the first breath of this new life, to be more wicked, tenfold more wicked, sold a slave to my original evil; and the thought, in that moment, braced and delighted me like wine. I stretched out my hands, exulting in the freshness of these sensations; and in the act, I was suddenly aware that I had lost in stature.

There was no mirror, at that date, in my room; that which stands beside me as I write, was brought there later on and for the very purpose of these transformations. The night, however, was far gone into the morning—the morning, black as it was, was nearly ripe for the conception of the day—the inmates of my house were locked in the most rigorous hours of slumber; and I determined, flushed as I was with hope and triumph, to venture in my new shape as far as to my bedroom. I crossed the yard, wherein the constellations looked down upon me, I could have thought, with wonder, the first creature of that sort that their unsleeping vigilance had yet disclosed to them; I stole through the corridors, a stranger in my own house; and coming to my room, I saw for the first time the appearance of Edward Hyde.

I must here speak by theory alone, saying not that which I know, but that which I suppose to be most probable. The evil side of my nature, to which I had now transferred the stamping efficacy, was less robust and less developed than the good which I had just deposed. Again, in the course of my life, which had been, after all, nine tenths a life of effort, virtue and control, it had been much less exercised and much less exhausted. And hence, as I think, it came about that Edward Hyde was so much smaller, slighter and younger than Henry Jekyll. Even as good shone upon the countenance of the

---

1   The canal in which water is conveyed to a mill wheel.

one, evil was written broadly and plainly on the face of the other. Evil besides (which I must still believe to be the lethal side of man) had left on that body an imprint of deformity and decay. And yet when I looked upon that ugly idol in the glass, I was conscious of no repugnance, rather of a leap of welcome. This, too, was myself. It seemed natural and human. In my eyes it bore a livelier image of the spirit, it seemed more express and single, than the imperfect and divided countenance, I had been hitherto accustomed to call mine. And in so far I was doubtless right. I have observed that when I wore the semblance of Edward Hyde, none could come near to me at first without a visible misgiving of the flesh. This, as I take it, was because all human beings, as we meet them, are commingled out of good and evil: and Edward Hyde, alone in the ranks of mankind, was pure evil.

I lingered but a moment at the mirror: the second and conclusive experiment had yet to be attempted; it yet remained to be seen if I had lost my identity beyond redemption and must flee before daylight from a house that was no longer mine; and hurrying back to my cabinet, I once more prepared and drank the cup, once more suffered the pangs of dissolution, and came to myself once more with the character, the stature and the face of Henry Jekyll.

That night I had come to the fatal cross roads. Had I approached my discovery in a more noble spirit, had I risked the experiment while under the empire of generous or pious aspirations, all must have been otherwise, and from these agonies of death and birth, I had come forth an angel instead of a fiend. The drug had no discriminating action; it was neither diabolical nor divine; it but shook the doors of the prison-house of my disposition; and like the captives of Philippi,[1] that which stood within ran forth. At that time my virtue slumbered; my evil, kept awake by ambition, was alert and swift to seize the occasion; and the thing that was projected was Edward Hyde. Hence, although I had now two characters as well as two appearances, one was wholly evil, and the other was still the old Henry Jekyll, that incongruous compound of whose reformation and improvement I had already learned to despair. The movement was thus wholly toward the worse.

Even at that time, I had not yet conquered my aversion to the dryness of a life of study. I would still be merrily disposed at times; and as my pleasures were (to say the least) undignified, and I was not only well known and highly considered, but

---

1   A reference to the divinely induced earthquake that rocks the Macedonian city of Philippi, collapsing the walls of the prison where the apostle Paul and his companion Silas are confined (Acts 16:26). Rather than flee, however, the men hand themselves over to their jailor, thereby inspiring him to convert to Christianity.

growing towards the elderly man, this incoherency of my life was daily growing more unwelcome. It was on this side that my new power tempted me until I fell in slavery. I had but to drink the cup, to doff at once the body of the noted professor, and to assume, like a thick cloak, that of Edward Hyde. I smiled at the notion; it seemed to me at the time to be humorous; and I made my preparations with the most studious care. I took and furnished that house in Soho, to which Hyde was tracked by the police; and engaged as housekeeper a creature whom I well knew to be silent and unscrupulous. On the other side, I announced to my servants that a Mr. Hyde (whom I described) was to have full liberty and power about my house in the square; and to parry mishaps, I even called and made myself a familiar object, in my second character. I next drew up that will to which you so much objected; so that if anything befell me in the person of Doctor Jekyll, I could enter on that of Edward Hyde without pecuniary loss. And thus fortified, as I supposed, on every side, I began to profit by the strange immunities of my position.

Men have before hired bravos[1] to transact their crimes, while their own person and reputation sat under shelter. I was the first that ever did so for his pleasures. I was the first that could thus plod in the public eye with a load of genial respectability, and in a moment, like a schoolboy, strip off these lendings[2] and spring headlong into the sea of liberty. But for me, in my impenetrable mantle, the safety was complete. Think of it—I did not even exist! Let me but escape into my laboratory door, give me but a second or two to mix and swallow the draught that I had always standing ready; and whatever he had done, Edward Hyde would pass away like the stain of breath upon a mirror; and there in his stead, quietly at home, trimming the midnight lamp in his study, a man who could afford to laugh at suspicion, would be Henry Jekyll.

The pleasures which I made haste to seek in my disguise were, as I have said, undignified; I would scarce use a harder term. But in the hands of Edward Hyde, they soon began to turn towards the monstrous. When I would come back from these excursions, I was often plunged into a kind of wonder at my vicarious depravity. This familiar[3] that I called out of my own soul, and sent forth alone to do his good pleasure, was a being inherently malign and villainous; his every act and thought centered on self; drinking pleasure with bestial avidity from any degree of torture to another; relentless like a man of stone. Henry Jekyll stood at times aghast before the acts of Edward Hyde; but the situation was apart from ordinary laws, and insidiously relaxed the grasp of conscience. It was Hyde, after all, and Hyde alone, that was guilty.

---

1   Hit men.
2   Borrowed clothes.
3   Attendant spirit, often demonic.

Jekyll was no worse; he woke again to his good qualities seemingly unimpaired; he would even make haste, where it was possible, to undo the evil done by Hyde. And thus his conscience slumbered.

Into the details of the infamy at which I thus connived (for even now I can scarce grant that I committed it) I have no design of entering I mean but to point out the warnings and the successive steps with which my chastisement approached. I met with one accident which, as it brought on no consequence, I shall no more than mention. An act of cruelty to a child aroused against me the anger of a passer by, whom I recognised the other day in the person of your kinsman; the doctor and the child's family joined him; there were moments when I feared for my life; and at last, in order to pacify their too just resentment, Edward Hyde had to bring them to the door, and pay them in a cheque drawn in the name, of Henry Jekyll. But this danger was easily eliminated from the future, by opening an account at another bank in the name of Edward Hyde himself; and when, by sloping my own hand backward, I had supplied my double with a signature, I thought I sat beyond the reach of fate.

Some two months before the murder of Sir Danvers, I had been out for one of my adventures, had returned at a late hour, and woke the next day in bed with somewhat odd sensations. It was in vain I looked about me; in vain I saw the decent furniture and tall proportions of my room in the square; in vain that I recognised the pattern of the bed curtains and the design of the mahogany frame; something still kept insisting that I was not where I was, that I had not wakened where I seemed to be, but in the little room in Soho where I was accustomed to sleep in the body of Edward Hyde. I smiled to myself, and, in my psychological way, began lazily to inquire into the elements of this illusion, occasionally, even as I did so, dropping back into a comfortable morning doze. I was still so engaged when, in one of my more wakeful moments, my eye fell upon my hand. Now the hand of Henry Jekyll (as you have often remarked) was professional in shape and size: it was large, firm, white and comely. But the hand which I now saw, clearly enough, in the yellow light of a mid-London morning, lying half shut on the bed clothes, was lean, corded, knuckly, of a dusky pallor and thickly shaded with a swart growth of hair. It was the hand of Edward Hyde.

I must have stared upon it for near half a minute, sunk as I was in the mere stupidity of wonder, before terror woke up in my breast as sudden and startling as the crash of cymbals; and bounding from my bed, I rushed to the mirror. At the sight that met my eyes, my blood was changed into something exquisitely thin and icy. Yes, I had gone to bed Henry Jekyll, I had awakened Edward Hyde. How was this to be explained? I asked myself; and then, with another bound of terror— how was it to be remedied? It was well on in the morning; the servants were up; all my drugs were in the cabinet—a long journey, down two pair of stairs, through the back passage, across the open court and through the anatomical theatre, from where I was then standing horror-struck. It might indeed be possible to cover my face; but of what use was that, when I was unable to conceal the alteration in my stature? And then with an overpowering sweetness of relief, it came back upon my mind that the servants were already used to the coming and going of my second self. I had soon dressed, as well as I was able, in clothes of my own size: had soon passed through the house, where Bradshaw stared and drew back at seeing Mr. Hyde at such an hour and in such a strange array; and ten minutes later, Dr. Jekyll had returned to his own shape and was sitting down, with a darkened brow, to make a feint of breakfasting.

Small indeed was my appetite. This inexplicable incident, this reversal of my previous experience, seemed, like the Babylonian finger on the wall,[1] to be spelling out the letters of my judgment; and I began to reflect more seriously than ever before on the issues and possibilities of my double existence. That part of me which I had the power of projecting, had lately been much exercised and nourished; it had seemed to me of late as though the body of Edward Hyde had grown in stature, as though (when I wore that form) I were conscious of a more generous tide of blood; and I began to spy a danger that, if this were much prolonged, the balance of my nature might be permanently overthrown, the power of voluntary change be forfeited, and the character of Edward Hyde become irrevocably mine. The power of the drug had not been always equally displayed. Once, very early in my career, it had totally failed me; since then I had been obliged on more than one occasion to double, and once, with infinite risk of death, to treble the amount; and these rare uncertainties had cast hitherto the sole shadow on my contentment. Now, however, and in the light of that morning's accident, I was led to remark that whereas, in the beginning, the difficulty had been to throw off the body of Jekyll, it had of late, gradually but decidedly transferred itself to the other side. All things therefore seemed to point to this: that I was slowly losing hold of my original and better self, and becoming slowly incorporated with my second and worse.

Between these two, I now felt I had to choose. My two natures had memory in common, but all other faculties were most unequally shared between them. Jekyll (who was composite) now with the most sensitive apprehensions, now with a greedy gusto, projected and shared in the pleasures and adventures of Hyde; but Hyde was

---

1   The writing on the wall, i.e., a portent of doom; a reference to the vision of handwriting that King Belshazzar of Babylon sees on his wall—informing him of his imminent destruction—after he profanes the sacred vessels from Solomon's Temple in Jerusalem (Daniel 5:5, 5:24–28).

indifferent to Jekyll, or but remembered him as the mountain bandit remembers the cavern in which he conceals himself from pursuit. Jekyll had more than a father's interest; Hyde had more than a son's indifference. To cast in my lot with Jekyll, was to die to those appetites which I had long secretly indulged and had of late begun to pamper. To cast it in with Hyde, was to die to a thousand interests and aspirations, and to become, at a blow and forever, despised and friendless. The bargain might appear unequal; but there was still another consideration in the scales; for while Jekyll would suffer smartingly in the fires of abstinence, Hyde would be not even conscious of all that he had lost. Strange as my circumstances were, the terms of this debate are as old and commonplace as man; much the same inducements and alarms cast the die for any tempted and trembling sinner; and it fell out with me, as it falls with so vast a majority of my fellows, that I chose the better part and was found wanting in the strength to keep to it.

Yes, I preferred the elderly and discontented doctor, surrounded by friends and cherishing honest hopes; and bade a resolute farewell to the liberty, the comparative youth, the light step, leaping pulses and secret pleasures, that I had enjoyed in the disguise of Hyde. I made this choice perhaps with some unconscious reservation, for I neither gave up the house in Soho, nor destroyed the clothes of Edward Hyde, which still lay ready in my cabinet. For two months, however, I was true to my determination; for two months, I led a life of such severity as I had never before attained to, and enjoyed the compensations of an approving conscience. But time began at last to obliterate the freshness of my alarm; the praises of conscience began to grow into a thing of course; I began to be tortured with throes and longings, as of Hyde struggling after freedom; and at last, in an hour of moral weakness, I once again compounded and swallowed the transforming draught.

I do not suppose that, when a drunkard reasons with himself upon his vice, he is once out of five hundred times affected by the dangers that he runs through his brutish, physical insensibility; neither had I, long as I had considered my position, made enough allowance for the complete moral insensibility and insensate readiness to evil, which were the leading characters of Edward Hyde. Yet it was by these that I was punished. My devil had been long caged, he came out roaring. I was conscious, even when I took the draught, of a more unbridled, a more furious propensity to ill. It must have been this, I suppose, that stirred in my soul that tempest of impatience with which I listened to the civilities of my unhappy victim; I declare at least, before God, no man morally sane could have been guilty of that crime upon so pitiful a provocation; and that I struck in no more reasonable spirit than that in which a sick child may break a plaything. But I had voluntarily stripped myself of all those balancing instincts, by which even the worst of us continues to walk with some degree of steadiness among temptations; and in my case, to be tempted, however slightly, was to fall.

Instantly the spirit of hell awoke in me and raged. With a transport of glee, I mauled the unresisting body, tasting delight from every blow; and it was not till weariness had begun to succeed, that I was suddenly, in the top fit of my delirium, struck through the heart by a cold thrill of terror. A mist dispersed; I saw my life to be forfeit; and fled from the scene of these excesses, at once glorying and trembling, my lust of evil gratified and stimulated, my love of life screwed to the topmost peg. I ran to the house in Soho, and (to make assurance doubly sure) destroyed my papers; thence I set out through the lamplit streets, in the same divided ecstasy of mind, gloating on my crime, light-headedly devising others in the future, and yet still hastening and still hearkening in my wake for the steps of the avenger. Hyde had a song upon his lips as he compounded the draught, and as he drank it, pledged the dead man. The pangs of transformation had not done tearing him, before Henry Jekyll, with streaming tears of gratitude and remorse, had fallen upon his knees and lifted his clasped hands to God. The veil of self-indulgence was rent from head to foot, I saw my life as a whole: I followed it up from the days of childhood, when I had walked with my father's hand, and through the self-denying toils of my professional life, to arrive again and again, with the same sense of unreality, at the damned horrors of the evening. I could have screamed aloud; I sought with tears and prayers to smother down the crowd of hideous images and sounds with which my memory swarmed against me; and still, between the petitions, the ugly face of my iniquity stared into my soul. As the acuteness of this remorse began to die away, it was succeeded by a sense of joy. The problem of my conduct was solved. Hyde was thenceforth impossible; whether I would or not, I was now confined to the better part of my existence; and O, how I rejoiced to think it! with what willing humility, I embraced anew the restrictions of natural life! with what sincere renunciation, I locked the door by which I had so often gone and come, and ground the key under my heel!

The next day, came the news that the murder had been overlooked,[1] that the guilt of Hyde was patent to the world, and that the victim was a man high in public estimation. It was not only a crime, it had been a tragic folly. I think I was glad to know it; I think I was glad to have my better impulses thus buttressed and guarded

---

1   Seen from above.

by the terrors of the scaffold. Jekyll was now my city of refuge;[1] let but Hyde peep out an instant, and the hands of all men would be raised to take and slay him.

I resolved in my future conduct to redeem the past; and I can say with honesty that my resolve was fruitful of some good. You know yourself how earnestly in the last months of last year, I laboured to relieve suffering;[2] you know that much was done for others, and that the days passed quietly, almost happily for myself. Nor can I truly say that I wearied of this beneficent and innocent life; I think instead that I daily enjoyed it more completely; but I was still cursed with my duality of purpose; and as the first edge of my penitence wore off, the lower side of me, so long indulged, so recently chained down, began to growl for license. Not that I dreamed of resuscitating Hyde; the bare idea of that would startle me to frenzy: no, it was in my own person, that I was once more tempted to trifle with my conscience; and it was as an ordinary secret sinner, that I at last fell before the assaults of temptation.

There comes an end to all things; the most capacious measure is filled at last; and this brief condescension to my evil finally destroyed the balance of my soul. And yet I was not alarmed; the fall seemed natural, like a return to the old days before I had made my discovery. It was a fine, clear, January day, wet under foot where the frost had melted, but cloudless overhead; and the Regent's Park[3] was full of winter chirrupings and sweet with Spring odours. I sat in the sun on a bench; the animal within me licking the chops of memory; the spiritual side a little drowsed, promising subsequent penitence, but not yet moved to begin. After all, I reflected I was like my neighbours; and then I smiled, comparing myself with other men, comparing my active goodwill with the lazy cruelty of their neglect. And at the very moment of that vainglorious thought, a qualm came over me, a horrid nausea and the most deadly shuddering. These passed away, and left me faint; and then as in its turn the faintness subsided, I began to be aware of a change in the temper of my thoughts, a greater boldness, a contempt of danger, a solution of the bonds of obligation. I looked down; my clothes hung formlessly on my shrunken limbs; the hand that lay on my knee was corded and hairy. I was once more Edward Hyde. A moment before I had been safe of all men's respect, wealthy, beloved—the cloth laying for me in

---

1   Six cities in ancient Israel where those guilty of manslaughter could seek asylum.
2   Worked as a volunteer at a charity.
3   Large park north of Marylebone in London's West End. The image of frost melting underfoot and the sudden tonal shift from January idyll to "horrid nausea" might be an allusion on Stevenson's part to another horrid transformation that took place on the same spot: the famous Regent's Park Ice-skating Disaster of January 15, 1867, in which 40 ice-skaters died when the ice collapsed beneath their feet. 160 others were injured.

the dining room at home; and now I was the common quarry of mankind, hunted, houseless, a known murderer, thrall to the gallows.

My reason wavered, but it did not fail me utterly. I have more than once observed that, in my second character, my faculties seemed sharpened to a point and my spirits more tensely elastic; thus it came about that, where Jekyll perhaps might have succumbed, Hyde rose to the importance of the moment. My drugs were in one of the presses of my cabinet; how was I to reach them? That was the problem that (crushing my temples in my hands) I set myself to solve. The laboratory door I had closed. If I sought to enter by the house, my own servants would consign me to the gallows. I saw I must employ another hand, and thought of Lanyon. How was he to be reached? how persuaded? Supposing that I escaped capture in the streets, how was I to make my way into his presence? and how should I, an unknown and displeasing visitor, prevail on the famous physician to rifle the study of his colleague, Dr. Jekyll? Then I remembered that of my original character, one part remained to me: I could write my own hand; and once I had conceived that kindling spark, the way that I must follow became lighted up from end to end.

Thereupon, I arranged my clothes as best I could, and summoning a passing hansom; drove to an hotel in Portland Street,[1] the name of which I chanced to remember. At my appearance (which was indeed comical enough, however tragic a fate these garments covered) the driver could not conceal his mirth. I gnashed my teeth upon him with a gust of devilish fury; and the smile withered from his face—happily for him—yet more happily for myself, for in another instant I had certainly dragged him from his perch. At the inn, as I entered, I looked about me with so black a countenance as made the attendants tremble; not a look did they exchange in my presence; but obsequiously took my orders, led me to a private room, and brought me wherewithal to write. Hyde in danger of his life was a creature new to me: shaken with inordinate anger, strung to the pitch of murder, lusting to inflict pain. Yet the creature was astute; mastered his fury with a great effort of the will; composed his two important letters, one to Lanyon and one to Poole; and that he might receive actual evidence of their being posted, sent them out with directions that they should be registered.

Thenceforward, he sat all day over the fire in the private room, gnawing his nails; there he dined, sitting alone with his fears, the waiter visibly quailing before his eye; and thence, when the night was fully come, he set forth in the corner of a closed

---

1   Great Portland Street, between Marylebone and Fitzrovia neighborhoods, south of Regent's Park.

cab, and was driven to and fro about the streets of the city. He, I say—I cannot say, I. That child of Hell had nothing human; nothing lived in him but fear and hatred. And when at last, thinking the driver had begun to grow suspicious, he discharged the cab and ventured on foot, attired in his misfitting clothes, an object marked out for observation, into the midst of the nocturnal passengers, these two base passions raged within him like a tempest. He walked fast, hunted by his fears, chattering to himself, skulking through the less frequented thoroughfares, counting the minutes that still divided him from midnight. Once a woman spoke to him, offering, I think, a box of lights. He smote her in the face, and she fled.

When I came to myself at Lanyon's, the horror of my old friend perhaps affected me somewhat: I do not know; it was at least but a drop in the sea to the abhorrence with which I looked back upon these hours. A change had come over me. It was no longer the fear of the gallows, it was the horror of being Hyde that racked me. I received Lanyon's condemnation partly in a dream; it was partly in a dream that I came home to my own house and got into bed. I slept after the prostration of the day, with a stringent and profound slumber which not even the nightmares that wrung me could avail to break. I awoke in the morning shaken, weakened, but refreshed. I still hated and feared the thought of the brute that slept within me, and I had not of course forgotten the appalling dangers of the day before; but I was once more at home, in my own house and close to my drugs; and gratitude for my escape shone so strong in my soul that it almost rivalled the brightness of hope.

I was stepping leisurely across the court after breakfast, drinking the chill of the air with pleasure, when I was seized again with those indescribable sensations that heralded the change; and I had but the time to gain the shelter of my cabinet, before I was once again raging and freezing with the passions of Hyde. It took on this occasion a double dose to recall me to myself; and alas, six hours after, as I sat looking sadly in the fire, the pangs returned, and the drug had to be re-administered. In short, from that day forth it seemed only by a great effort as of gymnastics, and only under the immediate stimulation of the drug, that I was able to wear the countenance of Jekyll. At all hours of the day and night, I would be taken with the premonitory shudder; above all, if I slept, or even dozed for a moment in my chair, it was always as Hyde that I awakened. Under the strain of this continually impending doom and by the sleeplessness to which I now condemned myself, ay, even beyond what I had thought possible to man, I became, in my own person, a creature eaten up and emptied by fever, languidly weak both in body and mind, and solely occupied by one thought: the horror of my other self. But when I slept, or when the virtue of the medicine wore off, I would leap almost without transition (for the pangs of transformation grew daily less marked) into the possession of a fancy brimming with images of terror, a soul boiling with causeless hatreds, and a body that seemed not strong enough to contain the raging energies of life. The powers of Hyde seemed to have grown with the sickliness of Jekyll. And certainly the hate that now divided them was equal on each side. With Jekyll, it was a thing of vital instinct. He had now seen the full deformity of that creature that shared with him some of the phenomena of consciousness, and was co-heir with him to death: and beyond these links of community, which in themselves made the most poignant part of his distress, he thought of Hyde, for all his energy of life, as of something not only hellish but inorganic. This was the shocking thing; that the slime of the pit seemed to utter cries and voices; that the amorphous dust gesticulated and sinned; that what was dead, and had no shape, should usurp the offices of life. And this again, that that insurgent horror was knit to him closer than a wife, closer than an eye; lay caged in his flesh, where he heard it mutter and felt it struggle to be born; and at every hour of weakness, and in the confidence of slumber, prevailed against him, and deposed him out of life. The hatred of Hyde for Jekyll, was of a different order. His terror of the gallows drove him continually to commit temporary suicide, and return to his subordinate station of a part instead of a person; but he loathed the necessity, he loathed the despondency into which Jekyll was now fallen, and he resented the dislike with which he was himself regarded. Hence the apelike tricks that he would play me, scrawling in my own hand blasphemies on the pages of my books, burning the letters and destroying the portrait of my father; and indeed, had it not been for his fear of death, he would long ago have ruined himself in order to involve me in the ruin. But his love of life is wonderful; I go further: I, who sicken and freeze at the mere thought of him, when I recall the abjection and passion of this attachment, and when I know how he fears my power to cut him off by suicide, I find it in my heart to pity him.

It is useless, and the time awfully fails me, to prolong this description; no one has ever suffered such torments, let that suffice; and yet even to these, habit brought—no, not alleviation—but a certain callousness of soul, a certain acquiescence of despair; and my punishment might have gone on for years, but for the last calamity which has now fallen, and which has finally severed me from my own face and nature. My provision of the salt, which had never been renewed since the date of the first experiment, began to run low. I sent out for a fresh supply, and mixed the draught; the ebullition followed, and the first change of colour, not the second; I drank it and it was without efficiency. You will learn from Poole how I have had London ransacked; it was in vain; and I am now persuaded that my first supply was impure, and that it was that unknown impurity which lent efficacy to the draught.

About a week has passed, and I am now finishing this statement under the influence of the last of the old powders. This, then, is the last time, short of a miracle, that Henry Jekyll can think his own thoughts or see his own face (now how sadly altered!) in the glass. Nor must I delay too long to bring my writing to an end; for if my narrative has hitherto escaped destruction, it has been by a combination of great prudence and great good luck. Should the throes of change take me in the act of writing it, Hyde will tear it in pieces; but if some time shall have elapsed after I have laid it by, his wonderful selfishness and circumscription to the moment will probably save it once again from the action of his apelike spite. And indeed the doom that is closing on us both, has already changed and crushed him. Half an hour from now, when I shall again and forever reindue[1] that hated personality, I know how I shall sit shuddering and weeping in my chair, or continue, with the most strained and fearstruck ecstasy[2] of listening, to pace up and down this room (my last earthly refuge) and give ear to every sound of menace. Will Hyde die upon the scaffold? or will he find the courage to release himself at the last moment? God knows; I am careless; this is my true hour of death, and what is to follow concerns another than myself. Here then, as I lay down the pen and proceed to seal up my confession, I bring the life of that unhappy Henry Jekyll to an end.

---

1 Adopt, put on.
2 Frenzy.

THE ELEPHANT MAN

FREDERICK TREVES

Frederick Treves (1853–1923) was born in Dorchester, the son of a prosperous furniture salesman. The boyhood friend of Thomas Hardy, Treves was educated at the Merchant Taylor's School in London and the London Hospital Medical School, where he began his illustrious career as abdominal surgeon, performing the first appendectomy in England, a procedure that he would perform on King Edward VII in 1901. But Treves's most famous—and most tragic—patient was Joseph Carey Merrick (1852–1890), the man known to the world as the Elephant Man. In 1884, Treves discovered the severely deformed Merrick, who suffered from either neurofibromatosis or (more likely) Proteus syndrome, in a crude "freakshop" on Mile End Road across from the hospital. Two years later, having been abandoned by his employer, a desperate Merrick sought Treves's protection. Merrick lived out the remaining four years of his life at London Hospital, a *cause célèbre*, suffocating in his sleep on April 11, 1890. His best friend, Frederick Treves, dissected his body. The following account of their first encounter comes from Treves's *The Elephant Man and Other Reminiscences* (1923).

IN the Mile End Road,[1] opposite to the London Hospital, there was (and possibly still is) a line of small shops. Among them was a vacant greengrocer's which was to let. The whole of the front of the shop, with the exception of the door, was hidden by a hanging sheet of canvas on which was the announcement that the Elephant Man was to be seen within and that the price of admission was twopence. Painted on the canvas in primitive colours was a life-size portrait of the Elephant Man. This very crude production depicted a frightful creature that could only have been possible in a nightmare. It was the figure of a man with the characteristics of

---

[1] In London's East End.

an elephant. The transfiguration was not far advanced. There was still more of the man than of the beast. This fact—that it was still human—was the most repellent attribute of the creature. There was nothing about it of the pitiableness of the misshapen or the deformed, nothing of the grotesqueness of the freak, but merely the loathing insinuation of a man being changed into an animal. Some palm trees in the background of the picture suggested a jungle and might have led the imaginative to assume that it was in this wild that the perverted object had roamed.

When I first became aware of this phenomenon the exhibition was closed, but a well-informed boy sought the proprietor in a public house and I was granted a private view on payment of a shilling. The shop was empty and grey with dust. Some old tins and a few shrivelled potatoes occupied a shelf and some vague, vegetable refuse the window. The light in the place was dim, being obscured by the painted placard outside. The far end of the shop—where I expect the late proprietor sat at a desk—was cut off by a curtain or rather by a red tablecloth suspended from a cord by a few rings. The room was cold and dank, for it was the month of November. The year, I might say, was 1884.

The showman pulled back the curtain and revealed a bent figure crouching on a stool and covered by a brown blanket. In front of it, on a tripod, was a large brick heated by a Bunsen burner. Over this the creature was huddled to warm itself. It never moved when the curtain was drawn back. Locked up in an empty shop and lit by the faint blue light of the gas jet, this hunched-up figure was the embodiment of loneliness. It might have been a captive in a cavern or a wizard watching for unholy manifestations in the ghostly flame. Outside the sun was shining and one could hear the footsteps of the passers-by, a tune whistled by a boy and the commonplace hum of traffic in the road.

The showman—speaking as if to a dog—called out harshly: "Stand up!" The thing arose slowly and let the blanket that covered its head and back fall to the ground. There stood revealed the most disgusting specimen of humanity that I have ever seen. In the course of my profession I had come upon lamentable deformities of the face due to injury or disease, as well as mutilations and contortions of the body depending upon like causes; but at no time had I met with such a degraded or perverted version of a human being as this lone figure displayed. He was naked to the waist, his feet were bare, he wore a pair of threadbare trousers that had once belonged to some fat gentleman's dress suit.

From the intensified painting in the street I had imagined the Elephant Man to be of gigantic size. This, however, was a little man below the average height and made to look shorter by the bowing of his back. The most striking feature about him was the enormous and misshapened head. From the brow there projected a huge bony mass like a loaf, while from the back of the head hung a bag of spongy, fungous-looking skin, the surface of which was comparable to brown cauliflower. On the top of the skull were a few long lank hairs. The osseous growth on the forehead almost occluded one eye. The circumference of the head was no less than that of the man's waist. From the upper jaw there projected another mass of bone. It protruded from the mouth like a pink stump, turning the upper lip inside out and making the mouth a mere slobbering aperture. This growth from the jaw had been so exaggerated in the painting as to appear to be a rudimentary trunk or tusk. The nose was merely a lump of flesh, only recognizable as a nose from its position. The face was no more capable of expression than a block of gnarled wood. The back was horrible, because from it hung, as far down as the middle of the thigh, huge, sack-like masses of flesh covered by the same loathsome cauliflower skin.

The right arm was of enormous size and shapeless. It suggested the limb of the subject of elephantiasis.[1] It was overgrown also with pendent masses of the same cauliflower-like skin. The hand was large and clumsy—a fin or paddle rather than a hand. There was no distinction between the palm and the back. The thumb had the appearance of a radish, while the fingers might have been thick, tuberous roots. As a limb it was almost useless. The other arm was remarkable by contrast. It was not only normal but was, moreover, a delicately shaped limb covered with fine skin and provided with a beautiful hand which any woman might have envied. From the chest hung a bag of the same repulsive flesh. It was like a dewlap suspended from the neck of a lizard. The lower limbs had the characters of the deformed arm. They were unwieldy, dropsical looking and grossly misshapened.

To add a further burden to his trouble the wretched man, when a boy, developed hip disease, which had left him permanently lame, so that he could only walk with a stick. He was thus denied all means of escape from his tormentors. As he told me later, he could never run away. One other feature must be mentioned to emphasize his isolation from his kind. Although he was already repellent enough, there arose from the fungous skin-growth with which he was almost covered a very sickening stench which was hard to tolerate. From the showman I learnt nothing about the Elephant Man, except that he was English, that his name was John Merrick[2] and that he was twenty-one years of age.

---

1   Extreme swelling of the limbs or other body parts caused by obstruction of the lymphatic vessels by parasitic worms.
2   Because he likely addressed Merrick by his last name, Treves misremembers his first name as "John."

As at the time of my discovery of the Elephant Man I was the Lecturer on Anatomy at the Medical College opposite, I was anxious to examine him in detail and to prepare an account of his abnormalities. I therefore arranged with the showman that I should interview his strange exhibit in my room at the college. I became at once conscious of a difficulty. The Elephant Man could not show himself in the streets. He would have been mobbed by the crowd and seized by the police. He was, in fact, as secluded from the world as the Man with the Iron Mask.[1] He had, however, a disguise, although it was almost as startling as he was himself. It consisted of a long black cloak which reached to the ground. Whence the cloak had been obtained I cannot imagine. I had only seen such a garment on the stage wrapped about the figure of a Venetian bravo. The recluse was provided with a pair of bag-like slippers in which to hide his deformed feet. On his head was a cap of a kind that never before was seen. It was black like the cloak, had a wide peak, and the general outline of a yachting cap. As the circumference of Merrick's head was that of a man's waist, the size of this head-gear may be imagined. From the attachment of the peak a grey flannel curtain hung in front of the face. In this mask was cut a wide horizontal slit through which the wearer could look out. This costume, worn by a bent man hobbling along with a stick, is probably the most remarkable and the most uncanny that has as yet been designed. I arranged that Merrick should cross the road in a cab, and to insure his immediate admission to the college I gave him my card. This card was destined to play a critical part in Merrick's life.

I made a careful examination of my visitor the result of which I embodied in a paper. I made little of the man himself. He was shy, confused, not a little frightened and evidently much cowed. Moreover, his speech was almost unintelligible. The great bony mass that projected from his mouth blurred his utterance and made the articulation of certain words impossible. He returned in a cab to the place of exhibition, and I assumed that I had seen the last of him, especially as I found next day that the show had been forbidden by the police and that the shop was empty.

I supposed that Merrick was imbecile and had been imbecile from birth. The fact that his face was incapable of expression, that his speech was a mere spluttering and his attitude that of one whose mind was void of all emotions and concerns gave grounds for this belief. The conviction was no doubt encouraged by the hope that his intellect was the blank I imagined it to be. That he could appreciate his position was unthinkable. Here was a man in the heyday of youth who was so vilely

---

1   A mysterious masked prisoner held at the Fortress of Pinerolo and the Bastille in the late seventeenth and early eighteenth centuries, and rumored to be a rival to the throne of Louis XIV of France.

deformed that everyone he met confronted him with a look of horror and disgust. He was taken about the country to be exhibited as a monstrosity and an object of loathing. He was shunned like a leper, housed like a wild beast, and got his only view of the world from a peephole in a showman's cart. He was, moreover, lame, had but one available arm, and could hardly make his utterances understood. It was not until I came to know that Merrick was highly intelligent, that he possessed an acute sensibility and—worse than all—a romantic imagination that I realized the overwhelming tragedy of his life.

The episode of the Elephant Man was, I imagined, closed; but I was fated to meet him again—two years later—under more dramatic conditions. In England the showman and Merrick had been moved on from place to place by the police, who considered the exhibition degrading and among the things that could not be allowed. It was hoped that in the uncritical retreats of Mile End a more abiding peace would be found. But it was not to be. The official mind there, as elsewhere, very properly decreed that the public exposure of Merrick and his deformities transgressed the limits of decency. The show must close.

The showman, in despair, fled with his charge to the Continent. Whither he roamed at first I do not know; but he came finally to Brussels. His reception was discouraging. Brussels was firm; the exhibition was banned; it was brutal, indecent and immoral, and could not be permitted within the confines of Belgium. Merrick was thus no longer of value. He was no longer a source of profitable entertainment. He was a burden. He must be got rid of. The elimination of Merrick was a simple matter. He could offer no resistance. He was as docile as a sick sheep. The impresario, having robbed Merrick of his paltry savings, gave him a ticket to London, saw him into the train and no doubt in parting condemned him to perdition.

His destination was Liverpool Street. The journey may be imagined. Merrick was in his alarming outdoor garb. He would be harried by an eager mob as he hobbled along the quay. They would run ahead to get a look at him. They would lift the hem of his cloak to peep at his body. He would try to hide in the train or in some dark corner of the boat, but never could he be free from that ring of curious eyes or from those whispers of fright and aversion. He had but a few shillings in his pocket and nothing either to eat or drink on the way. A panic-dazed dog with a label on his collar would have received some sympathy and possibly some kindness. Merrick received none.

What was he to do when he reached London? He had not a friend in the world. He knew no more of London than he knew of Pekin. How could he find a lodging, or what lodging-house keeper would dream of taking him in? All he wanted was to hide. What most he dreaded were the open street and the gaze of his fellow-men. If even he crept into a cellar the horrid eyes and the still more dreaded whispers would follow him to its depths. Was there ever such a home-coming!

At Liverpool Street he was rescued from the crowd by the police and taken into the third-class waiting-room. Here he sank on the floor in the darkest corner. The police were at a loss what to do with him. They had dealt with strange and mouldy tramps, but never with such an object as this. He could not explain himself. His speech was so maimed that he might as well have spoken in Arabic. He had, however, something with him which he produced with a ray of hope. It was my card.

The card simplified matters. It made it evident that this curious creature had an acquaintance and that the individual must be sent for. A messenger was dispatched to the London Hospital which is comparatively near at hand. Fortunately I was in the building and returned at once with the messenger to the station. In the waiting-room I had some difficulty in making a way through the crowd, but there, on the floor in the corner, was Merrick. He looked a mere heap. It seemed as if he had been thrown there like a bundle. He was so huddled up and so helpless looking that he might have had both his arms and his legs broken. He seemed pleased to see me, but he was nearly done. The journey and want of food had reduced him to the last stage of exhaustion. The police kindly helped him into a cab, and I drove him at once to the hospital. He appeared to be content, for he fell asleep almost as soon as he was seated and slept to the journey's end. He never said a word, but seemed to be satisfied that all was well.

In the attics of the hospital was an isolation ward with a single bed. It was used for emergency purposes—for a case of delirium tremens, for a man who had become suddenly insane or for a patient with an undetermined fever. Here the Elephant Man was deposited on a bed, was made comfortable and was supplied with food. I had been guilty of an irregularity in admitting such a case, for the hospital was neither a refuge nor a home for incurables. Chronic cases were not accepted, but only those requiring active treatment, and Merrick was not in need of such treatment. I applied to the sympathetic chairman of the committee, Mr. Carr Gomm, who not only was good enough to approve my action but who agreed with me that Merrick must not again be turned out into the world.

Mr. Carr Gomm wrote a letter to *The Times* detailing the circumstances of the refugee and asking for money for his support. So generous is the English public that in a few days—I think in a week—enough money was forthcoming to maintain Merrick for life without any charge upon the hospital funds. There chanced to be two empty rooms at the back of the hospital which were little used. They were on the ground floor, were out of the way, and opened upon a large courtyard called Bedstead Square, because here the iron beds were marshalled for cleaning and painting. The front room was converted into a bed-sitting room and the smaller chamber into a bathroom. The condition of Merrick's skin rendered a bath at least once a day a necessity, and I might here mention that with the use of the bath the unpleasant odour to which I have referred ceased to be noticeable. Merrick took up his abode in the hospital in December, 1886.

LETTER TO CENTRAL NEWS OFFICE FROM "JACK THE RIPPER"

On August 8, 1888, at 4:50 a.m., a laborer stumbled upon the body of a woman on the first-floor landing of a working-class apartment complex in Whitechapel, in London's densely populated East End. She had been stabbed thirty-nine times. She was identified as Martha Tabram, thirty-nine, a prostitute. Even in a neighborhood infamous for violent crime, the brutality of the murder shocked police. Three weeks later, the body of Polly Nichols, another Whitechapel prostitute, was discovered at 3:45 a.m. in Buck's Row. She had been nearly decapitated. From late August to early November, the bodies of four more working-class women—Annie Chapman, Lizzie Stride, Catherine Eddowes, and Mary Kelly—would be discovered mutilated in an increasingly ritualistic manner. Most frightening of all, however, was the killer's preternatural ability, in the dead of night, mere yards from bedroom windows and drunken passers-by, to *dismantle* his victims, opening their bodies, rearranging their internal organs on the ground, then escaping unseen, presumably covered in blood. The monstrous acts, police determined, took mere minutes to complete, leading many to conclude that the killer was an insane medical student or physician. Fed by a ravenous press, the murders sent the nation into a panic, a frenzy of recrimination, as the middle class confronted the violent truth of poverty, the plight of working women, and the predatory aspects of male sexuality. Theories about the killer's identity abounded. Some were far-fetched. Most, however, were opportunities for the British to indulge—under veil of moral concern—in bigotry toward marginalized communities: Jews, immigrants, and homosexuals, for instance.

On Thursday, September 27, 1888, the Whitechapel murderer, whom the press dubbed "Leather Apron," was officially re-christened, when the following letter—likely a hoax—was received at the offices of the Central News.

Dear Boss.

I keep on hearing the police have caught me but they wont fix me just yet. I have laughed when they look so clever and talk about being on the right track.

That joke about Leather Apron gave me real fits. I am down on whores and I shant quit ripping them till I do get buckled. Grand work the last job was, I gave the lady no time to squeal. How can they catch me now, I love my work and want to start again. You will soon hear of me with my funny little games. I saved some of the proper red stuff in a ginger beer bottle over the last job to write with but it went thick like glue and I cant use it. Red ink is fit enough I hope ha. ha. The next job I do I shall clip the ladys ears off and send to the police officers just for jolly wouldnt you. Keep this letter back till I do a bit more work then give it out straight. My knife's so nice and sharp I want to get to work right away if I get a chance, good luck.

Yours truly

Jack the Ripper

Dont mind me giving the trade name.

Wasnt good enough to post this before I got all the red ink off my hands curse it. No luck yet. They say I'm a doctor now ha ha.

Terrible Love

John Barlas

Oscar Wilde's friend, fellow Decadent, and the author of eight volumes of verse, which he wrote under the pseudonym "Evelyn Douglas," John Barlas (1860–1914) led a life of trouble. The schizophrenic son of a wealthy Scottish merchant, who died when Barlas was a boy, he spent his adolescence in London with his mother, who died when he was eighteen. He began writing poetry in 1876. After burning through his inheritance, Barlas became a teacher of languages. He embraced Marxism and anarchism, worked as an advocate for workers' rights, and travelled the country, lecturing on behalf of the socialist cause. Though his organizational skills were often impressive, he showed distressing signs of self-destruction and obsession, firing a loaded gun at a government building, spending an inordinate amount of time with prostitutes, beating his wife, assaulting strangers in the street, antagonizing police officers at political rallies. His participation in the demonstrations at Trafalgar Square in 1887 resulted in a severe head wound; complications from this wound, including depression and dementia, combined with a serious case of syphilis, caused his already precarious mental health to deteriorate further. He spent the last twenty years of his life at Gartnavel Asylum.

    The marriage of two murderers in the gloom
    Of a dark fane[1] to hymns of blackest night;
    Before a priest who keeps his hands from sight
    Hidden away beneath his robe of doom,
    Lest any see the flowers of blood that bloom   5
    For gems upon the fingers, red on white;
    The while far up in domes of dizzy height

---

1   Shrine.

The trumpets[1] of the organ peal and boom:
Such is our love. Oh sweet delicious lips
From which I fancy all the world's blood drips!   10
Oh supple waist, pale cheek, and eyes of fire,
Hard little breasts and white gigantic hips,
And blue-black hair with serpent coils that slips
Out of my hand in hours of red desire.

1887

---

1   Pipes.

The True Story of a Vampire

Stanislaus Eric Stenbock

The eccentric son of a Baltic-German count and a Manchester cotton heiress, Stanislaus Eric Stenbock (1860–1895) was the author of several books of macabre poetry and short stories in the Decadent style, including the homoerotic "The True Story of a Vampire" (1894). Though he never attained a degree, Stenbock attended Baillol College at Oxford, where he became a fixture of the underground gay scene, falling in love, at one point, with the teenage son of a Berkshire clergyman. An alcoholic in his later years, an avid pianist, convert to Catholicism, and collector of animals, Stenbock dwells in his writings upon themes of death and sexuality with a voice both mischievous and tragic.

VAMPIRE stories are generally located in Styria;[1] mine is, also. Styria is by no means the romantic kind of place described by those who have certainly never been there. It is a flat, uninteresting country, only celebrated by its turkeys, its capons, and the stupidity of its inhabitants. Vampires generally arrive at night, in carriages drawn by two black horses.

Our Vampire arrived by the commonplace means of the railway train, and in the afternoon. You must think I am joking, or perhaps that by the word "Vampire" I mean a financial vampire. No, I am quite serious. The Vampire of whom I am speaking, who laid waste our hearth and home, was a *real* vampire.

Vampires are generally described as dark, sinister-looking, and singularly handsome. Our Vampire was, on the contrary, rather fair, and certainly was not at first sight sinister-looking, and though decidedly attractive in appearance, not what one would call singularly handsome.

---

1   A state in southeastern Austria.

Yes, he desolated our home, killed my brother—the one object of my adoration—also my dear father. Yet, at the same time, I must say that I myself came under the spell of his fascination, and, in spite of all, have no ill-will towards him now.

Doubtless you have read in the papers *passim* of "the Baroness and her beasts." It is to tell how I came to spend most of my useless wealth on an asylum for stray animals that I am writing this.

I am old now; what happened then was when I was a little girl of about thirteen. I will begin by describing our household. We were Poles; our name was Wronski. We lived in Styria, where we had a castle. Our household was very limited. It consisted, with the exclusion of domestics, of only my father, our governess—a worthy Belgian named Mademoiselle Vonnaert—my brother, and myself. Let me begin with my father: he was old, and both my brother and I were children of his old age. Of my mother I remember nothing: she died in giving birth to my brother, who is only one year, or not as much, younger than myself. Our father was studious, continually occupied in reading books, chiefly on recondite subjects and in all kinds of unknown languages. He had a long white beard, and wore habitually a black velvet skull-cap.

How kind he was to us! It was more than I could tell. Still it was not I who was the favourite. His whole heart went out to Gabriel—Gabryel as we spelt it in Polish. He was always called by the Russian abbreviation Gavril—I mean, of course, my brother, who had a resemblance to the only portrait of my mother, a slight chalk sketch which hung in my father's study. But I was by no means jealous: my brother was and has been the only love of my life. It is for his sake that I am now keeping in Westbourne Park[1] a home for stray cats and dogs.

I was at that time, as I said before, a little girl; my name was Carmela.[2] My long tangled hair was always all over the place, and never would be combed straight. I was not pretty—at least, looking at a photograph of me at that time, I do not think I could describe myself as such. Yet at the same time, when I look at the photograph, I think my expression may have been pleasing to some people: irregular features, large mouth, and large wild eyes.

I was by way of being naughty—not so naughty as Gabriel in the opinion of Mlle. Vonnaert. Mlle. Vonnaert, I may intercalate, was a wholly excellent person, middle-aged, who really *did* speak good French, although she was a Belgian, and could also make herself understood in German, which, as you may or may not know, is the current language of Styria.

---

1   Neighborhood in West London, north of Notting Hill.
2   An allusion to Sheridan Le Fanu's lesbian vampire novel, *Carmilla*, which was serialized in 1871–1872, and which is also set in Styria.

I find it difficult to describe my brother Gabriel; there was something about him strange and superhuman, or perhaps I should rather say præter-human, something between the animal and the divine. Perhaps the Greek idea of the Faun might illustrate what I mean; but that will not do either. He had large, wild, gazelle-like eyes: his hair, like mine, was in a perpetual tangle—that point he had in common with me, and indeed, as I have afterwards heard, our mother having been of gipsy race, it will account for much of the innate wildness there was in our natures. I was wild enough, but Gabriel was much wilder. Nothing would induce him to put on shoes and stockings, except on Sundays—when he also allowed his hair to be combed, but only by me. How shall I describe the grace of that lovely mouth, shaped verily "en arc d'amour."[1] I always think of the text in the Psalm, "Grace is shed forth on thy lips, therefore has God blessed thee eternally"[2]—lips that seemed to exhale the very breath of life. Then that beautiful, lithe, living, elastic form!

He could run faster than any deer: spring like a squirrel to the topmost branch of a tree: he might have stood for the sign and symbol of vitality itself. But seldom could he be induced by Mlle. Vonnaert to learn lessons; but when he did so, he learnt with extraordinary quickness. He would play upon every conceivable instrument, holding a violin here, there, and everywhere, except the right place: manufacturing instruments for himself out of reeds—even sticks. Mlle. Vonnaert made futile efforts to induce him to learn to play the piano. I suppose he was what was called spoilt, though merely in the superficial sense of the word. Our father allowed him to indulge in every caprice.

One of his peculiarities, when quite a little child, was a horror at the sight of meat. Nothing on earth would induce him to taste it. Another thing which was particularly remarkable about him was his extraordinary power over animals. Everything seemed to come tame to his hand. Birds would sit on his shoulder. Then sometimes Mlle. Vonnaert and I would lose him in the woods— he would suddenly dart away. Then we would find him singing softly or whistling to himself, with all manner of woodland creatures around him—hedgehogs, little foxes, wild rabbits, marmots, squirrels, and such like. He would frequently bring these things home with him and insist on keeping them. This strange menagerie was the terror of poor Mlle. Vonnaert's heart. He chose to live in a little room at the top of a turret; but which,

---

1   Literally, "like an arc of love": an oblique reference perhaps—considering Gabriel's propensity to collect animals—to the rainbow in Genesis (*arc-en-ciel* in French) that eventually greets Noah's Ark.

2   "Thou art fairer than the children of men: grace is poured into thy lips: therefore God hath blessed thee for ever" (Psalms 45:2).

instead of going upstairs, he chose to reach by means of a very tall chestnut-tree, through the window. But in contradiction to all this, it was his custom to serve every Sunday Mass in the parish church, with hair nicely combed and with white surplice and red cassock. He looked as demure and tamed as possible. Then came the element of the divine. What an expression of ecstacy there was in those glorious eyes!

Thus far I have not been speaking about the Vampire. However, let me begin with my narrative at last. One day my father had to go to the neighbouring town—as he frequently had. This time he returned accompanied by a guest. The gentleman, he said, had missed his train, through the late arrival of another at our station, which was a junction, and he would therefore, as trains are not frequent in our parts, have had to wait there all night. He had joined in conversation with my father in the too-late-arriving train from the town: and had consequently accepted my father's invitation to stay the night at our house. But of course, you know, in these out-of-the-way parts we are almost patriarchal in our hospitality.

He was announced under the name of Count Vardalek[1]—the name being Hungarian. But he spoke German well enough: not with the monotonous accentuation of Hungarians, but rather, if anything, with a slight Slavonic intonation. His voice was peculiarly soft and insinuating. We soon afterwards found out he could talk Polish, and Mlle. Vonnaert vouched for his good French. Indeed he seemed to know all languages. But let me give my first impressions. He was rather tall, with fair wavy hair, rather long, which accentuated a certain effeminacy about his smooth face. His figure had something—I cannot say what—serpentine about it. The features were refined; and he had long, slender, subtle, magnetic-looking hands, a somewhat long sinuous nose, a graceful mouth, and an attractive smile, which belied the intense sadness of the expression of the eyes. When he arrived his eyes were half closed—indeed they were habitually so—so that I could not decide their colour. He looked worn and wearied. I could not possibly guess his age.

Suddenly Gabriel burst into the room: a yellow butterfly was clinging to his hair. He was carrying in his arms a little squirrel. Of course he was bare-legged as usual. The stranger looked up at his approach; then I noticed his eyes. They were green: they seemed to dilate and grow larger. Gabriel stood stock-still, with a startled look, like that of a bird fascinated by a serpent. But nevertheless he held out his hand to the newcomer. Vardalek, taking his hand—I don't know why I noticed this trivial thing—pressed the pulse with his forefinger. Suddenly Gabriel darted from the room

---

1   A possible allusion to James Malcolm Rymer's 1845 serial *Varney the Vampire; or, The Feast of Blood.*

and rushed upstairs, going to his turret-room this time by the staircase instead of the tree. I was in terror what the Count might think of him. Great was my relief when he came down in his velvet Sunday suit, and shoes and stockings. I combed his hair, and set him generally right.

When the stranger came down to dinner his appearance had somewhat altered; he looked much younger. There was an elasticity of the skin, combined with a delicate complexion, rarely to be found in a man. Before, he had struck me as being very pale.

Well, at dinner we were all charmed with him, especially my father. He seemed to be thoroughly acquainted with all my father's particular hobbies. Once when my father was relating some of his military experiences, he said something about a drummer-boy who was wounded in battle. His eyes opened completely again and dilated: this time with a particularly disagreeable expression, dull and dead, yet at the same time animated by some horrible excitement. But this was only momentary.

The chief subject of his conversation with my father was about certain curious mystical books which my father had just lately picked up, and which he could not make out, but Vardalek seemed completely to understand. At dessert-time my father asked him if he were in a great hurry to reach his destination: if not, would he not stay with us a little while: though our place was out of the way, he would find much that would interest him in his library.

He answered, "I am in no hurry. I have no particular reason for going to that place at all, and if I can be of service to you in deciphering these books, I shall be only too glad." He added with a smile which was bitter, very very bitter: "You see I am a cosmopolitan, a wanderer on the face of the earth."

After dinner my father asked him if he played the piano. He said, "Yes, I can a little," and he sat down at the piano. Then he played a Hungarian csardas[1]—wild, rhapsodic, wonderful.

That is the music which makes men mad. He went on in the same strain.

Gabriel stood stock-still by the piano, his eyes dilated and fixed, his form quivering. At last he said very slowly, at one particular motive—for want of a better word you may call it the *relâche*[2] of a csardas, by which I mean that point where the original quasi-slow movement begins again—"Yes, I think I could play that."

Then he quickly fetched his fiddle and self-made xylophone, and did actually, alternating the instruments, render the same very well indeed.

---

1   Hungarian dance, beginning slowly, ending with a flourish.
2   Loosening, slackening.

Vardalek looked at him, and said in a very sad voice, "Poor child! you have the soul of music within you."[1]

I could not understand why he seemed to commiserate instead of congratulate Gabriel on what certainly showed an extraordinary talent.

* * *

GABRIEL was shy even as the wild animals who were tame to him. Never before had he taken to a stranger. Indeed, as a rule, if any stranger came to the house by any chance, he would hide himself, and I had to bring him up his food to the turret chamber. You may imagine what was my surprise when I saw him walking about hand in hand with Vardalek the next morning, in the garden, talking livelily with him, and showing his collection of pet animals, which he had gathered from the woods, and for which we had had to fit up a regular zoological gardens. He seemed utterly under the domination of Vardalek. What surprised us was (for otherwise we liked the stranger, especially for being kind to him) that he seemed, though not noticeably at first—except perhaps to me, who noticed everything with regard to him—to be gradually losing his general health and vitality. He did not become pale as yet; but there was a certain languor about his movements which certainly there was by no means before.

My father got more and more devoted to Count Vardalek. He helped him in his studies: and my father would hardly allow him to go away, which he did sometimes—to Trieste, he said: he always came back, bringing us presents of strange Oriental jewellery or textures.

I knew all kinds of people came to Trieste, Orientals included. Still, there was a strangeness and magnificence about these things which I was sure even then could not possibly have come from such a place as Trieste, memorable to me chiefly for its necktie shops.

When Vardalek was away, Gabriel was continually asking for him and talking about him. Then at the same time he seemed to regain his old vitality and spirits. Vardalek always returned looking much older, wan, and weary. Gabriel would rush to meet him, and kiss him on the mouth. Then he gave a slight shiver: and after a little while began to look quite young again.

---

1 In late Victorian gay or "Uranian" subculture, "being musical" euphemistically referred to "being same-sex oriented."

Things continued like this for some time. My father would not hear of Vardalek's going away permanently. He came to be an inmate of our house. I indeed, and Mlle. Vonnaert also, could not help noticing what a difference there was altogether about Gabriel. But my father seemed totally blind to it.

One night I had gone downstairs to fetch something which I had left in the drawing-room. As I was going up again I passed Vardalek's room. He was playing on a piano, which had been specially put there for him, one of Chopin's nocturnes,[1] very beautifully: I stopped, leaning on the banisters to listen.

Something white appeared on the dark staircase. We believed in ghosts in our part. I was transfixed with terror and clung to the banisters. What was my astonishment to see Gabriel walking slowly down the staircase, his eyes fixed as though in a trance! This terrified me even more than a ghost would. Could I believe my senses? Could that be Gabriel?

I simply could not move. Gabriel, clad in his long white night-shirt, came downstairs and opened the door. He left it open. Vardalek still continued playing, but talked as he played.

He said—this time speaking in Polish—*Nie umiem wyrazic jak ciehie kocham*—"My darling, I fain would spare thee; but thy life is my life, and I must live, I who would rather die. Will God not have *any* mercy on me? Oh! oh! Life; oh, the torture of life!" Here he struck one agonised and strange chord, then continued playing softly, "O Gabriel, my beloved! my life, yes *life*—oh, why life? I am sure that this is but a little that I demand of thee. Surely thy superabundance of life can spare a little to one who is already dead. No, stay," he said now almost harshly, "what must be, must be!"

Gabriel stood there quite still, with the same fixed vacant expression, in the room. He was evidently walking in his sleep. Vardalek played on: then said, "Ah!" with a sigh of terrible agony. Then very gently, "Go now, Gabriel; it is enough." And Gabriel went out of the room and ascended the staircase at the same slow pace, with the same unconscious stare. Vardalek struck the piano, and although he did not play loudly, it seemed as though the strings would break. You never heard music so strange and so heart-rending!

I only know I was found by Mlle. Vonnaert in the morning, in an unconscious state, at the foot of the stairs. Was it a dream after all? I am sure now that it was not.

---

1 Polish composer Frédéric Chopin (1810–1849) wrote twenty-one "nocturnes," a musical form meant to evoke the night.

I thought then it might be, and said nothing to anyone about it. Indeed, what could I say?

Well, to let me cut a long story short, Gabriel, who had never known a moment's sickness in his life, grew ill: and we had to send to Gratz[1] for a doctor, who could give no explanation of Gabriel's strange illness. Gradually wasting away, he said: absolutely no organic complaint. What could this mean?

My father at last became conscious of the fact that Gabriel was ill. His anxiety was fearful. The last trace of grey faded from his hair, and it became quite white. We sent to Vienna for doctors. But all with the same result.

Gabriel was generally unconscious, and when conscious, only seemed to recognise Vardalek, who sat continually by his bedside, nursing him with the utmost tenderness.

One day I was alone in the room: and Vardalek cried suddenly, almost fiercely, "Send for a priest at once, at once," he repeated. "It is now almost too late!"

Gabriel stretched out his arms spasmodically, and put them round Vardalek's neck. This was the only movement he had made for some time. Vardalek bent down and kissed him on the lips. I rushed downstairs: and the priest was sent for. When I came back Vardalek was not there. The priest administered extreme unction. I think Gabriel was already dead, although we did not think so at the time.

Vardalek had utterly disappeared; and when we looked for him he was nowhere to be found; nor have I seen or heard of him since.

My father died very soon afterwards: suddenly aged, and bent down with grief. And so the whole of the Wronski property came into my sole possession. And here I am, an old woman, generally laughed at for keeping, in memory of Gabriel, an asylum for stray animals—and—people do not, as a rule, believe in Vampires!

---

1   Graz, a city in Styria, Austria.

Part VI
Hauntings

THE BELLS

LEOPOLD LEWIS

Born in London to an Anglo-Jewish family, Leopold David Lewis (1828–1890) attended the prestigious King's College School as a boy. Dante Gabriel Rossetti, whose father taught Italian at the school, was his classmate. At the age of twenty-two, Lewis embarked on a solid if unremarkable career as a solicitor. His true love, however, was the theatre. Though several of his plays and adaptations were performed at reputable venues, including *The Wandering Jew* (1873) at the Adelphi and *The Foundlings* (1881) at Sadler's Wells, his only real success was *The Bells* (1871), his translation of the 1867 French play *Le Juif Polonais* (The Polish Jew) by Émile Erkmann (1822–1899) and Alexandre Chatrian (1826–1890). *The Bells* ran for 150 nights at the Lyceum, breathing new life into the fading playhouse. Notable for its blend of melodrama and crude psychological realism, as well as for its pioneering use of gauze scrims to dramatize the unconscious life of Burgomaster Mathias, *The Bells* made its lead actor Henry Irving, who played Mathias, an instant celebrity. Indeed, by the turn of the century, "Irving's Mathias," as Mathias was known, had become one of the most memorable characters ever to have walked the Victorian stage. At the age of forty-seven, Lewis ended his legal career in order to devote his time to writing. In his final years, he became financially dependant upon an annual stipend from Irving.

First produced at the Royal Lyceum Theatre, London, 25 November 1871, with the following cast:

MATHIAS	Mr. Henry Irving
WALTER	Mr. Frank Hall
HANS	Mr. F. W. Irish
CHRISTIAN	Mr. H. Crellin
MESMERIST	Mr. A. Tapping
DOCTOR ZIMMER	Mr. Dyas
NOTARY	Mr. Collett
TONY	Mr. Fredericks
FRITZ	Mr. Fotheringham
JUDGE OF THE COURT	Mr. Gaston Murray
CLERK OF THB COURT	Mr. Branscombe
CATHERINE	Miss G. Pauncefort
ANNETTE	Miss Fanny Heywood
SOZEL	Miss Ellen Mayne

PERIOD—*December 24th & 26th, 1833*

THE BELLS

ACT 1

Interior of a Village Inn in Alsace.[1] *Table and chairs, R. 1 E.; L. 1 E., an old-fashioned sideboard, with curious china upon it, and glasses; door, R.; door, L.; large window at back, cut in scene, R.; large door at back, cut in scene, L.; a candle or lamp burns upon the table; a stove at back, R., with kettle on it; the pipe of stove going off through the wing at R. The country covered with snow is seen through the window; snow is falling; a large clock in L. corner, at back—hands to work. The Inn is the residence of the Burgomaster.*[2] *It is Christmas Eve.*

CATHERINE, *the Burgomaster's wife, discovered seated at a spinning-wheel,* L. 1 E. *Music upon rising of curtain.* HANS *passes window; enters through door at back; he is covered with snow; he carries a gun, and a large game-bag is slung across his shoulders.*

Hans [*taking off his hat and shaking away the snow*]. More snow, Madame Mathias, more snow! [*He places his gun by the stove.*
Catherine. Still in the village, Hans?
Hans. Yes, on Christmas Eve one may be forgiven some small indulgence.
Catherine. You know your sack of flour is ready for you at the mill?
Hans. Oh, yes; but I am not in a hurry. Father Walter will take charge of it for me in his cart. Now one glass of wine, madame, and then I'm off.
[*He sits at table,* R., *laughing.*
Catherine. Father Walter still here? I thought he had left long ago.
Hans. No, no. He is still at the Golden Fleece emptying his bottle. As I came along, I saw his cart standing outside the grocer's, with the coffee, the cinnamon, and the sugar, all covered with snow, he, he, he! He is a jolly old fellow. Fond of good wine, and I don't blame him, you may be sure. We shall leave together.

---

1   A traditionally German-speaking region in northeast France on the German border, Alsace saw heavy fighting during the Franco-Prussian War (1870–71). It was annexed by a unified and ascendant Germany in 1871, mere months before Lewis wrote *The Bells*. Though the play's action takes place nearly four decades prior to the Franco-Prussian War, its setting would have had freshly violent connotations for English audiences.
2   Mayor.

Catherine. And you have no fear of being upset?

Hans. What does it matter? As I said before, on Christmas Eve one may be forgiven some small indulgence.

Catherine. I will lend you a lanthorn[1] when you go. [*Calling without moving from her wheel.*] Sozel!

Sozel [*from within*, L.]. Madame!

Catherine. Some wine for Hans!

Sozel [*the same*]. Yes, madame.

Hans. That's the sort. Considering the festive character of weather like this, one really must take something.

Catherine. Yes, but take care, our white wine is very strong.

Hans. Oh, never fear, madame! But, where is our Burgomaster? How is it he is not to be seen? Is he ill?

Catherine. He went to Ribeauville five days ago.

Enter SOZEL, *carrying a decanter of white wine and glass; she places it on table*, R.; *she enters, door*, L.U.E.

Here is the wine, Master Hans. [*Exit* SOZEL, L.

Hans. Good, good! [*He pours out a glass, and drinks with gusto.*] I wager, now, that the Burgomaster has gone to buy the wine for the wedding.

Catherine [*laughing*]. Not at all improbable.

Hans. Only, just now, when I was at the Golden Fleece, it was talked about publicly, that the pretty Annette, the daughter of the Burgomaster, and Christian, the Quarter-master of Gendarmes, were going to be married! I could scarcely believe my ears. Christian is certainly a brave man, and an honest man, and a handsome man! I do not wish to maintain anything to the contrary. Our village is rather distinguished in that respect. [*Pulls up his shirt collar.*] But he has nothing but his pay to live upon, whilst Annette is the richest match in the village.

Catherine. Do you believe then, Hans, that money ought always to be the one consideration?

Hans. No, no, certainly not—on the contrary. Only, I thought that the Burgomaster—

Catherine. Well, you have been mistaken; Mathias did not even ask, "What have you?" He said at once, "Let Annette give her free consent, and I give mine!"

---

1   Lantern.

Hans. And did she give her free consent?

Catherine. Yes; she loves Christian, and as we have no other thought but the happiness of our child, we do not look for wealth!

Hans. Oh, if the Burgomaster consents and you consent, and Annette consents, why, I suppose I cannot refuse my consent either. Only, I may make this observation, I think Christian a very lucky dog, and I wish I was in his place!

Music, Enter ANNETTE, L., she crosses and looks
through window, then turns to HANS.

Annette. Good evening, Hans! [*Music ceases.*]

Hans [*rising from table and turning round*]. Ah, it is you. Good evening! Good evening! We were just talking about you!

Annette. About me!

Hans. Yes! [*He takes off his game-bag and hangs on back of chair, then looking at* ANNETTE *with admiration.*] Oh, oh! How smiling you look, and how prettily dressed; one would almost think that you were going to a wedding.

Annette. Ah, you are always joking.

Hans. No, no, I am not joking! I say what I think, that's all! That pretty cap, and that pretty dress, and those pretty shoes were not put on for the pleasure of a tough middle-aged forest-keeper like myself. It has been all arranged for another—for another I say, and I know who that particular "another" happens to be—he, he, he!

Annette [*blushing*]. How can you talk such nonsense!

Hans. Oh, yes, it is nonsense to say that you are fascinating, merry, good and pretty, no doubt; and it is nonsense to say that the particular another I refer to—you know the one I mean—the tall one with the handsome moustaches, is a fellow to be envied. Yes, it is nonsense to say it, for I for one do not envy him at all—no, not at all !

[FATHER WALTER has passed the window, now opens
door at back and puts his head in. ANNETTE turns to
look at him.

Walter [*laughing and coming in—he is covered with snow*]. Ah, she turned her head! It's not he you expect!

Annette. Who, Father Walter?

Walter. Ha, ha, ha! That's right. Up to the last minute she will pretend that she knows nothing. [*Crosses to* R.

Annette [*simply*]. I do not understand what you mean.

[WALTER *and* HANS *both laugh.*

Catherine. You are a couple of old fools!

Walter [*still laughing*]. You're not such an old fool as you look, are you, Hans?

Hans. No; and you don't look such an old fool as you are, do you, Walter?

Enter SOZEL, L., *with a lighted lanthorn, which she places upon the sideboard, L., then exits.*

Walter. No. What is the meaning of that lanthorn?

Hans. Why, to act as a light for the cart.

Annette. You can go by moonlight!

[*She opens the lanthorn and blows out the candle.*

Walter. Yes, yes; certainly we will go by the light of the moon! Let us empty a glass in honour of the young couple. [*They fill glasses.*] Here's to the health of Christian and Annette!

[*They drink—*HANS *taking a long time in drinking the contents of his glass, and then heaving a deep sigh, and Music commences.*

Walter [*seriously*]. And now listen, Annette; as I entered I saw Christian returning with two gendarmes, and I am sure that in a quarter of an hour—

Annette. Listen! [*Wind, off.*

Catherine. The wind is rising. I hope that Mathias is not now on the road!

Annette. No, no, it is Christian! [*Music, forte.*

CHRISTIAN *passes the window enters the door at back, covered with snow.*

All. Christian! [*Music ceases.*

Christian. Good evening, all. [ANNETTE *runs to him.*] Good evening, Annette.

Annette. Where have you come from, Christian?

Christian. From the Hôvald![1] From the Hôvald! What a snow-storm! I have seen many in Auvergne or the Pyrenees, but never anything like this.

[*He sits by the stove, and warms his hands. After hanging up his hat,* ANNETTE *goes out and returns with a jug of wine, which she places upon the stove.*

---

1   Hochwald, military outpost in a forested region near Alsatian border with Germany.

Walter [lighting his pipe and smoking, to HANS, *who is also smoking]*. There, look at that! What care she takes of him! It would not be for us that she would fetch the sugar and the cinnamon and warm the wine.

Christian [to ANNETTE, *laughing]*. Do not allow me, Annette, to be crushed by the satire of Father Walter, who knows how to defy the wind and the snow by the side of a good fire. I should like to see the figure he would present, if he had been five hours on duty as I have been in the snow, on the Hôvald.

Catherine. You have been five hours in the snow, Christian! Your duties must be terribly severe.

Christian. How can it be helped? At two o'clock we received information that smugglers had passed the river the previous night with tobacco and gunpowder; so we were bound to be off at once.

[*Music.* ANNETTE *pours out hot wine into glass and hands it to* CHRISTIAN, *C.*

Annette. Drink this, Christian, it will warm you.

Christian [standing, C.]. Thank you, Annette. [*Takes glass—looks at her tenderly, and drinks.*] Ah! that's good!

Walter. The Quarter-master is not difficult to please.

[*Music ceases.*

Catherine [to CHRISTIAN]. Never mind, Christian, you are fortunate to have arrived thus early! [*Wind heard, off.*] Listen to the wind! I hope that Mathias will have the prudence to stop for shelter somewhere on the road. [*To* HANS *and* WALTER.] I was right, you see, in advising you to go; you would now have been safely at home!

Hans [laughing]. Annette was the cause of our stopping. Why did she blow out the lanthorn?

Annette. Oh, you were glad enough to stop!

Christian. Your winters are very severe here.

Walter. Oh, not every year, Quarter-master! For fifteen years we have not had a winter so severe as this.

Hans. No—I do not remember to have seen so much snow since what is called "The Polish Jew's Winter." In that year the Schnieberg[1] was covered in the first days of November, and the frost lasted till the end of March.

Christian. And for that reason it is called "The Polish Jew's Winter"?

---

1   "Snowy Mountain," a generic mountain. It is unlikely that Lewis is referring to the famous Schneeberg in Austria.

Walter. No—it is for another and terrible reason, which none of us will ever forget. Madame Mathias remembers it well, I am sure.

Catherine [*solemnly*]. You are right, Walter, you are right.

Hans. Had you been here at that time, Quarter-master, you might have won your cross.

Christian. How?

> [ANNETTE *at work in* C., *on stool—*CATHERINE *at spinning-wheel, and* HANS *at table,* R., *smoking.*

Walter [*at last, to* CHRISTIAN, *in* C., *seated*]. I can tell you all about this affair from the beginning to the end, since I saw it nearly all myself. Curiously enough, it was this very day, just fifteen years ago, that I was seated at this very table. There was Mathias, who sat there, and who had only bought his mill just six months before; there was old John Roebec, who sat there—they used to call him "the Little Shoemaker"; and several others, who are now sleeping under the turf—we shall all go there some day! Happy are those who have nothing upon their conscience! We were just beginning a game of cards, when, just as the old clock struck ten, the sound of horse-bells was heard; a sledge stopped before the door, and almost immediately afterwards a Polish Jew entered. He was a well-made, vigorous man, between forty and fifty years of age. I fancy I can see him even now entering at that door with his green cloak and his fur cap, his large black beard and his great boots covered with hare skin. He was a seed merchant. He said as he came in, "Peace be with you!" Everybody turned to look at him, and thought, "Where has he come from? What does he want?" Because you must know that the Polish Jews who come to dispose of seed do not arrive in this province till the month of February. Mathias said to him, "What can I do for you?" But the Jew, without replying, first opened his cloak, and then unbuckled a girdle which he wore round his waist. This he threw upon the table, and we all heard the ringing sound of the gold it contained. Then he said, "The snow is deep; the road difficult; put my horse in the stable. In one hour I shall continue my journey." After that he drank his wine without speaking to anyone, and sat like a man depressed, and who is anxious about his affairs. At eleven o'clock the Night Watchman came in. Everyone went his way, and the Jew was left alone!

> [*Chord of Music—loud gust of wind—crash of glass off at* L.*—hurried music.* ALL. *start to their feet. Music continued.*

Catherine. What has happened? I must go and see.

Annette. Oh! no, you must not go!

Catherine. I will return immediately. Don't be alarmed.

> [*Exit* CATHERINE, *at* L. *During the following,* ANNETTE *takes up the spinning-wheel, and listens at the door for her mother.*

Christian. But I do not yet see how I could have gained the cross in this affair—

Walter. Stop a minute. The next morning they found the Jew's horse dead under the Bridge of Vechem, and a hundred yards further on, the green cloak and the fur cap, deeply stained with blood. As to what became of the Jew himself has never to this day been discovered. [*Music ceases.*

Hans. Everything that Walter has stated is strictly true. The gendarmes came here the next morning, notwithstanding the snow; and, in fact, it is since that dreadful time that the brigade has been established here.

Christian. But was no inquiry instituted?

Hans. Inquiry! I should think there was. It was the former Quarter-master, Kelz, who undertook the case. How he travelled about! What witnesses he badgered! What clues he discovered! What information and reports were written! and how the coat and the cap were analysed, and examined by magistrates and doctors!—but it all came to nothing!

Christian. But, surely, suspicion fell on someone.

Hans. Oh, of course, the gendarmes are never at a loss for suspicions in such cases. But proofs are required. About that time, you see, there were two brothers living in the village who had an old bear, with his ears all torn, two big dogs, and a donkey, that they took about with them to the fairs, and made the dogs bait the bear. This brought them a great deal of money; and they lived a rollicking dissipated life. When the Jew disappeared, they happened to be at Vechem; suspicions fastened upon them, and the report was, that they had caused the Jew to be eaten by the dogs and the bear, and that they only refrained from swallowing the cloak and cap, because they had had enough. They were arrested, and it would have gone hard with the poor devils, but Mathias interested himself in their case, and they were discharged, after being in prison fifteen months. That was the specimen of suspicion of the case.

Christian. What you have told me greatly astonishes me. I never heard a word of this before.

Re-enter CATHERINE, L.

Catherine. I was sure that Sozel had left the windows in the kitchen open. Now every pane of glass in them is broken. [*To* CHRISTIAN.] Fritz is outside. He wishes to speak with you.
Christian. Fritz, the gendarme!
Catherine. Yes, I asked him to come in, but he would not. It is upon some matter of duty.
Christian. Ah! good, I know what it is!
[*He rises, takes down his hat, and is going to the door.*
Annette. You will return, Christian?
Christian. In a few minutes. [*Music to take him off.*]
[*Exit, door,* C.
Walter. Ah! there goes a brave young fellow—gentle in character, I will admit, but not a man to trifle with rogues.
Hans. Yes, Mathias is fortunate in finding so good a son-in-law; but everything has succeeded with Mathias for the last fifteen years. [*Music commences.*] He was comparatively poor then, and now he is one of the richest men in the village, and the Burgomaster. He was born under a lucky star.
Walter. Well, and he deserves all the success he has achieved.
Catherine. Hark!
Annette. It is, perhaps, Christian returning as he promised.
[*Hurried music,* MATHIAS *passes the window, then enters at* C. *door; he wears a long cloak covered with snow, large cap made of otter's skin, gaiters and spurs, and carries a large riding-whip in his hand—chord—tableau.*
Mathias. It is I—It is I! [*Music ceases.*
Catherine [*rising*]. Mathias!
Hans and Walter [*Starting up*]. The Burgomaster!
Annette [*running and embracing him*]. At last you have come.
Mathias. Yes, yes! Heaven be praised! What a snow-storm. I was obliged to leave the carriage at Vechem. It will be brought over tomorrow.
Catherine [*embracing him and taking off his coat*]. Let me take this off for you. It was very kind of you not to stop away. We were becoming so anxious about you.
Mathias. So I thought, Catherine; and that was the reason I determined to reach home tonight. [*Looking round.*] Ha, ha! Father Walter and Hans, you will have

nice weather in which to go home. [*He takes off his hat, &c., and gives them to his* WIFE *and* DAUGHTER.] There! You will have to get all those things dried.

Catherine [*at door*, L.]. Sozel, get ready your master's supper at once, and tell Nickel to take the horse to the stable!

Sozel [*within*]. Yes, madame. [MATHIAS *sits* R., *by table*.

Annette. We thought perhaps that your cousin Bôth would have detained you.

Mathias [*unbuttoning his gaiters*]. Oh, I had finished all my business yesterday morning, and I wished to come away; but Bôth made me stop to see a performance in the town.

Annette. A performance! Is Punchinello[1] at Ribeauville?

Mathias. No, it was not Punchinello. It was a Parisian who did extraordinary tricks. He sent people to sleep.

Annette. Sent people to sleep!

Mathias. Yes.

Catherine. He gave them something to drink, no doubt

Mathias. No; he simply looked at them and made signs, and they went fast asleep.—It certainly was an astonishing performance. If I had not myself seen it I should never have believed it.

Hans. Ah! the Brigadier Stenger was telling me about it the other day. He had seen the same thing at Saverne. This Parisian sends people to sleep, and when they are asleep he makes them tell him everything that weighs upon their consciences.

Mathias. Exactly. [*To* ANNETTE] Annette?

Annette. What, father?

Mathias. Look in the big pocket of my cloak.

Enter SOZEL.

Sozel! take these gaiters and spurs; hang them in the stable with the harness.

Sozel. Yes, Burgomaster. [*Exit.*

ANNETTE, *who has taken a small box out of the pocket of the cloak, approaches her father,* C. *Music.*

Annette. What is it, father?

---

1 Anglicized name of Pulcinella, the clownish stock character from seventeenth-century Italian street and puppet theatre, and the crude star of Punch and Judy shows.

Mathias [*rising*]. Open the box.

> [*She opens the box, and takes out a handsome Alsatian hat, with gold and silver stars upon it—the others approach to look at it.*

Annette. Oh, how pretty! Is it for me?

Mathias. For whom else could it be? Not for Sozel, I fancy.

> [ANNETTE *puts on the hat after taking off her ribbon, and looks at herself in glass on sideboard—all express admiration.*

Annette. Oh! what will Christian say?

Mathias. He will say you are the prettiest girl in the province.

Annette [*kissing her father*]. Thank you, dear father. How good you are!

Mathias. It is my wedding present, Annette. The day of your marriage I wish you to wear it, and to preserve it forever. In fifteen or twenty years hence, will you remember your father gave it you?

Annette [*with emotion*]. Yes, dear father!

Mathias. All that I wish is to see you happy with Christian. [*Music ceases.*] And now for supper and some wine. [*To* WALTER *and* HANS.] You will stop and take a glass of wine with me?

Walter. With pleasure, Burgomaster.

Hans. For you, Burgomaster, we will try and make that little effort.

> [SOZEL *has entered, L., with tray of supper and wine which she has placed upon table.* MATHIAS *now sits at table, helps wine, and then commences to eat with a good appetite.* SOZEL *draws the curtains across window at back, and exits, L.*

Mathias. There is one advantage about the cold. It gives you a good appetite. Here's to your health! [*He drinks.*]

Walter and Hans. Here's yours, Burgomaster! [*They touch glasses and drink.*]

Mathias. Christian has not been here this evening?

Annette. Yes; they came to fetch him, but he will return presently.

Mathias. Ah! Good! good!

Catherine. He came late today, in consequence of some duty he had to perform in the Hôvald, in the capture of smugglers.

Mathias [*eating*]. Nice weather for such a business. By the side of the river, I found the snow five feet deep.

Walter. Yes; we were talking about that. We were telling the Quarter-master, that since the "Polish Jew's Winter" we had never seen weather like this.

[MATHIAS, *who was raising the glass to his lips—places it on the table again without drinking.*

Mathias. Ah! you were talking of that?

[*Distant sound of Bells heard. To himself—*"Bells! Bells!" *His whole aspect changes, and he leaves off eating, and sits listening. The Bells continue louder.*

Hans. That winter, you remember, Burgomaster, the whole valley was covered several feet deep with snow, and it was a long time before the horse of the Polish Jew could be dug out.

Mathias [*with indifference*]. Very possibly; but that tale is too old! It is like an old woman's story now, and is thought about no more. [*Watching them and starting up.*] Do you not hear the sound of Bells upon the road?

[*The Bells still go on.*

Walter and Hans [*listening*]. Bells? No!

Catherine. What is the matter, Mathias? you appear ill. You are cold; some warm wine will restore you. The fire in the stove is low; come, Annette, we will warm your father his wine in the kitchen.

[*Exeunt* CATHERINE *and* ANNETTE, *door* L.

Mathias. Thank you; it is nothing.

Walter. Come, Hans, let us go and see to the horse. At the same time, it is very strange that it was never discovered who did the deed.

Mathias. The rogues have escaped, more's the pity. Here's your health!

[*Music.*

Walter and Hans. Thank you!

Hans. It is just upon the stroke of ten!

[*They drink, and go out together at door* R.

Mathias [*alone—comes forward and listens with terror. Music with frequent chords*]. Bells! Bells! [*He runs to the window and slightly drawing the curtains, looks out.*] No one on the road. [*Comes forward.*] What is this jangling in my ears? What is tonight? Ah, it is the very night—the very hour! [*Clock strikes ten.*] I feel a darkness coming over me. [*Stage darkens.*] A sensation of giddiness seizes me. [*He staggers to chair.*] Shall I call for help? No, no, Mathias. Have courage! The Jew is dead!

[*Sinks on chair, the Bells come closer, then the back of the Scene rises and sinks, disclosing the Bridge of Vechem, with the snow-covered country and frozen rivulet; lime-kiln burning in the distance; the* JEW *is discovered seated in sledge dressed as described in speech in Act I; the horse carrying Bells; the* JEW's *face is turned away; the snow is falling fast; the scene is seen through a gauze; lime light; L., vision of a* MAN *dressed in a brown blouse and hood over his head, carrying an axe, stands in an attitude of following the sledge; when the picture is fully disclosed the Bells cease.*]

Mathias [*his back to scene*]. Oh, it is nothing. It is the wine and cold that have overcome me!

[*He rises and turns, goes up stage; starts violently upon seeing the vision before him; at the same time the* JEW *in the sledge suddenly turns his face, which is ashy pale, and fixes his eyes sternly upon him;* MATHIAS *utters a prolonged cry of terror, and falls senseless. Hurried Music.*]

END OF THE FIRST ACT

ACT II

SCENE. *Best room in the Burgomaster's house. Door, L.; door, R.; three large windows at back, looking out upon a street of the village, the church and the buildings covered with snow; large stove in the centre of room, practicable door to stove, tongs in grate; arm-chair near the stove; at L. (1st grooves), an old escritoire; near L., a table and armchair; chairs about room. It is morning; the room and street bright with sunlight.*

As the Curtain rises to Music, MATHIAS *is discovered seated in arm-chair at table;* CATHERINE *and* DOCTOR ZIMMER *standing at back by stove contemplating him. They advance.*

Doctor. You feel better, Burgomaster?

Mathias. Yes, I am quite well.

Doctor. No more pains in the head?

Mathias. No.

Doctor. No more strange noises in the ears?

Mathias. When I tell you that I am quite well—that I never was better—that is surely enough.

Catherine. For a long time he has had bad dreams. He talks in his sleep, and his thirst at night is constant, and feverish.

Mathias. Is there anything extraordinary in being thirsty during the night?

Doctor. Certainly not: but you must take more care of yourself. You drink too much white wine, Burgomaster. Your attack of the night before last arose from this cause. You had taken too much wine at your cousin's, and then the severe cold having seized you, the blood had flown to the head.

Mathias. I *was* cold, but that stupid gossip about the Polish Jew was the cause of all.

Doctor. How was that?

Mathias. Well, you must know, when the Jew disappeared, they brought me the cloak and cap that had belonged to the poor devil, and the sight of them quite upset me, remembering he had, the night before, stopped at our house. Since that time I had thought no more of the matter until the night before last, when some gossip brought the affair again to my mind. It was as if I had seen the ghost of the Jew. We all know that there are no such things, but—[*suddenly to his* WIFE]. Have you sent for the Notary?

Catherine. Yes; but you must be calm.

Mathias. I am calm. But Annette's marriage must take place at once. When a man in robust health and strength is liable to such an attack as I have had, nothing should be postponed till the morrow. What occurred to me the night before last might again occur tonight. I might not survive the second blow, and then I should not have seen my dear children happy. And now leave me. Whether it was the wine, or the cold, or the gossip about the Polish Jew, it comes to the same thing. It is all past and over now.

Doctor. But, perhaps, Burgomaster, it would be better to adjourn the signing of the marriage contract for a few days. It is an affair of so much interest and importance that the agitation might—

Mathias [*angrily*]. Good heavens, why will not people attend to their own business! I was ill, you bled me—I am well again—so much the better. Let the Notary be sent for at once. Let Father Walter and Hans be summoned as witnesses, and let the whole affair be finished without further delay.

Doctor [*to* CATHERINE, *aside*]. His nerves are still very much shaken. Perhaps it will be better to let him have his own way. [*To* MATHIAS.] Well, well, we'll say no more about it. Only don't forget what I have said—be careful of the white wine.

Mathias [*angrily striking the table, turning his back*]. Good! Good! Ah!

> [*The* DOCTOR *looks with pity towards him, bows to* CATHERINE, *and exits, door* L. *The church bell commences to ring. Music.*

Catherine [*at door* R., *calling*]. Annette! Annette!

Annette [*off* R.]. I am coming.

Catherine [*impatiently*]. Be quick. Be quick.

Annette [*off*]. Directly—directly!

Mathias. Don't hurry the poor child. You know that she is dressing.

Catherine. But I don't take two hours to dress.

Mathias. You; oh! that is different. She expects Christian. He was to have been here this morning. Something has detained him.

> *Enter* ANNETTE, *door* R., *she is in gala dress, and wears the golden heart upon her breast, and the hat given her by* MATHIAS *in the First Act.*

Catherine. At last, you are ready!

Annette. Yes, I am ready.

Mathias [*with affection*]. How beautiful you look, Annette.

Annette. You see, dear father, I have put on the hat.

Mathias. You did right—you did right.

Catherine [*impatiently*]. Are you not coming, Annette? The service will have commenced. [*Takes book off table.*] Come, come.

Annette. Christian has not yet been here.

Mathias. No, you may be sure some business detains him.

Catherine. Do come, Annette; you will see Christian by and by.

> [*Exit*, R., ANNETTE *is following.*

Mathias. Annette, Annette! Have you nothing to say to me?

> [ANNETTE *runs to him, and kisses him—he embraces her with affection.*

Annette. You know, dear father, how much I love you.

Mathias. Yes, yes. There, go now, dear child! your mother is impatient.

> [*Exit* ANNETTE, *door* R.

The villagers, MEN *and* WOMEN *in Sunday clothes, pass the window in couples,* MATHIAS *goes up and looks through the window,* ANNETTE *and* CATHERINE *pass and kiss hands to him—a* WOMAN *in the group says* "Good morning, Burgomaster." *Church bell ceases. Music ceases.*

Mathias [*coming forward to R. of stage, taking pinch of snuff*]. All goes well! Luckily all is over. But what a lesson, Mathias,—what a lesson! Would anyone believe that the mere talk about the Jew could bring on such a fit? Fortunately the people about here are such idiots they suspect nothing. [*Seats himself in chair by table.*] But it was that Parisian fellow at the fair who was the real cause of all. The rascal had really made me nervous. When he wanted to send me to sleep as well as the others, I said to myself, "Stop, stop, Mathias—this sending you to sleep may be an invention of the devil, you might relate certain incidents in your past life! You must be cleverer than that, Mathias; you mustn't run your neck into a halter; you must be cleverer than that—ah! you must be cleverer than that." [*Starting up and crossing to R.*] You will die an old man yet, Mathias, and the most respected in the Province—[*takes snuff*]—only this, since you dream and are apt to talk in your dreams, for the future you will sleep alone in the room above, the door locked, and the key safe in your pocket. They say walls have ears—let them hear me as much as they please. [*Music. Takes bunch of keys out of his pocket.*] And now to count the dowry of Annette, to be given to our dear son-in-law, in order that our dear son-in-law may love us. [*He crosses to L., unlocks the escritoire, takes out a large leather bag, unties it and empties the contents, consisting of gold pieces and rouleaux, upon the table.*] Thirty thousand francs. [*He sits at table, front to the audience, and commences to count the money.*] Thirty thousand francs—a fine dowry for Annette. Ah! it is pleasant to hear the sound of gold! A fine dowry for the husband of Annette. He's a clever fellow, is Christian. He's not a Kelz—half deaf and half blind; no, no—he's a clever fellow is Christian, and quite capable of getting on a right track. [*A pause.*] The first time I saw him I said to myself, "You shall be my son-in-law, and if anything should be discovered, you will defend me." [*Continues to count, weighing piece upon his finger—takes up a piece and examines it.*] A piece of old gold! [*Looks at it more closely—starts.*] Ah! that came from the girdle; not for them—no, no, not for them, for me. [*Places the piece of gold in his waistcoat pocket—he goes to the escritoire, opens a drawer, takes out another piece of gold and throws it upon the table in substitution.*] That girdle did us a good turn—without it—without it we were ruined. If Catherine only knew— poor, poor Catherine [*He sobs—his head sinks on his breast. Music ceases—the*

Bells heard off L., *he starts.*] The Bells! the Bells again! They must come from the mill. [*Rushes across to door* R., *calling.*] Sozel! Sozel, I say, Sozel!

Enter SOZEL, *door* R., *holding an open book, she is in her Sunday dress.*

Mathias. Is there anyone at the mill?
Sozel. No, Burgomaster. They have all gone to church, and the wheel is stopped.
Mathias. Don't you hear the sound of Bells?
Sozel. No, Burgomaster, I hear nothing. [*The Bells cease.*
Mathias [*aside*]. Strange—strange. [*Rudely.*] What were you doing?
Sozel. I was reading, Burgomaster.
Mathias. Reading—what? Ghost stories, no doubt.
Sozel. Oh, no, Burgomaster! I was reading such a curious story, about a band of robbers being discovered after twenty-three years had passed, and all through the blade of an old knife having been found in a blacksmith's shop, hidden under some rusty iron. They captured the whole of them, consisting of the mother, two sons, and the grandfather, and they hanged them all in a row. Look, Burgomaster, there's the picture.
[*Shows book—he strikes it violently out of her hand.*
Mathias. Enough, enough! It's a pity you have nothing better to do. There, go—go!
[*Exit* SOZEL, *door* R.

Seats himself at the table and puts remaining money into the bag.

The fools!—not to destroy all evidence against them. To be hanged through the blade of an old knife. Not like that—not like that am *I* to be caught!
[*Music—a sprightly military air.* CHRISTIAN *passes at back, stops at centre window and taps upon it.* MATHIAS *looks round, with a start, is reassured upon seeing who it is, and says, "Ah, it is Christian!"—he ties up the bag and places it in the escritoire.* CHRISTIAN *enters at door* R. MATHIAS *meets him half way—they shake hands. Music ceases.* CHRISTIAN *is in the full dress of a Quarter-master of Gendarmes.*
Christian. Good morning, Burgomaster, I hope you are better.
Mathias. Oh, yes, I am well, Christian. I have just been counting Annette's dowry, in good sounding gold. It was a pleasure to me to do so, as it recalled to me the

days gone by, when by industry and good fortune I had been enabled to gain it; and I thought that in the future my children would enjoy and profit by all that I had so acquired.

Christian. You are right, Burgomaster. Money gained by honest labour is the only profitable wealth. It is the good seed which in time is sure to bring a rich harvest.

Mathias. Yes, yes; especially when the good seed is sown in good ground. The contract must be signed today.

Christian. Today?

Mathias. Yes, the sooner the better. I hate postponements. Once decided, why adjourn the business? It shows a great want of character.

Christian. Well, Burgomaster, nothing to me could be more agreeable.

Mathias. Annette loves you.

Christian. Ah, she does.

Mathias. And the dowry is ready—then why should not the affair be settled at once? I hope, my boy, you will be satisfied.

Christian. You know, Burgomaster, I do not bring much.

Mathias. You bring courage and good conduct—I will take care of the rest; and now let us talk of other matters. You are late today. I suppose you were busy. Annette waited for you, and was obliged to go without you.

[*He goes up and sits by stove in arm-chair, opens stove door, takes up tongs and arranges fire.*

Christian [*unbuckling his sword and sitting in chair*]. Ah, it was a very curious business that detained me. Would you believe it, Burgomaster, I was reading old depositions from five o'clock till ten? The hours flew by, but the more I read the more I wished to read.

Mathias. And what was the subject of the depositions?

Christian. They were about the case of the Polish Jew who was murdered on the Bridge of Vechem fifteen years ago.

Mathias [*dropping the tongs*]. Ah!

Christian. Father Walter told me the story the night before last. It seems to me very remarkable that nothing was ever discovered.

Mathias. No doubt—no doubt.

Christian. The man who committed that murder must have been a clever fellow.

Mathias. Yes, he was not a fool.

Christian. A fool! He would have made one of the cleverest gendarmes in the department.

Mathias [*with a smile*]. Do you really think so?

Christian. I am sure of it. There are so many ways of detecting criminals, and so few escape, that to have committed a crime like this, and yet to remain undiscovered, showed the possession of extraordinary address.

Mathias. I quite agree with you, Christian; and what you say shows your good sense. When a man has committed a crime, and by it gained money, he becomes like a gambler, and tries his second and his third throw. I should think it requires a great amount of courage to resist the first success in crime.

Christian. You are right, but what is most remarkable to me in the case is this, that no trace of the murdered man was ever found. Now do you know what my idea is?

Mathias [*rising*]. No, no! What is your idea?

[*They come forward.*

Christian. Well, I find at that time there were a great many lime-kilns in the neighbourhood of Vechem. Now it is my idea that the murderer, to destroy all traces of his crime, threw the body of the Jew into one of these kilns. Old Kelz, my predecessor, evidently never thought of that.

Mathias. Very likely—very likely. Do you know that idea never occurred to me. You are the first who ever suggested it.

Christian. And this idea leads to many others. Now suppose—suppose inquiry had been instituted as to those persons who were burning lime at that time.

Mathias. Take care, Christian—take care. Why, I, myself, had a lime-kiln burning at the time the crime was committed.

Christian [*laughing*]. Oh, you, Burgomaster!

[MATHIAS *laughs heartily—they go up together.* ANNETTE *and* CATHERINE *pass the window.*

Annette [*as she passes the window before entering*]. He is there!

Enter ANNETTE *and* CATHERINE, *door* R.

Mathias [*to* CATHERINE]. Is the Notary here?

Catherine. Yes, he is in the next room with Father Walter and Hans, and the others. He is reading the contract to them now.

Mathias. Good—good!

Christian [*to* ANNETTE]. Oh, Annette, how that pretty hat becomes you!

Annette. Yes; it was dear father who gave it to me.

[*Music.*

Christian. It is today, Annette.

Annette. Yes, Christian, it is today.

Mathias [*coming between them*]. Well; you know what is customary when father, mother, and all consent.

Christian. What, Burgomaster?

Mathias [*smiling*]. You embrace your intended wife.

Christian. Is that so, Annette?

Annette. I don't know, Christian.

[*He kisses her forehead, and leads her up to stove, talking.*

Mathias [*to* CATHERINE, *who is seated in arm-chair L., by table*]. Look at our children, Catherine; how happy they are! When I think that we were once as happy! It's true; yes, it's true, we were once as happy as they are now! Why are you crying, Catherine? Are you sorry to see our children happy?

Catherine. No, no, Mathias; these are tears of joy, and I can't help them.

[*Throws herself upon* MATHIAS's *shoulder. Music ceases.*

Mathias. And now to sign the contract! [*Crosses to R. door and throws it open.*] Walter, Hans, come in! Let everyone present come in! The most important acts in life should always take place in the presence of all. It is an old and honest custom of Alsace. [*Music—"The Lauterbach," played forte.*

Enter at door R., HANS *with two* GIRLS *on his arm—*FATHER WALTER *with two* GIRLS*—*MEN *and* WOMEN VILLAGERS *arm-in-arm—they wear ribbons in their button-holes—The* NOTARY *with papers—*SOZEL. *The* MEN *wear their hats through the whole scene.* MATHIAS *advances and shakes hands with the* NOTARY *and conducts him to table on which is spread out the contract—pen and ink on table. The* COMPANY *fill the stage in groups.*

Notary. Gentlemen and witnesses,—You have just heard read the marriage contract between Christian Berne, Quarter-master of Gendarmes, and Annette Mathias. Has anyone any observations to make?

Several Voices. No, no.

Notary. Then we can at once proceed to take the signatures. [MATHIAS *goes to the escritoire and takes out the bag of gold which he places on the table before the*

NOTARY.] There is the dowry. It is not in promises made on paper, but in gold. Thirty thousand francs in good French gold.

All. Thirty thousand francs!

Christian. It is too much, Burgomaster.

Mathias. Not at all, not at all. When Catherine and myself are gone there will be more. And now, Christian—[*Music commences*]—I wish you to make me one promise.

Christian. What promise?

Mathias. Young men are ambitious. It is natural they should be. You must promise me that you will remain in this village while both of us live. [*Takes* CATHERINE's *hand.*] You know Annette is our only child; we love her dearly, and to lose her altogether would break our hearts. Do you promise?

Christian [*looks to* ANNETTE; *she returns a glance of approval*]. I do promise.

Mathias. Your word of honour, given before all?

Christian. My word of honour, given before all.

[*They shake hands. Music ceases.*

Mathias [*crossing to L. corner, and taking pinch of snuff—aside*]. It was necessary. And now to sign the contract. [*He goes to table; the* NOTARY *hands him the pen, and points to the place where he is to sign his name,* MATHIAS *is about to write. The Bells heard off.* MATHIAS *stops, listens with terror—his face to the audience, and away from the persons upon the stage—aside.*] Bells! Courage, Mathias! [*After an effort he signs rapidly—the Bells cease—he throws the pen down.*] Come, Christian, sign!

[CHRISTIAN *approaches the table to sign—as he is about to do so* WALTER *taps him on the shoulder.* MATHIAS *starts at the interruption.*

Walter. It is not every day you sign a contract like that.

[ALL *laugh.* MATHIAS *heaves a sigh and is reassured.* CHRISTIAN *signs—the* NOTARY *hands the pen to* CATHERINE, *who makes her cross—she then takes* ANNETTE *to table, who signs her name.* CATHERINE *kisses her affectionately and gives her to* CHRISTIAN.

Mathias [*aside*]. And now should the Jew return to this world, Christian must drive him back again. [*Aloud.*] Come, come, just one waltz and then dinner.

Walter. Stop! stop! Before we go we must have the song of the betrothal.

All. Yes, yes, Annette! Annette! the song of the betrothal.

Song, ANNETTE. *Air—"The Lauterbach."*

Suitors of wealth and high degree,
    In style superbly grand,
Tendered their love on bended knee
    And sought to win my hand.
        [*Tyrolienne by all, and waltz.*
But a soldier brave came to woo.
    No maid such love could spurn—
Proving his heart was fond and true.
    Won my love in return.

[*Tyrolienne as before by all, and waltz.* MATHIAS *is seated—in the midst of the waltz Bells are heard off.* MATHIAS *starts up and rushes into the midst of the* WALTZERS.

Mathias. The Bells! The Bells!
Catherine. Are you mad?

[MATHIAS *seizes her by the waist and waltzes wildly with her.*

Mathias. Ring on! Ring on! Houp! Houp!

[*Music, forte—while the waltz is at its height the Act Drop falls.*

END OF THE SECOND ACT

ACT III

SCENE. *Bedroom in the Burgomaster's house. The whole back of scene painted on a gauze; alcove on left; door, R.; two windows at back; small table by bed; chair, L. Night.*

Music.—Enter at door R., MATHIAS, FATHER WALTER, HANS, CHRISTIAN, ANNETTE, *and* CATUERINE; SOZEL *carrying a lighted candle, bottle of water and glass, which she places on table; they enter suddenly, the* MEN *appear to be slightly excited by wine; lights down at rising of curtain; lights turned up upon entrance of* SOZEL.

Hans [*laughing*]. Ha, ha! Everything has gone off admirably. We only wanted something to wind up with, and I may say that we are all as capitally wound up as the great clock at Strasbourg.

Walter. Yes, and what wine we have consumed! For many a day we shall remember the signing of Annette's marriage contract. I should like to witness such a contract every second day.

Hans. There, I object to your argument. Every day, I say!

Christian [*to* MATHIAS]. And so you are determined, Mathias, to sleep here tonight?

Mathias. Yes, I am decided. I wish for air. I know what is necessary for my condition. The heat was the cause of my accident. This room is cooler, and will prevent its recurrence. [*Laughter heard outside.*

Hans. Listen, how they are still revelling! Come, Father Walter, let us rejoin the revels!

Walter. But Mathias already deserts us, just at the moment when we were beginning to thoroughly enjoy ourselves.

Mathias. What more do you wish me to do? From noon till midnight is surely enough!

Walter. Enough, it may be, but not too much; never too much of such wine.

Hans. There, again, I object to your argument—never enough, I say.

Catherine. Mathias is right. You remember that Doctor Zimmer told him to be careful of the wine he took, or it would one day play him false. He has already taken too much since this morning.

Mathias. One glass of water before I go to rest is all I require. It will calm me—it will calm me.

KARL, FRITZ, *and* TONY, *three of the guests of the previous Act, enter suddenly, slightly merry, pushing each other.*

Guests. Good night, Burgomaster. Good night.

Tony. I say, Hans! don't you know that the Night Watchman is below?

Hans. The Night Watchman! What in the name of all that is political, does he want?

Karl. He requires us all to leave, and the house to be closed. It is past hours.

Mathias. Give him a bumper of wine, and then good night all!

Walter. Past hours! For a Burgomaster no regulations ought to exist.
Hans and Others. Certainly not.
Mathias [*with fierceness*]. Regulations made for all must be obeyed by all.
Walter [*timidly*]. Well, then, shall we go?
Mathias. Yes, yes, go! Leave me to myself,
Catherine [*to* WALTER]. Don't thwart his wish. Follow his directions.
Walter [*shaking hands with* MATHIAS]. Good night, Mathias. I wish you calm repose, and no unpleasant dreams.
Mathias [*fiercely*]. I never dream. [*Mildly.*] Good night, all. Go, friends, go.

> [*Music. Exeunt* WALTER, HANS, *and the three* GUESTS, *saying* "Good night, Burgomaster." CATHERINE, ANNETTE, *and* CHRISTIAN *remain.*

Mathias. Good night, Catherine. [*Embracing her.*] I shall be better here. The wine, the riot, those songs have quite dazed my brain. I shall sleep better here, I shall sleep better.
Christian. Yes, this room is fresh and cool. Good night.
Mathias. The same to you, Christian; the same to you.

> [*They shake hands.*

Annette [*running to her father and kissing him*]. Good night, dear father; may you sleep well!
Mathias [*kissing her with affection*]. Good night, dear child; do not fear for me—do not fear.

> [*Music. Exeunt all but* MATHIAS. *Music ceases. He goes up cautiously, locks the door* R., *and puts the key in his pocket.*

At last I am alone! Everything goes well. Christian the gendarme is caught! Tonight I shall sleep without a fear haunting me! If any new danger should threaten the father-in-law of the Quarter-master, it would soon be averted. Ah! What a power it is to know how to guide your destiny in life. You must hold good cards in your hands. Good cards! as I have done, and if you play them well you may defy ill fortune.

> *Chorus of* REVELLERS, *outside (without accompaniment).*

> Now, since we must part, let's drain a last glass:
>   Let's drink!
> Let us first drink to this gentle young lass;

    Let's drink!
From drinking this toast, we'll none of us shrink:
Others shall follow, when we've time to think.
    Our burden shall be, let us drink!
    The burden to bear is good drink.

                                                                           [Loud laughter heard outside.

Mathias [*taking off his coat*]. Ha, ha, ha! Those jolly topers[1] have got all they want. What holes in the snow they will make before they reach their homes! Drink! Drink! Is it not strange? To drink and drown every remorse! Yes, everything goes well! [*He drinks a glass of water.*] Mathias, you can at least boast of having well managed your affairs—the contract signed—rich—prosperous—respected—happy! [*Takes off waistcoat.*] No one now will hear you, if you dream. No one! No more folly!—no more Bells! Tonight, I triumph; for conscience is at rest!

          [*He enters the alcove. The Chorus of* REVELLERS *heard again, in the distance. A hand is extended from alcove and extinguishes the candle—stage dark. Curtain at back of gauze rises, disclosing an extensive set of a Court of Justice, arched, brilliantly lighted—at back, three* JUDGES *on the bench, dressed in black caps and red robes—at* R. *and* L., *the* PUBLIC, *in Alsatian costumes—in front of the* JUDGES, *but beneath them, a table, on which lies the Jew's cloak and cap—on* R., *the* PUBLIC PROSECUTOR *and* BARRISTERS—*on* L., *the* CLERK *or* REGISTRAR OF THE COURT, *and* BARRISTERS—*a* GENDARME *at each corner of the Court,* MATHIAS *is discovered seated on a stool in C. of Court—he is dressed in the brown blouse and hood worn by the* MAN *in the vision in Act I—he has his back to the* AUDIENCE, *face to* JUDGES.

The Clerk of the Court [L., *standing, reading the Act of Accusation*]. Therefore, the prisoner, Mathias, is accused of having, on the night of the 24th December, 1818, between midnight and one o'clock, assassinated the Jew Koveski, upon the Bridge of Vechem, to rob him of his gold.

President. Prisoner, you have heard the Act of Accusation read; you have already heard the depositions of the witnesses. What have you to say in answer?

---

1   Heavy drinkers.

Mathias [*violently—throws back hood, and starting up*]. Witnesses! People who saw nothing; people who live miles from the place where the crime was committed; at night, and in the winter time! You call such people witnesses!

President. Answer with calmness; these gestures—this violence will avail you nothing. You are a man full of cunning.

Mathias [*with humility*]. No, I am a man of simplicity.

President. You knew well the time to select; you knew well how to evade all suspicion; you knew well how to destroy all direct evidence. You are a dangerous man!

Mathias [*derisively*]. Because nothing can be proved against me I am dangerous! Every honest man then is dangerous when nothing can be proved against him! A rare encouragement for honesty!

President. The public voice accuses you. Answer me this: How is it that you hear the noise of Bells?

Mathias [*passionately*]. I do not hear the noise of Bells!

[*Music. Bells heard off as before,* MATHIAS *trembles.*

President. Prisoner, you speak falsely. At this moment you hear that noise. Tell us why is this?

Mathias. It is nothing. It is simply a jangling in my ears.

President. Unless you acknowledge the true cause of this noise you hear, we shall summon the Mesmerist to explain the matter to us.

Mathias [*with defiance*]. It is true then that I hear this noise.

[*Bells cease.*

President [*to the* CLERK OF THE COURT]. It is well; write that down.

Mathias. Yes; but I hear it in a dream.

President. Write, that he hears it in a dream.

Mathias [*furiously*]. Is it a crime to dream?

The Crowd [*murmur very softly among themselves, and move simultaneously, each person performing exactly the same movement of negation*]. N—N—N—o!

Mathias [*with confidence*]. Listen, friends! Don't fear for me! All this is but a dream—I am in a dream. If it were not a dream should I be clothed in these rags? Should I have before me such judges as these? Judges who, simply acting upon their own empty ideas, would hang a fellow creature. Ha, ha, ha! It is a dream—a dream!

[*He bursts into a loud derisive laugh.*

President. Silence, prisoner—silence! [*Turning to his companion* JUDGES.] Gentlemen—this noise of Bells arises in the prisoner's mind from the remembrance of what is past. The prisoner hears this noise because there rankles in his heart the memory of that he would conceal from us. The Jew's horse carried Bells.

Mathias. It is false, I have no memories.

President. Be silent!

Mathias [*with rage*]. A man cannot be condemned upon such suppositions. You must have proofs. I do not hear the noise of Bells.

President. You see, gentlemen, the prisoner contradicts himself. He has already made the avowal—now he retracts it.

Mathias. No! I hear nothing. [*The Bells heard.*] It is the blood rushing to my brain—this jangling in my ears. [*The Bells increase in sound.*] I ask for Christian. Why is not Christian here?

President. Prisoner! do you persist in your denial?

Mathias [*with force*]. Yes. There is nothing proved against me. It is a gross injustice to keep an honest man in prison. I suffer in the cause of justice.

[*The Bells cease.*

President. You persist. Well! Considering that since this affair took place fifteen years have passed, and that it is impossible to throw light upon the circumstances by ordinary means—first, through the cunning and audacity of the prisoner, and second, through the deaths of witnesses who could have given evidence—for these reasons we decree that the Court hear the Mesmerist. Officer, summon the Mesmerist.

Mathias [*in a terrible voice*]. I oppose it! I oppose it! Dreams prove nothing.

President. Summon the Mesmerist!

[*Exit* GENDARME, R.

Mathias [*striking the table*]. It is abominable! It is in defiance of all justice!

President. If you are innocent, why should you fear the Mesmerist, because he can read the inmost secrets of your heart? Be calm, or, believe me, your own indiscretion will prove that you are guilty.

Mathias. I demand an advocate. I wish to instruct the advocate Linder of Saverne. In a case like this, I do not care for cost. I am calm—as calm as any man who has no reproach against himself. I fear nothing; but dreams are dreams. [*Loudly.*] Why is Christian not here? My honour is his honour. Let him be sent for. He is an honest man. [*With exultation.*] Christian, I have made you rich. Come, and defend me!

[*Music. The* GENDARME *who had gone out, returns with the* MESMERIST.

Mesmerist [*bending to the Court respectfully*]. Your honours, the President and Judges of the Court, it is your decree that has brought me before your tribunal; without such direction, terror alone would have kept me far from here.

Mathias. Who can believe in the follies of the Mesmerist? They deceive the public for the purpose of gaining money! They merely perform the tricks of conjurers. I have seen this fellow already at my cousin Bôth's, at Ribeauville.

President [*to the* MESMERIST]. Can you send this man to sleep?

Mesmerist [*looking full at* MATHIAS, *who sinks upon chair, unable to endure the* MESMERIST'S *gaze*]. I can!

Mathias [*starting up*]. I will not be made the subject of this conjurer's experiments.

President. I command it!

Mathias. Christian—where is Christian? He will prove that I am an honest man.

President. Your resistance betrays you.

Mathias [*with defiance*]. I have no fear. [*Sits.*]

[*The* MESMERIST *goes up stage to back of* MATHIAS, *makes some passes. Music.*]

Mathias [*to himself*]. Mathias, if you sleep you are lost. [*His eyes are fixed as if struck with horror—in a hollow voice.*] No—no—I will not sleep—I—will—[*in a hesitating voice*] I will—not—no—

[*Falls asleep. Music ceases.*]

Mesmerist [*to the* PRESIDENT]. He sleeps. What shall I ask him?

President. Ask him what he did on the night of the 24th of December, fifteen years ago.

Mesmerist [*to* MATHIAS, *in a firm voice*]. You are at the night of the 24th December, 1818?

Mathias [*in a low voice*]. Yes.

Mesmerist. What time is it?

Mathias. Half-past eleven.

Mesmerist. Speak on, I command you!

Mathias [*still in the same attitude, speaking as if he were describing a vision presented to his sight*]. The people are leaving the inn—Catherine and little Annette have gone to rest. Our man Kasper comes in. He tells me the lime-kiln is lighted. I answer him, it is well; go to bed, I will see to the kiln. He leaves me; I am alone with the Jew, who warms himself at the stove. Outside, everything sleeps. Nothing is heard, except from time to time the Jew's horse under the shed, when he shakes his bells.

Mesmerist. Of what are you thinking?

Mathias. I am thinking that I must have money—that if I have not three thousand francs by the 31st, the inn will be taken from me. I am thinking that no one is stirring; that it is night; that there are two feet of snow upon the ground, and that the Jew will follow the high road quite alone!

Mesmerist. Have you already decided to attack him?

Mathias [*after a short silence*]. That man is strong. He has broad shoulders. I am thinking that he would defend himself well, should any one attack him.

[*He makes a movement.*

Mesmerist. What ails you?

Mathias [*in a low voice*]. He looks at me. He has grey eyes. [*As if speaking to himself.*] I must strike the blow!

Mesmerist. You are decided?

Mathias. Yes—yes; I will strike the blow! I will risk it!

Mesmerist. Go on!

Mathias [*continuing*]. I must, however, look round. I go out; all is dark! It still snows; no one will trace my footsteps in the snow.

[*He raises his hand as if feeling for something.*

Mesmerist. What are you doing?

Mathias. I am feeling in the sledge—should he carry pistols! There is nothing—I will strike the blow! [*He listens.*] All is silent in the village! Little Annette is crying; a goat bleats in the stable; the Jew is walking in his room!

Mesmerist. You re-enter?

Mathias. Yes. The Jew has placed six francs upon the table; I return him his money; he fixes his eyes steadily upon me!

Mesmerist. He speaks to you?

Mathias. He asks me how far it is to Mutzig. Four leagues. I wish him well on his journey! He answers—"God bless you!" He goes out—He is gone! [MATHIAS, *with body bent, takes several steps forward as if following and watching his victim, he extends his hands.*] The axe! Where is the axe? Ah, here, behind the door! How cold it is! [*He trembles.*] The snow falls—not a star! Courage, Mathias, you shall possess the girdle—courage!

Mesmerist. You follow him?

Mathias. Yes, yes. I have crossed the fields! [*Pointing.*] Here is the old bridge, and there below, the frozen rivulet! How the dogs howl at Daniel's farm—how they howl! And old Finck's forge, how brightly it glows upon the hillock. [*Low, as if speaking to himself.*] Kill a man!—kill a man! You will not do that, Mathias—you will not do that! Heaven forbids it. [*Proceeding to walk with measured steps and bent body.*]

You are a fool! Listen, you will be rich, your wife and child will no longer want for anything! The Jew came; so much the worse—so much the worse. He ought not to have come! You will pay all you owe; you will no more be in debt. [*Loud, in a broken tone.*] It must be, Mathias, that you kill him! [*He listens.*] No one on the road—no one! [*With an expression of terror.*] What dreadful silence! [*He wipes his forehead with his hand.*] One o'clock strikes, and the moon shines. Ah! The Jew has already passed! Thank God! thank God! [*He kneels—a pause—he listens—the Bells heard without as before.*] No! The Bells! The Bells! He comes! [*He bends down in a watching attitude, and remains still—a pause—in a low voice.*] You will be rich—you will be rich—you will be rich! [*The noise of the Bells increase—the* CROWD *express alarm simultaneously—all at once* MATHIAS *springs forward, and with a species of savage roar, strikes a terrible blow with his right hand.*] Ah! Ah! I have you now, Jew! [*He strikes again—the* CROWD *simultaneously express horror,* MATHIAS *leans forward and gazes anxiously on the ground—he extends his hand as if to touch something, but draws it back in horror.*] He does not move! [*He raises himself, utters a deep sigh of relief and looks round.*] The horse has fled with the sledge! [*The Bells cease—kneeling down.*] Quick, quick! The girdle! I have it. Ha! [*He performs the action in saying this of taking it from the Jew's body and buckling it round his own.*] It is full of gold, quite full. Be quick, Mathias, be quick! Carry him away.

> [*He bends low down and appears to lift the body upon his back; then he walks across stage, his body bent, his step slow as a man who carries a heavy load.*

Mesmerist. Where are you going?

Mathias [*stopping*]. To the lime-kiln. I am there. [*He appears to throw the body upon the kiln.*] How heavy he was! [*He breathes with force, then he again bends down to take up a pole—in a hoarse voice.*] Go into the fire, Jew, go into the fire! [*He appears to push the body with the pole, using his whole force, suddenly he utters a cry of horror and staggers away, his face covered with his hands.*] Those eyes, oh, those eyes! How he glares at me.

> [*He sinks on to stool, and takes the same attitude as when first thrown into sleep.*

President [*with a sign to the* MESMERIST]. It is well. [*To the* CLERK OF THE COURT.] You have written all?

Clerk. All!

President [*to* MESMERIST]. It is well—awake him now, and let him read himself.

Mesmerist. Awake! I command you!

Mathias [*awakes gradually—he appears bewildered*]. Where am I? [*He looks round.*] Ah! Yes; what is going on?

Clerk [*handing him paper*]. Here is your deposition—read it.

Mathias [*takes it and, before reading it, aside*]. Wretched, wretched fool! I have told all; I am lost! [*With rage, after reading the paper.*] It is false! [*Tears the paper into pieces.*] You are a set of rogues! Christian—where is Christian? It is a crime against justice! They will not let my only witness speak. Christian! They would kill the father of your wife! Help me—help me!

President. You force me to speak of an event of which I had wished to remain silent. Your son-in-law Christian, upon hearing of the crimes with which you are charged, by his own hand sought his death. He is no more.

Mathias. Ah!

[*He appears stupefied with dismay.*

President [*after consulting the other* JUDGES, *rises, speaks in a solemn tone of voice*]. Considering that on the night of the 24th December, 1818, between midnight and one o'clock, Mathias committed the crime of assassination upon the person of one Koveski, and considering that this crime was committed under circumstances which aggravates its enormity—such as premeditation, and for the purpose of highway robbery; the Court condemns the said Mathias to be hanged by the neck until he is dead!

[MATHIAS *staggers and falls on his knees. The* CROWD *make a movement of terror—the death-bell tolls—lights lowered gradually—then curtain at back of gauze descends, disclosing the scene as at commencement—lights up. Music—a peal of joy, bells heard ringing.*

Crowd [*without*]. Annette! Annette! The bride!

[*Hurried steps are heard upon the stairs outside, and then a loud knocking at the door of the room.*

Catherine [*without*]. Mathias! Mathias! get up at once. It is late in the morning, and all our guests are below.

[*More knocking.*

Christian [*without*]. Mathias! Mathias! [*Silence.*] How soundly he sleeps!

Walter [*without*]. Ho! Mathias, the wedding has commenced—Houp, houp!

[*More knocking.*

The Crowd [*outside*]. Burgomaster! Burgomaster!

[*Loud knocking.*

Catherine [*in an anxious voice*]. He does not answer. It is strange. Mathias!

[*A discussion among many voices is heard without.*
Christian. No—it is useless. Leave it to me!

At the same moment several violent blows are struck upon the door, which falls into the room from its hinges. Enter CHRISTIAN, *hurriedly—he runs to the alcove. Hurried music.*

Christian. Mathias! [*Looks into alcove and staggers back into room.*] Ah!

Enter CATHERINE *and* ANNETTE, *followed by* WALTER, HANS, *and the* CROWD, *all dressed for the wedding.*

Catherine. What has happened, Christian, what has happened?
[*She is rushing to alcove.*
Christian [*stopping her*]. Don't come near—don't come near.
Catherine [*endeavouring to pass*]. I will see what it is. Let me pass; do not fear for me.

[MATHIAS *appears from the alcove—he is dressed in the same clothes as when he retired into the alcove at the commencement of the scene, but his face is haggard, and ghastly pale—he comes out, his eyes fixed, his arms extended—as he rushes forward with uncertain steps, the* CROWD *fall back with horror, and form groups of consternation, with a general exclamation of terror.*

Mathias [*in a voice of strangulation*]. The rope! the rope! Take the rope from my neck!

[*He falls suddenly, and is caught in the arms of* HANS *and* WALTER, *who carry him to the chair in centre of stage. The Bells heard off. Music, the melody played in the Second Act when promise given. His hands clutch at his throat as if to remove something that strangles him—he looks pitifully round as if trying to recognize those about him, and then his head falls on his breast.* CATHERINE, *kneeling, places her hand on* MATHIAS'S *heart.*

Catherine. Dead! [*The Bells cease.*]

[ANNETTE *bursts into tears. The* WOMEN *in the crowd kneel, the* MEN *remove their hats and bend their heads upon their breasts—tableau.*

CURTAIN

A Beleaguered City

Margaret Oliphant

One of the most prolific writers of the nineteenth century, Scottish author Margaret Oliphant (1828–1897) produced nearly 100 novels, in addition to numerous biographies, histories, travel books, essays, reviews, short stories, and translations. She spent her childhood in Glasgow and Liverpool, published her first novel when she was twenty-one, and then married her cousin Frank Wilson Oliphant, an artist, in 1852. Her prodigious literary output was driven, in part, by personal tragedy. First, three of her children died in infancy. Then in 1859 Frank Oliphant died in Rome, where the couple had moved for the sake of his fragile health. Only thirty-one, Oliphant found herself in debt with three small children to support. Her circle of dependents widened considerably, however, when one of her brothers became bankrupt and merged his family with her household. Then another brother, an alcoholic, became dependent upon her financially. In response to these crises, Oliphant embraced her vocation with a new vigor and produced, among other popular works, her highly successful *Chronicles of Carlingford* series (1862–1876), published in *Blackwood's Magazine*. Queen Victoria cited Oliphant as her favorite novelist. In 1864, tragedy struck again, when Oliphant's ten-year-old daughter, her only daughter, died suddenly of gastric fever in Rome. Paralyzed by this loss, happening as it did in the city that claimed her husband, Oliphant traveled Europe with her two young sons, spending considerable time in France, where she witnessed firsthand the devastation wrought by the Franco-Prussian War and by the suppression of the Paris Commune in 1871. For fifteen years, Oliphant was unable to write about her daughter's death. She became engrossed in thoughts of the afterlife and the possibility of communicating with the so-called spirit world: the space between "the seen and the unseen." Written in 1879 and published in 1880, Oliphant's short novel *A Beleaguered City* is her attempt to come to terms with her loss. Her sympathetic exploration of spiritual questions struck a chord with Victorian readers. Robert Louis Stevenson told Oliphant that *A Beleaguered City* moved him to tears. Oliphant lived the last thirty years of her life at Windsor, in England, near her sons. Her eldest died in 1890, her youngest, in 1894. Brokenhearted, her fiction out of style, Oliphant died three years later, leaving behind literary progeny, however, in the form of 120 books.

Chapter One

THE NARRATIVE OF M. LE MAIRE
THE CONDITION OF THE CITY

I, MARTIN Dupin (de la Clairière), had the honour of holding the office of Maire[1] in the town of Semur, in the Haute Bourgogne,[2] at the time when the following events occurred. It will be perceived therefore, that no one could have more complete knowledge of the facts—at once from my official position, and from the place of eminence in the affairs of the district generally which my family has held for many generations—by what citizen-like virtues and unblemished integrity I will not be vain enough to specify. Nor is it necessary; for no one who knows Semur can be ignorant of the position held by the Dupins, from father to son. The estate La Clairière has been so long in the family that we might very well, were we disposed, add its name to our own, as so many families in France do;[3] and, indeed, I do not prevent my wife (whose prejudices I respect) from making this use of it upon her cards. But, for myself, bourgeois I was born and bourgeois I mean to die. My residence, like that of my father and grandfather, is at No. 29 in the Grande Rue, opposite the Cathedral,

---

1 Mayor.
2 Built on a rocky hillside overlooking the Armançon River, the medieval town of Semur-en-Auxois—located between Avallon to the west and Dijon to the east—is in Upper Burgundy, in central France. Oliphant visited Semur-en-Auxois in 1871 and took note of the fact that many of the religious images had been ripped from the façade of the cathedral by anti-clerical partisans.
3 Upper-middle-class French families incorporated the names of their estates into their family names in order to suggest that their antecedents had been nobles.

and not far from the Hospital of St. Jean. We inhabit the first floor, along with the *rez-de-chaussée*,[1] which has been turned into domestic offices suitable for the needs of the family. My mother, holding a respected place in my household, lives with us in the most perfect family union. My wife (*née* de Champfleurie) is everything that is calculated to render a household happy; but, alas! One only of our two children survives to bless us. I have thought these details of my private circumstances necessary, to explain the following narrative; to which I will also add, by way of introduction, a simple sketch of the town itself and its general conditions before these remarkable events occurred.

It was on a summer evening about sunset, the middle of month of June, that my attention was attracted by an incident of no importance which occurred in the street, when I was making my way home, after an inspection of the young vines in my new vineyard to the left of La Clairière. All were in perfectly good condition, and none of the many signs which point to the arrival of the insect[2] were apparent. I had come back in good spirits, thinking of the prosperity which I was happy to believe I had merited by a conscientious performance of all my duties. I had little with which to blame myself; not only my wife and relations, but my dependants and neighbours, approved my conduct as a man; and even my fellow-citizens, exacting as they are, had confirmed in my favour the good opinion which my family had been fortunate enough to secure from father to son. These thoughts were in my mind as I turned the corner of the Grande Rue and approached my own house. At this moment the tinkle of a little bell warned all the bystanders of the procession which was about to pass, carrying the rites of the Church to some dying person. Some of the women, always devout, fell on their knees. I did not go so far as this, for I do not pretend, in these days of progress, to have retained the same attitude of mind as that which it is no doubt becoming to behold in the more devout sex, but I stood respectfully out of the way, and took off my hat, as good breeding alone, if nothing else, demanded of me. Just in front of me, however, was Jacques Richard, always a troublesome individual, standing doggedly, with his hat upon his head and his hands in his pockets, straight in the path of M. le Curé.[3] There is not in all France a more obstinate fellow. He stood there, notwithstanding the efforts of a good woman to draw him away, and though I myself called to him. M. le Curé is not the man to flinch; and as he passed, walking as usual very quickly

---

1   Ground floor.
2   Phylloxera, a plant louse native to North America that devastated the European wine-making industry in the late nineteenth century.
3   Priest.

and straight, his soutane[1] brushed against the blouse of Jacques. He gave one quick glance from beneath his eyebrows at the profane interruption, but he would not distract himself from his sacred errand at such a moment. It *is* a sacred errand when any one, be he priest or layman, carries the best he can give to the bedside of the dying. I said this to Jacques when M. le Curé had passed and the bell went tinkling on along the street. "Jacques," said I, "I do not call it impious, like this good woman, but I call it inhuman. What! a man goes to carry help to the dying, and you show him no respect!"

This brought the colour to his face; and I think, perhaps, that he might have become ashamed of the part he had played; but the women pushed in again, as they are so fond of doing. "Oh, M. le Maire, he does not deserve that you should lose your words upon him!" they cried; "and, besides, is it likely he will pay any attention to you when he tries to stop even the *bon Dieu*?"[2]

"The *bon Dieu*!" cried Jacques. "Why doesn't He clear the way for himself? Look here. I do not care one farthing for your bon Dieu. Here is mine; I carry him about with me." And he took a piece of a hundred sous out of his pocket (how had it got there?) "*Vive l'argent!*"[3] he said. "You know it yourself, though you will not say so. There is no bon Dieu but money. With money you can do anything. *L'argent c'est le bon Dieu.*"[4]

"Be silent," I cried, "thou profane one!" And the women were still more indignant than I. "We shall see, we shall see; when he is ill and would give his soul for something to wet his lips, his bon Dieu will not do much for him," cried one; and another said, clasping her hands with a shrill cry, "It is enough to make the dead rise out of their graves!"

"The dead rise out of their graves!" These words, though one has heard them before, took possession of my imagination. I saw the rude fellow go along the street as I went on, tossing the coin in his hand. One time it fell to the ground and rang upon the pavement, and he laughed more loudly as he picked it up. He was walking towards the sunset, and I too, at a distance after. The sky was full of rose-tinted clouds floating across the blue, floating high over the grey pinnacles of the Cathedral, and filling the long open line of the Rue St. Etienne down which he was going. As I crossed to my own house I caught him full against the light, in his blue blouse,[5]

---

1 Cassock.
2 Good Lord.
3 Long live money!
4 Money is God.
5 The uniform of a working man.

tossing the big silver piece in the air, and heard him laugh and shout "*Vive l'argent!* This is the only *bon Dieu*." Though there are many people who live as if this were their sentiment, there are few who give it such brutal expression; but some of the people at the corner of the street laughed too. "Bravo, Jacques!" they cried; and one said, "You are right, *mon ami*,[1] the only god to trust in nowadays." "It is a short *credo*, M. le Maire," said another, who caught my eye. He saw I was displeased, this one, and his countenance changed at one.

"Yes, Jean Pierre," I said, "it is worse than short—it is brutal. I hope no man who respects himself will ever countenance it. It is against the dignity of human nature, if nothing more."

"Ah, M. le Maire!" cried a poor woman, one of the good ladies of the market, with entrenchments of baskets all round her, who had been walking my way; "ah, M. le Maire! Did not I say true? It is enough to bring the dead out of their graves."

"That would be something to see," said Jean Pierre, with a laugh; "and I hope, *ma bonne femme*,[2] that if you have any interest with them, you will entreat these gentlemen to appear before I go away."

"I do not like such jesting," said I. "The dead are very dead and will not disturb anybody, but even the prejudices of respectable persons ought to be respected. A ribald like Jacques counts for nothing, but I did not except this from you."

"What would you, M. le Maire?" he said, with a shrug of his shoulders. "We are made like that. I respect prejudices as you say. My wife is a good woman, she prays for two—but me! How can I tell that Jacques is not right after all? A *gross pièce*[3] of a hundred sous, one sees that, one knows what it can do—but for the other!" He thrust up one shoulder to his ear, and turned up the palms of his hands.

"It is our duty at all times to respect the convictions of others," I said, severely; and passed on to my own house, having no desire to encourage discussion at the street corner. A man in my position is obliged to be always mindful of the example he ought to set: But I had not yet done with this phrase, which had, as I have said, caught my ear and my imagination. My mother was in the great sale of the *rez-de-chaussée*, as I passed, in altercation with a peasant who had just brought us in some loads of wood. There is often, it seems to me, a sort of refrain in conversation, which one catches everywhere as one comes and goes. Figure my astonishment when I heard from the lips of my good mother the same words with which that good-for-

---

1 My friend.
2 My good woman.
3 A fat (or high-value) coin.

nothing Jacques Richard had made the profession of his brutal faith. "Go!" she cried, in anger; "you are all the same. Money is your god. *De grosses pièces*, that is all you think of in these days."

"*Eh, bien*, madame," said the peasant; "and if so, what then? Don't you others, gentlemen and ladies, do just the same? What is there in the world but money to think of? If it is a question of marriage, you demand what is the *dot*;[1] if it is a question of office, you ask, Monsieur Untel, is he rich? And it is perfectly just. We know what money can do; but as for *le bon Dieu*, whom our grandmothers used to talk about—"

And lo! Our *gros paysan*[2] made exactly the same gesture as Jean Pierre. He put up his shoulders to his ears, and spread out the palms of his hands, as who should say, There is nothing further to be said.

Then there occurred a still more remarkable repetition. My mother, as may be supposed, being a very respectable person, and more or less *dévote*,[3] grew red with indignation and horror.

"Oh, these poor grandmothers!" she cried; "God give them rest! It is enough to make the dead rise out of their graves."

"Oh, I will answer for *les morts!*[4] They will give nobody any trouble," he said with a laugh. I went in and reproved the man severely, finding that, as I supposed, he had attempted to cheat my good mother in the price of the wood. Fortunately she had been quite as clever as he was. She went upstairs shaking her head, while I gave the man to understand that no one should speak to her but with the profoundest respect in my house. "She has her opinions, like all respectable ladies," I said, "but under this roof these opinions shall always be sacred." And, to do him justice, I will add that when it was put to him in this way Gros-Jean was ashamed of himself.

When I talked over these incidents with my wife, as we gave each other the narrative of our day's experiences, she was greatly distressed, as may be supposed. "I try to hope they are not so bad as Bonne Maman[5] thinks. But oh, *mon ami*!" she said, "what will the world come to if this is what really believe?"

---

1   Dowry.
2   Fat peasant.
3   Devout.
4   The dead.
5   Granny.

"Take courage," I said; "the world will never come to anything much different from what it is. So long as there are *des anges*[1] like thee to pray for us, the scale will not go down to the wrong side."

I said this, of course, to please my Agnès, who is the best of wives; but on thinking it over after, I could not but be struck with the extreme justice (not to speak of the beauty of the sentiment) of this thought. The *bon Dieu*—if, indeed, that great Being is as represented to us by the Church—must naturally care as much for one-half of His creatures as for the other, though they have not the same weight in the world; and consequently the faith of the women must hold the balance straight, especially if, as is said, they exceed us in point of numbers. This leaves a little margin for those of them who profess the same freedom of thought as is generally accorded to men—a class, I must add, which I abominate from the bottom of my heart.

I need not dwell upon other little scenes which impressed the same idea still more upon my mind. Semur, I need not say, is not the center of the world, and might, therefore, be supposed likely to escape the full current of worldliness. We amuse ourselves little, and we have not any opportunity of rising to the heights of ambition; for our town is not even the *chef-lieu*[2] of the department,— though this is a subject upon which I cannot trust myself to speak. Figure to yourself that La Rochette—a place of yesterday, without either the beauty or the antiquity of Semur—has been chosen as the center of affairs, the residence of M. le Préfet![3] But I will not enter upon this question. What I was saying was, that, notwithstanding the fact that we amuse ourselves but little, that there is no theatre to speak of, little society, few distractions, and none of those inducements to strive for gain and to indulge the senses, which exist, for instance, in Paris—that capital of the world—yet, nevertheless, the thirst for money and for pleasure has increased among us to an extent which I cannot but consider alarming, Gros-Jean, our peasant, toils for money, and hoards; Jacques, who is a cooper and maker of wine casks, gains and drinks; Jean Pierre snatches at every sous that comes in his way, and spends it in yet worse dissipations. He is one who quails when he meets my eye; he sins *en cachette*;[4] but Jacques is bold, and

---

1   Angels.
2   County or department seat.
3   Chief administrator of the department.
4   Behind one's back.

defies opinion; and Gross-Jean is firm in the belief that to hoard money is the highest of mortal occupations. These three are types of what the population is at Semur. The men would all sell their souls for a *grosse pièce* of fifty sous—indeed, they would laugh, and express their delight that any one should believe them to have souls, if they could but have a chance of selling them: and the devil, who was once supposed to deal in that commodity, would be very welcome among us. And as for the *bon Dieu—pouff!* that was an affair of the grandmothers—*le bon Dieu c'est l'argent.* This is their creed. I was very near the beginning of my official year as Maire when my attention was called to these matters as I have described above. A man may go on for years keeping quiet himself—keeping out of tumult, religious or political—and make no discovery of the general current of feeling; but when you are forced to serve your country in any official capacity, and when your eyes are opened to the state of affairs around you, then I allow that an inexperienced observer might well cry out, as my wife did, "What will become of the world?" I am not prejudiced myself—unnecessary to say that the foolish scruples of the women do not move me. But the devotion of the community at large to this pursuit to gain—money without any grandeur, and pleasure without any refinement—that is a thing which cannot fail to wound all who believe in human nature. To be a millionaire—that, I grant, would be pleasant. A man as rich as Monte Christo,[1] able to do whatever he would, with the equipage of an English duke, the palace of an Italian prince, the retinue of a Russian noble—he, indeed, might be excused if his money seemed to him a kind of god. But Gros-Jean, who lays up two sous at a time, and lives on black bread and an onion; and Jacques, whose *gross pièce* but secures him the headache of a drunkard next morning—what to them could be this miserable deity? As for myself, however, it was my business, as Maire of the commune, to take as little notice as possible of the follies these people might say, and to hold the middle course between the prejudices of the respectable and the levities of the foolish. With this, without more, to think of, I had enough to keep all my faculties employed.

---

1 Hero of the novel *The Count of Monte Cristo* (1844–45) by Alexandre Dumas (1802–1870).

Chapter Two

THE NARRATIVE OF M. LE MAIRE CONTINUED: BEGINNING OF THE LATE REMARKABLE EVENTS

I DO not attempt to make out any distinct connection between the simple incidents above recorded, and the extraordinary events that followed. I have related them as they happened; chiefly by way of showing the state of feeling in the city, and the sentiment which pervaded the community—a sentiment, I fear, too common in my country. I need not say that to encourage superstition is far from my wish. I am a man of my century, and proud of being so; very little disposed to yield to the domination of the clerical party, though desirous of showing all just tolerance for conscientious faith, and every respect for the prejudices of the ladies of my family. I am, moreover, all the more inclined to be careful of giving in my adhesion to any prodigy, in consequence of a consciousness that the faculty of imagination has always been one of my characteristics. It usually is so, I am aware, in superior minds, and it has procured me many pleasures unknown to the common herd. Had it been possible for me to believe that I had been misled by this faculty, I should have carefully refrained from putting upon record any account of my individual impressions; but my attitude here is not that of a man recording his personal experiences only, but of one who is the official mouthpiece and representative of the commune, and whose duty it is to render to government and to the human race a true narrative of the very wonderful facts to which every citizen of Semur can bear witness. In this capacity it has become my duty so to arrange and edit the different accounts of the mystery, as to present one coherent and trustworthy chronicle to the world.

To proceed, however, with my narrative. It is not necessary for me to describe what summer is in the Haute Bourgogne. Our generous wines, our glorious fruits, are sufficient proof, without any assertion on my part. The summer with us is as a perpetual *fête*[1]—at least, before the insect appeared it was so, though now anxiety about the condition of our vines may cloud our enjoyment of the glorious sunshine which ripens them hourly before our eyes. Judge, then, of the astonishment of the world when there suddenly came upon us a darkness as in the depth of winter,

---

1 Holiday.

falling, without warning, into the midst of the brilliant weather to which we are accustomed, and which had never failed us before in the memory of man! It was the month of July, when, in ordinary seasons, a cloud is so rare that it is a joy to see one, merely as a variety upon the brightness. Suddenly, in the midst of our summer delights, this darkness came. Its first appearance took us so entirely by surprise that life seemed to stop short, and the business of the whole town was delayed by an hour or two; nobody being able to believe that at six o'clock in the morning the sun had not risen. I do not assert that the sun did not rise; all I mean to say is that at Semur it was still dark, as in a morning of winter, and when it gradually and slowly became day many hours of the morning were already spent. And never shall I forget the aspect of day when it came. It was like a ghost or pale shadow of the glorious days of July with which we are usually blessed. The barometer did not go down, nor was there any rain, but an unusual greyness wrapped earth and sky. I heard people say in the streets, and I am aware that the same words came to my own lips; "If it were not full summer, I should say it was going to snow." We have much snow in the Haute Bourgogne, and we are well acquainted with this aspect of the skies. Of the depressing effect which this greyness exercised upon myself personally, I will not speak. I was aware instinctively that such a state of the atmosphere must mean something more than was apparent on the surface. But, as the danger was of an entirely unprecedented character, it is not to be wondered at that I should be completely at a loss to divine what its meaning was. It was a blight some people said; and many were of opinion that it was caused by clouds of animalculæ[1] coming, as is described in ancient writing, to destroy the crops, and even to affect the health of the population. The doctors scoffed at this; but they talked about malaria, which, as far as I could understand, was likely to produce exactly the same effect. The night close in early as the day had dawned late; the lamps were lighted before six o'clock and daylight had only begun about ten! Figure to yourself, a July day! There ought to have been a moon almost at the full; but no moon was visible, no stars—nothing but a grey veil of clouds, growing darker and darker as the moments went on; such I have heard are the days and the nights in England, where the sea-fogs so often blot out the sky. But we are unacquainted with anything of the kind in our *plaisant pays de France*.[2] There was nothing else talked of in Semur all that night, as may well be imagined. I could not deliver myself from a sense of something dreadful in the air which was neither malaria nor animalculæ, I took a promenade through

---

1   Microscopic animals or insects.
2   Pleasant land of France.

the streets that evening, accompanied by M. Barbou, my *adjoint*,[1] to make sure that all was safe; and the darkness was such that we almost lost our way, though we were both born in the town and had known every turning from our boyhood. It cannot be denied that Semur is very badly lighted. We retain still the lanterns slung by cords across the streets which once were general in France, but which, in most places, have been superseded by the modern institution of gas. Gladly would I have distinguished my term of office by bringing gas to Semur. But the expense would have been great, and there were a hundred objections. In summer generally, the lanterns were of little consequence because of the brightness of the sky; but to see them now, twinkling dimly here and there, making us conscious how dark it was, was strange indeed. It was in the interests of order that we took our round, with a fear, in my mind at least, of I knew not what. M. l'Adjoint said nothing, but no doubt he thought as I did.

While we were thus patrolling the city with a special eye to the prevention of all seditious assemblages, such as are too apt to take advantage of any circumstances that may disturb the ordinary life of a city, or throw discredit on its magistrates, we were accosted by Paul Lecamus, a man whom I have always considered as something of a visionary, though his conduct is irreproachable, and his life honourable and industrious. He entertains religious convictions of a curious kind; but, as the man is quite free from revolutionary sentiments, I have never considered it to be my duty to interfere with him, or to investigate his creed. Indeed, he has been treated generally in Semur as a dreamer of dreams—one who holds a great many impracticable and foolish opinions—though the respect which I always exact for those whose lives are respectable and worthy has been a protection to him. He was, I think, aware that he owed something to my good offices, and it was to me accordingly that he addressed himself.

"Good evening, M. le Maire," he said; "you are groping about, like myself, in this strange night."

"Good evening M. Paul," I replied. "It is, indeed, a strange night. It indicates, I fear, that a storm is coming."

M. Paul shook his head. There is a solemnity about even his ordinary appearance. He has a long face, pale, and adorned with a heavy, drooping moustache, which adds much to the solemn impression made by his countenance. He looked at me with great gravity as he stood in the shadow of the lamp, and slowly shook his head.

---

1   Deputy mayor.

"You do not agree with me? Well! the opinion of a man like M. Paul Lecamus is always worthy to be heard."

"Oh!" he said, "I am called visionary. I am not supposed to be a trustworthy witness. Nevertheless, if M. le Maire will come with me, I will show him something that is very strange—something that is almost more wonderful than the darkness—more strange," he went on with great earnestness, "than any storm that ever ravaged Burgundy."

"That is much to say. A tempest now when the vines are in full bearing—"

"Would be nothing, nothing to what I can show you. Only come with me to the Porte St. Lambert."

"If M. le Maire will excuse me," said M. Barbou, "I think I will go home. It is a little cold, and you are aware that I am always afraid of the damp." In fact, our coats were beaded with a cold dew as in November, and I could not but acknowledge that my respectable colleague had reason. Besides, we were close to his house, and he had, no doubt, the sustaining consciousness of having done everything that was really incumbent upon him. "Our ways lie together as far as my house," he said, with a slight chattering of his teeth. No doubt it was the cold. After we had walked with him to his door, we proceeded to the Porte St. Lambert. By this time almost everybody had re-entered their houses. The streets were very dark, and they were also very still. When we reached the gates, at that hour of the night, we found them shut as a matter of course. The officers of the *octroi*[1] were standing close together at the door of their office, in which the lamp was burning. The very lamp seemed oppressed by the heavy air; it burnt dully, surrounded with a yellow haze. The men had the appearance of suffering greatly from cold. They received me with a satisfaction which was very gratifying to me. "At length here is M. le Maire himself," they said.

"My good friends," said I, "you have a cold post to-night. The weather has changed in the most extraordinary way. I have no doubt the scientific gentlemen at the Musée[2] will be able to tell us all about it—M. de Clairon—"

"Not to interrupt M. le Maire," said Riou, of the *octroi*, "I think there is more in it than any scientific gentleman can explain."

"Ah! You think so. But they explain everything," I said, with a smile. "They tell us how the wind is going to blow."

As I said this, there seemed to pass, us from the direction of the closed gates, a breath of air so cold that I could not restrain a shiver. They looked at each other. It

---

1 Toll house or gatehouse.
2 Athenaeum.

was not a smile that passed between them—they were too pale, too cold, to smile: but a look of intelligence. "M. le Maire," said one of them, "perceives it too;" but they did not shiver as I did. They were like men turned into ice who could feel no more.

"It is, without doubt, the most extraordinary weather," I said. My teeth chattered like Barbou's. It was all I could do to keep myself steady. No one made any reply; but Lecamus said, "Have the goodness to open the little postern for foot-passengers: M. le Maire wishes to make an inspection outside."

Upon these words, Riou, who knew me well, caught me by the arm. "A thousand pardons," he said, "M. le Maire; but I entreat you, do not go. Who can tell what is outside? Since this morning there is something very strange on the other side of the gates. If M. le Maire would listen to me, he would keep them shut night and day till that is gone, he would not go out into the midst of it. Mon Dieu! a man may be brave. I know the courage of M. le Maire; but to march without necessity into the jaws of hell: mon Dieu!" cried the poor man again. He crossed himself, and none of us smiled. Now a man may sign himself at the church door—one does so out of respect; but to use that ceremony for one's own advantage, before other men, is rare—except in the case of members of a very decided party.[1] Riou was not one of these. He signed himself in sight of us all, and not one of us smiled.

The other was less familiar—he knew me only in my public capacity—he was one Gallais of the Quartier St. Médon. He said, taking off his hat: "If I were M. le Maire, saving your respect, I would not go out into an unknown danger with this man here, a man who is known as a pietest,[2] as a clerical, as one who sees visions—"

"He is not a clerical, he is a good citizen," I said; "come, lend us your lantern. Shall I shrink from my duty wherever it leads me? Nay, my good friends, the Maire of a French commune fears neither man nor devil in the exercise of his duty. M. Paul, lead on." When I said the word "devil" a spasm of alarm passed over Riou's face. He crossed himself again. This time I could not but smile. "My little Riou," I said, "do you know that you are a little imbecile with your piety? There is a time for everything."

"Except religion, M. le Maire; that is never out of place," said Gallais.

I could not believe my senses. "Is it a conversion?" I said. "Some of our *Carmes déchaussés*[3] must have passed this way."

---

1   An oblique reference, perhaps, to the Legitimists, a royalist political party that attracted many traditionalist Catholics.
2   One who exhibits exaggerated or sentimental piety.
3   Barefooted Carmelite friars.

"M. le Maire will soon see other teachers more wonderful than the *Carmes déchaussés*," said Lecamus. He went and took down the lantern from its nail, and opened the little door. When it opened, I was once more penetrated by the same icy breath; once, twice, thrice, I cannot tell how many times this crossed me, as if some one passed. I looked round upon, the others—I gave way a step. I could not help it. In spite of me, the hair seemed to rise erect on my head. The two officers stood close together, and Riou, collecting his courage, made an attempt to laugh. "M. le Maire perceives," he said, his lips trembling almost too much to form the words, "that the winds are walking about," "Hush, for God's sake!" said the other, grasping him by the arm.

This recalled me to myself; and I followed Lecamus, who stood waiting for me holding the door a little ajar. He went on strangely, like—I can use no other words to express it—a man making his way in the face of a crowd, a thing very surprising to me. I followed him close; but the moment I emerged from the doorway something caught my breath. The same feeling seized me also. I gasped; a sense of suffocation came upon me; I put out my hand to lay hold upon my guide. The solid grasp I got of his arm re-assured me a little, and he did not hesitate, but pushed his way on. We got out clear of the gate and the shadow of the wall, keeping close to the little watch—tower on the west side. Then he made a pause, and so did I. We stood against the tower and looked out before us. There was nothing there. The darkness was great, yet through the gloom of the night I could see the division of the road from the broken ground on either side; there was nothing there. I gasped, and drew myself up close against the wall, as Lecamus had also done. There was in the air, in the night, sensation the most strange I have ever experienced. I have felt the same thing indeed at other times, in face of a great crowd, when thousands of people were moving, rustling, struggling, breathing around me, thronging all the vacant space, filling up every spot. This was the sensation that overwhelmed me here—a crowd; yet nothing to be seen but the darkness, the indistinct line of the road. We could not move for them, so close were they round us. What do I say? There was nobody—nothing—not a form to be seen, not a face but his and mine. I am obliged to confess that the moment was to me an awful moment. I could not speak. My heart beat wildly as if trying to escape from my breast—every breath I drew was with an effort. I clung to Lecamus with deadly and helpless error, and forced myself back upon the wall, crouching against it; I did not turn and fly, as would have been natural. What say I? *did* not! I *could* not! They pressed round us so. Ah! you would think I must be mad to use such words, for there was nobody near me—not a shadow even upon the road.

Lecamus would have gone farther on; he would have pressed his way boldly into the midst; but my courage was not equal to this. I clutched and clung to him, dragging myself along against the wall, my whole mind intent upon getting back. I was stronger than he, and he had no power to resist me. I turned back, stumbling blindly, keeping my face to that crowd (there was no one), but struggling back again, tearing the skin off my hands as I groped my way along the wall. Oh, the agony of seeing the door closed! I have buffeted my way through a crowd before now, but I may say that I never before knew what terror was. When I fell upon the door, dragging Lecamus with me, it opened, thank God! I stumbled in, clutching at Riou with my disengaged hand, and fell upon the floor of the *octroi*, where they thought I had fainted. But this was not the case. A man of resolution may give way to the overpowering sensations of the moment. His bodily faculties may fail him; but his mind will not fail. As in every really superior intelligence, my force collected for the emergency. While the officers ran to bring me water, to search for the eau-de-vie[1] which they had in a cupboard, I astonished them all by rising up, pale, but with full command of myself. "It is enough," I said, raising my hand. "I thank you, Messieurs, but nothing more is necessary;" and I would not take any of their restoratives. They were impressed, as was only natural, by the sight of my perfect self-possession: it helped them to acquire for themselves a demeanour befitting the occasion; and I felt, though still in great physical weakness and agitation, the consoling consciousness of having fulfilled my functions as head of the community.

"M. le Maire has seen a—a—what there is outside?" Riou cried, stammering in his excitement; and the other fixed upon me eyes which were hungering with eagerness—if, indeed, it is permitted to use such words.

"I have seen—nothing, Riou," I said.

They looked at me with the utmost wonder. "M le Maire has seen—nothing?" said Riou. "Ah, I see! you say so to spare us. We have proved ourselves cowards; but if you will pardon me, M. le Maire, you, too, re-entered precipitately—you too! There are facts which may appall the bravest—but I implore you to tell us what you have seen."

"I have seen nothing," I said. As I spoke, my natural clam composure returned, my heart resumed its usual tranquil beating. "There is nothing to be seen—it is dark, and one can perceive the line of the road for but a little way—that is all. There is nothing to been seen—"

---

1   Brandy.

They looked at me, startled and incredulous. They did not know what to think. How could they refuse to believe me, sitting there calmly raising my eyes to them, making my statement with what they felt to be an air of perfect truth? But, then, how account for the precipitate return which they had already noted, the supposed faint, the pallor of my looks? They did not know what to think.

And here, let me remark, as in my conduct throughout these remarkable events, may be seen the benefit, the high advantage, of truth. Had not this been the truth, I could not have borne the searching of their looks. But it was true. There was nothing—nothing to be seen; in one sense, this was the thing of all others which overwhelmed my mind. But why insist upon these matters of detail to unenlightened men? There was nothing, and I had seen nothing. What I said was the truth.

All this time Lecamus had said nothing. As I raised myself from the ground, I had vaguely perceived him hanging up the lantern where it had been before; now he became distinct to me as I recovered the full possession of my faculties. He had seated himself upon a bench by the wall. There was no agitation about him; no sign of the thrill of departing excitement, which I felt going through my veins as through the strings of a harp. He was sitting against the wall, with his head drooping, his eyes cast down, an air of disappointment and despondency about him—nothing more. I got up as soon as I felt that I could go away with perfect propriety; but, before I left the place, called him. He got up when he heard his name, but he did it with reluctance. He came with me because I asked him to do so, not from any wish of his own. Very different were the feelings of Riou and Gallais. They did their utmost to engage me in conversation, to consult me about a hundred trifles, to ask me with the greatest deference what they ought to do in such and such cases, pressing close to me, trying every expedient to delay my departure. When we went away they stood at the door of their little office close together, looking after us with looks which I found it difficult to forget; they would not abandon their post; but their faces were pale and contracted, their eyes wild with anxiety and distress.

It was only as I walked away, hearing my own steps and those of Lecamus ringing upon the pavement, that I began to realise what had happened. The effort of recovering my composure, the relief from the extreme excitement of terror (which, dreadful as the idea is, I am obliged to confess I had actually felt), the sudden influx of life and strength to my brain, had pushed away for the moment the recollection of what lay outside. When I thought of it again, the blood began once more to course in my veins. Lecamus went on by my side with this head down, the eyelids drooping over his eyes, not saying a word. He followed me when I called him: but cast a regretful look at the postern by which we had gone out, through which I had dragged him back in a panic (I confess it) unworthy of me. Only when we had left at some distance behind us that door into the unseen, did my senses come fully back to me, and I ventured to ask myself what it meant. "Lecamus," I said—I could scarcely put my question into words—"what do you think? what is your idea?—how do you explain—" Even then I am glad to think I had sufficient power of control not to betray all that I felt.

"One does not try to explain," he said slowly; "one longs to know—that is all. If M. le Maire had not been—in such haste—had he been willing to go farther—to investigate—"

"God forbid!" I said; and the impulse to quicken my steps, to get home and put myself in safety, was almost more than I could restrain. But I forced myself to go quietly, to measure my steps by his, which were slow and reluctant, as if he dragged himself away with difficulty from that which was behind.

What was it? "Do not ask, do not ask!" Nature seemed to say in my heart. Thoughts came into my mind in such a dizzy crowd, that the multitude of them seemed to take away my senses. I put up my hands to my ears, in which they seemed to be buzzing and rustling like bees, to stop the sound. When I did so, Lecamus turned and looked at me—grave and wondering. This recalled me to a sense of my weakness. But how I got home I can scarcely say. My mother and wife met me with anxiety. They were greatly disturbed about the Hospital of St. Jean, in respect to which it had been recently decided that certain changes should be made. The great ward of the hospital, which was the chief establishment for the sick in the town, had hitherto been so placed in communication with the chapel that mass was heard daily by all the patients—a thing which some had complained of as an annoyance disturbing their rest. So many, indeed, had been the complaints received, that we had come to the conclusion either that the opening should be built up, or the office suspended. Against, this decision, it is needless to say, the Sisters of St. Jean were moving heaven and earth. Equally unnecessary for me to add, that having so decided in my public capacity, as at once the representative of popular opinion and its guide, the covert reproaches which were breathed in my presence, and even the personal appeals made to me, had failed of any result. I respect the Sisters of St. Jean. They are good women and excellent nurses, and the commune owes them much. Still, justice must be impartial; and so long as I retain my position at the head of the community, it is my duty to see that all have their due. My opinions as a private individual, were I allowed to return to that humble position, are entirely a different matter; but this is a thing which ladies, however excellent, are slow to allow or to understand.

I will not pretend that this was to me a night of rest. In the darkness, when all is still, any anxiety which may afflict the soul is apt to gain complete possession and mastery, as all who have had true experience of life will understand. The night was very dark and very still, the clocks striking out the hours which went so slowly, and not another sound audible. The streets of Semur are always quiet, but they were more still than usual that night. Now and then, in a pause of my thoughts, I could hear the soft breathing of my Agnès in the adjoining room, which gave me a little comfort. But this was only by intervals, when I was able to escape from the grasp of the recollections that held me fast. Again I seemed to see under my closed eyelids the faint line of the high road which led from the Porte St. Lambert, the broken ground with its ragged bushes on either side, and no one—no one there—not a soul, not a shadow; yet a multitude! When I allowed myself to think of this, my heart leaped into my throat again, my blood ran in my veins like a river in flood. I need not say that I resisted this transport of the nerves with all my might. As the night grew slowly into morning my power of resistance increased; I turned my back, so to speak, upon my recollections, and said to myself, with growing firmness, that all sensations of the body must have their origin in the body. Some derangement of the system—easily explainable, no doubt, if one but held the due—must have produced the impression which otherwise it would be impossible to explain. As I turned this over and over in my mind, carefully avoiding all temptations to excitement—which is the only wise course in the case of a strong impression on the nerves—I gradually became able to believe that this was the cause. It is one of the penalties, I said to myself, which one has to pay for an organization more finely tempered than that of the crowd.

This long struggle with myself made the night less tedious, though, perhaps, more terrible; and when at length I was overpowered by sleep, the short interval of unconsciousness restored me like a cordial. I woke in the early morning, feeling almost able to smile at the terrors of the night. When one can assure oneself that the day has really begun, even while it is yet dark, there is a change of sensation, an increase of strength and courage. One by one the dark hours went on. I heard them pealing from the Cathedral clock—four, five, six, seven—all dark, dark. I had got up and dressed before the last, but found no one else awake when I went out—no one stirring in the house,—no one moving in the street. The Cathedral doors were shut fast, a thing I have never seen before since I remember. Get up early who will, Père Laserques the sacristan is always up still earlier. He is a good old man, and I have often heard him say God's house should be open first of all houses, in case there might be any miserable ones about who had found no shelter in the dwellings of men. But the darkness had cheated even Père Laserques. To see those great doors closed which stood always open gave me a shiver, I cannot well tell why. Had they been open, there was an inclination in my mind to have gone in, though I cannot tell why; for I am not in the habit of attending mass, save on Sunday to set an example. There were no shops open, not a sound about. I went out upon the ramparts to the Mont St. Lambert, where the band plays on Sundays. In all the trees there was not so much as the twitter of a bird. I could hear the river flowing swiftly below the wall, but I could not see it, except as something dark, a ravine of gloom below, and beyond the walls I did not venture to look. Why should I look? There was nothing, nothing as I knew. But fancy is so uncontrollable, and one's nerves so little to be trusted, that it was a wise precaution to refrain. The gloom itself was oppressive enough; the air seemed to creep with apprehensions, and from time to time my heart fluttered with a sick movement, as if it would escape from my control. But everything was still, still as the dead who had been so often in recent days called out of their graves by one or another. "Enough to bring the dead out their graves." What strange words to make use of! It was rather now as if the world had become a grave in which we, though living, were held fast.

Soon after this the dark world began to lighten faintly, and with the rising of a little white mist, like a veil rolling upwards, I at last saw the river and the fields beyond. To see anything at all lightened my heart a little, and I turned homeward when this faint daylight appeared. When I got back into the street, I found that the people at last were stirring. They had all a look of half panic, half shame upon their faces. Many were yawning and stretching themselves. "Good morning, M. le Maire," said one and another; "you are early astir." "Not so early either," I said; and then they added, almost every individual, with a look of shame, "We were so late this morning; we overslept ourselves—like yesterday. The weather is extraordinary." This was repeated to me by all kinds of people. They were half frightened, and they were ashamed. Père Laserques was sitting moaning on the Cathedral steps. Such a thing had never happened before. He had not rung the bell for early mass; he had not opened the Cathedral; he had not called M. le Curé. "I think I must be going out of my senses," he said; "but then, M. le Maire, the weather! Did anyone ever see such weather! Did anyone ever see such weather? I think there must be some evil brewing. It is not for nothing that the seasons change—that winter comes in the midst of summer."

After this I went home. My mother came running to one door when I entered, and my wife to another. "*O mon fils!*" and "*O mon ami!*"[1] they said, rushing upon me. They wept, these dear women. I could not at first prevail upon them to tell me what was the matter. At last they confessed that they believed something to have happened to me, in punishment for the wrong done to the Sisters at the hospital. "Make haste, my son, to amend this error," my mother cried, "lest a worse thing befall us!" And then I discovered that among the women, and among many of the poor people, it had come to be believed that the darkness was a curse upon us for what we had done in respect to the hospital. This roused me to indignation. "If they think I am to be driven from my duty by their magic," I cried; "it is no better than witchcraft!" not that I believed for a moment that it was they who had done it. My wife wept, and my mother became angry with me; but when a thing is duty, it is neither wife nor mother who will move me out of my way.

It was a miserable day. There was not light enough to see anything—scarcely to see each other's faces; and to add to our alarm, some travellers arriving by the diligence[2] (we are still three leagues from a railway, while that miserable little place, La Rochette, being the *chef-lieu*, has a terminus) informed me that the darkness only existed in Semur and the neighbourhood, and that within a distance of three miles the sun was shining. The sun was shining! Was it possible? It seemed so long since we had seen the sunshine; but this made our calamity more mysterious and more terrible. The people began to gather into little knots in the streets to talk of the strange thing that was happening. In the course of the day M. Barbou came to ask whether I did not think it would be well to appease the popular feeling by conceding what they wished to the Sisters of the hospital. I would not hear of it. "Shall we own than we are in the wrong? I do not think we are in the wrong," I said, and I would not yield. "Do you think the good Sisters have it in their power to darken the sky with their incantations?" M. l'Adjoint shook his head. He went away with a troubled countenance; but then he was not like myself, a man of natural firmness. All the efforts that were employed to influence him were also employed with me; but to yield to the women was not in my thoughts.

We are now approaching, however, the first important incident in this narrative. The darkness increased as the afternoon came on; and it became a kind of thick

---

1 Oh, my son! Oh, my love!
2 Stagecoach.

twilight, no lighter than many a night. It was between five and six o'clock, just the time when our streets are the most crowded, when, sitting at my window, from which I kept a watch upon the Grande Rue, not knowing what might happen—I saw that some fresh incident had taken place. Very dimly through the darkness I perceived a crowd, which increased every moment, in front of the Cathedral. After watching it for a few minutes, I got my hat and went out. The people whom I saw—so many that they covered the whole middle of the *Place*, reaching almost to the pavement on the other side—had their heads all turned towards the Cathedral. "What are you gazing at, my friend?" I said to one by whom I stood. He looked up at me with a face which looked ghastly in the gloom. "Look, M. le Maire!" he said; "cannot you see it on the great door?"

"I see nothing," said I; but as I uttered these words I did indeed see something which was very startling. Looking towards the great door of the Cathedral, as they all were doing, it suddenly seemed to me that I saw an illuminated placard attached to it, headed with the word "*Sommation*"[1] in gigantic letters. "*Tiens!*"[2] I cried; but when I looked again there was nothing. "What is this? It is some witchcraft!" I said, in spite of myself. "Do you see anything, Jean Pierre?"

"M. le Maire," he said, "one moment one sees something—the next, one sees nothing. Look! it comes again." I have always considered myself a man of courage, but when I saw this extraordinary appearance the panic which had seized upon me the former night returned, though in another form. Fly I could not, but I will not deny that my knees smote together. I stood for some minutes without being able to articulate a word—which, indeed, seemed the case with most of those before me. Never have I seen a more quiet crowd. They were all gazing, as if it was life or death that was set before them—while I, too, gazed with a shiver going over me. It was as I have seen an illumination of lamps in a stormy night; one moment the whole seems black as the wind sweeps over it, the next it springs into life again; and thus you go on, by turns losing and discovering the device formed by the lights. Thus from moment to moment there appeared before us, in letters that seemed to blaze and flicker, something that looked like a great official placard. "*Sommation!*"—this was how it was headed. I read a few words at a time, as it came and went; and who can describe the chill that ran through my veins as I made it out? It was a summons to the people of Semur by name—myself at the head as Maire (and I heard afterwards that every man who saw it saw his own name, though the whole *façade* of the Cathedral would

---

1   Summons.
2   Well now!

not have held a full list of all the people of Semur)—to yield their places, which they had not filled aright, to those who knew the meaning of life, being dead. NOUS AUTRES MORTS[1]—these were the words which blazed out oftenest of all, so that every one saw them. And "Go!" this terrible placard said—"Go! Leave this place to us who know the true signification of life." These words I remember, but not the rest; and even at this moment it struck me that there was no explanation, nothing but this *vraie signification de la vie*.[2] I felt like one in a dream; the light coming and going before me; one word, then another, appearing—sometimes a phrase like that I have quoted, blazing out, then dropping into darkness. For the moment I was struck dumb; but then it came back to my mind that I had an example to give, and that for me, eminently a man of my century, to yield credence to a miracle was something not to be thought of. Also I knew the necessity of doing something to break the impression of awe and terror on the mind of the people. "This is a trick," I cried loudly, that all might hear. "Let some one go and fetch M. de Clairon from the Musée. He will tell us how it has been done." This, boldly uttered, broke the spell. A number of pale faces gathered round me. "Here is M. le Maire—he will clear it up," they cried, making room for me that I might approach nearer. "M. le Maire is a man of courage—he has judgment. Listen to M. le Maire." It was a relief to everybody that I had spoken. And soon I found myself by the side of M. le Curé, who was standing among the rest, saying nothing, and with the air of one as much bewildered as any of us. He gave me one quick look from under his eyebrows to see who it was that approached him, as was his way, and made room for me, but said nothing. I was in too much emotion myself to keep silence—indeed, I was in that condition of wonder, alarm, and nervous excitement, that I had to speak or die; and there seemed an escape from something too terrible for flesh and blood to contemplate in the idea that there was trickery here. "M. le Curé," I said, "this is a strange ornament that you have placed on the front of your church. You are standing here to enjoy the effect. Now that you have seen how successful it has been, will not you tell me in confidence how it is done?"

I am conscious that there was a sneer in my voice, but I was too much excited to think of politeness. He gave me another of his rapid, keen looks.

"M. le Maire," he said, "you are injurious to a man who is as little fond of tricks as yourself."

---

1 WE OTHER DEAD.
2 True meaning of life.

His tone, his glance, gave me a certain sense of shame, but I could not stop myself. "One knows," I said, "that there are many things which an ecclesiastic may do without harm, which are not permitted to an ordinary layman—one who is an honest man, and no more."

M. le Curé made no reply. He gave me another of his quick glances, with an impatient turn of his head. Why should I have suspected him? for no harm was known of him. He was the Curé, that was all; and perhaps we men of the world have our prejudices too. Afterwards, however, as we waited for M. de Clairon—for the crisis was too exciting for personal resentment—M. le Curé himself let drop something which made it apparent that it was the ladies of the hospital upon whom his suspicions fell. "It is never well to offend women, M. le Maire," he said. "Women do not discriminate the lawful from the unlawful; so long as they produce an effect, it does not matter to them." This gave me a strange impression, for it seemed to me that M. le Curé was abandoning his own side. However, all other sentiments were, as may be imagined, but as shadows compared with the overwhelming power that held all our eyes and our thoughts to the wonder before us. Every moment seemed an hour till M. de Clairon appeared. He was pushed forward through the crowd as by magic, all making room for him; and many of us thought that when science thus came forward capable of finding out everything, the miracle would disappear. But instead of this it seemed to glow brighter than ever. That great word "*Sommation*" blazed out, so that we saw his figure waver against the light as if giving way before the flames that scorched him. He was so near that his outline was marked out dark against the glare they gave. It was as though his close approach rekindled every light. Then, with a flicker and trembling, word by word and letter by letter went slowly out before our eyes.

M. de Clairon came down very pale, but with a sort of smile on his face. "No, M. le Maire," he said, "I cannot see how it is done. It is clever. I will examine the door further, and try the panels. Yes, I have left some one to watch that nothing is touched in the meantime, with the permission of M. le Curé—"

"You have my full permission," M. le Curé said; and M. de Clairon laughed, though he was still very pale. "You saw my name there," he said. "I am amused—I who am not one of your worthy citizens, M. le Maire. What can Messieurs les Morts of Semur want with a poor man of science like me? But you shall have my report before the evening is out."

With this I had to be content. The darkness which succeeded to that strange light seemed more terrible than ever. We all stumbled as we turned to go away, dazzled by it, and stricken dumb, though some kept saying that it was a trick, and some murmured exclamations with voices full of terror. The sound of the crowd breaking up was like a regiment marching—all the world had been there. I was thankful, however, that neither my mother nor my wife had seen anything; and though they were anxious to know why I was so serious, I succeeded fortunately in keeping the secret from them.

M. de Clairon did not appear till late, and then he confessed to me he could make nothing of it. "If it is a trick (as of course it must be), it has been most cleverly done," he said; and admitted that he was baffled altogether. For my part, I was not surprised. Had it been the Sisters of the hospital, as M. le Curé thought, would they have let the opportunity pass of preaching a sermon to us, and recommending their doctrines? Not so; here there were no doctrines, nothing but that pregnant phrase, *la vraie signification de la vie*. This made a more deep impression upon me than anything else. The Holy Mother herself (whom I wish to speak of with profound respect), and the saints, and the forgiveness of sins, would have all been there had it been the Sisters, or even M. le Curé. This, though I had myself suggested an imposture, made it very unlikely to my quiet thoughts. But if not an imposture, what was it supposed to be?

Chapter Three

EXPULSION OF THE INHABITANTS

I WILL not attempt to give any detailed account of the state of the town during this evening. For myself I was utterly worn out, and went to rest as soon as M. de Clairon left me, having satisfied, as well as I could, the questions of the women. Even in the intensest excitement weary nature will claim her dues. I slept. I can even remember the grateful sense of being able to put all anxieties and perplexities aside for the moment, as I went to sleep. I felt the drowsiness gain upon me, and I was glad. To forget was of itself a happiness.

I woke up, however, intensely awake, and in perfect possession of all my faculties, while it was yet dark; and at once got up and began to dress. The moment of hesitation which generally follows waking—the little interval of thought in which one turns over perhaps that which is past, perhaps that which is to come—found no place within me. I got up without a moment's pause, like one who has been called to go on a journey; nor did it surprise me at all to see my wife moving about, taking a cloak from her wardrobe, and putting up linen in a bag. She was already fully dressed; but she asked no questions of me any more than I did of her. We were in haste, though we said nothing. When I had dressed, I looked round me to see if I had forgotten anything, as one does when one leaves a place. I saw my watch suspended to its usual hook, and my pocket-book, which I had taken from my pocket on the previous night. I took up also the light overcoat which I had worn when I made my rounds through the city on the first night of the darkness. "Now," I said, "Agnès, I am ready." I did not speak to her of where we were going, nor she to me. Little Jean and my mother met us at the door. Nor did *she* say anything, contrary to her custom; and the child was quite quiet. We went downstairs together without saying a word. The servants, who were all astir, followed us. I cannot give any description of the feelings that were in my mind. I had not any feelings. I was only hurried out, hastened by something which I could not define—a sense that I must go; and perhaps I was too much astonished to do anything but yield. It seemed, however, to be no force or fear that was moving me, but a desire of my own; though I could not tell how it was, or why I should be so anxious to get away. All the servants, trooping after me, had the same look in their faces; they were anxious to be gone—it seemed their business to go—there was no question, no consultation. And when we came out into the street, we encountered a stream of processions similar to our own. The children went quite steadily by the side of their parents. Little Jean, for example, on an ordinary occasion would have broken away—would have run to his comrades of the Bois-Sombre family, and they to him. But no; the little ones, like ourselves, walked along quite gravely. They asked no questions, neither did we ask any questions of each other, as, "Where are you going?" or, "What is the meaning of so early a promenade?" Nothing of the kind: my mother took my arm, and my wife, leading little Jean by the hand, came to the other side. The servants followed. The street was quite full of people; but there was no noise except the sound of their footsteps. All of us turned the same way—turned towards the gates—and though I was not conscious of any feeling except the wish to go on, there were one or two things which took a place in my memory. The first was, that my wife suddenly turned round as we were coming out of the *porte-cochère*,[1] her face lighting up. I need not say to any one who knows Madame Dupin de la Clairière, that she is a beautiful woman. Without any partiality on my part, it would be impossible for me to ignore this fact: for it is perfectly well known and acknowledged by all. She was pale this morning—a little paler than usual; and her

---

1   Carriage-entrance.

blue eyes enlarged, with a serious look, which they always retain more or less. But suddenly, as we went out of the door, her face lighted up, her eyes were suffused with tears—with light—how can I tell what it was?—they became like the eyes of angels. A little cry came from her parted lips—she lingered a moment stooping down as if talking to some one less tall than herself, then came after us, with that light still in her face. At the moment I was too much occupied to enquire what it was; but I noted it, even in the gravity of the occasion. The next thing I observed was M. le Curé, who, as I have already indicated, is a man of great composure of manner and presence of mind, coming out of the door of the Presbytery.[1] There was strange look on his face of astonishment and reluctance. He walked very slowly, not as we did, but with a visible desire to turn back, folding his arms across his breast, and holding himself as if against the wind, resisting some gale which blew behind him, and forced him on. We felt no gale; but there seemed to be a strange wind blowing along the side of the street on which M. le Curé was. And there was an air of concealed surprise in his face—great astonishment, but a determination not to let any one see that he was astonished, or that the situation was strange to him. And I cannot tell how it was, but I, too, though pre-occupied, was surprised to perceive that M. le Curé was going with the rest of us, though I could not have told why.

Behind M. le Curé there was another whom I remarked. This was Jacques Richard, he of whom I have already spoken. He was like a figure I have seen somewhere in sculpture. No one was near him, nobody touching him, and yet it was only necessary to look at the man to perceive that he was being forced along against his will. Every limb was in resistance; his feet were planted widely yet firmly upon the pavement; one of his arms was stretched out as if to lay hold on anything that should come within reach. M le Curé resisted passively; but Jacques resisted with passion, laying his back to the wind, and struggling not to be carried away. Notwithstanding his resistance, however, this rough figure was driven along slowly, struggling at every step. He did not make one movement that was not against his will, but still he was driven on. On our side of the street all went, like ourselves, calmly. My mother uttered now and then a low moan, but said nothing. She clung to my arm, and walked on, hurrying a little, sometimes going quicker than I intended to go. As for my wife, she accompanied us with her light step, which scarcely seemed to touch the ground, little Jean pattering by her side. Our neighbours were all round us. We streamed down, as in a long procession, to the Porte St. Lambert. It was only when we got there the strange character of the step we were all taking

---

1   Priest's house.

suddenly occurred to me. It was still a kind of grey twilight, not yet day. The bells of the Cathedral had begun to toll, which was very startling—not ringing in their cheerful way, but tolling as if for a funeral, and no other sound was audible but the noise of footsteps, like an army making a silent march into an enemy's country. We had reached the gate when a sudden wondering came over me. Why were we all going out of our houses in the wintry dusk to which our July day had turned? I stopped, and turning round, was about to say something to the others, when I became suddenly aware that here I was not my own master. My tongue clave to the roof of my mouth; I could not say a word. Then I myself was turned round, and softly, firmly, irresistibly pushed out of the gate. My mother, who clung to me, added a little, no doubt, to the force against me, whatever it was, for she was frightened, and opposed herself to any endeavour on my part to regain freedom of movement; but all that her feeble force could do against mine must have been little. Several other men around me seemed to be moved as I was. M. Barbou, for one, made a still more decided effort to turn back, for, being a bachelor, he had no one to restrain him. Him I saw turned round as you would turn a *roulette*. He was thrown against my wife in his tempestuous course, and but that she was so light and elastic in her tread, gliding out straight and softly like one of the saints, I think he must have thrown her down. And at that moment, silent as we all were, his "*Pardon, Madame, mille pardons, Madame*,"[1] and his tone of horror at his own indiscretion, seemed to come to me like a voice out of another life. Partially roused before by the sudden impulse of resistance I have described, I was yet more roused now. I turned round, disengaging myself from my mother. "Where are we going? Why are we thus cast forth? My friends, help!" I cried. I looked round upon the others, who, as I have said, had also awakened to a possibility of resistance. M. de Bois-Sombre, without a word, came and placed himself by my side; others started from the crowd. We turned to resist this mysterious impulse which had sent us forth. The crowd surged round us in the uncertain light.

Just then there was a dull soft sound, once, twice, thrice repeated. We rushed forward, but too late. The gates were closed upon us. The two folds of the great Porte St. Lambert, and the little postern for foot-passengers, all at once, not hurriedly, as from any fear of us, but slowly, softly, rolled on their hinges and shut—in our faces. I rushed forward with all my force and flung myself upon the gate. To what use? It was so closed as no mortal could open it. They told me after, for I was not aware at the moment, that I burst forth with cries and exclamations, bidding them "Open,

---

1 Pardon, Madame, a thousand pardons, Madame.

open in the name of God!" I was not aware of what I said, but it seemed to me that I heard a voice of which nobody said anything to me, so that it would seem to have been unheard by the others, saying with a faint sound as of a trumpet, "Closed—in the name of God." It might be only an echo, faintly brought back to me, of the words I had myself said.

There was another change, however, of which no one could have any doubt. When I turned round from these closed doors, though the moment before the darkness was such that we could not see the gates closing, I found the sun shining gloriously round us, and all my fellow-citizens turning with one impulse, with a sudden cry of joy, to hail the full day.

Le grand jour![1] Never in my life did I feel the full happiness of it, the full sense of the words before. The sun burst out into shining, the birds into singing. The sky stretched over us—deep and unfathomable and blue,—the grass grew under our feet, a soft air of morning blew upon us, waving the curls of the children, the veils of the women, whose faces were lit up by the beautiful day. After three days of darkness what a resurrection! It seemed to make up to us for the misery of being thus expelled from our homes. It was early, and all the freshness of the morning was upon the road and the fields, where the sun had just dried the dew. The river ran softly, reflecting the blue sky. How black it had been, deep and dark as a stream of ink, when I had looked down upon it from Mont St. Lambert! And now it ran as clear and free as the voice of a little child. We all shared this moment of joy—for to us of the South the sunshine is as the breath of life, and to be deprived of it had been terrible. But when that first pleasure was over, the evidence of our strange position forced itself upon us with overpowering reality and force, made stronger by the very light. In the dimness it had not seemed so certain; now, gazing at each other in the clear light of the natural morning, we saw what had happened to us. No more delusion was possible. We could not flatter ourselves now that it was a trick or a deception. M. de Clairon stood there like the rest of us, staring at the closed gates which science could not open. And there stood M. le Curé, which was more remarkable still. The Church herself had not been able to do anything. We stood, a crowd of houseless exiles, looking at each other, our children clinging to us, our hearts failing us, expelled from our homes. As we looked in each other's faces we saw our own trouble. Many of the women sat down and wept; some upon the stones in the road, some on the grass. The children took fright from them, and began to cry too. What was to become of us? I looked round upon this crowd with despair

---

1   Broad daylight!

in my heart. It was I to whom every one would look—for lodging, for direction—everything that human creatures want. It was my business to forget myself, though I also had been driven from my home and my city. Happily there was one thing I had left. In the pocket of my overcoat was my scarf of office.[1] I stepped aside behind a tree, and took it out, and tied it upon me. That was something. There was thus a representative of order and law in the midst of the exiles, whatever might happen. This action, which a great number of the crowd saw, restored confidence. Many of the poor people gathered round me, and placed themselves near me, especially those women who had no natural support. When M. le Curé saw this, it seemed to make a great impression upon him. He changed colour, he who was usually so calm. Hitherto he had appeared bewildered, amazed to find himself as others. This, I must add, though you may perhaps think is superstitious, surprised me very much too. But now he regained his self-possession. He stepped upon a piece of wood that lay in front of the gate. "My children"—he said. But just then the Cathedral bells, which had gone on tolling, suddenly burst into a wild peal. I do not know what it sounded like. It was a clamour of notes all run together, tone upon tone, without time or measure, as though a multitude had seized upon the bells and pulled all the ropes at once. If it was joy, what strange and terrible joy! It froze the very blood in our veins. M le Curé became quite pale. He stepped down hurriedly from the piece of wood. We all made a hurried movement farther off from the gate.

It was now that I perceived the necessity of doing something, of getting this crowd disposed of, especially the women and the children. I am not ashamed to own that I trembled like the others; and nothing less than the consciousness that all eyes were upon me, and that my scarf of office marked me out among all who stood around, could have kept me from moving with precipitation as they did. I was enabled, however to retire at a deliberate pace, and being thus slightly detached from the crowd, I took advantage of the opportunity to address them. Above all things, it was my duty to prevent a tumult in these unprecedented circumstances. "My friends," I said, "the event which has occurred is beyond explanation for the moment. The very nature of it is mysterious; the circumstances are such as require the closest investigation. But take courage. I pledge myself not to leave this place till the gates are open, and you can return to your homes; in the meantime, however, the women and the children cannot remain here. Let those who have friends in the villages near, go and ask for shelter; and let all who will, go to my house of la Clairière. My mother,

---

1   French mayors wear a tricolor sash over their shoulders as an emblem of authority.

my wife! recall to yourselves the position you occupy, and show an example. Lead our neighbours, I entreat you, to La Clairière."

My mother is advanced in years and no longer strong, but she has a great heart. "I will go," she said. "God bless thee, my son! There will no harm happen; for if this be true which we are told, thy father is in Semur."

There then occurred one of those incidents for which calculation never will prepare us. My mother's words seemed, as it were to open the flood-gates; my wife came up to me with the light in her face which I had seen when we left our own door. "It was our little Marie—our angel," she said, and then there arose a great cry and clamour of others, both men and women pressing round. "I saw my mother," said one, "who is dead twenty years come the St. Jean."[1] "And I my little René," said another. "And I my Camille, who was killed in Africa." And lo, what did they do, but rush towards the gate in a crowd—that gate from which they had this moment fled in terror—beating upon it, and crying out, "Open to us, open to us, our most dear! Do you think we have forgotten you? We have never forgotten you!" What could we do with them, weeping thus, smiling, holding out their arms to—we knew not what. Even my Agnès was beyond my reach. Marie was our little girl who was dead. Those who were thus transported by a knowledge beyond ours were the weakest among us; most of them were women, the men old or feeble, and some children. I can recollect that I looked for Paul Lecamus among them, with wonder not to see him there. But though they were weak, they were beyond our strength to guide. What could we do with them? How could we force them away while they held to the fancy that those they loved were there? As it happens in times of emotion, it was those who were most impassioned who took the first place. We were at our wits' end.

But while we stood waiting, not knowing what to do, another sound suddenly came from the walls, which made them all silent in a moment. The most of us ran to this point and that (some taking flight altogether; but with the greater part anxious; curiosity and anxiety had for the moment extinguished fear), in a wild eagerness to see who or what it was. Bu there was nothing to be seen, though the sound came from the wall close to the Mont St. Lambert, which I have already described. It was to me like the sound of a trumpet, and so I heard others say; and along with the trumpet were sounds as of words, though I could not make them out. But those others seemed to understand—they grew calmer—they ceased to weep. They raised their faces, all with that light upon them—that light I had seen in my Agnès. Some of them fell upon their knees. Imagine to yourself what a sight it was, all of us standing

---

1 Feast of Saint John the Baptist, June 24th.

round, pale, stupefied, without a word to say! Then the women suddenly burst forth into replies—"*Oui, ma chérie! Oui, mon ange!*"[1] they cried. And while we looked they rose up; they came back, calling the children around them. My Agnès took that place which I had bidden her take. She had not hearkened to me, to leave me—but she hearkened now; and though I had bidden her to do this, yet to see her do it bewildered me, made my heart stand still. "*Mon ami*," she said, "I must leave thee; it is commanded: they will not have the children suffer." What could we do? We stood pale and looked on, while all the little ones, all the feeble, were gathered in a little army. My mother stood like me—to her nothing had been revealed. She was very pale, and there was a quiver of pain in her lips. She was the one who had been ready to do my bidding: but there was a rebellion in her heart now. When the procession was formed (for it was my care to see that everything was done in order), she followed, but among the last. Thus they went away, many of them weeping, looking back, waving their hands to us. My Agnès covered her face, she could not look at me; but she obeyed. They went some to this side, some to that, leaving us gazing. For a long time we did nothing but watch them, going along the roads. What had their angels said to them? Nay, but God knows. I heard the sound; it was like the sound of the silver trumpets that travelers talk of; it was like music from heaven.[2] I turned to M. le Curé, who was standing by. "What is it?" I cried, "you are their director—you are an ecclesiastic—you know what belongs to the unseen. What is this that has been said to them?" I have always thought well of M. le Curé. There were tears running down his cheeks. "I know not," he said. "I am a miserable like the rest. What they know is between God and them. Me! I have been of the world, like the rest."

This is how we were left alone—the men of the city—to take what means were best to get back to our homes. There were several left among us who had shared the enlightenment of the women, but these were not persons of importance who could put themselves at the head of affairs. And there were women who remained with us, but these not of the best. To see our wives go was very strange to us; it was the thing we wished most to see, the women and children in safety; yet it was a strange sensation to see them go. For me, who had the charge of all on my hands, the relief was beyond description—yet was it strange; I cannot describe it. Then I called upon M. Barbou, who was trembling like a leaf, and gathered the chief of the citizens about me, including M. le Curé, that we should consult together what we should do.

---

1   Yes, my dear! Yes, my angel!
2   "Make thee two trumpets of silver; of a whole piece shalt thou make them: that thou mayest use them for the calling of the assembly, and for the journeying of the camps" (Numbers 10:2).

I know no words that can describe our state in the strange circumstances we were now placed in. The women and the children were safe; that was much. But we—we were like an army suddenly formed, but without arms, without any knowledge of how to fight, without being able to see our enemy. We Frenchmen have not been without knowledge of such perils. We have seen the invader[1] enter our doors; we have been obliged to spread our table for him, and give him of our best. But to be put forth by forces no man could resist—to be left outside, with the doors of our own houses closed upon us—to be confronted by nothing—by a mist, a silence, a darkness,—this was enough to paralyse the heart of any man. And it did so, more or less, according to the nature of those who were exposed to the trial. Some altogether failed us, and fled, carrying the news into the country, where most people laughed at them, as we understood afterwards. Some could do nothing but sit and gaze, huddled together in crowds, at the cloud over Semur, from which they expected to see fire burst and consume the city altogether. And a few, I grieve to say, took possession of the little *cabaret*,[2] which stands at about half a kilometre from the St. Lambert gate, and established themselves there, in hideous riot, which was the worst thing of all for serious men to behold. Those upon whom I could rely I formed into patrols to go round the city, that no opening of a gate, or movement of those who were within, should take place without our knowledge. Such an emergency shows what men are. M. Barbour, though in ordinary times he discharges his duties as *adjoint* satisfactorily enough (though, it need not be added, a good Maire who is acquainted with his duties, makes the office of *adjoint* of but little importance), was now found entirely useless. He could not forget how he had been spun round and tossed forth from the city gates. When I proposed to put him at the head of a patrol, he had an attack of the nerves. Before nightfall he deserted me altogether, going off to his country-house, and taking a number of his neighbours with him. "How can we tell when we may be permitted to return to the town?" he said, with his teeth chattering. "M. le Maire, I adjure you to put yourself in a place of safety."

"Sir," I said to him, sternly, "for one who deserts his post there is no place of safety."

But I do not think he was capable of understanding me. Fortunately, I found in M. le Curé a much more trustworthy coadjutor. He was indefatigable; he had the habit of sitting up to all hours, of being called at all hours, in which our *bourgeoisie*, I cannot but acknowledge, is wanting. The expression I have before described of

---

[1] Prussians—a reference to the Franco-Prussian War (1870–71), which led to the humiliating collapse of the Second Empire in France.
[2] Tavern.

astonishment—but of astonishment which he wished to conceal—never left his face. He did not understand how such a thing could have been permitted to happen while he had no share in it; and, indeed, I will not deny that this was a matter of great wonder to myself too.

The arrangements I have described gave us occupation; and this had a happy effect upon us in distracting our minds from what had happened; for I think that if we had sat still and gazed at the dark city we should soon have gone mad, as some did. In our ceaseless patrols and attempts to find a way of entrance, we distracted ourselves from the enquiry: "Who would dare to go in if the entrance were found?" In the meantime not a gate was opened, not a figurer was visible. We saw nothing, no more than if Semur had been a picture painted upon a canvas. Strange sights indeed met our eyes—sights which made event the bravest quail. The strangest of them was the boats that would go down and up the river, shooting forth from under the fortified bridge, which is one of the chief features of our town, sometimes with sails perfectly well managed, sometimes impelled by oars, but with no one visible in them—no one conducting them. To see one of these boats impelled up the stream, with no rower visible, was a wonderful sight. M. de Clairon, who was by my side, murmured something about a magnetic current; but when I asked him sternly by what set in motion, his voice died away in his moustache. M. le Curé said very little: one saw his lips move as he watched with us the passage of those boats. He smiled when it was proposed by some one to fire upon them. He read his Hours[1] as he went round at the head of his patrol. My fellow townsmen and I conceived a great respect for him; and he inspired pity in me also. He had been the teacher of the Unseen among us, till the moment when the Unseen was thus, as it were, brought within our reach; but with the revelation he had nothing to do; and it filled him with pain and wonder. It made him silent; he said little about his religion, but signed himself, and his lips moved. He thought (I imagine) that he had displeased Those who are over all.

When night came the bravest of us were afraid. I speak for myself. It was bright moonlight where we were, and Semur lay like a blot between the earth and the sky, all dark; even the Cathedral towers were lost in it; nothing visible but the line of the ramparts, whitened outside by the moon. One knows what black and strange shadows are cast by the moonlight; and it seemed to all of us that we did not know what might be lurking behind every tree. The shadows of the branches looked like terrible faces. I sent all my people out on the patrols, though they were dropping

---

1   Liturgy of the Hours, set of daily prayers.

with fatigue. Rather that than to be mad with terror. For myself, I took up my post as near the bank of the river as we could approach; for there was a limit beyond which we might not pass. I made the experiment often; and it seemed to me, and to all that attempted it, that we did reach the very edge of the stream; but the next moment perceived that we were at a certain distance, say twenty metres or thereabout. I placed myself there very often, wrapping a cloak about me to preserve me from the dew. (I may say that food had been sent us, and wine from La Clairière and many other houses in the neighbourhood, where the women had gone for this among other reasons, that we might be nourished by them.) And I must here relate a personal incident, though I have endeavoured not to be egotistical. While I sat watching, I distinctly saw a boat, a boat which belonged to myself, lying on the very edge of the shadow. The prow, indeed, touched the moonlight where it was cut clean across by the darkness; and this was how I discovered that it was the *Marie*, a pretty pleasure-boat which had been made for my wife. The sight of it made my heart beat; for what could it mean but that some one who was dear to me, some one in whom I took an interest, was there? I sprang up from where I sat to make another effort to get nearer; but my feet were as lead, and would not move; and there came a singing in my ears, and my blood coursed through my veins as in a fever, Ah! was it possible? I, who am a man, who have resolution, who have courage, who can lead the people, *I was afraid!* I sat down again and wept like a child. Perhaps it was my little Marie that was in the boat. God, He knows if I loved thee, my little angel! but I was afraid. O how mean is man! though we are so proud. They came near to me who were my own, and it was borne in upon my spirit that my good father was with the child; but because they had died I was afraid. I covered my face with my hands. Then it seemed to me that I heard a long quiver of a sigh; a long, long breath, such as sometimes relieves a sorrow that is beyond words. Trembling, I uncovered my eyes. There was nothing on the edge of the moonlight; all was dark, and all was still, the white radiance making a clear line across the river, but nothing more.

If my Agnès had been with me she would have seen our child, she would have heard that voice! The great cold drops of moisture were on my forehead. My limbs trembled, my heart fluttered in my bosom. I could neither listen nor yet speak. And those who would have spoken to me, those who loved me, sighing, went away. It is not possible that such wretchedness should be credible to noble minds; and if it had not been for pride and for shame, I should have fled away straight to La Clairière, to put myself under shelter, to have some one near me who was less a coward than I. I, upon whom all the others relied, the Maire of the Commune! I make my confession. I was of no more force than this.

A voice behind me made me spring to my feet—the leap of a mouse would have driven me wild. I was altogether demoralized. "Monsieur le Maire, it is but I," said some one quite humble and frightened. "*Tiens!*—it is thou, Jacques!" I said. I could have embraced him, though it is well known how little I approve of him. But he was living, he was a man like myself. I put out my hand, and felt him warm and breathing, and I shall never forget the ease that came to my heart. Its beating calmed, I was restored to myself.

"M. le Maire," he said, "I wish to ask you something. Is it true all that is said about these people, I would say, these Messieurs? I do not wish to speak with disrespect, M. le Maire."

"What is it, Jacques, that is said?" I had called him "thou"[1] not out of contempt, but because, for the moment, he seemed to me as a brother, as one of my friends.

"M. le Maire, is it indeed *les morts* that are in Semur?"

He trembled, and so did I. "Jacques," I said, "you know all that I know."

"Yes, M. le Maire, it is so, sure enough. I do not doubt it. If it were the Prussians, a man could fight. But *ces Messieurs là!*[2] What I want to know is: is it because of what you did to those little Sisters, those good little ladies of St. Jean?"

"What I did? You were yourself one of the complainants. You were of those who said, when a man is ill, when he is suffering, they torment him with their mass; it is quiet he wants, not their mass. These were thy words, *vaurien*.[3] And now you say it was I!"

"True, M. le Maire," said Jacques; "but look you, when a man is better, when he has just got well, when he feels he is safe, then you should not take what he says for gospel. It would be strange if one had a new illness just when one is getting well of the old; and one feels now is the time to enjoy one's self, to kick up one's heels a little, while at least there is not likely to be much of a watch kept *up there*—the saints forgive me," cried Jacques, trembling and crossing himself, 'if I speak with levity at such a moment! And the little ladies were very kind. It was wrong to close their chapel, M. le Maire. From that comes all our trouble."

"You good-for-nothing!" I cried, "it is you and such as you that are the beginning of our trouble. You thought there was no watch kept *up there*; you thought God would not take the trouble to punish you; you went about the streets of Semur

---

1   In French, the informal *tu* ("thou") is used to address intimates and inferiors; the more formal and polite *vous* ("you") is used to address strangers, acquaintances, and those to whom one shows respect.
2   Those gentlemen there!
3   Good-for-nothing.

tossing a *grosse pièce* of a hundred sous, and calling out, 'There is no God—this is my god; *l'argent, c'est le bon Dieu.*' "

"M. le Maire, M. le Maire, be silent, I implore you! It is enough to bring down a judgment upon us."

"It has brought down a judgment upon us. Go thou and try what thy *grosse pièce* will do for thee now—worship thy god. Go, I tell you, and get help from your money."

"I have no money, M. le Maire, and what could money do here? We would do much better to promise a large candle for the next festival, and that the ladies of St. Jean—"

"Get away with thee to the end of the world, thou and thy ladies of St. Jean!" I cried; which was wrong, I do not deny it, for they are good women, not like this good-for-nothing fellow. And to think that this man, whom I despise, was more pleasant to me than the dear souls who loved me! Shame came upon me at the thought. I too, then, was like the others, fearing the Unseen—capable of understanding only that which was palpable. When Jacques slunk away, which he did for a few steps, not losing sight of me, I turned my face towards the river and the town. The moonlight fell upon the water, white as silver where that line of darkness lay, shining, as if it tried, and tried in vain, to penetrate Semur; and between that and the blue sky overhead lay the city out of which we had been driven forth—the city of the dead. "O God," I cried, "whom I know not, am not I to Thee as my little Jean is to me, a child and less than a child? Do not abandon me in this darkness. Would I abandon him were he ever so disobedient? And God, if thou art God, Thou art a better father than I." When I had said this, my heart was a little relieved. It seemed to me that I had spoken to some one who knew all of us, whether we were dead or whether we were living. That is a wonderful thing to think of, when it appears to one not as a thing to believe, but as something that is real. It gave me courage. I got up and went to meet the patrol which was coming in, and found that great good-for-nothing Jacques running close after me, holding my cloak. "Do not send me away, M. le Maire," he said, "I dare not stay by myself with *them* so near." Instead of his money, in which he had trusted, it was I who had become his god now.

Chapter Four

OUTSIDE THE WALLS

THERE are few who have not heard something of the sufferings of a siege. Whether within or without, it is the most terrible of all the experiences of war. I am old enough to recollect the trenches before Sebastopol,[1] and all that my countrymen and the English endured there. Sometimes I endeavoured to think of this to distract me from what we ourselves endured. But how different was it! We had neither shelter nor support. We had no weapons, nor any against whom to wield them. We were cast out of our home in the midst of our lives, in the midst of our occupations, and left there helpless, to gaze at each other, to blind our eyes trying to penetrate the darkness before us. Could we have done anything, the oppression might have been less terrible—but what was there that we could do? Fortunately (though I do not deny that I felt each desertion) our band grew less and less every day. Hour by hour some one stole away—first one, then another, dispersing themselves among the villages near, in which many had friends. The accounts which these men gave were, I afterwards learnt, of the most vague description. Some talked of wonders they had seen, and were laughed at—and some spread reports of internal division among us. Not till long after did I know all the reports that went abroad. It was said that there had been fighting in Semur, and that we were divided into two factions, one of which had gained the mastery, and driven the other out. This was the story current in La Rochette, where they are always glad to hear anything to the discredit of the people of Semur; but no credence could have been given to it by those in authority, otherwise M. le Préfet, however indifferent to our interests, must necessarily have taken some steps for our relief. Our entire separation from the world was indeed one of the strangest details of this terrible period. Generally the diligence, though conveying on the whole few passengers, returned with two or three, at least, visitors or commercial persons, daily—and the latter class frequently arrived in carriages of their own; but during this period no stranger came to see our miserable plight. We made shelter for ourselves under the branches of the few trees that grew in the uncultivated ground on either side of the road—and a hasty erection, half tent half shed, was put up for a place to assemble in, or for those who were unable to bear the heat of

---

1 The Siege of Sebastopol (1844–45) during the Crimean War.

the day or the occasional chills of the night. But the most of us were too restless to seek repose, and could not bear to be out of sight of the city. At any moment it seemed to us the gate might open, or some loophole be visible by which we might throw ourselves upon the darkness and vanquish it. This was what we said to ourselves, forgetting how we shook and trembled whenever any contact had been possible with those who were within. But one thing was certain, that though we feared, we could not turn our eyes from the place. We slept leaning against a tree, or with our heads on our hands, and our faces toward Semur. We took no count of day or night, but ate the morsel the women brought to us, and slept thus, not sleeping, when want or weariness overwhelmed us. There was scarcely an hour in the day that some of the women did not come to ask what news. They crept along the roads in twos and threes, and lingered for hours sitting by the way weeping, starting at every breath of wind.

Meanwhile all was not silent within Semur. The Cathedral bells rang often, at first filling us with hope, for how familiar was that sound! The first time, we all gathered together and listened, and many wept. It was as if we heard our mother's voice. M. de Bois-Sombre burst into tears. I have never seen him within the doors of the Cathedral since his marriage; but he burst into tears. "*Mon Dieu!* If I were but there!" he said. We stood and listened, our hearts melting, some falling on their knees. M. le Curé stood up in the midst of us and began to intone the psalm; [He has a beautiful voice. It is sympathetic, it goes to the heart.] "I was glad when they said to me, Let us go up—" And though there were few of us who could have supposed themselves capable of listening to that sentiment a little while before with any sympathy, yet a vague hope rose up within us while we heard him, while we listened to the bells. What man is there to whom the bells of his village, the *carillon*[1] of his city, is not most dear? It rings for him through all his life; it is the first sound of home in the distance when he comes back—the last that follows him like a long farewell when he goes away. While we listened, we forgot our fears. They were as we were, they were also our brethren, who rang those bells. We seemed to see them trooping into our beautiful Cathedral. Ah! Only to see it again, to be within its shelter, cool and calm as in our mother's arms! It seemed to us that we should wish for nothing more.

When the sound ceased we looked into each other's faces, and each man saw that his neighbour was pale. Hope died in us when the sound died away, vibrating sadly through the air. Some men threw themselves on the ground in their despair.

---

1   Pealing.

And from this time forward many voices were heard, calls and shouts within the walls, and sometimes a sound like a trumpet, and other instruments of music. We thought, indeed, that noises as of bands patrolling along the ramparts were audible as our patrols worked their way round and round. This was a duty which I never allowed to be neglected, not because I put very much faith in it, but because it gave us a sort of employment. There is a story somewhere which I recollect dimly of an ancient city[1] which its assailants did not touch, but only marched round and round till the walls fell, and they could enter. Whether this was a story of classic times or out of our own remote history, I could not recollect. But I thought of it many times while we made our way like a procession of ghosts, round and round, straining our ears to hear what those voices were which sounded above us, in tones that were familiar, yet so strange. This story got so much into my head (and after a time all our heads seemed to get confused and full of wild and bewildering expedients) that I found myself suggesting—I, a man known for sense and reason—that we should blow trumpets at some time to be fixed, which was a thing the ancients had done in the strange tale which had taken possession of me. M. le Curé looked at me with disapproval. He said, "I did not expect from M. le Maire anything that was disrespectful to religion." Heaven forbid that I should be disrespectful to religion at any time of life, but then it was impossible to me. I remembered after that the tale of which I speak, which had so seized upon me, was in the sacred writings; but those who know me will understand that no sneer at these writings or intention of wounding the feelings of M. le Curé was in my mind.

I was seated one day upon a little inequality of the ground, leaning my back against a half-withered hawthorn, and dozing with my head in my hands, when a soothing, which always diffuses itself from her presence, shed itself over me, and opening my eyes, I saw my Agnès sitting by me. She had come with some food and a little linen, fresh and soft like her own touch. My wife was not gaunt and worn like me, but she was pale and as thin as a shadow. I woke with a start, and seeing her there, there suddenly came a dread over me that she would pass away before my eyes, and go over to Those who were within Semur. I cried "*Non, mon Agnès; non, mon Agnès*: before you ask, No!" seizing her and holding her fast in this dream, which was not altogether a dream. She looked at me with a smile, that has always been to me as the rising of the sun over the earth.

"*Mon ami*," she said surprised, "I ask nothing, except that you should take a little rest and spare thyself." Then she added, with haste, what I knew she would say,

---

1 Jericho.

"Unless it were this, *mon ami*. If I were permitted, I would go into the city—I would ask those who are there, what is their meaning: and if no way can be found—no act of penitence.—Oh! do not answer in haste! I have no fear; and it would be to save thee."

A strong throb of anger came into my throat. Figure to yourself that I looked at my wife with anger, with the same feeling which had moved me when the deserters left us; but far more hot and sharp. I seized her soft hands and crushed them in mine. "You would leave me!" I said. "You would desert your husband. You would go over to our enemies!"

"O Martin, say not so," she cried, with tears, "Not enemies. There is our little Marie, and my mother, who died when I was born."

"You love these dead tyrants. Yes," I said, "you love them best. You will go to—the majority, to the majority, to the strongest. Do not speak to me! Because your God is on their side, you will forsake us too."

Then she threw herself upon me and encircled me with her arms. The touch of them stilled my passion; but yet I held her, clutching her gown, so terrible a fear came over me that she would go and come back no more.

"Forsake thee!" she breathed out over me with a moan. Then, putting her cool cheek to mine, which burned, "But I would die for thee, Martin."

"Silence, my wife: that is what you shall not do," I cried, beside myself. I rose up; I put her away from me. That is, I know it, what has been done. Their God does this, they do not hesitate to say—takes from you what you love best, to make you better—*you!* and they ask you to love Him when He has thus despoiled you! "Go home, Agnès," I said, hoarse with terror. "Let us face them as we may; you shall not go among them, or put thyself in peril. Die for me! *Mon Dieu!* and what then, what should I do then? Turn your face from them; turn from them; go! go! and let me not see thee here again."

My wife did not understand the terror that seized me. She obeyed me, as she always does, but, with the tears falling from her white cheeks, fixed upon me the most piteous look. "*Mon ami*," she said, "you are disturbed, you are not in possession of yourself; this cannot be what you mean."

"Let me not see thee here again!" I cried. "Would you make me mad in the midst of my trouble? No! I will not have you look that way. Go home! go home!" Then I took her into my arms and wept, though I am not a man given to tears. "Oh! my Agnès," I said, "give me thy counsel. What you tell me I will do; but rather than risk thee, I would live thus for ever, and defy them."

She put her hand upon my lips. "I will not ask this again," she said, bowing her head; "but defy them—why should you defy them? Have they come for nothing? Was Semur a city of the saints? They have come to convert our people, Martin—thee too, and the rest. If you will submit your hearts, they will open the gates, will go back to their sacred homes: and we to ours. This has been borne in upon me sleeping and waking; and it seemed to me that if I could but go, and say, 'Oh! my fathers, oh! my brothers, they submit,' all would be well. For I do not fear them, Martin. Would they harm me that love us? I would but give our Marie one kiss—"

"You are a traitor!" I said. "You would steal yourself from me, and do me the worst wrong of all—"

But I recovered my calm. What she said reached my understanding at last. "Submit!" I said, "but to what? To come and turn us from our homes, to wrap our town in darkness, to banish our wives and our children, to leave us here to be scorched by the sun and drenched by the rain,—this is not to convince us, my Agnès. And to what then do you bid us submit—?"

"It is to convince you, *mon ami,* of the love of God, who has permitted this great tribulation to be, that we might be saved," said Agnès. Her face was sublime with faith. It is possible to these dear women; but for me the words she spoke were but words without meaning. I shook my head. Now that my horror and alarm were passed, I could well remember often to have heard words like these before.

"My angel!" I said, "all this I admire, I adore in thee; but how is it the love of God?—and how shall we be saved by it? Submit! I will do anything that is reasonable; but of what truth have we here the proof—?"

Some one had come up behind as we were talking. When I heard his voice I smiled notwithstanding my despair. It was natural that the Church should come to the woman's aid. But I would not refuse to give ear to M. le Curé, who had proved himself a man, had he been ten times a priest.

"I have not heard what Madame has been saying, M. le Maire, neither would I interpose but for your question. You ask of what truth have we the proof here? It is the Unseen that has revealed itself. Do we see anything, you and I! Nothing, nothing, but a cloud. But that which we cannot see, that which we know not, that which we dread—look! it is there."

I turned unconsciously as he pointed with his hand. Oh, heaven, what did I see! Above the cloud that wrapped Semur there was a separation, a rent in the darkness, and in mid heaven the Cathedral towers, pointing to the sky. I paid no more attention to M. le Curé. I sent forth a shout that roused all, even the weary line of the patrol that was marching slowly with bowed heads round the walls;

and there went up such a cry of joy as shook the earth. "The towers, the towers!" I cried. These were the towers that could be seen leagues off, the first sign of Semur; our towers, which we had been born to love like our father's name. I have had joys in my life, deep and great. I have loved, I have won honours, I have conquered difficulty; but never had I felt as now. It was if one had been born again.

When we had gazed upon them, blessing them and thanking God, I gave orders that all our company should be called to the tent, that we might consider whether any new step could now be taken: Agnès with the other women sitting apart on one side and waiting. I recognized even in the excitement of such a time that theirs was no easy part. To sit there silent, to wait till we had spoken, to be bound by what we decided, and to have no voice—yes, that was hard. They thought they knew better than we did: but they were silent, devouring us with their eager eyes. I love one woman more than all the world; I count her the best thing that God has made; yet would I not be as Agnès for all that life Could give me. It was her part to be silent, and she was so, like the angel she is, while even Jacques Richard had the right to speak. *Mon Dieu!* But it is hard, I allow it; they have need to be angels. This thought passed through my mind even at the crisis which had now arrived. For at such moments one sees everything, one thinks of everything, though it is only after that one remembers what one has seen and thought. When my fellow-citizens gathered together (we were now less than a hundred in number, so many had gone from us), I took it upon myself to speak. We were a haggard, worn-eyed company, having had neither shelter nor sleep nor even food, save in hasty snatches. I stood at the door of the tent and they below, for the ground sloped a little. Beside me were M. le Curé, M. de Bois-Sombre, and one or two others of the chief citizens. "My friends," I said, "you have seen that a new circumstance has occurred. It is not within our power to tell what its meaning is, yet it must be a symptom of good. For my own part, to see these towers makes the air lighter. Let us think of the Church as we may, no one can deny that the towers of Semur are dear to our hearts."

"M. le Maire," said M. de Bois-Sombre, interrupting, "I speak I am sure the sentiments of my fellow-citizens when I say that there is no longer any question among us concerning the Church; it is an admirable institution, a universal advantage—"

"Yes, yes," said the crowd, "yes, certainly!" and some added, "It is the only safe-guard, it is our protection," and some signed themselves. In the crowd I saw Riou, who had done this at the *octroi*. But the sign did not surprise me now.

M. le Curé stood by my side, but he did not smile. His countenance was dark, almost angry. He stood quite silent, with his eyes on the ground. It gave him no pleasure, this profession of faith.

"It is well, my friends," said I, "we are all in accord; and the good God has permitted us again to see these towers. I have called you together to collect your ideas. This change must have a meaning. It has been suggested to me that we might send an ambassador—a messenger. If that is possible, into the city—"

Here I stopped short; and a shiver ran through me—a shiver which went over the whole company. We were all pale as we looked in each other's faces; and for a moment no one ventured to speak. After this pause it was perhaps natural that he who first found his voice should be the last who had any right to give an opinion. Who should it be but Jacques Richard? "M. le Maire," cried the fellow, "speaks at his ease—but who will thus risk himself?" Probably he did not mean that his grumbling should be heard, but in the silence every sound was audible; there was a gasp, a catching of the breath, and all turned their eyes again upon me. I did not pause to think what answer I should give. "I!" I cried. "Here stands one who will risk himself, who will perish if need be—"

Something stirred behind me. It was Agnès who had risen to her feet, who stood with her lips parted and quivering, with her hands clasped, as if about to speak. But she did not speak. Well! She had proposed to do it. Then why not I?

"Let me make the observation," said another of our fellow-citizens, Bordereau the banker, "that this would not be just. Without M. le Maire we should be a mob without a head. If a messenger is to be sent, let it be some one not so indispensable—"

"Why send a messenger?" said another, Philip Leclerc. "Do we know that these Messieurs will admit any one? and how can you speak, how can you parley with those—" and he too, was seized with a shiver—"whom you cannot see?"

Then there came another voice out of the crowd. It was one who would not show himself, who was conscious of the mockery in his tone. "If there is any one sent, let it be M. le Curé," it said.

M. le Curé stepped forward. His pale countenance flushed red. "Here am I," he said, "I am ready; but he who spoke speaks to mock me. Is it befitting in this presence?"

There was a struggle among the men. Whoever it was who had spoken (I did not wish to know), I had no need to condemn the mocker; they themselves silenced him; then Jacques Richard (still less worthy of credit) cried out again with a voice that was husky. What are men made of? Notwithstanding everything, it was from the *cabaret,* from the wineshop, that he had come. He said,

"Though M. le Maire will not take my opinion, yet it is this. Let them reopen the chapel in the hospital. The ladies of St. Jean—"

"Hold thy peace," I said, "miserable!" But a murmur rose. "Though it is not his part to speak, I agree," said one. "And I." "And I." There was well-nigh a tumult of consent; and this made me angry. Words were on my lips which might have been foolish to utter, when M. de Bois-Sombre, who is a man of judgment, interfered.

"M. le Maire," he said, "as there are none of us here who would show disrespect to the Church and holy things—that is understood—it is not necessary to enter into details. Every restriction that would wound the most susceptible is withdrawn; not one more than another, but all. We have been indifferent in the past, but for the future you will agree with me that everything shall be changed. The ambassador—whoever he may be—" he added with a catching of his breath, "must be empowered to promise—everything—submission to all may be required."

Here the women could not restrain themselves; they all rose up with a cry, and many of them began to weep. "Ah!" said one with a hysterical sound of laughter in her tears. "*Sante Mère!*[1] it will be heaven upon earth."

M. le Curé said nothing; a keen glance of wonder, yet of subdued triumph, shot from under his eyelids. As for me, I wrung my hands: "What you say will be superstition; it will be hypocrisy," I cried.

But at that moment a further incident occurred. Suddenly, while we deliberated, a long loud peal of a trumpet sounded into the air. I have already said that many sounds had been heard before; but this was different; there was not one of us that did not feel that this was addressed to himself. The agitation was extreme; it was a summons, the beginning of some distinct communication. The crowd scattered; but for myself, after a momentary struggle, I went forward resolutely. I did not even look back at my wife. I was no longer Martin Dupin, but the Maire of Semur, the saviour of the community. Even Bois-Sombre quailed: but I felt that it was in me to hold head against death itself; and before I had gone two steps I felt rather than saw that M. le Curé had come to my side. We went on without a word; gradually the others collected behind us, following yet straggling here and there upon the inequalities of the ground.

Before us lay the cloud that was Semur, a darkness defined by the shining of the summer day around, the river escaping from that gloom as from a cavern, the towers piercing through, but the sunshine thrown back on every side from that darkness. I have spoken of the walls as if we saw them, but there were no walls

---

1   Blessed Mother.

visible, nor any gate, though we all turned like blind men to where the Porte St. Lambert was. There was the broad vacant road leading up to it, leading into the gloom. We stood there at a little distance. Whether it was human weakness or an invisible barrier, how can I tell? We stood thus immovable, with the trumpet pealing out over us, out of the cloud. It summoned every man as by his name. To me it was not wonderful that this impression should come, but afterwards it was elicited from all that this was the feeling of each. We all waited in such a supreme agitation as I cannot describe for some communication that was to come.

When suddenly, in a moment, the trumpet ceased; there was an interval of dead and terrible silence; then, each with a leap of his heart as if it would burst from his bosom, we saw a single figure slowly detach itself out of the gloom. "My God!" I cried. My senses went from me; I felt my head go round like a straw tossed on the winds.

To know them so near, those mysterious visitors—to feel them, to hear them, was not that enough? But, to see! Who could bear it? Our voices rang like broken chords, like a tearing and rending of sound. Some covered their faces with their hands; for our very eyes seemed to be drawn out of their sockets, fluttering like things with a separate life.

Then there fell upon us a strange and wonderful calm. The figure advanced slowly; there was weakness in it. The step, though solemn, was feeble; and if you can figure to yourself our consternation, the pause, the cry—our hearts dropping back as it might into their places—the sudden stop of the wild panting in our breasts: when there became visible to us a human face well known, a man as we were. "Lecamus!" I cried; and all the men round took it up, crowding nearer, trembling yet delivered from their terror; some even laughed in the relief. There was but one who had an air of discontent, and that was M. le Curé. As he said "Lecamus!" like the rest, there was impatience, disappointment, anger in his tone.

And I, who had wondered where Lecamus had gone; thinking sometimes that he was one of the deserters who had left us! But when he came nearer his face was as the face of a dead man, and a cold chill came over us. His eyes, which were cast down, flickered under the thin eyelids in which all the veins were visible. His face was gray like that of the dying. "Is he dead?" I said. But, except M. le Curé, no one knew that I spoke.

"Not even so," said M. le Curé, with a mortification in his voice, which I have never forgotten. "Not even so. That might be something. They teach us not by angels—by the fools and of scourings of the earth."

And he would have turned away. It was a humiliation. Was not he the representative of the Unseen, the vicegerent,[1] with power over heaven and hell? But something was here more strong than he. He stood by my side in spite of himself to listen to the ambassador. I will not deny that such a choice was strange, strange beyond measure, to me also.

"Lecamus," I said, my voice trembling in my throat, "have you been among the dead, and do you live?"

"I live," he said; then looked around with tears upon the crowd. "Good neighbours, good friends." he said, and put out his hand and touched them; he was as much agitated as they.

"M. Lecamus." Said I, "we are in very strange circumstances, as you know: do not trifle with us. If you have indeed been with those who have taken the control of our city, do not keep us in suspense. You will see by the emblems of my office that it is to me you must address yourself; if you have a mission, speak."

"It is just," he said, "it is just—but bear with me one moment. It is good to behold those who draw breath; if I have not loved you enough, my good neighbours, forgive me now!"

"Rouse yourself, Lecamus," said I with some anxiety. "Three days we have been suffering here; we are distracted with the suspense. Tell us your message—if you have anything to tell."

"Three days!" he said, wondering; "I should have said years. Time is long when there is neither night nor day." Then, uncovering himself, he turned towards the city. "They who have sent me would have you know that they come, not in anger but in friendship: for the love they bear you, and because it has been permitted—"

As he spoke his feebleness disappeared. He held his head high; and we clustered closer and closer round him, not losing a half word, not a tone, not a breath.

"They are not the dead. They are the immortal. They are those who dwell—elsewhere. They have other work, which has been interrupted because of this trial. They ask, 'Do you know now—do you know now?' This is what I am bidden to say."

"What"—I said (I tried to say it, but my lips were dry), "What would they have us to know?"

But a clamour interrupted me. "Ah! yes, yes, yes!" the people cried, men and women; some wept aloud, some signed themselves, some held up their hands to the skies. "Never more will we deny religion," they cried, "never more fail in our duties. They shall see how we will follow every office, how the churches shall be full, how

---

1   Earthly representative of God.

we will observe the feasts and the days of the saints! M. Lecamus," cried two or three together; "go, tell these Messieurs that we will have masses said for them, that we will obey in everything. We have seen what comes of it when a city is without piety. Never more will we neglect the holy functions; we will vow ourselves to the holy Mother and the saints—"

"And if those ladies wish it," cried Jacques Richard, "there shall be as many masses as there are Priests to say them in the Hospital of St. Jean."

"Silence, fellow!" I cried; "is it for you to promise in the name of the Commune?" I was almost beside myself. "M. Lecamus, is it for this that they have come?"

His head had begun to droop again, and a dimness came over his face. "Do I know?" he said. "It was them I longed for, not to know their errand; but I have not yet said all. You are to send two—two whom you esteem the highest—to speak with them face to face."

Then at once there rose a tumult among the people—an eagerness which nothing could subdue. There was a cry that the ambassadors were already elected, and we were pushed forward, M. le Curé and myself, towards the gate. They would not hear us speak. "We promise," they cried, "we promise everything; let us but get back." Had it been to sacrifice us they would have done the same; they would have killed us in their passion, in order to return to their city—and afterwards mourned us and honoured us as martyrs. But for the moment they had neither ruth nor fear. Had it been they who were going to reason not with flesh and blood, it would have been different; but it was we, not they; and they hurried us on as not willing that a moment should be lost. I had to struggle, almost to fight, in order to provide them with a leader, which was indispensable, before I myself went away. For who could tell if we should ever come back? For a moment I hesitated, thinking that it might be well to invest M. de Bois Sombre as my deputy with my scarf of office; but then I reflected that when a man goes to battle, when he goes to risk his life, perhaps to lose it, for his people, it is his right to bear those signs which distinguish him from common men, which show in what office, for what cause, he is ready to die.

Accordingly I paused, struggling against the pressure of the people, and said in loud voice, "In the absence of M. Barbou, who has forsaken us, I constitute the excellent M. Félix de Bois-Sombre my representative. In my absence my fellow-citizens will respect and obey him as myself." There was a cry of assent. They would have given their assent to anything that we might but go on. What was it to them? They took no thought of the heaving of my bosom, the beating of my heart. They left us on the edge of the darkness with our faces towards the gate. There we stood one breathless moment. Then the little postern slowly opened before us, and once more we stood within Semur.

Chapter Five

THE NARRATIVE OF PAUL LECAMUS

M. LE Maire having requested me, on his entrance into Semur, to lose no time in drawing up an account of my residence in the town, to be placed with his own narrative, I have promised to do so to the best of my ability, feeling that explanation may be short. Many things, needless to enumerate, press this upon my mind. It was a pleasure to me to see my neighbors when I first came out of the city; but their voices, their touch, their vehemence and eagerness wear me out. From my childhood up I have shrunk from close contact with my fellow-men. My mind has been busy with other thoughts; I have desired to investigate the mysterious and unseen. When I have walked abroad I have heard whispers in the air; I have felt the movement of wings, the gliding of unseen feet. To my comrades these have been a source of alarm and disquiet, but not to me; is not God in the unseen with all His angels? and not only so, but the best and wisest of men. There was a time indeed, when life acquired for me a charm. There was a smile which filled me with blessedness, and made the sunshine more sweet. But when she died my earthly joys died with her. Since then I have thought of little but the depths profound, into which she has disappeared like the rest.

I was in the garden of my house on that night when all the others left Semur. I was restless, my mind was disturbed. It seemed to me that I approached the crisis of my life. Since the time when I led M. le Maire beyond the walls, and we felt both of us the rush and pressure of that crowd, a feeling of expectation had been in my mind. I knew not what I looked for—but something I looked for that should change the world. The "Sommation" on the Cathedral doors did not surprise me. Why should it be a matter of wonder that the dead should come back? The wonder is that they do not. Ah! that is the wonder. How one can go away who loves you, and never return nor speak, nor send any message—that is the miracle; not that the heavens should bend down and the gates of Paradise roll back and those who have left us return.

All my life it has been a marvel to me how they could be kept away. I could not stay in-doors on this strange night. My mind was full of agitation. I came out into the garden though it was dark. I sat down upon the bench under the trellis—she loved it. Often had I spent half the night there thinking of her.

It was very dark that night: the sky all veiled, no light anywhere—a night like November. One would have said there was snow in the air. I think I must have slept toward morning (I have observed throughout that the preliminaries of these occurrences have always been veiled in sleep), and when I woke suddenly it was to find myself, if I may so speak, the subject of a struggle. The struggle was within me, yet it was not I. In my mind there was a desire to rise from where I sat and go away, I could not tell where or why; but something in me said stay, and my limbs were as heavy as lead. I could not move; I sat still against my will; against one part of my will—but the other was obstinate and would not let me go. Thus a combat took place within me of which I knew not the meaning. While it went on I began to hear the sound of many feet, the opening of doors, the people pouring out into the streets. This gave me no surprise; it seemed to me that I understood why it was; only in my own case, I knew nothing. I listened to the steps pouring past, going on and on, faintly dying away in the distance, and there was a great stillness. I then became convinced, though I cannot tell how, that I was the only living man left in Semur; but neither did this trouble me. The struggle within me came to an end, and I experienced a great calm.

I cannot tell how long it was till I perceived a change in the air, in the darkness round me. It was like the movement of some one unseen. I have felt such a sensation in the night, when all was still, before now. I saw nothing. I heard nothing. Yet I was aware, I cannot tell how, that there was a great coming and going, and the sensation as of a multitude in the air. I then rose and went into my house, where Leocadie, my old housekeeper, had shut all the doors so carefully when she went to bed. They were now all open, even the door of my wife's room of which I kept always the key, and where no one entered but myself; the windows also were open. I looked out upon the Grande Rue, and all the other houses were like mine. Everything was open, doors and windows, and the streets were full. There was in them a flow and movement of the unseen, without a sound, sensible only to the soul. I cannot describe it, for I neither heard nor saw, but felt. I have often been in crowds; I have lived in Paris, and once passed into England, and walked about the London streets. But never, it seemed to me, never was I aware of so many, of so great a multitude. I stood at my open window, and watched as in a dream. M. le Maire is aware that his house is visible from mine. Towards that a stream seemed to be always going, and at the windows and in the doorways was a sensation of multitudes like that which I have already described. Gazing out thus upon the revolution which was happening before my eyes, I did not think of my own house or what was passing there, till suddenly, in a moment, I was aware that some one had come in to me. Not a crowd as elsewhere; one. My heart leaped up like a bird let loose; it grew faint within me with joy and fear. I was giddy so that I could not stand. I called out her name, but low, for I was too happy, I had no voice. Besides was it needed, when heart already spoke to heart?

I had no answer, but I needed none. I laid myself down on the floor where her feet would be. Her presence wrapped me round and round. It was beyond speech. Neither did I need to see her face, nor to touch her hand. She was more near to me, more near, than when I held her in my arms. How long it was so, I cannot tell; it was long as love, yet short as the drawing of a breath. I knew nothing, felt nothing but Her, alone; all my wonder and desire to know departed from me. We said to each other everything without words—heart overflowing into heart. It was beyond knowledge or speech.

But this is not of public signification that I should occupy with it the time of M. le Maire.

After a while my happiness came to an end. I can no more tell how, than I can tell how it came. One moment, I was warm in her presence; the next, I was alone. I rose up staggering with blindness and woe—could it be that already, already it was over? I went out blindly following after her. My God, I shall follow, I shall follow, till life is over. She loved me; but she was gone.

Thus, despair came to me at the very moment when the longing of my soul was satisfied and I found myself among the unseen; but I cared for knowledge no longer, I sought only her. I lost a portion of my time so. I regret to have to confess it to M. le Maire. Much that I might have learned will thus remain lost to my fellow-citizens and the world. We are made so. What we desire eludes us at the moment of grasping it—or those affections which are the foundation of our lives preoccupy us, and blind the soul. Instead of endeavouring to establish my faith and enlighten my judgment as to those mysteries which have been my life-long study, all higher purpose departed from me; and I did nothing but rush through the city, groping among those crowds, seeing nothing, thinking of nothing—save of One.

From this also I awakened at out of a dream. What roused me was the pealing of the Cathedral bells. I was made to pause and stand still, and return to myself. Then I perceived, but dimly, that the thing which had happened to me was that which I had desired all my life. I leave this explanation of my failure[1] in public duty to the charity of M. le Maire.

The bells of the Cathedral brought me back to myself—to that which we call reality in our language; but of all that was around me when I regained consciousness, it now appeared to me that I only was a dream. I was in the midst of a world where all was in movement. What the current was which flowed around me I know not; if it was thought which becomes sensible among spirits, if it was action, I cannot tell. But the energy, the force, the living that was in them, that could no one misunderstand. I stood in the streets, lagging and feeble, scarcely able to wish, much less to think. They pushed against me, put me aside, took no note of me. In the unseen world described by a poet[2] whom M. le Maire has probably heard of, the man who traverses Purgatory (to speak of no other place) is seen by all, and is a wonder to all he meets—his shadow, his breath separate him from those around him. But whether the unseen life has changed, or if it is I who am not worthy their attention, this I know that I stood in our city like a ghost, and no one took any heed of me. When there came back upon me slowly my old desire to inquire, to understand, I was met with this difficulty at the first—that no one heeded me. I went through and through the streets, sometimes I paused to look round, to implore that which swept by me to make itself known. But the stream went along like soft air, like the flowing of a river, setting me aside from time to time, as the air will displace a straw, or the water a stone, but no more. There was neither languor nor lingering. I was the only passive thing, the being without occupation. Would you have paused in your labours to tell an idle traveler the meaning of our lives, before the day when you left Semur? Nor would they: I was driven hither and thither by the current of that life, but no one stepped forth out of the unseen to hear my questions or to answer me how this might be.

You have been made to believe that all was darkness in Semur. M. le Maire, it was not so. The darkness wrapped the walls in a winding sheet; but within, soon after you were gone, there arose a sweet and wonderful light—a light that was neither of the sun nor of the moon; and presently, after the ringing of the bells, the silence departed as the darkness had departed. I began to hear, first a murmur, then the sound of the going which I had felt without hearing it—then a faint tinkle of voices—and at the last, as my mind grew attuned to these wonders, the very words they said. If

---

1 The reader will remember that the ringing of the Cathedral bells happened in fact very soon after the exodus of the citizens; so that the self-reproaches of M. Lecamus had less foundation than he thought. [*Oliphant*]
2 Dante.

they spoke in our language or in another, I cannot tell; but I understood. How long it was before the sensation of their presence was aided by the happiness of hearing I know not, nor do I know how the time has passed, or how long it is, whether years or days, that I have been in Semur with those who are now there; for the light did not vary—there was no night or day. All I know is that suddenly, on awakening from a sleep (for the wonder was that I could sleep, sometimes sitting on the Cathedral steps, sometimes in my own house; where sometimes also I lingered and searched about for the crusts that Leocadie had left), I found the whole world full of sound. They sang going in bands about the streets; they talked to each other as they went along every way. From the houses, all open, where everyone could go who would, there came the soft chiming of those voices. And at first every sound was full of gladness and hope. The song they sang first was like this: "Send, us, send to our father's house. Many are our brethren, many and dear. They have forgotten, forgotten, forgotten! But when we speak, then will they hear." And the others answered: "We have come, we have come to the house of our fathers. Sweet are the homes, the homes we were born in. As we remember, so will they, remember. When we speak, when we speak, they will hear." Do not think that these were the words they sang; but it was like this. And as they sang there was joy and expectation everywhere. It was more beautiful than any of our music, for it was full of desire and longing, yet hope and gladness; whereas among us, where there is longing, it is always sad. Later a great singer, I know not who he was, one going past as on a majestic soft wind, sang another song, of which I shall tell you by and by. I do not think he was one of them. They came out to the windows, to the doors, into all the streets and byways to hear him as he went past.

M. le Maire will, however, be good enough to remark that I did not understand all that I heard. In the middle of a phrase, in a word half breathed, a sudden barrier would rise. For a time I laboured after their meaning, trying hard and vainly to understand; but afterwards I perceived that only when they spoke of Semur, of you who were gone forth, and of what was being done, could I make it out. At first this made me only more eager to hear; but when thought came, then I perceived that of all my longing nothing was satisfied. Though I was alone with the unseen, I comprehended it not; only when it touched upon what I knew, then I understood.

At first all went well. Those who were in the streets, and at the doors and windows of the houses, and on the Cathedral steps, where they seemed to throng, listening to the sounding of the bells, spoke only of this that they had come to do. Of you and you only I heard. They said to each other, with great joy, that the women had been instructed, that they had listened, and were safe. There was pleasure in all the city.

The singers were called forth, those who were best instructed (so I judged from what I heard), to take the place of the warders on the walls; and all, as they went along sang that song: "Our brothers have forgotten; but when we speak, they will hear." How was it, how was it that you did not hear? One time I was by the river *porte*[1] in a boat; and this song came to me from the walls as sweet as Heaven. Never have I heard such a song. The music was beseeching, it moved the very heart. "We have come out of the unseen," they sang; "for love of you; believe us, believe us! Love brings us back to earth; believe us believe us!" How was it that you did not hear? When I heard those singers sing, I wept; they beguiled the heart out of my bosom. They sang, they shouted, the music swept about all the walls: "Love brings us back to earth, believe us!" M. le Maire, I saw you from the river gate; there was a look of perplexity upon your face; and one put his curved hand to his ear as if to listen to some thin far-off sound, when it was like a storm, like a tempest of music!

After that there was a great change in the city. The choirs came back from the walls marching more slowly, and with a sighing through all the air. A sigh, nay, something like a sob breathed through the streets. "They cannot hear us, or they will not hear us." Wherever I turned, this was what I heard: "They cannot hear us." The whole town, and all the houses that were teeming with souls, and all the street, where so many were coming and going, was full of wonder and dismay. (If you will take my opinion, they know pain as well as joy, M. le Maire, Those who are in Semur. They are not as gods, perfect and sufficing to themselves, nor are they all-knowing and all-wise, like the good God. They hope like us, and desire, and are mistaken; but do no wrong. This is my opinion. I am no more than other men, that you should accept it without support; but I have lived among them, and this is what I think.) They were taken by surprise; they did not understand it any more than we understand when we have put forth all our strength and fail. They were confounded, if I could judge rightly. Then there arose cries from one to another: "Do you forget what was said to us?" and, "We were warned, we were warned." There went a sighing over all the city: "They cannot hear us, our voices are not as their voices; they cannot see us. We have taken their homes from them, and they know not the reason." My heart was wrung for their disappointment. I longed to tell them that neither had I heard at once; but it was only after a time that I ventured upon this. And whether I spoke, and was heard; or if it was read in my heart, I cannot tell. There was a pause made round me as if of wondering and listening, and then, in a moment, in the twinkling of an eye, a face suddenly turned and looked into my face.

---

1   Gate.

M. le Maire, it was the face of your father, Martin Dupin, whom I remember as well as I remember my own father. He was the best man I ever knew. It appeared to me for a moment, that face alone, looking at me with questioning eyes.

There seemed to be agitation and doubt for a time after this; some went out (so I understood) on embassies among you, but could get no hearing; some through the gates, some by the river. And the bells were rung that you might hear and know; but neither could you understand the bells. I wandered from one place to another, listening and watching—till the unseen became to me as the seen, and I thought of the wonder no more. Sometimes there came to me vaguely a desire to question them, to ask whence they came and what was the secret of their living, and why they were here? But if I had asked who would have heard me? And desire had grown faint in my heart; all I wished for was that you should hear, that you should understand; with this wish Semur was full. They thought but of this. They went to the walls in bands, each in their order, and as they came all the others rushed to meet them, to ask, "What news?" I following, now with one, now with another, breathless and footsore as they glided along. It is terrible when flesh and blood live with those who are spirits. I toiled after them. I sat on the Cathedral steps, and slept and waked, and heard the voices still in my dream. I prayed, but it was hard to pray. Once following a crowd I entered your house, M. le Maire, and went up, though I scarcely could drag myself along. There many were assembled as in council. Your father was at the head of all. He was the one, he only, who knew me. Again he looked at me and I saw him, and in the light of his face an assembly such as I have seen in pictures. One moment it glimmered before me and then it was gone. There were the captains of all the bands waiting to speak, men and women. I heard them repeating from one to another the same tale. One voice was small and soft like a child's; it spoke of you. "We went to him," it said; and your father, M. le Maire, he too joined in, and said: "We went to him—but he could not hear us." And some said it was enough—that they had no commission from on high, that they were but permitted,—that it was their own will to do it—and that the time had come to forbear.

Now, while I listened, my heart was grieved that they should fail. This gave me a wound for myself who had trusted in them, and also for them. But I, who am I, a poor man without credit among my neighbours, a dreamer, one whom many despise, that I should come to their aid? Yet I could not listen and take no part. I cried out: "Send me. I will tell them in words they understand." The sound of my voice was like a roar in that atmosphere. It sent a tremble into the air. It seemed to rend me as it came forth from me, and made me giddy, so that I would have fallen had not there been a support afforded me. As the light was going out of my eyes I saw again the faces looking at each other, questioning, benign, beautiful heads one over another, eyes that were clear as the heavens, but sad. I trembled while I gazed: there was the bliss of heaven in their faces, yet they were sad. Then everything faded. I was led away, I know not how, and brought to the door and put forth. I was not worthy to see the blessed grieve. That is a sight upon which the angels look with awe, and which bring those tears which are salvation into the eyes of God.

I went back to my house, weary yet calm. There were many in my house; but because my heart was full of one who was not there, I knew not those who were there. I sat me down where she had been. I was weary, more weary than ever before, but calm. Then I bethought me that I knew no more than at the first, that I had lived among the unseen as if they were my neighbours, neither fearing them, nor hearing those wonders which they have to tell. As I sat with my head in my hands, two talked to each other close by: "Is it true that we have failed?" said one; and the other answered, "Must not all fail that is not sent of the Father?" I was silent; but I knew them, they were the voices of my father and my mother. I listened as out of a faint, in a dream.

While I sat thus, with these voices in my ears, which a little while before would have seemed to me more worthy of note than anything on earth, but which now lulled me and comforted me, as a child is comforted by the voices of its guardians in the night, there occurred a new thing in the city like nothing I had heard before. It roused me notwithstanding my exhaustion and stupor. It was the sound as of some one passing through the city suddenly and swiftly, whether in some wonderful chariot, whether on some sweeping mighty wind, I cannot tell. The voices stopped that were conversing beside me, and I stood up, and with an impulse I could not resist went out, as if a king were passing that way. Straight, without turning to the right or left, through the city, from one gate of another, this passenger seemed going; and as he went there was the sound as of a proclamation, as if it were a herald denouncing war or ratifying peace. Whosoever he was, the sweep of his going moved my hair like a wind. At first the proclamation was but as a great shout, and I could not understand it; but as he came nearer the words became distinct. "Neither will they believe—though one rose from the dead." As it passed a murmur went up from the city, like the voice of a great multitude. Then there came sudden silence.

At this moment, for a time—M. le Maire will take my statement for what it is worth—I became unconscious of what passed further. Whether weariness overpowered me and I slept, as at the most terrible moment nature will demand to do, or if I fainted I cannot tell; but for a time I knew no more. When I came to myself, I was seated on the Cathedral steps with everything silent around me. From thence I rose up, moved by a will which was not mine, and was led softly across the Grande Rue, through the great square, with my face towards the Porte St. Lambert, I went steadily on without hesitation, never doubting that the gates would open to me, doubting nothing, though I had never attempted to withdraw from the city before. When I came to the gate I said not a word, nor any one to me; but the door rolled slowly open before me, and I was put forth into the morning light, into the shining of the sun. I have now said everything I had to say. The message I delivered was said through me; I can tell no more. Let me rest a little; figure to yourselves, I have known no night of rest, nor eaten a morsel of bread for—did you say it was but there days?

Chapter Six

M. LE MARIE RESUMES HIS NARRATIVE

We re-entered by the door for foot-passengers which is by the side of the great Porte St. Lambert.

I will not deny that my heart was, as one may say, in my throat. A man does what is his duty, what his fellow-citizens expect of him; but that is not to say that he renders himself callous to natural emotion. My veins were swollen, the blood coursing through them like a high-flowing river; my tongue was parched and dry. I am not ashamed to admit that from head to foot my body quivered and trembled. I was afraid—but I went forward; no man can do more. As for M. le Curé he said not a word. If he had any fears the concealed them as I did. But his occupation is with the ghostly and spiritual. To see men die, to accompany them to the verge of the grave, to create for them during the time of their suffering after death (if it is true that they suffer), an interest in heaven, this his profession must necessarily give him courage. My position is very different. I have not made up my mind upon these subjects. When one can believe frankly in all the Church says, many things become simple, which otherwise cause great difficulty in the mind. The mysterious and wonderful then find their natural place in the course of affairs; but when a man thinks for himself, and has to take everything on his own responsibility, and make all the necessary explanations, there is often great difficulty. So many things will not fit into their places, they straggle like weary men on a march. One cannot put them together, or satisfy one's self.

The sun was shining outside the walls when we re-entered Semur; but the first step we took was into a gloom as black as night, which did not re-assure us, it is unnecessary to say. A chill was in the air, of night and mist. We shivered, not with the nerves only but with the cold. And as all was dark, so all was still. I had expected to feel the presence of those who were there, as I had felt the crowd of the invisible before they entered the city. But the air was vacant, there was nothing but darkness and cold. We went on for a little way with a strange fervour of expectation. At each moment, at each step, it seemed to me that some great call must be made upon my self-possession and courage, some event happen; but there was nothing. All was calm, the houses on either side of the way were open, all but the office of the *octroi* which was black as night with its closed door. M. le Curé has told me since that he believed Them to be there, though unseen. This idea, however, was not in my mind. I had felt the unseen multitude; but here the air was free, there was no one interposing between us, who breathed as men, and the walls that surrounded us. Just within the gate a lamp was burning, hanging to its rope over our heads; and the lights were in the houses as if some one had left them there; they threw a strange glimmer into the darkness, flickering in the wind. By and by as we went on the gloom lessened, and by the time we had reached the Grande Rue, there was a clear steady pale twilight by which we saw everything, as by the light of day.

We stood at the corner of the square and looked round. Although still I heard the beating of my own pulses loudly working in my ears, yet it was less terrible than at first. A city when asleep is wonderful to look on, but in all the closed doors and windows one feels the safety and repose sheltered there which no man can disturb; and the air has in it a sense of life, subdued, yet warm. But here all was open, and all deserted. The house of the miser Grosgain was exposed from the highest to the lowest, but nobody was there to search for what was hidden. The hotel de Bois-Sombre, with its great *porte-cochère*, always so jealously closed; and my own house, which my mother and wife have always guarded so carefully, that damp nor breath of night might enter, had every door and window wide open. Desolation seemed seated in all these empty places. I feared to go into my own dwelling. It seemed to me as if the dead must be lying within. *Bon Dieu*! Not a soul, not a shadow; all vacant in this soft twilight; nothing moving, nothing visible. The great doors of the Cathedral were wide open, and every little entry. How spacious the city looked, how silent, how wonderful! There was room for a squadron to wheel in the great square, but not so much as a bird, not a dog; all pale and empty. We stood for a long time (or it seemed a long time) at the corner, looking right and left. We were afraid to make a step farther. We knew not what to do. Nor could I speak; there was much I wished to say, but something stopped my voice.

At last M. le Curé found utterance. His voice so moved the silence, that at first my heart was faint with fear; it was hoarse, and the sound rolled round the great square like muffled thunder. One did not seem to know what strange faces might rise at the open windows, what terrors might appear. But all he said was, "We are ambassadors in vain."

What was it that followed? My teeth chattered. I could not hear. It was as if "in vain! in vain!" came back in echoes, more and more distant from every opening. They breathed all around us, then were still, then returned louder from beyond the river. M. le Curé, though he is a spiritual person, was no more courageous than I. With one impulse, we put out our hands and grasped each other. We retreated back to back, like men hemmed in by foes, and I felt his heart beating wildly, and he mine. Then silence, silence settled all around.

It was now my turn to speak. I would not be behind, come what might, though my lips were parched with mental trouble.

I said, "Are we indeed too late? Lecamus must have deceived himself."

To this there came no echo and no reply, which would be a relief, you may suppose; but it was not so. It was well-nigh more appalling, more terrible than the sound; for though we spoke thus, we did not believe the place was empty. Those whom we approached seemed to be wrapping themselves in silence, invisible, waiting to speak with some awful purpose when their time came.

There we stood for some minutes, like two children, holding each other's hands, leaning against each other at the corner of the square—as helpless as children, waiting for what should come next. I say it frankly, my brain and my heart were one throb. They plunged and beat so wildly that I could scarcely have heard any other sound. In this respect I think he was more calm. There was on his face that look of intense listening which strains the very soul. But neither he nor I heard anything, not so much as a whisper. At last, "Let us go on," I said. We stumbled as we went, with agitation and fear. We were afraid to turn our backs to those empty houses, which seemed to gaze at us with all their empty windows pale and glaring. Mechanically, scarce knowing what I was doing, I made towards my own house.

There was no one there. The rooms were all open and empty. I went from one to another, with a sense of expectation which made my heart faint; but no one was there, nor anything changed. Yet I do wrong to say that nothing was changed. In my library, where I keep my books, where my father and grandfather conducted their affairs, like me, one little difference struck me suddenly, as if some one had dealt me a blow. The old bureau which my grandfather had used, at which I remember standing by his knee, had been drawn from the corner where I had placed it out of the way (to make room for the furniture I preferred), and replaced, as in old times, in the middle of the room. It was nothing; yet how much was in this! though only myself could have perceived it. Some of the old drawers were open, full of old papers. I glanced over them in my agitation, to see if there might be any writing, any message addressed to me; but there was nothing, nothing but this silent sign of those who has been here. Naturally M. le Curé, who kept watch at the door, was unacquainted with the cause of my emotion. The last room I entered was my wife's. Her veil was lying on the white bed, as if she had gone out that moment, and some of her ornaments were on the table. It seemed to me that the atmosphere of mystery which filled the rest of the house was not here. A ribbon, a little ring, what nothings are these? Yet they make even emptiness sweet. In my Agnès's room there is a little shrine, more sacred to us than any altar. There is the picture of our little Marie. It is covered with a veil, embroidered with needlework which it is a wonder to see. Not always can even Agnès bear to look upon the face of this angel, whom God has taken from her.[1] She has worked the little curtain with lilies, with white and virginal flowers; and no hand, not even mine, ever draws it aside. What did I see? The veil was boldly folded away; the face of the child looked at me across her mother's bed, and upon the frame of the picture was laid a branch of olive, with silvery leaves. I know no more but that I uttered a great cry, and flung myself upon my knees before this angel-gift. What stranger could know what was in my heart? M. le Curé, my friend, my brother, came hastily to me, with a pale countenance; but when he looked at me, he drew back and turned a way his face, and a sob came from his breast. Never child had called him father, were it in heaven, were it on earth. Well I knew whose tender fingers had placed the branch of olive there.

I went out of the room and locked the door. It was just that my wife should find it where it had been laid.

---

1   Many late nineteenth-century middle-class families would memorialize a deceased infant or toddler with an artfully arranged postmortem photograph, called a "sleeping beauty."

I put my arm into his as we went out once more into the street. That moment had made us brother and brother. And this union made us more strong. Besides, the silence and the emptiness began to grow less terrible to us. We spoke in our natural voices as we came out, scarcely knowing how great was the difference between them and the whispers which had been all we dared at first to employ. Yet the sound of these louder tones scared us when we heard them for we were still trembling, not assured of deliverance. It was he who showed himself a man, not I; for my heart was overwhelmed, the tears stood in my eyes, I had no strength to resist my impressions.

"Martin Dupin," he said suddenly, "it is enough. We are frightening ourselves with shadows. We are afraid even of our own voices. This must not be. Enough! Whosoever they were who have been in Semur, their visitation is over, and they are gone."

"I think so," I said faintly; "but God knows." Just then something passed me as sure as ever man passed me. I started back out of the way and dropped my friend's arm, and covered my eyes with my hands. It was nothing that could be seen; it was an air, a breath. M. le Curé looked at me wildly; he was as a man beside himself. He struck his foot upon the pavement and gave a loud and bitter cry.

"Is it delusion?" he said, "O my God! or shall not even this, not even so much as this be revealed to me?"

To see a man who had so ruled himself, who had resisted every disturbance and stood fast when all gave way, moved thus at the very last to cry out with passion against that which had been denied to him, brought me back to myself. How often had I read it in his eyes before! He—the priest—the servant of the unseen—yet to all of us lay persons had that been revealed which was hid from him. A great pity was within me, and gave me strength. "Brother," I said, "We are weak. If we saw heaven opened, could we trust to our vision now? Our imaginations are masters of us. So far as mortal eye can see, we are alone in Semur. Have you forgotten your psalm,[1] and how you sustained us at the first? And now, your Cathedral is open to you, my brother. *Lœtatus sum*,"[2] I said. It was an inspiration from above, and no thought of mine; for it is well known, that though deeply respectful, I have never professed religion. With one impulse we turned, we went together, as in a procession, across the silent *place*, and up the great steps. We said not a word to each other of what we meant to do. All was fair and silent in the holy place; a breath of incense still in

---

1   "I was glad when they said unto me, Let us go into the house of the Lord. Our feet shall stand within the gates, O Jerusalem" (Psalms 122:1–2).
2   I am glad.

the air; a murmur of psalms (as one could imagine) far up in the high roof. There I served, while he said his mass. It was for my friend that this impulse came to my mind; but I was rewarded. The days of my childhood seemed to come back to me. All trouble, and care, and mystery, and pain, seemed left behind. All I could see was the glimmer on the altar of the great candlesticks, the sacred pyx[1] in its shrine, the chalice, and the book. I was again an *enfant de chœur*[2] robed in white, like the angels, no doubt, no disquiet in my Soul—and my father kneeling behind among the faithful, bowing his head, with a sweetness which I too knew, being a father, because it was his child that tinkled the bell and swung the censer. Never since those days have I served the mass. My heart grew soft within me as the heart of a little child. The voice of M. le Curé was full of tears—it swelled out into the air and filled the vacant place. I knelt behind him on the steps of the altar and wept.

Then there came a sound that made our hearts leap in our bosoms. His voice wavered as if it had been struck by a strong wind; but he was a brave man, and he went on. It was the bells of the Cathedral that pealed out over our heads. In the midst of the office, while we knelt all alone, they began to ring as at Easter or some great festival. At first softly, almost sadly, like choirs of distant singers, that died away and were echoed and died again; then taking up another strain, they rang out into the sky with hurrying notes and clang of joy. The effect upon myself was wonderful. I no longer felt any fear. The illusion was complete. I was a child again, serving the mass in my little surplice—aware that all who loved me were kneeling behind, that the good God was smiling, and the Cathedral bells ringing out their majestic Amen.

M. le Curé came down the altar steps when his mass was ended. Together we put away the vestments and the holy vessels. Our hearts were soft; the weight was taken from them. As we came out the bells were dying away in long and low echoes, now faint, now louder, like mingled voices of gladness and regret. And whereas it had been a pale twilight when we entered, the clearness of the day had rolled sweetly in, and now it was fair morning in all the streets. We did not say a word to each other, but arm and arm took our way to the gates, to open to our neighbours, to call all our fellow-citizens back to Semur.

If I record here an incident of another kind, it is because of the sequel that followed. As we passed by the hospital of St. Jean, we heard distinctly, coming from within, the accents of a feeble yet impatient voice. The sound revived for a moment the troubles that were stilled within us—but only for a moment. This was

---

1   The container that holds the consecrated bread of the Eucharist.
2   Choirboy.

no visionary voice. It brought a smile to the grave face of M. le Curé and tempted me well nigh to laughter, so strangely did this sensation of the actual, break and disperse the visionary atmosphere. We went in without any timidity, with a conscious relaxation of the great strain upon us. In a little nook, curtained off from the great ward, lay a sick man upon his bed. "Is it M. le Maire?" he said; "*à la bonne heure!*[1] I have a complaint to make of the nurses for the night. They have gone out to amuse themselves; they take no notice of poor sick people. They have known for a week that I could not sleep; but neither have they given me a sleeping draught, nor endeavoured to distract me with cheerful conversation. And to-day, look you, M. le Maire, not one of the sisters has come near me!"

"Have you suffered, my poor fellow?" I said; but he would not go so far as this.

"I don't want to make complaints, M. le Maire; but the sisters do not come themselves as they used to do. One does not care to have a strange nurse, when one knows that if the sisters did their duty—But if it does not occur any more I do not wish it to be thought that I am the one to complain."

"Do not fear, *Mon ami*," I said. "I will say to the Reverend Mother that you have been left too long alone."

"And listen, M. le Maire," cried the man; "those bells, will they never be done? My head aches with the din they make. How can one go to sleep with all that riot in one's ears?"

We looked at each other, we could not but smile. So that which is joy and deliverance to one is vexation to another. As we went out again into the street the lingering music of the bells died out, and (for the first time for all these terrible days and nights) the great clock struck the hour. And as the clock struck, the last cloud rose like a mist and disappeared in flying vapours, and the full sunshine of noon burst on Semur.

---

1   Just at the right moment!

Chapter Seven

SUPPLEMENT BY M. DE BOIS-SOMBRE

WHEN M. le Maire disappeared within the mist, we all remained behind with troubled hearts. For my own part I was alarmed for my friend. M. Martin Dupin is not noble. He belongs, indeed, to the *haute bourgeoisie*,[1] and all his antecedents are most respectable; but it is his personal character and admirable qualities which justify me in calling him my friend. The manner in which he has performed his duties to his fellow-citizens during this time of distress has been sublime. It is not my habit to take any share in public life; the unhappy circumstances of France[2] have made this impossible for years. Nevertheless, I put aside my scruples when it became necessary, to leave him free for his mission. I gave no opinion upon that mission itself, or how far he was right in obeying the advice of a hare-brained enthusiast like Lecamus. Nevertheless the moment had come at which our banishment had become intolerable. Another day, and I should have proposed an assault upon the place. Our dead forefathers, though I would speak of them with every respect, should not presume upon their privilege. I do not pretend to be braver than other men, nor have I shown myself more equal than others to cope with the present emergency. But I have the impatience of my countrymen, and rather than rot here outside the gates, parted from Madame de Bois-Sombre and my children, who, I am happy to state, are in safety at the country house of the brave Dupin, I should have dared any hazard. This being the case, a new step of any kind called for my approbation, and I could not refuse under the circumstances—especially as no ceremony of installation was required or profession of loyalty to one government or another—to take upon me the office of coadjutor and act as deputy for my friend Martin outside the walls of Semur.

The moment at which I assumed the authority was one of great discouragement and depression. The men were tired to death. Their minds were worn out as well as their bodies. The excitement and fatigue had been more than they could bear. Some were for giving up the contest and seeking new homes for themselves. These were they, I need not remark, who had but little to lose; some seemed to care for nothing

---

1 Upper middle class.
2 The defeat of Napoleon III in 1870 by the Prussians, the subsequent collapse of the Second Empire in France, and the emergence and then brutal suppression of the revolutionary Paris Commune in 1871.

but to lie down and rest. Though it produced a great movement among us when Lecamus suddenly appeared coming out of the city; and the undertaking of Dupin and the excellent Curé was viewed with great interest, yet there could not but be signs apparent that the situation had lasted too long. It was *tendu*[1] in the strongest degree, and when that is the case a reaction must come. It is impossible to say, for one thing, how great was our personal discomfort. We were as soldiers campaigning without a commissariat, or any precautions taken for our welfare; no food save what was sent to us from La Clairière and other places; no means of caring for our personal appearance, in which lies so much of the materials of self-respect. I say nothing of the chief features of all—the occupation of our homes by others—the forcible expulsion of which we had been the objects. No one could have been more deeply impressed than myself at the moment of these extraordinary proceedings; but we cannot go on with one monotonous impression, however serious, we other Frenchmen. Three days is a very long time to dwell in one thought; I myself had become impatient, I do not deny. To go away, which would have been very natural, and which Agathe proposed, was contrary to my instincts and interests both. I trust I can obey the logic of circumstances as well as another; but to yield is not easy, and to leave my hotel[2] at Semur—now the chief residence, alas! of the Bois-Sombres—probably to the licence of a mob—for one can never tell at what moment Republican institutions may break down and sink back into the chaos from which they arose—was impossible. Nor would I forsake the brave Dupin without the strongest motive; but that the situation was extremely *tendu,* and a reaction close at hand, was beyond dispute.

I resisted the movement which my excellent friend made to take off and transfer to me his scarf of office. These things are much thought of among the bourgeoisie. "*Mon ami*," I said, "you cannot tell what use you may have for it; whereas our townsmen know me, and that I am not one to take up an unwarrantable position." We then accompanied him to the neighbourhood of the Porte St. Lambert. It was at that time invisible; we could but judge approximately. My men were unwilling to approach too near, neither did I myself think it necessary. We parted, after giving the two envoys an honourable escort, leaving a clear space between us and the darkness. To see them disappear gave us all a startling sensation. Up to the last moment I had doubted whether they would obtain admittance. When they disappeared from our eyes, there came upon all of us an impulse of alarm. I myself was so far moved by it, that I called out after them in a sudden panic. For if any catastrophe had happened, how could I ever

---

1 Tense.
2 Town mansion.

have forgiven myself, especially as Madame Dupin de la Clairière, a person entirely *comme il faut*,[1] and of the most distinguished character, went after her husband, with a touching devotion, following him to the very edge of the darkness? I do not think, so deeply possessed was he by his mission, that he saw her. Dupin is very determined in his way; but he is imaginative and thoughtful, and it is very possible that, as he required all his powers to brace him for this enterprise, he made it a principle neither to look to the right hand nor the left. When we paused, and following after our two representatives, Madame Dupin stepped forth, a thrill ran through us all. Some would have called to her, for I heard many broken exclamations; but most of us were too much startled to speak. We thought nothing less than that she was about to risk herself by going after them into the city. If that was her intention—and nothing is more probable; for women are very daring, though they are timid—she was stopped, it is most likely, by that curious inability to move a step farther which we have all experienced. We saw her pause, clasp her hands in despair (or it might be in token of farewell to her husband), then, instead of returning, seat herself on the road on the edge of the darkness. It was a relief to all who were looking on to see her there.

In the reaction after that excitement I found myself in face of a great difficulty—what to do with my men, to keep them from demoralization. They were greatly excited; and yet there was nothing to be done for them, for myself, for any of us, but to wait. To organise the patrol again, under the circumstances, would have been impossible. Dupin, perhaps, might have tried it with the *bourgeois* determination which so often carries its point in spite of all higher intelligence; but to me, who have not this commonplace way of looking at things, it was impossible. The worthy soul did not think in what a difficulty he left us. That intolerable, good-for-nothing Jacques Richard (whom Dupin protects unwisely, I cannot tell why), and who was already half-seas-over,[2] had drawn several of his comrades with him towards the *cabaret*, which was always a danger to us. "We will drink success to M. le Maire," he said, "*mes bons amis*! That can do no one any harm; and as we have spoken up, as we have empowered him to offer handsome terms, to *Messieurs les Morts*—"

It was intolerable. Precisely at the moment when our fortune hung in the balance, and when, perhaps, an indiscreet word—"Arrest that fellow," I said. "Riou, you are an official; you understand your duty. Arrest him on the spot, and confine him in the tent out of the way of mischief. Two of you mount guard over him. And let a

---

1 Proper.
2 British slang for "drunk."

party be told off, of which you will take the command, Louis Bertin, to go at once to La Clairière and beg the Reverend Mothers of the hospital to favour us with their presence. It will be well to have those excellent ladies in our front whatever happens; and you may communicate to them the unanimous decision about their chapel. You Robert Lemaire, with an escort, will proceed to the *campagne*[1] of M. Barbou, and put him in possession of the circumstances. Those of you who have a natural wish to seek a little repose will consider yourselves as discharged from duty and permitted to do so. Your Maire having confided to me his authority—not without your consent—(this I avow I added with some difficulty, for who cared for their assent? But a Republican Government offers a premium to every insincerity), I wait with confidence to see these dispositions carried out."

This, I am happy to say, produced the best effect. They obeyed me without hesitation; and, fortunately for me, slumber seized upon the majority. Had it not been for this, I can scarcely tell how I should have got out of it. I felt drowsy myself, having been with the patrol the greater part of the night; but to yield to such weakness was, in my position, of course impossible.

This, then, was our attitude during the last hours of suspense, which were perhaps the most trying of all. In the distance might be seen the little bands marching towards La Clairière, on one side, and M. Barbou's country-house ("La Corbeille des Raisins")[2] on the other. It goes without saying that I did not want M. Barbou, but it was the first errand I could think of. Towards the city, just where the darkness began that enveloped it, sat Madame Dupin. That *sainte-femme*[3] was praying for her husband, who could doubt? And under the trees, wherever they could find a favourable spot, my men lay down on the grass, and most of them fell asleep. My eyes were heavy enough, but responsibility drives away rest. I had but one nap of five minutes' duration, leaning against a tree, when it occurred to me that Jacques Richard, whom I sent under escort half-drunk to the tent, was not the most admirable companion for that poor visionary Lecamus, who had been accommodated there. I roused myself, therefore, though unwillingly, to see whether these two, so discordant, could agree.

I met Lecamus at the tent-door. He was coming out, very feeble and tottering, with that dazed look which (according to me) has always been characteristic of him. He had a bundle of papers in his hand. He had been setting in order his report of what had happened to him, to be submitted to the Maire. "Monsieur," he said, with

---

1   Country house.
2   The Basket of Grapes.
3   Saintly woman.

some irritation (which I forgave him), "you have always been unfavourable to me. I owe it to you that this unhappy drunkard has been sent to disturb me in my feebleness and the discharge of a public duty."

"My good Monsieur Lecamus," said I, "you do my recollection too much honour. The fact is, I had forgotten all about you and your public duty. Accept my excuses. Though indeed your supposition that I should have taken the trouble to annoy you, and your description of that good-for-nothing as an unhappy drunkard, are signs of intolerance which I should not have expected in a man so favoured."

This speech, though too long, pleased me, for a man of this species, a revolutionary (are not all visionaries revolutionaries?) is always, when occasion offers, to be put down. He disarmed me, however, by his humility. He gave a look round. "Where can I go?" he said, and there was pathos in his voice. At length he perceived Madame Dupin sitting almost motionless on the road. "Ah!" he said, "there is my place." The man, I could not but perceive, was very weak. His eyes were twice their natural size, his face was the colour of ashes; through his whole frame there was a trembling; the papers shook in his hand. A compunction seized my mind: I regretted to have sent that piece of noise and folly to disturb a poor man so suffering and weak. "Monsieur Lecamus," I said, "forgive me. I acknowledge that it was inconsiderate. Remain here in comfort, and I will find for this unruly fellow another place of confinement."

"Nay," he said, "there is my place," pointing to where Madame Dupin sat. I felt disposed for a moment to indulge in a pleasantry, to say that I approved his taste; but on second thoughts I forebore. He went tottering slowly across the broken ground, hardly able to drag himself along. "Has he had any refreshment?" I asked of one of the women who were about. They told me yes, and this restored my composure; for after all I had not meant to annoy him, I had forgotten he was there—a trivial fault in circumstances so exciting. I was more easy in my mind, however, I confess it, when I saw that he had reached his chosen position safely. The man looked so weak. It seemed to me that he might have died on the road.

I thought I could almost perceive the gate, with Madame Dupin seated under the battlements, her charming figure relieved against the gloom, and that poor Lecamus lying, with his papers fluttering at her feet. This was the last thing I was conscious of.

Chapter Eight

EXTRACT FROM THE NARRATIVE OF MADAME DUPIN DE LA CLAIRIÉRE (née DE CHAMPFLEURIE)

I WENT with my husband to the city gate. I did not wish to distract his mind from what he had undertaken, therefore I took care he should not see me; but to follow close, giving the sympathy of your whole heart, must not that be a support? If I am asked whether I was content to let him go, I cannot answer yes; but had another than Martin been chosen, I could not have borne it. What I desired, was to go myself. I was not afraid: and if it had proved dangerous, if I had been broken and crushed to pieces between the seen and the unseen, one could not have had a more beautiful fate. It would have made me happy to go. But perhaps it was better that the messenger should not be a woman; they might have said it was delusion, an attack of the nerves. We are not trusted in these respects, though I find it hard to tell why.

But I went with Martin to the gate. To go as far as was possible, to be as near as possible, that was something. If there had been room for me to pass, I should have gone, and with such gladness! for God He knows that to help to thrust my husband into danger, and not share it, was terrible to me. But no; the invisible line was still drawn, beyond which I could not stir. The door opened before him, and closed upon me. But though to see him disappear into the gloom was anguish, yet to know that he was the man by whom the city should be saved was sweet. I sat down on the spot where my steps were stayed. It was close to the wall, where there is a ledge of stonework round the basement of the tower. There I sat down to wait till he should come again.

If any one thinks, however, that we, who were under the shelter of the roof of La Clairière were less tried than our husbands, it is a mistake; our chief grief was that we were parted from them, not knowing what suffering, what exposure they might have to bear, and knowing that they would not accept, as most of us were willing to accept, the interpretation of the mystery; but there was a certain comfort in the fact that we had to be very busy, preparing a little food to take to them, and feeding the others. La Clairière is a little country house, not a great château, and it was taxed to the utmost to afford some covert to the people. The children were all sheltered and cared for; but as for the rest of us we did as we could. And how gay they were, all the little ones! What was it to them all that had happened? It was a fête for them to be in the country, to be so many together, to run in the fields and the gardens. Sometimes their laughter and their happiness were more than we could bear. Agathe de Bois-Sombre, who takes life hardly, who is more easily deranged than I, was one who was much disturbed by this. But was it not to preserve the children that we were commanded to go to La Clairière? Some of the women also were not easy to bear with. When they were put into our rooms they too found it a fête, and sat down among the children, and ate and drank, and forgot what it was; what awful reason had driven us out of our homes. These were not, oh let no one think so! the majority; but there were some, it cannot be denied; and it was difficult for me to calm down Bonne Maman, and keep her from sending them away with their babes. "But they are *misérables*," she said. "If they were to wander and be lost, if they were to suffer as thou sayest, where would be the harm? I have no patience with the idle, with those who impose upon thee." It is possible that Bonne Maman was right—but what then? "Preserve the children and the sick," was the mission that had been given to me. My own room was made the hospital. Nor did this please Bonne Maman. She bid me if I did not stay in it myself to give it to the Bois-Sombres, to some who deserved it. But is it not they who need most who deserve most? Bonne Maman cannot bear that the poor and wretched should live in her Martin's chamber. He is my Martin no less. But to give it up to our Lord is not that to sanctify it? There are [those] who have put Him into their own bed when they imagined they were but sheltering a sick beggar there; that He should have the best was sweet to me: and could not I pray all the better that our Martin should be enlightened, should come to the true sanctuary? When I said this Bonne Maman wept. It was the grief of her heart that Martin thought otherwise than as we do. Nevertheless she said, "He is so good; the *bon Dieu* knows how good he is;" as if even his mother could know that so well as I!

But with the women and the children crowding everywhere, the sick in my chamber, the helpless in every corner, it will be seen that we, too, had much to do. And our hearts were elsewhere, with those who were watching the city, who were face to face with those in whom they had not believed. We were going and coming all day long with food for them, and there never was a time of the night or day that there were not many of us watching on the brow of the hill to see if any change came in Semur. Agathe and I, and our children, were all together in one little room. She believed in God, but it was not any comfort to her; sometimes she would weep and pray all day long; sometimes entreat her husband to abandon the city, to go elsewhere and live, and fly from this strange fate. She is one who cannot endure to be unhappy—not to have what she wishes. As for me, I was brought up in poverty and it is no wonder if I can more easily submit. She was not willing that I should come this morning to Semur. In the night the Mère Julie[1] had roused us, saying she had seen a procession of angels coming to restore us to the city. Ah! to those who have no knowledge it is easy to speak of processions of angels. But to those who have seen what an angel is—how they flock upon us unawares in the darkness, so that one is confused, and scarce can tell if it is reality or a dream; to those who have heard a little voice soft as the dew coming out of heaven! I said to them—for all were in a great tumult—that the angels do not come in processions, they steal upon us unaware, they reveal themselves in the soul. But they did not listen to me; even Agathe took pleasure in hearing of the revelation. As for me, I had denied myself, I had not seen Martin for a night and a day. I took one of the great baskets, and I went with the women who were the messengers for the day. A purpose formed itself in my heart, it was to make my way into the city, I know not how, and implore them to have pity upon us before the people were distraught. Perhaps, had I been able to refrain from speaking to Martin, I might have found the occasion I wished; but how could I conceal my desire from my husband? And now all is changed, I am rejected and he is gone. He was more worthy. Bonne Maman is right. Our good God, who is our father, does He require that one should make profession of faith, that all should be alike? He sees the heart; and to choose my Martin, does not that prove that He loves best that which is best, not I, or a priest, or one who makes professions? Thus, I sat down at the gate with a great confidence, though also a trembling in my heart. He who had known how to choose him among all the others, would not He guard him? It was a proof to me once again that heaven is true, that the good God loves and comprehends us all, to see how His wisdom, which is unerring, had chosen the best man in Semur.

And M. le Curé, that goes without saying, he is a priest of priests, a true servant of God.

I saw my husband go: perhaps, God knows, into danger, perhaps to some encounter such as might fill the world with awe—to meet those who read the thought in your mind before it comes to your lips. Well! there is no thought in Martin that is not noble and true. Me, I have follies in my heart, every kind of folly; but he!—the tears came in a flood to my eyes, but I would not shed them, as if I were weeping for fear and sorrow—no—but for happiness to know that falsehood was not in him. My little Marie, a holy virgin, may look into her father's heart—I do not fear the test.

---

1 Mother, used here in the sense of "village matriarch."

The sun came warm to my feet as I sat on the foundation of our city, but the projection of the tower gave me a little shade. All about was a great peace. I thought of the psalm which say, "He will give it to His beloved sleeping"[1]—that is true; but always there are some who are used as instruments, who are not permitted to sleep. The sounds that came from the people gradually ceased; they were all very quiet. M. de Bois-Sombre I saw at a distance making his dispositions. Then M. Paul Lecamus, whom I had long known, came up across the field, and seated himself close to me upon the road. I have always had a great sympathy with him since the death of his wife; ever since there has been an abstraction in his eyes, a look of desolation. He has no children or any one to bring him back to life. Now, it seemed to me that he had the air of a man who was dying. He had been in the city while all of us had been outside.

"Monsieur Lecamus," I said, "you look very ill, and this is not a place for you. Could not I take you somewhere, where you might be more at ease?"

"It is true, Madame," he said, "the road is hard, but the sunshine is sweet; and when I have finished what I am writing for M. le Maire, it will be over. There will be no more need—"

I did not understand what he meant. I asked him to let me help him, but he shook his head. His eyes were very hollow, in great caves, and his face was the colour of ashes. Still he smiled. "I thank you, Madame," he said, "infinitely; everyone knows that Madame Dupin is kind; but when it is done, I shall be free."

"I am sure, M. Lecamus, that my husband—that M. le Maire—would not wish you to trouble yourself, to be hurried—"

"No," he said, "not he, but I. Who else could write what I have to write? It must be done while it is day."

"Then there is plenty of time, M. Lecamus. All the best of the day is yet to come; it is still morning. If you could but get as far as La Clairière. There we would nurse you—restore you."

He shook his head. "You have enough on your hands at La Clairière," he said; and then, leaning upon the stones, he began to write again with his pencil. After a time, when he stopped, I ventured to ask—"Monsieur Lecamus, is it, indeed, Those—whom we have known, who are in Semur?"

He turned his dim eyes upon me. "Does Madame Dupin," he said, "require to ask?"

---

1   "It is vain for you to rise up early, to sit up late, to eat the bread of sorrows: for so he giveth his beloved sleep" (Psalms 127:2).

"No, no. It is true. I have seen and heard. But yet, when a little time passes, you know? one wonders; one asks one's self, was it dream?"

"That is what I fear," he said. "I, too, if life went on, might ask, notwithstanding all that has occurred to me, Was it a dream?"

"M. Lecamus, you will forgive me if I hurt you. You saw—her?"

"No. Seeing—what is seeing? It is but a vulgar sense, it is not all; but I sat at her feet. She was with me. We were one, as of old—." A gleam of strange light came into his dim eyes. "Seeing is not everything, Madame."

"No, M. Lecamus. I heard the dear voice of my little Marie."

"Nor is hearing everything," he said hastily. "Neither did she speak; but she was there. We were one; we had no need to speak. What is speaking or hearing when heart wells into heart? For a very little moment, only for a moment, Madame Dupin."

I put out my hand to him; I could not say a word. How was it possible that she could go away again, and leave him so feeble, so worn, alone?

"Only a very little moment," he said, slowly. "There were other voices—but not hers. I think I am glad it was in the spirit we met, she and I—I prefer not to see her till—after—"

"Oh, M. Lecamus, I am too much of the world! To see them, to hear them—it is for this I long."

"No, dear Madame. I would not have it till—after—. But I Must make haste, I must write, I hear the hum approaching—"

I could not tell what he meant; but I asked no more. How still everything was! The people lay asleep on the grass, and, I, too, was overwhelmed by the great quiet. I do not know if I slept, but I dreamed. I saw a child very fair and tall always near me, but hiding her face. It appeared to me in my dream that all I wished for was to see this hidden countenance, to know her name; and that I followed and watched her, but for a long time in vain. All at once she turned full upon me, held out her arms to me. Do I need to say who it was? I cried out in my dream to the good God, that He had done well to take her from me—that this was worth it all. Was it a dream? I would not give that dream for years of waking life. Then I started and came back, in a moment, to the still morning sunshine, the sight of the men asleep, the roughness of the wall against which I leant. Some one laid a hand on mine. I opened my eyes, not knowing what it was—if it might be my husband coming back, or her whom I had seen in my dream. It was M. Lecamus. He had risen up upon his knees—his papers were all laid aside. His eyes in those hollow caves were opened wide, and quivering with a strange light. He had caught my wrist with his worn hand. "Listen!" he said;

his voice fell to a whisper; a light broke over his face, "Listen!" he cried; "they are coming." While he thus grasped my wrist, holding up his weak and wavering body in that strained attitude, the moments passed very slowly. I was afraid of him, of his worn face and thin hands, and the wild eagerness about him. I am ashamed to say it, but so it was. And for this reason it seemed long to me, though I think not more than a minute, till suddenly the bells rang out, sweet and glad as they ring at Easter for the resurrection. There had been ringing of bells before, but not like this. With a start and universal movement the sleeping men got up from where they lay—not one but every one, coming out of the little hollows and from under the trees as if from graves. They all sprang up to listen, with one impulse; and as for me, knowing that Martin was in the City, can it be wondered at if my heart beat so loud that I was incapable of thought of others! What brought me to myself was the strange weight of M. Lecamus on my arm. He put his other hand upon me, all cold in the brightness, all trembling. He raised himself thus slowly to his feet. When I looked at him I shrieked aloud. I forgot all else. His face was transformed—a smile came upon it that was ineffable—the light blazed up, and then quivered and flickered in his eyes like a dying flame. All this time he was leaning his weight upon my arm. Then suddenly he loosed his hold of me, stretched out his hands, stood up, and—died. My God! shall I ever forget him as he stood—his head raised, his hands held out, his lips moving, the eyelids opened wide with a quiver, the light flickering and dying! He died first, standing up, saying something with his pale lips—then fell. And it seemed to me all at once, and for a moment, that I heard a sound of many people marching past, the murmur and hum of a great multitude; and softly, softly I was put out of the way, and a voice said, "*Adieu, ma sœur,*"[1] "*Ma sœur!*" Who called me "*Ma sœur*"? I have no sister. I cried out, saying I know not what. They told me after that I wept and wrung my hands, and said, "Not thee, not thee, Marie!" But after that I knew no more.

---

1   Farewell, my sister.

Chapter Nine

THE NARRATIVE OF MADAME VEUVE[1] DUPIN (née LEPELLETIER)

To complete the *Procés verbal*,[2] my son wishes me to give my account of the things which happened out of Semur during its miraculous occupation, as it is his desire, in the interests of truth, that nothing should be left out. In this I fine a great difficulty for many reasons; in the first place, because I have not the aptitude of expressing myself in writing, and it may well be that the phrases I employ may fail in the correctness which good French requires; and again, because it is my misfortune not to agree in all points with my Martin, though I am proud to think that he is, in every relation of life, so good a man, that the women of his family need not hesitate to follow his advice—but necessarily there are some points which one reserves; and I cannot but feel the closeness of the connection between the late remarkable exhibition of the power of Heaven and the outrage done upon the good Sisters of St. Jean by the administration, of which unfortunately my son is at the head. I say unfortunately, since it is the spirit of independence and pride in him which has resisted all the warnings offered by Divine Providence, and which refuses even now to right the wrongs of the Sisters of St. Jean; though, if it may be permitted to me to say it, as his mother, it was very fortunate in the late troubles that Martin Dupin found himself at the head of the Commune of Semur—since who else could have kept his self-control as he did?—caring for all things and forgetting nothing; who else would, with so much courage, have entered the city? and what other man, being a person of the world and secular in all his thoughts, as, alas! it is so common for men to be, would have so nobly acknowledged his obligations to the good God when our misfortunes were over? My constant prayers for his conversion do not make me incapable of perceiving the nobility of his conduct. When the evidence has been incontestable he has not hesitated to make a public profession of his gratitude, which all will acknowledge to be the sign of a truly noble mind and a heart of gold.

I have long felt that the times were ripe for some exhibition of the power of God. Things have been going very badly among us. Not only have the powers of darkness

---

1 Widow.
2 Verbal record.

triumphed over our holy church, in a manner ever to be wept and mourned by all the faithful, and which might have been expected to bring down fire from Heaven upon our heads, but the corruption of popular manners (as might also have been expected) has been daily arising to a pitch unprecedented. The fêtes[1] may indeed be said to be observed, but in what manner? In the cabarets rather than in the churches; and as for the fasts and the vigils, who thinks of them? Who attends to those sacred moments of penitence? Scarcely even a few ladies are found to do so, instead of the whole population, as in duty bound. I have even seen it happen that my daughter-in-law and myself, and her friend Madame de Bois-Sombre, and old Mère Julie from the market, have formed the whole congregation. Figure to yourself the *bon Dieu* and all the blessed saints looking down from heaven to hear—four persons only in our great Cathedral! I trust that I know that the good God does not despise even two or three; but if any one will think of it—the great bells rung, and the candles lighted, and the curé in his beautiful robes, and all the companies of heaven looking on—and only us four! This shows the neglect of all sacred ordinances that was in Semur. While, on the other hand, what grasping there was for money; what fraud and deceit; what foolishness and dissipation! Even the Mère Julie herself, though a devout person, the pears she sold to us on the last market day before these events, were far, very far, as she must have known, from being satisfactory. In the same way Gros-Jean, though a peasant from our own village near La Clairière, and a man for whom we have often done little services, attempted to impose upon me about the wood for the winter's use, the very night before these occurrences. "It is enough," I cried out, "to bring the dead out of their graves." I did not know—the holy saints forgive me!—how near it was to the moment when this should come true.

And perhaps it is well that I should admit without concealment that I am not one of the women to whom it has been given to see those who came back. There are moments when I will not deny I have asked myself why those others should have been so privileged and never I. Not even in a dream do I see those whom I have lost; yet I think that I too have loved them as well as any have been loved. I have stood by their beds to the last; I have closed their beloved eyes. *Mon Dieu! Mon Dieu!* Have not I drunk of that cup to the dregs?[2] But never to me, never to me, has it been permitted either to see or to hear. *Bien!*[3] It has been so ordered. Agnès, my daughter-in-law, is a good woman. I have not a word to say against her; and if there are moments when

---
1 Feast days.
2 "Awake, awake, stand up, O Jerusalem, which hast drunk at the hand of the Lord the cup of his fury; thou hast drunken the dregs of the cup of trembling, and wrung them out" (Isaiah 51:17).
3 Well!

my heart rebels, when I ask myself why she should have her eyes opened and not I, the good God knows that I do not complain against His will—it is in His hand to do as He pleases. And if I receive no privileges, yet have I the privilege which is best, which is, as M. le Curé justly observes, the highest of all—that of doing my duty. In this I thank the good Lord our Seigneur that my Martin has never needed to be ashamed of his mother.

I will also admit that when it was first made apparent to me—not by the sounds of voices which the others heard, but by the use of my reason which I humbly believe is also a gift of God—that the way in which I could best serve both those of the city and my son Martin, who is over them, was to lead the way with the children and all the helpless to La Clairière, thus relieving the watchers, there was for a time a great struggle in my bosom. What were they all to me, that I should desert my Martin, my only son, the child of my old age; he who is as his father, as dear, and yet more dear, because he is his father's son? "What! (I said in my heart) abandon thee, my child? nay, rather abandon life and every consolation; for what is life to me but thee?" But while my heart swelled with this cry, suddenly it became apparent to me how many there were holding up their hands helplessly to him, clinging to him so that he could not move. To whom else could they turn? He was the one among all who preserved his courage, who neither feared nor failed. When those voices rang out from the walls—which some understood, but which I did not understand, and many more with me—though my heart was wrung with straining my ears to listen if there was not a voice for me too, yet at the same time this thought was working in my heart. There was a poor woman close to me with little children clinging to her; neither did she know what those voices said. Her eyes turned from Semur, all lost in the darkness, to the sky above us and to me beside her, all confused and bewildered; and the children clung to her, all in tears, crying with that wail which is endless—the trouble of childhood which does not know why it is troubled. "Maman! Maman!" they cried "let us go home." "Oh! be silent, my little ones," said the poor woman; "be silent; we will go to M. le Maire—he will not leave us without a friend." It was then that I saw what my duty was. But it was with a pang—*bon Dieu!*—when I turned my back upon my Martin, when I went away to shelter, to peace, leaving my son thus in face of an offended Heaven and all the invisible powers, do you suppose it was a whole heart I carried in my breast? But no! it was nothing save a great ache—a struggle as of death. But what of that? I had my duty to do, as he had—and as he did not flinch, so did not I; otherwise he would have been ashamed of his mother—and I? I Should have felt that the blood was not mine which ran in his veins.

No one can tell what it was, that march to La Clairière. Agnès first was like an angel. I hope I always do Madame Martin justice. She is a saint. She is good to the bottom of her heart. Nevertheless, with those natures which are enthusiast—which are upborne by excitement—there is also a weakness. Though she was brave as the holy Pucelle[1] when we set out, after a while she flagged like another. The colour went out of her face, and though she smiled still, yet the tears came to her eyes, and she would have wept with the other women, and with the wail of the weary children, and all the agitation, and the weariness, and the length of the way, had not I recalled her to herself. "Courage!" I said to her. "Courage, *ma fille!*[2] We will throw open all the chambers. I will give up even that one in which my Martin Dupin, the father of thy husband, died." "*Ma mère,*"[3] she said, holding my hand to her bosom, "he is not dead—he is in Semur." Forgive me, dear Lord! It gave me a pang that she could see him and not I. "For me," I cried, "It is enough to know that my good man is in heaven: his room, which I have kept sacred, shall be given up to the poor." But oh! the confusion of the stumbling, weary feet; the little children that dropped by the way, and caught at our skirts, and wailed and sobbed; the poor mothers with babes upon each arm, with sick hearts and failing limbs. One cry seemed to rise round us as we went, each infant moving the others to sympathy, till it rose like one breath, a wail of "*Maman! Maman!*"[4] a cry that had no meaning, through having so much meaning. It was difficult not to cry out too in the excitement, in the labouring of the long, long, confused, and tedious way. "*Maman! Maman!*" The Holy Mother could not but hear it. It is not possible but that she must have looked out upon us, and heard us, so helpless as we were, where she sits in heaven.

When we got to La Clairière we were ready to sink down with fatigue like all the rest—nay, even more than the rest, for we were not used to it, and for my part I had altogether lost the habitude of long walks. But then you could see what Madame Martin was. She is slight and fragile and pale, not strong, as any one can perceive; but she rose above the needs of the body. She was the one among us who rested not. We threw open all the rooms, and the poor people thronged in. Old Léontine, who is the *garde*[5] of the house, gazed upon us and the crowd whom we brought with us with great eyes full of fear and trouble. "But, Madame," she cried, "Madame!"

---

1   "The Maid," the sobriquet of Saint Joan of Arc (ca.1412–1431), national heroine of France who led the French armies against the English in the Hundred Years War.
2   My daughter.
3   My mother.
4   Mommy! Mommy!
5   Caretaker, keeper.

following me as I went above to the better rooms. She pulled me by my robe. She pushed the poor women with their children away. "*Allez donc, allez!*[1]—rest outside till these ladies have time to speak to you," she said; and pulled me by my sleeve. Then "Madame Martin is putting all this *canaille*[2] into our very chambers," she cried. She had always distrusted Madame Martin, who was taken by the peasants for a clerical and *dévote*,[3] because she was noble. "The *bon Dieu* be praised that Madame also is here, who has sense and will regulate everything." "These are no *canaille*," I said: "be silent, *ma bonne* Léontine, here is something which you cannot understand. This is Semur which has come out to us for lodging." She let the keys drop out of her hands. It was not wonderful if she was amazed. All day long she followed me about, her very mouth open with wonder. "Madame Martin, that understands itself," she would say. "She is romanesque—she has imagination—but Madame, Madame has *bon sens*[4]—who would have believed it of Madame?" Léontine had been my *femme de ménage*[5] long before there was a Madame Martin, when my son was young; and naturally it was of me she still thought. But I cannot put down all the trouble we had ere we found shelter for every one. We filled the stables and the great barn, and all the cottages near; and to get them food, and to have something provided for those who were watching before the city, and who had no one but us to think of them, was a task which was almost beyond our powers. Truly it was beyond our powers—but the Holy Mother of heaven and the good angels helped us. I cannot tell to any one how it was accomplished, yet it was accomplished. The wail of the little ones ceased. They slept that first night as if they had been in heaven. As for us, when the night came, and the dews and the darkness, it seemed to us as if we were out of our bodies, so weary were we, so weary that we could not rest. From La Clairière on ordinary occasions it is a beautiful sight to see the lights of Semur shining in all the high windows, and the streets throwing up a faint whiteness upon the sky; but how strange it was now to look down and see nothing but a darkness—a cloud, which was the city! The lights of the watchers in their camp were invisible to us,—they were so small and low upon the broken ground that we could not see them. Our Agnès crept close to me; we went with one accord to the seat before the door. We did not say "I will go," but went by one impulse, for our hearts were there; and we were glad to taste the freshness of the night and be silent after all our labours. We leant upon each other in

---

1 Go, then, go!
2 Riffraff.
3 Enthusiast, in the religious sense of the word.
4 Good sense.
5 Housekeeper.

our weariness. "*Ma mère*," she said, "where is he now, our Martin?" and wept. "He is where there is the most to do, be thou sure of that," I cried, but wept not. For what did I bring him into the world but for this end?

Were I to go day by day and hour by hour over that time of trouble, the story would not please any one. Many were brave and forgot their own sorrows to occupy themselves with those of others, but many also were not brave. There were those among us who murmured and complained. Some would contend with us to let them go and call their husbands, and leave the miserable country where such things could happen. Some would rave against the priests and the government, and some against those who neglected and offended the Holy Church. Among them there were those who did not hesitate to say it was our fault, though how we were answerable they could not tell. We were never at any time of the day or night without a sound of some one weeping or bewailing herself, as if she were the only sufferer, or crying out against those who had brought her here, far from all her friends. By times it seemed to me that I could bear it no longer, that it was but justice to turn those murmurers (*pleureuses*) away, and let them try what better they could do for themselves. But in this point Madame Martin surpassed me. I do not grudge to say it. She was better than I was, for she was more patient. She wept with the weeping women, then dried her eyes and smiled upon them without a thought of anger—whereas I could have turned them to the door. One thing, however, which I could not away with, was that Agnès filled her own chamber with the poorest of the poor. "How," I cried, "thyself and thy friend Madame de Bois-Sombre, were you not enough to fill it, that you should throw open that chamber to good-for-nothings, to *va-nu-pieds*,[1] to the very rabble?" "*Ma mère*," said Madame Martin, "our good Lord died for them." "And surely for thee too, thou *saint-imbécile*!"[2] I cried out in my indignation. What, my Martin's chamber which he had adorned for his bride! I was beside myself. And they have an obstinacy these enthusiasts! But for that matter her friend Madame de Bois-Sombre thought the same. She would have been one of the *pleureuses* herself had it not been for shame. "Agnès wishes to aid the *bon Dieu*, Madame," she said, "to make us suffer still a little more." The tone in which she spoke, and the contraction in her forehead, as if our hospitality was not enough for her, turned my heart again to my daughter-in-law. "You have reason, Madame," I cried; "there are indeed many ways in which Agnès does the work of the good God." The Bois-Sombres are poor, they have not a roof to shelter them save that of the old *hôtel* in Semur, from

---

1 Ragamuffins—literally, "those who go barefoot."
2 Saintly fool.

whence they were sent forth like the rest of us. And she and her children owed all to Agnès. Figure to yourself then my resentment when this lady directed her scorn at my daughter-in-law. I am not myself noble, though of the *haute bourgeoisie*, which some people think a purer race.

Long and terrible were the days we spent in this suspense. For ourselves it was well that there was so much to do—the food to provide for all this multitude, the little children to care for, and to prepare the provisions for our men who were before Semur. I was in the Ardennes[1] during the war,[2] and I saw some of its perils—but these were nothing to what we encountered now. It is true that my son Martin was not in the war, which made it very different to me; but here the dangers were such as we could not understand, and they weighed upon our spirits. The seat at the door, and that point where the road turned, where there was always so beautiful a view of the valley and of the town of Semur—were constantly occupied by groups of poor people gazing at the darkness in which their homes lay. It was strange to see them, some kneeling and praying with moving lips; some taking but one look, not able to endure the sight. I was of these last. From time to time, whenever I had a moment I came out, I know not why, to see if there was any change. But to gaze upon that altered prospect for hours, as some did, would have been intolerable to me. I could not linger nor try to imaging what might be passing there, either among those who were within (as was believed), or those who were without the walls. Neither could I pray as many did. My devotions of every day I will never, I trust, forsake or forget, and that my Martin was always in my mind is it needful to say? But to go over and over all the vague fears that were in me, and all those thoughts which would have broken my heart had they been put into words, I could not do this even to the good Lord Himself. When I suffered myself to think, my heart grew sick, my head swam round, the light went from my eyes. They are happy who can do so, who can take the *bon Dieu* into their confidence, and say all to Him; but me, I could not do it. I could not dwell upon that which was so terrible, upon my home abandoned, my son—Ah? now that it is past, it is still terrible to think of. And then it was all I was capable of, to trust my God and do what was set before me. God, He knows what it is we can do and what we cannot. I could not tell even to Him all the terror and the misery and the darkness there was in me; but I put my faith in Him. It was all of which I was capable. We are not made alike, neither in the body nor in the soul.

---

1 Forested region in northeastern France and Belgium.
2 Franco-Prussian War.

And there were many women like me at La Clairière. When we had done each piece of work we would look out with a kind of hope, then go back to find something else to do—not looking at each other, not saying a word. Happily there was a great deal to do. And to see how some of the women, and those the most anxious, would work, never resting, going on from one thing to another, as if they were hungry for more and more! Some did it with their mouths shut close, with their countenances fixed, not daring to pause or meet another's eyes; but some, who were more patient, worked with a soft word, and sometimes a smile, and sometimes a tear; but ever working on. Some of them were an example to us all. In the morning, when we got up, some from beds, some from the floor,—I insisted that all should lie down, by turns at least, for we could not make room for every one at the same hours,—the very first thought of all was to hasten to the window, or, better, to the door. Who could tell what might have happened while we slept? For the first moment no one would speak,—it was the moment of hope—and then there would be a cry, a clasping of the hands, which told—what we all knew. The one of the women who touched my heart most was the wife of Riou of the *octroi*. She had been almost rich for her condition in life, with a good house and a little servant whom she trained admirably, as I have had occasion to know. Her husband and her son were both among those whom we had left under the walls of Semur; but she had three children with her at La Clairière. Madame Riou slept lightly, and so did I. Sometimes I heard her stir in the middle of the night, though so softly that no one woke. We were in the same room, for it may be supposed that to keep a room to one's self was not possible. I did not stir, but lay and watched her as she went to the window, her figure visible against the pale dawning of the light, with an eager quick movement as of expectation—then turning back with slower step and a sigh. She was always full of hope. As the days went on, there came to be a kind of communication between us. We understood each other. When one was occupied and the other free, that one of use who went out to the door to look across the valley where Semur was would look at the other as if to say, "I go." When it was Madame Riou who did this, I shook my head, and she gave me a smile which awoke at every repetition (though I knew it was vain) a faint expectation, a little hope. When she came back, it was she who would shake her head, with her eyes full of tears. "Did I not tell thee?" I said, speaking to her as if she were my daughter. "It will be for next time, Madame," she would say, and smile, yet put her apron to her eyes. There were many who were like her, and there were those of whom I have spoken who were *pleureuses*, never hoping anything, doing little, bewailing themselves and their hard fate. Some of them we employed to carry the provisions to Semur, and this amused them, though the heaviness of the baskets made again a complaint.

As for the children, thank God! they were not disturbed as we were—to them it was a beautiful holiday—it was like Heaven. There is no place on earth that I love like Semur, yet it is true that the streets are narrow, and there is not much room for the children. Here they were happy as the day; they strayed over all our gardens and the meadows, which were full of flowers; they sat in companies upon the green grass, as thick as the daisies themselves, which they loved. Old Sister Mariette, who is called Marie de la Consolation, sat out in the meadow under an acacia-tree and watched over them. She was the one among us who was happy. She had no son, no husband, among the watchers, and though, no doubt, she loved her convent and her hospital, yet she sat all day long in the shade and in the full air, and smiled, and never looked towards Semur. "The good Lord will do as He wills," she said, "and that will be well." It was true—we all knew it was true; but it might be—who could tell?—that it was His will to destroy our town, and take away our bread, and perhaps the lives of those who were dear to us; and something came in our throats which prevented a reply. "*Ma sœur*,"[1] I said, "we are of the world, we tremble for those we love; we are not as you are." Sister Mariette did nothing but smile upon us. "I have known my Lord these sixty years," she said, "and He has taken everything from me." To see her smile as she said this was more than I could bear. From me He had taken something, but not all. Must we be prepared to give up all if we would be perfected? There were many of the others also who trembled at these words. "And now He gives me my consolation," she said, and called the little ones round her, and told them a tale of the Good Shepherd, which is out of the holy Gospel. To see all the little ones round her knees in a crowd, and the peaceful face with which she smiled upon them, and the meadows all full of flowers, and the sunshine coming and going through the branches: and to hear that tale of Him who went forth to seek the lamb that was lost, was like a tale out of a holy book, where all was peace and goodness and joy. But on the other side, not twenty steps off, was the house full of those who wept, and at all doors and windows anxious faces gazing down upon that cloud in the valley where Semur was. A procession of our women was coming back, many with lingering steps, carrying the baskets which were empty. "Is there any news?" we asked, reading their faces before they could answer. And some shook their heads, and some wept. There was no other reply.

---

1   My sister.

On the last night before our deliverance, suddenly, in the middle of the night, there was a great commotion in the house. We all rose out of our beds at the sound of the cry, almost believing that some one at the window had seen the lifting of the cloud, and rushed together, frightened, yet all in an eager expectation to hear what it was. It was in the room where the old Mère Julie slept that the disturbance was. Mère Julie was one of the market-women of Semur, the one I have mentioned who was devout, who never missed the *Salut*[1] in the afternoon, besides all masses which are obligatory. But there were other matters in which she had not satisfied my mind, as I have before said. She was the mother of Jacques Richard, who was a good-for-nothing, as is well known. At La Clairière Mère Julie had enacted a strange part. She had taken no part in anything that was done, but had established herself in the chamber allotted to her, and taken the best bed in it, where she kept her place night and day, making the others wait upon her. She had always expressed a great devotion for St. Jean; and the Sisters of the Hospital had been very kind to her, and also to her *vaurien* of a son, who was indeed, in some manner, the occasion of all our troubles—being the first who complained of the opening of the chapel into the chief ward, which was closed up by the administration, and thus became, as I and many others think, the cause of all the calamities that have come upon us. It was her bed that was the center of the great commotion we had heard, and a dozen voices immediately began to explain to us as we entered. "Mère Julie has had a dream. She has been a vision," they said. It was a vision of angels in the most beautiful robes, all shining with gold and whiteness.

"The dress of the Holy Mother which she wears on the great *fêtes* was nothing to them," Mère Julie told us, when she had composed herself. For all had run here and there at her first cry, and procured for her a *tisane*,[2] and a cup of *bouillon*,[3] and all that was good for an attack of the nerves, which was what it was at first supposed to be. "Their wings were like the wings of the great peacock on the terrace, but also like those of eagles. And each one had a collar of beautiful jewels about his neck, and robes whiter than those of any bride." This was the description she gave: and to see the women how they listened, head above head, a cloud of eager faces, all full of awe and attention! The angels had promised her that they would come again, when we had bound ourselves to observe all the functions of the Church, and when all these Messieurs had been converted, and made their submission—to lead us back gloriously to Semur. There was a great tumult in the chamber, and all cried out that

---

1 A prayer, the Salutation of the Virgin Mary.
2 Herbal tea.
3 Cup of beef broth.

they were convinced, that they were ready to promise. All except Madame Martin, who stood and looked at them with a look which surprised me, which was of pity rather than sympathy. As there was no one else to speak, I took the word, being the mother of the present Maire, and wife of the last, and in part mistress of the house. Had Agnès spoken I would have yielded to her, but as she was silent I took my right. "Mère Julie," I said, "and *mes bonnes femmes*,[1] my friends, know you that it is the middle of the night, the hour at which we must rest if we are to be able to do the work that is needful, which the *bon Dieu* has laid upon us? It is not from us—my daughter and myself—who, it is well known, have followed all the functions of the Church, that you will meet with an opposition to your promise. But what I desire is that you should calm yourselves, that you should retire and rest till the time of work, husbanding your strength, since we know not what claim may be made upon it. The holy angels," I said, "will comprehend, or if not they, then the *bon Dieu*, who understands everything."

But it was with difficulty that I could induce them to listen to me, to do that which was reasonable. When, however, we had quieted the agitation, and persuaded the good women to repose themselves, it was no longer possible for me to rest. I promised to myself a little moment of quiet, for my heart longed to be alone. I stole out as quietly as I might, not to disturb any one, and sat down upon the bench outside the door. It was still a kind of half-dark, nothing visible, so that if any one should gaze and gaze down the valley, it was not possible to see what was there: and I was glad that it was not possible, for my very soul was tired. I sat down and leant my back upon the wall of our house, and opened my lips to draw in the air of the morning. How still it was! the very birds not yet begun to rustle and stir in the bushes; the night air hushed, and scarcely the first faint tint of blue beginning to steal into the darkness. When I had sat there a little, closing my eyes, lo, tears began to steal into them like rain when there has been a fever of heat. I have wept in my time many tears, but the time of weeping is over with me, and through all these miseries I had shed none. Now they came without asking, like a benediction refreshing my eyes. Just then I felt a soft pressure upon my shoulder, and there was Agnès coming close, putting her shoulder to mine, as was her way, that we might support each other.

"You weep, *ma mère*," she said.

"I think it is one of the angels Mère Julie has seen," said I. "It is a refreshment—a blessing; my eyes were dry with weariness."

---

1   Good women.

"Mother," said Madame Martin, "do you think it is angels with wings like peacocks and jeweled collars that our Father sends to us? Ah, not so—one of those whom we love has touched your dear eyes," and with that she kissed me upon my eyes, taking me in her arms. My heart is sometimes hard to my son's wife, but not always—not with my will, God knows! Her kiss was soft as the touch of any angel could be.

"God bless thee, my child," I said.

"Thanks, thanks, *ma mère!*" she cried. "Now I am resolved; now will I go and speak to Martin—of something in my heart."

"What will you do, my child?" I said, for as the light increased I could see the meaning in her face, and that it was wrought up for some great thing. "Beware, Agnès; risk not my son's happiness by risking thyself; thou art more to Martin than all the world beside."

"He loves thee dearly, mother," she said. My heart was comforted. I was able to remember that I too had had my day. "He loves his mother, thank God, but not as he loves thee. Beware, *ma fille*. If you risk my son's happiness, neither will I forgive you." She smiled upon me, and kissed my hands.

"I will go and take him his food and some linen, and carry him your love and mine."

"*You* will go, and carry one of those heavy baskets with the others!"

"Mother," cried Agnès, "now you shame me that I have never done it before."

What could I say? Those whose turn it was were preparing their burdens to set out. She had her little packet made up, besides, of our cool white linen, which I knew would be so grateful to my son. I went with her to the turn of the road, helping her with her basket; but my limbs trembled, what with the long continuance of the trial, what with the agitation of the night. It was but just daylight when they went away, disappearing down the long slope of the road that led to Semur. I went back to the bench at the door, and there I sat down and thought. Assuredly it was wrong to close up the chapel, to deprive the sick of the benefit of the holy mass. But yet I could not but reflect that the *bon Dieu* had suffered still more great scandals to take place without such a punishment. When, however, I reflected on all that has been done by those who have no cares of this world as we have, but are brides of Christ, and upon all they resign by their dedication, and the claim they have to be furthered, not hindered, in their holy work: and when I bethought myself how many and great are the powers of evil, and that, save in us poor women who can do so little, the Church has few friends: then it came back to me how heinous was the offence that had been committed, and that it might well be that the saints out of heaven should return to earth to take the part and avenge the cause of the weak. My husband would have been the first to do it, had he seen with my eyes; but though in the flesh he did not do so, is it to be doubted that in heaven their eyes are enlightened—those who have been subjected to the cleansing fires[1] and have ascended into final bliss? This all became clear to me as I sat and pondered, while the morning light grew around me, and the sun rose and shed his first rays, which are as precious gold, on the summits of the mountains—for at La Clairière we are nearer the mountains than at Semur.

The house was more still than usual, and all slept to a later hour because of the agitation of the past night. I had been seated, like old sister Mariette, with my eyes turned rather towards the hills than to the valley, being so deep in my thoughts that I did not look, as it was our constant wont to look, if any change had happened over Semur. Thus blessings come unawares when we are not looking for them. Suddenly I lifted my eyes—but not with expectation—languidly, as one looks without thought. Then it was that I gave that great cry which brought all crowding to the windows, to the gardens, to every spot from whence that blessed sight was visible; for there before us, piercing through the clouds, were the beautiful towers of Semur, the Cathedral with all its pinnacles, that are as if they were carved out of foam, and the solid tower of St. Lambert, and the others, every one. They told me after that I flew, though I am past running, to the farmyard to call the labourers and servants of the farm bidding them prepare every carriage and waggon, and even the *charrettes*,[2] to carry back the children, and those who could not walk to the city.

"The men will be wild with privation and trouble," I said to myself; "they will want the sight of their little children, the comfort of their wives."

I did not wait to reason nor to ask myself if I did well; and my son has told me since that he scarcely was more thankful for our great deliverance than, just when the crowd of gaunt and weary men returned into Semur, and there was a moment when excitement and joy were at their highest, and danger possible, to hear the roll of the heavy farm waggons, and to see me arrive, with all the little ones and their mothers, like a new army, to take possession of their homes once more.

---

1   Purgatory.
2   Carts.

Chapter Ten

M. LE MAIRE CONCLUDES HIS RECORD

THE narratives which I have collected from the different eye-witnesses during the time of my own absence, will show how everything passed while I, with M. le Cure, was recovering possession of our city. Many have reported to me verbally the occurrences of the last half-hour before my return; and in their accounts there are naturally discrepancies, owing to their different points of view and different ways of regarding the subject. But all are agreed that a strange and universal slumber had seized upon all. M. de Bois-Sombre even admits that he, too, was overcome by this influence. They slept while we were performing our dangerous and solemn duty in Semur. But all are agreed that a strange and universal slumber had seized upon all. M. de Bois-Sombre even admits that he, too, was overcome by this influence. But when the Cathedral bells began to ring, with one impulse all awoke, and starting from the places where they lay, from the shade of the trees and bushes and sheltering hollows, saw the cloud and the mist and the darkness which had enveloped Semur suddenly rise from the walls. It floated up into the higher air before their eyes, then was caught and carried away, and flung about into shreds upon the sky by a strong wind, of which down below no influence was felt. They all gazed, not able to get their breath, speechless, beside themselves with joy, and saw the walls reappear, and the roofs of the houses, and our glorious Cathedral against the blue sky. They stood for a moment spell-bound. M. de Bois-Sombre informs me that he was afraid of a wild rush into the city, and himself hastened to the front to lead and restrain it; when suddenly a great cry rang through the air, and some one was seen to fall across the high road, straight in front of the Porte St. Lambert. M. de Bois-Sombre was at once aware who it was, for he himself had watched Lecamus taking his place at the feet of my wife, who awaited my return there. This checked the people in their first rush towards their homes; and when it was seen that Madame Dupin had also sunk down fainting on the ground after her more than human exertions for the comfort of all, there was but one impulse of tenderness and pity. When I reached the gate on my return, I found my wife lying there in all the pallor of death, and for a moment my heart stood still with sudden terror. What mattered Semur to me, if it had cost me my Agnès? or how could I think of Lecamus or any other, while she lay between life and death? I had her carried back to our own house. She was first to re-enter Semur; and after a time, thanks be to

God, she came back to herself. But Paul Lecamus was a dead man. No need to carry him in, to attempt unavailing cares. "He has gone, that one; he has marched with the others," said the old doctor, who had served in his day, and sometimes would use the language of the camp. He cast but one glance at him, and laid his hand upon his heart in passing. "Cover his face," was all he said.

It is possible that this check was good for the restraint of the crowd. It moderated the rush with which they returned to their homes. The sight of the motionless figures stretched out by the side of the way overawed them. Perhaps it may seem strange, to any one who has known what had occurred, that the state of the city should have given me great anxiety the first night of our return. The withdrawal of the oppression and awe which had been on the men, the return of everything to its natural state, the sight of their houses unchanged, so that the brain turned round of these common people, who seldom reflect upon anything, and they already began to ask themselves was it all a delusion—added to the exhaustion of their physical condition, and the natural desire for ease and pleasure after the long strain upon all their faculties—produced an excitement which might have led to very disastrous consequences. Fortunately I had foreseen this. I have always been considered to possess great knowledge of human nature, and this has been matured by recent events. I sent off messengers instantly to bring home the women and children, and called around me the men in whom I could most trust. Though I need not say that the excitement and suffering of the past three days had told not less upon myself than upon others, I abandoned all idea of rest. The first thing that I did, aided by my respectable fellow-townsmen, was to take possession of all *cabarets* and wine-shops, allowing indeed the proprietors to return, but preventing all assemblages within them. We then established a patrol of respectable citizens throughout the city, to preserve the public peace. I calculated, with great anxiety, how many hours it would be before my messengers could reach La Clairière, to bring back the women—for in such a case the wives are the best guardians, and can exercise an influence more general and less suspected than that of the magistrates; but this was not be hoped for for three or four hours at least. Judge, then, what was my joy and satisfaction when the sound of wheels (in itself a pleasant sound, for no wheels had been audible on the high-road since these events began) came briskly to us from the distance; and looking out from the watch tower over the Porte St. Lambert, I saw the strangest procession. The wine-carts and all the farm vehicles of La Clairière, and every kind of country waggon, were jolting along the road, all in a tumult and babble of delicious voices; and from under the rude canopies and awnings and roofs of vine branches, made up to shield them from the sun, lo! there were the children like birds in a nest, one little head peeping over the other. And the cries and songs, the laughter, and the shoutings! As they came along the air grew sweet, the world was made new. Many of us, who had borne all the terrors and sufferings of the past without fainting, now felt their strength fail them. Some broke out into tears, interrupted with laughter. Some called out aloud the names of their little ones. We went out to meet them, every man there present, myself at the head. And I will not deny that a sensation of pride came over me when I saw my mother stand up in the first waggon, with all those happy ones fluttering around her. "My son," she said, "I have discharged the trust that was given me. I bring thee back the blessing of God." "And God bless thee, my mother!" I cried. The other men, who were fathers, like me, came round me, crowding to kiss her hand. It is not among the women of my family that you will find those who abandon their duties.

And then to lift down in armfuls, those flowers of paradise, all fresh with the air of the fields, all joyous like the birds! We put them down by twos and threes, some of us sobbing with joy. And to see them dispersing hand in hand, running here and there, each to its home, carrying peace, and love, and gladness, through the streets—that was enough to make the most serious smile. No fear was in them, or care. Every haggard man they met—some of them feverish, restless, beginning to think of riot and pleasure after forced abstinence—there was a new shout, a rush of little feet, a shower of soft kisses. The women were following after, some packed into the carts and waggons, pale and worn, yet happy; some walking behind in groups; the more strong, or the more eager, in advance, and a long line of stragglers behind. There was anxiety in their faces, mingled with their joy. How did they know what they might find in the houses from which they had been shut out? And many felt, like me, that in the very return, in the relief, there was danger. But the children feared nothing; they filled the streets with their dear voices, and happiness came back with them. When I felt my little Jean's cheek against mine, then for the first time did I know how much anguish I had suffered—how terrible was parting, and how sweet was life. But strength and prudence melt away when one indulges one's self, even in one's dearest affections. I had to call my guardians together, to put mastery upon myself, that a just vigilance might not be relaxed. M. de Bois-Sombre, though less anxious than myself, and disposed to believe (being a soldier) that a little license would do no harm, yet stood by me; and, thanks to our precautions, all went well.

Before night three parts of the population had returned to Semur, and the houses were all lighted up as for a great festival. The Cathedral stood open—even the great west doors, which are only opened on great occasions—with a glow of tapers gleaming out on every side. As I stood in the twilight watching, and glad at heart to think that all was going well, my mother and my wife—still pale, but now recovered from her fainting and weakness—came out into the great square, leading my little Jean. They were on their way to the Cathedral, to thank God for their return. They looked at me, but did not ask me to go with them, those dear women; they respect my opinions, as I had always respected theirs. But this silence moved me more than words; there came into my heart a sudden inspiration. I was still in my scarf of office, which had been, I say it without vanity, the standard of authority and protection during all our trouble; and thus marked out as representative of all, I uncovered myself, after the ladies of my family had passed, and, without joining them, silently followed with a slow and solemn step. A suggestion, a look, is enough for my countrymen; those who were in the Place with me perceived in a moment what I meant. One by one they uncovered, they put themselves behind me. Thus we made such a procession as had never been seen in Semur. We were gaunt and worn with watching and anxiety, which only added to the solemn effect. Those who were already in the Cathedral, and especially M. le Cure, informed me afterwards that the tramp of our male feet as we came up the great steps gave to all a thrill of expectation and awe. It was at the moment of the exposition of the Sacrament that we entered. Instinctively, in a moment, all understood—a thing which could happen nowhere but in France, where intelligence is swift as the breath on our lips. Those who were already there yielded their places to us, most of the women rising up, making as it were a ring round us, the tears running down their faces. When the Sacrament was replaced upon the altar, M. le Cure, perceiving our meaning, began at once in his noble voice to intone the *Te Deum*.[1] Rejecting all other music, he adopted the plain song in which all could join, and with one voice, every man in unison with his brother, we sang with him. The great Cathedral walls seemed to throb with the sound that rolled upward, *mâle*[2] and deep, as no song has ever risen from Semur in the memory of man. The women stood up around us, and wept and sobbed with pride and joy.

When this wonderful moment was over, and all the people poured forth out of the Cathedral walls into the soft evening, with stars shining above, and all the friendly lights below, there was such a tumult of emotion and gladness as I have never seen before. Many of the poor women surrounded me, kissed my hand notwithstanding my resistance, and called upon God to bless me; while some of the older persons made remarks full of justice and feeling.

---

1   Hymn of praise to God.
2   Manly.

"The *bon Dieu* is not used to such singing," one of them cried, her old eyes streaming with tears. "It must have surprised the saints up in heaven!"

"It will bring a blessing," cried another. "It is not like our little voices, that perhaps only reach half-way."

This was figurative language, yet it was impossible to doubt there was much truth in it. Such a submission of our intellects, as I felt in determining to make it, must have been pleasing to heaven. The women, they are always praying; but when we thus presented ourselves to give thanks, it meant something, a real homage; and with a feeling of solemnity we separated, aware that we had contented both earth and heaven.

Next morning there was a great function in the Cathedral, at which the whole city assisted. Those who could not get admittance crowded upon the steps, and knelt halfway across the Place. It was an occasion long remembered in Semur, though I have heard many say not in itself so impressive as the *Te Deum* on the evening of our return. After this we returned to our occupations, and life was resumed under its former conditions in our city.

It might be supposed, however, that the place in which events so extraordinary had happened would never again be as it was before. Had I not been myself so closely involved, it would have appeared to me certain, that the streets, trod once by such inhabitants as those who for these nights and days abode within Semur, would have always retained some trace of their presence; that life there would have been more solemn than in other places; and that those families for whose advantage the dead had risen out of their graves, would have henceforward carried about with them some sign of that interposition. It will seem almost incredible when I now add that nothing of this kind has happened at Semur. The wonderful manifestation which interrupted our existence has passed absolutely as if it had never been. We had not been twelve hours in our houses ere we had forgotten, or practically forgotten, our expulsion from them. Even myself, to whom everything was so vividly brought home, I have to enter my wife's room to put aside the curtain from little Marie's picture, and to see and touch the olive branch which is there, before I can recall to myself anything that resembles the feeling with which I re-entered that sanctuary. My grandfather's bureau still stands in the middle of my library, where I found it on my return; but I have got used to it, and it no longer affects me. Everything is as it was; and I cannot persuade myself that, for a time, I and mine were shut out, and our places taken by those who neither eat nor drink, and whose life is invisible to our eyes. Everything, I say, is as it was—everything goes on as if it would endure for ever. We know this cannot be, yet it does not move us. Why, then, should the other move us? A little time, we are aware, and we, too, shall be as they are—as shadows, and unseen. But neither has the one changed us, and neither does the other. There was, for some time, a greater respect shown to religion in Semur, and a more devout attendance at the sacred functions; but I regret to say this did not continue. Even in my own case—I say it with sorrow—it did not continue. M. le Curé is an admirable person. I know no more excellent ecclesiastic. He is indefatigable in the performance of his spiritual duties; and he has, besides, a noble and upright soul. Since the days when we suffered and laboured together, he has been to me as a brother. Still, it is undeniable that he makes calls upon our credulity, which a man obeys with reluctance. There are ways of surmounting this; as I see in Agnès for one, and in M. de Bois-Sombre for another. My wife does not question, she believes much; and in respect to that which she cannot acquiesce in, she is silent. "There are many things I hear you talk of, Martin, which are strange to me," she says, "of myself I cannot believe in them; but I do not oppose, since it is possible you may have reason to know better than I; and so with some things that we hear from M. le Curé." This is how she explains herself—but she is a woman. It is a matter of grace to yield to our better judgment. M. de Bois-Sombre has another way. "*Ma foi*,"[1] he says, "I have not the time for all your delicacies, my good people; I have come to see that these things are for the advantage of the world, and it is not my business to explain them. If M. le Curé attempted to criticise me in military matters, or thee, my excellent Martin, in affairs of business, or in the culture of your vines, I should think him not a wise man; and in like manner, faith and religion, these are his concern." Félix de Bois-Sombre is an excellent fellow; but he smells a little of the *mousquetaire*.[2] I, who am neither a soldier nor a woman, I have hesitations. Nevertheless, so long as I am Maire of Semur, nothing less than the most absolute respect shall ever be shown to all truly religious persons, with whom it is my earnest desire to remain in sympathy and fraternity, so far as that may be.

It seemed, however, a little while ago as if my tenure of this office would not be long, notwithstanding the services which I am acknowledged, on every hand, to have done to my fellow-townsmen. It will be remembered that when M. le Curé and myself found Semur empty, we heard a voice of complaining from the hospital of St. Jean, and found a sick man who had been left there, and who grumbled against the Sisters, and accused them of neglecting him, but remained altogether unaware, in the meantime, of what had happened in the city. Will it be believed that after a

---

1   My faith.
2   Musketeer.

time this fellow was put faith in as a seer, who had heard and beheld many things of which we were all ignorant? It must be said that, in the meantime, there had been a little excitement in the town on the subject of the Chapel in the hospital, to which repeated reference has already been made. It was insisted on behalf of these ladies that a promise had been given, taking, indeed, the form of a vow, that, as soon as we were again in possession of Semur, their full privileges should be restored to them. Their advocates even went so far as to send to me a deputation of those who had been nursed in the hospital, the leader of which was Jacques Richard, who since he has been, as he says, "converted," thrusts himself to the front of every movement.

"Permit me to speak, M. le Maire," he said; "me, who was one of those so misguided as to complain, before the great lesson we have all received. The mass did not disturb any sick person who was of right dispositions. I was then a very bad subject, indeed—as, alas! M. le Maire too well knows. It annoyed me only as all pious observances annoyed me. I am now, thank heaven, of a very different way of thinking—"

But I would not listen to the fellow. When he was a *mauvais sujet*[1] he was less abhorrent to me than now.

The men were aware that when I pronounced myself so distinctly on any subject there was nothing more to be said, for, though gentle as a lamb and open to all reasonable arguments, I am capable of making the most obstinate stand for principle; and to yield to popular superstition, is that worthy of a man who has been instructed? At the same time it raised a great anger in my mind that all that should be thought of was a thing so trivial. That they should have given themselves, soul and body, for a little money; that they should have scoffed at all that was noble and generous, both in religion and in earthly things; all that was nothing to them. And now they would insult the Great God Himself by believing that all He cared for was a little mass in a convent chapel. What desecration! What debasement! When I went to M. le Curé, he smiled at my vehemence. There was pain in his smile, and it might be indignation; but he was not furious like me.

"They will conquer you, my friend," he said.

"Never," I cried. "Before I might have yielded. But to tell me the gates of death have been rolled back, and Heaven revealed, and the great God stooped down from Heaven, in order that mass should be said according to the wishes of the community

---

1 Bad character.

in the midst of the sick wards! They will never make me believe this, if I were to die for it."

"Nevertheless, they will conquer," M. le Curé said.

It angered me that he should say so. My heart was sore as if my friend had forsaken me. And then it was that the worst step was taken in this crusade of false religion. It was from my mother that I heard of it first. One day she came home in great excitement, saying that now indeed a real light was to be shed upon all that had happened to us.

"It appears," she said, "that Pierre Plastron was in the hospital all the time, and heard and saw many wonderful things. Sister Génevieve had just told me. It is wonderful beyond anything you could believe. He has spoken with our holy patron himself, St. Lambert, and has received instructions for a pilgrimage—"

"Pierre Plastron!" I cried; "Pierre Plastron saw nothing, *ma mére*. He was not even aware that anything remarkable had occurred. He complained to us of the Sisters that they neglected him: he knew nothing more."

"My son," she said, looking upon me with reproving eyes, "what have the good Sisters done to thee? Why is it that you look so unfavourably upon everything that comes from the community of St. Jean?"

"What have I to do with the community?" I cried—"when I tell thee, Maman, that this Pierre Plastron knows nothing! I heard it from the fellow's own lips, and M. le Curé was present and heard him too. He had seen nothing, he knew nothing. Inquire of M. le Curé, if you have doubts of me."

"I do not doubt you, Martin," said my mother with severity, "when you are not biased by prejudice. And, as for M. le Curé, it is well known that the clergy are often jealous of the good Sisters, when they are not under their own control."

Such was the injustice with which we were treated. And next day nothing was talked of but the revelation of Pierre Plastron. What he had seen and what he had heard was wonderful. All the saints had come and talked with him, and told him what he was to say to his townsmen. They told him exactly how everything had happened: how St. Jean himself had interfered on behalf of the Sisters, and how, if we were not more attentive on the duties of religion, certain among us would be bound hand and foot and cast into the jaws of hell.

That I was one, nay the chief, of these denounced persons, no one could have any doubt. This exasperated me; and as soon as I knew that this folly had been printed and was in every house, I hastened to M. le Curé, and entreated him in his next Sunday's sermon to tell the true story of Pierre Plastron, and reveal the imposture. But M. le Curé shook his head. "It will do no good," he said.

"But how no good?" said I. "What good are we looking for? These are lies, nothing but lies. Either he has deceived the poor ladies basely, or they themselves—but this is what I cannot believe."

"Dear friend," he said, "compose thyself. Have you never discovered yet how strong is self-delusion? There will be no lying of which they are aware. Figure to yourself what a stimulus to the imagination to know that he was here, actually here. Even I—it suggests a hundred things to me. The Sisters will have said to him (meaning no evil, nay meaning the edification of the people), 'But, Pierre, reflect! You must have seen this and that. Recall thy recollections a little.' And by degrees Pierre will have found out that he remembered—more than could have been hoped."

"*Mon Dieu!*" I cried, out of patience, "and you know all this, yet you will not tell them the truth—the very truth."

"To what good?" he said. Perhaps M. le Curé was right: but, for my part, had I stood up in that pulpit, I should have contradicted their lies and given no quarter. This, indeed, was what I did both in my private and public capacity; but the people, though they loved me, did not believe me. They said, "The best men have their prejudices. M. le Maire is an excellent man; but what will you? He is but human after all."

M. le Curé and I said no more to each other on this subject. He was a brave man, yet here perhaps he was not quite brave. And the effect of Pierre Plastron's revelations in other quarters was to turn the awe that had been in many minds into mockery and laughter. "*Ma foi,*" said Félix de Bois-Sombre, "Monseigneur St. Lambert had bad taste, *mon ami* Martin, to choose Pierre Plastron for his confidant when he might have had thee." "M. de Bois-Sombre does ill to laugh," said my mother (even my mother! she was not on my side), "when it is known that the foolish are often chosen to confound the wise."[1] But Agnès, my wife, it was she who gave me the best consolation. She turned to me with the tears in her beautiful eyes.

"*Mon ami,*" she said, "let Monseigneur St. Lambert say what he will. He is not God that we should put him above all. There were other saints with other thoughts that came for thee and for me!"

All this contradiction was over when Agnès and I together took our flowers on the *jour des morts*[2] to the graves we love. Glimmering among the rest was a new cross which I had not seen before. This was the inscription upon it:—

---

1   "But God hath chosen the foolish things of the world to confound the wise; and God hath chosen the weak things of the world to confound the things which are mighty" (1 Corinthians 1:27).
2   All Soul's Day, November 2nd.

À PAUL LECAMUS
PARTI
LE 20 JUILLET, 1875
AVEC LES BIEN-AIMÉS[1]

On it was wrought in the marble a little branch of olive. I turned to look at my wife as she laid underneath this cross a handful of violets.[2] She gave me her hand still fragrant with the flowers. There was none of his family left to put up for him any token of human remembrance. Who but she should have done it, who had helped him to join that company and army of the beloved? "This was our brother," she said; "he will tell my Marie what use I made of her olive leaves."

---

1 To Paul Lecamus, departed 20 July 1875, with the well-beloved.
2 Traditional symbols of humility and mourning.

A Phantom Lover

Vernon Lee

"Vernon Lee" was the pseudonym of Violet Paget (1856–1935), the brilliant and precocious daughter of English expatriates living on the Continent. Her formative years were spent in the south of France, where she formed a life-long friendship with the future painter John Singer Sargent, and in Florence, Italy, where she resided from 1873 to her death. At thirteen, Paget published her first short story, a tale in French titled "Les aventures d'une pièce de monnaie." Her *Studies of the Eighteenth Century in Italy*, however, published when she was twenty-four, established her reputation as an art critic, essayist, and scholar of formidable intellect. During her annual visits to England, her intellectual circle would often include such luminaries as Robert Browning, Oscar Wilde, William Morris, Henry James, and the aesthetic philosopher Walter Pater, whose heady prose and subtle explorations of the power of sensation proved especially appealing to Paget. Over the course of her distinguished career, Paget authored over forty books on a wide range of topics, including travel, music, aesthetics, and folklore. Her most popular works, however, were her supernatural or "fantastic" tales, in which she explores the connection between the spectral and the aesthetic: the sensation of being haunted and the experience of art. The following story, written in 1886, was her first published ghost story. It was reprinted as "Oke of Okehurst" four years later in *Hauntings: Fantastic Stories*. Because Paget never married, and because she cultivated close, romantic friendships with a number of women over the course of her life, scholarly interest has recently turned to the subject of her sexuality and to sexual themes in her writings. Known for her sharp conversation, her cosmopolitanism, and for the circle of young female fans she inspired, Paget was drawn in the early twentieth century to feminist and pacifist causes.

I

THAT sketch up there with the boy's cap? Yes; that's the same woman. I wonder whether you could guess who she was. A singular being, is she not? The most marvelous creature, quite, that I have ever met: a wonderful elegance, exotic, far-fetched, poignant; an artificial perverse sort of grace and research in every outline and movement and arrangement of head and neck, and hands and fingers. Here are a lot of pencil sketches I made while I was preparing to paint her portrait. Yes; there's nothing but her in the whole sketchbook. Mere scratches, but they may give some idea of her marvelous, fantastic kind of grace. Here she is leaning over the staircase, and here sitting in the swing. Here she is walking quickly out of the room. That's her head. You see she isn't really handsome; her forehead is too big, and her nose too short. This gives no idea of her. It was altogether a question of movement. Look at the strange cheeks, hollow and rather flat; well, when she smiled she had the most marvelous dimples here. There was something exquisite and uncanny about it. Yes; I began the picture, but it was never finished. I did the husband first. I wonder who has his likeness now? Help me to move these pictures away from the wall. Thanks. This is her portrait; a huge wreck. I don't suppose you can make much of it; it is merely blocked in, and seems quite mad. You see my idea was to make her leaning against a wall—there was one hung with yellow that seemed almost brown—so as to bring out the silhouette.

It was very singular I should have chosen that particular wall. It does look rather insane in this condition, but I like it; it has something of her. I would frame it and hang it up, only people would ask questions. Yes; you have guessed quite right—it is Mrs. Oke of Okehurst. I forgot you had relations in that part of the country; besides, I suppose the newspapers were full of it at the time. You didn't know that it all took place under my eyes? I can scarcely believe now that it did: it all seems so distant, vivid but unreal, like a thing of my own invention. It really was much stranger than any one guessed. People could no more understand it than they could understand her. I doubt whether anyone ever understood Alice Oke besides myself. You mustn't think me unfeeling. She was a marvelous, weird, exquisite creature, but one couldn't feel sorry for her. I felt much sorrier for the wretched creature of a husband. It seemed such an appropriate end for her; I fancy she would have liked it could she have known. Ah! I shall never have another chance of painting such a portrait as I wanted. She seemed sent me from heaven or the other place. You have never heard the story in detail? Well, I don't usually mention it, because people are so brutally stupid or sentimental; but I'll tell it you. Let me see. It's too dark to paint any more today, so I can tell it you now. Wait; I must turn her face to the wall. Ah, she was a marvelous creature!

II

YOU remember, three years ago, my telling you I had let myself in for painting a couple of Kentish squireen?[1] I really could not understand what had possessed me to say yes to that man. A friend of mine had brought him one day to my studio—Mr. Oke of Okehurst, that was the name on his card. He was a very tall, very well-made, very good-looking young man, with a beautiful fair complexion, beautiful fair moustache, and beautifully fitting clothes; absolutely like a hundred other young men you can see any day in the Park, and absolutely uninteresting from the crown of his head to the tip of his boots. Mr. Oke, who had been a lieutenant in the Blues[2] before his marriage, was evidently extremely uncomfortable on finding himself in a studio. He felt misgivings about a man who could wear a velvet coat in town,[3] but at the same time he was nervously anxious not to treat me in the very least like a tradesman. He walked round my place, looked at everything with the most scrupulous attention, stammered out a few complimentary phrases, and then, looking at his friend for assistance, tried to come to the point, but failed. The point, which the friend kindly explained, was that Mr. Oke was desirous to know whether my engagements would allow of my painting him and his wife, and what my terms would be. The poor man blushed perfectly crimson during this explanation, as if he had come with the most improper proposal; and I noticed—the only interesting thing about him—a very odd nervous frown between his eyebrows, a perfect double gash—a thing which usually means something abnormal: a mad-doctor[4] of my acquaintance calls it the maniac-frown. When I had answered, he suddenly burst out into rather confused explanations: his wife—Mrs. Oke—had seen some of my—pictures—paintings—portraits—at the—the—what d'you call it?—Academy. She had—in short, they had made a very great impression upon her. Mrs. Oke had a great taste for art; she was, in short, extremely desirous of having her portrait and his painted by me, *etcetera*.

---

1   A slightly derisive term for the landed gentry.
2   The Royal Horse Guards.
3   Suggests that the artist-narrator's clothes are less than formal.
4   A doctor who treats the mad.

"My wife," he suddenly added, "is a remarkable woman. I don't know whether you will think her handsome—she isn't exactly, you know. But she's awfully strange," and Mr. Oke of Okehurst gave a little sigh and frowned that curious frown, as if so long a speech and so decided an expression of opinion had cost him a great deal.

It was a rather unfortunate moment in my career. A very influential sitter of mine—you remember the fat lady with the crimson curtain behind her?—had come to the conclusion or been persuaded that I had painted her old and vulgar, which, in fact, she was. Her whole clique had turned against me, the newspapers had taken up the matter, and for the moment I was considered as a painter to whose brushes no woman would trust her reputation. Things were going badly. So I snapped but too gladly at Mr. Oke's offer, and settled to go down to Okehurst at the end of a fortnight. But the door had scarcely closed upon my future sitter when I began to regret my rashness; and my disgust at the thought of wasting a whole summer upon the portrait of a totally uninteresting Kentish squire, and his doubtless equally uninteresting wife, grew greater and greater as the time for execution approached. I remember so well the frightful temper in which I got into the train for Kent, and the even more frightful temper in which I got out of it at the little station nearest to Okehurst. It was pouring floods. I felt a comfortable fury at the thought that my canvases would get nicely wetted before Mr. Oke's coachman had packed them on the top of the waggonette. It was just what served me right for coming to this confounded place to paint these confounded people. We drove off in the steady downpour. The roads were a mass of yellow mud; the endless flat grazing-grounds under the oak-trees, after having been burnt to cinders in a long drought, were turned into a hideous brown sop; the country seemed intolerably monotonous.

My spirits sank lower and lower. I began to meditate upon the modern Gothic country-house, with the usual amount of Morris furniture,[1] Liberty rugs,[2] and Mudie novels,[3] to which I was doubtless being taken. My fancy pictured very vividly the five or six little Okes—that man certainly must have at least five children—the aunts, and sisters-in-law, and cousins; the eternal routine of afternoon tea and lawn-tennis; above all, it pictured Mrs. Oke, the bouncing, well-informed, model housekeeper, electioneering, charity-organising young lady, whom such an individual as Mr. Oke would regard in the light of a remarkable woman. And my spirit sank within me, and I cursed my avarice in accepting the commission, my spiritlessness in not throwing it

---

1   William Morris (1834–1896), British poet, essayist, book-binder, printer, socialist activist, and prolific designer of lush neo-medieval furniture, tapestries, and wallpaper.
2   Rugs from the fashionable West End store Liberty.
3   Charles Edward Mudie (1818–1890), British bookseller of popular novels.

over while yet there was time. We had meanwhile driven into a large park, or rather a long succession of grazing-grounds, dotted about with large oaks, under which the sheep were huddled together for shelter from the rain. In the distance, blurred by the sheets of rain, was a line of low hills, with a jagged fringe of bluish firs and a solitary windmill. It must be a good mile and a half since we had passed a house, and there was none to be seen in the distance—nothing but the undulation of sere grass, sopped brown beneath the huge blackish oak-trees, and whence arose, from all sides, a vague disconsolate bleating. At last the road made a sudden bend, and disclosed what was evidently the home of my sitter. It was not what I had expected. In a dip in the ground a large red-brick house, with the rounded gables and high chimney-stacks of the time of James I[1]—a forlorn, vast place, set in the midst of the pasture-land, with no trace of garden before it, and only a few large trees indicating the possibility of one to the back; no lawn either, but on the other side of the sandy dip, which suggested a filled-up moat, a huge oak, short, hollow, with wreathing, blasted, black branches, upon which only a handful of leaves shook in the rain. It was not at all what I had pictured to myself the home of Mr. Oke of Okehurst.

My host received me in the hall, a large place, panelled and carved, hung round with portraits up to its curious ceiling—vaulted and ribbed like the inside of a ship's hull. He looked even more blond and pink and white, more absolutely mediocre in his tweed suit; and also, I thought, even more good-natured and duller. He took me into his study, a room hung round with whips and fishing-tackle in place of books, while my things were being carried upstairs. It was very damp, and a fire was smouldering. He gave the embers a nervous kick with his foot, and said, as he offered me a cigar—

"You must excuse my not introducing you at once to Mrs. Oke. My wife—in short, I believe my wife is asleep."

"Is Mrs. Oke unwell?" I asked, a sudden hope flashing across me that I might be off the whole matter.

"Oh no! Alice is quite well; at least, quite as well as she usually is. My wife," he added, after a minute, and in a very decided tone, "does not enjoy very good health—a nervous constitution. Oh no! not at all ill, nothing at all serious, you know. Only nervous, the doctors say; mustn't be worried or excited, the doctors say; requires lots of repose—that sort of thing."

---

1   King James I (1566–1625).

There was a dead pause. This man depressed me, I knew not why. He had a listless, puzzled look, very much out of keeping with his evident admirable health and strength.

"I suppose you are a great sportsman?" I asked from sheer despair, nodding in the direction of the whips and guns and fishing-rods.

"Oh no! not now. I was once. I have given up all that," he answered, standing with his back to the fire, and staring at the polar bear beneath his feet. "I—I have no time for all that now," he added, as if an explanation were due. "A married man—you know. Would you like to come up to your rooms?" he suddenly interrupted himself. "I have had one arranged for you to paint in. My wife said you would prefer a north light. If that one doesn't suit, you can have your choice of any other."

I followed him out of the study, through the vast entrance-hall. In less than a minute I was no longer thinking of Mr. and Mrs. Oke and the boredom of doing their likeness; I was simply overcome by the beauty of this house, which I had pictured modern and philistine. It was, without exception, the most perfect example of an old English manor-house that I had ever seen; the most magnificent intrinsically, and the most admirably preserved. Out of the huge hall, with its immense fireplace of delicately carved and inlaid grey and black stone, and its rows of family portraits, reaching from the wainscoting to the oaken ceiling, vaulted and ribbed like a ship's hull, opened the wide, flat-stepped staircase, the parapet surmounted at intervals by heraldic monsters, the wall covered with oak carvings of coats-of-arms, leafage, and little mythological scenes, painted a faded red and blue, and picked out with tarnished gold, which harmonised with the tarnished blue and gold of the stamped leather that reached to the oak cornice, again delicately tinted and gilded. The beautifully damascened suits of court armour looked, without being at all rusty, as if no modem hand had ever touched them; the very rugs under foot were of sixteenth-century Persian make; the only things of today were the big bunches of flowers and ferns, arranged in majolica dishes upon the landings. Everything was perfectly silent; only from below came the chimes, silvery like an Italian palace fountain, of an old-fashioned clock.

It seemed to me that I was being led through the palace of the Sleeping Beauty.

"What a magnificent house!" I exclaimed as I followed my host through a long corridor, also hung with leather, wainscoted with carvings, and furnished with big wedding coffers, and chairs that looked as if they came out of some Vandyck[1] portrait.

---

1 Anthony Van Dyck (1599–1641), Flemish portrait-painter and leading court painter in England during the reign of Charles I (1625–1649).

In my mind was the strong impression that all this was natural, spontaneous—that it had about it nothing of the picturesqueness which swell studios have taught to rich and aesthetic houses. Mr. Oke misunderstood me.

"It is a nice old place," he said, "but it's too large for us. You see, my wife's health does not allow of our having many guests; and there are no children."

I thought I noticed a vague complaint in his voice; and he evidently was afraid there might have seemed something of the kind, for he added immediately—

"I don't care for children one jackstraw, you know, myself; can't understand how anyone can, for my part."

If ever a man went out of his way to tell a lie, I said to myself, Mr. Oke of Okehurst was doing so at the present moment.

When he had left me in one of the two enormous rooms that were allotted to me, I threw myself into an arm-chair and tried to focus the extraordinary imaginative impression which this house had given me.

I am very susceptible to such impressions; and besides the sort of spasm of imaginative interest sometimes given to me by certain rare and eccentric personalities, I know nothing more subduing than the charm, quieter and less analytic, of any sort of complete and out-of-the-common-run sort of house. To sit in a room like the one I was sitting in, with the figures of the tapestry glimmering grey and lilac and purple in the twilight, the great bed, columned and curtained, looming in the middle, and the embers reddening beneath the overhanging mantelpiece of inlaid Italian stonework, a vague scent of rose-leaves and spices, put into the china bowls by the hands of ladies long since dead, while the clock downstairs sent up, every now and then, its faint silvery tune of forgotten days, filled the room;—to do this is a special kind of voluptuousness, peculiar and complex and indescribable, like the half-drunkenness of opium or haschisch,[1] and which, to be conveyed to others in any sense as I feel it, would require a genius, subtle and heady, like that of Baudelaire.[2]

After I had dressed for dinner I resumed my place in the arm-chair, and resumed also my reverie, letting all these impressions of the past—which seemed faded like the figures in the arras, but still warm like the embers in the fireplace, still sweet and subtle like the perfume of the dead rose-leaves and broken spices in the china bowls—permeate me and go to my head. Of Oke and Oke's wife I did not think; I seemed quite alone, isolated from the world, separated from it in this exotic enjoyment.

---

1   Hashish.
2   Charles Baudelaire (1821–1867), French poet, critic, dandy, and author of the groundbreaking *Fleur du Mal* (1857), which explores narcotic use, among other things.

Gradually the embers grew paler; the figures in the tapestry more shadowy; the columned and curtained bed loomed out vaguer; the room seemed to fill with greyness; and my eyes wandered to the mullioned bow-window, beyond whose panes, between whose heavy stonework, stretched a greyish-brown expanse of sore and sodden park grass, dotted with big oaks; while far off, behind a jagged fringe of dark Scotch firs, the wet sky was suffused with the blood-red of the sunset. Between the falling of the raindrops from the ivy outside, there came, fainter or sharper, the recurring bleating of the lambs separated from their mothers, a forlorn, quavering, eerie little cry.

I started up at a sudden rap at my door.

"Haven't you heard the gong for dinner?" asked Mr. Oke's voice.

I had completely forgotten his existence.

III

I FEEL that I cannot possibly reconstruct my earliest impressions of Mrs. Oke. My recollection of them would be entirely coloured by my subsequent knowledge of her; whence I conclude that I could not at first have experienced the strange interest and admiration which that extraordinary woman very soon excited in me. Interest and admiration, be it well understood, of a very unusual kind, as she was herself a very unusual kind of woman; and I, if you choose, am a rather unusual kind of man. But I can explain that better anon.

This much is certain, that I must have been immeasurably surprised at finding my hostess and future sitter so completely unlike everything I had anticipated. Or no—now I come to think of it, I scarcely felt surprised at all; or if I did, that shock of surprise could have lasted but an infinitesimal part of a minute. The fact is, that, having once seen Alice Oke in the reality, it was quite impossible to remember that one could have fancied her at all different: there was something so complete, so completely unlike everyone else, in her personality, that she seemed always to have been present in one's consciousness, although present, perhaps, as an enigma.

Let me try and give you some notion of her: not that first impression, whatever it may have been, but the absolute reality of her as I gradually learned to see it. To begin with, I must repeat and reiterate over and over again, that she was, beyond all comparison, the most graceful and exquisite woman I have ever seen, but with a grace and an exquisiteness that had nothing to do with any preconceived notion or previous experience of what goes by these names: grace and exquisiteness recognised at once as perfect, but which were seen in her for the first, and probably, I do believe, for the last time. It is conceivable, is it not, that once in a thousand years there may arise a combination of lines, a system of movements, an outline, a gesture, which is new, unprecedented, and yet hits off exactly our desires for beauty and rareness? She was very tall; and I suppose people would have called her thin. I don't know, for I never thought about her as a body—-bones, flesh, that sort of thing; but merely as a wonderful series of lines, and a wonderful strangeness of personality. Tall and slender, certainly, and with not one item of what makes up our notion of a well-built woman. She was as straight—I mean she had as little of what people call figure—as a bamboo; her shoulders were a trifle high, and she had a decided stoop; her arms and her shoulders she never once wore uncovered. But this bamboo figure of hers had a suppleness and a stateliness, a play of outline with every step she took, that I can't compare to anything else; there was in it something of the peacock and something also of the stag; but, above all, it was her own. I wish I could describe her. I wish, alas!—I wish, I wish, I have wished a hundred thousand times—I could paint her, as I see her now, if I shut my eyes—even if it were only a silhouette. There! I see her so plainly, walking slowly up and down a room, the slight highness of her shoulders; just completing the exquisite arrangement of lines made by the straight supple back, the long exquisite neck, the head, with the hair cropped in short pale curls, always drooping a little, except when she would suddenly throw it back, and smile, not at me, nor at any one, nor at anything that had been said, but as if she alone had suddenly seen or heard something, with the strange dimple in her thin, pale cheeks, and the strange whiteness in her full, wide-opened eyes: the moment when she had something of the stag in her movement. But where is the use of talking about her? I don't believe, you know, that even the greatest painter can show what is the real beauty of a very beautiful woman in the ordinary sense: Titian's and Tintoretto's[1] women must have been miles handsomer than they have made them. Something—and that the very essence—always escapes, perhaps because real beauty is as much a thing in time—a thing like music, a succession, a series—as in space. Mind you, I am speaking of a woman beautiful in the conventional sense. Imagine, then, how much more so in the case of a woman like Alice Oke; and if the pencil and brush, imitating each line and tint, can't succeed, how is it possible to give even the vaguest notion with mere wretched words—words possessing only a wretched abstract meaning, an impotent conventional association? To make a

---

1 Tiziano Vecellio (1477–1576), called "Titian," and Jacopo Comin (1518–1594), called "Tintoretto," were Italian Renaissance painters from Venice.

long story short, Mrs. Oke of Okehurst was, in my opinion, to the highest degree exquisite and strange—an exotic creature, whose charm you can no more describe than you could bring home the perfume of some newly discovered tropical flower by comparing it with the scent of a cabbage-rose or a lily.

That first dinner was gloomy enough. Mr. Oke—Oke of Okehurst, as the people down there called him—was horribly shy, consumed with a fear of making a fool of himself before me and his wife, I then thought. But that sort of shyness did not wear off; and I soon discovered that, although it was doubtless increased by the presence of a total stranger, it was inspired in Oke, not by me, but by his wife. He would look every now and then as if he were going make a remark, and then evidently restrain himself, and remain silent. It was very curious to see this big, handsome, manly young fellow, who ought to have had any amount of success with women, suddenly stammer and grow crimson in the presence of his own wife. Nor was it the consciousness of stupidity; for when you got him alone, Oke, although always slow and timid, had a certain amount of ideas, and very defined political and social views, and a certain childlike earnestness and desire to attain certainty and truth which was rather touching. On the other hand, Oke's singular shyness was not, so far as I could see, the result of any kind of bullying on his wife's part. You can always detect, if you have any observation, the husband or the wife who is accustomed to be snubbed, to be corrected, by his or her better-half: there is a self-consciousness in both parties, a habit of watching and fault-finding, of being watched and found fault with. This was clearly not the case at Okehurst. Mrs. Oke evidently did not trouble herself about her husband in the very least; he might say or do any amount of silly things without rebuke or even notice; and he might have done so, had he chosen, ever since his wedding-day. You felt that at once. Mrs. Oke simply passed over his existence. I cannot say she paid much attention to any one's, even to mine. At first I thought it an affectation on her part—for there was something farfetched in her whole appearance, something suggesting study, which might lead one to tax her with affectation at first; she was dressed in a strange way, not according to any established aesthetic eccentricity, but individually, strangely, as if in the clothes of an ancestress of the seventeenth century. Well, at first I thought it a kind of pose on her part, this mixture of extreme graciousness and utter indifference which she manifested towards me. She always seemed to be thinking of something else; and although she talked quite sufficiently, and with every sign of superior intelligence, she left the impression of having been as taciturn as her husband.

In the beginning, in the first few days of my stay at Okehurst, I imagined that Mrs. Oke was a highly superior sort of flirt; and that her absent manner, her look, while speaking to you, into an invisible distance, her curious irrelevant smile, were so many means of attracting and baffling adoration. I mistook it for the somewhat similar manners of certain foreign women—it is beyond English ones—which mean, to those who can understand, "pay court to me." But I soon found I was mistaken. Mrs. Oke had not the faintest desire that I should pay court to her; indeed she did not honour me with sufficient thought for that; and I, on my part, began to be too much interested in her from another point of view to dream of such a thing. I became aware, not merely that I had before me the most marvelously rare and exquisite and baffling subject for a portrait, but also one of the most peculiar and enigmatic of characters. Now that I look back upon it, I am tempted to think that the psychological peculiarity of that woman might be summed up in an exorbitant and absorbing interest in herself—a Narcissus attitude—curiously complicated with a fantastic imagination, a sort of morbid daydreaming, all turned inwards, and with no outer characteristic save a certain restlessness, a perverse desire to surprise and shock, to surprise and shock more particularly her husband, and thus be revenged for the intense boredom which his want of appreciation inflicted upon her.

I got to understand this much little by little, yet I did not seem to have really penetrated the something mysterious about Mrs. Oke. There was a waywardness, a strangeness, which I felt but could not explain—a something as difficult to define as the peculiarity of her outward appearance, and perhaps very closely connected therewith. I became interested in Mrs. Oke as if I had been in love with her; and I was not in the least in love. I neither dreaded parting from her, nor felt any pleasure in her presence. I had not the smallest wish to please or to gain her notice. But I had her on the brain. I pursued her, her physical image, her psychological explanation, with a kind of passion which filled my days, and prevented my ever feeling dull. The Okes lived a remarkably solitary life. There were but few neighbours, of whom they saw but little; and they rarely had a guest in the house. Oke himself seemed every now and then seized with a sense of responsibility towards me. He would remark vaguely, during our walks and after-dinner chats, that I must find life at Okehurst horribly dull; his wife's health had accustomed him to solitude, and then also his wife thought the neighbours a bore. He never questioned his wife's judgment in these matters. He merely stated the case as if resignation were quite simple and inevitable; yet it seemed to me, sometimes, that this monotonous life of solitude, by the side of a woman who took no more heed of him than of a table or chair, was producing a vague depression and irritation in this young man, so evidently cut out for a cheerful, commonplace life. I often wondered how he could endure it at all, not having, as I had, the interest of a strange psychological riddle to solve, and of a great portrait to paint. He was, I found, extremely good—the type of the perfectly conscientious young Englishman, the sort of man who ought to have been the Christian soldier kind of thing; devout, pure-minded, brave, incapable of any baseness, a little intellectually dense, and puzzled by all manner of moral scruples. The condition of his tenants and of his political party—he was a regular Kentish Tory[1]—lay heavy on his mind. He spent hours every day in his study, doing the work of a land agent and a political whip, reading piles of reports and newspapers and agricultural treatises; and emerging for lunch with piles of letters in his hand, and that odd puzzled look in his good healthy face, that deep gash between his eyebrows, which my friend the mad-doctor calls the *maniac-frown*. It was with this expression of face that I should have liked to paint him; but I felt that he would not have liked it, that it was more fair to him to represent him in his mere wholesome pink and white and blond conventionality. I was perhaps rather unconscientious about the likeness of Mr. Oke; I felt satisfied to paint it no matter how, I mean as regards character, for my whole mind was swallowed up in thinking how I should paint Mrs. Oke, how I could best transport on to canvas that singular and enigmatic personality. I began with her husband, and told her frankly that I must have much longer to study her. Mr. Oke couldn't understand why it should be necessary to make a hundred and one pencil-sketches of his wife before even determining in what attitude to paint her; but I think he was rather pleased to have an opportunity of keeping me at Okehurst; my presence evidently broke the monotony of his life. Mrs. Oke seemed perfectly indifferent to my staying, as she was perfectly indifferent to my presence. Without being rude, I never saw a woman pay so little attention to a guest; she would talk with me sometimes by the hour, or rather let me talk to her, but she never seemed to be listening. She would lie back in a big seventeenth-century armchair while I played the piano, with that strange smile every now and then in her thin cheeks, that strange whiteness in her eyes; but it seemed a matter of indifference whether my music stopped or went on. In my portrait of her husband she did not take, or pretend to take, the very faintest interest; but that was nothing to me. I did not want Mrs. Oke to think me interesting; I merely wished to go on studying her.

The first time that Mrs. Oke seemed to become at all aware of my presence as distinguished from that of the chairs and tables, the dogs that lay in the porch, or the clergyman or lawyer or stray neighbour who was occasionally asked to dinner, was one day—I might have been there a week—when I chanced to remark to her upon the very singular resemblance that existed between herself and the portrait of a lady

---

1   Member of the Conservative Party.

that hung in the hall with the ceiling like a ship's hull. The picture in question was a full length, neither very good nor very bad, probably done by some stray Italian of the early seventeenth century. It hung in a rather dark corner, facing the portrait, evidently painted to be its companion, of a dark man, with a somewhat unpleasant expression of resolution and efficiency, in a black Vandyck dress. The two were evidently man and wife; and in the corner of the woman's portrait were the words, "Alice Oke, daughter of Virgil Pomfret, Esq., and wife to Nicholas Oke of Okehurst," and the date 1626—"Nicholas Oke" being the name painted in the corner of the small portrait. The lady was really wonderfully like the present Mrs. Oke, at least so far as an indifferently painted portrait of the early days of Charles I, can be like a living woman of the nineteenth century. There were the same strange lines of figure and face, the same dimples in the thin cheeks, the same wide-opened eyes, the same vague eccentricity of expression, not destroyed even by the feeble painting and conventional manner of the time. One could fancy that this woman had the same walk, the same beautiful line of nape of the neck and stooping head as her descendant; for I found that Mr. and Mrs. Oke, who were first cousins, were both descended from that Nicholas Oke and that Alice, daughter of Virgil Pomfret. But the resemblance was heightened by the fact that, as I soon saw, the present Mrs. Oke distinctly made herself up to look like her ancestress, dressing in garments that had a seventeenth-century look; nay, that were sometimes absolutely copied from this portrait.

"You think I am like her," answered Mrs. Oke dreamily to my remark, and her eyes wandered off to that unseen something, and the faint smile dimpled her thin cheeks.

"You are like her, and you know it. I may even say you wish to be like her, Mrs. Oke," I answered, laughing.

"Perhaps I do."

And she looked in the direction of her husband. I noticed that he had an expression of distinct annoyance besides that frown of his.

"Isn't it true that Mrs. Oke tries to look like that portrait?" I asked, with a perverse curiosity.

"Oh, fudge!" he exclaimed, rising from his chair and walking nervously to the window. "It's all nonsense, mere nonsense. I wish you wouldn't, Alice."

"Wouldn't what?" asked Mrs. Oke, with a sort of contemptuous indifference. "If I am like that Alice Oke, why I am; and I am very pleased anyone should think so. She and her husband are just about the only two members of our family—our most flat, stale, and unprofitable family—that ever were in the least degree interesting."

Oke grew crimson, and frowned as if in pain.

"I don't see why you should abuse our family, Alice," he said. "Thank God, our people have always been honourable and upright men and women!"

"Excepting always Nicholas Oke and Alice his wife, daughter of Virgil Pomfret, Esq.," she answered, laughing, as he strode out into the park.

"How childish he is!" she exclaimed when we were alone. "He really minds, really feels disgraced by what our ancestors did two centuries and a half ago. I do believe William would have those two portraits taken down and burned if he weren't afraid of me and ashamed of the neighbours. And as it is, these two people really are the only two members of our family that ever were in the least interesting. I will tell you the story some day."

As it was, the story was told to me by Oke himself. The next day, as we were taking our morning walk, he suddenly broke a long silence, laying about him all the time at the sere grasses with the hooked stick that he carried, like the conscientious Kentishman he was, for the purpose of cutting down his and other folk's thistles.

"I fear you must have thought me very ill-mannered towards my wife yesterday," he said shyly; "and indeed I know I was."

Oke was one of those chivalrous beings to whom every woman, every wife—and his own most of all—appeared in the light of something holy. "But—but—I have a prejudice which my wife does not enter into, about raking up ugly things in one's own family. I suppose Alice thinks that it is so long ago that it has really got no connection with us; she thinks of it merely as a picturesque story. I daresay many people feel like that; in short, I am sure they do, otherwise there wouldn't be such lots of discreditable family traditions afloat. But I feel as if it were all one whether it was long ago or not; when it's a question of one's own people, I would rather have it forgotten. I can't understand how people can talk about murders in their families, and ghosts, and so forth."

"Have you any ghosts at Okehurst, by the way?" I asked. The place seemed as if it required some to complete it.

"I hope not," answered Oke gravely.

His gravity made me smile.

"Why, would you dislike it if there were?" I asked.

"If there are such things as ghosts," he replied, "I don't think they should be taken lightly. God would not permit them to be, except as a warning or a punishment."

We walked on some time in silence, I wondering at the strange type of this commonplace young man, and half wishing I could put something into my portrait that should be the equivalent of this curious unimaginative earnestness. Then Oke told me the story of those two pictures—told it me about as badly and hesitatingly as was possible for mortal man.

He and his wife were, as I have said, cousins, and therefore descended from the same old Kentish stock. The Okes of Okehurst could trace back to Norman, almost to Saxon times, far longer than any of the titled or better-known families of the neighbourhood. I saw that William Oke, in his heart, thoroughly looked down upon all his neighbours. "We have never done anything particular, or been anything particular—never held any office," he said; "but we have always been here, and apparently always done our duty. An ancestor of ours was killed in the Scotch wars,[1] another at Agincourt[2]—mere honest captains." Well, early in the seventeenth century, the family had dwindled to a single member, Nicholas Oke, the same who had rebuilt Okehurst in its present shape. This Nicholas appears to have been somewhat different from the usual run of the family. He had, in his youth, sought adventures in America, and seems, generally speaking, to have been less of a nonentity than his ancestors. He married, when no longer very young, Alice, daughter of Virgil Pomfret, a beautiful young heiress from a neighbouring county. "It was the first time an Oke married a Pomfret," my host informed me, "and the last time. The Pomfrets were quite different sort of people—restless, self-seeking; one of them had been a favourite of Henry VIII." It was clear that William Oke had no feeling of having any Pomfret blood in his veins; he spoke of these people with an evident family dislike—the dislike of an Oke, one of the old, honourable, modest stock, which had quietly done its duty, for a family of fortune-seekers and Court minions. Well, there had come to live near Okehurst, in a little house recently inherited from an uncle, a certain Christopher Lovelock, a young gallant and poet, who was in momentary disgrace at Court for some love affair. This Lovelock had struck up a great friendship with his neighbours of Okehurst—too great a friendship, apparently, with the wife, either for her husband's taste or her own. Anyhow, one evening as he was riding home alone, Lovelock had been attacked and murdered, ostensibly by highwaymen, but as was afterwards rumoured, by Nicholas Oke, accompanied by his wife dressed as a groom. No legal evidence had been got, but the tradition had remained. "They used to tell it us when we were children," said my host, in a hoarse voice, "and to frighten my cousin—I mean my wife—and me with stories about Lovelock. It is merely a tradition, which I hope may die out, as I sincerely pray to heaven

---

1   Wars of Scottish Independence in the thirteenth and fourteenth centuries.
2   A battle in 1415 during the Hundred Years War (1337–1453), which ended with the defeat of the French by the English.

that it may be false." "Alice—Mrs. Oke—you see," he went on after some time, "doesn't feel about it as I do. Perhaps I am morbid. But I do dislike having the old story raked up."

And we said no more on the subject.

IV

FROM that moment I began to assume a certain interest in the eyes of Mrs. Oke; or rather, I began to perceive that I had a means of securing her attention. Perhaps it was wrong of me to do so; and I have often reproached myself very seriously later on. But after all, how was I to guess that I was making mischief merely by chiming in, for the sake of the portrait I had undertaken, and of a very harmless psychological mania, with what was merely the fad, the little romantic affectation or eccentricity, of a scatter-brained and eccentric young woman? How in the world should I have dreamed that I was handling explosive substances? A man is surely not responsible if the people with whom he is forced to deal, and whom he deals with as with all the rest of the world, are quite different from all other human creatures.

So, if indeed I did at all conduce to mischief, I really cannot blame myself. I had met in Mrs. Oke an almost unique subject for a portrait-painter of my particular sort, and a most singular, *bizarre* personality. I could not possibly do my subject justice so long as I was kept at a distance, prevented from studying the real character of the woman. I required to put her into play. And I ask you whether any more innocent way of doing so could be found than talking to a woman, and letting her talk, about an absurd fancy she had for a couple of ancestors of hers of the time of Charles I, and a poet whom they had murdered?—particularly as I studiously respected the prejudices of my host, and refrained from mentioning the matter, and tried to restrain Mrs. Oke from doing so, in the presence of William Oke himself.

I had certainly guessed correctly. To resemble the Alice Oke of the year 1626 was the caprice, the mania, the pose, the you may call it, of the Alice Oke of 1880; and to perceive this resemblance was the sure way of gaining her good graces. It was the most extraordinary craze, of all the extraordinary crazes of childless and idle women, that I had ever met; but it was more than that, it was admirably characteristic. It finished off the strange figure of Mrs. Oke, as I saw it in my imagination—this *bizarre* creature of enigmatic, far-fetched exquisiteness—that she should have no interest in the present, but only an eccentric passion in the past. It seemed to give the meaning to the absent look in her eyes, to her irrelevant and far-off smile. It was like the words to a weird piece of gipsy music, this that she, who was so different, so distant from all women of her own time, should try and identify herself with a woman of the past—that she should have a kind of flirtation—But of this anon.

I told Mrs. Oke that I had learnt from her husband the outline of the tragedy, or mystery, whichever it was, of Alice Oke, daughter of Virgil Pomfret, and the poet Christopher Lovelock. That look of vague contempt, of a desire to shock, which I had noticed before, came into her beautiful, pale, diaphanous[1] face.

"I suppose my husband was very shocked at the whole matter," she said—"told it you with as little detail as possible, and assured you very solemnly that he hoped the whole story might be a mere dreadful calumny? Poor Willie! I remember already when we were children, and I used to come with my mother to spend Christmas at Okehurst, and my cousin was down here for his holidays, how I used to horrify him by insisting upon dressing up in shawls and waterproofs, and playing the story of the wicked Mrs. Oke; and he always piously refused to do the part of Nicholas, when I wanted to have the scene on Cotes Common. I didn't know then that I was like the original Alice Oke; I found it out only after our marriage. You really think that I am?"

She certainly was, particularly at that moment, as she stood in a white Vandyck dress, with the green of the park-land rising up behind her, and the low sun catching her short locks and surrounding her head, her exquisitely bowed head, with a pale-yellow halo. But I confess I thought the original Alice Oke, siren and murderess though she might be, very uninteresting compared with this wayward and exquisite creature whom I had rashly promised myself to send down to posterity in all her unlikely wayward exquisiteness.

One morning while Mr. Oke was despatching his Saturday heap of Conservative manifestoes and rural decisions—he was justice of the peace in a most literal sense, penetrating into cottages and huts, defending the weak and admonishing the ill-conducted—one morning while I was making one of my many pencil-sketches (alas, they are all that remain to me now!) of my future sitter, Mrs. Oke gave me her version of the story of Alice Oke and Christopher Lovelock.

"Do you suppose there was anything between them?" I asked—"that she was ever in love with him? How do you explain the part which tradition ascribes to her in the supposed murder? One has heard of women and their lovers who have killed the husband; but a woman who combines with her husband to kill her lover, or at least

---

1   Delicate and translucent: a key concept in Paterian aesthetics and the subject of his 1864 essay "Diaphaneitè."

the man who is in love with her—that is surely very singular." I was absorbed in my drawing, and really thinking very little of what I was saying.

"I don't know," she answered pensively, with that distant look in her eyes. "Alice Oke was very proud, I am sure. She may have loved the poet very much, and yet been indignant with him, hated having to love him. She may have felt that she had a right to rid herself of him, and to call upon her husband to help her to do so."

"Good heavens! what a fearful idea!" I exclaimed, half laughing. "Don't you think, after all, that Mr. Oke may be right in saying that it is easier and more comfortable to take the whole story as a pure invention?"

"I cannot take it as an invention," answered Mrs. Oke contemptuously, "because I happen to know that it is true."

"Indeed!" I answered, working away at my sketch, and enjoying putting this strange creature, as I said to myself, through her paces; "how is that?"

"How does one know that anything is true in this world?" she replied evasively; "because one does, because one feels it to be true, I suppose."

And, with that far-off look in her light eyes, she relapsed into silence.

"Have you ever read any of Lovelock's poetry?" she asked me suddenly the next day.

"Lovelock?" I answered, for I had forgotten the name. "Lovelock, who" —But I stopped, remembering the prejudices of my host, who was seated next to me at table.

"Lovelock who was killed by Mr. Oke's and my ancestors."

And she looked full at her husband, as if in perverse enjoyment of the evident annoyance which it caused him.

"Alice," he entreated in a low voice, his whole face crimson, "for mercy's sake, don't talk about such things before the servants."

Mrs. Oke burst into a high, light, rather hysterical laugh, the laugh of a naughty child.

"The servants! Gracious heavens! do you suppose they haven't heard the story? Why, it's as well known as Okehurst itself in the neighbourhood. Don't they believe that Lovelock has been seen about the house? Haven't they all heard his footsteps in the big corridor? Haven't they, my dear Willie, noticed a thousand times that you never will stay a minute alone in the yellow drawing-room—that you run out of it, like a child, if I happen to leave you there for a minute?"

True! How was it I had not noticed that? or rather, that I only now remembered having noticed it? The yellow drawing-room was one of the most charming rooms in the house: a large, bright room, hung with yellow damask and panelled with carvings, that opened straight out on to the lawn, far superior to the room in which we habitually sat, which was comparatively gloomy. This time Mr. Oke struck me as really too childish. I felt an intense desire to badger him.

"The yellow drawing-room!" I exclaimed. "Does this interesting literary character haunt the yellow drawing-room? Do tell me about it. What happened there?"

Mr. Oke made a painful effort to laugh.

"Nothing ever happened there, so far as I know," he said, and rose from the table.

"Really?" I asked incredulously.

"Nothing did happen there," answered Mrs. Oke slowly, playing mechanically with a fork, and picking out the pattern of the tablecloth. "That is just the extraordinary circumstance, that, so far as any one knows, nothing ever did happen there; and yet that room has an evil reputation. No member of our family, they say, can bear to sit there alone for more than a minute. You see, William evidently cannot."

"Have you ever seen or heard anything strange there?" I asked of my host.

He shook his head. "Nothing," he answered curtly, and lit his cigar.

"I presume you have not," I asked, half laughing, of Mrs. Oke, "since you don't mind sitting in that room for hours alone? How do you explain this uncanny reputation, since nothing ever happened there?"

"Perhaps something is destined to happen there in the future," she answered, in her absent voice. And then she suddenly added, "Suppose you paint my portrait in that room?"

Mr. Oke suddenly turned round. He was very white, and looked as if he were going to say something, but desisted.

"Why do you worry Mr. Oke like that?" I asked, when he had gone into his smoking-room with his usual bundle of papers. "It is very cruel of you, Mrs. Oke. You ought to have more consideration for people who believe in such things, although you may not be able to put yourself in their frame of mind."

"Who tells you that I don't believe in *such things,* as you call them?" she answered abruptly.

"Come," she said, after a minute, "I want to show you why I believe in Christopher Lovelock. Come with me into the yellow room."

V

WHAT Mrs. Oke showed me in the yellow room was a large bundle of papers, some printed and some manuscript, but all of them brown with age, which she took out of an old Italian ebony inlaid cabinet. It took her some time to get them, as a complicated arrangement of double locks and false drawers had to be put in play; and while she was doing so, I looked round the room, in which I had been only three or four times before. It was certainly the most beautiful room in this beautiful house, and, as it seemed to me now, the most strange. It was long and low, with something that made you think of the cabin of a ship, with a great mullioned window that let in, as it were, a perspective of the brownish green park-land, dotted with oaks, and sloping upwards to the distant line of bluish firs against the horizon. The walls were hung with flowered damask, whose yellow, faded to brown, united with the reddish colour of the carved wainscoting and the carved oaken beams. For the rest, it reminded me more of an Italian room than an English one. The furniture was Tuscan of the early seventeenth century, inlaid and carved; there were a couple of faded allegorical pictures, by some Bolognese master, on the walls; and in a corner, among a stack of dwarf orange-trees, a little Italian harpsichord of exquisite curve and slenderness, with flowers and landscapes painted upon its cover. In a recess was a shelf of old books, mainly English and Italian poets of the Elizabethan time; and close by it, placed upon a carved wedding-chest, a large and beautiful melon-shaped lute. The panes of the mullioned window were open, and yet the air seemed heavy, with an indescribable heady perfume, not that of any growing flower, but like that of old stuff that should have lain for years among spices.

"It is a beautiful room!" I exclaimed. "I should awfully like to paint you in it"; but I had scarcely spoken the words when I felt I had done wrong. This woman's husband could not bear the room, and it seemed to me vaguely as if he were right in detesting it.

Mrs. Oke took no notice of my exclamation, but beckoned me to the table where she was standing sorting the papers.

"Look!" she said, "these are all poems by Christopher Lovelock"; and touching the yellow papers with delicate and reverent fingers, she commenced reading some of them out loud in a slow, half-audible voice. They were songs in the style of those of Herrick, Waller, and Drayton,[1] complaining for the most part of the cruelty of a lady called Dryope,[2] in whose name was evidently concealed a reference to that of the mistress of Okehurst. The songs were graceful, and not without a certain faded passion: but I was thinking not of them, but of the woman who was reading them to me.

Mrs. Oke was standing with the brownish yellow wall as a background to her white brocade dress, which, in its stiff seventeenth-century make, seemed but to bring out more clearly the slightness, the exquisite suppleness, of her tall figure. She held the papers in one hand, and leaned the other, as if for support, on the inlaid cabinet by her side. Her voice, which was delicate, shadowy, like her person, had a curious throbbing cadence, as if she were reading the words of a melody, and restraining herself with difficulty from singing it; and as she read, her long slender throat throbbed slightly, and a faint redness came into her thin face. She evidently knew the verses by heart, and her eyes were mostly fixed with that distant smile in them, with which harmonised a constant tremulous little smile in her lips.

"That is how I would wish to paint her!" I exclaimed within myself; and scarcely noticed, what struck me on thinking over the scene, that this strange being read these verses as one might fancy a woman would read love-verses addressed to herself.

"Those are all written for Alice Oke—Alice the daughter of Virgil Pomfret," she said slowly, folding up the papers. "I found them at the bottom of this cabinet. Can you doubt of the reality of Christopher Lovelock now?"

The question was an illogical one, for to doubt of the existence of Christopher Lovelock was one thing, and to doubt of the mode of his death was another; but somehow I did feel convinced.

"Look!" she said, when she had replaced the poems, "I will show you something else." Among the flowers that stood on the upper storey of her writing-table—for I found that Mrs. Oke had a writing-table in the yellow room—stood, as on an altar, a small black carved frame, with a silk curtain drawn over it: the sort of thing behind which you would have expected to find a head of Christ or of the Virgin Mary. She drew the curtain and displayed a large-sized miniature, representing a young man, with auburn curls and a peaked auburn beard, dressed in black, but with lace about his neck, and large pear-shaped pearls in his ears: a wistful, melancholy face. Mrs. Oke took the miniature religiously off its stand, and showed me, written in faded characters upon the back, the name "Christopher Lovelock," and the date 1626.

---

1   Robert Herrick (1591–1674), Edmund Waller (1606–1687), and Michael Drayton (1563–1631), English lyric poets.
2   The name of a mythological Greek girl who metamorphoses into a tree.

"I found this in the secret drawer of that cabinet, together with the heap of poems," she said, taking the miniature out of my hand.

I was silent for a minute.

"Does—does Mr. Oke know that you have got it here?" I asked; and then wondered what in the world had impelled me to put such a question.

Mrs. Oke smiled that smile of contemptuous indifference. "I have never hidden it from anyone. If my husband disliked my having it, he might have taken it away, I suppose. It belongs to him, since it was found in his house."

I did not answer, but walked mechanically towards the door. There was something heady and oppressive in this beautiful room; something, I thought, almost repulsive in this exquisite woman. She seemed to me, suddenly, perverse and dangerous.

I scarcely know why, but I neglected Mrs. Oke that afternoon. I went to Mr. Oke's study, and sat opposite to him smoking while he was engrossed in his accounts, his reports, and electioneering papers. On the table, above the heap of paper-bound volumes and pigeon-holed documents, was, as sole ornament of his den, a little photograph of his wife, done some years before. I don't know why, but as I sat and watched him, with his florid, honest, manly beauty, working away conscientiously, with that little perplexed frown of his, I felt intensely sorry for this man.

But this feeling did not last. There was no help for it: Oke was not as interesting as Mrs. Oke; and it required too great an effort to pump up sympathy for this normal, excellent, exemplary young squire, in the presence of so wonderful a creature as his wife. So I let myself go to the habit of allowing Mrs. Oke daily to talk over her strange craze, or rather of drawing her out about it. I confess that I derived a morbid and exquisite pleasure in doing so: it was so characteristic in her, so appropriate to the house! It completed her personality so perfectly and made it so much easier to conceive a way of painting her. I made up my mind little by little, while working at William Oke's portrait (he proved a less easy subject than I had anticipated, and, despite his conscientious efforts, was a nervous, uncomfortable sitter, silent and brooding)—I made up my mind that I would paint Mrs. Oke standing by the cabinet in the yellow room, in the white Vandyck dress copied from the portrait of her ancestress. Mr. Oke might resent it, Mrs. Oke even might resent it; they might refuse to take the picture, to pay for it, to allow me to exhibit; they might force me to run my umbrella through the picture. No matter. That picture should be painted, if merely for the sake of having painted it; for I felt it was the only thing I could do, and that it would be far away my best work. I told neither of my resolution, but prepared sketch after sketch of Mrs. Oke, while continuing to paint her husband.

Mrs. Oke was a silent person, more silent even than her husband, for she did not feel bound, as he did, to attempt to entertain a guest or to show any interest in him. She seemed to spend her life—a curious, inactive, half-invalidish life, broken by sudden fits of childish cheerfulness—in an eternal daydream, strolling about the house and grounds, arranging the quantities of flowers that always filled all the rooms, beginning to read and then throwing aside novels and books of poetry, of which she always had a large number; and, I believe, lying for hours, doing nothing, on a couch in that yellow drawing-room, which, with her sole exception, no member of the Oke family had ever been known to stay in alone. Little by little I began to suspect and to verify another eccentricity of this eccentric being, and to understand why there were stringent orders never to disturb her in that yellow room.

It had been a habit at Okehurst, as at one or two other English manor-houses, to keep a certain amount of the clothes of each generation, more particularly wedding dresses. A certain carved oaken press, of which Mr. Oke once displayed the contents to me, was a perfect museum of costumes, male and female, from the early years of the seventeenth to the end of the eighteenth century—a thing to take away the breath of a *bric-a-brac* collector, an antiquary, or a *genre* painter. Mr. Oke was none of these, and therefore took but little interest in the collection, save in so far as it interested his family feeling. Still he seemed well acquainted with the contents of that press.

He was turning over the clothes for my benefit, when suddenly I noticed that he frowned. I know not what impelled me to say, "By the way, have you any dresses of that Mrs. Oke whom your wife resembles so much? Have you got that particular white dress she was painted in, perhaps?"

Oke of Okehurst flushed very red.

"We have it," he answered hesitatingly, "but—it isn't here at present—I can't find it. I suppose," he blurted out with an effort, "that Alice has got it. Mrs. Oke sometimes has the fancy of having some of these old things down. I suppose she takes ideas from them."

A sudden light dawned in my mind. The white dress in which I had seen Mrs. Oke in the yellow room, the day that she showed me Lovelock's verses, was not, as I had thought, a modern copy; it was the original dress of Alice Oke, the daughter of Virgil Pomfret—the dress in which, perhaps, Christopher Lovelock had seen her in that very room.

The idea gave me a delightful picturesque shudder. I said nothing. But I pictured to myself Mrs. Oke sitting in that yellow room—that room which no Oke of Okehurst save herself ventured to remain in alone, in the dress of her ancestress, confronting, as it were, that vague, haunting something that seemed to fill the place—that vague presence, it seemed to me, of the murdered cavalier poet.

Mrs. Oke, as I have said, was extremely silent, as a result of being extremely indifferent. She really did not care in the least about anything except her own ideas and day-dreams, except when, every now and then, she was seized with a sudden desire to shock the prejudices or superstitions of her husband. Very soon she got into the way of never talking to me at all, save about Alice and Nicholas Oke and Christopher Lovelock; and then, when the fit seized her, she would go on by the hour, never asking herself whether I was or was not equally interested in the strange craze that fascinated her. It so happened that I was. I loved to listen to her, going on discussing by the hour the merits of Lovelock's poems, and analysing her feelings and those of her two ancestors. It was quite wonderful to watch the exquisite, exotic creature in one of these moods, with the distant look in her grey eyes and the absent-looking smile in her thin cheeks, talking as if she had intimately known these people of the seventeenth century, discussing every minute mood of theirs, detailing every scene between them and their victim, talking of Alice, and Nicholas, and Lovelock as she might of her most intimate friends. Of Alice particularly, and of Lovelock. She seemed to know every word that Alice had spoken, every idea that had crossed her mind. It sometimes struck me as if she were telling me, speaking of herself in the third person, of her own feelings—as if I were listening to a woman's confidences, the recital of her doubts, scruples, and agonies about a living lover. For Mrs. Oke, who seemed the most self-absorbed of creatures in all other matters, and utterly incapable of understanding or sympathising with the feelings of other persons, entered completely and passionately into the feelings of this woman, this Alice, who, at some moments, seemed to be not another woman, but herself.

"But how could she do it—how could she kill the man she cared for?" I once asked her.

"Because she loved him more than the whole world!" she exclaimed, and rising suddenly from her chair, walked towards the window, covering her face with her hands.

I could see, from the movement of her neck, that she was sobbing. She did not turn round, but motioned me to go away.

"Don't let us talk any more about it," she said. "I am ill to-day, and silly."

I closed the door gently behind me. What mystery was there in this woman's life? This listlessness, this strange self-engrossment and stranger mania about people long dead, this indifference and desire to annoy towards her husband—did it all mean that Alice Oke had loved or still loved some one who was not the master of

Okehurst? And his melancholy, his preoccupation, the something about him that told of a broken youth—did it mean that he knew it?

VI

THE following days Mrs. Oke was in a condition of quite unusual good spirits. Some visitors—distant relatives—were expected, and although she had expressed the utmost annoyance at the idea of their coming, she was now seized with a fit of housekeeping activity, and was perpetually about arranging things and giving orders, although all arrangements, as usual, had been made, and all orders given, by her husband.

William Oke was quite radiant.

"If only Alice were always well like this!" he exclaimed; "if only she would take, or could take, an interest in life, how different things would be! But," he added, as if fearful lest he should be supposed to accuse her in any way, "how can she, usually, with her wretched health? Still, it does make me awfully happy to see her like this."

I nodded. But I cannot say that I really acquiesced in his views. It seemed to me, particularly with the recollection of yesterday's extraordinary scene, that Mrs. Oke's high spirits were anything but normal. There was something in her unusual activity and still more unusual cheerfulness that was merely nervous and feverish; and I had, the whole day, the impression of dealing with a woman who was ill and who would very speedily collapse.

Mrs. Oke spent her day wandering from one room to another, and from the garden to the greenhouse, seeing whether all was in order, when, as a matter of fact, all was always in order at Okehurst. She did not give me any sitting, and not a word was spoken about Alice Oke or Christopher Lovelock. Indeed, to a casual observer, it might have seemed as if all that craze about Lovelock had completely departed, or never existed. About five o'clock, as I was strolling among the red-brick round-gabled outhouses—each with its armorial oak—and the old-fashioned spalliered[1] kitchen and fruit garden, I saw Mrs. Oke standing, her hands full of York and Lancaster roses,[2] upon the steps facing the stables. A groom was currycombing a horse, and outside the coach-house was Mr. Oke's little high-wheeled cart.

---

1   Built of rough-hewn paving stones.
2   White and red roses, respectively: heraldic symbols of the warring houses of York and Lancaster during the War of the Roses (ca.1455–ca.1487), and symbols more generally of the English counties Yorkshire and Lancashire.

"Let us have a drive!" suddenly exclaimed Mrs. Oke, on seeing me. "Look what a beautiful evening—and look at that dear little cart! It is so long since I have driven, and I feel as if I must drive again. Come with me. And you, harness Jim at once and come round to the door."

I was quite amazed; and still more so when the cart drove up before the door, and Mrs. Oke called to me to accompany her. She sent away the groom, and in a minute we were rolling along, at a tremendous pace, along the yellow-sand road, with the sere pasturelands, the big oaks, on either side.

I could scarcely believe my senses. This woman, in her mannish little coat and hat, driving a powerful young horse with the utmost skill, and chattering like a school-girl of sixteen, could not be the delicate, morbid, exotic, hot-house creature, unable to walk or to do anything, who spent her days lying about on couches in the heavy atmosphere, redolent with strange scents and associations, of the yellow drawing-room. The movement of the light carriage, the cool draught, the very grind of the wheels upon the gravel, seemed to go to her head like wine.

"It is so long since I have done this sort of thing," she kept repeating; "so long, so long. Oh, don't you think it delightful, going at this pace, with the idea that any moment the horse may come down and we two be killed?" and she laughed her childish laugh, and turned her face, no longer pale, but flushed with the movement and the excitement, towards me.

The cart rolled on quicker and quicker, one gate after another swinging to behind us, as we flew up and down the little hills, across the pasture lands, through the little red-brick gabled villages, where the people came out to see us pass, past the rows of willows along the streams, and the dark-green compact hop-fields, with the blue and hazy tree-tops of the horizon getting bluer and more hazy as the yellow light began to graze the ground. At last we got to an open space, a high-lying piece of common-land, such as is rare in that ruthlessly utilised country of grazing-grounds and hop-gardens. Among the low hills of the Weald,[1] it seemed quite preternaturally high up, giving a sense that its extent of flat heather and gorse, bound by distant firs, was really on the top of the world. The sun was setting just opposite, and its lights lay flat on the ground, staining it with the red and black of the heather, or rather turning it into the surface of a purple sea, canopied over by a bank of dark purple clouds—the jet-like sparkle of the dry ling[2] and gorse tipping the purple like sunlit wavelets. A cold wind swept in our faces.

---

1   Rolling upland.
2   Heather.

"What is the name of this place?" I asked. It was the only bit of impressive scenery that I had met in the neighbourhood of Okehurst.

"It is called Cotes Common," answered Mrs. Oke, who had slackened the pace of the horse, and let the reins hang loose about his neck. "It was here that Christopher Lovelock was killed."

There was a moment's pause; and then she proceeded, tickling the flies from the horse's ears with the end of her whip, and looking straight into the sunset, which now rolled, a deep purple stream, across the heath to our feet—

"Lovelock was riding home one summer evening from Appledore, when, as he had got half-way across Cotes Common, somewhere about here—for I have always heard them mention the pond in the old gravel-pits as about the place—he saw two men riding towards him, in whom he presently recognised Nicholas Oke of Okehurst accompanied by a groom. Oke of Okehurst hailed him; and Lovelock rode up to meet him. 'I am glad to have met you, Mr. Lovelock,' said Nicholas, 'because I have some important news for you'; and so saying, he brought his horse close to the one that Lovelock was riding, and suddenly turning round, fired off a pistol at his head. Lovelock had time to move, and the bullet, instead of striking him, went straight into the head of his horse, which fell beneath him. Lovelock, however, had fallen in such a way as to be able to extricate himself easily from his horse; and drawing his sword, he rushed upon Oke, and seized his horse by the bridle. Oke quickly jumped off and drew his sword; and in a minute, Lovelock, who was much the better swordsman of the two, was having the better of him. Lovelock had completely disarmed him, and got his sword at Oke's throat, crying out to him that if he would ask forgiveness he should be spared for the sake of their old friendship, when the groom suddenly rode up from behind and shot Lovelock through the back. Lovelock fell, and Oke immediately tried to finish him with his sword, while the groom drew up and held the bridle of Oke's horse. At that moment the sunlight fell upon the groom's face, and Lovelock recognised Mrs. Oke, He cried out, 'Alice, Alice! it is you who have murdered me!' and died. Then Nicholas Oke sprang into his saddle and rode off with his wife, leaving Lovelock dead by the side of his fallen horse. Nicholas Oke had taken the precaution of removing Lovelock's purse and throwing it into the pond, so the murder was put down to certain highwaymen who were about in that part of the country. Alice Oke died many years afterwards, quite an old woman, in the reign of Charles II; but Nicholas did not live very long, and shortly before his death got into a very strange condition, always brooding, and sometimes threatening to kill his wife. They say that in one of these fits, just shortly before his death, he told the whole story of the murder, and made a prophecy that when the head of his house and master of Okehurst should marry another Alice Oke descended from himself and his wife, there should be an end of the Okes of Okehurst. You see, it seems to be coming true. We have no children, and I don't suppose we shall ever have any. I, at least, have never wished for them."

Mrs. Oke paused, and turned her face towards me with the absent smile in her thin cheeks: her eyes no longer had that distant look; they were strangely eager and fixed. I did not know what to answer; this woman positively frightened me. We remained for a moment in that same place, with the sunlight dying away in crimson ripples on the heather, gilding the yellow banks, the black waters of the pond, surrounded by thin rushes, and the yellow gravel-pits; while the wind blew in our faces and bent the ragged warped bluish tops of the firs. Then Mrs. Oke touched the horse, and off we went at a furious pace. We did not exchange a single word, I think, on the way home. Mrs. Oke sat with her eyes fixed on the reins, breaking the silence now and then only by a word to the horse, urging him to an even more furious pace. The people we met along the roads must have thought that the horse was running away, unless they noticed Mrs. Oke's calm manner and the look of excited enjoyment in her face. To me it seemed that I was in the hands of a madwoman, and I quietly prepared myself for being upset or dashed against a cart. It had turned cold, and the draught was icy in our faces when we got within sight of the red gables and high chimney-stacks of Okehurst. Mr. Oke was standing before the door. On our approach I saw a look of relieved suspense, of keen pleasure come into his face.

He lifted his wife out of the cart in his strong arms with a kind of chivalrous tenderness.

"I am so glad to have you back, darling," he exclaimed—"so glad! I was delighted to hear you had gone out with the cart, but as you have not driven for so long, I was beginning to be frightfully anxious, dearest. Where have you been all this time?"

Mrs. Oke had quickly extricated herself from her husband, who had remained holding her, as one might hold a delicate child who has been causing anxiety. The gentleness and affection of the poor fellow had evidently not touched her—she seemed almost to recoil from it.

"I have taken him to Cotes Common," she said, with that perverse look which I had noticed before, as she pulled off her driving-gloves. "It is such a splendid old place."

Mr. Oke flushed as if he had bitten upon a sore tooth, and the double gash painted itself scarlet between his eyebrows.

Outside, the mists were beginning to rise, veiling the park-land dotted with big black oaks, and from which, in the watery moonlight, rose on all sides the eerie little cry of the lambs separated from their mothers. It was damp and cold, and I shivered.

VII

THE next day Okehurst was full of people, and Mrs. Oke, to my amazement, was doing the honours of it as if a house full of commonplace, noisy young creatures, bent upon flirting and tennis, were her usual idea of felicity.

The afternoon of the third day—they had come for an electioneering ball, and stayed three nights—the weather changed; it turned suddenly very cold and began to pour. Every one was sent indoors, and there was a general gloom suddenly over the company. Mrs. Oke seemed to have got sick of her guests, and was listlessly lying back on a couch, paying not the slightest attention to the chattering and piano-strumming in the room, when one of the guests suddenly proposed that they should play charades. He was a distant cousin of the Okes, a sort of fashionable artistic Bohemian, swelled out to intolerable conceit by the amateur-actor vogue of a season.

"It would be lovely in this marvelous old place," he cried, "just to dress up, and parade about, and feel as if we belonged to the past. I have heard you have a marvelous collection of old costumes, more or less ever since the days of Noah, somewhere, Cousin Bill."

The whole party exclaimed in joy at this proposal. William Oke looked puzzled for a moment, and glanced at his wife, who continued to lie listless on her sofa.

"There is a press full of clothes belonging to the family," he answered dubiously, apparently overwhelmed by the desire to please his guests; "but—but—I don't know whether it's quite respectful to dress up in the clothes of dead people."

"Oh, fiddlestick!" cried the cousin." What do the dead people know about it? Besides," he added, with mock seriousness, "I assure you we shall behave in the most reverent way and feel quite solemn about it all, if only you will give us the key, old man."

Again Mr. Oke looked towards his wife, and again met only her vague, absent glance.

"Very well," he said, and led his guests upstairs.

An hour later the house was filled with the strangest crew and the strangest noises. I had entered, to a certain extent, into William Oke's feeling of unwillingness to let his ancestors' clothes and personality be taken in vain; but when the masquerade was complete, I must say that the effect was quite magnificent. A dozen youngish men and women—those who were staying in the house and some neighbours who had come for lawn-tennis and dinner—were rigged out, under the direction of the theatrical cousin, in the contents of that oaken press: and I have never seen a more beautiful sight than the panelled corridors, the carved and escutcheoned staircase, the dim drawing-rooms with their faded tapestries, the great hall with its vaulted and ribbed ceiling, dotted about with groups or single figures that seemed to have come straight from the past. Even William Oke, who, besides myself and a few elderly people, was the only man not masqueraded, seemed delighted and fired by the sight. A certain schoolboy character suddenly came out in him; and finding that there was no costume left for him, he rushed upstairs and presently returned in the uniform he had worn before his marriage. I thought I had really never seen so magnificent a specimen of the handsome Englishman; he looked, despite all the modern associations of his costume, more genuinely old-world than all the rest, a knight for the Black Prince or Sidney,[1] with his admirably regular features and beautiful fair hair and complexion. After a minute, even the elderly people had got costumes of some sort—dominoes arranged at the moment, and hoods and all manner of disguises made out of pieces of old embroidery and Oriental stuffs and furs; and very soon this rabble of masquers had become, so to speak, completely drunk with its own amusement—with the childishness, and, if I may say so, the barbarism, the vulgarity underlying the majority even of well-bred English men and women—Mr. Oke himself doing the mountebank like a schoolboy at Christmas.

"Where is Mrs. Oke? Where is Alice?" some one suddenly asked.

Mrs. Oke had vanished. I could fully understand that to this eccentric being, with her fantastic, imaginative, morbid passion for the past, such a carnival as this must be positively revolting; and, absolutely indifferent as she was to giving offence, I could imagine how she would have retired, disgusted and outraged, to dream her strange day-dreams in the yellow room.

But a moment later, as we were all noisily preparing to go in to dinner, the door opened and a strange figure entered, stranger than any of these others who were profaning the clothes of the dead: a boy, slight and tall, in a brown riding-coat, leathern belt, and big buff boots, a little grey cloak over one shoulder, a large grey

---

1   Edward, Prince of Wales (1343–1376), a renowned military leader, who wore a black suit of armor; Sir Philip Sidney (1554–1586), poet, soldier, and courtier during the reign of Elizabeth I.

hat slouched over the eyes, a dagger and pistol at the waist. It was Mrs. Oke, her eyes preternaturally bright, and her whole face lit up with a bold, perverse smile.

Every one exclaimed, and stood aside. Then there was a moment's silence, broken by faint applause. Even to a crew of noisy boys and girls playing the fool in the garments of men and women long dead and buried, there is something questionable in the sudden appearance of a young married woman, the mistress of the house, in a riding-coat and jackboots; and Mrs. Oke's expression did not make the jest seem any the less questionable.

"What is that costume?" asked the theatrical cousin, who, after a second, had come to the conclusion that Mrs. Oke was merely a woman of marvelous talent whom he must try and secure for his amateur troop next season.

"It is the dress in which an ancestress of ours, my namesake Alice Oke, used to go out riding with her husband in the days of Charles I," she answered, and took her seat at the head of the table. Involuntarily my eyes sought those of Oke of Okehurst. He, who blushed as easily as a girl of sixteen, was now as white as ashes, and I noticed that he pressed his hand almost convulsively to his mouth.

"Don't you recognise my dress, William?" asked Mrs. Oke, fixing her eyes upon him with a cruel smile.

He did not answer, and there was a moment's silence, which the theatrical cousin had the happy thought of breaking by jumping upon his seat and emptying off his glass with the exclamation—

"To the health of the two Alice Okes, of the past and the present!"

Mrs. Oke nodded, and with an expression I had never seen in her face before, answered in a loud and aggressive tone—

"To the health of the poet, Mr. Christopher Lovelock, if his ghost be honouring this house with its presence!"

I felt suddenly as if I were in a madhouse. Across the table, in the midst of this room full of noisy wretches, tricked out red, blue, purple, and parti-coloured, as men and women of the sixteenth, seventeenth, and eighteenth centuries, as improvised Turks and Eskimos, and dominoes, and clowns, with faces painted and corked and floured over, I seemed to see that sanguine sunset, washing like a sea of blood over the heather, to where, by the black pond and the wind-warped firs, there lay the body of Christopher Lovelock, with his dead horse near him, the yellow gravel and lilac ling soaked crimson all around; and above emerged, as out of the redness, the pale blond head covered with the grey hat, the absent eyes, and strange smile of Mrs. Oke. It seemed to me horrible, vulgar, abominable, as if I had got inside a madhouse.

VIII

FROM that moment I noticed a change in William Oke; or rather, a change that had probably been coming on for some time got to the stage of being noticeable.

I don't know whether he had any words with his wife about her masquerade of that unlucky evening. On the whole I decidedly think not. Oke was with every one a diffident and reserved man, and most of all so with his wife; besides, I can fancy that he would experience a positive impossibility of putting into words any strong feeling of disapprobation towards her, that his disgust would necessarily be silent. But be this as it may, I perceived very soon that the relations between my host and hostess had become exceedingly strained. Mrs. Oke, indeed, had never paid much attention to her husband, and seemed merely a trifle more indifferent to his presence than she had been before. But Oke himself, although he affected to address her at meals from a desire to conceal his feeling, and a fear of making the position disagreeable to me, very clearly could scarcely bear to speak to or even see his wife. The poor fellow's honest soul was quite brimful of pain, which he was determined not to allow to overflow, and which seemed to filter into his whole nature and poison it. This woman had shocked and pained him more than was possible to say, and yet it was evident that he could neither cease loving her nor commence comprehending her real nature. I sometimes felt, as we took our long walks through the monotonous country, across the oak-dotted grazing-grounds, and by the brink of the dull-green, serried hop-rows, talking at rare intervals about the value of the crops, the drainage of the estate, the village schools, the Primrose League,[1] and the iniquities of Mr. Gladstone,[2] while Oke of Okehurst carefully cut down every tall thistle that caught his eye—I sometimes felt, I say, an intense and impotent desire to enlighten this man about his wife's character. I seemed to understand it so well, and to understand it well seemed to imply such a comfortable acquiescence; and it seemed so unfair that just he should be condemned to puzzle for ever over this enigma, and wear out his soul trying to comprehend what now seemed so plain to me. But how would it ever be possible to get this serious, conscientious, slow-brained representative of English simplicity and honesty and thoroughness to understand the mixture of

---

1   A political organization (1883–2004) devoted to strengthening and expanding the British Conservative Party; named in honor of the favorite flower of Benjamin Disraeli (1804–1881), British Prime Minister, leader of the Conservative Party.
2   William Gladstone (1809–1898), four-time Prime Minister of Great Britain and leader of the Liberal Party.

self-engrossed vanity, of shallowness, of poetic vision, of love of morbid excitement, that walked this earth under the name of Alice Oke?

So Oke of Okehurst was condemned never to understand; but he was condemned also to suffer from his inability to do so. The poor fellow was constantly straining after an explanation of his wife's peculiarities; and although the effort was probably unconscious, it caused him a great deal of pain. The gash—the maniac-frown, as my friend calls it—between his eyebrows, seemed to have grown a permanent feature of his face.

Mrs. Oke, on her side, was making the very worst of the situation. Perhaps she resented her husband's tacit reproval of that masquerade night's freak, and determined to make him swallow more of the same stuff, for she clearly thought that one of William's peculiarities, and one for which she despised him, was that he could never be goaded into an outspoken expression of disapprobation; that from her he would swallow any amount of bitterness without complaining. At any rate she now adopted a perfect policy of teasing and shocking her husband about the murder of Lovelock. She was perpetually alluding to it in her conversation, discussing in his presence what had or had not been the feelings of the various actors in the tragedy of 1626, and insisting upon her resemblance and almost identity with the original Alice Oke. Something had suggested to her eccentric mind that it would be delightful to perform in the garden at Okehurst, under the huge ilexes and elms, a little masque which she had discovered among Christopher Lovelock's works; and she began to scour the country and enter into vast correspondence for the purpose of effectuating this scheme. Letters arrived every other day from the theatrical cousin, whose only objection was that Okehurst was too remote a locality for an entertainment in which he foresaw great glory to himself. And every now and then there would arrive some young gentleman or lady, whom Alice Oke had sent for to see whether they would do.

I saw very plainly that the performance would never take place, and that Mrs. Oke herself had no intention that it ever should. She was one of those creatures to whom realisation of a project is nothing, and who enjoy plan-making almost the more for knowing that all will stop short at the plan. Meanwhile, this perpetual talk about the pastoral, about Lovelock, this continual attitudinising as the wife of Nicholas Oke, had the further attraction to Mrs. Oke of putting her husband into a condition of frightful though suppressed irritation, which she enjoyed with the enjoyment of a perverse child. You must not think that I looked on indifferent, although I admit that this was a perfect treat to an amateur student of character like myself. I really did feel most sorry for poor Oke, and frequently quite indignant with his wife. I was several times on the point of begging her to have more consideration for him, even of suggesting that this kind of behavior, particularly before a comparative stranger like me, was very poor taste. But there was something elusive about Mrs. Oke, which made it next to impossible to speak seriously with her; and besides, I was by no means sure that any interference on my part would not merely animate her perversity.

One evening a curious incident took place. We had just sat down to dinner, the Okes, the theatrical cousin, who was down for a couple of days, and three or four neighbours. It was dusk, and the yellow light of the candles mingled charmingly with the greyness of the evening. Mrs. Oke was not well, and had been remarkably quiet all day, more diaphanous, strange, and far-away than ever; and her husband seemed to have felt a sudden return of tenderness, almost of compassion, for this delicate, fragile creature. We had been talking of quite indifferent matters, when I saw Mr. Oke suddenly turn very white, and look fixedly for a moment at the window opposite to his seat.

"Who's that fellow looking in at the window, and making signs to you, Alice? Damn his impudence!" he cried, and jumping up, ran to the window, opened it, and passed out into the twilight. We all looked at each other in surprise; some of the party remarked upon the carelessness of servants in letting nasty-looking fellows hang about the kitchen, others told stories of tramps and burglars. Mrs. Oke did not speak; but I noticed the curious, distant-looking smile in her thin cheeks.

After a minute William Oke came in, his napkin in his hand. He shut the window behind him and silently resumed his place.

"Well, who was it?" we all asked.

"Nobody. I—I must have made a mistake," he answered, and turned crimson, while he busily peeled a pear.

"It was probably Lovelock," remarked Mrs. Oke, just as she might have said, "It was probably the gardener," but with that faint smile of pleasure still in her face. Except the theatrical cousin, who burst into a loud laugh, none of the company had ever heard Lovelock's name, and, doubtless imagining him to be some natural appanage[1] of the Oke family, groom or farmer, said nothing, so the subject dropped.

From that evening onwards things began to assume a different aspect. That incident was the beginning of a perfect system—a system of what? I scarcely know how to call it. A system of grim jokes on the part of Mrs. Oke, of superstitious fancies on the part of her husband—a system of mysterious persecutions on the part of some less earthly tenant of Okehurst. Well, yes, after all, why not? We have all heard of

---

1   Adjunct.

ghosts, had uncles, cousins, grandmothers, nurses, who have seen them; we are all a bit afraid of them at the bottom of our soul; so why shouldn't they be? I am too sceptical to believe in the impossibility of anything, for my part!

Besides, when a man has lived throughout a summer in the same house with a woman like Mrs. Oke of Okehurst, he gets to believe in the possibility of a great many improbable things, I assure you, as a mere result of believing in her. And when you come to think of it, why not? That a weird creature, visibly not of this earth, a reincarnation of a woman who murdered her lover two centuries and a half ago, that such a creature should have the power of attracting about her (being altogether superior to earthly lovers) the man who loved her in that previous existence, whose love for her was his death—what is there astonishing in that? Mrs. Oke herself, I feel quite persuaded, believed or half believed it; indeed she very seriously admitted the possibility thereof, one day that I made the suggestion half in jest. At all events, it rather pleased me to think so; it fitted in so well with the woman's whole personality; it explained those hours and hours spent all alone in the yellow room, where the very air, with its scent of heady flowers and old perfumed stuffs, seemed redolent of ghosts. It explained that strange smile which was not for any of us, and yet was not merely for herself—that strange, far-off look in the wide pale eyes. I liked the idea, and I liked to tease, or rather to delight her with it. How should I know that the wretched husband would take such matters seriously?

He became day by day more silent and perplexed-looking; and, as a result, worked harder, and probably with less effect, at his land-improving schemes and political canvassing. It seemed to me that he was perpetually listening, watching, waiting for something to happen: a word spoken suddenly, the sharp opening of a door, would make him start, turn crimson, and almost tremble; the mention of Lovelock brought a helpless look, half a convulsion, like that of a man overcome by great heat, into his face. And his wife, so far from taking any interest in his altered looks, went on irritating him more and more. Every time that the poor fellow gave one of those starts of his, or turned crimson at the sudden sound of a footstep, Mrs. Oke would ask him, with her contemptuous indifference, whether he had seen Lovelock. I soon began to perceive that my host was getting perfectly ill. He would sit at meals never saying a word, with his eyes fixed scrutinisingly on his wife, as if vainly trying to solve some dreadful mystery; while his wife, ethereal, exquisite, went on talking in her listless way about the masque, about Lovelock, always about Lovelock. During our walks and rides, which we continued pretty regularly, he would start whenever in the roads or lanes surrounding Okehurst, or in its grounds, we perceived a figure in the distance. I have seen him tremble at what, on nearer approach, I could scarcely restrain my laughter on discovering to be some well-known farmer or neighbour or servant. Once, as we were returning home at dusk, he suddenly caught my arm and pointed across the oak-dotted pastures in the direction of the garden, then started off almost at a run, with his dog behind him, as if in pursuit of some intruder.

"Who was it?" I asked. And Mr. Oke merely shook his head mournfully. Sometimes in the early autumn twilights, when the white mists rose from the park-land, and the rooks formed long black lines on the palings, I almost fancied I saw him start at the very trees and bushes, the outlines of the distant oast-houses,[1] with their conical roofs and projecting vanes, like gibing fingers in the half light.

"Your husband is ill," I once ventured to remark to Mrs. Oke, as she sat for the hundred-and-thirtieth of my preparatory sketches (I somehow could never get beyond preparatory sketches with her). She raised her beautiful, wide, pale eyes, making as she did so that exquisite curve of shoulders and neck and delicate pale head that I so vainly longed to reproduce.

"I don't see it," she answered quietly. "If he is, why doesn't he go up to town and see the doctor? It's merely one of his glum fits."

"You should not tease him about Lovelock," I added, very seriously. "He will get to believe in him."

"Why not? If he sees him, why he sees him. He would not be the only person that has done so"; and she smiled faintly and half perversely, as her eyes sought that usual distant indefinable something.

But Oke got worse. He was growing perfectly unstrung, like a hysterical woman. One evening that we were sitting alone in the smoking-room, he began unexpectedly a rambling discourse about his wife; how he had first known her when they were children, and they had gone to the same dancing-school near Portland Place;[2] how her mother, his aunt-in-law, had brought her for Christmas to Okehurst while he was on his holidays; how finally, thirteen years ago, when he was twenty-three and she was eighteen, they had been married; how terribly he had suffered when they had been disappointed of their baby, and she had nearly died of the illness.

"I did not mind about the child, you know," he said in an excited voice; "although there will be an end of us now, and Okehurst will go to the Curtises. I minded only about Alice." It was next to inconceivable that this poor excited creature, speaking almost with tears in his voice and in his eyes, was the quiet, well-got-up,

---
1   Kilns for drying hops.
2   Majestic avenue south of Regent's Park in London's West End.

irreproachable young ex-Guardsman who had walked into my studio a couple of months before.

Oke was silent for a moment, looking fixedly at the rug at his feet, when he suddenly burst out in a scarce audible voice—

"If you knew how I cared for Alice—how I still care for her. I could kiss the ground she walks upon. I would give anything—my life any day—if only she would look for two minutes as if she liked me a little—as if she didn't utterly despise me"; and the poor fellow burst into a hysterical laugh, which was almost a sob. Then he suddenly began to laugh outright, exclaiming, with a sort of vulgarity of intonation which was extremely foreign to him—

"Damn it, old fellow, this is a queer world we live in!" and rang for more brandy and soda, which he was beginning, I noticed, to take pretty freely now, although he had been almost a blue-ribbon man[1]—as much so as is possible for a hospitable country gentleman—when I first arrived.

IX

IT became clear to me now that, incredible as it might seem, the thing that ailed William Oke was jealousy. He was simply madly in love with his wife, and madly jealous of her. Jealous—but of whom? He himself would probably have been quite unable to say. In the first place—to clear off any possible suspicion—certainly not of me. Besides the fact that Mrs. Oke took only just a very little more interest in me than in the butler or the upper-housemaid, I think that Oke himself was the sort of man whose imagination would recoil from realising any definite object of jealousy, even though jealously might be killing him inch by inch. It remained a vague, permeating, continuous feeling—the feeling that he loved her, and she did not care a jackstraw about him, and that everything with which she came into contact was receiving some of that notice which was refused to him—every person, or thing, or tree, or stone: it was the recognition of that strange far-off look in Mrs. Oke's eyes, of that strange absent smile on Mrs. Oke's lips—eyes and lips that had no look and no smile for him.

Gradually his nervousness, his watchfulness, suspiciousness, tendency to start, took a definite shape. Mr. Oke was for ever alluding to steps or voices he had heard, to figures he had seen sneaking round the house. The sudden bark of one of the dogs

---

1 Teetotaler (The Blue Ribbon Association was a nineteenth-century temperance organization.).

would make him jump up. He cleaned and loaded very carefully all the guns and revolvers in his study, and even some of the old fowling-pieces and holster-pistols in the hall. The servants and tenants thought that Oke of Okehurst had been seized with a terror of tramps and burglars. Mrs. Oke smiled contemptuously at all these doings.

"My dear William," she said one day, "the persons who worry you have just as good a right to walk up and down the passages and staircase, and to hang about the house, as you or I. They were there, in all probability, long before either of us was born, and are greatly amused by your preposterous notions of privacy."

Mr. Oke laughed angrily. "I suppose you will tell me it is Lovelock—your eternal Lovelock—whose steps I hear on the gravel every night. I suppose he has as good a right to be here as you or I." And he strode out of the room.

"Lovelock—Lovelock! Why will she always go on like that about Lovelock?" Mr. Oke asked me that evening, suddenly staring me in the face.

I merely laughed.

"It's only because she has that play of his on the brain," I answered; "and because she thinks you superstitious, and likes to tease you."

"I don't understand," sighed Oke.

How could he? And if I had tried to make him do so, he would merely have thought I was insulting his wife, and have perhaps kicked me out of the room. So I made no attempt to explain psychological problems to him, and he asked me no more questions until once—But I must first mention a curious incident that happened.

The incident was simply this. Returning one afternoon from our usual walk, Mr. Oke suddenly asked the servant whether anyone had come. The answer was in the negative; but Oke did not seem satisfied. We had hardly sat down to dinner when he turned to his wife and asked, in a strange voice which I scarcely recognised as his own, who had called that afternoon.

"No one," answered Mrs. Oke; "at least to the best of my knowledge."

William Oke looked at her fixedly.

"No one?" he repeated, in a scrutinising tone; "no one, Alice?"

Mrs. Oke shook her head. "No one," she replied.

There was a pause.

"Who was it, then, that was walking with you near the pond, about five o'clock?" asked Oke slowly.

His wife lifted her eyes straight to his and answered contemptuously—

"No one was walking with me near the pond, at five o'clock or any other hour."

Mr. Oke turned purple, and made a curious hoarse noise like a man choking.

"I—I thought I saw you walking with a man this afternoon, Alice," he brought out with an effort; adding, for the sake of appearances before me, "I thought it might have been the curate come with that report for me."

Mrs. Oke smiled.

"I can only repeat that no living creature has been near me this afternoon," she said slowly. "If you saw any one with me, it must have been Lovelock, for there certainly was no one else."

And she gave a little sigh, like a person trying to reproduce in her mind some delightful but too evanescent impression.

I looked at my host; from crimson his face had turned perfectly livid, and he breathed as if some one were squeezing his windpipe.

No more was said about the matter. I vaguely felt that a great danger was threatening. To Oke or to Mrs. Oke? I could not tell which; but I was aware of an imperious inner call to avert some dreadful evil, to exert myself, to explain, to interpose. I determined to speak to Oke the following day, for I trusted him to give me a quiet hearing, and I did not trust Mrs. Oke. That woman would slip through my fingers like a snake if I attempted to grasp her elusive character.

I asked Oke whether he would take a walk with me the next afternoon, and he accepted to do so with a curious eagerness. We started about three o'clock. It was a stormy, chilly afternoon, with great balls of white clouds rolling rapidly in the cold blue sky, and occasional lurid gleams of sunlight, broad and yellow, which made the black ridge of the storm, gathered on the horizon, look blue-black like ink.

We walked quickly across the sere and sodden grass of the park, and on to the highroad that led over the low hills, I don't know why, in the direction of Cotes Common. Both of us were silent, for both of us had something to say, and did not know how to begin. For my part, I recognised the impossibility of starting the subject: an uncalled-for interference from me would merely indispose Mr. Oke, and make him doubly dense of comprehension. So, if Oke had something to say, which he evidently had, it was better to wait for him.

Oke, however, broke the silence only by pointing out to me the condition of the hops, as we passed one of his many hop-gardens. "It will be a poor year," he said, stopping short and looking intently before him—"no hops at all. No hops this autumn."

I looked at him. It was clear that he had no notion what he was saying. The dark-green bines were covered with fruit; and only yesterday he himself had informed me that he had not seen such a profusion of hops for many years.

I did not answer, and we walked on. A cart met us in a dip of the road, and the carter touched his hat and greeted Mr. Oke. But Oke took no heed; he did not seem to be aware of the man's presence.

The clouds were collecting all round; black domes, among which coursed the round grey masses of fleecy stuff.

"I think we shall be caught in a tremendous storm," I said; "hadn't we better be turning?" He nodded, and turned sharp round.

The sunlight lay in yellow patches under the oaks of the pasture-lands, and burnished the green hedges. The air was heavy and yet cold, and everything seemed preparing for a great storm. The rooks whirled in black clouds round the trees and the conical red caps of the oast-houses which give that country the look of being studded with turreted castles; then they descended—a black line—upon the fields, with what seemed an unearthly loudness of caw. And all round there arose a shrill quavering bleating of lambs and calling of sheep, while the wind began to catch the topmost branches of the trees.

Suddenly Mr. Oke broke the silence.

"I don't know you very well," he began hurriedly, and without turning his face towards me; "but I think you are honest, and you have seen a good deal of the world—much more than I. I want you to tell me—but truly, please—what do you think a man should do if"—and he stopped for some minutes.

"Imagine," he went on quickly, "that a man cares a great deal—a very great deal for his wife, and that he finds out that she—well, that—that she is deceiving him. No—don't misunderstand me; I mean—that she is constantly surrounded by some one else and will not admit it—some one whom she hides away. Do you understand? Perhaps she does not know all the risk she is running, you know, but she will not draw back—she will not avow it to her husband"—

"My dear Oke," I interrupted, attempting to take the matter lightly, "these are questions that can't be solved in the abstract, or by people to whom the thing has not happened. And it certainly has not happened to you or me."

Oke took no notice of my interruption. "You see," he went on, "the man doesn't expect his wife to care much about him. It's not that; he isn't merely jealous, you know. But he feels that she is on the brink of dishonouring herself—because I don't think a woman can really dishonour her husband; dishonour is in our own hands, and depends only on our own acts. He ought to save her, do you see? He must, must save her, in one way or another. But if she will not listen to him, what can he do? Must he seek out the other one, and try and get him out of the way? You see it's all the fault of the other—not hers, not hers. If only she would trust in her husband, she would be safe. But that other one won't let her."

"Look here, Oke," I said boldly, but feeling rather frightened; "I know quite well what you are talking about. And I see you don't understand the matter in the very least. I do. I have watched you and watched Mrs. Oke these six weeks, and I see what is the matter. Will you listen to me?"

And taking his arm, I tried to explain to him my view of the situation—that his wife was merely eccentric, and a little theatrical and imaginative, and that she took a pleasure in teasing him. That he, on the other hand, was letting himself get into a morbid state; that he was ill, and ought to see a good doctor. I even offered to take him to town with me.

I poured out volumes of psychological explanations. I dissected Mrs. Oke's character twenty times over, and tried to show him that there was absolutely nothing at the bottom of his suspicions beyond an imaginative *pose* and a garden-play on the brain. I adduced twenty instances, mostly invented for the nonce, of ladies of my acquaintance who had suffered from similar fads. I pointed out to him that his wife ought to have an outlet for her imaginative and theatrical over-energy. I advised him to take her to London and plunge her into some set where every one should be more or less in a similar condition. I laughed at the notion of there being any hidden individual about the house. I explained to Oke that he was suffering from delusions, and called upon so conscientious and religious a man to take every step to rid himself of them, adding innumerable examples of people who had cured themselves of seeing visions and of brooding over morbid fancies. I struggled and wrestled, like Jacob with the angel, and I really hoped I had made some impression. At first, indeed, I felt that not one of my words went into the man's brain—that, though silent, he was not listening. It seemed almost hopeless to present my views in such a light that he could grasp them. I felt as if I were expounding and arguing at a rock. But when I got on to the tack of his duty towards his wife and himself, and appealed to his moral and religious notions, I felt that I was making an impression.

"I daresay you are right," he said, taking my hand as we came in sight of the red gables of Okehurst, and speaking in a weak, tired, humble voice. "I don't understand you quite, but I am sure what you say is true. I daresay it is all that I'm seedy. I feel sometimes as if I were mad, and just fit to be locked up. But don't think I don't struggle against it. I do, I do continually, only sometimes it seems too strong for me. I pray God night and morning to give me the strength to overcome my suspicions, or to remove these dreadful thoughts from me. God knows, I know what a wretched creature I am, and how unfit to take care of that poor girl."

And Oke again pressed my hand. As we entered the garden, he turned to me once more.

"I am very, very grateful to you," he said, "and, indeed, I will do my best to try and be stronger. If only," he added, with a sigh, "if only Alice would give me a moment's breathing-time, and not go on day after day mocking me with her Lovelock."

X

I HAD begun Mrs. Oke's portrait, and she was giving me a sitting. She was unusually quiet that morning; but, it seemed to me, with the quietness of a woman who is expecting something, and she gave me the impression of being extremely happy. She had been reading, at my suggestion, the "Vita Nuova,"[1] which she did not know before, and the conversation came to roll upon that, and upon the question whether love so abstract and so enduring was a possibility. Such a discussion, which might have savoured of flirtation in the case of almost any other young and beautiful woman, became in the case of Mrs. Oke something quite different; it seemed distant, intangible, not of this earth, like her smile and the look in her eyes.

"Such love as that," she said, looking into the far distance of the oak-dotted parkland, "is very rare, but it can exist. It becomes a person's whole existence, his whole soul; and it can survive the death, not merely of the beloved, but of the lover. It is unextinguishable, and goes on in the spiritual world until it meet a reincarnation of the beloved; and when this happens, it jets out and draws to it all that may remain of that lover's soul, and takes shape and surrounds the beloved one once more."

Mrs. Oke was speaking slowly, almost to herself, and I had never, I think, seen her look so strange and so beautiful, the stiff white dress bringing out but the more the exotic exquisiteness and incorporealness of her person.

I did not know what to answer, so I said half in jest—

"I fear you have been reading too much Buddhist literature, Mrs. Oke. There is something dreadfully esoteric in all you say."

She smiled contemptuously.

---

1   Book of courtly love poetry and commentary by medieval Italian poet Dante Alighieri (1265–1321).

"I know people can't understand such matters," she replied, and was silent for some time. But, through her quietness and silence, I felt, as it were, the throb of a strange excitement in this woman, almost as if I had been holding her pulse.

Still, I was in hope that things might be beginning to go better in consequence of my interference. Mrs. Oke had scarcely once alluded to Lovelock in the last two or three days; and Oke had been much more cheerful and natural since our conversation. He no longer seemed so worried; and once or twice I had caught in him a look of great gentleness and loving-kindness, almost of pity, as towards some young and very frail thing, as he sat opposite his wife.

But the end had come. After that sitting Mrs. Oke had complained of fatigue and retired to her room, and Oke had driven off on some business to the nearest town. I felt all alone in the big house, and after having worked a little at a sketch I was making in the park, I amused myself rambling about the house.

It was a warm, enervating, autumn afternoon: the kind of weather that brings the perfume out of everything, the damp ground and fallen leaves, the flowers in the jars, the old woodwork and stuffs; that seems to bring on to the surface of one's consciousness all manner of vague recollections and expectations, a something half pleasurable, half painful, that makes it impossible to do or to think. I was the prey of this particular, not at all unpleasurable, restlessness. I wandered up and down the corridors, stopping to look at the pictures, which I knew already in every detail, to follow the pattern of the carvings and old stuffs, to stare at the autumn flowers, arranged in magnificent masses of colour in the big china bowls and jars. I took up one book after another and threw it aside; then I sat down to the piano and began to play irrelevant fragments. I felt quite alone, although I had heard the grind of the wheels on the gravel, which meant that my host had returned. I was lazily turning over a book of verses—I remember it perfectly well, it was Morris's "Love is Enough"—in a corner of the drawing-room, when the door suddenly opened and William Oke showed himself. He did not enter, but beckoned to me to come out to him. There was something in his face that made me start up and follow him at once. He was extremely quiet, even stiff, not a muscle of his face moving, but very pale.

"I have something to show you," he said, leading me through the vaulted hall, hung round with ancestral pictures, into the gravelled space that looked like a filled-up moat, where stood the big blasted oak, with its twisted, pointing branches. I followed him on to the lawn, or rather the piece of park-land that ran up to the house. We walked quickly, he in front, without exchanging a word. Suddenly he stopped, just where there jutted out the bow-window of the yellow drawing-room, and I felt Oke's hand tight upon my arm.

"I have brought you here to see something," he whispered hoarsely; and he led me to the window.

I looked in. The room, compared with the out door, was rather dark; but against the yellow wall I saw Mrs. Oke sitting alone on a couch in her white dress, her head slightly thrown back, a large red rose in her hand.

"Do you believe now?" whispered Oke's voice hot at my ear. "Do you believe now? Was it all my fancy? But I will have him this time. I have locked the door inside, and, by God! he shan't escape."

The words were not out of Oke's mouth. I felt myself struggling with him silently outside that window. But he broke loose, pulled open the window, and leapt into the room, and I after him. As I crossed the threshold, something flashed in my eyes; there was a loud report, a sharp cry, and the thud of a body on the ground.

Oke was standing in the middle of the room, with a faint smoke about him; and at his feet, sunk down from the sofa, with her blond head resting on its seat, lay Mrs. Oke, a pool of red forming in her white dress. Her mouth was convulsed, as if in that automatic shriek, but her wide-open white eyes seemed to smile vaguely and distantly.

I know nothing of time. It all seemed to be one second, but a second that lasted hours. Oke stared, then turned round and laughed.

"The damned rascal has given me the slip again!" he cried; and quickly unlocking the door, rushed out of the house with dreadful cries.

That is the end of the story. Oke tried to shoot himself that evening, but merely fractured his jaw, and died a few days later, raving. There were all sorts of legal inquiries, through which I went as through a dream; and whence it resulted that Mr. Oke had killed his wife in a fit of momentary madness. That was the end of Alice Oke. By the way, her maid brought me a locket which was found round her neck, all stained with blood. It contained some very dark auburn hair, not at all the colour of William Oke's. I am quite sure it was Lovelock's.

A Chilly Night

Christina Rossetti

I rose at the dead of night
    And went to the lattice alone
To look for my Mother's ghost
    Where the ghostly moonlight shone.

My friends had failed one by one,
    Middleaged, young, and old,
Till the ghosts were warmer to me
    Than my friends that had grown cold.

I looked and I saw the ghosts
    Dotting plain and mound: 10
They stood in the blank moonlight
    But no shadow lay on the ground;
They spoke without a voice
    And they leapt without a sound.

I called: "O my Mother dear,"—
    I sobbed: "O my Mother kind,
Make a lonely bed for me
    And shelter it from the wind:

"Tell the others not to come
    To see me night or day;   20
But I need not tell my friends
    To be sure to keep away."

My Mother raised her eyes,
    They were blank and could not see;
Yet they held me with their stare
    While they seemed to look at me.

She opened her mouth and spoke,
   I could not hear a word
While my flesh crept on my bones
   And every hair was stirred.   30

She knew that I could not hear
   The message that she told
Whether I had long to wait
   Or soon should sleep in the mould:[1]
I saw her toss her shadowless hair
   And wring her hands in the cold.

I strained to catch her words
   And she strained to make me hear,
But never a sound of words
   Fell on my straining ear.   40

From midnight to the cockcrow
   I kept my watch in pain
While the subtle ghosts grew subtler
   In the sad night on the wane.

From midnight to the cockcrow
   I watched till all were gone,
Some to sleep in the shifting sea
   And some under turf and stone:
Living had failed and dead had failed
   And I was indeed alone.   50

                1856

---

1   Loose soil.

Cobwebs

Christina Rossetti

It is a land with neither night nor day,
    Nor heat nor cold, nor any wind, nor rain,
    Nor hills nor valleys; but one even plain
Stretches thro' long unbroken miles away:
While thro' the sluggish air a twilight grey   5
    Broodeth; no moons or seasons wax and wane,
    No ebb and flow are there along the main,
No bud-time no leaf-falling there for aye:—
No ripple on the sea, no shifting sand,
    No beat of wings to stir the stagnant space,   10
No pulse of life thro' all the loveless land:
And loveless sea; no trace of days before,
    No guarded home, no toil-won resting place,
No future hope, no fear for evermore.

                1855

FURISODÉ

LAFCADIO HEARN

Born in Greece, the illegitimate son of an Anglo-Irish father and a Greek mother, Patrick Lafcadio Hearn (1850–1904) was raised by his aunt in Dublin and educated by Jesuits. At nineteen, he became a drifter, working as a dishwasher in London, New York, and Cincinnati, before breaking into the newspaper business. He soon made a name for himself with his lurid stories of death and physical mutilation. Repelled by the materialism of the West, Hearn became increasingly obsessed with Eastern societies. One week after *Harper's Weekly* sent him to Japan in 1890 to work as a journalist, he quit his job and accepted a position as an English teacher in a small coastal town. He took a Japanese name—Yakumo Koizumi—and renounced his British citizenship, marrying a Japanese woman from a samurai family. His many writings on Japan, including *Glimpses of Unfamiliar Japan* (1894), *Exotics and Retrospectives* (1898), and *In Ghostly Japan* (1898), from which the following short tale comes, combine touristic impressions with traditional Japanese myths, stories, and beliefs.

RECENTLY, while passing through a little street tenanted chiefly by dealers in old wares, I noticed a *furisodé*, or long-sleeved robe, of the rich purple tint called *murasaki*, hanging before one of the shops. It was a robe such as might have been worn by a lady of rank in the time of the Tokugawa.[1] I stopped to look at the five crests upon it; and in the same moment there came to my recollection this legend of a similar robe said to have once caused the destruction of Yedo.[2]

Nearly two hundred and fifty years ago, the daughter of a rich merchant of the city of the Shoguns,[3] while attending some temple-festival, perceived in the crowd

---

1 The Edo Period (1603–1868).
2 Edo, the former name of Tokyo. In March 1657, over 100,000 people died in the Great Fire of Meireki, which destroyed two-thirds of the city.
3 Military leaders of Japan.

a young samurai[1] of remarkable beauty, and immediately fell in love with him. Unhappily for her, he disappeared in the press before she could learn through her attendants who he was or whence he had come. But his image remained vivid in her memory,—even to the least detail of his costume. The holiday attire then worn by samurai youths was scarcely less brilliant than that of young girls; and the upper dress of this handsome stranger had seemed wonderfully beautiful to the enamoured maiden. She fancied that by wearing a robe of like quality and color, bearing the same crest, she might be able to attract his notice on some future occasion.

Accordingly she had such a robe made, with very long sleeves, according to the fashion of the period; and she prized it greatly. She wore it whenever she went out; and when at home she would suspend it in her room, and try to imagine the form of her unknown beloved within it. Sometimes she would pass hours before it,—dreaming and weeping by turns. And she would pray to the gods and the Buddhas[2] that she might win the young man's affection,—often repeating the invocation of the Nichiren sect: *Namu myō hō rengé kyō!*[3]

But she never saw the youth again; and she pined with longing for him, and sickened, and died, and was buried. After her burial, the long-sleeved robe that she had so much prized was given to the Buddhist temple of which her family were parishioners. It is an old custom to thus dispose of the garments of the dead.

The priest was able to sell the robe at a good price; for it was a costly silk, and bore no trace of the tears that had fallen upon it. It was bought by a girl of about the same age as the dead lady. She wore it only one day. Then she fell sick, and began to act strangely,—crying out that she was haunted by the vision of a beautiful young man, and that for love of him she was going to die. And within a little while she died; and the long-sleeved robe was a second time presented to the temple.

Again the priest sold it; and again it became the property of a young girl, who wore it only once. Then she also sickened, and talked of a beautiful shadow, and died, and was buried. And the robe was given a third time to the temple; and the priest wondered and doubted.

Nevertheless he ventured to sell the luckless garment once more. Once more it was purchased by a girl and once more worn; and the wearer pined and died. And the robe was given a fourth time to the temple.

---

1 Member of Japanese warrior-nobility.
2 People who have achieved Buddhahood, or full enlightenment through Buddhism.
3 Nichiren (1222–1282) was a Buddhist monk and founder of a major school of Japanese Buddhism. The practice of chanting the mantra *Nam-myoho-renge-kyo*—"devotion to the law of the lotus flower scripture"—is a central component of Nichiren Buddhism and a path to enlightenment.

Then the priest felt sure that there was some evil influence at work; and he told his acolytes to make a fire in the temple-court, and to burn the robe.

So they made a fire, into which the robe was thrown. But as the silk began to burn, there suddenly appeared upon it dazzling characters of flame,—the characters of the invocation, *Namu myō hō rengé kyō*;—and these, one by one, leaped like great sparks to the temple roof; and the temple took fire.

Embers from the burning temple presently dropped upon neighbouring roofs; and the whole street was soon ablaze. Then a sea-wind, rising, blew destruction into further streets; and the conflagration spread from street to street, and from district into district, till nearly the whole of the city was consumed. And this calamity, which occurred upon the eighteenth day of the first month of the first year of Meiréki (1655),[1] is still remembered in Tōkyō as the *Furisodé-Kwaji*,—the Great Fire of the Long-sleeved Robe.

According to a story-book called *Kibun-Daijin*, the name of the girl who caused the robe to be made was O-Samé; and she was the daughter of Hikoyémon, a wine-merchant of Hyakushō-machi,[2] in the district of Azabu.[3] Because of her beauty she was also called Azabu-Komachi,[4] or the Komachi of Azabu.[5] The same book says that the temple of the tradition was a Nichiren temple called Hon-myoji, in the district of Hongo;[6] and that the crest upon the robe was a *kikyō*-flower.[7] But there are many different versions of the story; and I distrust the *Kibun-Daijin* because it asserts that the beautiful samurai was not really a man, but a transformed dragon, or water-serpent, that used to inhabit the lake at Uyéno,—*Shinobazu-no-Iké*.[8]

---

1 Hearn is not quite correct here. The Meireki Era began in 1655, but the Great Fire occurred in its third year, in 1657.
2 Farmer's town.
3 Area of Tokyo south of the city center, formerly an agricultural district.
4 Town beauty of Azabu.
5 After more than a thousand years, the name of Komachi, or Ono-no-Komachi, is still celebrated in Japan. She was the most beautiful woman of her time, and so great a poet that she could move heaven by her verses, and cause rain to fall in time of drought. Many men loved her in vain; and many are said to have died for love of her. But misfortunes visited her when her youth had passed; and, after having been reduced to the uttermost want, she became a beggar, and died at last upon the public highway, near Kyōto. As it was thought shameful to bury her in the foul rags found upon her, some poor person gave a worn-out summer-robe *(katabira)* to wrap her body in; and she was interred near Arashiyama at a spot still pointed out to travellers as the "Place of the Katabira" (*Katabira-no-Tsuchi*). [Hearn]
6 Former ward in central Tokyo, now called Bunkyō.
7 Chinese bellflower, symbol of undying love.
8 Shinobazu Pond in Tokyo.

Part VII

Chaos

FROM
THE FRENCH REVOLUTION

THOMAS CARLYLE

The most influential cultural critic of the Victorian period, a man revered during his lifetime as a modern mystic, Thomas Carlyle (1795–1881) was born in the tiny Scottish village of Ecclefechan, far away from the London intellectual scene over which he would one day preside. After leaving Edinburgh University without finishing his degree, Carlyle worked reluctantly as a teacher and private tutor, immersing himself all the while in German idealist philosophy, in which he became an expert, and which replaced the Christian faith he lost as a young man. A fierce critic of utilitarianism, laissez-faire capitalism, and the cultural and moral chaos unleashed, in his eyes, by democracy, Carlyle railed against the excesses and emptiness of modern life in a series of stylish and bombastic texts—*Sartor Resartus* (1833–1834), *On Heroes and Hero-Worship* (1841), and *Past and Present* (1843)—that left his contemporaries reeling. It is his monumental *The French Revolution* (1837), however, a prose-poem masquerading as a history book, that stands as his masterpiece. Obsessed with the text, Dickens wrote a novelistic adaptation: *A Tale of Two Cities* (1859). Equally repelled by revolutionaries and by their aristocratic oppressors, Carlyle viewed the events in France as a metaphor for the tragic birth of modernity, in which the organic moral energy holding society together suddenly and irrevocably disappears. In the passage that follows, a mob of Parisian women march on city hall.

THE MENADS[1]

IF Voltaire[2] once, in splenetic humour, asked his countrymen: "But you, *Gualches*,[3] what have you invented?" they can now answer: The Art of Insurrection. It was an art needed in these last singular times:[4] an art for which the French nature, so full of vehemence, so free from depth, was perhaps of all others the fittest.

Accordingly, to what a height, one may well say of perfection, has this branch of human industry been carried by France, within the last half-century! Insurrection, which, Lafayette[5] thought, might be "the most sacred of duties," ranks now, for the French people, among the duties which they can perform. Other mobs are dull masses; which roll onwards with a dull fierce tenacity, a dull fierce heat, but emit no light-flashes of genius as they go. The French mob, again, is among the liveliest phenomena of our world. So rapid, audacious; so clear-sighted, inventive, prompt to seize the moment; instinct with life to its finger-ends! That talent, were there no other, of spontaneously standing in queue, distinguishes, as we said, the French People from all Peoples, ancient and modern.

Let the Reader confess too that, taking one thing with another, perhaps few terrestrial Appearances are better worth considering than mobs. Your mob is a genuine outburst of Nature; issuing from, or communicating with, the deepest deep of Nature. When so much goes grinning and grimacing as a lifeless Formality, and under the stiff buckram[6] no heart can be felt beating, here once more, if nowhere else, is a Sincerity and Reality. Shudder at it; or even shriek over it, if thou must; nevertheless consider it. Such a Complex of human Forces and Individualities hurled forth, in their transcendental mood, to act and react, on circumstances and on one another; to work out what it is in them to work. The thing they will do is known to no man; least of all to themselves. It is the inflammablest immeasurable Fire-work, generating, consuming itself. With what phases, to what extent, with what results it will burn off, Philosophy and Perspicacity conjecture in vain.

---

1 Maenads were violent, drunken, ecstatic female followers of the Greek god Dionysus.
2 François-Marie Arouet Voltaire (1694–1778), French Enlightenment philosopher and author.
3 Reactionary self-important Frenchmen.
4 In 1789, when the Revolution began.
5 Marie-Joseph Paul Yves Roch du Motier, Marquis de la Fayette (1757–1834), an early leader of the Revolution.
6 Stiff linen used in bookbinding.

"Man," as has been written, "is for ever interesting to man; nay properly there is nothing else interesting."¹ In which light also, may we not discern why most Battles have become so wearisome? Battles, in these ages, are transacted by mechanism; with the slightest possible development of human individuality or spontaneity: men now even die, and kill one another, in an artificial manner. Battles ever since Homer's time, when they were Fighting Mobs, have mostly ceased to be worth looking at, worth reading of or remembering. How many wearisome bloody Battles does History² strive to represent; or even, in a husky way, to sing:—and she would omit or carelessly slur-over this one Insurrection of Women?

A thought, or dim raw-material of a thought, was fermenting all night, universally in the female head, and might explode. In squalid garret, on Monday morning Maternity awakes, to hear children weeping for bread. Maternity must forth to the streets, to the herb-markets and Bakers'-queues; meets there with hunger-stricken Maternity, sympathetic, exasperative. O we unhappy women! But, instead of Bakers'-queues, why not to Aristocrats' palaces, the root of the matter? *Allons!*³ Let us assemble. To the Hôtel-de-Ville;⁴ to Versailles;⁵ to the Lanterne!⁶

In one of the Guardhouses of the Quartier Saint-Eustache,⁷ "a young woman" seizes a drum,—for how shall National Guards give fire on women, on a young woman? The young woman seizes the drum; sets forth, beating it, "uttering cries relative to the dearth of grains."⁸ Descend, O mothers; descend, ye Judiths,⁹ to food and revenge!—All women gather and go; crowds storm all stairs, force out all women: the female Insurrectionary Force, according to Camille,¹⁰ resembles the English Naval one;¹¹ there is a universal "Press of women." Robust Dames of the

---

1   Johann Wolfgang von Goethe (1749–1832), in *Wilhelm Meister's Apprenticeship* (1795–96): "Man is properly the *only* object that interests man" (II.iv).
2   Clio, Greek muse of history.
3   Let's go!
4   City hall.
5   The royal residence outside Paris.
6   Lamp in the Place de la Grève used as a gibbet.
7   In central Paris.
8   Wheat.
9   Jewish heroine who attempts to rally her countrymen against a foreign conqueror.
10 Camille Desmoulins (1760–1794), revolutionary journalist and chronicler of the early days of the Revolution.
11 The mob of women invoke the British Navy insofar as they act as a press gang, conscripting recruits.

Halle,[1] slim Mantua-makers,[2] assiduous, risen with the dawn; ancient Virginity tripping to matins; the Housemaid, with early broom; all must go. Rouse ye, O women; the laggard men will not act; they say, we ourselves may act!

And so, like snowbreak from the mountains, for every staircase is a melted brook, it storms; tumultuous, wild-shrilling, towards the Hôtel-de-Ville. Tumultuous; with or without drum-music: for the Faubourg Saint-Antoine[3] also has tucked up its gown; and with besom-staves,[4] fire-irons, and even rusty pistols (void of ammunition), is flowing on. Sound of it flies, with a velocity of sound, to the utmost Barriers. By seven o'clock, on this raw October morning, fifth of the month, the Townhall will see wonders. Nay, as chance would have it, a male party are already there; clustering tumultuously round some National Patrol, and a Baker who has been seized with short weights. They are there; and have even lowered the rope of the Lanterne. So that the official persons have to smuggle forth the short-weighing Baker by back doors, and even send "to all the Districts" for more force.

Grand it was, says Camille, to see so many Judiths, from eight to ten thousand of them in all, rushing out to search into the root of the matter! Not unfrightful it must have been; ludicro-terrific, and most unmanageable. At such hour the overwatched Three Hundred are not yet stirring: none but some Clerks, a company of National Guards; and M. de Gouvion, the Major-general. Gouvion has fought in America for the cause of civil Liberty; a man of no inconsiderable heart, but deficient in head. He is, for the moment, in his back apartment; assuaging Usher Maillard, the Bastille-sergeant, who has come, as too many do, with "representations." The assuagement is still incomplete when our Judiths arrive.

The National Guards form on the outer stairs, with levelled bayonets; the ten thousand Judiths press up, resistless; with obtestations,[5] with outspread hands,—merely to speak to the Mayor. The rear forces them; nay, from male hands in the rear, stones already fly: the National Guard must do one of two things; sweep the Place de Grève[6] with cannon, or else open to right and left. They open; the living deluge rushes in. Through all rooms and cabinets, upwards to the topmost belfry: ravenous; seeking arms, seeking Mayors, seeking justice;—while, again, the better-

---

1   Market district in central Paris.
2   Seamstresses.
3   Neighborhood in Eastern Paris, in the vicinity of the Bastille, inhabited by the poor.
4   Brooms used as walking sticks.
5   Entreaties.
6   The public square in front of the Hôtel de Ville.

dressed speak kindly to the Clerks; point out the misery of these poor women; also their ailments, some even of an interesting sort.[1]

Poor M. de Gouvion is shiftless in this extremity;—a man shiftless, perturbed: who will one day commit suicide. How happy for him that Usher Maillard the shifty was there, at the moment, though making representations! Fly back, thou shifty Maillard: seek the Bastille Company; and O return fast with it; above all, with thy own shifty head! For, behold, the Judiths can find no Mayor or Municipal; scarcely, in the topmost belfry, can they find poor Abbé Lefevre the Powder-distributor. Him, for want of a better, they suspend there: in the pale morning light; over the top of all Paris, which swims in one's failing eyes:—a horrible end? Nay, the rope broke, as French ropes often did; or else an Amazon[2] cut it. Abbé Lefevre falls, some twenty feet, rattling among the leads; and lives long years after, though always with "a *tremblement* in the limbs."[3]

And now doors fly under hatchets; the Judiths have broken the Armory; have seized guns and cannons, three money-bags, paper-heaps; torches flare: in few minutes, our brave Hôtel-de-Ville, which dates from the Fourth Henry,[4] will, with all that it holds, be in flames!

---

1 Deux Amis, iii, 141–66. [*Carlyle*]
2 Female warrior from Greek mythology.
3 Dusaulx, Prise de la Bastille, note, p. 281. [*Carlyle*]
4 Henri de Bourbon, King of France, 1589–1610.

FROM
THE LAST DAYS OF POMPEII

Edward Bulwer-Lytton

Culminating in the natural disaster described below, Bulwer-Lytton's *The Last Days of Pompeii*, his popular historical novel from 1834, presents the eruption of Mount Vesuvius in 79 CE as a metaphor for the cataclysmic shift in the ancient world from paganism to Christianity. A towering cloud of ash and gas forms above the mountain in the days preceding the tragic event. With its decidedly arm-like formations, the angry cloud points accusingly at Pompeii's decadent population. As Roman civilization collapses under an initial rain of pumice, then beneath a pyroclastic flow, the city's persecuted Christians bask vicariously in God's wrath. The volcano kills debauched polytheistic villains, one by one. Bulwer-Lytton's protagonist, a Greek named Glaucus, who exhibits many of the attributes of a Victorian gentleman, escapes to Athens, where he converts to Christianity and tempers the militancy of the fledgling faith with his respectability.

THE PROGRESS OF THE DESTRUCTION[1]

THE cloud, which had scattered so deep a murkiness over the day, had now settled into a solid and impenetrable mass. It resembled less even the thickest gloom of a night in the open air than the close and blind darkness of some narrow room.[2] But in proportion as the blackness gathered, did the lightnings around Vesuvius increase in their vivid and scorching glare. Nor was their horrible beauty confined to the usual hues of fire; no rainbow ever rivalled their varying and prodigal dyes. Now brightly blue as the most azure depth of a

---

1   Book V, Chapter vii.
2   Pliny. [*Bulwer-Lytton*]

southern sky—now of a livid and snakelike green, darting restlessly to and fro as the folds of an enormous serpent—now of a lurid and intolerable crimson, gushing forth through the columns of smoke, far and wide, and lighting up the whole city from arch to arch,—then suddenly dying into a sickly paleness, like the ghost of their own life!

In the pauses of the showers, you heard the rumbling of the earth beneath, and the groaning waves of the tortured sea; or, lower still, and audible but to the watch of intensest fear, the grinding and hissing murmur of the escaping gases through the chasms of the distant mountain. Sometimes the cloud appeared to break from its solid mass, and, by the lightning, to assume quaint and vast mimicries of human or of monster shapes, striding across the gloom, hurtling one upon the other, and vanishing swiftly into the turbulent abyss of shade; so that, to the eyes and fancies of the affrighted wanderers, the unsubstantial vapours were as the bodily forms of gigantic foes,—the agents of terror and of death.[1]

The ashes in many places were already knee-deep; and the boiling showers which came from the steaming breath of the volcano forced their way into the houses, bearing with them a strong and suffocating vapour. In some places, immense fragments of rock, hurled upon the house roofs, bore down along the streets masses of confused ruin, which yet more and more, with every hour, obstructed the way; and, as the day advanced, the motion of the earth was more sensibly felt—the footing seemed to slide and creep—nor could chariot or litter be kept steady, even on the most level ground.

Sometimes the huger stones striking against each other as they fell, broke into countless fragments, emitting sparks of fire, which caught whatever was combustible within their reach; and along the plains beyond the city the darkness was now terribly relieved; for several houses, and even vineyards, had been set on flames; and at various intervals the fires rose suddenly and fiercely against the solid gloom. To add to this partial relief of the darkness, the citizens had, here and there, in the more public places, such as the porticos of temples and the entrances to the forum, endeavoured to place rows of torches; but these rarely continued long; the showers and the winds extinguished them, and the sudden darkness into which their sudden birth was converted had something in it doubly terrible and doubly impressing on the impotence of human hopes, the lesson of despair.

---

1   Dion Cassius. [*Bulwer-Lytton*]

Frequently, by the momentary light of these torches, parties of fugitives encountered each other, some hurrying towards the sea, others flying from the sea back to the land; for the ocean had retreated rapidly from the shore—an utter darkness lay over it, and upon its groaning and tossing waves the storm of cinders and rock fell without the protection which the streets and roofs afforded to the land. Wild—haggard—ghastly with supernatural fears, these groups encountered each other, but without the leisure to speak, to consult, to advise; for the showers fell now frequently, though not continuously, extinguishing the lights, which showed to each band the deathlike faces of the other, and hurrying all to seek refuge beneath the nearest shelter. The whole elements of civilisation were broken up. Ever and anon, by the flickering lights, you saw the thief hastening by the most solemn authorities of the law, laden with, and fearfully chuckling over, the produce of his sudden gains. If, in the darkness, wife was separated from husband, or parent from child, vain was the hope of reunion. Each hurried blindly and confusedly on. Nothing in all the various and complicated machinery of social life was left save the primal law of self-preservation! * * *

THE KRAKEN

ALFRED TENNYSON

The most popular poet of his era and one of the most oft-quoted poets in the world, Alfred Tennyson (1809–1892) seemed to many of his contemporaries an eccentric figure: a tall, shy man, fond of cloaks and wide-brimmed hats, the wistful voice of a rapidly modernizing age. At eighteen, the socially awkward Tennyson left home for Cambridge, leaving behind his bitter father, a disgruntled clergyman. There he joined a circle of talented undergraduate poets who called themselves the "Apostles," becoming the intimate friend of their charismatic leader, Arthur Hallam, whose untimely death in 1833—in conjunction with Tennyson's growing religious uncertainty and his study of geology—left him spiritually and emotionally rudderless. In much of the poetry that followed, including *In Memoriam A.H.H.* (1850) and his Arthurian epic, *Idylls of the King* (1859–1885), Tennyson struggled to process the loss of his friend and of the purpose and promise he represented. Tennyson succeeded William Wordsworth as poet laureate in 1850, becoming for the first time in his life financially secure. His new title only reinforced, however, his sense that he stood at the crossroads of history, haunted by the passage of time. To the generation of poets that followed him, Tennyson seemed a prisoner of his times. He held the post of poet laureate for forty-two years.

    Below the thunders of the upper deep,
    Far, far beneath in the abysmal sea,
    His ancient, dreamless, uninvaded sleep
    The Kraken[1] sleepeth: faintest sunlights flee
    About his shadowy sides; above him swell   5
    Huge sponges of millennial growth and height;

---

1   Monstrous giant squid from Scandinavian folklore.

And far away into the sickly light,
From many a wondrous grot and secret cell
Unnumber'd and enormous polypi[1]
Winnow with giant arms the slumbering green.   10
There hath he lain for ages, and will lie
Battening upon huge sea-worms in his sleep.
Until the latter fire[2] shall heat the deep;
Then once by man and angels to be seen,
In roaring he shall rise and on the surface die.[3]   15

                                1830

---

1   Tentacled sea animals, such as the octopus, cuttlefish, and squid.
2   The Apocalypse.
3   An allusion to the seven judgments heralded by the seven angels in Revelation: at the sound of the second angel's trumpet one-third of all sea creatures die (Revelation 8:9).

Jack Straw's Castle

Bithia Mary Croker

Bithia Mary Croker (ca.1849–1920) was born in County Roscommon, Ireland, the daughter of William Sheppard, an Anglican rector. In 1871, she married Lt. Col. John Stokes Croker of the Royal Scots and Royal Munster Fusiliers and moved to County Kildare. Her most life-changing move, however, occurred in 1877, when she and her husband travelled to Madras. During the fourteen years that she spent in India and Bengal, Croker began a prolific career as a novelist. She is the author of numerous short stories, including ghost stories, and nearly fifty novels, many of which have Anglo-Irish and Anglo-Indian themes and settings. Twenty of her novels are set in India. She lived in England the last twenty-three years of her life. "Jack Straw's Castle" first appeared in Croker's *In the Kingdom of Kerry and Other Stories* (1896).

> I have supp'd full with horrors.[1]
> *Macbeth*

MAJOR Blewe, of the Honourable East India Company's Service,[2] hated all manner of men and loved all blends of whisky; the result of this idiosyncrasy was that, after suffering many things from him for many

---

1   I have almost forgot the taste of fears:
   The time has been, my senses would have cooled
   To hear a night-shriek, and my fell of hair
   Would at a dismal treatise rouse and stir
   As life were in't. I have supped full with horrors.
   Direness, familiar to my slaughterous thoughts,
   Cannot once start me. (V.v.9–15)

2   An English trading company founded in 1600, the East India Company ruled India from 1757 to 1858, at which time the British Crown assumed direct control, following the Indian Rebellion

years, the officers of the South Nellore[1] Regiment revolted *en masse*. Endurance has its limits. If a comrade is a smart soldier and a good fellow, much is overlooked; but Major Blewe was neither, and, after an outrageous scene at an inspection dinner, he received a strong official hint to go.

He left with a substantial pension. He was not "broke"—and carried away with him the detestation of a large body of men, an unparalleled grievance, and a deathless thirst for strong waters. The Major did not return to his native land, but settled down on a hill station in Madras—whether it was on the Nilgherries, the Pulneys, the Shevaroys,[2] or elsewhere, is immaterial. Suffice to say, that he rented a four-roomed bungalow near a small station. It was cheap, in good repair, out of the way, and solitary—standing on a bare hillside, almost surrounded and concealed by rows of funereal pines, and known by the name of "Jack Straw's Castle."[3]

Here Major Blewe took up his abode, and made, as was his custom, life a purgatory to his miserable retainers. He had joined the Service in the days when, among a certain set, cursing and beating one's servants was a fashionable and laudable action, and he prided himself that he was conservative, had never discarded old habits, and that every domestic in his employment had been conscientiously and soundly thrashed. He failed, however, to mention the one grand occasion on which, having dragged an able-bodied *chokra*[4] into his bathroom—there to belabour him privately and at ease—that too vigorous young man had administered to his employer such a drubbing that he was unable to leave his bed for weeks—and meanwhile the delinquent had decamped with the Major's gold watch, silver spoons, and his pet cane!

This had *not* been a lesson, and was an old story now. Major Blewe was a notoriously bad master; his name was well noted in various bazaars. Why, then, did Hassan, his butler, and Ahmed, his cook (brothers), remain with him year after year? It was true that the wages were considerable, but what wages can repay a man for blows, kicks, curses, and insults? Major Blewe had the gift of tongues, and his invectives were as glib and as coarse as those of any old Tamil grass-cutter. The water-man and *dhoby*[5] had a better time than the indoor domestics, not being so

---

of 1857. The events depicted in Croker's story take place approximately 5–9 years after the Indian Mutiny, as it was called.
1 City north of Chennai (Madras).
2 Anglicized names of the Nilgiri, Palni, and Servarayan Hills in southern India.
3 Jack Straw's Castle is a historic pub on wooded Hampstead Heath, London. Built in the early eighteenth century, it takes its name from the famous comrade of Wat Tyler, who led the 1381 Peasants' Revolt against Richard II.
4 Male servant.
5 Washerman.

constantly *en evidence,* but no horsekeeper born of woman would remain two days, and the Major kept no pony—fortunately for that quadruped.

He invariably began the day with a hoarse, savage roar, when his early morning peg was first introduced to him. As the hours went by, these roars increased and multiplied—accompanied by kicks and blows. Attendance on him was almost as dangerous as waiting on a wild beast. In fact, he was worse than some, for he threw bottles with a deadly aim—also lamps, and scalding water. Rash, indeed, the bill collector who ventured within his reach. To be brief, Major Blewe was a degraded old savage, and yet some people declared "that he could be a gentleman when he chose." Now and then he appeared in the local reading-room and at church—red-faced, beetle-browed, blustering—but clothed, not to say dressed, and dapper, and in his right mind. But what about those other—alas! too frequent—occasions when he was to be met, singing and staggering along the highroad, with the top button of his coat fastened in the lowest button-hole of the said garment, and a guilty black bottle protruding from his pocket?

He had no occupation; he made no attempt at gardening, beyond cultivating some red chillies; and his reading was confined to the local paper, which often accumulated unopened for weeks. He spent his days in swallowing strong pegs, smoking rank "Trichys,"[1] and harrying his staff by night and day. Foolhardy, indeed, the man who dared to call his soul his own!

The owner of Jack Straw's Castle was a slender, narrow-chested Eurasian,[2] named Ezra Pedro. He collected his rents monthly, and in person. Occasionally he arrived at Major Blewe's at some desperate domestic crisis; and once, when he found his tenant tearing off the butler's turban and coat, he ventured to expostulate, and privately asked the Major "if he was not afraid of appearing before the cantonment magistrate—not afraid of law proceedings?"

"Law action? I'd like to see them try to bully old Joe Blewe! I am in my own house, where I do as I please! My house is my castle—Joe Blewe's Castle!"

"If I were you, my honoured sir, I would send away your cook and butler, and the water-man. I have heard things"—lowering his voice—"in the bazaar—hints, whispers—"

"That they rob me? Of course they do!"

"If I may humbly venture to suggest, I would counsel more gentle and polite treatment, honourable sir; and I implore you to get rid of your present servants at

---

1 Cigarettes (possibly narcotic-laced) from southern Indian city of Tiruchirapalli, called Trichy for short.
2 Of mixed race.

once. You may be sorry if you keep them—and—so may I. I do not wish to lose an excellent tenant, now you have been here thirteen years."

"Who the devil said I was going to leave?'" bawled the Major. "Wait till I give you notice! Keep your opinions to yourself, you snivelling, meddling, pudding-faced black brute! Here! Get out of the place at once, or I'll help you!"

And poor, timid, well-meaning Mr. Ezra Pedro was fain to retire with undignified celerity.

After a short time, there were whispers and vague rumours that Major Blewe—Blue Devil, as he was called—had been worse than usual with respect to violence, language, and liquor. He had broken the water-man's head, kicked the cook's wife's mother, and drowned the butler's beloved and only dog. Of late he had not been encountered slanting about the highways, and his absence was a relief; nor had he appeared in church or reading-room. The individual most interested in his welfare was his landlord, who arrived punctually on the first day of the month, receipt in hand.

He rapped timidly—no answer. Then he hammered boldly. After all, there was a month's rent due, and it was *his* house. Still dead silence. He called to a passing acquaintance, and together they peeped around, listened, whispered, wondered, and finally climbed in through an ill-secured window.

The bungalow proved to be as neat as a new pin, and in apple-pie order (it was let furnished, as are all hill houses). The Major's bedroom was beautifully tidy; long double rows of empty bottles stood as if "dressed" on parade; his clothes were folded up, his topee[1] and cap hung below his sword-scabbard; his shaving apparatus (razor included) was arranged in tempting order; and a clock was briskly ticking on the chimney-piece. The tiny sitting-room was chiefly filled by a long chair, a teapoy,[2] pipes, and peg tumblers. It was vacant. The little dining-room—ah! here was a promising sign. The cloth was laid in preparation for a meal. There were appointments for two, a cruet-stand and well-filled decanter were set by the Major's seat, and a good-sized covered dish was placed before it. The flies were swarming around this, and some rash impulse of curiosity tempted Pedro to raise the electroplated lid. He gave a shrill, wild scream as he let it fall with a frightful clang; for, grinning at him, on the dish, was Major Blewe's head!

The landlord and his companion tore out of the bungalow, and, in the language of old story-books, they ran, and they ran, and they ran. They ultimately brought the

---

1   Pith helmet.
2   Small table.

police, and a vast and excited crowd, to inspect that ghastly dinner-table. The police looked wise—as usual—asked questions, examined the premises, and made copious entries. But from that day to this—a matter of thirty years and more—no trace has ever been found of Major Blewe's servants, or of Major Blewe's body.

Jack Straw's Castle was to let, a bargain, for many seasons; and for many seasons it "has stood, a roofless ruin."

FROM
DEGENERATION

MAX NORDAU

The son of a rabbi, Max Nordau (1849–1923) was born in Pest, Hungary. He broke his mother's heart by changing his surname from Südfeld (southern field) to Nordau (northern meadow) in an effort to escape his Orthodox Jewish upbringing, rejecting religion in favor of evolutionary theory. He worked as a journalist before attending medical school at the University of Pest. Shortly after moving to Paris to practice medicine, he published his first book, *The Conventional Lies of Our Civilization* (1883), in which he renounced the "religious lie" and insisted that human solidarity should be prized over meaningless religious principles. This work won Nordau immediate global attention; it was translated into fifteen languages and banned in several countries. It is his controversial—and decidedly sexphobic—*Degeneration* (1892), however, for which he is remembered today. The concept of "degeneration" was first popularized in the late 1850s by French psychiatrist B. A. Morel, who used it to describe a diseased and deviant nervous system triggered by unhealthy behavior and living conditions. Cesare Lombroso, Nordau's colleague and the dedicatee of *Degeneration*, diagnosed criminals as "degenerate." Nordau went even further, suggesting that Western culture as a whole suffered from a modernity-induced state of degeneration, an apocalyptic disaster looming, he warned, in mankind's future. In the wake of the anti-Semitic Dreyfus Affair in the 1890s, Nordau embraced his Jewish identity, becoming a co-founder of the World Zionist Organization. He championed efforts to relocate hundreds of thousands of Jews to Palestine but died twenty-five years before his vision of an independent Jewish state was realized.

THE DUSK OF THE NATIONS

FIN-DE-SIÈCLE is a name covering both what is characteristic of many modern phenomena, and also the underlying mood which in them finds expression. Experience has long shown that an idea usually derives its designation from the language of the nation which first formed it. This, indeed, is a law of constant application when historians of manners and customs inquire into language, for the purpose of obtaining some notion, through the origins of some verbal root, respecting the home of the earliest inventions and the line of evolution in different human races. *Fin-de-siècle* is French, for it was in France that the mental state so entitled was first consciously realized. The word has flown from one hemisphere to the other, and found its way into all civilized languages. A proof this that the need of it existed. The *fin-de-siècle* state of mind is to-day everywhere to be met with; nevertheless, it is in many cases a mere imitation of a foreign fashion gaining vogue, and not an organic evolution. It is in the land of its birth that it appears in its most genuine form, and Paris is the right place in which to observe its manifold expressions.

No proof is needed of the extreme silliness of the term. Only the brain of a child or of a savage could form the clumsy idea that the century is a kind of living being, born like a beast or a man, passing through all the stages of existence, gradually ageing and declining after blooming childhood, joyous youth, and vigorous maturity, to die with the expiration of the hundredth year, after being afflicted in its last decade with all the infirmities of mournful senility. Such a childish anthropomorphism or zoomorphism never stops to consider that the arbitrary division of time, rolling ever continuously along, is not identical amongst all civilized beings, and that while this nineteenth century of Christendom is held to be a creature reeling to its death presumptively in dire exhaustion, the fourteenth century of the Mahommedan world is tripping along in the baby-shoes of its first decade, and the fifteenth century of the Jews strides gallantly by in the full maturity of its fifty-second year. Every day on our globe 130,000 human beings are born, for whom the world begins with this same day, and the young citizen of the world is neither feebler nor fresher for leaping into life in the midst of the death-throes of 1900, nor on the birthday of the twentieth century. But it is a habit of the human mind to project externally its own subjective states. And it is in accordance with this naïvely egoistic tendency that the

French ascribe their own senility to the century, and speak of *fin-de-siècle* when they ought correctly to say *fin-de-race*.¹

But however silly a term *fin-de-siècle* may be, the mental constitution which it indicates is actually present in influential circles. The disposition of the times is curiously confused, a compound of feverish restlessness and blunted discouragement, of fearful presage and hang-dog renunciation. The prevalent feeling is that of imminent perdition and extinction. *Fin-de-siècle* is at once a confession and a complaint. The old Northern faith contained the fearsome doctrine of the Dusk of the Gods.² In our days there have arisen in more highly-developed minds vague qualms of a Dusk of the Nations, in which all suns and all stars are gradually waning, and mankind with all its institutions and creations is perishing in the midst of a dying world.

It is not for the first time in the course of history that the horror of world-annihilation has laid hold of men's minds. A similar sentiment took possession of the Christian peoples at the approach of the year 1000. But there is an essential difference between chiliastic³ panic and *fin-de-siècle* excitement. The despair at the turn of the first millennium of Christian chronology proceeded from a feeling of fulness of life and joy of life. Men were aware of throbbing pulses, they were conscious of unweakened capacity for enjoyment, and found it unmitigatedly appalling to perish together with the world, when there were yet so many flagons⁴ to drain and so many lips to kiss, and when they could yet rejoice so vigorously in both love and wine. Of all this in the *fin-de-siècle* feeling there is nothing. Neither has it anything in common with the impressive twilight-melancholy of an aged Faust,⁵ surveying the work of a lifetime, and who, proud of what has been achieved, and contemplating what is begun but

---

1   This passage has been misunderstood. It has been taken to mean that all the French nation had degenerated, and their race was approaching its end. However, from the concluding paragraph of this chapter, it may be clearly seen that I had in my eye only the upper ten thousand. The peasant population, and a part of the working classes and the *bourgeoisie*, are sound. I assert only the decay of the rich inhabitants of great cities and the leading classes. It is they who have discovered *fin-de-siècle*, and it is to them also that *fin-de-race* applies. [Nordau]

2   In Norse mythology, *Ragnorök*, or "twilight of the gods," refers to the destruction of the world and the death of the gods. Two of the thinkers whom Nordau most loathed, composer Richard Wagner (1813–1883) and philosopher Friedrich Nietzsche (1844–1900), invoke the *Ragnorök* myth as a metaphor for modernity: Wagner, most notably, in his opera *Götterdämmerung* (1876), which means "Twilight of the Gods" in German; and Nietzsche, in his philosophical treatise *Götzendämmerung* (1888), which translates "Twilight of the Idols."

3   Chiliasm is the belief that Christ will return to earth and reign for 1000 years.

4   Jugs of wine.

5   Legendary German scholar who makes a pact with Satan in exchange for scientific knowledge.

not completed, is seized with vehement desire to finish his work, and, awakened from sleep by haunting unrest, leaps up with the cry: "Was ich gedacht, ich eil' es zu vollbringen."[1]

Quite otherwise is the *fin-de-siècle* mood. It is the impotent despair of a sick man, who feels himself dying by inches in the midst of an eternally living nature blooming insolently for ever. It is the envy of a rich, hoary voluptuary, who sees a pair of young lovers making for a sequestered forest nook; it is the mortification of the exhausted and impotent refugee from a Florentine plague, seeking in an enchanted garden the experiences of a Decamerone,[2] but striving in vain to snatch one more pleasure of sense from the uncertain hour. The reader of Turgenieff's[3] *A Nest of Nobles* will remember the end of that beautiful work. The hero, Lavretzky, comes as a man advanced in years to visit at the house where, in his young days, he had lived his romance of love. All is unchanged. The garden is fragrant with flowers. In the great trees the happy birds are chirping; on the fresh turf the children romp and shout. Lavretzky alone has grown old, and contemplates, in mournful exclusion, a scene where nature holds on its joyous way, caring nought that Lisa the beloved is vanished, and Lavretzky, a broken-down man, weary of life. Lavretzky's admission that, amidst all this ever-young, ever-blooming nature, for him alone there comes no morrow; Alving's dying cry for "The sun—the sun!" in Ibsen's *Ghosts*[4]—these express rightly the *fin-de-siècle* attitude of to-day.

This fashionable term has the necessary vagueness which fits it to convey all the half-conscious and indistinct drift of current ideas. Just as the words "freedom," "ideal," "progress" seem to express notions, but actually are only sounds, so in itself *fin-de-siècle* means nothing, and receives a varying signification according to the diverse mental horizons of those who use it.

The surest way of knowing what *fin-de-siècle* implies, is to consider a series of particular instances where the word has been applied. Those which I shall adduce are drawn from French books and periodicals of the last two years.[5]

---

1   "My thought I hasten to fulfil." [*Nordau*] The quote is from *Faust* (1806–32) by Johann Wolfgang von Goethe (1749–1832).
2   *The Decameron* (ca.1353), by Italian author Giovanni Boccaccio, is a collection of one hundred love stories, narrated by ten young Florentines who have fled their plague-infested city.
3   Ivan Sergeyevich Turgenev (1818–1883), Russian novelist.
4   Henrik Ibsen (1828–1906), Norwegian playwright, whose psychological realism and unflattering representations of bourgeois family life shocked audiences in the last decades of the nineteenth century.
5   A four-act comedy, by H. Micard and F. de Jouvenot, named *Fin-de-Siècle,* which was played in Paris in 1890, hardly avails to determine the sense of the word as the French use it. The authors were

A king abdicates, leaves his country, and takes up his residence in Paris, having reserved certain political rights. One day he loses much money at play, and is in a dilemma. He therefore makes an agreement with the Government of his country, by which, on receipt of a million francs, he renounces for ever every title, official position and privilege remaining to him. *Fin-de-siècle* king.

A bishop is prosecuted for insulting the minister of public worship. The proceedings terminated, his attendant canons distribute amongst the reporters in court a defence, copies of which he has prepared beforehand. When condemned to pay a fine, he gets up a public collection, which brings in tenfold the amount of the penalty. He publishes a justificatory volume containing all the expressions of support which have reached him. He makes a tour through the country, exhibits himself in every cathedral to the mob curious to see the celebrity of the hour, and takes the opportunity of sending round the plate. *Fin-de-siècle* bishop.

The corpse of the murderer Pranzini after execution underwent autopsy. The head of the secret police cuts off a large piece of skin, has it tanned, and the leather made into cigar-cases and card-cases for himself and some of his friends. *Fin-de-siècle* official.

An American weds his bride in a gas-factory, then gets with her into a balloon held in readiness, and enters on a honeymoon in the clouds. *Fin-de-siècle* wedding.

An *attaché* of the Chinese Embassy publishes high-class works in French under his own name. He negotiates with banks respecting a large loan for his Government, and draws large advances for himself on the unfinished contract. Later it comes out that the books were composed by his French secretary, and that he has swindled the banks. *Fin-de-siècle* diplomatist.

A public schoolboy walking with a chum passes the gaol where his father, a rich banker, has repeatedly been imprisoned for fraudulent bankruptcy, embezzlement and similar lucrative misdemeanours. Pointing to the building, he tells his friend with a smile: "Look, that's the governor's school." *Fin-de-siècle* son.

Two young ladies of good family, and school friends, are chatting together. One heaves a sigh. "What's the matter?" asks the other. "I'm in love with Raoul, and he with me." "Oh, that's lovely! He's handsome, young, elegant; and yet you're sad?" "Yes, but he has nothing, and is nothing, and my parents want me to marry the baron, who is fat, bald, and ugly, but has a huge lot of money." "Well, marry the

---

concerned, not to depict a phase of the age or a psychological state, but only to give an attractive title to their piece. [*Nordau*]

baron without any fuss, and make Raoul acquainted with him, you goose." *Fin-de-siècle* girls.

Such test-cases show how the word is understood in the land of its birth. Germans who ape Paris fashions, and apply *fin-de-siècle* almost exclusively to mean what is indecent and improper, misuse the word in their coarse ignorance as much as, in a previous generation, they vulgarized the expression *demi-monde*,[1] misunderstanding its proper meaning, and giving it the sense of *fille de joie*,[2] whereas its creator Dumas[3] intended it to denote persons whose lives contained some dark period, for which they were excluded from the circle to which they belong by birth, education, or profession, but who do not by their manner betray, at least to the inexperienced, that they are no longer acknowledged as members of their own caste.

Prima facie, a king who sells his sovereign rights for a big cheque seems to have little in common with a newly-wedded pair who make their wedding-trip in a balloon, nor is the connection at once obvious between an episcopal Barnum[4] and a well-brought-up young lady who advises her friend to a wealthy marriage mitigated by a *cicisbeo*.[5] All these *fin-de-siècle* cases have, nevertheless, a common feature, to wit, a contempt for traditional views of custom and morality.

Such is the notion underlying the word *fin-de-siècle*. It means a practical emancipation from traditional discipline, which theoretically is still in force. To the voluptuary this means unbridled lewdness, the unchaining of the beast in man; to the withered heart of the egoist, disdain of all consideration for his fellow-men, the trampling under foot of all barriers which enclose brutal greed of lucre and lust of pleasure; to the contemner of the world it means the shameless ascendency of base impulses and motives, which were, if not virtuously suppressed, at least hypocritically hidden; to the believer it means the repudiation of dogma, the negation of a super-sensuous world, the descent into flat phenomenalism;[6] to the sensitive nature yearning for aesthetic thrills, it means the vanishing of ideals in art, and no more power in its accepted forms to arouse emotion. And to all, it means the end of an

---

1   A person on the fringes of high society.
2   A woman of pleasure.
3   Alexandre Dumas, *fils* (1824–1895), French novelist and playwright, author of *Le Demi-monde* (1855), and the illegitimate son of novelist Alexandre Dumas, *père* (1802–1870).
4   Phineas Taylor Barnum (1810–1891), American showman, businessman, and renowned self-promoter.
5   In eighteenth- and nineteenth-century Venice, a *cicisbeo* was the publicly acknowledged lover and chaperone of a married woman: an arrangement approved by her husband.
6   A materialist or non-metaphysical explanation of existence.

established order, which for thousands of years has satisfied logic, fettered depravity, and in every art matured something of beauty.

One epoch of history is unmistakably in its decline, and another is announcing its approach. There is a sound of rending in every tradition, and it is as though the morrow would not link itself with to-day. Things as they are totter and plunge, and they are suffered to reel and fall, because man is weary, and there is no faith that it is worth an effort to uphold them. Views that have hitherto governed minds are dead or driven hence like disenthroned kings, and for their inheritance they that hold the titles and they that would usurp are locked in struggle. Meanwhile interregnum in all its terrors prevails; there is confusion among the powers that be; the million, robbed of its leaders, knows not where to turn; the strong work their will; false prophets arise, and dominion is divided amongst those whose rod is the heavier because their time is short. Men look with longing for whatever new things are at hand, without presage whence they will come or what they will be. They have hope that in the chaos of thought, art may yield revelations of the order that is to follow on this tangled web. The poet, the musician, is to announce, or divine, or at least suggest in what forms civilization will further be evolved. What shall be considered good to-morrow—what shall be beautiful? What shall we know to-morrow—what believe in? What shall inspire us? How shall we enjoy? So rings the question from the thousand voices of the people, and where a market-vendor sets up his booth and claims to give an answer, where a fool or a knave suddenly begins to prophesy in verse or prose, in sound or colour, or professes to practise his art otherwise than his predecessors and competitors, there gathers a great concourse, crowding around him to seek in what he has wrought, as in oracles of the Pythia,[1] some meaning to be divined and interpreted. And the more vague and insignificant they are, the more they seem to convey of the future to the poor gaping souls gasping for revelations, and the more greedily and passionately are they expounded.

Such is the spectacle presented by the doings of men in the reddened light of the Dusk of the Nations. Massed in the sky the clouds are aflame in the weirdly beautiful glow which was observed for the space of years after the eruption of Krakatoa.[2] Over the earth the shadows creep with deepening gloom, wrapping all objects in a mysterious dimness, in which all certainty is destroyed and any guess seems plausible.

---

1   Priestess presiding at the Oracle of Delphi in Greece.
2   A volcanic island in the Indonesian Archipelago, Krakatoa erupted in 1883, causing devastating tsunamis and a sonic boom heard 3000 miles away. So much pumice and ash entered the atmosphere, that weather patterns were changed for years; temperatures fell around the world; skies turned an eerie orange.

Forms lose their outlines, and are dissolved in floating mist. The day is over, the night draws on. The old anxiously watch its approach, fearing they will not live to see the end. A few amongst the young and strong are conscious of the vigour of life in all their veins and nerves, and rejoice in the coming sunrise. Dreams, which fill up the hours of darkness till the breaking of the new day, bring to the former comfortless memories, to the latter high-souled hopes. And in the artistic products of the age we see the form in which these dreams become sensible.

Here is the place to forestall a possible misunderstanding. The great majority of the middle and lower classes is naturally not *fin-de-siècle*. It is true that the spirit of the times is stirring the nations down to their lowest depths, and awaking even in the most inchoate and rudimentary human being a wondrous feeling of stir and upheaval. But this more or less slight touch of moral sea-sickness does not excite in him the cravings of travailing women, nor express itself in new æsthetic needs. The Philistine or the Proletarian still finds undiluted satisfaction in the old and oldest forms of art and poetry, if he knows himself unwatched by the scornful eye of the votary of fashion, and is free to yield to his own inclinations. He prefers Ohnet's[1] novels to all the symbolists,[2] and Mascagni's *Cavalleria Rusticana*[3] to all Wagnerians and to Wagner himself; he enjoys himself royally over slap-dash farces and music-hall melodies, and yawns or is angered at Ibsen; he contemplates gladly chromos[4] of paintings depicting Munich beer-houses and rustic taverns, and passes the open-air painters without a glance. It is only a very small minority who honestly find pleasure in the new tendencies, and announce them with genuine conviction as that which alone is sound, a sure guide for the future, a pledge of pleasure and of moral benefit. But this minority has the gift of covering the whole visible surface of society, as a little oil extends over a large area of the surface of the sea. It consists chiefly of rich educated people, or of fanatics. The former give the *ton*[5] to all the snobs, the fools, and the blockheads; the latter make an impression upon the weak and dependent, and intimidate the nervous. All snobs affect to have the same taste as the select and exclusive minority, who pass by everything that once was considered beautiful

---

1   Georges Ohnet (1848–1918), French bourgeois novelist and opponent of literary realism.
2   A group of late nineteenth-century French poets whose unconventional subject matter, decadent psychology, and experimental language irked detractors.
3   Pietro Mascagni (1863–1945), Italian composer, whose opera *Cavalleria Rusticana* (1890) romanticizes Sicilian village life.
4   Color prints.
5   Aura of fashion.

with an air of the greatest contempt. And thus it appears as if the whole of civilized humanity were converted to the æsthetics of the Dusk of the Nations.

HERMAPHRODITUS

ALGERNON CHARLES SWINBURNE

A son of privilege, educated at Eton and Oxford, Algernon Charles Swinburne (1837–1909)—with his shocking mane of red hair—waged a one-man war against Victorian respectability through his decadent poetry and scandalous life. He worked tirelessly to cultivate a bad reputation; he flirted with political radicalism; he hinted that he had experimented with every variety of sexual vice, though he was particularly fond, his friends knew, of erotic spankings. Influenced by the poetry of Percy Bysshe Shelley and Charles Baudelaire, as well as by the political and philosophical erotica of the Marquis de Sade, Swinburne's poetry—including his anti-Christian "Hymn to Proserpine," his homoerotic "Anactoria," and his tribute to Baudelaire, "Ave Atque Vale"—combines an exquisite sense of meter and rhyme, a pagan sensuousness, and an elegiac wistfulness. Swinburne's riotous life eventually caught up with him, however, his alcoholism taking a heavy toll on his health in 1879. Nursed back to health by his friend Theodore Watts-Dunton, in whose custody he lived for the rest of his life, a chastened Swinburne continued to write, but never again with the exhilarating decadence that once made him so popular with Victorian undergraduates. The following poem first appeared in *Poems and Ballads* (1866).

I.

Lift up thy lips, turn round, look back for love,
    Blind love that comes by night and casts out rest;
    Of all things tired thy lips look weariest,
Save the long smile that they are wearied of.
Ah sweet, albeit no love be sweet enough,
    Choose of two loves and cleave unto the best;
    Two loves at either blossom of thy breast

Strive until one be under and one above.
    Their breath is fire upon the amorous air,
    Fire in thine eyes and where thy lips suspire: 10
And whosoever hath seen thee, being so fair,
    Two things turn all his life and blood to fire;
A strong desire begot on great despair,
    A great despair cast out by strong desire.

II.

Where between sleep and life some brief space is,
    With love like gold bound round about the head,
    Sex to sweet sex with lips and limbs is wed,
Turning the fruitful feud of hers and his
To the waste wedlock of a sterile kiss;
    Yet from them something like as fire is shed   20
    That shall not be assuaged till death be dead,
Though neither life nor sleep can find out this.
Love made himself of flesh that perisheth
    A pleasure-house for all the loves his kin;
But on the one side sat a man like death,
    And on the other a woman sat like sin.
So with veiled eyes and sobs between his breath
    Love turned himself and would not enter in.

III.

Love, is it love or sleep or shadow or light
    That lies between thine eyelids and thine eyes?   30
    Like a flower laid upon a flower it lies,
Or like the night's dew laid upon the night.
Love stands upon thy left hand and thy right,
    Yet by no sunset and by no moonrise
    Shall make thee man and ease a woman's sighs,
Or make thee woman for a man's delight.
To what strange end hath some strange god made fair
    The double blossom of two fruitless flowers?

    Hid love in all the folds of all thy hair,
        Fed thee on summers, watered thee with showers,   40
    Given all the gold that all the seasons wear
        To thee that art a thing of barren hours?

IV.

Yea, love, I see; it is not love but fear.
    Nay, sweet, it is not fear but love, I know;
    Or wherefore should thy body's blossom blow
So sweetly, or thine eyelids leave so clear
Thy gracious eyes that never made a tear—
    Though for their love our tears like blood should flow,
    Though love and life and death should come and go,
So dreadful, so desirable, so dear?   50
Yea, sweet, I know; I saw in what swift wise[1]
    Beneath the woman's and the water's kiss
    Thy moist limbs melted into Salmacis,[2]
And the large light turned tender in thine eyes,
And all thy boy's breath softened into sighs;
    But Love being blind, how should he know of this?

Au Musée du Louvre,[3] *Mars* 1863.

1866

---

1   Manner.
2   Ovid tells the story of Salmacis and Hermaphroditus in *Metamorphoses*. Overcome with lust for the beautiful Hermaphroditus, the water nymph Salmacis attempts to rape him as he bathes in a pool. When he struggles against her grasp, she implores the gods to prevent his escape. They grant her wish by fusing their bodies forever into a new two-sexed creature.
3   As Swinburne's note indicates, the poem was inspired by his visit in March 1863 to the Louvre in Paris, where he saw the *Borghese Hermaphroditus*, a marble statue of a nude hermaphrodite turning in sleep on a mattress. The statue is a Roman copy from the second century CE of a Greek original from the second century BCE.

Hap

Thomas Hardy

Thomas Hardy (1840–1928) was born in Dorset, in southwest England, the son of a stonemason. Though he trained as an architect and worked for a time in London, Hardy's true loves were poetry and the rolling countryside of western England, which he immortalized in his novels as the fictional world of "Wessex." He wrote numerous novels, including *Under the Greenwood Tree* (1872), *Far from the Madding Crowd* (1874), *The Return of the Native* (1878), *The Mayor of Casterbridge* (1886), and *Tess of the D'Urbervilles* (1891), all the while composing poetry, including "Hap," a brutal reflection upon the arbitrary yet seemingly inescapable nature of suffering. After critics attacked *Jude the Obscure* as pornography in 1895, he abandoned novels, devoting himself thenceforth to poetry. Perhaps the only writer to find success as both a nineteenth-century novelist and a twentieth-century poet, Hardy produced nearly a thousand poems in the second half of his career.

If but some vengeful god would call to me
From up the sky, and laugh: "Thou suffering thing,
Know that thy sorrow is my ecstasy,
That thy love's loss is my hate's profiting!"

Then would I bear it, clench myself, and die, 5
Steeled by the sense of ire unmerited;
Half-eased in that a Powerfuller[1] than I
Had willed and meted[2] me the tears I shed.

---

1 One more powerful.
2 Given, measured out.

> But not so. How arrives it joy lies slain,
> And why unblooms the best hope ever sown? 10
> —Crass Casualty¹ obstructs the sun and rain,
> And dicing Time² for gladness casts a moan . . .
> These purblind³ Doomsters⁴ had as readily strown
> Blisses about my pilgrimage as pain.
>
> 1866

---

1   Crude mishap or random accident.
2   Instead of operating on an astral plan, the motions of the cosmos unfold by chance, like the throw of cosmic dice.
3   Half-blind
4   Doomsayers, judges.

NEURASTHENIA

A. MARY F. ROBINSON

Agnes Mary Frances Robinson (1857–1944) was celebrated as the new Letitia Landon when she published her first volume of poetry, *A Handful of Honeysuckle*, in 1878. She had grown up in a cultured household and studied classics and literature at University College, London, where she was the only female student in a course on advanced Greek. Her early work reflects the values and philosophies of the Aesthetic movement epitomized by the theories of Walter Pater, a family friend. Her critique of rural England, *A New Arcadia, Idylls of Country Life* (1884), marked a shift in Robinson's work from the purely aesthetic to the socially invested. She was involved in an intimate relationship with the writer Vernon Lee throughout the 1880s, during which time she published a study of Emily Brontë, but she shocked everyone in 1888 by marrying James Darmesteter, a professor of Persian literature in Paris. After Darmesteter's death, Robinson married Émile Duclaux, the director of the Pasteur Institute; during her marriages, she published under her married names. The following poem, published in 1902 under the name "Mary Duclaux," describes the experience of having neurasthenia: a disease of the nervous system, similar to hysteria, with symptoms that include depression, anxiety, and chronic fatigue. The stress of modern civilization and urban life in particular, it was believed, caused the disease.

I watch the happier people of the house
    Come in and out, and talk, and go their ways;
I sit and gaze at them; I cannot rouse
    My heavy mind to share their busy days.

> I watch them glide, like skaters on a stream, 5
>   Across the brilliant surface of the world.
> But I am underneath: they do not dream
>   How deep below the eddying flood is whirl'd.
>
> They cannot come to me, nor I to them;
>   But, if a mightier arm could reach and save, 10
> Should I forget the tide I had to stem?[1]
>   Should I, like these, ignore the abysmal wave?
>
> Yes! in the radiant air how could I know
>   How black it is, how fast[2] it is, below?

1902

---

1 To make headway against.
2 Fixed and unchanging.

FROM
SUICIDE: A STUDY IN SOCIOLOGY

ÉMILE DURKHEIM

Born into a rabbinical family in Lorraine, France, David Émile Durkheim (1858–1917) flirted with the idea of becoming a rabbi, so attracted was he to the power of community, but ultimately pursued what remains a profoundly influential academic career. Durkheim was one of the founders of modern sociology, which was only beginning to emerge as an independent academic discipline in the late nineteenth century. After studying philosophy in France and social science at several universities in Germany, Durkheim took a teaching position at the University of Bordeaux, where he founded Europe's first department of sociology, as well as the groundbreaking journal *L'Année Sociologique*. His works include *The Division of Labor in Society* (1893), *The Rules of Sociological Method* (1895), *Suicide: A Study in Sociology* (1897), and *The Elementary Forms of Religious Life* (1912), in which Durkheim maps the social underpinnings of seemingly personal and hence subjective experience. The nationalism sparked by World War I in France alienated Durkheim, who became the occasional target of anti-Semitic tirades. His son's death on the front lines in 1915 devastated him; he died of a stroke less than two years later.

ANOMIC SUICIDE[1]

IT is a well-known fact that economic crises have an aggravating effect on the suicidal tendency. In Vienna, in 1873 a financial crisis occurred which reached its height in 1874; the number of suicides immediately rose. From 141 in 1872, they rose to 153 in 1873 and 216 in 1874. The increase in 1874 is 53% above 1872 and 41% above 1873. What proves this catastrophe to have been the sole cause of the increase is the special prominence of the increase when the crisis was acute, or during the first four months of 1874. From January 1 to April 30 there had been 48 suicides in 1871, 44 in 1872, 43 in 1873; there were 73 in 1874. The increase is 70%.[2] The same crisis occurring at the same time in Frankfurt-on-Main[3] produced the same effects there. In the years before 1874, 22 suicides were committed annually on the average; in 1874 there were 32, or 45% more.

The famous crash is unforgotten which took place on the Paris Bourse[4] during the winter of 1882. Its consequences were felt not only in Paris but throughout France. From 1874 to 1886 the average annual increase was only 2%; in 1882 it was 7%. Moreover, it was unequally distributed among the different times of year, occurring principally during the first three months or at the very time of the crash. Within these three months alone 59% of the total rise occurred. So distinctly is the rise the result of unusual circumstances that it not only is not encountered in 1881 but has disappeared in 1883, although on the whole the latter year had a few more suicides than the preceding one:

	1881	1882	1883
Annual total	6,741	7,213 (plus 7%)	7,267
First three months	1,589	1,770 (plus 11%)	1,604

This relation is found not only in some exceptional cases, but is the rule. The number of bankruptcies is a barometer of adequate sensitivity, reflecting the

---

1 Translated by John A. Spaulding and George Simpson.
2 In 1874 over 1873. [*Simpson*]
3 Frankfurt, Germany.
4 Stock market.

variations of economic life. When they increase abruptly from year to year, some serious disturbance has *certainly* occurred. From 1845 to 1869 there were sudden rises, symptomatic of crises, on three occasions. While the annual increase in the number of bankruptcies during this period is 3.2%, it is 26% in 1847, 37% in 1854 and 20% in 1861. At these three moments, there is also to be observed an unusually rapid rise in the number of suicides. While the average annual increase during these 24 years was only 2%, it was 17% in 1847, 8% in 1854 and 9% 1861.

But to what do these crises owe their influence? Is it because they increase poverty by causing public wealth to fluctuate? Is life more readily renounced as it becomes more difficult? The explanation is seductively simple; and it agrees with the popular idea of suicide. But it is contradicted by facts.

Actually, if voluntary deaths increased because life was becoming more difficult, they should diminish perceptibly as comfort increases. Now, although when the price of the most necessary foods rises excessively, suicides generally do the same, they are not found to fall below the average in the opposite case. In Prussia, in 1850 wheat was quoted at the lowest point it reached during the entire period of 1848–81; it was at 6.91 marks per 50 kilograms; yet at this very time suicides rose from 1,527 where they were in 1849 to 1,736, or an increase of 13%, and continued to increase during the years 1851, 1852 and 1853 although the cheap market held. In 1858-59 a new fall took place; yet suicides rose from 2,038 in 1857 to 2,126 in 1858, and to 2,146 in 1859. From 1863 to 1866 prices which had reached 11.04 marks in 1861 fell progressively to 7.95 marks in 1864 and remained very reasonable for the whole period; suicides during the same time increased 17% (2,112 in 1862, 2,485 in 1866).[1] Similar facts are observed in Bavaria. According to a curve constructed by Mayr[2] for the period 1835-61, the price of rye was lowest during the years 1857-58 and 1858-59; now suicides, which in 1857 numbered only 286, rose to 329 in 1858, to 387 in 1859. The same phenomenon had already occurred during the years 1848-50; at that time wheat had been very cheap in Bavaria as well as throughout Europe. Yet, in spite of a slight temporary drop due to political events, which we have mentioned, suicides remained at the same level. There were 217 in 1847, there were still 215 in 1848, and if they dropped for a moment to 189 in 1849, they rose again in 1850 and reached 250.

---

1 See Starck, *Verbrechen und Vergehen in Preussen*, Berlin, 1884, p. 55. [Durkheim]
2 *Die Gesetzmässigkeit im Gesellschaftsleben*, p. 345. [Durkheim]

So far is the increase in poverty from causing the increase in suicide that even fortunate crises, the effect of which is abruptly to enhance a country's prosperity, affect suicide like economic disasters.

The conquest of Rome by Victor-Emmanuel in 1870, by definitely forming the basis of Italian unity, was the starting point for the country of a process of growth which is making it one of the great powers of Europe. Trade and industry received a sharp stimulus from it and surprisingly rapid changes took place. Whereas in 1876, 4,459 steam boilers with a total of 54,000 horse-power were enough for industrial needs, the number of machines in 1887 was 9,983 and their horse-power of 167,000 was threefold more. Of course the amount of production rose proportionately during the same time.[1] Trade followed the same rising course; not only did the merchant marine, communications and transportation develop, but the number of persons and things transported doubled.[2] As this generally heightened activity caused an increase in salaries (an increase of 35% is estimated to have taken place from 1873 to 1889), the material comfort of workers rose, especially since the price of bread was falling at the same time.[3] Finally, according to calculations by Bodio,[4] private wealth rose from 45 and a half billions on the average during the period 1875-80 to 51 billions during the years 1880-85 and 54 billions and a half in 1885-90.[5]

Now, an unusual increase in the number of suicides is observed parallel with this collective renaissance. From 1866 to 1870 they were roughly stable; from 1871 to 1877 they increased 36%. There were in

1864–70	29 suicides per million	1874	37 suicides per million
1871	31 suicides per million	1875	34 suicides per million
1872	33 suicides per million	1876	36.5 suicides per million
1873	36 suicides per million	1877	40.6 suicides per million

---

1 See Fornasari di Verce, *La criminalita e le vicende economiche d'Italia*, Turin, 1894, pp. 77–83. [*Durkheim*]
2 *Ibid.*, pp. 108–117. [*Durkheim*]
3 *Ibid.*, pp. 86–104. [*Durkheim*]
4 Luigi Bodio (1840–1920), Italian statistician and economist.
5 The increase is less during the period 1885–90 because of a financial crisis. [*Durkheim*]

And since then the movement has continued. The total figure, 1,139 in 1877, was 1,463 in 1889, a new increase of 28%.

In Prussia the same phenomenon occurred on two occasions. In 1866 the kingdom received a first enlargement. It annexed several important provinces, while becoming the head of the Confederation of the North. Immediately this growth in glory and power was accompanied by a sudden rise in the number of suicides. There had been 123 suicides per million during the period 1856-60 per average year and only 122 during the years 1861-65. In the five years, 1866-70, in spite of the drop in 1870, the average rose to 133. The year 1867, which immediately followed victory, was that in which suicide achieved the highest point it had reached since 1816 (1 suicide per 5,432 inhabitants, while in 1864 there was only one case per 8,739).

On the morrow of the war of 1870 a new accession of good fortune took place. Germany was unified and placed entirely under Prussian hegemony. An enormous war indemnity added to the public wealth; commerce and industry made great strides. The development of suicide was never so rapid. From 1875 to 1886 it increased 90%, from 3,278 cases to 6,212.

World expositions, when successful, are considered favorable events in the existence of a society. They stimulate business, bring more money into the country and are thought to increase public prosperity, especially in the city where they take place. Yet, quite possibly, they ultimately take their toll in a considerably higher number of suicides. Especially does this seem to have been true of the Exposition of 1878. The rise that year was the highest occurring between 1874 and 1886. It was 8%, that is, higher than the one caused by the crash of 1882. And what almost proves the Exposition to have been the cause of this increase is that 86% of it took place precisely during the six months of the Exposition.

In 1889 things were not identical all over France. But quite possibly the Boulanger crisis[1] neutralized the contrary effects of the Exposition by its depressive influence on the growth of suicides. Certainly at Paris, although the political feeling aroused must have had the same effect as in the rest of the country, things happened as in 1878. For the 7 months of the Exposition, suicides increased almost 10%, 9.66 to be exact, while through the remainder of the year they were below what they had been in 1888 and what they afterwards were in 1890.

---

1   Georges Ernest Boulanger (1837–1891), reactionary French general and politician, whose dictatorial aspirations threatened to destabilize the Third Republic and eventually led to his downfall, his flight from France, and his suicide in a Belgian cemetery.

	1888	1889	1890
The seven months of the Exposition	517	567	540
The five other months	319	311	356

It may well be that but for the Boulanger influence the rise would have been greater.

What proves still more conclusively that economic distress does not have the aggravating influence often attributed to it, is that it tends rather to produce the opposite effect. There is very little suicide in Ireland, where the peasantry leads so wretched a life. Poverty-stricken Calabria has almost no suicides; Spain has a tenth as many as France. Poverty may even be considered a protection. In the various French departments the more people there are who have independent means, the more numerous are suicides.

Departments Where, per 100,000 Inhabitants, Suicides Were Committed (1878–1887)		*Average Number of Persons of Independent Means per 1,000 Inhabitants in Each Group of Departments (1886)*
Suicides	Number of Departments	
From 48 to 43	5	127
From 38 to 31	6	73
From 30 to 24	6	69
From 23 to 18	15	59
From 17 to 13	18	49
From 12 to 8	26	49
From 7 to 3	10	42

Comparison of the maps confirms that of the averages.

If therefore industrial or financial crises increase suicides, this is not because they cause poverty, since crises of prosperity have the same result; it is because they are crises, that is, disturbances of the collective order.[1] Every disturbance of equilibrium, even though it achieves greater comfort and a heightening of general vitality, is an impulse to voluntary death. Whenever serious readjustments take place in the social order, whether or not due to a sudden growth or to an unexpected catastrophe, men are more inclined to self-destruction. How is this possible? How can something considered generally to improve existence serve to detach men from it?

For the answer, some preliminary considerations are required.

II

NO living being can be happy or even exist unless his needs are sufficiently proportioned to his means. In other words, if his needs require more than can be granted, or even merely something of a different sort, they will be under continual friction and can only function painfully. Movements incapable of production without pain tend not to be reproduced. Unsatisfied tendencies atrophy, and as the impulse to live is merely the result of all the rest, it is bound to weaken as the others relax.

In the animal, at least in a normal condition, this equilibrium is established with automatic spontaneity because the animal depends on purely material conditions. All the organism needs is that the supplies of substance and energy constantly employed in the vital process should be periodically renewed by equivalent quantities; that replacement be equivalent to use. When the void created by existence in its own resources is filled, the animal, satisfied, asks nothing further. Its power of reflection is not sufficiently developed to imagine other ends than those implicit in its physical nature. On the other hand, as the work demanded of each organ itself

---

1   To prove that an increase in prosperity diminishes suicides, the attempt has been made to show that they become less when emigration, the escape-valve of poverty, is widely practiced (See Legoyt, pp. 257–259). But cases are numerous where parallelism instead of inverse proportions exist between the two. In Italy from 1876 to 1890 the number of emigrants rose from 76 per 100,000 inhabitants to 335, a figure itself exceeded between 1887 and 1889. At the same time suicides did not cease to grow in numbers. [*Durkheim*]

depends on the general state of vital energy and the needs of organic equilibrium, use is regulated in turn by replacement and the balance is automatic. The limits of one are those of the other; both are fundamental to the constitution of the existence in question, which cannot exceed them.

This is not the case with man, because most of his needs are not dependent on his body or not to the same degree. Strictly speaking, we may consider that the quantity of material supplies necessary to the physical maintenance of a human life is subject to computation, though this be less exact than in the preceding case and a wider margin left for the free combinations of the will; for beyond the indispensable minimum which satisfies nature when instinctive, a more awakened reflection suggests better conditions, seemingly desirable ends craving fulfillment. Such appetites, however, admittedly sooner or later reach a limit which they cannot pass. But how determine the quantity of well-being, comfort or luxury legitimately to be craved by a human being? Nothing appears in man's organic nor in his psychological constitution which sets a limit to such tendencies. The functioning of individual life does not require them to cease at one point rather than at another; the proof being that they have constantly increased since the beginnings of history, receiving more and more complete satisfaction, yet with no weakening of average health. Above all, how establish their proper variation with different conditions of life, occupations, relative importance of services, etc.? In no society are they equally satisfied in the different stages of the social hierarchy. Yet human nature is substantially the same among all men, in its essential qualities. It is not human nature which can assign the variable limits necessary to our needs. They are thus unlimited so far as they depend on the individual alone. Irrespective of any external regulatory force, but capacity for feeling is in itself an insatiable and bottomless abyss.

But if nothing external can restrain this capacity, it can only be a source of torment to itself. Unlimited desires are insatiable by definition and insatiability is rightly considered a sign of morbidity. Being unlimited, they constantly and infinitely surpass the means at their command; they cannot be quenched. Inextinguishable thirst is constantly renewed torture. It has been claimed, indeed, that human activity naturally aspires beyond assignable limits and sets itself unattainable goals. But how can such an undetermined state be any more reconciled with the conditions of mental life than with the demands of physical life? All man's pleasure in acting, moving and exerting himself implies the sense that his efforts are not in vain and that by walking he has advanced. However, one does not advance when one walks toward no goal, or—which is the same thing—when his goal is infinity. Since the distance between us and it is always the same, whatever road we take, we might as well have made the motions without progress from the spot. Even our glances behind and our feeling of pride at the distance covered can cause only deceptive satisfaction, since the remaining distance is not proportionately reduced. To pursue a goal which is by definition unattainable is to condemn oneself to a state of perpetual unhappiness. Of course, man may hope contrary to all reason, and hope has its pleasures even when unreasonable. It may sustain him for a time; but it cannot survive the repeated disappointments of experience indefinitely. What more can the future offer him than the past, since he can never reach a tenable condition nor even approach the glimpsed ideal? Thus, the more one has, the more one wants, since satisfactions received only stimulate instead of filling needs. Shall action as such be considered agreeable? First, only on condition of blindness to its uselessness. Secondly, for this pleasure to be felt and to temper and half veil the accompanying painful unrest, such unending motion must at least always be easy and unhampered. If it is interfered with only restlessness is left, with the lack of ease which it, itself, entails. But it would be a miracle if no insurmountable obstacle were never encountered. Our thread of life on these conditions is pretty thin, breakable at any instant.

To achieve any other result, the passions first must be limited. Only then can they be harmonized with the faculties and satisfied. But since the individual has no way of limiting them, this must be done by some force exterior to him. A regulative force must play the same role for moral needs which the organism plays for physical needs. This means that the force can only be moral. The awakening of conscience interrupted the state of equilibrium of the animal's dormant existence; only conscience, therefore, can furnish the means to re-establish it. Physical restraint would be ineffective; hearts cannot be touched by physio-chemical forces. So far as the appetites are not automatically restrained by physiological mechanisms, they can be halted only by a limit that they recognize as just. Men would never consent to restrict their desires if they felt justified in passing the assigned limit. But, for reasons given above, they cannot assign themselves this law of justice. So they must receive it from an authority which they respect, to which they yield spontaneously. Either directly and as a whole, or through the agency of one of its organs, society alone can play this moderating role; for it is the only moral power superior to the individual, the authority of which he accepts. It alone has the power necessary to stipulate law and to set the point beyond which the passions must not go. Finally, it alone can estimate the reward to be prospectively offered to every class of human functionary, in the name of the common interest.

As a matter of fact, at every moment of history there is a dim perception, in the moral consciousness of societies, of the respective value of different social services, the relative reward due to each, and the consequent degree of comfort appropriate on the average to workers in each occupation. The different functions are graded in public opinion and a certain coefficient of well-being assigned to each, according to its place in the hierarchy. According to accepted ideas, for example, a certain way of living is considered the upper limit to which a workman may aspire in his efforts to improve his existence, and there is another limit below which he is not willingly permitted to fall unless he has seriously bemeaned himself. Both differ for city and country workers, for the domestic servant and the day-laborer, for the business clerk and the official, etc. Likewise the man of wealth is reproved if he lives the life of a poor man, but also if he seeks the refinements of luxury overmuch. Economists may protest in vain; public feeling will always be scandalized if an individual spends too much wealth for wholly superfluous use, and it even seems that this severity relaxes only in times of moral disturbance.[1] A genuine regimen exists, therefore, although not always legally formulated, which fixes with relative precision the maximum degree of ease of living to which each social class may legitimately aspire. However, there is nothing immutable about such a scale. It changes with the increase or decrease of collective revenue and the changes occurring in the moral ideas of society. Thus what appears luxury to one period no longer does so to another; and the well-being which for long periods was granted to a class only by exception and supererogation, finally appears strictly necessary and equitable.

Under this pressure, each in his sphere vaguely realizes the extreme limit set to his ambitions and aspires to nothing beyond. At least if he respects regulations and is docile to collective authority, that is, has a wholesome moral constitution, he feels that it is not well to ask more. Thus, an end and goal are set to the passions. Truly, there is nothing rigid nor absolute about such determination. The economic ideal assigned each class of citizens is itself confined to certain limits, within which the desires have free range. But it is not infinite. This relative limitation and the moderation it involves, make men contented with their lot while stimulating them moderately to improve it; and this average contentment causes the feeling of calm, active happiness, the pleasure in existing and living which characterizes health for societies as well as for individuals. Each person is then at least, generally speaking, in harmony with his condition, and desires only what he may legitimately hope for as the normal reward of his activity. Besides, this does not condemn man to a sort of immobility. He may seek to give beauty to his life; but his attempts in this

---

1 Actually, this is a purely moral reprobation and can hardly be judicially implemented. We do not consider any reestablishment of sumptuary laws desirable or even possible. [*Durkheim*]

direction may fail without causing him to despair. For, loving what he has and not fixing his desire solely on what he lacks, his wishes and hopes may fail of what he has happened to aspire to, without his being wholly destitute. He has the essentials. The equilibrium of his happiness is secure because it is defined, and a few mishaps cannot disconcert him.

But it would be of little use for everyone to recognize the justice of the hierarchy of functions established by public opinion, if he did not also consider the distribution of these functions just. The workman is not in harmony with his social position if he is not convinced that he has his deserts. If he feels justified in occupying another, what he has would not satisfy him. So it is not enough for the average level of needs for each social condition to be regulated by public opinion, but another, more precise rule, must fix the way in which these conditions are open to individuals. There is no society in which such regulation does not exist. It varies with times and places. Once it regarded birth as the almost exclusive principle of social classification; today it recognizes no other inherent inequality than hereditary fortune and merit. But in all these various forms its object is unchanged. It is also only possible, everywhere, as a restriction upon individuals imposed by superior authority, that is, by collective authority. For it can be established only by requiring of one or another group of men, usually of all, sacrifices and concessions in the name of the public interest.

Some, to be sure, have thought that this moral pressure would become unnecessary if men's economic circumstances were only no longer determined by heredity. If inheritance were abolished, the argument runs, if everyone began life with equal resources and if the competitive struggle were fought out on a basis of perfect equality, no one could think its results unjust. Each would instinctively feel that things are as they should be.

Truly, the nearer this ideal equality were approached, the less social restraint will be necessary. But it is only a matter of degree. One sort of heredity will always exist, that of natural talent. Intelligence, taste, scientific, artistic, literary or industrial ability, courage and manual dexterity are gifts received by each of us at birth, as the heir to wealth receives his capital or as the nobleman formerly received his title and function. A moral discipline will therefore still be required to make those less favored by nature accept the lesser advantages which they owe to the chance of birth. Shall it be demanded that all have an equal share and that no advantage be given those more useful and deserving? But then there would have to be a discipline far stronger to make these accept a treatment merely equal to that of the mediocre and incapable.

But like the one first mentioned, this discipline can be useful only if considered just by the peoples subject to it. When it is maintained only by custom and force, peace and harmony are illusory; the spirit of unrest and discontent are latent; appetites superficially restrained are ready to revolt. This happened in Rome and Greece when the faiths underlying the old organization of the patricians and plebeians were shaken, and in our modern societies when aristocratic prejudices began to lose their old ascendancy. But this state of upheaval is exceptional; it occurs only when society is passing through some abnormal crisis. In normal conditions the collective order is regarded as just by the great majority of persons. Therefore, when we say that an authority is necessary to impose this order on individuals, we certainly do not mean that violence is the only means of establishing it. Since this regulation is meant to restrain individual passions, it must come from a power which dominates individuals; but this power must also be obeyed through respect, not fear.

It is not true, then, that human activity can be released from all restraint. Nothing in the world can enjoy such a privilege. All existence being a part of the universe is relative to the remainder; its nature and method of manifestation accordingly depend not only on itself but on other beings, who consequently restrain and regulate it. Here there are only differences of degree and form between the mineral realm and the thinking person. Man's characteristic privilege is that the bond he accepts is not physical but moral; that is, social. He is governed not by a material environment brutally imposed on him, but by a conscience superior to his own, the superiority of which he feels. Because the greater, better part of his existence transcends the body, he escapes the body's yoke, but is subject to that of society.

But when society is disturbed by some painful crisis or by beneficent but abrupt transitions, it is momentarily incapable of exercising this influence; thence come the sudden rises in the curve of suicides which we have pointed out above.

In the case of economic disasters, indeed, something like a declassification occurs which suddenly casts certain individuals into a lower state than their previous one. Then they must reduce their requirements, restrain their needs, learn greater self-control. All the advantages of social influence are lost so far as they are concerned; their moral education has to be recommenced. But society cannot adjust them instantaneously to this new life and teach them to practice the increased self-repression to which they are unaccustomed. So they are not adjusted to the condition forced on them, and its very prospect is intolerable; hence the suffering which detaches them from a reduced existence even before they have made trial of it.

It is the same if the source of the crisis is an abrupt growth of power and wealth. Then, truly, as the conditions of life are changed, the standard according to which needs were regulated can no longer remain the same; for it varies with social resources, since it largely determines the share of each class of producers. The scale is upset; but a new scale cannot be immediately improvised. Time is required for the public conscience to reclassify men and things. So long as the social forces thus freed have not regained equilibrium, their respective values are unknown and so all regulation is lacking for a time. The limits are unknown between the possible and the impossible, what is just and what is unjust, legitimate claims and hopes and those which are immoderate. Consequently, there is no restraint upon aspirations. If the disturbance is profound, it affects even the principles controlling the distribution of men among various occupations. Since the relations between various parts of society are necessarily modified, the ideas expressing these relations must change. Some particular class especially favored by the crisis is no longer resigned to its former lot, and, on the other hand, the example of its greater good fortune arouses all sorts of jealousy below and about it. Appetites, not being controlled by a public opinion become disoriented, no longer recognize the limits proper to them. Besides, they are at the same time seized by a sort of natural erethism simply by the greater intensity of public life. With increased prosperity desires increase. At the very moment when traditional rules have lost their authority, the richer prize offered these appetites stimulates them and makes them more exigent and impatient of control. The state of de-regulation or anomy is thus further heightened by passions being less disciplined, precisely when they need more disciplining.

But then their very demands make fulfillment impossible. Overweening ambition always exceeds the results obtained, great as they may be, since there is no warning to pause here. Nothing gives satisfaction and all this agitation is uninterruptedly maintained without appeasement. Above all, since this race for an unattainable goal can give no other pleasure but that of the race itself, if it is one, once it is interrupted the participants are left empty-handed. At the same time the struggle grows more violent and painful, both from being less controlled and because competition is greater. All classes contend among themselves because no established classification any longer exists. Effort grows, just when it becomes less productive. How could the desire to live not be weakened under such conditions?

This explanation is confirmed by the remarkable immunity of poor countries. Poverty protects against suicide because it is a restraint in itself. No matter how one acts, desires have to depend upon resources to some extent; actual possessions are partly the criterion of those aspired to. So the less one has the less he is tempted to extend the range of his needs indefinitely. Lack of power, compelling moderation, accustoms men to it, while nothing excites envy if no one has superfluity. Wealth, on the other hand, by the power it bestows, deceives us into believing that we depend on ourselves only. Reducing the resistance we encounter from objects, it suggests the possibility of unlimited success against them. The less limited one feels, the more intolerable all limitation appears. Not without reason, therefore, have so many religions dwelt on the advantages and moral value of poverty. It is actually the best school for teaching self-restraint. Forcing us to constant self-discipline, it prepares us to accept collective discipline with equanimity, while wealth, exalting the individual, may always arouse the spirit of rebellion which is the very source of immorality. This, of course, is no reason why humanity should not improve its material condition. But though the moral danger involved in every growth of prosperity is not irremediable, it should not be forgotten.

III

If anomy never appeared except, as in the above instances, in intermittent spurts, and acute crisis, it might cause the social suicide-rate to vary from time to time, but it would not be a regular, constant factor. In one sphere of social life, however—the sphere of trade and industry—it is actually in a chronic state.

For a whole century, economic progress has mainly consisted in freeing industrial relations from all regulation. Until very recently it was the function of a whole system of moral forces to exert this discipline. First, the influence of religion was felt alike by worker and masters, the poor and the rich. It consoled the former and taught them contentment with their lot by informing them of the providential nature of the social order, that the share of each class was assigned by God himself, and by holding out the hope for just compensation in a world to come in return for the inequalities of this world. It governed the latter, recalling that worldly interests are not man's entire lot, that they must be subordinate to other and higher interests, and that they should therefore not be pursued without rule or measure. Temporal power, in turn, restrained the scope of economic functions by its supremacy over them and by the relatively subordinate role it assigned them. Finally, within the business world proper, the occupational groups by regulating salaries, the price of products and production itself, indirectly fixed the average level of income on which needs are partially based by the very force of circumstances. However, we do not mean to propose this organization as a model. Clearly it would be inadequate to existing societies without great changes. What we stress is its existence, the fact of its useful influence, and that nothing today has come to take its place.

Actually, religion has lost most of its power. And government, instead of regulating economic life, has become its tool and servant. The most opposite schools, orthodox economists and extreme socialists, unite to reduce government to the role of a more or less passive intermediary among the various social functions. The former wish to make it simply the guardian of individual contracts; the latter leave it the task of doing the collective bookkeeping, that is, of recording the demands of consumers, transmitting them to producers, inventorying the total revenue and distributing it according to a fixed formula. But both refuse it any power to subordinate other social organs to itself and to make them converge toward one dominant aim. On both sides nations are declared to have the single or chief purpose of achieving industrial prosperity; such is the implication of the dogma of economic materialism, the basis of both apparently opposed systems. And as these theories merely express the state of opinion, industry, instead of being still regarded as a means to an end transcending itself, has become the supreme end of individuals and societies alike. Thereupon the appetites thus excited have become freed of any limiting authority. By sanctifying them, so to speak, this apotheosis of well-being has placed them above all human law. Their restraint seems like a sort of sacrilege. For this reason, even the purely utilitarian regulation of them exercised by the industrial world itself through the medium of occupational groups has been unable to persist. Ultimately, this liberation of desires has been made worse by the very development of industry and the almost infinite extension of the market. So long as the producer could gain his profits only in his immediate neighborhood, the restricted amount of possible gain could not much overexcite ambition. Now that he may assume to have almost the entire world as his customer, how could passions accept their former confinement in the face of such limitless prospects?

Such is the source of the excitement predominating in this part of society, and which has thence extended to the other parts. There, the state of crisis and anomy is constant and, so to speak, normal. From top to bottom of the ladder, greed is aroused without knowing where to find ultimate foothold. Nothing can calm it, since its goal is far beyond all it can attain. Reality seems valueless by comparison with the dreams of fevered imaginations; reality is therefore abandoned, but so too is possibility abandoned when it in turn becomes reality. A thirst arises for novelties, unfamiliar pleasures, nameless sensations, all of which lose their savor once known. Henceforth one has no strength to endure the least reverse. The whole fever subsides and the sterility of all the tumult is apparent, and it is seen that all these new sensations in their infinite quantity cannot form a solid foundation of happiness to support one during days of trial. The wise man, knowing how to enjoy achieved results without having constantly to replace them with others, finds in them an attachment to life in the hour of difficulty. But the man who has always pinned all his hopes on the future and lived with his eyes fixed upon it, has nothing in the past as a comfort against the present's afflictions, for the past was nothing to him but a series of hastily experienced stages. What blinded him to himself was his expectation always to find further on the happiness he had so far missed. Now he is stopped in his tracks; from now on nothing remains behind or ahead of him to fix his gaze upon. Weariness alone, moreover, is enough to bring disillusionment, for he cannot in the end escape the futility of an endless pursuit.

We may even wonder if this moral state is not principally what makes economic catastrophes of our day so fertile in suicides. In societies where a man is subjected to a healthy discipline, he submits more readily to the blows of chance. The necessary effort for sustaining a little more discomfort costs him relatively little, since he is used to discomfort and constraint. But when every constraint is hateful in itself, how can closer constraint not seem intolerable? There is no tendency to resignation in the feverish impatience of men's lives. When there is no other aim but to outstrip constantly the point arrived at, how painful to be thrown back! Now this very lack of organization characterizing our economic condition throws the door wide to every sort of adventure. Since imagination is hungry for novelty, and ungoverned, it gropes at random. Setbacks necessarily increase with risks and thus crises multiply, just when they are becoming more destructive.

Yet these dispositions are so inbred that society has grown to accept them and is accustomed to think them normal. It is everlastingly repeated that it is man's nature to be eternally dissatisfied, constantly to advance, without relief or rest, toward an indefinite goal. The longing for infinity is daily represented as a mark of moral distinction, whereas it can only appear within unregulated consciences which elevate to a rule the lack of rule from which they suffer. The doctrine of the most ruthless and swift progress has become an article of faith. But other theories appear parallel with those praising the advantages of instability, which, generalizing the situation that gives them birth, declare life evil, claim that it is richer in grief than in pleasure and that it attracts men only by false claims. Since this disorder is greatest in the economic world; it has most victims there.

Industrial and commercial functions are really among the occupations which furnish the greatest number of suicides (see Table). Almost on a level with the liberal professions, they sometimes surpass them; they are especially more afflicted than agriculture, where the old regulative forces still make their appearance felt most and where the fever of business has least penetrated. Here is best recalled what was once the general constitution of the economic order. And the divergence would be yet greater if, among the suicides of industry, employers were distinguished from workmen, for the former are probably most stricken by the state of anomy. The enormous rate of those with independent means (720 per million) sufficiently shows that the possessors of most comfort suffer most. Everything that enforces subordination attenuates the effects of this state. At least the horizon of the lower classes is limited by those above them, and for this same reason their desires are more modest. Those who have only empty space above them are almost inevitably lost in it, if no force restrains them.

TABLE—Suicides per Million Persons of Different Occupations					
	Trade	Transportation	Industry	Agriculture	Liberal Profession*
France (1878–87)†	440	...	340	240	300
Switzerland (1876)	664	1,514	577	304	558
Italy (1866–76)	277	152.6	80.4	26.7	618 ‡
Prussia (1883–90)	754		456	315	832
Bavaria (1884–91)	465	...	369	153	454
Belgium (1885–90)	421	...	160	160	100
Wurttemberg (1873–78)	273	...	190	206	...
Saxony (1878)		341.59 §		71.17	...

* When statistics distinguish several different sorts of liberal occupations, we show as a specimen the one in which the suicide-rate is highest.
† From 1826 to 1880 economic functions seem less affected (see Compte-rendu of 1880); but were occupational statistics very accurate?
‡ This figure is reached only by men of letters.
§ Figure represents Trade, Transportation and Industry combined for Saxony. [Simpson]

Anomy, therefore, is a regular and specific factor in suicide in our modern societies; one of the springs from which the annual contingent feeds. So we have here a new type to distinguish from the others. It differs from them in its dependence, not on the way in which individuals are attached to society, but on how it regulates them. Egoistic suicide results from man's no longer finding a basis for existence in life; altruistic suicide, because this basis for existence appears to man situated beyond life itself. The third sort of suicide, the existence of which has just been shown, results from man's activity's lacking regulation and his consequent sufferings. By virtue of its origin we shall assign this last variety the name of *anomic suicide*.

Certainly, this and egoistic suicide have kindred ties. Both spring from society's insufficient presence in individuals. But the sphere of its absence is not the same in both cases. In egoistic suicide it is deficient in truly collective activity, thus depriving the latter of object and meaning. In anomic suicide, society's influence is lacking in the basically individual passions, thus leaving them without a check-rein. In spite of their relationship, therefore, the two types are independent of each other. We may offer society everything social in us, and still be unable to control our desires; one may live in an anomic state without being egoistic, and vice versa. These two sorts of suicide therefore do not draw their chief recruits from the same social environments; one has its principal field among intellectual careers, the world of thought—the other, the industrial or commercial world. * * *

THE SUICIDE CLUB

ROBERT LOUIS STEVENSON

Stevenson's first collection of short stories, *New Arabian Nights* (1882), published when he was thirty-two, opens with the three interlocking tales that comprise "The Suicide Club." With his simultaneously cheeky and tributary choice of title, Stevenson announced to the world in his characteristically playful way that he had achieved the modern equivalent of *A Thousand and One Nights*, or *The Arabian Nights*, as it is commonly known: a ribald, romantic, and wildly popular collection of medieval Arabic, Persian, and Indian tales. The one thousand and one stories in *The Arabian Nights* are narrated by Queen Scheherazade, whose new husband, the king, plans to execute her after their wedding night, his custom with all his wives. To save her life and the lives of hundreds of other women, Scheherazade turns storyteller, entertaining her rapt husband with a new tale each night, withholding its ending, however, until the next evening. Her execution is thereby postponed one thousand and one times, until her husband finally spares her. The palindromic number 1001 symbolizes infinity in the Arabic tradition. Stevenson, too, uses the conceit of a framing narrator at the end of each story: a generic editor who compiles the literary creations of an unnamed "Arabian author." The implication is that Stevenson's financial life depends upon his ability to tell entertaining stories to a volatile audience. The four-part "The Rajah's Diamond" followed "The Suicide Club" in the original collection; it describes the further adventures of Prince Florizel and Colonel Geraldine.

STORY OF THE YOUNG MAN WITH THE CREAM TARTS

DURING his residence in London, the accomplished Prince Florizel of Bohemia[1] gained the affection of all classes by the seduction of his manner and by a well-considered generosity. He was a remarkable man even by what was known of him; and that was but a small part of what he actually did. Although of a placid temper in ordinary circumstances, and accustomed to take the world with as much philosophy as any ploughman, the Prince of Bohemia was not without a taste for ways of life more adventurous and eccentric than that to which he was destined by his birth. Now and then, when he fell into a low humour, when there was no laughable play to witness in any of the London theatres, and when the season of the year was unsuitable to those field sports in which he excelled all competitors, he would summon his confidant and Master of the Horse,[2] Colonel Geraldine, and bid him prepare himself against an evening ramble. The Master of the Horse was a young officer of a brave and even temerarious[3] disposition. He greeted the news with delight, and hastened to make ready. Long practice and a varied acquaintance of life had given him a singular facility in disguise, he could adapt not only his face and bearing, but his voice and almost his thoughts, to those of any rank, character, or nation; and in this way he diverted attention from the Prince and sometimes gained admission for the pair into strange societies. The civil authorities were never taken into the secret of these adventures; the imperturbable courage of the one and the ready invention and chivalrous devotion of the other had brought them through a score of dangerous passes; and they grew in confidence as time went on.

---

1 Though Stevenson chose to name his protagonist after Shakespeare's Prince Florizel of Bohemia from *The Winter's Tale*, the character might have been inspired, in part, by King Ludwig II of Bavaria (1845–1886), the great castle-builder and the patron of composer Richard Wagner (1813–1883). A highly eccentric man, Ludwig II—called Mad King Ludwig—was fond, like Florizel, of wearing disguises and embarking on reckless adventures. He was notorious for his homosexual escapades, ordering his groomsmen, according to one report, to dance nude for his pleasure. After being deposed, Ludwig died in 1886 under mysterious circumstances, purportedly drowning himself and his private physician in Lake Starnberg
2 Manager of the Royal Stables, a largely ceremonial post in this case.
3 Recklessly daring.

One evening in March they were driven by a sharp fall of sleet into an Oyster Bar in the immediate neighbourhood of Leicester Square.[1] Colonel Geraldine was dressed and painted[2] to represent a person connected with the Press in reduced circumstances; while the Prince had, as usual, travestied his appearance by the addition of false whiskers and a pair of large adhesive eyebrows. These lent him a shaggy and weather-beaten air, which, for one of his urbanity, formed the most impenetrable disguise. Thus equipped, the commander and his satellite sipped their brandy and soda in security.

The bar was full of guests, male and female; but though more than one of these offered to fall into talk with our adventurers, none of them promised to grow interesting upon a nearer acquaintance. There was nothing present but the lees[3] of London and the commonplace of disrespectability; and the Prince had already fallen to yawning, and was beginning to grow weary of the whole excursion, when the swing doors were pushed violently open, and a young man, followed by a couple of commissionaires,[4] entered the bar. Each of the commissionaires carried a large dish of cream tarts under a cover, which they at once removed; and the young man made the round of the company, and pressed these confections upon everyone's acceptance with an exaggerated courtesy. Sometimes his offer was laughingly accepted; sometimes it was firmly, or even harshly, rejected. In these latter cases the newcomer always ate the tart himself, with some more or less humorous commentary.

At last he accosted Prince Florizel.

"Sir," said he, with a profound obeisance, proffering the tart at the same time between his thumb and forefinger, "will you so far honour an entire stranger? I can answer for the quality of the pastry, having eaten two dozen and three of them myself since five o'clock."

"I am in the habit," replied the Prince, "of looking not so much to the nature of a gift as to the spirit in which it is offered."

"The spirit, sir," returned the young man, with another bow, "is one of mockery."

"Mockery?" repeated Florizel. And whom do you propose to mock?"

"I am not here to expound my philosophy," replied the other, "but to distribute these cream tarts. If I mention that I heartily include myself in the ridicule of the transaction, I hope you will consider honour satisfied and condescend. If not,

---

1 Square in central London near Covent Garden; an entertainment district at night.
2 With stage makeup.
3 Dregs, the sediment of wine at the bottom of a barrel.
4 Uniformed door attendants at theatres and hotels.

you will constrain me to eat my twenty-eighth, and I own to being weary of the exercise."

"You touch me," said the Prince, "and I have all the will in the world to rescue you from this dilemma, but upon one condition. If my friend and I eat your cakes—for which we have neither of us any natural inclination—we shall expect you to join us at supper by way of recompense."

The young man seemed to reflect.

"I have still several dozen upon hand," he said at last; "and that will make it necessary for me to visit several more bars before my great affair is concluded. This will take some time; and if you are hungry——"

The Prince interrupted him with a polite gesture.

"My friend and I will accompany you," he said; "for we have already a deep interest in your very agreeable mode of passing an evening. And now that the preliminaries of peace are settled, allow me to sing the treaty for both."

And the Prince swallowed the tart with the best grace imaginable.

"It is delicious," said he.

"I perceive you are a connoisseur," replied the young man.

Colonel Geraldine likewise did honour to the pastry; and everyone in that bar having now either accepted or refused his delicacies, the young man with the cream tarts led the way to another and similar establishment. The two commissionaires, who seemed to have grown accustomed to their absurd employment, followed immediately after; and the Prince and the Colonel brought up the rear, arm in arm, and smiling to each other as they went. In this order the company visited two other taverns, where scenes were enacted of a like nature to that already described—some refusing, some accepting, the favours of this vagabond hospitality, and the young man himself eating each rejected tart.

On leaving the third saloon the young man counted his store. There were but nine remaining, three in one tray and six in the other.

"Gentlemen," said he, addressing himself to his two new followers,

"I am unwilling to delay your supper. I am positively sure you must be hungry. I feel that I owe you a special consideration. And on this great day for me, when I am closing a career of folly by my most conspicuously silly action, I wish to behave handsomely to all who give me countenance. Gentlemen, you shall wait no longer. Although my constitution is shattered by previous excesses, at the risk of my life I liquidate the suspensory condition."

With these words he crushed the nine remaining tarts into his mouth, and swallowed them at a single movement each. Then, turning to the commissionaires, he gave them a couple of sovereigns.

"I have to thank you," said he, "for your extraordinary patience."

And he dismissed them with a bow apiece. For some seconds he stood looking at the purse from which he had just paid his assistants, then, with a laugh, he tossed it into the middle of the street, and signified his readiness for supper.

In a small French restaurant in Soho,[1] which had enjoyed an exaggerated reputation for some little while, but had already begun to be forgotten, and in a private room up two pair[2] of stairs, the three companions made a very elegant supper, and drank three or four bottles of champagne, talking the while upon indifferent subjects. The young man was fluent and gay, but he laughed louder than was natural in a person of polite breeding; his hands trembled violently, and his voice took sudden and surprising inflections, which seemed to be independent of his will. The dessert had been cleared away, and all three had lighted their cigars, when the Prince addressed him in these words:

"You will, I am sure, pardon curiosity. What I have seen of you has greatly pleased but even more puzzled me. And though I should be loth[3] to seem indiscreet, I must tell you that my friend and I are persons very well worthy to be entrusted with a secret. We have many of our own, which we are continually revealing to improper ears. And if, as I suppose, your story is a silly one, you need have no delicacy with us, who are two of the silliest men in England. My name is Godall, Theophilus Godall; my friend is major Alfred Hammersmith—or at least, such is the name by which he chooses to be known. We pass our lives entirely in the search for extravagant adventures; and there is no extravagance with which we are not capable of sympathy."

"I like you, Mr. Godall," returned the young man; "you inspire me with a natural confidence; and I have not the slightest objection to your friend the Major, whom I take to be a nobleman in masquerade. At least, I am sure he is no soldier."

The Colonel smiled at this compliment to the perfection of his art; and the young man went on in a more animated manner.

"There is every reason why I should not tell you my story. Perhaps that is just the reason why I am going to do so. At least, you seem so well prepared to hear a tale of silliness that I cannot find it in my heart to disappoint you. My name in spite of

---

1 Entertainment district in central London, famous for its nightclubs, dancing halls, and houses of ill repute.
2 Flights.
3 Loath.

your example, I shall keep to myself. My age is not essential to the narrative. I am descended from my ancestors by ordinary generation,[1] and from them I inherited the very eligible human tenement[2] which I still occupy and a fortune of three hundred pounds a year. I suppose they also handed on to me a harebrain humour, which it has been my chief delight to indulge. I received a good education. I can play the violin nearly well enough to earn money in the orchestra of a penny gaff,[3] but not quite. The same remark applies to the flute and the French horn. I learned enough of whist to lose about a hundred a year at that scientific game. My acquaintance with French was sufficient to enable me to squander money in Paris with almost the same facility as in London. In short, I am a person full of manly accomplishments. I have had every sort of adventure including a duel about nothing. Only two months ago I met a young lady exactly suited to my taste in mind and body; I found my heart melt; I saw that I had come upon my fate at last, and was in the way to fall in love. But when I came to reckon up what remained to me of my capital, I found it amounted to something less than four hundred pounds! I ask you fairly—can a man who respects himself fall in love on four hundred pounds? I concluded, certainly not; left the presence of my charmer, and slightly accelerating my usual rate of expenditure, came this morning to my last eighty pounds. This I divided into two equal parts; forty I reserved for a particular purpose; the remaining forty I was to dissipate before the night. I have passed a very entertaining day, and played many farces besides that of the cream tarts which procured me the advantage of your acquaintance; for I was determined, as I told you, to bring a foolish career to a still more foolish conclusion; and when you saw me throw my purse into the street, the forty pounds were at an end. Now you know me as well as I know myself: a fool but consistent in his folly; and, as I will ask you to believe, neither a whimperer nor a coward."

From the whole tone of the young man's statement it was plain that he harboured very bitter and contemptuous thoughts about himself. His auditors were led to imagine that his love affair was nearer his heart than he admitted, and that he had a design on his own life. The farce of the cream tarts began to have very much the air of a tragedy in disguise.

"Why, is this not odd," broke out Geraldine, giving a look to Prince Florizel, "that we three fellows should have met by the merest accident in so large a wilderness as London, and should be so nearly in the same condition?"

---

1   He is not an aristocrat, in other words.
2   I.e., highly desirable rented rooms. He is being facetious.
3   Tawdry music hall.

"How?" cried the young man. "Are you, too, ruined? Is this supper a folly like my cream tarts? Has the devil brought three of his own together for a last carouse?"

"The devil, depend upon it, can sometimes do a very gentlemanly thing," returned Prince Florizel; "and I am so much touched by this coincidence, that, although we are not entirely in the same case, I am going to put an end to the disparity. Let your heroic treatment of the last cream tarts be my example."

So saying, the Prince drew out his purse and took from it a small bundle of banknotes.

"You see, I was a week or so behind you, but I mean to catch you up and come neck and neck into the winningpost,"[1] he continued. "This," laying one of the notes upon the table, will suffice for the bill. As for the rest—"

He tossed them into the fire, and they went up the chimney in single blaze.

The young man tried to catch his arm, but as the table was between them his interference came too late.

"Unhappy man," he cried, "you should not have burned them all! You should have kept forty pounds."

"Forty pounds!" repeated the Prince. "Why, in heaven's name, forty pounds?"

"Why not eighty?" cried the Colonel; "for to my certain knowledge there must have been a hundred in the bundle."

"It was only forty pounds he needed," said the young man gloomily. "But without them there is no admission. The rule is strict. Forty pounds for each. Accursed life, where a man cannot even die without money!"

The Prince and the Colonel exchanged glances.

"Explain yourself," said the latter. "I have still a pocketbook tolerably well lined, and I need not say how readily I should share my wealth with Godall. But I must know to what end: you must certainly tell us what you mean."

The young man seemed to awaken; he looked uneasily from one to the other, and his face flushed deeply.

"You are not fooling me?" he asked. "You are indeed ruined men like me?"

"Indeed, I am for my part," replied the Colonel.

"And for mine," said the Prince, "I have given you proof. Who but a ruined man would throw his notes into the fire? The action speaks for itself."

"A ruined man—yes," returned the other suspiciously, "or else a millionaire."

"Enough, sir," said the Prince; "I have said so, and I am not accustomed to have my word remain in doubt."

---

1   Post at the end of a racecourse.

"Ruined?" said the young man "Are you ruined, like me? Are you, after a life of indulgence, come to such a pass that you can only indulge yourself in one thing more? Are you"—he kept lowering his voice as he went on—"are you going to give yourselves that last indulgence? Are you going avoid the consequences of your folly by the one infallible and easy path? Are you going to give the slip to the sheriff's officers of conscience by the one open door?"

Suddenly he broke off and attempted to laugh.

"Here is your health!" he cried, emptying his glass, "and good night to you, my merry ruined men."

Colonel Geraldine caught him by the arm as he was about to rise.

"You lack confidence in us," he said, "and you are wrong. To all your questions I make answer in the affirmative. But I am not so timid, and can speak the Queen's English plainly. We too, like yourself, have had enough of life, and are determined to die. Sooner or later, alone or together, we meant to seek out death and beard[1] him where he lies ready. Since we have met you, and your case is more pressing, let it be tonight—and at once—and, if you will, all three together. Such a penniless trio," he cried, "should go arm in arm into the halls of Pluto,[2] and give each other some countenance among the shades!"[3]

Geraldine had hit exactly on the manners and intonations that became the part he was playing. The Prince himself was disturbed, and looked over at his confidant with a shade of doubt. As for the young man, the flush came back darkly into his cheek, and his eyes threw out a spark of light.

"You are the men for me!" he cried, with an almost terrible gaiety. "Shake hands upon the bargain!" (his hand was cold and wet.) "You little know in what a company you will begin the march! You little know in what a happy moment for yourselves you partook of my cream tarts! I am only a unit, but I am a unit in an army. I know Death's private door. I am one of his familiars, and can show you into eternity without ceremony and yet without scandal."

They called upon him eagerly to explain his meaning.

"Can you muster eighty pounds between you?" he demanded.

Geraldine ostentatiously consulted his pocket-book, and replied in the affirmative.

"Fortunate beings!" cried the young man. "Forty pounds is the entry money of the Suicide Club."

---

1   Confront.
2   Roman god of the underworld.
3   Disembodied spirits, ghosts.

"The Suicide Club," said the Prince, "why, what the devil is that?"

"Listen," said the young man; "this is the age of conveniences, and I have to tell you of the last perfection of the sort. We have affairs in different places; and hence railways were invented. Railways separated us infallibly from our friends; and so telegraphs were made that we might communicate speedily at great distances. Even in hotels we have lifts to spare us a climb of some hundred steps. Now, we know that life is only a stage to play the fool upon as long as the part amuses us.[1] There was one more convenience lacking to modern comfort; a decent, easy way to quit that stage; the back stairs to liberty; or as I said this moment, Death's private door. This, my two fellow rebels, is supplied by the Suicide Club. Do not suppose that you and I are alone, or even exceptional, in the highly reasonable desire that we profess. A large number of our fellowmen, who have grown heartily sick of the performance in which they are expected to join daily and all their lives long, are only kept from flight by one or two considerations. Some have families who would be shocked, or even blamed, if the matter became public; others have a weakness at heart and recoil from the circumstances of death. That is, to some extent, my own experience. I cannot put a pistol to my head and draw the trigger; for something stronger than myself withholds the act; and although I loathe life, I have not strength enough in my body to take hold of death and be done with it. For such as I, and for all who desire to be out of the coil[2] without posthumous scandal, the Suicide Club has been inaugurated. How this has been managed, what is its history, or what may be its ramifications[3] in other lands, I am myself uninformed; and what I know of its constitution, I am not at liberty to communicate to you. To this extent, however, I am at your service. If you are truly tired of life, I will introduce you tonight to a meeting; and if not tonight, at least some time within the week, you will be easily relieved of your existences. It is now (consulting his watch) eleven; by half-past, at latest, we must leave this place; so that you have half an hour before you to consider my proposal. It is more serious than a cream tart," he added, with a smile; "and I suspect more palatable."

"More serious, certainly," returned Colonel Geraldine; "and as it is so much more so, will you allow me five minutes' speech in private with my friend, Mr. Godall?"

"It is only fair," answered the young man. "If you will permit, I will retire."

---

1   An echo of Jaques's words in *As You Like It*: "All the world's a stage, / And all the men and women merely players" (II.vii.38–39).
2   "For in that sleep of death what dreams may come / When we have shuffled off this mortal coil" (*Hamlet*, III.i.74–75).
3   Branches.

"You will be very obliging," said the Colonel.

As soon as the two were alone—"What," said Prince Florizel, "is the use of this confabulation,[1] Geraldine? I see you are flurried, whereas my mind is very tranquilly made up. I will see the end of this."

"Your Highness," said the Colonel turning pale; "let me ask you to consider the importance of your life, not only to your friends, but to the public interest. 'If not tonight,' said this madman; but supposing that tonight some irreparable disaster were to overtake your Highness's person, what, let me ask you, what would be my despair, and what the concern and disaster of a great nation?"

"I will see the end of this," repeated the Prince in his most deliberate tones; "and have the kindness, Colonel Geraldine, to remember and respect your word of honour as a gentleman. Under no circumstances, recollect, nor without my special authority, are you to betray the incognito under which I choose to go abroad. These were my commands, which I now reiterate. And now," he added, "let me ask you to call for the bill."

Colonel Geraldine bowed in submission; but he had a very white face as he summoned the young man of the cream tarts, and issued his directions to the waiter. The Prince preserved his undisturbed demeanour, and described a Palais Royal[2] farce to the young suicide with great humour and gusto. He avoided the Colonel's appealing looks without ostentation, and selected another cheroot[3] with more than usual care. Indeed, he was now the only man of the party who kept any command over his nerves.

The bill was discharged, the Prince giving the whole change of the note to the astonished waiter; and the three drove off in a four-wheeler.[4] They were not long upon the way before the cab stopped at the entrance to a rather dark court. Here all descended.

After Geraldine had paid the fare, the young man turned, and addressed Prince Florizel as follows:

"It is still time, Mr. Godall, to make good your escape into thraldom.[5] And for you too, Major Hammersmith. Reflect well before you take another step; and if your hearts say no—here are the crossroads."

---

1 Chat.
2 Théâtre du Palais-Royal in Paris.
3 Cigar.
4 Four-wheel hackney carriage.
5 Servitude, bondage; in other words, the daily grind.

"Lead on, sir," said the Prince. "I am not the man to go back from a thing once said."

"Your coolness does me good," replied their guide. "I have never seen anyone so unmoved at this conjuncture; and yet you are not the first whom I have escorted to this door. More than one of my friends has preceded me, where I knew I must shortly follow. But this is of no interest to you. Wait me here for only a few moments; I shall return as soon as I have arranged the preliminaries of your introduction."

And with that the young man, waving his hand to his companions, turned into the court, entered a doorway and disappeared.

"Of all our follies," said Colonel Geraldine in a low voice, "this is the wildest and most dangerous."

"I perfectly believe so," returned the Prince.

"We have still," pursued the Colonel, "a moment to ourselves. Let me beseech your Highness to profit by the opportunity and retire. The consequences of this step are so dark, and may be so grave, that I feel myself justified in pushing a little farther than usual the liberty which your Highness is so condescending as to allow me in private."

"Am I to understand that Colonel Geraldine is afraid?" asked his Highness, taking his cheroot from his lips, and looking keenly into the other's face.

"My fear is certainly not personal," replied the other proudly; "of that your Highness may rest well assured."

"I had supposed as much," returned the Prince, with undisturbed good humour; "but I was unwilling to remind you of the difference in our stations. No more—no more," he added, seeing Geraldine about to apologise, "you stand excused."

And he smoked placidly, leaning against a railing, until the young man returned.

"Well," he asked, "has our reception been arranged?"

"Follow me," was the reply. "The President will see you in the cabinet.[1] And let me warn you to be frank in your answers. I have stood your guarantee; but the club requires a searching inquiry before admission; for the indiscretion of a single member would lead to the dispersion of the whole society for ever."

The Prince and Geraldine put their heads together for a moment. "Bear me out in this," said the one; and "bear me out in that," said the other; and by boldly taking up the characters of men with whom both were acquainted, they had come to an

---

1   His private office.

agreement in a twinkling, and were ready to follow their guide into the President's cabinet.

There were no formidable obstacles to pass. The outer door stood open; the door of the cabinet was ajar; and there, in a small but very high apartment, the young man left them once more.

"He will be here immediately," he said with a nod, as he disappeared.

Voices were audible in the cabinet through the folding doors which formed one end; and now and then the noise of a champagne cork, followed by a burst of laughter, intervened among the sounds of conversation. A single tall window looked out upon the river and the embankment; and by the disposition of the lights they judged themselves not far from Charing Cross station.[1] The furniture was scanty, and the coverings worn to the thread; and there was nothing movable except a handbell in the centre of a round table, and the hats and coats of a considerable party hung round the wall on pegs.

"What sort of a den is this?" said Geraldine.

"That is what I have come to see," replied the Prince. "If they keep live devils on the premises, the thing may grow amusing."

Just then the folding door was opened no more than was necessary for the passage of a human body; and there entered at the same moment a louder buzz of talk, and the redoubtable President of the Suicide Club. The President was a man of fifty or upwards; large and rambling in his gait, with shaggy side whiskers, a bald top to his head, and a veiled grey eye, which now and then emitted a twinkle. His mouth, which embraced a large cigar, he kept continually screwing round and round and from side to side, as he looked sagaciously and coldly at the strangers. He was dressed in light tweeds, with his neck very open in a striped shirt collar; and carried a minute book[2] under one arm.

"Good evening," said he, after he had closed the door behind him. "I am told you wish to speak with me."

"We have a desire, sir, to join the Suicide Club," replied the Colonel.

The President rolled his cigar about in his mouth.

"What is that?" he said abruptly.

"Pardon me," returned the Colonel, "but I believe you are the person best qualified to give us information on that point."

---

1 Busy train station on the Strand, near Trafalgar Square.
2 Notebook.

"I?" cried the President. "A Suicide Club? Come, come! this is a frolic for All Fools'-Day,[1] I can make allowances for gentlemen who get merry in their liquor, but let there be an end to this."

"Call your Club what you will," said the Colonel, "you have some company behind these doors, and we insist on joining it."

"Sir," returned the President, curtly, "you have made a mistake. This is a private house, and you must leave it instantly."

The Prince had remained quietly in his seat throughout this little colloquy; but now, when the Colonel looked over to him, as much as to say, "Take your answer and come away, for God's sake!" he drew his cheroot from his mouth, and spoke—

"I have come here," said he, "upon the invitation of a friend of yours. He has doubtless informed you of my intention in thus intruding on your party. Let me remind you that a person in my circumstances has exceedingly little to bind him, and is not at all likely to tolerate much rudeness. I am a very quiet man, as a usual thing; but, my dear sir, you are either going to oblige me in the little matter of which you are aware, or you shall very bitterly repent that you ever admitted me to your antechamber."

The President laughed aloud.

"That is the way to speak," said he. "You are a man who is a man. You know the way to my heart, and can do what you like with me. Will you," he continued, addressing Geraldine, "will you step aside for a few minutes? I shall finish first with your companion, and some of the club's formalities require to be fulfilled in private."

With these words he opened the door of a small closet,[2] into which he shut the colonel.

"I believe in you," he said to Florizel, as soon as they were alone; "but are you sure of your friend?"

"Not so sure as I am of myself, though he has more cogent reasons," answered Florizel, "but sure enough to bring him here without alarm. He has had enough to cure the most tenacious man of life. He was cashiered[3] the other day for cheating at cards."

"A good reason, I daresay," replied the President; "at least, we have another in the same case, and I feel sure of him. Have you also been in the Service, may I ask?"

"I have," was the reply; "but I was too lazy, I left it early."

"What is your reason for being tired of life?" pursued the President.

---

1 April Fool's Day.
2 Small private chamber.
3 Dishonorably discharged.

"The same as near as I can make out," answered the Prince; "unadulterated laziness."

The President started. "D—n it," said he, "you must have something better than that."

"I have no more money," added Florizel. "That is also a vexation, without doubt. It brings my sense of idleness to an acute point."

The President rolled his cigar round in his mouth for some seconds, directing his gaze straight into the eyes of this unusual neophyte;[1] but the Prince supported his scrutiny with unabashed good temper.

"If I had not a deal of experience," said the President at last, "I should turn you off. But I know the world; and this much any way, that the most frivolous excuses for a suicide are often the toughest to stand by. And when I downright like a man, as I do you, sir, I would rather strain the regulation than deny him."

The Prince and the Colonel, one after the other, were subjected to a long and particular interrogatory: the Prince alone; but Geraldine in the presence of the Prince, so that the President might observe the countenance of the one while the other was being warmly cross-examined. The result was satisfactory; and the President, after having booked a few details of each case, produced a form of oath to be accepted. Nothing could be conceived more passive than the obedience promised, or more stringent than the terms by which the juror[2] bound himself. The man who forfeited a pledge so awful could scarcely have a rag of honour or any of the consolations of religion left to him. Florizel signed the document, but not without a shudder; the Colonel followed his example with an air of great depression. Then the President received the entry money; and without more ado, introduced the two friends into the smoking-room of the Suicide Club.

The smoking room of the Suicide Club was the same height as the cabinet into which it opened, but much larger, and papered from top to bottom with an imitation of oak wainscot. A large and cheerful fire and a number of gas jets illuminated the company. The Prince and his follower made the number up to eighteen. Most of the party were smoking, and drinking champagne; a feverish hilarity reigned, with sudden and rather ghastly pauses.

"Is this a full meeting?" asked the Prince.

---

1 Convert.
2 Oath-taker.

"Middling," said the President. "By the way," he added, "if you have any money, it is usual to offer some champagne. It keeps up a good spirit, and is one of my own little perquisites."[1]

"Hammersmith," said Florizel, "I may leave the champagne to you."

And with that he turned away and began to go round among the guests. Accustomed to play the host in the highest circles, he charmed and dominated all whom he approached; there was something at once winning and authoritative in his address; and his extraordinary coolness gave him yet another distinction in this half maniacal society. As he went from one to another he kept both his eyes and ears open, and soon began to gain a general idea of the people among whom he found himself. As in all other places of resort, one type predominated: people in the prime of youth, with every show of intelligence and sensibility in their appearance, but with little promise of strength or the quality that makes success. Few were much above thirty, and not a few were still in their teens. They stood, leaning on tables and shifting on their feet; sometimes they smoked extraordinarily fast, and sometimes they let their cigars go out; some talked well, but the conversation of others was plainly the result of nervous tension, and was equally without wit or purport. As each new bottle of champagne was opened, there was a manifest improvement in gaiety. Only two were seated—one in a chair in the recess of the window, with his head hanging and his hands plunged deep into his trouser pockets, pale, visibly moist with perspiration, saying never a word, a very wreck of soul and body; the other sat on the divan close by the chimney, and attracted notice by a trenchant dissimilarity from all the rest. He was probably upwards of forty, but he looked fully ten years older; and Florizel thought he had never seen a man more naturally hideous, nor one more ravaged by disease and ruinous excitements. He was no more than skin and bone, was partly paralysed, and wore spectacles of such unusual power, that his eyes appeared through the glasses greatly magnified and distorted in shape. Except the Prince and the President, he was the only person in the room who preserved the composure of ordinary life.

There was little decency among the members of the dub. Some boasted of the disgraceful actions, the consequences of which had reduced them to seek refuge in death; and the others listened without disapproval. There was a tacit understanding against moral judgments; and whoever passed the club doors enjoyed already some of the immunities of the tomb: They drank to each other's memories, and to those of notable suicides in the past. They compared and developed their different views

---

1   Perks.

of death—some declaring that it was no more than blackness and cessation; others full of a hope that that very night they should be scaling the stars and commercing[1] with the mighty dead.

"To the eternal memory of Baron Trenck,[2] the type of suicides!" cried one. "He went out of a small cell into a smaller, that he might come forth again to freedom."

"For my part," said a second, "I wish no more than a bandage for my eyes and cotton for my ears. Only they have no cotton thick enough in this world."

A third was for reading the mysteries of life in a future state; and a fourth professed that he would never have joined the club, if he had not been induced to believe in Mr. Darwin.

"I could not bear," said this remarkable suicide, "to be descended from an ape."

Altogether, the Prince was disappointed by the bearing and conversation of the members.

"It does not seem to me," he thought, "a matter for so much disturbance. If a man has made up his mind to kill himself, let him do it, in God's name, like a gentleman. This flutter and big talk is out of place."

In the meanwhile Colonel Geraldine was a prey to the blackest apprehensions; the club and its rules were still a mystery, and he looked round the room for some one who should be able to set his mind at rest. In this survey his eye lighted on the paralytic person with the strong spectacles; and seeing him so exceedingly tranquil, he besought the President, who was going in and out of the room under a pressure of business, to present him to the gentleman on the divan.

The functionary explained the needlessness of all such formalities within the club, but nevertheless presented Mr. Hammersmith to Mr. Malthus.[3]

Mr. Malthus looked at the Colonel curiously, and then requested him to take a seat upon his right.

"You are a newcomer," he said, "and wish information? You have come to the proper source. It is two years since I first visited this charming club."

The Colonel breathed again. If Mr. Malthus had frequented the place for two years there could be little danger for the Prince in a single evening. But Geraldine was none the less astonished, and began to suspect a mystification.

---

1   Socially interacting.
2   Baron Franz von der Trenck (1711–1749), corrupt and misanthropic Austrian mercenary who died in prison.
3   A nominal echo of Thomas Robert Malthus (1766–1834), British economist and demographer whose *An Essay on the Principle of Population* (1798) warned that human reproduction rates would eventually outstrip the food supply.

"What!" cried he, "two years! I thought—but indeed I see I have been made the subject of a pleasantry."

"By no means," replied Mr. Malthus mildly. "My case is peculiar. I am not, properly speaking, a suicide at all; but, as it were, an honorary member. I rarely visit the club twice in two months. My infirmity and the kindness of the President have procured me these little immunities, for which besides I pay at an advanced rate. Even as it is my luck has been extraordinary."

"I am afraid," said the Colonel, "that I must ask you to be more explicit. You must remember that I am still most imperfectly acquainted with the rules of the club."

"An ordinary member who comes here in search of death like yourself," replied the paralytic, "returns every evening until fortune favours him. He can even, if he is penniless, get board and lodging from the President: very fair, I believe, and clean, although, of course, not luxurious; that could hardly be, considering the exiguity[1] (if I may so express myself) of the subscription. And then the President's company is a delicacy in itself."

"Indeed!" cried Geraldine, "he had not greatly prepossessed me."

"Ah!" said Mr. Malthus, "you do not know the man: the drollest fellow! What stories! What cynicism! He knows life to admiration and, between ourselves, is probably the most corrupt rogue in Christendom."

"And he also," asked the Colonel, "is a permanency—like yourself, if I may say so without offence?"

"Indeed, he is a permanency in a very different sense from me," replied Mr. Malthus. "I have been graciously spared, but I must go at last. Now he never plays. He shuffles and deals for the club, and makes the necessary arrangements. That man, my dear Mr. Hammersmith, is the very soul of ingenuity. For three years he has pursued in London his useful and, I think I may add, his artistic calling; and not so much as a whisper of suspicion has been once aroused. I believe him myself to be inspired. You doubtless remember the celebrated case, six months ago, of the gentleman who was accidentally poisoned in a chemist's shop? That was one of the least rich, one of the least racy, of his notions; but then, how simple! and how safe!"

"You astound me," said the Colonel. "Was that unfortunate gentleman one of the—" He was about to say "victims"; but bethinking himself in time, he substituted—"members of the club?"

In the same flash of thought, it occurred to him that Mr. Malthus himself had not at all spoken in the tone of one who is in love with death; and he added hurriedly:

---

1 Smallness, modesty.

"But I perceive I am still in the dark. You speak of shuffling and dealing; pray for what end? And since you seem rather unwilling to die than otherwise, I must own that I cannot conceive what brings you here at all."

"You say truly that you are in the dark," replied Mr. Malthus with more animation. "Why, my dear sir, this club is the temple of intoxication. If my enfeebled health could support the excitement more often, you may depend upon it I should be more often here. It requires all the sense of duty engendered by a long habit of ill-health and careful regimen, to keep me from excess in this, which is, I may say, my last dissipation. I have tried them all, sir," he went on, laying his hand on Geraldine's arm, "all without exception, and I declare to you, upon my honour, there is not one of them that has not been grossly and untruthfully overrated. People trifle with love. Now, I deny that love is a strong passion. Fear is the strong passion; it is with fear that you must trifle, if you wish to taste the intensest joys of living. Envy me—envy me, sir," he added with a chuckle, "I am a coward!"

Geraldine could scarcely repress a movement of repulsion for this deplorable wretch; but he commanded himself with an effort, and continued his inquiries.

"How, sir," he asked, "is the excitement so artfully prolonged? and where is there any element of uncertainty?"

"I must tell you how the victim for every evening is selected," returned Mr. Malthus; "and not only the victim, but another member, who is to be the instrument in the club's hands, and death's high priest for that occasion."

"Good God!" said the Colonel, "do they then kill each other?"

"The trouble of suicide is removed in that way," returned Malthus with a nod.

"Merciful Heavens!" ejaculated the Colonel, "and may you—may I—may the—my friend I mean—may any of us be pitched upon this evening as the slayer of another man's body and immortal spirit? Can such things be possible among men born of women? Oh! infamy of infamies!"

He was about to rise in his horror, when he caught the Prince's eye. It was fixed upon him from across the room with a frowning and angry stare. And in a moment Geraldine recovered his composure:

"After all," he added, "why not? And since you say the game is interesting, *vogue la galère*[1]—I follow the club!"

Mr. Malthus had keenly enjoyed the Colonel's amazement and disgust. He had the vanity of wickedness; and it pleased him to see another man give way to a gen-

---

1 Come what may; literally, let the galley be kept rowing.

erous movement, while he felt himself, in his entire corruption, superior to such emotions.

"You now, after your first moment of surprise," said he, "are in a position to appreciate the delights of our society. You can see how it combines the excitement of a gaming table, a duel and a Roman amphitheatre. The Pagans did well enough; I cordially admire the refinement of their minds; but it has been reserved for a Christian country to attain this extreme, this quintessence, this absolute of poignancy. You will understand how vapid are all amusements to a man who has acquired a taste for this one. The game we play," he continued, "is one of extreme simplicity. A full pack—but I perceive you are about to see the thing in progress. Will you lend me the help of your arm? I am unfortunately paralysed."

Indeed, just as Mr. Malthus was beginning his description, another pair of folding-doors was thrown open, and the whole club began to pass, not without some hurry, into the adjoining room. It was similar in every respect to the one from which it was entered, but somewhat differently furnished. The centre was occupied by a long green table, at which the President sat shuffling a pack of cards with great particularity. Even with the stick and the Colonel's arm; Mr. Malthus walked with so much difficulty that everyone was seated before this pair and the Prince, who had waited for them, entered the apartment; and, in consequence, the three took seats close together at the lower end of the board.

"It is a pack of fifty-two," whispered Mr. Malthus, "Watch for the ace of spades, which is the sign of death, and the ace of clubs, which designates the official of the night. Happy young men!" he added. "You have good eyes, and can follow the game. Alas! I cannot tell an ace from deuce across the table."

And he proceeded to equip himself with a second pair of spectacles.

"I must at least watch the faces," he explained.

The Colonel rapidly informed his friend of all that he had learned from the honorary member, and of the horrible alternative that lay before them. The Prince was conscious of a deadly chill and a contraction about his heart; he swallowed with difficulty, and looked from side to side like a man in a maze.

"One bold stroke," whispered the Colonel, "and we may still escape."

But the suggestion recalled the Prince's spirits.

"Silence!" said he. "Let me see that you can play like a gentleman for any stake, however serious."

And he looked about him, once more to all appearance at his ease, although his heart beat thickly, and he was conscious of an unpleasant heat in his bosom. The members were all very quiet and intent; everyone was pale, but none so pale as Mr. Malthus. His eyes protruded; his head kept nodding involuntarily upon his spine; his hands found their way, one after the other, to his mouth, where they made clutches at his tremulous and ashen lips. It was plain that the honorary member enjoyed his membership on very startling terms.

"Attention, gentlemen!" said the President.

And he began slowly dealing the cards about the table in the reverse direction, pausing until each man had shown his card. Nearly everyone hesitated; and sometimes you would see a player's fingers stumble more than once before he could turn over the momentous slip of pasteboard. As the Prince's turn drew nearer, he was conscious of a growing and almost suffocating excitement; but he had somewhat of the gambler's nature, and recognised almost with astonishment that there was a degree of pleasure in his sensations. The nine of clubs fell to his lot; the three of spades was dealt to Geraldine; and the queen of hearts to Mr. Malthus, who was unable to suppress a sob of relief. The young man of the cream tarts almost immediately afterwards turned over the ace of clubs, and remained frozen with horror, the card still resting on his finger; he had not come there to kill, but to be killed; and the Prince in his generous sympathy with his position almost forgot the peril that still hung over himself and his friend.

The deal was coming round again, and still Death's card had not come out. The players held their respiration, and only breathed by gasps. The Prince received another club; Geraldine had a diamond; but when Mr. Malthus turned up his card a horrible noise, like that of something breaking, issued from his mouth; and he rose from his seat and sat down again, with no sign of his paralysis. It was the ace of spades. The honorary member had trifled once too often with his terrors.

Conversation broke out again almost at once. The players relaxed their rigid attitudes, and began to rise from the table and stroll back by twos and threes into the smoking room. The President stretched his arms and yawned, like a man who has finished his day's work. But Mr. Malthus sat in his place, with his head in his hands, and his hands upon the table, drunk and motionless—a thing stricken down.

The Prince and Geraldine made their escape at once. In the cold night air their horror of what they had witnessed was redoubled.

"Alas!" cried the Prince, "to be bound by an oath in such a matter! to allow this wholesale trade in murder to be continued with profit and impunity! If I but dared to forfeit my pledge!"

"That is impossible for your Highness," replied the Colonel, "whose honour is the honour of Bohemia. But I dare, and may with propriety, forfeit mine."

"Geraldine," said the Prince, "if your honour suffers in any of the adventures into which you follow me, not only will I never pardon you, but—what I believe will much more sensibly affect you—I should never forgive myself."

"I receive your Highness's commands," replied the Colonel. "Shall we go from this accursed spot?"

"Yes," said the Prince. "Call a cab in Heaven's name, and let me try to forget in slumber the memory of this night's disgrace."

But it was notable that he carefully read the name of the court before he left it.

The next morning, as soon as the Prince was stirring, Colonel Geraldine brought him a daily newspaper, with the following paragraph marked:

"MELANCHOLY ACCIDENT—This morning, about two o'clock, Mr. Bartholomew Malthus, of 16, Chepstow Place, Westbourne Grove, on his way home from a party at a friend's house, fell over the upper parapet in Trafalgar Square,[1] fracturing his skull and breaking a leg and an arm. Death was instantaneous. Mr. Malthus, accompanied by a friend, was engaged in looking for a cab at the time of the unfortunate occurrence. As Mr. Malthus was paralytic, it is thought that his fall may have been occasioned by another seizure. The unhappy gentleman was well known in the most respectable circles, and his loss will be widely and deeply deplored."

"If ever a soul went straight to Hell," said Geraldine solemnly, "it was that paralytic man's."

The Prince buried his face in his hands, and remained silent.

"I am almost rejoiced," continued the Colonel, "to know that he is dead. But for our young man of the cream tarts I confess my heart bleeds."

"Geraldine," said 'the Prince, raising his face, "that unhappy lad was last night as innocent as you and I; and this morning the guilt of blood is on his soul. When I think of the President, my heart grows sick within me. I do not know how it shall be done, but I shall have that scoundrel at my mercy as there is a God in heaven. What an experience, what a lesson, was that game of cards!"

"One," said the Colonel, "never to be repeated."

The Prince remained so long without replying, that Geraldine grew alarmed.

"You cannot mean to return," he said. "You have suffered too much and seen too much horror already. The duties of your high position forbid the repetition of the hazard."

"There is much in what you say," replied Prince Florizel, "and I am not altogether pleased with my own determination. Alas! in the clothes of the greatest potentate,

---

1 Large public square in the heart of London.

what is there but a man? I never felt my weakness more acutely than now, Geraldine, but it is stronger than I. Can I cease to interest myself in the fortunes of the unhappy young man who supped with us some hours ago? Can I leave the President to follow his nefarious career unwatched? Can I begin an adventure so entrancing, and not follow it to an end? No, Geraldine: you ask of the Prince more than the man is able to perform. Tonight, once more, we take our places at the table of the Suicide Club."

Colonel Geraldine fell upon his knees.

"Will your Highness take my life?" he cried. "It is his—his freely; but do not, O do not! let him ask me to countenance so terrible a risk."

"Colonel Geraldine," replied the Prince, with some haughtiness of manner, "your life is absolutely your own. I only look for obedience; and when that is unwillingly rendered, I shall look for that no longer. I add one word: your importunity in this affair has been sufficient."

The Master of the Horse regained his feet at once.

"Your Highness," he said, "may I be excused in my attendance this afternoon? I dare not, as an honourable man, venture a second time into that fatal house until I have perfectly ordered my affairs. Your Highness shall meet, I promise him, with no more opposition from the most devoted and grateful of his servants."

"My dear Geraldine," returned Prince Florizel, "I always regret when you oblige me to remember my rank. Dispose of your day as you think fit, but be here before eleven in the same disguise."

The club, on this second evening, was not so fully attended; and when Geraldine and the Prince arrived, there were not above half-a-dozen persons in the smoking-room. His Highness took the President aside and congratulated him warmly on the demise of Mr. Malthus.

"I like," he said, "to meet with capacity, and certainly find much of it in you. Your profession is of a very delicate nature, but I see you are well qualified to conduct it with success and secrecy."

The President was somewhat affected by these compliments from one of his Highness's superior bearing. He acknowledged them almost with humility.

"Poor Malthy!" he added, "I shall hardly know the club without him. The most of my patrons are boys, sir, and poetical boys, who are not much company for me. Not but what Malthy had some poetry, too; but it was of a kind that I could understand."

"I can readily imagine you should find yourself in sympathy with Mr. Malthus," returned the Prince. "He struck me as a man of a very original disposition."

The young man of the cream tarts was in the room, but painfully depressed and silent. His late companions sought in vain to lead him into conversation.

"How bitterly wish," he cried, "that I had never brought you to this infamous abode! Begone, while you are clean-handed. If you could have heard the old man scream as he fell, and the noise of his bones upon the pavement! Wish me, if you have any kindness to so fallen a being—wish the ace of spades for me tonight!"

A few more members dropped in as the evening went on, but the club did not muster more than the devil's dozen[1] when they took their places at the table. The prince was again conscious of a certain joy in his alarms, but he was astonished to see Geraldine so much more self-possessed than on the night before.

"It is extraordinary," thought the Prince, "that a will, made or unmade, should so greatly influence a young man's spirit."

"Attention, gentlemen!" said the President, and he began to deal.

Three times the cards went all round the table, and neither of the marked cards had yet fallen from his hand. The excitement as he began the fourth distribution was overwhelming. There were just cards enough to go once more entirely round. The Prince, who sat second from the dealer's left, would receive, in the reverse mode of dealing practised at the club, the second last card. The third player turned up a black ace—it was the ace of clubs. The next received a diamond, the next a heart, and so on; but the ace of spades was still undelivered. At last Geraldine, who sat upon the Prince's left, turned his card; it was an ace, but the ace of hearts.

When Prince Florizel saw his fate upon the table in front of him, his heart stood still. He was a brave man, but the sweat poured off his face. There were exactly fifty chance out of a hundred that he was doomed. He reversed the table card; it was the ace of spades. A loud roaring filled his brain, and the table swam before his eyes. He heard the player on his right break into a fit of laughter that sounded between mirth and disappointment; he saw the company rapidly dispersing, but his mind was full of other thoughts. He recognised how foolish, how criminal, had been his conduct. In perfect health in the prime of his years, the heir to a throne, he had gambled away his future and that of a brave and loyal country. "God," he cried, "God forgive me!" And with that, the confusion of his senses passed away, and he regained his self-possession in a moment.

To his surprise Geraldine had disappeared. There was no one in the cardroom but his destined butcher consulting with the President, and the young man of the cream tarts, who slipped up to the Prince and whispered in his ear:

---

1   Thirteen.

"I would give a million, if I had it, for your luck." His Highness could not help reflecting, as the young man departed, that he would have sold his opportunity for a much more moderate sum.

The whispered conference now came to an end. The holder of the ace of clubs left the room with a look of intelligence, and the President, approaching the unfortunate Prince, proffered him his hand.

"I am pleased to have met you, sir," said he, "and pleased to have been in a position to do you this trifling service. At least, you cannot complain of delay. On the second evening—what a stroke of luck!"

The Prince endeavoured in vain to articulate something in response, but his mouth was dry and his tongue seemed paralysed.

"You feel a little sickish?" asked the President, with some show of solicitude. "Most gentlemen do. Will you take a little brandy?"

The Prince signified in the affirmative, and the other immediately filled some of the spirit into a tumbler.

"Poor old Malthy!" ejaculated the President, as the Prince drained the glass. "He drank near upon a pint, and little enough good it seemed to do him!"

"I am more amenable to treatment," said the Prince, a good deal revived. "I am my own man again at once, as you perceive. And so, let me ask you, what are my directions?"

"You will proceed along the Strand[1] in the direction of the City, and on the left-hand pavement, until you meet the gentleman who has just left the room. He will continue your instructions, and him you will have the kindness to obey; the authority of the club is vested in his person for the night. And now," added the President, "I wish you a pleasant walk."

Florizel acknowledged the salutation rather awkwardly, and took his leave. He passed through the smoking room, where the bulk of the players were still consuming champagne, some of which he had himself ordered and paid for; and he was surprised to find himself cursing them in his heart. He put on his hat and greatcoat in the cabinet, and selected his umbrella from a corner. The familiarity of these acts, and the thought that he was about them for the last time, betrayed him into a fit of laughter which sounded unpleasantly in his own ears. He conceived a reluctance to leave the cabinet, and turned instead to the window. The sight of the lamps and the darkness recalled him to himself.

---

1   Busy street in central London extending from Trafalgar Square in the west to Fleet Street in the east.

"Come, come, I must be a man," he thought, "and tear myself away."

At the corner of Box Court three men fell upon Prince Florizel and he was unceremoniously thrust into a carriage, which at once drove rapidly away. There was already an occupant.

"Will your Highness pardon my zeal?" said a well-known voice. The Prince threw himself upon the Colonel's neck in a passion of relief.

"How can I ever thank you?" he cried. "And how was this effected?"

Although he had been willing to march upon his doom, he was overjoyed to yield to friendly violence, and return once more to life and hope.

"You can thank me effectually enough," replied the Colonel, "by avoiding all such dangers in the future. And as for your second question, all has been managed by the simplest means. I arranged this afternoon with a celebrated detective. Secrecy has been promised and paid for. Your own servants have been principally engaged in the affair. The house in Box Court has been surrounded since nightfall, and this, which is one of your own carriages, has been awaiting you for nearly an hour."

"And the miserable creature who was to have slain me—what of him?" inquired the Prince.

"He was pinioned[1] as he left the club," replied the Colonel, "and now awaits your sentence at the Palace, where he will soon be joined by his accomplices."

"Geraldine," said the Prince, "you have saved me against my explicit orders, and you have done well. I owe you not only my life, but a lesson; and I should be unworthy of my rank if I did not show myself grateful to my teacher. Let it be yours to choose the manner."

There was a pause, during which the carriage continued to speed through the streets, and the two men were each buried in his own reflections. The silence was broken by Colonel Geraldine.

"Your Highness," said he, "has by this time a considerable body of prisoners. There is at least one criminal among the number to whom justice should be dealt. Our oath forbids us all recourse to law; and discretion would forbid it equally if the oath were loosened. May I inquire your Highness's intention?"

"It is decided," answered Florizel; "the President must fall in duel. It only remains to choose his adversary."

"Your Highness has permitted me to name my own recompense," said the colonel. "Will he permit me to ask the appointment of my brother? It is an honourable post, but I dare assure your Highness that the lad will acquit himself with credit."

---

1 Restrained.

"You ask me an ungracious favour," said the prince, "but I must refuse you nothing."

The colonel kissed his hand with the greatest affection; and at that moment the carriage rolled under the archway of the Prince's splendid residence.

An hour after, Florizel in his official robes, and covered with all the orders[1] of Bohemia, received the members of the Suicide Club.

"Foolish and wicked men," said he, "as many of you as have been driven into this strait by the lack of fortune shall receive employment and remuneration from my officers. Those who suffer under a sense of guilt must have recourse to a higher and more generous Potentate than I. I feel pity for all of you, deeper than you can imagine; tomorrow you shall tell me your stories; and as you answer more frankly, I shall be the more able to remedy your misfortunes. As for you," he added, turning to the President, "I should only offend a person of your parts by any offer of assistance; but I have instead a piece of diversion to propose to you. Here," laying his hand on the shoulder of Colonel Geraldine's young brother, "is an officer of mine who desires to make a little tour upon the Continent; and I ask you, as a favour, to accompany him on this excursion. Do you," he went on, changing his tone, "do you shoot well with the pistol? Because you may have need of that accomplishment. When two men go travelling together, it is best to be prepared for all. Let me add that, if by any chance you should lose young Mr. Geraldine upon the way, I shall always have another member of my household to place at your disposal; and I am known, Mr. President, to have long eyesight, and as long an arm."

With these words, said with much sternness, the Prince concluded his address. Next morning the members of the club were suitably provided for by his munificence, and the President set forth upon his travels, under the supervision of Mr. Geraldine, and a pair of faithful and adroit lackeys, well trained in the Prince's household. Not content with this, discreet agents were put in possession of the house in Box Court, and all letters or visitors for the Suicide Club or its officials were to be examined by Prince Florizel in person.

Here (says my Arabian author) *ends* THE STORY OF THE YOUNG MAN WITH THE CREAM TARTS, *who is now a comfortable householder in Wigmore Street, Cavendish Square.*[2] *The number, for obvious reasons, I suppress. Those who care to pursue the adventures of Prince Florizel and the*

---
1   Insignia.
2   Fashionable square in London's West End, near Oxford Circus.

President of the Suicide Club, may read the HISTORY OF THE PHYSICIAN AND THE SARATOGA TRUNK.

STORY OF THE PHYSICIAN AND THE SARATOGA TRUNK

MR. Silas Q. Scuddamore was a young American of a simple and harmless disposition, which was the more to his credit as he came from New England—a quarter of the New World not precisely famous for those qualities. Although he was exceedingly rich, he kept a note of all his expenses in a little paper pocketbook; and he had chosen to study the attractions of Paris from the seventh story of what is called a furnished hotel, in the Latin Quarter.[1] There was a great deal of habit in his penuriousness; and his virtue, which was very remarkable among his associates, was principally founded upon diffidence and youth.

The next room to his was inhabited by a lady, very attractive in her air and very elegant in toilette,[2] whom, on his first arrival, he had taken for a Countess. In course of time he had learned that she was known by the name of Madame Zéphyrine, and that whatever station she occupied in life it was not that of a person of title. Madame Zéphyrine, probably in the hope of enchanting the young American, used to flaunt by him on the stairs with a civil inclination, a word of course, and a knock-down[3] look out of her black eyes, and disappear in a rustle of silk, and with the revelation of an admirable foot and ankle. But these advances, so far from encouraging Mr. Scuddamore, plunged him into the depths of depression and bashfulness. She had come to him several times for a light, or to apologise for the imaginary depredations of her poodle; but his mouth was closed in the presence of so superior a being, his French promptly left him, and he could only stare and stammer until she was gone. The slenderness of their intercourse did not prevent him from throwing out insinuations of a very glorious order when he was safely alone with a few males.

The room on the other side of the American's—for there were three rooms on a floor in the hotel—was tenanted by an old English physician of rather doubtful

---
1 Left bank of the Seine, near the Sorbonne University, and home in the nineteenth century to artists, students, intellectuals, as well as a raucous nightlife.
2 Dress and grooming.
3 Penetrating, unequivocal.

reputation. Dr. Noel, for that was his name, had been forced to leave London, where he enjoyed a large and increasing practice; and it was hinted that the police had been the instigators of this change of scene. At least he, who had made something of a figure in earlier life, now dwelt in the Latin Quarter in great simplicity and solitude, and devoted much of his time to study. Mr. Scuddamore had made his acquaintance, and the pair would now and then dine together frugally in a restaurant across the street.

Silas Q. Scuddamore had many little vices of the more respectable order, and was not restrained by delicacy from indulging them in many rather doubtful ways. Chief among his foibles stood curiosity. He was a born gossip; and life, and especially those parts of it in which he had no experience, interested him to the degree of passion. He was a pert, invincible questioner, pushing his inquiries with equal pertinacity and indiscretion; he had been observed, when he took a letter to the post, to weigh it in his hand, to turn it over and over, and to study the address with care; and when he found a flaw in the partition between his room and Madame Zéphyrine's, instead of filling it up he enlarged and improved the opening, and made use of it as a spy-hole on his neighbour's affairs.

One day, in the end of March, his curiosity growing as it was indulged, he enlarged the hole a little further, so that he might command another corner of the room. That evening, when he went as usual to inspect Madame Zéphyrine's movements, he was astonished to find the aperture obscured in an odd manner on the other side, and still more abashed when the obstacle was suddenly withdrawn and a titter of laughter reached his ears. Some of the plaster had evidently betrayed the secret of his spy-hole, and his neighbour had been returning the compliment in kind. Mr. Scuddamore was moved to a very acute feeling of annoyance; he condemned Madame Zéphyrine unmercifully; he even blamed himself; but when he found, next day, that she had taken no means to baulk[1] him of his favourite pastime, continued to profit by her carelessness, and gratify his idle curiosity.

That next day Madame Zéphyrine received a long visit from a tall, loosely-built man of fifty or upwards, whom Silas had not hitherto seen. His tweed suit and coloured shirt, no less than his shaggy side whiskers, identified him as a Britisher, and his dull grey eye affected Silas with a sense of cold. He kept screwing his mouth from side to side and round and round during the whole colloquy, which was carried on in whispers. More than once it seemed to the young New Englander as if their gestures indicated his own apartment; but the only thing definite he could

---

1   Balk, hinder.

gather by the most scrupulous attention was this remark made by the Englishman in a somewhat higher key, as if in answer to some reluctance or opposition.

"I have studied his taste to a nicety, and I tell you again and again you are the only woman of the sort that I can lay my hands on."

In answer to this, Madame Zéphyrine sighed, and appeared by a gesture to resign herself, like one yielding to unqualified authority.

That afternoon the observatory was finally blinded, a wardrobe having been drawn in front of it upon the other side; and while Silas was still lamenting over this misfortune, which he attributed to the Britisher's malign suggestion, the concierge brought him up a letter in a female handwriting. It was conceived in French of no very rigorous orthography,[1] bore no signature, and in the most encouraging terms invited the young American to be present in a certain part of the Bullier Ball at eleven o'clock that night. Curiosity and timidity fought a long battle in his heart; sometimes he was all virtue, sometimes all fire and daring; and the result of it was that, long before ten, Mr. Silas Q. Scuddamore presented himself in unimpeachable attire at the door of the Bullier Ball Rooms, and paid his entry money with a sense of reckless deviltry that was not without its charm.

It was Carnival time, and the Ball was very full and noisy. The lights and the crowd at first rather abashed our young adventurer, and then, mounting to his brain with a sort of intoxication, put him in possession of more than his own share of manhood. He felt ready to face the devil, and strutted in the ballroom with the swagger of a cavalier. While he was thus parading, he became aware of Madame Zéphyrine and her Britisher in conference behind a pillar. The catlike spirit of eavesdropping overcame him at once. He stole nearer and nearer on the couple from behind, until he was within earshot.

"That is the man," the Britisher was saying; "there—with the long blond hair—speaking to a girl in green."

Silas identified a very handsome young fellow of small stature, who was plainly the object of this designation.

"It is well," said Madame Zéphyrine. "I shall do my utmost. But, remember, the best of us may fail in such a matter."

"Tut!" returned her companion; "I answer for the result. Have I not chosen you from thirty? Go; but be wary of the prince. I cannot think what cursed accident brought him here tonight. As if there were not a dozen balls in Paris better worth his

---

1 Correct spelling.

notice than this riot of students and counterjumpers![1] See him where he sits, more like a reigning Emperor at home than a Prince upon his holidays!"

Silas was again lucky. He observed a person of rather a full build, strikingly handsome, and of a very stately and courteous demeanour, seated at table with another handsome young man, several years his junior, who addressed him with conspicuous deference. The name of Prince struck gratefully on Silas's Republican hearing, and the aspect of the person to whom that name was applied exercised its usual charm upon his mind. He left Madame Zéphyrine and her Englishman to take care of each other, and threading his way through the assembly, approached the table which the Prince and his confidant had honoured with their choice.

"I tell you, Geraldine," the former was saying, "the action is madness. Yourself (I am glad to remember it) chose your brother for this perilous service, and you are bound in duty to have a guard upon his conduct. He has consented to delay so many days in Paris; that was already an imprudence, considering the character of the man he has to deal with; but now, when he is within eight-and-forty hours of his departure, when he is within two or three days of the decisive trial, I ask you, is this a place for him to spend his time? He should be in a gallery at practice; he should be sleeping long hours and taking moderate exercise on foot; he should be on rigorous diet, without white wines or brandy. Does the dog[2] imagine we are playing comedy? The thing is deadly earnest, Geraldine."

"I know the lad too well to interfere," replied Colonel Geraldine, "and well enough not to be alarmed. He is more cautious than you fancy, and of an indomitable spirit. If it had been a woman I should not say so much, but I trust the President to him and the two valets without an instant's apprehension."

"I am gratified to hear you say so," replied the Prince; "but my mind is not at rest. These servants are well-trained spies, and already has not this miscreant succeeded three times in eluding their observation and spending several hours on end in private, and most likely dangerous affairs? An amateur might have lost him by accident, but if Rudolph and Jérome were thrown off the scent, it must have been done on purpose, and by a man who had a cogent reason and exceptional resources."

"I believe the question is now one between my brother and myself," replied Geraldine, with a shade of offence in his tone.

---

1   Derogatory term for salesmen in shops.
2   Fellow.

"I permit it to be so, Colonel Geraldine," returned Prince Florizel. "Perhaps, for that very reason, you should be all the more ready to accept my counsels. But enough. That girl in yellow dances well."

And the talk veered into the ordinary topics of a Paris ballroom in the Carnival.

Silas remembered where he was, and that the hour was already near at hand when he ought to be upon the scene of his assignation. The more he reflected the less he liked the prospect, and as at that moment an eddy in the crowd began to draw him in the direction of the door he suffered it to carry him away without resistance. The eddy stranded him in a corner under the gallery, where his ear was immediately struck with the voice of Madame Zéphyrine. She was speaking in French with the young man of the blond locks who had been pointed out by the strange Britisher not half an hour before.

"I have a character at stake," she said, "or I would put no other condition than my heart recommends. But you have only to say so much to the porter, and he will let you go by without a word."

"But why this talk of debt?" objected her companion.

"Heavens!" said she, "do you think I do not understand my own hotel?"

And she went by, clinging affectionately to her companion's arm.

This put Silas in mind of his billet.[1]

"Ten minutes hence," thought he, "and I may be walking with as beautiful a woman as that, and even better dressed—perhaps a real lady, possibly a woman of title."

And then he remembered the spelling, and was a little downcast.

"But it may have been written by her maid," he imagined.

The clock was only a few minutes from the hour, and this immediate proximity set his heart beating at a curious and rather disagreeable speed. He reflected with relief that he was in no way bound to put in an appearance. Virtue and cowardice were together, and he made once more for the door, but this time of his own accord, and battling against the stream of people which was now moving in a contrary direction. Perhaps this prolonged resistance wearied him, or perhaps he was in that frame of mind when merely to continue in the same determination for a certain number of minutes produces a reaction and a different purpose. Certainly, at least, he wheeled about for a third time, and did not stop until he had found a place of concealment within a few yards of the appointed place.

---

1   Note.

Here he went through an agony of spirit, in which he several times prayed to God for help, for Silas had been devoutly educated. He had now not the least inclination for the meeting; nothing kept him from flight but a silly fear lest he should be thought unmanly but this was so powerful that it kept head against all other motives; and although it could not decide him to advance, prevented him from definitely running away. At last the clock indicated ten minutes past the hour. Young Scuddamore's spirit began to rise; he peered round the corner and saw no one at the place of meeting; doubtless his unknown correspondent had wearied and gone away. He became as bold as he had formerly been timid. It seemed to him that if he came at all to the appointment, however late, he was clear from the charge of cowardice. Nay, now he began to suspect a hoax, and actually complimented himself on his shrewdness in having suspected and outmanoeuvred his mystifiers. So very idle a thing is a boy's mind!

Armed with these reflections, he advanced boldly from his corner; but he had not taken above a couple of steps before a hand was laid upon his arm. He turned and beheld a lady cast in a very large mould and with somewhat stately features, but bearing no mark of severity in her looks.

"I see that you are a very self-confident lady-killer," said she; "for you make yourself expected. But I was determined to meet you. When a woman has once so far forgotten herself as to make the first advance, she has long ago left behind her all considerations of petty pride."

Silas was overwhelmed by the size and attractions of his correspondent and the suddenness with which she had fallen upon him. But she soon set him at his ease. She was very towardly[1] and lenient in her behaviour; she led him on to make pleasantries, and then applauded him to the echo; and in a very short time, between blandishments and a liberal exhibition of warm brandy, she had not only induced him to fancy himself in love, but to declare his passion with the greatest vehemence.

"Alas!" she said; "I do not know whether I ought not to deplore this moment, great as is the pleasure you give me by your words. Hitherto I was alone to suffer; now, poor boy, there will be two. I am not my own mistress. I dare not ask you to visit me at my own house, for I am watched by jealous eyes. Let me see," she added; "I am older than you, although so much weaker; and while I trust in your courage and determination, I must employ my own knowledge of the world for our mutual benefit. Where do you live?"

---

1   Promising.

He told her that he lodged in a furnished hotel, and named the street and number.

She seemed to reflect for some minutes, with an effort of mind. "I see," she said at last. "You will be faithful and obedient, will you not?"

Silas assured her eagerly of his fidelity.

"Tomorrow night, then," she continued, with an encouraging smile, "you must remain at home all the evening; and if any friends should visit you, dismiss them at once on any pretext that most readily presents itself. Your door is probably shut by ten?" she asked.

"By eleven," answered Silas.

"At a quarter past eleven," pursued the lady, "leave the house. Merely cry for the door to be opened, and be sure you fall into no talk with the porter, as that might ruin everything. Go straight to the corner where the Luxembourg Gardens[1] join the Boulevard;[2] there you will find me waiting you. I trust you to follow my advice from point to point: and remember, if you fail me in only one particular, you will bring the sharpest trouble on a woman whose only fault is to have seen and loved you."

"I cannot see the use of all these instructions," said Silas.

"I believe you are already beginning to treat me as a master," she cried, tapping him with her fan upon the arm. "Patience, patience! that should come in time. A woman loves to be obeyed at first, although afterwards she finds her pleasure in obeying. Do as I ask you, for Heaven's sake, or I will answer for nothing. Indeed, now I think of it," she added, with the manner of one who has just seen further into a difficulty, "I find a better plan of keeping importunate visitors away. Tell the porter to admit no one for you, except a person who may come that night to claim a debt; and speak with some feeling, as though you feared the interview, so that he may take your words in earnest."

"I think you may trust me to protect myself against intruders," he said, not without a little pique.

"That is how I should prefer the thing arranged," she answered, coldly. "I know you men; you think nothing of a woman's reputation."

Silas blushed and somewhat hung his head; for the scheme he had in view had involved a little vainglorying before his acquaintances.

"Above all," she added, "do not speak to the porter as you come out."

---

1 Public park near Paris's Latin Quarter.
2 Boulevard Saint Michel.

"And why?" said he. "Of all your instructions, that seems to me the least important."

"You at first doubted the wisdom of some of the others, which you now see to be very necessary," she replied. "Believe me, this also has its uses; in time you will see them; and what am I to think of your affection, if you refuse me such trifles at our first interview?"

Silas confounded himself in explanations and apologies; in the middle of these she looked up at the clock and clapped her hands together with a suppressed scream.

"Heavens!" she cried, "is it so late? I have not an instant to lose. Alas, we poor women, what slaves we are! What have I not risked for you already?"

And after repeating her directions, which she artfully combined with caresses and the most abandoned looks, she bade him farewell and disappeared among the crowd.

The whole of the next day Silas was filled with a sense of great importance; he was now sure she was a countess; and when evening came he minutely obeyed her orders and was at the corner of the Luxembourg Gardens by the hour appointed. No one was there. He waited nearly half an hour, looking in the face of everyone who passed or loitered near the spot; he even visited the neighbouring corners of the Boulevard and made a complete circuit of the garden railings; but there was no beautiful countess to throw herself into his arms. At last, and most reluctantly, he began to retrace his steps towards his hotel. On the way he remembered the words he had heard pass between Madame Zéphyrine and the blond young man, and they gave him an indefinite uneasiness.

"It appears," he reflected, "that everyone has to tell lies to our porter."

He rang the bell, the door opened before him, and the porter in his bedclothes came to offer him a light.

"Has he gone?" inquired the porter.

"He? Whom do you mean?" asked Silas, somewhat sharply, for he was irritated by his disappointment.

"I did not notice him go out," continued the porter, "but I trust you paid him. We do not care, in this house, to have lodgers who cannot meet their liabilities."[1]

"What the devil do you mean?" demanded Silas, rudely. "I cannot understand a word of this farrago."[2]

---

1 Financial obligations.
2 Confused mixture, mishmash.

"The short, blond young man who came for his debt," returned the other. "Him it is I mean. Who else should it be, when I had your orders to admit no one else?"

"Why, good God, of course he never came," retorted Silas.

"I believe what I believe," returned the porter, putting his tongue into his cheek with a most roguish air.

"You are an insolent scoundrel," cried Silas, and, feeling that he had made a ridiculous exhibition of asperity, and at the same time bewildered by a dozen alarms, he turned and began to run upstairs.

"Do you not want a light then?" cried the porter.

But Silas only hurried the faster, and did not pause until he had reached the seventh landing and stood in front of his own door. There he waited a moment to recover his breath, assailed by the worst forebodings and almost dreading to enter the room.

When at last he did so he was relieved to find it dark, and to all appearance, untenanted. He drew a long breath. Here he was, home again in safety, and this should be his last folly as certainly as it had been his first. The matches stood on a little table by the bed, and he began to grope his way in that direction. As he moved, his apprehensions grew upon him once more, and he was pleased, when his foot encountered an obstacle, to find it nothing more alarming than a chair. At last he touched curtains. From the position of the window, which was faintly visible, he knew he must be at the foot of the bed, and had only to feel his way along it in order to reach the table in question.

He lowered his hand, but what it touched was not simply a counterpane[1]—it was a counterpane with something underneath it like the outline of a human leg. Silas withdrew his arm and stood a moment petrified.

"What, what," he thought, "can this betoken?"

He listened intently, but there was no sound of breathing. Once more, with a great effort, he reached out the end of his finger to the spot he had already touched; but this time he leaped back half a yard, and stood shivering and fixed with terror. There was something in his bed. What it was he knew not, but there was something there.

It was some seconds before he could move. Then, guided by an instinct, he fell straight upon the matches, and keeping his back towards the bed lighted a candle. As soon as the flame had kindled, he turned slowly round and looked for what he feared to see. Sure enough, there was the worst of his imaginations realised. The

---

1   Bedspread.

coverlid was drawn carefully up over the pillow, but it moulded the outline of a human body lying motionless; and when he dashed forward and flung aside the sheets, he beheld the blond young man whom he had seen in the Bullier Ball the night before, his eyes open and without speculation, his face swollen and blackened, and a thin stream of blood trickling from his nostrils.

Silas uttered a long, tremulous wail, dropped the candle, and fell on his knees beside the bed.

Silas was awakened from the stupor into which his terrible discovery had plunged him, by a prolonged but discreet tapping at the door. It took him some seconds to remember his position; and when he hastened to prevent anyone from entering it was already too late. Dr. Noel, in a tall nightcap, carrying a lamp which lighted up his long white countenance, sidling in his gait, and peering and cocking his head like some sort of bird, pushed the door slowly open, and advanced into the middle of the room.

"I thought I heard a cry," began the Doctor, "and fearing you might be unwell I did not hesitate to offer this intrusion."

Silas, with a flushed face and a fearful beating heart, kept between the Doctor and the bed; but he found no voice to answer.

"You are in the dark," pursued the Doctor; "and yet you have not even begun to prepare for rest. You will not easily persuade me against my own eyesight; and your face declares most eloquently that you require either a friend or a physician—which is it to be? Let me feel your pulse, for that is often a just reporter of the heart."

He advanced to Silas, who still retreated before him backwards, and sought to take him by the wrist; but the strain on the young American's nerves had become too great for endurance. He avoided the Doctor with a febrile movement, and, throwing himself upon the floor, burst into a flood of weeping.

As soon as Dr. Noel perceived the dead man in the bed his face darkened; and hurrying back to the door which he had left ajar, he hastily closed and double-locked it.

"Up!" he cried, addressing Silas in strident tones; "this is no time for weeping. What have you done? How came this body in your room? Speak freely to one who may be helpful. Do you imagine I would ruin you? Do you think this piece of dead flesh on your pillow can alter in any degree the sympathy with which you have inspired me? Credulous youth, the horror with which blind and unjust law regards an action never attaches to the doer in the eyes of those who love him; and if I saw the friend of my heart return to me out of seas of blood he would be in no way changed in my affection. Raise yourself," he said; "good and ill are a chimera; there is nought in life except destiny, and however you may be circumstanced there is one at your side who will help you to the last."

Thus encouraged, Silas gathered himself together, and in a broken voice, and helped out by the Doctor's interrogations, contrived at last to put him in possession of the facts. But the conversation between the Prince and Geraldine he altogether omitted, as he had understood little of its purport, and had no idea that it was in any way related to his own misadventure.

"Alas!" cried Dr. Noel, "I am much abused, or you have fallen innocently into the most dangerous hands in Europe. Poor boy, what a pit has been dug for your simplicity! into what a deadly peril have your unwary feet been conducted! This man," he said, "this Englishman, whom you twice saw, and whom I suspect to be the soul of the contrivance, can you describe him? Was he young or old? tall or short?"

But Silas, who, for all his curiosity, had not a seeing eye in his head, was able to supply nothing but meagre generalities, which it was impossible to recognise.

"I would have it a piece of education in all schools!" cried the Doctor angrily. "Where is the use of eyesight and articulate speech if a man cannot observe and recollect the features of his enemy? I, who know all the gangs of Europe, might have identified him, and gained new weapons for your defence. Cultivate this art in future, my poor boy; you may find it of momentous service."

"The future!" repeated Silas. "What future is there left for me except the gallows?"

"Youth is but a cowardly season," returned the Doctor; "and a man's own troubles look blacker than they are. I am old, and yet I never despair."

"Can I tell such a story to the police?" demanded Silas.

"Assuredly not," replied the Doctor. "From what I see already of the machination in which you have been involved, your case is desperate upon that side; and for the narrow eye of the authorities you are infallibly the guilty person. And remember that we only know a portion of the plot; and the same infamous contrivers have doubtless arranged many other circumstances which would be elicited by a police inquiry, and help to fix the guilt more certainly upon your innocence."

"I am then lost, indeed!" cried Silas.

"I have not said so," answered Dr. Noel, "for I am a cautious man."

"But look at this!" objected Silas, pointing to the body. "Here is this object in my bed: not to be explained, not to be disposed of, not to be regarded without horror."

"Horror?" replied the Doctor. "No. When this sort of clock has run down, it is no more to me than an ingenious piece of mechanism, to be investigated with the bistery.¹ When blood is once cold and stagnant, it is no longer human blood; when flesh is once dead, it is no longer that flesh which we desire in our lovers and respect in our friends. The grace, the attraction, the terror, have all gone from it with the animating spirit. Accustom yourself to look upon it with composure; for if my scheme is practicable you will have to live some days in constant proximity to that which now so greatly horrifies you."

"Your scheme?" cried Silas. "What is that? Tell me speedily Doctor; for I have scarcely courage enough to continue to exist."

Without replying, Dr. Noel turned towards the bed, and proceeded to examine the corpse.

"Quite dead," he murmured, "Yes as I had supposed, the pockets empty. Yes, and the name cut off the shirt. Their work has been done thoroughly and well. Fortunately, he is of small stature."

Silas followed these words with an extreme anxiety. At last the Doctor, his autopsy completed, took a chair and addressed the young American with a smile.

"Since I came into your room," said he, "although my ears and my tongue have been so busy, I have not suffered my eyes to remain idle. I noted a little while ago that you have there, in the corner, one of those monstrous constructions which your fellow countrymen carry with them into all quarters of the globe—in a word, a Saratoga trunk.² Until this moment I have never been able to conceive the utility of these erections; but then I began to have a glimmer. Whether it was for convenience in the slave trade, or to obviate the results of too ready an employment of the bowie knife, I cannot bring myself to decide. But one thing I see plainly—the object of such a box is to contain a human body."

"Surely," cried Silas, "surely this is not a time for jesting."

"Although I may express myself with some degree of pleasantry," replied the Doctor, "the purport of my words is entirely serious. And the first thing we have to do, my young friend, is to empty your coffer of all that it contains."

Silas, obeying the authority of Doctor Noel, put himself at his disposition. The Saratoga trunk was soon gutted of its contents, which made a considerable litter on the floor; and then—Silas taking the heels and the Doctor supporting the shoulders—the body of the murdered man was carried from the bed, and, after some difficulty, doubled up and inserted whole into the empty box. With an effort on the part of both, the lid was forced down upon this unusual baggage, and the

---

1   Scalpel.
2   Large traveling trunk, named after the spa town in upstate New York.

trunk was locked and corded by the Doctor's own hand, while Silas disposed of what had been taken out between the closet and a chest of drawers.

"Now," said the Doctor, "the first step has been taken on the way to your deliverance. Tomorrow, or rather today, it must be your task to allay the suspicions of your porter, paying him all that you owe; while you may trust me to make the arrangements necessary to a safe conclusion. Meantime, follow me to my room, where I shall give you a safe and powerful opiate; for, whatever you do, you must have rest."

The next day was the longest in Silas's memory; it seemed as if it would never be done. He denied himself to his friends, and sat in a corner with his eyes fixed upon the Saratoga trunk in dismal contemplation. His own former indiscretions were now returned upon him in kind; for the observatory had been once more opened, and he was conscious of an almost continual study from Madame Zéphyrine's apartment. So distressing did this become, that he was at last obliged to block up the spy-hole from his own side; and when he was thus secured from observation he spent a considerable portion of his time in contrite tears and prayer.

Late in the evening Dr. Noel entered the room carrying in his hand a pair of sealed envelopes without address, one somewhat bulky, and the other so slim as to seem without enclosure.

"Silas," he said, seating himself at the table, "the time has now come for me to explain my plan for your salvation. Tomorrow morning, at an early hour, Prince Florizel of Bohemia returns to London, after having diverted himself for a few days with the Parisian carnival. It was my fortune, a good while ago, to do Colonel Geraldine, his Master of the Horse, one of those services, so common in my profession, which are never forgotten upon either side. I have no need to explain to you the nature of the obligation under which he was laid; suffice it to say that I knew him ready to serve me in any practicable manner. Now, it was necessary for you to gain London with your trunk unopened. To this the Custom House seemed to oppose a fatal difficulty; but I bethought me that the baggage of so considerable a person as the Prince, is, as a matter of courtesy, passed without examination by the officers of Custom. I applied to Colonel Geraldine, and succeeded in obtaining a favourable answer. Tomorrow, if you go before six to the hotel where the Prince lodges, your baggage will be passed over as a part of his, and you yourself will make the journey as a member of his suite."

"It seems to me, as you speak, that I have already seen both the Prince and Colonel Geraldine; I even overheard some of their conversation the other evening at the Bullier Ball."

"It is probable enough; for the Prince loves to mix with all societies," replied the Doctor. "Once arrived in London," he pursued, "your task is nearly ended. In this more bulky envelope I have given you a letter which I dare not address; but in the other you will find the designation of the house to which you must carry it along with your box, which will there be taken from you and not trouble you any more."

"Alas!" said Silas, "I have every wish to believe you; but how is it possible? You open up to me a bright prospect, but, I ask you, is my mind capable of receiving so unlikely a solution? Be more generous, and let me farther understand your meaning."

The Doctor seemed painfully impressed.

"Boy," he answered, "you do not know how hard a thing you ask of me. But be it so. I am now inured to humiliation; and it would be strange if I refused you this, after having granted you so much. Know, then, that although I now make so quiet an appearance—frugal, solitary, addicted to study—when I was younger, my name was once a rallying cry among the most astute and dangerous spirits of London; and while I was outwardly an object for respect and consideration, my true power resided in the most secret, terrible, and criminal relations. It is to one of the persons who then obeyed me that I now address myself to deliver you from your burden. They were men of many different nations and dexterities, all bound together by a formidable oath, and working to the same purposes; the trade of the association was in murder; and I who speak to you, innocent as I appear, was the chieftain of this redoubtable crew."

"What?" cried Silas. "A murderer? And one with whom murder was a trade? Can I take your hand? Ought I so much as to accept your services? Dark and criminal old man, would you make an accomplice of my youth and my distress?"

The Doctor bitterly laughed.

"You are difficult to please, Mr. Scuddamore," said he; "but I now offer you your choice of company between the murdered man and the murderer. If your conscience is too nice to accept my aid, say so, and I will immediately leave you. Thenceforward you can deal with your trunk and its belongings as best suits your upright conscience."

"I own myself wrong," replied Silas. "I should have remembered how generously you offered to shield me, even before I had convinced you of my innocence, and I continue to listen to your counsels with gratitude."

"That is well," returned the Doctor; "and I perceive you are beginning to learn some of the lessons of experience."

"At the same time," resumed the New Englander, "as you confess yourself accustomed to this tragical business, and the people to whom you recommend me are your own former associates and friends, could you not yourself undertake the transport of the box, and rid me at once of its detested presence?"

"Upon my word," replied the Doctor, "I admire you cordially. If you do not think I have already meddled sufficiently in your concerns, believe me, from my heart I think the contrary. Take or leave my services as I offer them; and trouble me with no more words of gratitude, for I value your consideration even more lightly than I do your intellect. A time will come, if you should be spared to see a number of years in health of mind, when you will think differently of all this, and blush for your tonight's behaviour."

So saying, the Doctor arose from his chair, repeated his directions briefly and clearly, and departed from the room without permitting Silas any time to answer.

The next morning Silas presented himself at the hotel, where he was politely received by Colonel Geraldine, and relieved, from that moment, of all immediate alarm about his trunk and its grisly contents. The journey passed over without much incident, although the young man was horrified to overhear the sailors and railway porters complaining among themselves about the unusual weight of the Prince's baggage. Silas travelled in a carriage with the valets, for Prince Florizel chose to be alone with his Master of the Horse. On board the steamer, however, Silas attracted his Highness's attention by the melancholy of his air and attitude as he stood gazing at the pile of baggage; for he was still full of disquietude about the future.

"There is a young man," observed the Prince, "who must have some cause for sorrow."

"That," replied Geraldine, "is the American for whom I obtained permission to travel with your suite."

"You remind me that I have been remiss in courtesy," said Prince Florizel, and advancing to Silas, he addressed him with the most exquisite condescension in these words:

"I was charmed, young sir, to be able to gratify the desire you made known to me through Colonel Geraldine. Remember, if you please, that I shall be glad at any future time to lay you under a more serious obligation."

And he then put some questions as to the political condition of America, which Silas answered with sense and propriety.

"You are still a young man," said the Prince; "but I observe you to be very serious for your years. Perhaps you allow your attention to be too much occupied with grave studies. But, perhaps, on the other hand, I am myself indiscreet and touch upon a painful subject."

"I have certainly cause to be the most miserable of men," said Silas; "never has a more innocent person been more dismally abused."

"I will not ask you for your confidence," returned Prince Florizel, "But do not forget that Colonel Geraldine's recommendation is an unfailing passport; and that I am not only willing, but possibly more able than many others, to do you a service."

Silas was delighted with the amiability of this great personage; but his mind soon returned upon its gloomy preoccupations; for not even the favour of a prince to a Republican can discharge a brooding spirit of its cares.

The train arrived at Charing Cross, where the officers of the Revenue[1] respected the baggage of Prince Florizel in the usual manner. The most elegant equipages were in waiting; and Silas was driven, along with the rest, to the Prince's residence. There Colonel Geraldine sought him out, and expressed himself pleased to have been of any service to a friend of the physician's, for whom he professed a great consideration.

"I hope," he added, "that you will find none of your porcelain injured. Special orders were given along the line to deal tenderly with the Prince's effects."

And then, directing the servants to place one of the carriages at the young gentleman's disposal, and at once to charge the Saratoga trunk upon the dickey,[2] the Colonel shook hands and excused himself on account of his occupations in the princely household.

Silas now broke the seal of the envelope containing the address, and directed the stately footman to drive him to Box Court, opening off the Strand. It seemed as if the place were not at all unknown to the man, for he looked startled and begged a repetition of the order. It was with a heart full of alarms, that Silas mounted into the luxurious vehicle, and was driven to his destination. The entrance to Box Court was too narrow for the passage of a coach; it was a mere footway between railings, with a post at either end. On one of these posts was seated a man, who at once jumped down and exchanged a friendly sign with the driver, while the footman opened the door and inquired of Silas whether he should take down the Saratoga trunk, and to what number it should be carried.

"If you please," said Silas. "To number three."

---

1   Custom house.
2   The rear seat on a carriage reserved for servants.

The footman and the man who had been sitting on the post, even with the aid of Silas himself, had hard work to carry in the trunk; and before it was deposited at the door of the house in question, the young American was horrified to find a score of loiterers looking on. But he knocked with as good a countenance as he could muster up, and presented the other envelope to him who opened.

"He is not at home," said he, "but if you will leave your letter and return tomorrow early, I shall be able to inform you whether and when he can receive your visit. Would you like to leave your box?" he added.

"Dearly," cried Silas; and the next moment he repented his precipitation, and declared, with equal emphasis, that he would carry the box along with him to the hotel.

The crowd jeered at his indecision and followed him to the carriage with insulting remarks; and Silas, covered with shame and terror, implored the servants to conduct him to some quiet and comfortable house of entertainment in the immediate neighbourhood.

The Prince's equipage deposited Silas at the Craven Hotel in Craven Street, and immediately drove away, leaving him alone with the servants of the inn. The only vacant room, it appeared, was a little den up four pairs of stairs, and looking towards the back. To this hermitage, with infinite trouble and complaint, a pair of stout porters carried the Saratoga trunk. It is needless to mention that Silas kept closely at their heels throughout the ascent, and had his heart in his mouth at every corner. A single false step, he reflected, and the box might go over the bannisters and land its fatal contents, plainly discovered, on the pavement of the hall.

Arrived in the room, he sat down on the edge of his bed to recover from the agony that he had just endured; but he had hardly taken his position when he was recalled to a sense of his peril by the action of the boots,[1] who had knelt beside the trunk, and was proceeding officiously to undo its elaborate fastenings.

"Let it be!" cried Silas. "I shall want nothing from it while I stay here."

"You might have let it lie in the hall, then," growled the man; "a thing as big and heavy as a church. What you have inside, I cannot fancy. If it is all money, you are a richer man than me."

"Money?" repeated Silas, in a sudden perturbation. "What do you mean by money? I have no money, and you are speaking like a fool."

---

1   Hotel employee who performs menial jobs for guests, most notably shining their shoes.

"All right, captain," retorted the boots with a wink. "There's nobody will touch your lordship's money. I'm as safe as the bank," he added; "but as the box is heavy, I shouldn't mind drinking something to your lordship's health."

Silas pressed two Napoleons[1] upon his acceptance, apologising, at the same time, for being obliged to trouble him with foreign money, and pleading his recent arrival for excuse. And the man, grumbling with even greater fervour, and looking contemptuously from the money in his hand to the Saratoga trunk and back again from the one to the other, at last consented to withdraw. For nearly two days the dead body had been packed into Silas's box; and as soon as he was alone the unfortunate New Englander nosed all the cracks and openings with the most passionate attention. But the weather was cool, and the trunk still managed to contain his shocking secret.

He took a chair beside it, and buried his face in his hands, and his mind in the most profound reflection. If he were not speedily relieved, no question but he must be speedily discovered. Alone in a strange city, without friends or accomplices, if the Doctor's introduction failed him, he was indubitably a lost New Englander. He reflected pathetically over his ambitious designs for the future; he should not now become the hero and spokesman of his native place of Bangor, Maine; he should not, as he had fondly anticipated, move on from office to office, from honour to honour; he might as well divest himself at once of all hope of being acclaimed President of the United States, and leaving behind him a statue, in the worst possible style of art, to adorn the Capitol at Washington. Here he was, chained to a dead Englishman doubled up inside a Saratoga trunk; whom he must get rid of, or perish from the rolls of national glory!

I should be afraid to chronicle the language employed by this young man to the Doctor, to the murdered man, to Madame Zéphyrine, to the boots of the hotel, to the Prince's servants, and, in a word, to all who had been ever so remotely connected with his horrible misfortune.

He slunk down to dinner about seven at night; but the yellow coffee room appalled him, the eyes of the other diners seemed to rest on his with suspicion, and his mind remained upstairs with the Saratoga trunk. When the waiter came to offer him cheese, his nerves were already so much on edge that he leaped halfway out of his chair and upset the remainder of a pint of ale upon the tablecloth.

The fellow offered to show him to the smoking room when he had done; and although he would have much preferred to return at once to his perilous treasure, he

---

1 Two twenty-franc coins.

had not the courage to refuse, and was shown downstairs to the black, gas-lit cellar; which formed, and possibly still forms, the divan of the Craven Hotel.

Two very sad betting men were playing billiards attended by a moist, consumptive marker;[1] and for the moment Silas imagined that these were the only occupants of the apartment. But at the next glance his eye fell upon a person smoking in the farthest corner, with lowered eyes and a most respectable and modest aspect. He knew at once that he had seen the face before; and, in spite of the entire change of clothes, recognised the man whom he had found seated on a post at the entrance to Box Court, and who had helped him to carry the trunk to and from the carriage. The New Englander simply turned and ran, nor did he pause until he had locked and bolted himself into his bedroom.

There, all night long, a prey to the most terrible imaginations, he watched beside the fatal boxful of dead flesh. The suggestion of the boots that his trunk was full of gold inspired him with all manner of new terrors, if he so much as dared to close an eye; and the presence in the smoking room, and under an obvious disguise, of the loiterer from Box Court convinced him that he was once more the centre of obscure machinations.

Midnight had sounded some time, when, impelled by uneasy suspicions, Silas opened his bedroom door and peered into the passage. It was dimly illuminated by a single jet of gas; and some distance off he perceived a man sleeping on the floor in the costume of an hotel underservant, Silas drew near the man on tiptoe. He lay partly on his back, partly on his side, and his right forearm concealed his face from recognition. Suddenly, while the American was still bending over him, the sleeper removed his arm and opened his eyes, and Silas found himself once more face to face with the loiterer of Box Court.

"Good night, sir," said the man, pleasantly.

But Silas was too profoundly moved to find an answer, and regained his room in silence.

Towards morning, worn out by apprehension, he fell asleep on his chair, with his head forward on the trunk. In spite of so constrained an attitude and such a grisly pillow, his slumber was sound and prolonged, and he was only awakened at a late hour and by a sharp tapping at the door.

He hurried to open, and found the boots without.

"You are the gentleman who called yesterday at Box Court?" he asked.

Silas, with a quaver, admitted that he had done so.

---

1 Scorekeeper.

"Then this note is for you," added the servant, proffering a sealed envelope.

Silas tore it open, and found inside the words: "Twelve o'clock."

He was punctual to the hour; the trunk was carried before him by several stout servants; and he was himself ushered into a room, where a man sat warming himself before the fire with his back towards the door. The sound of so many persons entering and leaving, and the scraping of the trunk as it was deposited upon the bare boards, were alike unable to attract the notice of the occupant; and Silas stood waiting, in an agony of fear, until he should deign to recognise his presence.

Perhaps five minutes had elapsed before the man turned leisurely about, and disclosed the features of Prince Florizel of Bohemia.

"So, sir," he said, with great severity, "this is the manner in which you abuse my politeness. You join yourselves to persons of condition, I perceive, for no other purpose than to escape the consequences of your crimes; and I can readily understand your embarrassment when I addressed myself to you yesterday."

"Indeed," cried Silas, "I am innocent of everything except misfortune."

And in a hurried voice, and with the greatest ingenuousness, he recounted to the Prince the whole history of his calamity.

"I see I have been mistaken," said his Highness, when he had heard him to an end. "You are no other than a victim, and since I am not to punish you may be sure I shall do my utmost to help. And now," he continued, "to business. Open your box at once, and let me see what it contains."

Silas changed colour.

"I almost fear to look upon it," he exclaimed.

"Nay," replied the Prince, "have you not looked at it already? This is a form of sentimentality to be resisted. The sight of a sick man, whom we can still help, should appeal more directly to the feelings than that of a dead man who is equally beyond help or harm, love or hatred. Nerve yourself, Mr. Scuddamore," and then, seeing that Silas still hesitated, "I do not desire to give another name to my request," he added.

The young American awoke as if out of a dream, and with a shiver of repugnance addressed himself to loose the straps and open the lock of the Saratoga trunk. The Prince stood by, watching with a composed countenance and his hands behind his back. The body was quite stiff, and it cost Silas a great effort, both moral and physical, to dislodge it from its position, and discover the face.

Prince Florizel started back with an exclamation of painful surprise.

"Alas!" he cried, "you little know, Mr. Scuddamore, what a cruel gift you have brought me. This is a young man of my own suite, the brother of my trusted friend; and it was upon matters of my own service that he has thus perished at the hands of violent and treacherous men. Poor Geraldine," he went on, as if to himself, "in what words am I to tell you of your brother's fate? How can I excuse myself in your eyes, or in the eyes of God, for the presumptuous schemes that led him to this bloody and unnatural death? Ah, Florizel! Florizel! when will you learn the discretion that suits mortal life, and be no longer dazzled with the image of power at your disposal? Power!" he cried; "who is more powerless? I look upon this young man whom I have sacrificed, Mr. Scuddamore, and feel how small a thing it is to be a Prince."

Silas was moved at the sight of his emotion. He tried to murmur some consolatory words, and burst into tears. The Prince, touched by his obvious intention, came up to him and took him by the hand.

"Command yourself," said he. "We have both much to learn, and we shall both be better men for today's meeting."

Silas thanked him in silence with an affectionate look.

"Write me the address of Doctor Noel on this piece of paper," continued the Prince, leading him towards the table; "and let me recommend you, when you are again in Paris, to avoid the society of that dangerous man. He has acted in this matter on a generous inspiration; that I must believe; had he been privy to young Geraldine's death he would never have despatched the body to the care of the actual criminal."

"The actual criminal!" repeated Silas in astonishment.

"Even so," returned the Prince. "This letter, which the disposition of Almighty Providence has so strangely delivered into my hands, was addressed to no less a person than the criminal himself, the infamous President of the Suicide Club. Seek to pry no farther in these perilous affairs, but content yourself with your own miraculous escape, and leave this house at once. I have pressing affairs, and must arrange at once about this poor clay, which was so lately a gallant and handsome youth."

Silas took a grateful and submissive leave of Prince Florizel, but he lingered in Box Court until he saw him depart in a splendid carriage on a visit to Colonel Henderson of the police. Republican as he was, the young American took off his hat with almost a sentiment of devotion to the retreating carriage. And the same night he started by rail on his return to Paris.

Here (observes my Arabian author) *is the end of* THE HISTORY OF THE PHYSICIAN AND THE SARATOGA TRUNK. *Omitting some reflections on the power of Providence, highly pertinent in the original, but little suited to our occidental taste, I shall only add that Mr. Scuddamore has already begun to mount the ladder of political fame, and by last advices[1] was the Sheriff his native town.*

THE ADVENTURE OF THE HANSOM CABS

LIEUTENANT Brackenbury Rich had greatly distinguished himself in one of the lesser Indian hill wars. He it was who took the chieftain prisoner with his own hand; his gallantry was universally applauded; and when he came home, prostrated by an ugly sabre cut and a protracted jungle fever,[2] society was prepared to welcome the Lieutenant as a celebrity of minor lustre. But his was a character remarkable for unaffected modesty; adventure was dear to his heart, but he cared little for adulation; and he waited at foreign watering places and in Algiers until the fame of his exploits had run through its nine days' vitality[3] and begun to be forgotten. He arrived in London at last, in the early season, with as little observation as he could desire; and as he was an orphan and had none but distant relatives who lived in the provinces, it was almost as a foreigner that he installed himself in the capital of the country for which he had shed his blood.

On the day following his arrival he dined alone at a military club. He shook hands with a few old comrades, and received their warm congratulations; but as one and all had some engagement for the evening, he found himself left entirely to his own resources. He was in dress, for he had entertained the notion of visiting a theatre. But the great city was new to him; he had gone from a provincial school to a military college, and thence direct to the Eastern Empire; and he promised himself a variety of delights in this world for exploration. Swinging his cane, he took his way westward. It was a mild evening, already dark, and now and then threatening rain. The succession of faces in the lamplight stirred the Lieutenant's imagination; and it seemed to him as if he could walk for ever in that stimulating city atmosphere and surrounded by the mystery of four million private lives. He glanced at the houses, and marveled what was passing behind those warmly lighted windows; he looked into face after face, and saw them each intent upon some unknown interest, criminal or kindly.

---

1   News.
2   Malaria.
3   Victorian equivalent of "until his fifteen minutes of fame was up."

"They talk of war," he thought, "but this is the great battlefield of mankind."

And then he began to wonder that he should walk so long in this complicated scene, and not chance upon so much as the shadow of an adventure for himself.

"All in good time," he reflected. "I am still a stranger, and perhaps wear a strange air. But I must be drawn into the eddy before long."

The night was already well advanced when a plump[1] of cold rain fell suddenly out of the darkness. Brackenbury paused under some trees, and as he did so he caught sight of a hansom cabman making him a sign that he was disengaged. The circumstance fell in so happily to the occasion that he at once raised his cane in answer, and had soon ensconced himself in the London gondola.[2]

"Where to, sir?" asked the driver.

"Where you please," said Brackenbury.

And immediately, at a pace of surprising swiftness, the hansom drove off through the rain into a maze of villas. One villa was so like another, each with its front garden, and there was so little to distinguish the deserted lamplit streets and crescents[3] through which the flying hansom took its way, that Brackenbury soon lost all idea of direction. He would have been tempted to believe that the cabman was amusing himself by driving him round and round and in and out about a small quarter, but there was something businesslike in the speed which convinced him of the contrary. The man had an object in view, he was hastening towards a definite end; and Brackenbury was at once astonished at the fellow's skill in picking a way through such a labyrinth, and a little concerned to imagine what was the occasion of his hurry. He had heard tales of strangers falling ill in London. Did the driver belong to some bloody and treacherous association? and was he himself being whirled to a murderous death?

The thought had scarcely presented itself, when the cab swung sharply round a corner and pulled up before the garden gate of a villa in a long and wide road. The house was brilliantly lighted up. Another hansom had just driven away, and Brackenbury could see a gentleman being admitted at the front door and received by several liveried servants. He was surprised that the cabman should have stopped so immediately in front of a house where a reception was being held; but he did not doubt it was the result of accident, and sat placidly smoking where he was, until he heard the trap thrown open over his head.

"Here we are, sir," said the driver.

---

1 Drop.
2 Hansom cab, London's answer to the Venetian gondola.
3 A reference to the stately crescent-shaped streets that abound in London's West End.

"Here!" repeated Brackenbury. "Where?"

"You told me to take you where I pleased, sir," returned the man with a chuckle, "and here we are."

It struck Brackenbury that the voice was wonderfully smooth and courteous for a man in so inferior a position; he remembered the speed at which he had been driven; and now it occurred to him that the hansom was more luxuriously appointed than the common run of public conveyances.

"I must ask you to explain," said he, "Do you mean to turn me out into the rain? My good man, I suspect the choice is mine."

"The choice is certainly yours," replied the driver; "but when I tell you all, I believe I know how a gentleman of your figure will decide. There is a gentlemen's party in this house. I do not know whether the master be a stranger to London and without acquaintances of his own; or whether he is a man of odd notions. But certainly I was hired to kidnap single gentlemen in evening dress, as many as I pleased, but military officers by preference. You have simply to go in and say that Mr. Morris invited you."

"Are you Mr. Morris?" inquired the Lieutenant.

"Oh, no," replied the cabman. "Mr. Morris is the person of the house."

"It is not a common way of collecting guests," said Brackenbury: "but an eccentric man might very well indulge the whim without any intention to offend. And suppose that I refuse Mr. Morris's invitation," he went on, "what then?"

"My orders are to drive you back where I took you from," replied the man, "and set out to look for others up to midnight. Those who have no fancy for such an adventure, Mr. Morris said, were not the guests for him."

These words decided the Lieutenant on the spot.

"After all," he reflected, as he descended from the hansom, "I have not had long to wait for my adventure."

He had barely found footing on the sidewalk, and was still feeling in his pocket for the fare, when the cab swung about and drove off by the way it came at the former breakneck velocity. Brackenbury shouted after the man, who paid no heed, and continued to drive away; but the sound of his voice was overheard in the house, the door was again thrown open, emitting a flood of light upon the garden, and a servant ran down to meet him holding an umbrella.

"The cabman has been paid," observed the servant in a very civil tone; and he proceeded to escort Brackenbury along the path and up the steps. In the hall several other attendants relieved him of his hat, cane, and paletot,[1] gave him a ticket with a number in return, and politely hurried him up a stair adorned with tropical flowers, to the door of an apartment on the first storey.[2] Here a grave butler inquired his name, and announcing "Lieutenant Brackenbury Rich," ushered him into the drawing room of the house.

A young man, slender and singularly handsome, came forward and greeted him with an air at once courtly and affectionate. Hundreds of candles, of the finest wax, lit up a room that was perfumed, like the staircase, with a profusion of rare and beautiful flowering shrubs. A side table was loaded with tempting viands. Several servants went to and fro with fruits and goblets of champagne. The company was perhaps sixteen in number, all men, few beyond the prime of life, and with hardly an exception, of a dashing and capable exterior. They were divided into two groups one about a roulette board, and the other surrounding a table at which one of their number held a bank of baccarat.[3]

"I see," thought Brackenbury, "I am in a private gambling saloon, and the cabman was a tout."[4]

His eye had embraced the details, and his mind formed the conclusion, while his host was still holding him by the hand; and to him his looks returned from this rapid survey. At a second view Mr. Morris surprised him still more than on the first. The easy elegance of his manners, the distinction, amiability, and courage that appeared upon his features, fitted very ill with the Lieutenant's preconceptions on the subject of the proprietor of a hell;[5] and the tone of his conversation seemed to mark him out for a man of position and merit. Brackenbury found he had an instinctive liking for his entertainer; and though he chid himself for the weakness, he was unable to resist a sort of friendly attraction for Mr. Morris's person and character.

"I have heard of you, Lieutenant Rich," said Mr. Morris, lowering his tone; "and believe me I am gratified to make your acquaintance. Your looks accord with the reputation that has preceded you from India. And if you will forget for a while the irregularity of your presentation in my house, I shall feel it not only an honour, but a genuine pleasure besides. A man who makes a mouthful of barbarian cavaliers," he added with a laugh, "should not be appalled by a breach of etiquette, however serious."

---

1 Overcoat.
2 Floor above the ground floor.
3 Card game popular with the well-to-do.
4 Someone who sells inside information to bettors.
5 Gambling house.

And he led him towards the sideboard and pressed him to partake of some refreshment.

"Upon my word," the Lieutenant reflected, "this is one of the pleasantest fellows and, I do not doubt, one of the most agreeable societies in London."

He partook of some champagne, which he found excellent; and observing that many of the company were already smoking, he lit one of his own Manillas,[1] and strolled up to the roulette board, where he sometimes made a stake and sometimes looked on smilingly on the fortune of others. It was while he was thus idling that he became aware of a sharp scrutiny to which the whole of the guests were subjected. Mr. Morris went here and there, ostensibly busied on hospitable concerns; but he had ever a shrewd glance at disposal; not a man of the party escaped his sudden, searching looks; he took stock of the bearing of heavy losers, he valued the amount of the stakes, he paused behind couples who were deep in conversation; and, in a word, there was hardly a characteristic of anyone present but he seemed to catch and make a note of it. Brackenbury began to wonder if this were indeed a gambling hell: it had so much the air of a private inquisition. He followed Mr. Morris in all his movements; and although the man had a ready smile, he seemed to perceive, as it were under a mask, a haggard, careworn, and preoccupied spirit. The fellows around him laughed and made their game but Brackenbury had lost interest in the guests.

"This Morris," thought he, "is no idler in the room. Some deep purpose inspires him; let it be mine to fathom it."

Now and then Mr. Morris would call one of his visitors aside; and after a brief colloquy in an anteroom, he would return alone, and the visitors in question reappeared no more. After a certain number of repetitions, this performance excited Brackenbury's curiosity to a high degree. He determined to be at the bottom of this minor mystery at once; and strolling into the anteroom, found a deep window recess concealed by curtains of the fashionable green. Here he hurriedly ensconced himself; nor had he to wait long before the sound of steps and voices drew near him from the principal apartment. Peering through the division, he saw Mr. Morris escorting a fat and ruddy personage, with somewhat the look of a commercial traveller,[2] whom Brackenbury had already remarked for his coarse laugh and underbred behaviour at the table. The pair halted immediately before the window, so that Brackenbury lost not a word of the following discourse:

---

1   A cheroot made with tobacco grown in the Philippines.
2   Traveling salesman.

"I beg you a thousand pardons!" began Mr. Morris, with the most conciliatory manner; "and, if I appear rude, I am sure you will readily forgive me. In a place so great as London accidents must continually happen; and the best that we can hope is to remedy them with as small delay as possible. I will not deny that I fear you have made a mistake and honoured my poor house by inadvertence; for, to speak openly, I cannot at all remember your appearance. Let me put the question without unnecessary circumlocution—between gentlemen of honour a word will suffice—Under whose roof do you suppose yourself to be?"

"That of Mr. Morris," replied the other, with a prodigious display of confusion, which had been visibly growing upon him throughout the last few words.

"Mr. John or Mr. James Morris?" inquired the host.

"I really cannot tell you," returned the unfortunate guest. "I am not personally acquainted with the gentleman, any more than I am with yourself."

"I see," said Mr. Morris. "There is another person of the same name farther down the street; and I have no doubt the policeman will be able to supply you with his number. Believe me, I felicitate myself on the misunderstanding which has procured me the pleasure of your company for so long; and let me express a hope that we may meet again upon a more regular footing. Meantime, I would not for the world detain you longer from your friends. John," he added, raising his voice, "will you see that this gentleman finds his greatcoat?"

And with the most agreeable air Mr. Morris escorted his visitor as far as the anteroom door, where he left him under the conduct of the butler. As he passed the window, on his return to the drawing room, Brackenbury could hear him utter a profound sigh, as though his mind was loaded with a great anxiety, and his nerves already fatigued with the task on which he was engaged.

For perhaps an hour the hansoms kept arriving with such frequency, that Mr. Morris had to receive a new guest for every old one that he sent away, and the company preserved its number undiminished. But towards the end of that time the arrivals grew few and far between, and at length ceased entirely, while the process of elimination was continued with unimpaired activity. The drawing room began to look empty: the baccarat was discontinued for lack of a banker; more than one person said good night of his own accord, and was suffered to part without expostulation; and in the meanwhile Mr. Morris redoubled in agreeable attentions to those who stayed behind. He went from group to group and from person to person with looks of the readiest sympathy and the most pertinent and pleasing talk; he was not so much like a host as like a hostess, and there was a feminine coquetry and condescension in his manner which charmed the hearts of all.

As the guests grew thinner, Lieutenant Rich strolled for a moment out of the drawing room into the hall in quest of fresher air. But he had no sooner passed the threshold of the antechamber than he was brought to a dead halt by a discovery of the most surprising nature. The flowering shrubs had disappeared from the staircase; three large furniture waggons stood beside the garden gate; the servants were busy dismantling the house upon all sides; and some of them had already donned their greatcoats and were preparing to depart. It was like the end of a country ball, where everything has been supplied by contract. Brackenbury had indeed some matter for reflection. First, the guests, who were no real guests after all, had been dismissed; and now the servants, who could hardly be genuine servants, were actively dispersing.

"Was the whole establishment a sham?" he asked himself. "The mushroom of a single night which should disappear before morning?"

Watching a favourable opportunity, Brackenbury dashed upstairs to the higher regions of the house. It was as he had expected. He ran from room to room, and saw not a stick of furniture nor so much as a picture on the walls. Although the house had been painted and papered, it was not only uninhabited at present, but plainly had never been inhabited at all. The young officer remembered with astonishment its specious, settled, and hospitable air on his arrival. It was only at a prodigious cost that the imposture could have been carried out upon so great a scale.

Who, then, was Mr. Morris? What was his intention in thus playing the householder for a single night in the remove west of London? And did he collect his visitors at hazard from the streets?

Brackenbury remembered that he had already delayed too long, and hastened to join the company. Many had left during his absence; and counting the Lieutenant and his host, there were not more than five persons in the drawing room—recently so thronged. Mr. Morris greeted him, as he reentered the apartment, with a smile, and immediately rose to his feet.

"It is now time, gentlemen," said he, "to explain my purpose in decoying you from your amusements. I trust you did not find the evening hang very dully on your hands; but my object, I will confess it, was not to entertain your leisure, but to help myself in an unfortunate necessity. You are all gentlemen," he continued, "your appearance does you that much justice, and I ask for no better security. Hence, I speak it without concealment, I ask you to render me a dangerous and delicate service; dangerous because you may run the hazard of your lives, and delicate because I must ask an absolute discretion upon all that you shall see or hear. From an utter stranger the request is almost comically extravagant; I am well aware of this; and I would add at once, if there be anyone present who has heard enough, if there be one among the party who recoils from a dangerous confidence and a piece of Quixotic[1] devotion to he knows not whom—here is my hand ready, and I shall wish him good night and Godspeed with all the sincerity in the world."

A very tall, black man, with a heavy stoop, immediately responded to this appeal.

"I commend your frankness, Sir," said he; "and, for my part, I go. I make no reflections; but I cannot deny that you fill me with suspicious thoughts. I go myself, as I say; and perhaps you will think I have no right to add words to my example."

"On the contrary," replied Mr. Morris, "I am obliged to you for all you say. It would be impossible to exaggerate the gravity of my proposal."

"Well, gentlemen, what do you say?" said the tall man, addressing the others. "We have had our evening's frolic; shall we all go homeward peaceably in a body? You will think well of my suggestion in the morning, when you see the sun again in innocence and safety."

The speaker pronounced the last words with an intonation which added to their force; and his face wore a singular expression, full of gravity and significance. Another of the company rose hastily, and, with some appearance of alarm, prepared to take his leave. There were only two who held their ground, Brackenbury and an old red-nosed cavalry Major; but these two preserved a nonchalant demeanour, and, beyond a look of intelligence which they rapidly exchanged, appeared entirely foreign to the discussion that had just been terminated.

Mr. Morris conducted the deserters as far as the door, which he closed upon their heels; then he turned round, disclosing a countenance of mingled relief and animation, and addressed the two officers as follows.

"I have chosen my men like Joshua in the Bible,"[2] said Mr. Morris, "and I now believe I have the pick of London. Your appearance pleased my hansom cabmen; then it delighted me; I have watched your behaviour in a strange company, and under the most unusual circumstances: I have studied how you played and how you bore your losses; lastly, I have put you to the test of a staggering announcement, and you received it like an invitation to dinner. It is not for nothing," he cried, "that I have been for years the companion and the pupil of the bravest and wisest potentate in Europe."

---

1   Absurdly over-ambitious, a reference to the impractically chivalrous hero of Miguel de Cervantes's (1547–1616) novel *Don Quixote de la Mancha* (1605–1615).
2   Israelite leader who selects thirty thousand men to march with him on the city of Ai (Joshua 8:3).

"At the affair of Bunderchang,"[1] observed the Major, "I asked for twelve volunteers, and every trooper in the ranks replied to my appeal. But a gaming party is not the same thing as a regiment under fire. You may be pleased, I suppose, to have found two, and two who will not fail you at a push. As for the pair who ran away, I count them among the most pitiful hounds I ever met with. Lieutenant Rich," he added, addressing Brackenbury, "I have heard much of you of late; and I cannot doubt but you have also heard of me. I am Major O'Rooke."

And the veteran tendered his hand, which was red and tremulous, to the young Lieutenant.

"Who has not?" answered Brackenbury.

"When this little matter is settled," said Mr. Morris, "you will think I have sufficiently rewarded you; for I could offer neither a more valuable service than to make him acquainted with the other."

"And now," said Major O'Rooke, "is it a duel?"

"A duel after a fashion," replied Mr. Morris, "a duel with unknown and dangerous enemies, and as I gravely fear, a duel to the death. I must ask you," he continued, "to call me Morris no longer; call me, if you please, Hammersmith; my real name, as well as that of another person to whom I hope to present you before long, you will gratify me by not asking and not seeking to discover for yourselves. Three days ago the person of whom I speak disappeared suddenly from home; and, until this morning, I received no hint of his situation. You will fancy my alarm when I tell you that he is engaged upon a work of private justice. Bound by an unhappy oath, too lightly sworn, he finds it "necessary, without the help of law, to rid the earth of an insidious and bloody villain. Already two of our friends, and one of them my own born brother, have perished in the enterprise. He himself, or I am much deceived, is taken in the same fatal toils. But at least he still lives and still hopes, as this biller sufficiently proves."

And the speaker, no other than Colonel Geraldine, proffered a letter, thus conceived:

Major Hammersmith,—On Wednesday, at 3 A.M., you will be admitted by the small door to the gardens of Rochester House, Regent's Park,[2] by a man who is entirely in my interest. I must request you not to fail me by a second. Pray bring my case of swords, and, if you can find them, one or two gentlemen of

---

1   A reference to the region around Jhansi in Bundelkhand, the site of intense fighting and political unrest during the anti-imperial Indian Mutiny of 1857.
2   Large park in London's West End.

conduct and discretion to whom my person is unknown. My name must not be used in this affair.

T. GODALL.

"From his wisdom alone, if he had no other title," pursued Colonel Geraldine, when the others had each satisfied his curiosity, "my friend is a man whose directions should implicitly be followed. I need not tell you, therefore, that I have not so much as visited the neighbourhood of Rochester House; and that I am still as wholly in the dark as either of yourselves as to the nature of my friend's dilemma. I betook myself, as soon as I had received this order, to a furnishing contractor, and, in a few hours, the house in which we now are had assumed its late air of festival. My scheme was at least original; and I am far from regretting an action which has procured me the services of Major O'Rooke and Lieutenant Brackenbury Rich. But the servants in the street will have a strange awakening. The house which this evening was full of lights and visitors they will find uninhabited and for sale tomorrow morning. Thus even the most serious concerns," added the Colonel "have a merry side."

"And let us add a merry ending," said Brackenbury.

The Colonel consulted his watch.

"It is now hard on two," he said. "We have an hour before us, and a swift cab is at the door. Tell me if I may count upon your help."

"During a long life," replied Major O'Rooke, "I never took back my hand from anything, nor so much as hedged a bet."

Brackenbury signified his readiness in the most becoming terms; and after they had drunk a glass or two of wine, the Colonel gave each of them a loaded revolver, and the three mounted into the cab and drove off for the address in question.

Rochester House was a magnificent residence on the banks of the canal.[1] The large extent of the garden isolated it in an unusual degree from the annoyances of neighbourhood. It seemed the *parc aux cerfs*[2] of some great nobleman or millionaire. As far as could be seen from the street, there was not a glimmer of light in any of the numerous windows of the mansion; and the place had a look of neglect, as though the master had been long from home.

The cab was discharged, and the three gentlemen were not long in discovering the small door, which was a sort of postern[3] in a lane between two garden walls. It still wanted ten or fifteen minutes of the appointed time; the rain fell heavily, and the

---

1   Regent's Canal, part of which borders Regent's Park to the north.
2   Deer park.
3   Back or side entrance.

adventurers sheltered themselves below some pendant ivy, and spoke in low tones of the approaching trial.

Suddenly Geraldine raised his finger to command silence, and all three bent their hearing to the utmost. Through the continuous noise of the rain, the steps and voices of two men became audible from the other side of the wall; and, as they drew nearer, Brackenbury, whose sense of hearing was remarkably acute, could even distinguish some fragments of their talk.

"Is the grave dug?" asked one.

"It is," replied the other; "behind the laurel hedge. When the job is done, we can cover it with a pile of stakes."

The first speaker laughed, and the sound of his merriment was shocking to the listeners on the other side.

"In an hour from now," he said.

And by the sound of the steps it was obvious that the pair had separated, and were proceeding in contrary directions.

Almost immediately after the postern door was cautiously opened, a white face was protruded into the lane, and a hand was seen beckoning to the watchers. In dead silence the three passed the door, which was immediately locked behind them, and followed their guide through several garden alleys to the kitchen entrance of the house. A single candle burned in the great paved kitchen, which was destitute of the customary furniture; and as the party proceeded to ascend from thence by a flight of winding stairs, a prodigious noise of rats testified, still more plainly to the dilapidation of the house.

Their conductor preceded them, carrying the candle. He was a lean man, much bent, but still agile; and he turned from time to time and admonished silence and caution by his gestures. Colonel Geraldine followed on his heels, the case of swords under one arm, and a pistol ready in the other. Brackenbury's heart beat thickly. He perceived that they were still in time; but he judged from the alacrity of the old man that the hour of action must be near at hand; and the circumstances of this adventure were so obscure and menacing, the place seemed so well chosen for the darkest acts, that an older man than Brackenbury might have been pardoned a measure of emotion as he closed the procession up the winding stair.

At the top the guide threw open a door and ushered the three officers before him into a small apartment, lighted by a smoky lamp and the glow of a modest fire. At the chimney corner sat a man in the early prime of life, and of a stout but courtly and commanding appearance. His attitude and expression were those of the most unmoved composure; he was smoking a cheroot with much enjoyment and deliberation, and on a table by his elbow stood a long glass of some effervescing beverage which diffused an agreeable odour through the room.

"Welcome," said he, extending his hand to Colonel Geraldine. "I knew I might count on your exactitude."

"On my devotion," replied the Colonel, with a bow.

"Present me to your friends," continued the first; and, when that ceremony had been performed, "I wish, gentlemen," he added, with the most exquisite affability, "that I could offer you a more cheerful programme; it is ungracious to inaugurate an acquaintance upon serious affairs; but the compulsion of events is stronger than the obligations of good-fellowship. I hope and believe you will be able to forgive me this unpleasant evening; and for men of your stamp it will be enough to know that you are conferring a considerable favour."

"Your Highness," said the Major, "must pardon my bluntness. I am unable to hide what I know. For some time back I have suspected Major Hammersmith, but Mr. Godall is unmistakable. To seek two men in London unacquainted with Prince Florizel of Bohemia was to ask too much at Fortune's hands."

"Prince Florizel!" cried Brackenbury in amazement.

And he gazed with the deepest interest on the features of the celebrated personage before him.

"I shall not lament the loss of my incognito," remarked the Prince, "for it enables me to thank you with the more authority. You would have done as much for Mr. Godall, I feel sure, as for the Prince of Bohemia; but the latter can perhaps do more for you. The gain is mine," he added, with a courteous gesture.

And the next moment he was conversing with the two officers about the Indian army and the native troops, a subject on which, as on all others, he had a remarkable fund of information and the soundest views.

There was something so striking in this man's attitude at a moment of deadly peril that Brackenbury was overcome with respectful admiration; nor was he less sensible to the charm of his conversation or the surprising amenity of his address. Every gesture, every intonation, was not only noble in itself, but seemed to ennoble the fortunate mortal for whom it was intended; and Brackenbury confessed to himself with enthusiasm that this was a sovereign for whom a brave man might thankfully lay down his life.

Many minutes had thus passed, when the person who had introduced them into the house, and who had sat ever since in a corner, and with his watch in his hand, arose and whispered a word into the Prince's ear.

"It is well, Dr. Noel," replied Florizel, aloud; and then addressing the others, "You will excuse me, gentlemen," he added, "if I have to leave you in the dark. The moment now approaches."

Dr. Noel extinguished the lamp. A faint, gray light, premonitory of the dawn, illuminated the window, but was not sufficient to illuminate the room; and when the Prince rose to his feet, it was impossible to distinguish his features or to make a guess at the nature of the emotion which obviously affected him as he spoke. He moved towards the door, and placed himself at one side of it in an attitude of the wariest attention.

"You will have the kindness," he said, "to maintain the strictest silence, and to conceal yourselves in the densest of the shadow."

The three officers and the physician hastened to obey, and for nearly ten minutes the only sound in Rochester House was occasioned by the excursions of the rats behind the woodwork. At the end of that period, a loud creak of a hinge broke in with surprising distinctness on the silence; and shortly after, the watchers could distinguish a slow and cautious tread approaching up the kitchen stair. At every second step the intruder seemed to pause and lend an ear, and during these intervals, which seemed of an incalculable duration, a profound disquiet possessed the spirit of the listeners. Dr. Noel, accustomed as he was to dangerous emotions, suffered an almost pitiful physical prostration; his breath whistled in his lungs, his teeth grated one upon another, and his joints cracked aloud as he nervously shifted his position.

At last a hand was laid upon the door, and the bolt shot back with a slight report. There followed another pause, during which Brackenbury could see the Prince draw himself together noiselessly as if for some unusual exertion. Then the door opened, letting in a little more of the light of the morning; and the figure of a man appeared upon the threshold and stood motionless. He was tall, and carried a knife in his hand. Even in the twilight they could see his upper teeth bare and glistening, for his mouth was open like that of a hound about to leap. The man had evidently been over the head in water but a minute or two before; and even while he stood there the drops kept falling from his wet clothes and pattered on the floor.

The next moment he crossed the threshold. There was a leap, a stifled cry, an instantaneous struggle; and before Colonel Geraldine could spring to his aid, the Prince held the man, disarmed and helpless, by the shoulders.

"Dr. Noel," he said, "you will be so good as to relight the lamp."

And relinquishing the charge of his prisoner to Geraldine and Brackenbury, he crossed the room and set his back against the chimneypiece. As soon as the lamp had kindled, the party beheld an unaccustomed sternness on the Prince's features. It was no longer Florizel, the careless gentleman; it was the Prince of Bohemia, justly incensed and full of deadly purpose, who now raised his head and addressed the captive President of the Suicide Club.

"President," he said, "you have laid your last snare, and your own feet are taken in it. The day is beginning; it is your last morning. You have just swum the Regent's Canal; it is your last bathe in this world. Your old accomplice, Dr. Noel, so far from betraying me, has delivered you into my hands for judgment. And the grave you had dug for me this afternoon shall serve, in God's almighty providence, to hide your own just doom from the curiosity of mankind. Kneel and pray, sir, if you have a mind that way; for your time is short, and God is weary of your iniquities."

The President made no answer either by word or sign; but continued to hang his head and gaze sullenly on the floor, as though he were conscious of the Prince's prolonged and unsparing regard.

"Gentlemen," continued Florizel, resuming the ordinary tone of his conversation, "this is a fellow who has long eluded me, but whom, thanks to Dr. Noel, I now have tightly by the heels. To tell the story of his misdeeds would occupy more time than we can now afford; but if the canal had contained nothing but the blood of his victims, I believe the wretch would have been no drier than you see him. Even in an affair of, this sort I desire to preserve the forms of honour. But I make you the judges, gentleman—this is more an execution than a duel, and to give the rogue his choice of weapons would be to push too far a point of etiquette. I cannot afford to lose my life in such a business," he continued, unlocking the case of swords; "and as a pistol bullet travels so often on the wings of chance, and skill and courage may fall by the most trembling marksman, I have decided, and I feel sure you will approve my determination, to put this question to the touch of swords."

When Brackenbury and Major O'Rooke, to whom these remarks were particularly addressed, had each intimated his approval, "Quick, sir," added Prince Florizel to the President, "choose a blade and do not keep me waiting; I have an impatience to be done with you for ever."

For the first time since he was captured and disarmed the President raised his head, and it was plain that he began instantly to pluck up courage.

"Is it to be stand up?"[1] he asked eagerly, "and between you and me?"

"I mean so far to honour you," replied the Prince.

---

1 Honorable.

"Oh, come!" cried the President. "With a fair field,[1] who knows how things may happen? I must add that I consider it handsome behavior on your highness's part; and if the worst comes to the worst I shall die by one of the most gallant gentlemen in Europe."

And the President, liberated by those who had detained him, stepped up to the table and began, with minute attention, to select a sword. He was highly elated, and seemed to feel no doubt that he should issue victorious from the contest. The spectators grew alarmed in the face of so entire a confidence, and adjured prince Florizel to reconsider his intention.

"It is but a farce," he answered; "and I think I can promise you, gentlemen that it will not be long a-playing."

"Your Highness will be careful not to overreach," said Colonel Geraldine.

"Geraldine," returned the Prince, "did you ever know me fail in a debt of honour? I owe you this man's death, and you shall have it."

The President at last satisfied himself with one of the rapiers, and signified his readiness by a gesture that was not devoid of a rude[2] nobility. The nearness of peril, and the sense of courage, even to this obnoxious villain, lent an air of manhood and a certain grace.

The Prince helped himself at random to a sword.

"Colonel Geraldine and Doctor Noel," he said, "will have the goodness to await me in this room. I wish no personal friend of mine to be involved in this transaction. Major O'Rooke, you are a man of some years and a settled reputation—let me recommend the President to your good graces. Lieutenant Rich will be so good as lend me his attentions: a young man cannot have too much experience in such affairs."

"Your Highness," replied Brackenbury, "it is an honour I shall prize extremely."

"It is well," returned Prince Florizel; "I shall hope to stand your friend in more important circumstances."

And so saying he led the way out of the apartment and down the kitchen stairs.

The two men who were thus left alone threw open the window and leaned out, straining every sense to catch an indication of the tragical events that were about to follow. The rain was now over; day had almost come, and the birds were piping in the shrubbery and on the forest trees of the garden. The Prince and his companions were visible for a moment as they followed an alley between two flowering thickets;

---

1 Level playing field.
2 Crude.

but at the first corner a clump of foliage intervened, and they were again concealed from view. This was all that the Colonel and the Physician had an opportunity to see, and the garden was so vast, and the place of combat evidently so remote from the house, that not even the noise of swordplay reached their ears.

"He has taken him towards the grave," said Dr. Noel, with a shudder.

"God," cried the Colonel, "God defend the right!"

And they awaited the event in silence, the Doctor shaking with fear, the Colonel in an agony of sweat. Many minutes must have elapsed, the day was sensibly broader, and the birds were singing more heartily in the garden before a sound of returning footsteps recalled their glances towards the door. It was the Prince and the two Indian officers who entered. God had defended the right.

"I am ashamed of my emotion," said Prince Florizel; "I feel it is a weakness unworthy of my station, but the continued existence of that hound of hell had begun to prey upon me like a disease, and his death has more refreshed me than a night of slumber. Look, Geraldine," he continued, throwing his sword upon the floor, "there is the blood of the man who killed your brother. It should be a welcome sight. And yet," he added, "see how strangely we men are made! my revenge is not yet five minutes old, and already I am beginning to ask myself if even revenge be attainable on this precarious stage of life. The ill he did, who can undo it? The career in which he amassed a huge fortune (for the house itself in which we stand belonged to him)—that career is now a part of the destiny of mankind for ever; and I might weary myself making thrusts in carte[1] until the crack of Judgment, and Geraldine's brother would be none the less dead, and a thousand other innocent persons would be none the less dishonoured and debauched! The existence of a man is so small a thing to take, so mighty a thing to employ! Alas!" he cried, "is there anything in life so disenchanting as attainment?"

"God's justice has been done," replied the Doctor. "So much I behold. The lesson, your Highness, has been a cruel one for me; and I await my own turn with deadly apprehension."

"What was I saying?" cried the Prince. "I have punished, and here is the man beside us who can help me to undo. Ah, Dr. Noel! you and I have before us many a day of hard and honourable toil; and perhaps, before we have done, you may have more than redeemed your early errors."

"And in the meantime," said the Doctor, "let me go and bury my oldest friend."

---

1 Fencing motion.

(*And this,* observes the erudite Arabian, *is the fortunate conclusion of the tale. The Prince, it is superfluous to mention, forgot none of those who served him in this great exploit; and to this day his authority and influence help them forward in their public career, while his condescending friendship adds a charm to their private life.* To collect, continues my author, *all the strange events in which this Prince has played the part of Providence were to fill the habitable globe with books.* * * *)

Part VIII
Death

Childe Roland to the Dark Tower Came

Robert Browning

Born in the London suburb of Camberwell, the sensitive son of a bank clerk and a musical mother, Robert Browning (1812–1889) was educated primarily at home in the family's 6000-volume library, where he read widely in idiosyncratic subjects, modeling himself, in his early confessional poetry, on his hero, Percy Bysshe Shelley. After John Stuart Mill criticized his work as self-indulgent, a mortified Browning turned from poetry to playwriting. His sojourn in the theatre, where he found his creative voice in monologue-writing, resulted in the hybrid poetic form with which he became associated: the dramatic monologue, with its scrappy colloquialisms, grotesque and cryptogrammic psychology, and naturalistic employment of speech patterns. Though his first collection of monologues, *Dramatic Lyrics* (1842), was not well received, by the end of his life, following the publication of *Men and Women* (1855), *Dramatis Personae* (1864), and his novelistic epic *The Ring and the Book* (1868–1869), Browning's fame was solidly established, his talent thought by many to rival Tennyson's. His fifteen-year marriage to poet Elizabeth Barrett Browning, with whom he eloped to Florence, Italy against the wishes of her possessive father, were the happiest years of his life. An invalid six years his senior, Barrett Browning was a literary celebrity at the time, Browning, by contrast, an obscure, experimental poet. Returning to London after her death in 1861, Browning became a fixture in the literary scene.

(See Edgar's Song in "LEAR")[1]

I

My first thought was, he lied in every word,
    That hoary cripple, with malicious eye
    Askance to watch the working of his lie
On mine, and mouth scarce able to afford
Suppression of the glee, that pursed and scored
    Its edge, at one more victim gained thereby.

II

What else should he be set for, with his staff?
    What, save to waylay with his lies, ensnare
    All travelers who might find him posted there,
And ask the road? I guessed what skull-like laugh   10
Would break, what crutch 'gin write my epitaph
    For pastime in the dusty thoroughfare,

III

If at his counsel I should turn aside
    Into that ominous tract which, all agree,
    Hides the Dark Tower. Yet acquiescingly
I did turn as he pointed: neither pride
Nor hope rekindling at the end descried,
    So much as gladness that some end might be.

---

1   As Browning's directive indicates, the poem is inspired by a particular moment in Shakespeare's *King Lear*. Naked on the stormy heath, feigning madness, spouting gibberish, Edgar encounters the increasingly unbalanced Lear, who seems to find some solace in the young man's hodgepodge of epic and fairy-tale references. At the end of the scene, Edgar, who refers to himself throughout as "Poor Tom," sings the following song: "Child Rowland to the dark tower came; / His word was still, 'Fie, foh, and fum, / I smell the blood of a British man' " (III.iv.185–187). "Childe" is the title of a young man of noble birth awaiting knighthood. Rowland was Charlemagne's nephew and the hero of the twelfth-century French epic *The Song of Roland*.

IV

For, what with my whole world-wide wandering,
    What with my search drawn out thro' years, my hope   20
    Dwindled into a ghost not fit to cope
With that obstreperous joy success would bring,—
I hardly tried now to rebuke the spring
    My heart made, finding failure in its scope.

V

As when a sick man very near to death
    Seems dead indeed, and feels begin and end
    The tears and takes the farewell of each friend,
And hears one bid the other go, draw breath
Freelier outside, ("since all is o'er," he saith,
    "And the blow fallen no grieving can amend;")   30

VI

While some discuss if near the other graves
    Be room enough for this, and when a day
    Suits best for carrying the corpse away,
With care about the banners, scarves and staves:
And still the man hears all, and only craves
    He may not shame such tender love and stay.

VII

Thus, I had so long suffered in this quest,
    Heard failure prophesied so oft, been writ
    So many times among "The Band"—to wit,
The knights who to the Dark Tower's search addressed   40
Their steps—that just to fail as they, seemed best,
    And all the doubt was now—should I be fit?

VIII

So, quiet as despair, I turned from him,
    That hateful cripple, out of his highway
    Into the path he pointed. All the day
Had been a dreary one at best, and dim[1]
Was settling to its close, yet shot one grim
    Red leer to see the plain catch its estray.[2]

IX

For mark! no sooner was I fairly found
    Pledged to the plain, after a pace or two,   50
    Than, pausing to throw backward a last view
O'er the safe road, 'twas gone; grey plain all round:
Nothing but plain to the horizon's bound.
    I might go on; nought else remained to do.

X

So, on I went. I think I never saw
    Such starved ignoble nature; nothing throve:
    For flowers—as well expect a cedar grove!
But cockle,[3] spurge,[4] according to their law
Might propagate their kind, with none to awe,[5]
    You'd think; a burr[6] had been a treasure-trove.   60

XI

No! penury, inertness and grimace,
    In some strange sort, were the land's portion. "See
    Or shut your eyes," said Nature peevishly.

---

1   Dusk.
2   A stray animal.
3   Weed.
4   Poisonous plant with small flowers, causes vomiting when ingested.
5   Nothing to stop their spread.
6   A prickly seedpod.

"It nothing skills:[1] I cannot help my case:
'Tis the Last Judgment's fire must cure this place,[2]
   Calcine[3] its clods and set my prisoners free."

XII

If there pushed any ragged thistle-stalk
   Above its mates, the head was chopped; the bents[4]
   Were jealous else. What made those holes and rents
In the dock's[5] harsh swarth leaves, bruised as to baulk[6]   70
All hope of greenness? 'tis a brute must walk
   Pashing[7] their life out, with a brute's intents.

XIII

As for the grass, it grew as scant as hair
   In leprosy; thin dry blades pricked the mud
   Which underneath looked kneaded up with blood.
One stiff blind horse, his every bone a-stare,
Stood stupefied, however he came there:
   Thrust out past service from the devil's stud![8]

XIV

Alive? he might be dead for aught I know,
   With that red gaunt and colloped[9] neck a-strain,   80
   And shut eyes underneath the rusty mane;
Seldom went such grotesqueness with such woe;

---

1 It makes no difference.
2 The Apocalypse.
3 Incinerate.
4 Bent grass.
5 Sour grass.
6 Balk.
7 Smashing.
8 Collection of horses kept for breeding.
9 Having folds or ridges of flesh.

I never saw a brute I hated so;
   He must be wicked to deserve such pain.

XV

I shut my eyes and turned them on my heart.
   As a man calls for wine before he fights,
   I asked one draught of earlier, happier sights,
Ere fitly I could hope to play my part.
Think first, fight afterwards—the soldier's art:
   One taste of the old time sets all to rights.   90

XVI

Not it! I fancied Cuthbert's reddening face
   Beneath its garniture of curly gold,
   Dear fellow, till I almost felt him fold
An arm in mine to fix me to the place,
That way he used. Alas, one night's disgrace!
   Out went my heart's new fire and left it cold.

XVII

Giles then, the soul of honour—there he stands
   Frank as ten years ago when knighted first.
   What honest man should dare (he said) he durst.
Good—but the scene shifts—faugh! what hangman-hands   100
Pin to his breast a parchment? His own bands
   Read it. Poor traitor, spit upon and curst!

XVIII

Better this present than a past like that;
   Back therefore to my darkening path again!
   No sound, no sight as far as eye could strain.

Will the night send a howlet[1] or a bat?
I asked: when something on the dismal flat
    Came to arrest my thoughts and change their train.

XIX

A sudden little river crossed my path
    As unexpected as a serpent comes.   110
    No sluggish tide congenial to the glooms;
This, as it frothed by, might have been a bath
For the fiend's glowing hoof—to see the wrath
    Of its black eddy bespate[2] with flakes and spumes.[3]

XX

So petty yet so spiteful! All along,
    Low scrubby alders[4] kneeled down over it;
    Drenched willows flung them headlong in a fit
Of mute despair, a suicidal throng:
The river which had done them all the wrong,
    Whate'er that was, rolled by, deterred no whit.   120

XXI

Which, while I forded,—good saints, how I feared
    To set my foot upon a dead man's cheek,
    Each step, or feel the spear I thrust to seek
For hollows, tangled in his hair or beard!
—It may have been a water-rat I speared,
    But, ugh! it sounded like a baby's shriek.

---

1   Owl.
2   Bespattered.
3   River foam.
4   Trees.

XXII

Glad was I when I reached the other bank.
  Now for a better country. Vain presage!
  Who were the strugglers, what war did they wage,
Whose savage trample thus could pad the dank   130
Soil to a plash?[1] Toads in a poisoned tank,
  Or wild cats in a red-hot iron cage—

XXIII

The fight must so have seemed in that fell cirque.[2]
  What penned them there, with all the plain to choose?
  No foot-print leading to that horrid mews,[3]
None out of it. Mad brewage[4] set to work
Their brains, no doubt, like galley-slaves the Turk
  Pits for his pastime, Christians against Jews.

XXIV

And more than that—a furlong on—why, there!
  What bad use was that engine for, that wheel,   140
  Or brake,[5] not wheel—that harrow[6] fit to reel
Men's bodies out like silk? with all the air
Of Tophet's[7] tool, on earth left unaware,
  Or brought to sharpen its rusty teeth of steel.

XXV

Then came a bit of stubbed ground, once a wood,
  Next a marsh, it would seem, and now mere earth

---

1 Slush.
2 Brutal crater or sinister-looking hollow.
3 Pen, corral.
4 Intoxicating mixture.
5 Toothed machine for beating flax or hemp.
6 Farm implement with sharp teeth used to break clods.
7 Hell's.

Desperate and done with; (so a fool finds mirth,
Makes a thing and then mars it, till his mood
Changes and off he goes!) within a rood[1]—
    Bog, clay and rubble, sand and stark black dearth.   150

XXVI

Now blotches rankling,[2] coloured gay and grim,
    Now patches where some leanness of the soil's
    Broke into moss or substances like boils;
Then came some palsied oak, a cleft in him
Like a distorted mouth that splits its rim
    Gaping at death, and dies while it recoils.

XXVII

And just as far as ever from the end!
    Nought in the distance but the evening, nought
    To point my footstep further! At the thought,
A great black bird, Apollyon's[3] bosom-friend,   160
Sailed past, nor beat his wide wing dragon-penned[4]
    That brushed my cap—perchance the guide I sought.

XXVIII

For, looking up, aware I somehow grew,
    'Spite of the dusk, the plain had given place
    All round to mountains—with such name to grace
    Mere ugly heights and heaps now stolen in view.
How thus they had surprised me,—solve it, you!
    How to get from them was no clearer case.

---

1   A quarter acre.
2   Festering.
3   "The angel of the bottomless pit, whose name in the Hebrew tongue *is* Abaddon, but in the Greek tongue hath *his* name Apollyon" (Revelation 9:11).
4   In dragon-like motions.

XXIX

Yet half I seemed to recognize some trick
   Of mischief happened to me, God knows when—   170
   In a bad dream perhaps. Here ended, then,
Progress this way. When, in the very nick
Of giving up, one time more, came a click
   As when a trap shuts—you're inside the den!

XXX

Burningly it came on me all at once,
   This was the place! those two hills on the right,
   Crouched like two bulls locked horn in horn in fight;
While to the left, a tall scalped mountain ... Dunce,
Dotard, a-dozing at the very nonce,[1]
   After a life spent training for the sight!   180

XXXI

What in the midst lay but the Tower itself?
   The round squat turret, blind as the fool's heart,[2]
   Built of brown stone, without a counterpart
In the whole world. The tempest's mocking elf
Points to the shipman thus the unseen shelf[3]
   He strikes on, only when the timbers start.

XXXII

Not see? because of night perhaps?—why, day
   Came back again for that! before it left,
   The dying sunset kindled through a cleft:

---

1   Moment.
2   "The fool hath said in his heart, There is no God" (Psalms 14:1).
3   Sandbar.

The hills, like giants at a hunting, lay,　　　　　　　　　190
Chin upon hand, to see the game at bay,—
　　"Now stab and end the creature—to the heft!"¹

XXXIII

Not hear? when noise was everywhere! it tolled
　　Increasing like a bell. Names in my ears
　　Of all the lost adventurers my peers,—
How such a one was strong, and such was bold,
And such was fortunate, yet each of old
　　Lost, lost! one moment knelled the woe of years.

XXXIV

There they stood, ranged along the hill-sides, met
　　To view the last of me, a living frame　　　　　　200
　　For one more picture! in a sheet of flame
I saw them and I knew them all. And yet
Dauntless the slug-horn² to my lips I set,
　　And blew. *"Childe Roland to the Dark Tower came."*

　　　　　　　　　　　　　　　　　　　　1855

1　Hilt.
2　"Slug-horn" derives from the Scots Gaelic word for "war cry." Browning turns it into an actual trumpet.

TITHONUS

ALFRED TENNYSON

    The woods decay, the woods decay and fall,[1]
The vapors weep their burthen to the ground,
Man comes and tills the field and lies beneath,
And after many a summer dies the swan.
Me only cruel immortality
Consumes; I wither slowly in thine arms,
Here at the quiet limit of the world,
A white-hair'd shadow roaming like a dream
The ever-silent spaces of the East,[2]
Far-folded mists, and gleaming halls of morn.   10
    Alas! for this gray shadow, once a man—
So glorious in his beauty and thy choice,
Who madest him thy chosen, that he seem'd,
To his great heart none other than a God!
I ask'd thee, "Give me immortality,"
Then didst thou grant mine asking with a smile,
Like wealthy men who care not how they give.
But thy strong Hours indignant work'd their wills,
And beat me down and marr'd and wasted me,
And tho' they could not end me, left me maim'd   20
To dwell in presence of immortal youth,
Immortal age beside immortal youth,
And all I was in ashes. Can thy love,
Thy beauty, make amends, tho' even now,

---

1   A Trojan prince, Tithonus was the mortal husband of Eos, goddess of the dawn, who, every morning, drove her chariot across the sky, opening the gates for Apollo, the sun. Eos asked Zeus to grant Tithonus eternal life, but, tragically, forgot to specify eternal youth.
2   "Eos" in Greek means "East" as well as "dawn."

Close over us, the silver star,[1] thy guide,
Shines in those tremulous eyes that fill with tears
To hear me? Let me go; take back thy gift.
Why should a man desire in any way
To vary from the kindly race of men,
Or pass beyond the goal of ordinance[2]   30
Where all should pause, as is most meet[3] for all?
   A soft air fans the cloud apart; there comes
A glimpse of that dark world where I was born.
Once more the old mysterious glimmer steals
From thy pure brows, and from thy shoulders pure,
And bosom beating with a heart renew'd.
Thy cheek begins to redden thro' the gloom,
Thy sweet eyes brighten slowly close to mine.
Ere yet, they blind the stars, and the wild team[4]
Which love thee, yearning for thy yoke, arise,   40
And shake the darkness from their loosen'd manes,
And beat the twilight into flakes of fire.
   Lo! ever thus thou growest beautiful
In silence, then before thine answer given
Departest; and thy tears are on my cheek.[5]
   Why wilt thou ever scare me with thy tears,
And make me tremble lest a saying learnt,
In days far-off, on that dark earth, be true?
"The Gods themselves cannot recall their gifts."
   Ay me! ay me! with what another heart   50
In days far-off, and with what other eyes
I used to watch—if I be he that watch'd—
The lucid outline forming round thee; saw
The dim curls kindle into sunny rings;
Changed with thy mystic change, and felt my blood
Glow with the glow that slowly crimson'd all

---

1   Venus, the morning star.
2   That which is decreed by Fate.
3   Fitting.
4   The divine horses pulling her chariot.
5   Morning dew.

Thy presence and thy portals, while I lay,
Mouth, forehead, eyelids, growing dewy-warm
With kisses balmier than half-operating buds
Of April, and could hear the lips that kiss'd   60
Whispering I knew not what of wild and sweet,
Like that strange song I heard Apollo sing,
While Ilion like a mist rose into towers.[1]
   Yet hold me not for ever in thine East;
How can my nature longer mix with thine?
Coldly thy rosy shadows bathe me, cold
Are all thy lights, and cold my wrinkled feet
Upon thy glimmering thresholds, when the steam
Floats up from those fields about the homes
Of happy men that have the power to die,   70
And grassy barrows[2] of the happier dead.
Release me, and restore me to the ground.
Thou seest all things, thou wilt see my grave;
Thou wilt renew thy beauty morn by morn,
I earth in earth forget these empty courts,
And thee returning on thy silver wheels.

              1833

---

1   According to Ovid, Apollo built the towering walls of Troy (Ilion) with the music of his lyre.
2   Burial mounds.

Rizpah

Alfred Tennyson

17—[1]

1

Wailing, wailing, wailing, the wind over land and sea—
And Willy's voice in the wind, "O mother, come out to me!"
Why should he call me to-night, when he knows that I cannot go?
For the downs are as bright as day, and the full moon stares at the snow.

2

We should be seen, my dear; they would spy us out of the town.
The loud black nights for us, and the storm rushing over the down,
When I cannot see my own hand, but am led by the creak of the chain,
And grovel and grope for my son till I find myself drenched with the rain.

3

Anything fallen again? nay—what was there left to fall?
I have taken them home, I have number'd the bones, I have hidden them all.   10

---

1   The dramatic monologue is set in an unspecified year in the eighteenth century. It was inspired, however, by a gruesome incident from 1792 that Tennyson read about in a magazine. A young man robbed a mail coach in Sussex in southeastern England and was hanged, his chained body left to rot on the gibbet. Over a period of weeks and months, as bones dropped, one by one, from his decomposing corpse, his mother secretly gathered them and buried them in the churchyard, from which the remains of executed criminals were banned. The woman's actions reminded Tennyson of the biblical story of Rizpah, whose two sons and five nephews were executed by the Gibeonites. For five months she stood guard over the skeletonizing bodies, preventing birds from disturbing them by day, animals by night, until David ordered them buried (2 Samuel 21:8–14).

What am I saying? and what are *you*?[1] do you come as a spy?
Falls? what falls? who knows? As the tree falls so must it lie.[2]

4

Who let her in? how long has she been? you—what have you heard?
Why did you sit so quiet? you never have spoken a word.
O—to pray with me—yes—a lady—none of their spies—
But the night has crept into my heart, and begun to darken my eyes.

5

Ah—you, that have lived so soft, what should *you* know of the night,
The blast and the burning shame and the bitter frost and the fright?
I have done it, while you were asleep—you were only made for the day.
I have gather'd my baby together—and now you may go your way.   20

6

Nay—for it's kind of you, madam, to sit by an old dying wife.
But say nothing hard of my boy, I have only an hour of life.
I kiss'd my boy in the prison, before he went out to die.
"They dared me to do it," he said, and he never has told me a lie,
I whipt him for robbing an orchard once when he was but a child—
"The farmer dared me to do it," he said; he was always so wild—
And idle—and couldn't be idle—my Willy—he never could rest.
The King should have made him a soldier, he would have been one of his best.

7

But he lived with a lot of wild mates, and they never would let him be good;
They swore that he dare not rob the mail, and he swore that he would;   30
And he took no life, but he took one purse, and when all was done
He flung it among his fellows—"I'll none of it," said my son.

---
1   Spoken to the unnamed lady, a middle-class charity worker, most likely, who sits beside the speaker's hospital bed.
2   Ecclesiastes 11:3.

8

I came into court to the judge and the lawyers. I told them my tale,
God's own truth—but they kill'd him, they kill'd him for robbing the mail.
They hang'd him in chains for a show—we had always borne a good name—
To be hang'd for a thief—and then put away—isn't that enough shame?
Dust to dust[1]—low down—let us hide! but they set him, so high
That all the ships of the world[2] could stare at him, passing by.
God 'ill pardon the hell-black raven and horrible fowls of the air,
But not the black heart of the lawyer who kill'd him and hang'd him there.   40

9

And the jailer forced me away. I had bid him my last good-bye;
They had fasten'd the door of his cell. "O mother!" I heard him cry.
I couldn't get back tho' I tried, he had something further to say,
And now I never shall know it. The jailer forced me away.

10

Then since I couldn't but hear that cry of my boy that was dead,
They seized me and shut me up: they fasten'd me down on my bed.
"Mother, O mother!"—he call'd in the dark to me year after year—
They beat me for that, they beat me—you know that I couldn't but hear;
And then at the last they found I had grown so stupid and still
They let me abroad again—but the creatures had worked their will.   50

11

Flesh of my flesh was gone, but bone of my bone was left[3]—
I stole them all from the lawyers—and you, will you call it a theft?—

---

1   From the English Burial Service: "We now commit his body to the grave; earth to earth, ashes to ashes, dust to dust, in the sure and certain hope of the resurrection to eternal life for all who trust in Christ." See also Genesis 3:19.
2   The eighteenth-century incident that inspired Tennyson's dramatic monologue occurred in the coastal town of Shoreham-by-Sea.
3   Genesis 2:23.

My baby, the bones that had suck'd me, the bones that had laughed and had cried—
Theirs? O, no! they are mine—not theirs—they had moved in my side.

12

Do you think I was scared by the bones? I kiss'd 'em, I buried 'em all—
I can't dig deep, I am old—in the night by the churchyard wall.
My Willy 'ill rise up whole when the trumpet of judgment 'ill sound,[1]
But I charge you never to say that I laid him in holy ground.

13

They would scratch him up—they would hang him again on the cursed tree.
Sin? O, yes, we are sinners, I know—let all that be, 60
And read me a Bible verse of the Lord's goodwill toward men—
"Full of compassion and mercy, the Lord"[2]—let me hear it again;
"Full of compassion and mercy—long-suffering."[3] Yes, O, yes!
For the lawyer is born but to murder—the Saviour lives but to bless.
He'll never put on the black cap[4] except for the worst of the worst,
And the first may be last—I have heard it in church—and the last may be first.
Suffering—O, long-suffering—yes, as the Lord must know,
Year after year in the mist and the wind and the shower and the snow.

14

Heard, have you? what? they have told you he never repented his sin.
How do they know it? are *they* his mother? are *you* of his kin? 70
Heard! have you ever heard, when the storm on the downs began,
The wind that 'ill wail like a child and the sea that 'ill moan like a man?

---

1   Revelation 8:2.
2   Psalms 145:8.
3   Psalms 86:15.
4   When passing a sentence of death, the judge wore a loose black cap, a token of sorrow.

15

Election, Election, and Reprobation—it's all very well[1]
But I go to-night to my boy, and I shall not find him in hell.
For I cared so much for my boy that the Lord has look'd into my care,
And He means me I'm sure to be happy with Willy, I know not where.

16

And if *he* be lost—but to save *my* soul, that is all your desire—
Do you think that I care for *my* soul if my boy be gone to the fire?
I have been with God in the dark—go, go, you may leave me alone—
You never have borne a child—you are just as hard as a stone. 80

17

Madam, I beg your pardon! I mink that you mean to be kind,
But I cannot hear what you say for my Willy's voice in the wind—
The snow and the sky so bright—he used but to call in the dark,
And he calls to me now from the church and not from the gibbet—for hark!
Nay—you can hear it yourself—it is coming—shaking the walls—
Willy—the moon's in a cloud—Good-night. I am going. He calls.

1880

---

1 Here, the distraught speaker is tempering the deterministic Calvinist doctrine of predestination—namely, that God preordained the fate of the universe, including the salvation or damnation of every individual—with a maternal doctrine of unconditional love.

After Death

Christina Rossetti

The curtains were half drawn, the floor was swept
   And strewn with rushes,[1] rosemary[2] and may[3]
   Lay thick upon the bed on which I lay,
Where, thro' the lattice ivy-shadows[4] crept.
He leaned above me, thinking that I slept   5
   And could not hear him; but I heard him say:
   "Poor child, poor child": and as he turned away
Came a deep silence, and I knew he wept.
He did not touch the shroud, or raise the fold
   That hid my face, or take my hand in his,   10
      Or ruffle the smooth pillows for my head:
      He did not love me living; but once dead
   He pitied me; and very sweet it is
To know he still is warm tho' I am cold.

                1862

---

1   Bulrush, symbol of salvation due to its association with the baby Moses.
2   Rosemary, woven into funeral wreaths as symbol of remembrance.
3   Hawthorn, or "may," was once believed to cure a broken heart. It was also believed to be the tree from which Christ's crown of thorns was fashioned.
4   Ivy, symbol of eternal life.

My First Séance

Florence Marryat

The daughter of renowned naval officer and nautical novelist Captain Marryat, Florence Marryat (1837–1899) became quite famous in her own right. At sixteen, she married an officer in the British Army and moved to India. Upon her return in 1860, she embarked on a remarkably productive writing career, publishing over 70 novels, including numerous sensation novels, and editing the periodical *London Society* from 1872 to 1876. She claimed that she wrote her first novel, *Love's Conflict* (1865), to console herself while her children struggled with scarlet fever. She divorced and remarried in 1879. Marryat firmly believed in female financial independence, and her own professional ventures were considerable. At forty-three, her career took a new turn. She became a playwright, actress, and opera singer, eventually joining the D'Oyly Carte Opera Company. Marryat converted to Roman Catholicism late in life and developed a fascination with unorthodox spirituality and spiritualism. She describes her encounters with spiritual mediums, her contact with the spirit realm, and her initiation into the world of séances in *There is No Death* (1891), from which the following selection comes. When she met her own death in 1899, she mentioned neither husband in her will; she left everything to two of her children and a male friend.

I HAD returned from India and spent several years in England before the subject of Modern Spiritualism was brought under my immediate notice. Cursorily I had heard it mentioned by some people as a dreadfully wicked thing, diabolical to the last degree, by others as a most amusing pastime for evening parties, or when one wanted to get some "fun out of the table." But neither description charmed me, nor tempted me to pursue the occupation. I had already lost too many friends. Spiritualism (so it seemed to me) must either be humbug[1] or a very solemn thing, and I neither wished to trifle with it or to be trifled with by it. And after twenty years' continued experience I hold the same opinion. I have proved Spiritualism *not* to be humbug, therefore I regard it in a sacred light. For, *from whatever cause* it may proceed, it opens a vast area for thought to any speculative mind, and it is a matter of constant surprise to me to see the indifference with which the world regards it. That it *exists* is an undeniable fact. Men of science have acknowledged it, and the churches cannot deny it. The only question appears to be, "*What* is it, and *whence* does the power proceed?" If (as many clever people assert) from ourselves, then must these bodies and minds of ours possess faculties hitherto undreamed of, and which we have allowed to lie culpably fallow. If our bodies contain magnetic forces sufficient to raise substantial and apparently living forms from the bare earth, which our eyes are clairvoyant enough to see, and which can articulate words which our ears are clairaudient enough to hear—if, in addition to this, our minds can read each other's inmost thoughts, can see what is passing at a distance, and foretell what will happen in the future, then are our human powers greater than we have ever imagined, and we ought to do a great deal more with them than we do. And even regarding Spiritualism from *that* point of view, I cannot understand the lack of interest displayed in the discovery, to turn these marvelous powers of the human mind to greater account.

To discuss it, however, from the usual meaning given to the word, namely, as a means of communication with the departed, leaves me as puzzled as before. All Christians acknowledge they have spirits independent of their bodies, and that when their bodies die, their spirits will continue to live on. Wherein, then, lies the terror of the idea that these liberated spirits will have the privilege of roaming the universe as they will? And if they argue the *impossibility* of their return, they deny the records which form the only basis of their religion. No greater proof can be brought forward of the truth of Spiritualism than the truth of the Bible, which teems and bristles with accounts of it from beginning to end. From the period when the Lord God walked with Adam and Eve in the garden of Eden, and the angels came to Abram's[2] tent, and pulled Lot out of the doomed city;[3] when the witch of Endor raised up

---

1   Nonsense.
2   Abraham.
3   Sodom and Gomorrah.

Samuel,[1] and Balaam's ass[2] spoke, and Ezekiel[3] wrote that the hair of his head stood up because "a spirit" passed before him, to the presence of Satan with Jesus in the desert, and the reappearance of Moses and Elias,[4] the resurrection of Christ Himself, and His talking and eating with His disciples, and the final account of John being caught up to Heaven to receive the Revelations—*all is Spiritualism, and nothing else.* The Protestant Church that pins its faith upon the Bible, and nothing but the Bible, cannot deny that the spirits of mortal men have reappeared and been recognized upon this earth, as when the graves opened at the time of the Christ's crucifixion, and "many bodies of those that were dead arose and went into the city, and were seen of many."[5] The Catholic Church does not attempt to deny it. All her legends and miracles (which are disbelieved and ridiculed by the Protestants aforesaid) are founded on the same truth—the miraculous or supernatural return (as it is styled) of those who are gone, though I hope to make my readers believe, as I do, that there is nothing miraculous in it, and far from being *supernatural* it is only a continuation of Nature. Putting the churches and the Bible, however, on one side, the History of Nations proves it to be possible. There is not a people on the face of the globe that has not its (so-called) superstitions, nor a family hardly, which has not experienced some proofs of spiritual communion with earth. Where learning and science have thrust all belief out of sight, it is only natural that the man who does not believe in a God nor a Hereafter should not credit the existence of spirits, nor the possibility of communicating with them. But the lower we go in the scale of society, the more simple and childlike the mind, the more readily does such a faith gain credence, and the more stories you will hear to justify belief. It is just the same with religion, which is hid from the wise and prudent, and revealed to babes.

If I am met here with the objection that the term "Spiritualism" has been at times mixed up with so much that is evil as to become an offence, I have no better answer to make than by turning to the irrefragable testimony of the Past and Present to prove that in all ages, and of all religions, there have been corrupt and demoralized exponents whose vices have threatened to pull down the fabric they lived to raise. Christianity itself would have been overthrown before now, had we been unable to separate its doctrine from its practice.

---

1   1 Samuel 28:3–25.
2   Numbers 22:21–41.
3   Ezekiel 8:3.
4   Matthew 17:1–13.
5   Matthew 27:52–53.

I held these views in the month of February, 1873, when I made one of a party of friends assembled at the house of Miss Elizabeth Philip, in Gloucester Crescent,[1] and was introduced to Mr. Henry Dunphy of the *Morning Post,* both of them since gone to join the great majority. Mr. Dunphy soon got astride of his favorite hobby of Spiritualism, and gave me an interesting account of some of the *séances* he had attended. I had heard so many clever men and women discuss the subject before, that I had begun lo believe on their authority that there must be "something in it," but I held the opinion that sittings in the dark must afford so much liberty for deception, that I would engage in none where I was not permitted the use of my eyesight.

I expressed myself somewhat after this fashion to Mr. Dunphy. He replied, "Then the time has arrived for you to investigate Spiritualism, for I can introduce you to a medium who will show you the faces of the dead." This proposal exactly met my wishes, and I gladly accepted it. Annie Thomas (Mrs. Pender Cudlip,)[2] the novelist, who is an intimate friend of mine, was staying with me at the time and became as eager as I was to investigate the phenomena. We took the address Mr. Dunphy gave us of Mrs. Holmes, the American medium, then visiting London, and lodging in Old Quebec Street, Portman Square,[3] but we refused his introduction, preferring to go *incognito.* Accordingly, the next evening, when she held a public *séance,* we presented ourselves at Mrs. Holmes' door; and having first removed our wedding-rings, and tried to look as virginal as possible, sent up our names as Miss Taylor and Miss Turner. I am perfectly aware that this medium was said afterwards to be untrustworthy. So may a servant who was perfectly honest, whilst in my service, leave me for a situation where she is detected in theft. That does not alter the fact that she stole nothing from me. I do not think I know *a single medium* of whom I have not (at some time or other) heard the same thing, and I do not think I know a single woman whom I have not also, at some time or other, heard scandalized by her own sex, however pure and chaste she may imagine the world holds her. The question affects me in neither case. I value my acquaintances for what they are *to me,* not for what they may be to others; and I have placed trust in my media from what I individually have seen and heard, and proved to be genuine in their presence, and not from what others may imagine they have found out about them. It is no detriment to my witness that the media I sat with cheated somebody else, either before or after. My business was only to take care that *I* was not cheated, and I have

---

1 Crescent-shaped street near Regent's Park, London.
2 Annie Thomas (1838–1918), prolific author of popular novels, including *High Stakes* (1868), *Blotted Out* (1876), and *The Diva* (1901).
3 Elegant square in London's West End, near Hyde Park.

never, in Spiritualism, accepted anything at the hands of others that I could not prove for myself.

Mrs. Holmes did not receive us very graciously on the present occasion. We were strangers to her—probably sceptics, and she eyed us rather coldly. It was a bitter night, and the snow lay so thick upon the ground that we had some difficulty in procuring a hansom[1] to take us from Bayswater[2] to Old Quebec Street. No other visitors arrived, and after a little while Mrs. Holmes offered to return our money (ten shillings), as she said if she did sit with us, there would probably be no manifestations on account of the inclemency of the weather. (Often since then I have proved her assertion to be true, and found that any extreme of heat or cold is liable to make a *séance* a dead failure).

But Annie Thomas had to return to her home in Torquay[3] on the following day, and so we begged the medium to try at least to show us something, as we were very curious on the subject. I am not quite sure what I expected or hoped for on this occasion. I was full of curiosity and anticipation, but I am sure that I never thought I should see any face which I could recognize as having been on earth. We waited till nine o'clock in hopes that a circle would be formed, but as no one else came, Mrs. Holmes consented to sit with us alone, warning us, however, several times to prepare for a disappointment. The lights were therefore extinguished, and we sat for the usual preliminary dark *séance,* which was good, perhaps, but has nothing to do with a narrative of facts, proved to be so. When it concluded, the gas was re-lit and we sat for "Spirit Faces."

There were two small rooms connected by folding doors. Annie Thomas and I, were asked to go into the back room—to lock the door communicating with the landings, and secure it with our own seal, stamped upon a piece of tape stretched across the opening—to examine the window and bar the shutter inside—to search the room thoroughly, in fact, to see that no one was concealed in it—and we did all this as a matter of business. When we had satisfied ourselves that no one could enter from the back, Mr. and Mrs. Holmes, Annie Thomas, and I were seated on four chairs in the front room, arranged in a row before the folding doors, which were opened, and a square of black calico fastened across the aperture from one wall to the other. In this piece of calico was cut a square hole about the size of an ordinary window, at which we were told the spirit faces (if any) would appear. There was no singing, nor noise of any sort made to drown the sounds of preparation, and we

---

1   Two-wheel carriage that seats two passengers.
2   London neighborhood north of Kensington Gardens.
3   Seaside resort in southwestern England.

could have heard even a rustle in the next room. Mr. and Mrs. Holmes talked to us of their various experiences, until, we were almost tired of waiting, when something white and indistinct like a cloud of tobacco smoke, or a bundle of gossamer, appeared and disappeared again.

"They are coming! I *am* glad!" said Mrs. Holmes. "I didn't think we should get anything to-night,"—and my friend and I were immediately on the tiptoe of expectation. The white mass advanced and retreated several times, and finally settled before the aperture and opened in the middle, when a female face was distinctly to be seen above the black calico. What was our amazement to recognize the features of Mrs. Thomas, Annie Thomas' mother. Here I should tell my readers that Annie's father, who was a lieutenant in the Royal Navy and captain of the coastguard at Morston in Norfolk,[1] had been a near neighbor and great friend of my father, Captain Marryat,[2] and their children had associated like brothers and sisters. I had therefore known Mrs. Thomas well, and recognized her at once, as, of course, did her daughter. The witness of two people is considered sufficient in law. It ought to be accepted by society. Poor Annie was very much affected, and talked to her mother in the most incoherent manner. The spirit did not appear able to answer in words, but she bowed her head or shook it, according as she wished to say "yes" or "no." I could not help feeling awed at the appearance of the dear old lady, but the only thing that puzzled me was the cap she wore, which was made of white net, quilled closely round her face, and unlike any I had ever seen her wear in life. I whispered this to Annie, and she replied at once, "It is the cap she was buried in," which settled the question. Mrs. Thomas had possessed a very pleasant but very uncommon looking face, with bright black eyes, and a complexion of pink and white like that of a child. It was some time before Annie could be persuaded to let her mother go, but the next face that presented itself astonished her quite as much, for she recognized it as that of Captain Gordon, a gentleman whom she had known intimately and for a length of time. I had never seen Captain Gordon in the flesh, but I had heard of him, and knew he had died from a sudden accident. All I saw was the head of a good-looking, fair, young man, and not feeling any personal interest in his appearance, I occupied the time during which my friend conversed with him about olden days, by minutely examining the working of the muscles of his throat, which undeniably stretched when his head moved. As I was doing so, he leaned forward, and I saw a dark stain, which looked like a clot of blood, on his fair hair, on the left side of the forehead.

---

1   In eastern England.
2   Frederick Marryat (1792–1848), naval captain and popular author of novels with nautical settings and themes.

"Annie! what did Captain Gordon die of?" I asked. "He fell from a railway carriage," she replied, "and struck his head upon the line." I then pointed out to her the blood upon his hair. Several other faces appeared, which we could not recognize. At last came one of a gentleman, apparently moulded like a bust in plaster of Paris. He had a kind of smoking cap upon the head, curly hair, and a beard, but from being perfectly colorless, he looked so unlike nature, that I could not trace a resemblance to any friend of mine, though he kept on bowing in my direction, to indicate that I knew, or had known him. I examined this face again and again in vain. Nothing in it struck me as familiar, until the mouth broke into a grave, amused smile at my perplexity. In a moment I recognized it as that of my dear old friend, John Powles, whose history I shall relate *in extenso* further on. I exclaimed "Powles," and sprang towards it, but with my hasty action the figure disappeared. I was terribly vexed at my imprudence, for this was the friend of all others I desired to see, and sat there, hoping and praying the spirit would return, but it did not. Annie Thomas' mother and friend both came back several times; indeed, Annie recalled Captain Gordon so often, that on his last appearance the power was so exhausted, his face looked like a faded sketch in water-colors, but "Powles" had vanished altogether. The last face we saw that night was that of a little girl, and only her eyes and nose were visible, the rest of her head and face being enveloped in some white flimsy material like muslin. Mrs. Holmes asked her for whom she came, and she intimated that it was for me. I said she must be mistaken, and that I had known no one in life like her. The medium questioned her very closely, and tried to put her "out of court,"[1] as it were. Still, the child persisted that she came for me. Mrs. Holmes said to me, "Cannot you remember *anyone* of that age connected with you in the spirit world? No cousin, nor niece, nor sister, nor the child of a friend?" I tried to remember, but I could not, and answered, "No! no child of that age." She then addressed the little spirit. "You have made a mistake. There is no one here who knows you. You had better move on." So the child did move on, but very slowly and reluctantly. I could read her disappointment in her eyes, and after she had disappeared, she peeped round the corner again and looked at me, longingly. This was "Florence" my dear *lost* child (as I then called her), who had left me as a little infant of ten days old, and whom I could not at first recognize as a young girl of ten years. Her identity, however, has been proved to me since, beyond all doubt, as will be seen in the chapter which relates my reunion with her, and is headed "My Spirit Child." Thus ended the first *séance* at which I ever assisted, and it made a powerful impression upon my mind. Mrs. Holmes, in bidding

---

1   Out of bounds.

us good-night, said, "You two ladies must be very powerful mediums. I never held so successful a *séance* with strangers in my life before." This news elated us—we were eager to pursue our investigations, and were enchanted to think we could have *séances* at home, and as soon as Annie Thomas took up her residence in London, we agreed to hold regular meetings for the purpose. This was the *séance* that made me a student of the psychological phenomena, which the men of the nineteenth century term Spiritualism. Had it turned out a failure, I might now have been as most men are. *Quien sabe?*[1] As it was, it incited me to go on and on, until I have seen and heard things which at that moment would have seemed utterly impossible to me. And I would not have missed the experience I have passed through for all the good this world could offer me.

---

1   Who knows?

Cairo and the Plague

Alexander William Kinglake

Alexander William Kinglake (1809–1891) was born in Taunton, Somerset to a prosperous family of Scottish ancestry. Educated at Eton and Cambridge, Kinglake embarked on a career in law and politics, entering Parliament in 1856. Forced from office under a cloud of scandal twelve years later, an embittered Kinglake devoted his energies to an eight-volume history of the Crimean War. The passage that follows, however, comes from Kinglake's first literary endeavor, his highly popular and decidedly Orientalist travel narrative *Eothen*, which means "from the East" or "from dawn" in Greek. Published at his own expense in 1844, it recounts his harrowing journey in 1834 through the Ottoman Empire: present-day Turkey, the Levant, and Egypt, where plague was raging.

CAIRO and Plague! During the whole time of my stay the plague was so master of the city, and stared so plain in every street and every alley, that I can't now affect to dissociate the two ideas.[1]

---

1 There is some semblance of bravado in my manner of talking about the plague. I have been more careful to describe the terrors of other people than my own. The truth is that during the whole period of my stay at Cairo I remained thoroughly impressed with a sense of my danger. I may almost say that I lived under perpetual apprehension, for even in sleep, as I fancy, there remained with me some faint notion of the peril with which I was encompassed. But fear does not necessarily damp the spirits; on the contrary, it will often operate as an excitement, giving rise to unusual animation, and thus it affected me. If I had not been surrounded at this time by new faces, new scenes, and new sounds, the effect produced upon *my* mind by one unceasing cause of alarm may have been very different. As it was, the eagerness with which I pursued my rambles among the wonders of Egypt was sharpened and increased by the sting of the fear of death. Thus my account of the matter plainly conveys an impression that I remained at Cairo without losing my cheerfulness and buoyancy of spirits. And this is the truth; but it is also true, as I have freely confessed, that my sense of danger during the whole period was lively and continuous. [*Kinglake*]

When, coming from the desert, I rode through a village lying near to the city on the eastern side, there approached me, with busy face and earnest gestures, a personage in the Turkish dress.¹ His long flowing beard gave him rather a majestic look, but his briskness of manner and his visible anxiety to accost me seemed strange in an Oriental. The man, in fact, was French, or of French origin, and his object was to warn me of the plague, and prevent me from entering the city.

"Arrêtez-vous, monsieur, je vous en prie—arrêtez-vous; il ne faut pas entrer dans la ville; la peste y règne partout."

"Oui, je sais,² mais—"

"Mais, monsieur, je dis la peste—la peste; c'est de LA PESTE qu'il est question."

"Oui, je sais, mais—"

"Mais, monsieur, je dis encore LA PESTE—LA PESTE. Je vous conjure de ne pas entrer dans la ville—vous seriez dans une ville empestée."

"Oui, je sais, mais—"

"Mais, monsieur, je dois donc vous avertir tout bonnement que si vous entrez dans la ville, vous serez—enfin vous serez COMPROMIS!"³

"Oui, je sais, mais—"⁴

The Frenchman was at last convinced that it was vain to reason with a mere Englishman, who could not understand what it was to be "compromised." I thanked him most sincerely for his kindly meant warning; in hot countries it is very unusual indeed for a man to go out in the glare of the sun and give free advice to a stranger.

When I arrived at Cairo I summoned Osman Effendi, who was, as I knew, the owner of several houses, and would be able to provide me with apartments; he had no difficulty in doing this, for there was not one European traveler in Cairo besides myself. Poor Osman! he met me with a sorrowful countenance, for the fear of the plague sat heavily on his soul; he seemed as if he felt that he was doing wrong in

---

1   Baggy trousers and tunic, as opposed to a *galabaya* or robe.
2   *Anglicè* for "je le sais." These answers of mine as given above are not meant as specimens of mere French, but of that fine, terse, nervous *Continental English* with which I and my compatriots make our way through Europe. [Kinglake]
3   The import of the word "compromised," when used in reference to contagion, is explained in page 2. [Kinglake]
4   "Stop, sir, please—stop; you can't enter the city; the plague is spreading everywhere." "Yes, I know, but—" "But sir, I'm telling you it's the plague—plague; this is the PLAGUE we're talking about." "Yes, I know, but—" "But sir, I repeat: PLAGUE—PLAGUE. I implore you not to enter the city—you would be in a disease-stricken city." "Yes, I know, but—" "But sir, I must caution you (without beating around the bush) that if you enter the city you will be—well, you will be in serious jeopardy." "Yes, I know, but—."

lending me a resting-place, and he betrayed such a listlessness about temporal matters as one might look for in a man who believed that his days were numbered. He caught me, too, soon after my arrival, coming out from the public baths,[1] and from that time forward he was sadly afraid of me, for upon the subject of contagion he held European opinions.

Osman's history is a curious one. He was a Scotchman born, and when very young, being then a drummer-boy, he landed in Egypt with Fraser's[2] force. He was taken prisoner, and, according to Mohammedan custom, the alternative of death or the Koran was offered to him. He did not choose death, and, therefore, went through the ceremonies necessary for turning him into a good Mohammedan. But what amused me most in his history was this: that very soon after having embraced Islam he was obliged in practice to become curious and discriminating in his new faith—to make war upon Mohammedan dissenters, and follow the orthodox standard of the Prophet in fierce campaigns against the Wahabis,[3] the Unitarians[4] of the Mussulman world. The Wahabis were crushed, and Osman, returning home in triumph from his holy wars, began to flourish in the world; he acquired property, and became "effendi," or gentleman. At the time of my visit to Cairo, he seemed to be much respected by his brother Mohammedans, and gave pledge of his sincere alienation from Christianity by keeping a couple of wives. He affected the same sort of reserve in mentioning them as is generally shown by Orientals. He invited me, indeed, to see his harem, but he made both his wives bundle out before I was admitted; he felt, as it seemd to me, that neither of them would bear criticism, and I think that this idea, rather than any motive of sincere jealousy, induced him to keep them out of sight. The rooms of the harem reminded me of an English nursery rather than a Mohammedan paradise. One is apt to judge of a woman before one sees her by the air of elegance or coarseness with which she surrounds her home. I judged Osman's wives by this test, and condemned them both. But the strangest feature in Osman's character was his inextinguishable nationality. In vain they had brought

---

1   It is said that when a Mussulman finds himself attacked by the plague, he goes and takes a bath. The couches on which the bathers recline would carry infection, according to the notions of the Europeans. Whenever, therefore, I took the bath at Cairo (except the first time of my doing so), I avoided that part of the luxury which consists in being "put up to dry" upon a kind of bed. [Kinglake]
2   During the Anglo-Turkish War (1807–09), the forces of British general Alexander Mackenzie-Fraser (ca.1756–1809) briefly occupied north Egypt, which was then part of the Ottoman Empire.
3   Followers of a reformist movement in Sunni Islam that emerged in the mid eighteenth century.
4   Like Christian Unitarians, the Wahhabis or Muwahiddun adhere to a doctrine of the unity of God.

him over the seas in early boyhood; in vain had he suffered captivity, conversion, circumcision; in vain they had passed him through fire in their Arabian campaigns: they could not cut away or burn out poor Osman's inborn love of all that was Scotch. In vain men called him effendi; in vain he swept along in Eastern robes; in vain the rival wives adorned his harem: the joy of his heart still plainly lay in this, that he had three shelves of books, and that the books were thoroughbred Scotch—the Edinburgh this, the Edinburgh that, and above all, I recollect, he prided himself upon the "Edinburgh Cabinet Library."[1]

The fear of the plague is its forerunner. It is likely enough that at the time of my seeing poor Osman the deadly taint was beginning to creep through his veins, but it was not till after I had left Cairo that he was visibly stricken. He died.

As soon as I had seen all that interested me in Cairo and its neighborhood, I wished to make my escape from a city that lay under the terrible curse of the plague; but Mysseri[2] fell ill—in consequence, I believe of the hardships which he had been suffering in my service; after a while he recovered sufficiently to undertake a journey, but then there was some difficulty in procuring beasts of burden, and it was not till the nineteenth day of my sojourn that I quitted the city.

During all this time the power of the plague was rapidly increasing. When I first arrived, it was said that the daily number of "accidents" by plague, out of a population of about two hundred thousand, did not exceed four or five hundred; but before I went away, the deaths were reckoned at twelve hundred a day. I had no means of knowing whether the numbers (given out, as I believe they were, by officials) were at all correct, but I could not help knowing that from day to day the number of the dead was increasing. My quarters were in one of the chief thoroughfares of the city, and as the funerals in Cairo take place between daybreak and noon (a time during which I generally stayed in my rooms), I could form some opinion as to the briskness of the plague. I don't mean that I got up every morning with the sun. It was not so. But the funerals of most people in decent circumstances at Cairo are attended by singers and howlers, and the performances of these people woke me in the early morning, and prevented me from remaining in ignorance of what was going on in the street below.

These funerals were very simply conducted. The bier was a shallow wooden tray carried upon a light and weak wooden frame. The tray had, in general, no lid, but the body was more or less hidden from view by a shawl or scarf. The whole was

---

1   A popular series of books on scientific and technological subjects edited by Dionysius Lardner (1793–1859).
2   Kinglake's Turkish servant.

borne upon the shoulders of men, and hurried forward at a great pace. Two or three singers generally preceded the bier; the howlers (these are paid for their vocal labors) followed after; and last of all came such of the dead man's friends and relations as could keep up with such a rapid procession; these, especially the women, would get terribly blown,[1] and would struggle back into the rear; many were fairly "beaten off." I never observed any appearance of mourning in the mourners; the pace was too severe for any solemn affectation of grief.

When first I arrived at Cairo, the funerals that daily passed under my windows were many, but still there were frequent and long intervals without a single howl. Every day, however (except one, when I fancied that I observed a diminution of funerals), these intervals became less frequent and shorter, and at last the passing of the howlers from morn to noon was almost incessant. I believe that about one half of the whole people was carried off by this visitation. The Orientals, however, have more quiet fortitude than Europeans under afflictions of this sort, and they never allow the plague to interfere with their religious usages. I rode, one day, round the great burial-ground. The tombs are strewed over a great expanse, among the vast mountains of rubbish (the accumulation of many centuries) which surround the city. The ground, unlike the Turkish "cities of the dead," which are made so beautiful by their dark cypresses, has nothing to sweeten melancholy—nothing to mitigate the hatefulness of death. Carnivorous beasts and birds possess the place by night, and now in the fair morning it was all alive with fresh comers—alive with dead. Yet at this very time when the plague was raging so furiously, and on this very ground which resounded so mournfully with the howls of arriving funerals, preparations were going on for the religious festival called the Kourban Bairam.[2] Tents were pitched, and *swings hung for the amusement of children.* A ghastly holiday! but the Mohammedans take a pride, and a just pride, in following their ancient customs undisturbed by the shadow of death.

I did not hear, whilst I was at Cairo, that any prayer for a remission of the plague had been offered up in the mosques. I believe that, however frightful the ravages of the disease may be, the Mohammedans refrain from approaching Heaven with their complaints until the plague has endured for a long space, and then at last they pray God, not that the plague may cease, but that it may go to another city!

A good Mussulman seems to take pride in repudiating the European notion that the will of God can be eluded by shunning the touch of a sleeve. When I went to see

---

1 Winded.
2 Turkish name for Eid al-Adha ("Festival of Sacrifice"), celebrated seventy days after the end of the month of Ramadan.

the Pyramids of Sakkara,[1] I was the guest of a noble old fellow—an Osmanli[2] (how sweet it was to hear his soft, rolling language after suffering as I had suffered of late from the shrieking tongue of the Arabs!). This man was aware of the European ideas about contagion, and his first care, therefore, was to assure me that not a single instance of plague had occurred in his village. He then inquired as to the progress of the plague at Cairo. I had but a bad account to give. Up to this time my host had carefully refrained from touching me, out of respect to the European theory of contagion; but as soon as it was made plain that he, and not I, would be the person endangered by contact, he gently laid his hand upon my arm, in order to make me feel sure that the circumstance of my coming from an infected city did not occasion him the least uneasiness. In that touch there was true hospitality.

Very different is the faith and the practice of the Europeans, or rather, I mean, of the Europeans settled in the East, and commonly called Levantines. When I came to the end of my journey over the desert, I had been so long alone that the prospect of speaking to somebody at Cairo seemed almost a new excitement. I felt a sort of consciousness that I had a little of the wild beast about me, but I was quite in the humor to be charmingly tame, and to be quite engaging in my manners, if I should have an opportunity of holding communion with any of the human race whilst at Cairo. I knew no one in the place, and had no letters of introduction, but I carried letters of credit, and it often happens, in places remote from England, that those "advices" operate as a sort of introduction, and obtain for the bearer (if disposed to receive them) such ordinary civilities as it may be in the power of the banker to offer.

Very soon after my arrival, I found out the abode of the Levantine to whom my credentials were addressed. At his door several persons (all Arabs) were hanging about and keeping guard. It was not till after some delay, and the interchange of some communications with those in the interior of the citadel, that I was admitted. At length, however, I was conducted through the court, and up a flight of stairs, and finally into the apartment where business was transacted. The room was divided by a good, substantial fence of iron bars, and behind these defenses the banker had his station. The truth was that from fear of the plague he had adopted the course usually taken by European residents, and had shut himself up "in strict quarantine"—that is to say, that he had, as he hoped, cut himself off from all communication with infecting substances. The Europeans long resident in the East, without any or with scarcely

---

1   Saqqara, south of Cairo.
2   An Ottoman Turk.

any exception, are firmly convinced that the plague is propagated by contact, and by contact only—that if they can but avoid the touch of an infecting substance they are safe, and that if they cannot they die. This belief induces them to adopt the contrivance of putting themselves in that state of siege which they call "quarantine." It is a part of their faith that metals, and hempen rope, and also, I fancy, one or two other substances, will not carry the infection; and they likewise believe that the germ of pestilence lying in an infected substance may be destroyed by submersion in water, or by the action of smoke. They, therefore, guard the doors of their houses with the utmost care against intrusion, and condemn themselves, with all the members of their family, including European servants, to a strict imprisonment within the walls of their dwelling. Their native attendants are not allowed to enter at all, but they make the necessary purchases of provisions; these are hauled up through one of the windows by means of a rope, and are afterwards soaked in water.

I knew nothing of these mysteries, and was not, therefore, prepared for the sort of reception I met with. I advanced to the iron fence, and putting my letter between the bars, politely proffered it to Mr. Banker. Mr. Banker received me with a sad and dejected look, and not "with open arms," or with any arms at all, but with—a pair of tongs! I placed my letter between the iron fingers. These instantly picked it up as it were a viper, and conveyed it away to be scorched and purified by fire and smoke. I was disgusted at this reception, and at the idea that anything of mine could carry infection to the poor wretch who stood on the other side of the bars— pale and trembling, and already meet for death. I looked with something of the Mohammedan's feeling upon these little contrivances for eluding fate; and in this instance at least they were vain: a little while, and the poor money-changer,[1] who had strived to guard the days of his life (as though they were coins) with bolts and bars of iron—he was seized by the plague, and he died.

To people entertaining such opinions as these respecting the fatal effect of contact, the narrow and crowded streets of Cairo were terrible as the easy slope that leads to Avernus.[2] The roaring ocean and the beetling[3] crags owe something of their sublimity to this—that if they be tempted they can take the warm life of a man. To the contagionist, filled as he is with the dread of final causes, having no faith in destiny, nor in the fixed will of God, and with none of the devil-may-care indifference which might stand him instead of creeds—to such one every rag that shivers

---

1   A loaded word, evocative of the "moneychangers" Christ drove from the Temple (Mark 11:15).
2   Located in a crater, Lake Avernus in Italy was believed by the Romans to be the entrance to the underworld.
3   Jutting.

in the breeze of a plague-stricken city has this sort of sublimity. If, by any terrible ordinance, he be forced to venture forth, he sees death dangling from every sleeve, and as he creeps forward, he poises his shuddering limbs between the imminent jacket that is stabbing at his right elbow, and the murderous pelisse that threatens to mow him clean down as it sweeps along on his left. But most of all he dreads that which most of all he should love—the touch of a woman's dress; for mothers and wives, hurrying forth on kindly errands from the bedsides of the dying, go slouching along through the streets more wilfully and less courteously than the men. For a while it may be that the caution of the poor Levantine may enable him to avoid contact, but sooner or later, perhaps, the dreaded chance arrives. That bundle of linen, with the dark, tearful eyes at the top of it, that labors along with the voluptuous clumsiness of Grisi[1]—she has touched the poor Levantine with the hem of her sleeve! From that dread moment his peace is gone; his mind forever hanging upon the fatal touch, invites the blow which he fears; he watches for the symptoms of plague so carefully that, sooner or later, they come in truth. The parched mouth is a sign—his mouth *is* parched. The throbbing brain—his brain *does* throb. The rapid pulse—he touches his own wrist (for he dares not ask counsel of any man, lest he be deserted), he touches his wrist, and feels how his frighted blood goes galloping out of his heart. There is nothing but the fatal swelling that is wanting to make his sad conviction complete. Immediately he has an odd feel under the arm—no pain, but a little straining of the skin. He would to God it were his fancy that were strong enough to give him that sensation! This is the worst of all. It now seems to him that he could be happy and contented with his parched mouth, and his throbbing brain, and his rapid pulse, if only he could know that there were no swelling under the left arm; but dares he try? In a moment of calmness and deliberation he dares not, but when for a while he has writhed under the torture of suspense, a sudden strength of will drives him to seek and know his fate. He touches the gland, and finds the skin sane and sound, but under the cuticle there lies a small lump, like a pistol bullet, that moves as he pushes it. Oh! but is this for all certainty? is this the sentence of death? Feel the gland of the other arm; there is not the same lump exactly, yet something a little like it. Have not some people glands naturally enlarged? Would to Heaven he were one! So he does for himself the work of the plague, and when the Angel of Death, thus courted, does indeed and in truth come, he has only to finish that which has been so well begun. He passes his fiery hand over the brain of

---

1 Kinglake is referring to the melodramatic lurching and gesticulations of the famous Italian soprano Giulia Grisi (1811–1869).

the victim, and lets him rave for a season, but all chance-wise, of people and things once dear, or of people and things indifferent. Once more the poor fellow is back at his home in fair Provence, and sees the sun-dial that stood in his childhood's garden—sees part of his mother, and the long since forgotten face of that dear little sister (he sees her, he says, on a Sunday morning, for all the church bells are ringing); he looks up and down through the universe, and owns it well piled with bales upon bales of cotton and cotton eternal—so much so that he feels—he knows—he swears he could make that winning hazard, if the billiard-table would not slant upwards, and if the cue were a cue worth playing with; but it is not; it's a cue that won't move—his own arm won't move. In short, there's the devil to pay in the brain of the poor Levantine; and perhaps the next night but one he becomes the "life and the soul" of some squalling jackal family, who fish him out by the foot from his shallow and sandy grave.

Better fate was mine. By some happy perverseness (occasioned, perhaps, by my disgust at the notion of being received with a pair of tongs), I took it into my pleasant head that all the European notions about contagion were thoroughly unfounded—that the plague might be providential, or "epidemic" (as they phrase it), but was not contagious, and that I could not be killed by the touch of a woman's sleeve, nor yet by her blessed breath. I, therefore, determined that the plague should not alter my habits and amusements in any one respect. Though I came to this resolve from impulse, I think that I took the course which was in effect the most prudent; for the cheefulness of spirits which I was thus enabled to retain discouraged the yellow-winged angel, and prevented him from taking a shot at me. I, however, so far respected the opinion of the Europeans that I avoided touching, when I could do so without privation or inconvenience. This endeavor furnished me with a sort of amusement as I passed through the streets. The usual mode of moving from place to place in the city of Cairo is upon donkeys. Of these great numbers are always in readiness, with donkey-boys attached. I had two who constantly (until one of them died of the plague) waited at my door upon the chance of being wanted. I found this way of moving about exceedingly pleasant, and never attempted any other. I had only to mount my beast, and tell my donkey-boy the point for which I was bound, and instantly I began to glide on at a capital pace. The streets of Cairo are not paved in any way, but strewed with a dry, sandy soil, so deadening to sound that the footfall of my donkey could scarcely be heard. There is no trottoir,[1] and as you ride through the streets you mingle with the people on foot. Those who

---

1   Sidewalk.

are in your way, upon being warned by the shout of the donkey-boy, move very slightly aside, so as to leave you a narrow lane for your passage. Through this you move at a gallop, gliding on delightfully in the very midst of crowds, without being inconvenienced or stopped for a moment; it seems to you that it is not the donkey, but the donkey-boy, who wafts you along with his shouts through pleasant groups and air that comes thick with the fragrance of burial spice. "Eh, sheik! Eh, bint! reggalek, shumalek," etc. ("O old man, O virgin, get out of the way on the right! O virgin, O old man, get out of the way on the left! This Englishman comes, he comes, he comes!") The narrow alley which these shouts cleared for my passage made it possible, though difficult, to go on for a long way without touching a single person, and my endeavors to avoid such contact were a sort of game for me in my loneliness. If I got through a street without being touched, I won; if I was touched, I lost—lost a deuce of a stake, according to the theory of the Europeans, but that I deemed to be all nonsense; I only lost that game, and would certainly win the next. * * *

I ascended, one day, to the citadel, and gained from its ramparts a superb view of the town. The fanciful and elaborate gilt-work of the many minarets gives a light and florid grace to the city as seen from this height, but before you can look for many seconds at such things, your eyes are drawn westward—drawn westward and over the Nile, till they rest upon the massive enormities of the Gizeh Pyramids.

I saw within the fortress many yoke of men, all haggard and woebegone, and a kennel of very fine lions, well fed and flourishing; I say *yoke* of men, for the poor fellows were working together in bonds; I say a *kennel* of lions, for the beasts were not inclosed in cages, but simply chained up like dogs.

I went round the bazaars; it seemed to me that pipes and arms were cheaper here than at Constantinople, and I should advise you, therefore, if you reach both places, to prefer the market of Cairo. In the open slave market I saw about fifty girls exposed for sale, but all of them black or "invisible" brown. A slave agent took me to some rooms in the upper story of the building, and also into several obscure houses in the neighborhood, with a view to show me some white women. The owners raised various objections to the display of their ware, and well they might, for I had not the least notion of purchasing; some refused on account of the illegality of selling to unbelievers,[1] and others declared that all transactions of this sort were completely out of the question as long as the plague was raging. I only succeeded in seeing one white slave who was for sale, but on this treasure the owner affected to set an

---

1 It is not strictly lawful to sell *white* slaves to a Christian. [*Kinglake*]

immense value, and raised my expectations to a high pitch by saying that the girl was Circassian,[1] and was "fair as the full moon." There was a good deal of delay, but at last I was led into a long, dreary room, and there, after marching timidly forward for a few paces, I descried at the farther end that mass of white linen which indicates an Eastern woman. She was bid to uncover her face, and I presently saw that, though very far from being good-looking according to my notion of beauty, she had not been inaptly described by the man who compared her to the full moon, for her large face was perfectly round and perfectly white. Though very young, she was nevertheless extremely fat. She gave me the idea of having been got up for sale—of having been fattened and whitened by medicines or by some peculiar diet. I was firmly determined not to see any more of her than the face. She was perhaps disgusted at this my virtuous resolve, as well as with my personal appearance; perhaps she saw my distaste and disappointment; perhaps she wished to gain favor with her owner by showing her attachment to his faith; at all events, she holloed out very lustily and very decidedly that "she would not be bought by the infidel." * * *

Although the plague was now spreading quick and terrible havoc * * * I did not see very plainly any corresponding change in the looks of the streets until the seventh day after my arrival; I then first observed that the city was *silenced*. There were no outward signs of despair, nor of violent terror, but many of the voices that had swelled the busy hum of men were already hushed in death, and the survivors, so used to scream and screech in their earnestness whenever they bought or sold, now showed an unwonted indifference about the affairs of this world; it was less worth while for men to haggle and haggle, and crack the sky with noisy bargains, when the Great Commander was there, who could "pay all their debts with the roll of his drum."[2]

At this time I was informed that of twenty-five thousand people at Alexandria, twelve thousand had died already; the Destroyer had come rather later to Cairo, but there was nothing of weariness in his strides. The deaths came faster than ever they

---

1 From the Caucasus, between the Black and Caspian seas.
2 From "How Happy the Soldier," a military tune popular in the late eighteenth century:

> How happy the soldier who lives on his pay,
> And spends half a crown on six pence a day;
> He fears neither justices, warrants nor bums,
> But pays all his debts with a roll of the drums.

befell in the plague of London;[1] but the calmness of Orientals under such visitations, and their habit of using biers for interment, instead of burying coffins along with the bodies, rendered it practicable to dispose of the dead in the usual way, without shocking the people by any unaccustomed spectacle of horror. There was no tumbling of bodies into carts, as in the plague of Florence[2] and the plague of London; every man, according to his station, was properly buried, and that in the accustomed way, except that he went to his grave at a pace more than usually rapid.

The funerals pouring through the streets were not the only public evidence of deaths. In Cairo this custom prevails: at the instant of a man's death (if his property is sufficient to justify the expense) professional howlers are employed. I believe that these persons are brought near to the dying man when his end appears to be approaching, and the moment that life is gone, they lift up their voices and send forth a loud wail from the chamber of death. Thus I knew when my near neighbors died. Sometimes the howls were near, sometimes more distant. Once I was awakened in the night by the wail of death in the next house, and another time by a like howl from the house opposite; and there were two or three minutes, I recollect, during which the howl seemed to be actually *running* along the street.

I happened to be rather teased at this time by a sore throat, and I thought it would be well to get it cured, if I could, before I again started on my travels. I therefore inquired for a Frank[3] doctor, and was informed that the only one then at Cairo was a Bolognese refugee, a very young practitioner, and so poor that he had not been able to take flight, as the other medical men had done. At such a time as this it was out of the question to *send* for an European physician; a person thus summoned would be sure to suppose that the patient was ill of the plague, and would decline to come. I therefore rode to the young doctor's residence, ascended a flight or two of stairs, and knocked at his door. No one came immediately, but after some little delay the medico himself opened the door and admitted me. I, of course, made him understand that I had come to consult him, but before entering upon my throat grievance, I accepted a chair and exchanged a sentence or two of commonplace conversation. Now the natural commonplace of the city at this season was of a gloomy sort: "Comme va la peste?" ("How goes the plague?") And this was precisely the question I put. A deep sigh, and the words, "Sette cento per giorno, signor" ("Seven hundred a day"), pronounced in a tone of the deepest sadness and dejection, were the answer I received.

---

1   The Great Plague of London (1665–66).
2   The Black Death struck Florence in 1348.
3   European.

The day was not oppressively hot, yet I saw that the doctor was transpiring profusely, and even the outside surface of the thick shawl dressing-gown in which he had wrapped himself appeared to be moist. He was a handsome, pleasant-looking young fellow, but the deep melancholy of his tone did not tempt me to prolong the conversation, and without further delay, I requested that my throat might be looked at. The medico held my chin in the usual way, and examined my throat; he then wrote me a prescription, and almost immediately afterwards I bade him farewell; but as he conducted me towards the door I observed an expression of strange and unhappy watchfulness in his rolling eyes. It was not the next day, but the next day but one, if I rightly remember, that I sent to request another interview with my doctor. In due time Dthemetri, my messenger, returned, looking sadly aghast; he had "*met* the medico," for so he phrased it, "coming out from his house—in a bier!"

It was, of course, plain that when the poor Bolognese stood looking down my throat, and almost mingling his breath with mine, he was already stricken of the plague. I suppose that his violent sweat must have been owing to some medicine administered by himself in the faint hope of a cure. The peculiar rolling of his eyes which I had remarked is, I believe, to experienced observers, a pretty sure test of the plague. A Russian acquaintance of mine, speaking from the information of men who had made the Turkish campaigns of 1828 and 1829, told me that by this sign the officers of Sabalkansky's force were able to make out the plague-stricken soldiers with a good deal of certainty.

It so happened that most of the people with whom I had anything to do, during my stay at Cairo, were seized with plague, and all these died. Since I had been for a long time en route before I reached Egypt, and was about to start again for another long journey over the desert, there were of course, many little matters touching my wardrobe and my traveling equipments which required to be attended to whilst I remained in the city. It happened so many times that Dthemetri's orders in respect to these matters were frustrated by the deaths of the tradespeople and others whom he employed that at last I became quite accustomed to the peculiar manner of the man when he prepared to announce a new death to me. The poor fellow naturally supposed that I should feel some uneasiness at hearing of the "accidents" continually happening to persons employed by me, and he therefore communicated their deaths as though they were the deaths of friends. He would cast down his eyes and look like a man abashed, and then gently and with a mournful gesture allow the words, "Morto, signor," to come through his lips. I don't know how many of such instances occurred, but they were several, and besides these (as I told you before), my banker, my doctor, my landlord, and my magician all died of the plague. A lad who acted as a helper in the house I occupied lost a brother and a sister within a few hours. Out of my established donkey-boys one died. I did not hear of any instance in which a plague-stricken patient had recovered.

Going out one morning, I met unexpectedly the scorching breath of the khamsin wind,[1] and fearing that I should faint under the infliction, I returned to my rooms. Reflecting, however, that I might have to encounter this wind in the desert, where there would be no possibility of avoiding it, I thought it would be better to brave it once more in the city, and to try whether I could really bear it or not. I therefore mounted my ass, and rode to old Cairo and along the gardens by the banks of the Nile. The wind was hot to the touch, as though it came from a furnace; it blew strongly, but yet with such perfect steadiness that the trees bending under its force remained fixed in the same curves without perceptibly waving. The whole sky was obscured by a veil of yellowish gray, that shut out the face of the sun. The streets were utterly silent, being indeed almost entirely deserted, and not without cause, for the scorching blast, whilst it fevers the blood, closes up the pores of the skin, and is terribly distressing, therefore, to every animal that encounters it. I returned to my rooms dreadfully ill. My head ached with a burning pain, and my pulse bounded quick and fitfully, but perhaps (as in the instance of the poor Levantine whose death I was mentioning) the fear and excitement I felt in trying my own wrist may have made my blood flutter the faster.

It is a thoroughly well believed theory that during the continuance of the plague you can't be ill of any other febrile malady. An unpleasant privilege that! for ill I was, and ill of fever, and I anxiously wished that the ailment might turn out to be anything rather than plague. I had some right to surmise that my illness might have been merely the effect of the hot wind, and this notion was encouraged by the elasticity of my spirits, and by a strong forefeeling that much of my destined life in this world was yet to come and yet to be fulfilled. That was my instinctive belief; but when I carefully weighed the probabilities on the one side and on the other, I could not help seeing that the strength of argument was all against me. There was a strong antecedent likelihood in *favor* of my being struck by the same blow as the rest of the people who had been dying around me. Besides, it occurred to me that, after all, the universal opinion of the Europeans upon a medical question, such as that of contagion, might probably be correct, and *if it were,* I was so thoroughly "compromised," especially by the touch and breath of the dying medico, that I had no right to expect any other fate than that which now

---

1 A hot, sandy wind that blows in North Africa and on the Arabian Peninsula, similar to the Sirocco.

seemed to have overtaken me. Balancing, then, as well as I could all the considerations suggested by hope and fear, I slowly and reluctantly came to the conclusion that, according to all merely reasonable probability, the plague had come upon me.

You might suppose that this conviction would have induced me to write a few farewell lines to those who were dearest, and that having done that, I should have turned my thoughts towards the world to come. Such, however, was not the case. I believe that the prospect of death often brings with it strong anxieties about matters of comparatively trivial import, and certainly with me the whole energy of the mind was directed towards the one petty object of concealing my illness until the latest possible moment—until the delirious stage. I did not believe that either Mysseri or Dthemetri, who had served me so faithfully in all trials, would have deserted me (as most Europeans are wont to do) when they knew that I was stricken by plague, but I shrank from the idea of putting them to this test, and I dreaded the consternation which the knowledge of my illness would be sure to occasion.

I was very ill indeed at the moment when my dinner was served, and my soul sickened at the sight of the food, but I had luckily the habit of dispensing with the attendance of servants during my meal, and as soon as I was left alone, I made a melancholy calculation of the quantity of food I should have eaten if I had been in my usual health, and filled my plates accordingly, and gave myself salt, and so on, as though I were going to dine. I then transferred the viands to a piece of the omnipresent "Times" newspaper, and hid them away in a cupboard, for it was not yet night, and I dared not to throw the food into the street until darkness came. I did not at all relish this process of fictitious dining, but at length the cloth was removed, and I gladly reclined on my divan, (I would not lie down), with the "Arabian Nights"[1] in my hand.

I had a feeling that tea would be a capital thing for me, but I would not order it until the usual hour. When at last the time came, I drank deep draughts from the fragrant cup. The effect was almost instantaneous. A plenteous sweat burst through my skin, and watered my clothes through and through. I kept myself thickly covered. The hot, tormenting weight which had been loading my brain was slowly heaved away. The fever was extinguished. I felt a new buoyancy of spirits, and an unusual activity of mind. I went into my bed under a load of thick covering, and when morning came, and I asked myself how I was, I answered, "Perfectly well."

---

1 Popular in the West in the eighteenth and nineteenth centuries, *A Thousand and One Nights* is a collection of Persian, Indian, and Arabic folktales.

I was very anxious to procure, if possible, some medical advice for Mysseri, whose illness preventd my departure. Every one of the European practising doctors, of whom there had been many, had either died or fled; it was said, however, that there was an Englishman in the medical service of the Pasha[1] who quietly remained at his post, but that he never engaged in private practice. I determined to try if I could obtain assistance in this quarter. I did not venture at first, and at such a time as this, to ask him to visit a servant who was prostrate on the bed of sickness; but thinking that I might thus gain an opportunity of persuading him to attend Mysseri, I wrote a note mentioning my own affair of the sore throat, and asking for the benefit of his medical advice. He instantly followed back my messenger, and was at once shown up into my room. I entreated him to stand off, telling him fairly how deeply I was "compromised," and especially by my contact with a person actually ill and since dead of plague. The generous fellow, with a good-humored laugh at the terror of the contagionists, marched straight up to me, and forcibly seized my hand and shook it with manly violence. I felt grateful indeed, and swelled with fresh pride of race, because that my countryman could carry himself so nobly. He soon cured Mysseri, as well as me, and all this he did from no other motives than the pleasure of doing a kindness and the delight of braving a danger.

At length the great difficulty[2] I had had in procuring beasts for my departure was overcome, and now, too, I was to have the new excitement of traveling on dromedaries. With two of these beasts and three camels, I gladly wound my way from out of the pest-stricken city. As I passed through the streets, I observed a grave elder stretching forth his arms and lifting up his voice in a speech which seemed to have some reference to me; requiring an interpretation, I found that the man had said: "The Pasha seeks camels, and he finds them not; the Englishman says, 'Let camels be brought,' and behold, there they are!"

I no sooner breathed the free, wholesome air of the desert than I felt that a great burden which I had been scarcely conscious of bearing was lifted away from my mind. For nearly three weeks I had lived under peril of death; the peril ceased, and not till then did I know how much alarm and anxiety I had really been suffering.)

---

1   High-ranking civil or military official in the Ottoman Empire, here the Ottoman commander in Egypt.
2   The difficulty was occasioned by the immense exertions which the Pasha was making to collect camels for military purposes. [*Kinglake*]

Death

Emily Brontë

Emily Jane Brontë (1818–1848) died of complications from pulmonary disease at the age of thirty. Her short and reclusive life has proven as fascinating to readers as her only novel, *Wuthering Heights* (1847), which inspired hostile reviews upon its publication, and which was written, along with her poetry, under the male pseudonym Ellis Bell. Born in Thornton, Yorkshire, the fourth daughter of the Reverend Patrick Brontë and Maria Branwell Brontë, Brontë sought refuge from the sorrows of childhood—the deaths of her mother and two older sisters—in storytelling games about make-believe worlds with her sisters Charlotte and Anne and her brother Branwell. Unlike her siblings, however, Brontë refused to abandon her invented world. Until her death, she spent her free hours engrossed in an imaginary realm in the North Pacific called Gondal: the subject of much of her poetry. Written in 1845 as part of her Gondal saga, and published in 1846 in *Poems by Currer, Ellis, and Acton Bell*, the following poem was originally titled "Rosina Alcona to Julius Brenzaida."

DEATH! that struck when I was most confiding
In my certain faith of joy to be—
Strike again, Time's withered branch dividing
From the fresh root of Eternity!

Leaves, upon Time's branch, were growing brightly,
Full of sap, and full of silver dew;
Birds beneath its shelter gathered nightly;
Daily round its flowers the wild bees flew.

Sorrow passed, and plucked the golden blossom;
Guilt stripped off the foliage in its pride;
But within its parent's kindly bosom,
Flowed for ever Life's restoring tide.

Little mourned I for the parted gladness,
For the vacant nest and silent song—
Hope was there, and laughed me out of sadness;
Whispering, "Winter will not linger long!"

And, behold! with tenfold increase blessing,
Spring adorned the beauty-burdened spray;
Wind and rain and fervent heat, caressing,
Lavished glory on that second May!

High it rose—no winged grief could sweep it;
Sin was scared to distance with its shine;
Love, and its own life, had power to keep it
From all wrong—from every blight but thine!

Cruel Death! The young leaves droop and languish;
Evening's gentle air may still restore—
No! the morning sunshine mocks my anguish—
Time, for me, must never blossom more!

Strike it down, that other boughs may flourish
Where that perished sapling used to be;
Thus, at least, its mouldering corpse will nourish
That from which it sprung—Eternity.

1846

ACKNOWLEDGMENTS

Émile Durkheim, selection from *Suicide: A Study in Sociology,* translated by John Spaulding and George Simpson, pp. 241–263. Copyright © 1979 by The Free Press. Reprinted with permission.

Frederick Treves, "The Elephant Man" in *The True History of the Elephant Man* by Michael Howell and Peter Ford. Copyright © 1992 Allison and Busby. Reprinted with permission.

All other selections in this anthology copyright © 2010 by Matthew Kaiser.